THE VIKING PORTABLE LIBRARY

PAUL AND JANE BOWLES

JANE BOWLES was born in New York City in 1917. In 1932, having developed tuberculosis of the bone in her right knee, she was sent for treatment to a sanatorium in Leysin, Switzerland. She returned to the United States in 1934 and soon became part of the bohemian art and literary world of New York. In 1938 she married Paul Bowles and they set out on their travels to Central America, France, and Mexico. Her novel, *Two Serious Ladies*, was published in 1943. In 1948 she followed Paul to Tangier. Her play *In the Summer House* was performed on Broadway in 1953. In 1958 she suffered a debilitating stroke. She died in Málaga, Spain, in 1973. Though her published work—one novel, nine stories, and one play—is small in size, it has been highly praised by Tennessee Williams and Alan Sillitoe, among other writers. John Ashbery has written of her work: "It is to be hoped that she will be recognized for what she is: one of the finest modern writers of fiction, in any language."

PAUL BOWLES was born in Jamaica, New York, in 1910. He began composing music and writing stories at a very early age. When he was sixteen, his poetry was printed in the European literary magazine *transition*. At the age of eighteen he began his travels to Europe, North Africa, Mexico, and Central America. A student of Aaron Copland's, Bowles established his reputation early as a highly gifted composer. In 1945 he returned to writing short stories, and by 1947, when he went to Tangier, fiction had become his major focus. He is the author of four novels, *The Sheltering Sky*, *Let It Come Down*, *The Spider's House*, and *Up Above the World*; one hundred short stories; a book of poetry; and many travel essays. Internationally famous, he is regarded as one of the finest American prose writers of the century. He continues to live in Tangier.

MILLICENT DILLON is a novelist, short story writer, and biographer. Her biography of Jane Bowles, *A Little Original Sin*, was published in 1981. She is also the editor of *Out in the World: The Selected Letters of Jane Bowles*, published in 1985. A Guggenheim Fellow, she is currently at work on a book-length portrait of Paul Bowles.

Each volume in The Viking Portable Library either presents a representative selection from the works of a single outstanding writer or offers a comprehensive anthology on a special subject. Averaging 700 pages in length and designed for compactness and readability, these books fill a need not met by other compilations. All are edited by distinguished authorities, who have written introductory essays and included much other helpful material.

The Portable

PAUL AND JANE BOWLES

Edited and with an Introduction by

MILLICENT DILLON

PENGUIN BOOKS

PENGUIN BOOKS
Published by the Penguin Group
Penguin Books USA Inc., 375 Hudson Street,
New York, New York 10014, U.S.A.
Penguin Books Ltd, 27 Wrights Lane,
London W8 5TZ, England
Penguin Books Australia Ltd, Ringwood,
Victoria, Australia
Penguin Books Canada Ltd, 10 Alcorn Avenue,
Toronto, Ontario, Canada M4V 3B2
Penguin Books (N.Z.) Ltd, 182–190 Wairau Road,
Auckland 10, New Zealand

Penguin Books Ltd, Registered Offices:
Harmondsworth, Middlesex, England

First published in Penguin Books 1994

1 3 5 7 9 10 8 6 4 2

Page 613 constitutes an extension of this copyright page.

Library of Congress Cataloging in Publication Data
Bowles, Paul, 1910–
Portable Paul and Jane Bowles/edited by Millicent Dillon.
p. cm.
ISBN 0-14-016960-1
1. American literature—20th century. I. Bowles, Jane Auer,
1917–1973. II. Dillon, Millicent. III. Title.
PS3552.O874A6 1994
813'.54—dc20 93-33494

Printed in the United States of America
Set in Sabon

CONTENTS

PART THREE

INTRODUCTION

In a break from tradition this Viking Portable presents the work of two authors, Paul and Jane Bowles, husband and wife. At first glance the work of one seems to have little to do with the work of the other. Her writing is always on an edge; it thrives on disjunctions. His is smooth and flowing like a melody that goes on and on to its necessary completion. (He was, in fact, for many years a distinguished composer and continues to compose music to this day.) Her work is always surprising, often funny. His is almost exclusively dark and sinister.

His usual locale is at a distance from the United States—Morocco, Mexico, Central America. Submitting to an imagined vision of a primitive world, he ferrets out his characters' darkest urgings. All that we push away from us in daily life becomes the center, the common place of his narratives. Her material is the stuff of daily life, transformed by an odd, slanting vision. Even as they talk about food or plain pleasures, her characters are obsessed with thoughts of sin and salvation.

In his imaginative world the idea of salvation has no place and the pleasures are never plain. His characters inhabit a world of violence in which they are brought inescapably to a dire end; yet all this is done in a language of the most beautiful clarity and in a form that is classical in its essence. The tone of her writing is hard to pin down; it is ever shifting, even within a single sentence. Frequently one gets the sense in her prose not of an ongoing narrative but of a work of theme and variations.

The logic of his work is recognizable, even inescapable. It pins us down as readers, forcing us to share the terrible fate of his characters. Her logic seems to define its own rules. It is bewildering at times, yet tellingly consistent. Its effect is to throw us back upon our own lives to search for answers.

Yet despite these differences—or perhaps because of them—when selections from their work are placed side by side and interwoven, the resulting effect is unexpected and mysterious. The alternating voices of the two writers—so different in content and tone—seem to resonate, picking up aspects of themes and turns of phrase that double back upon one another. Curiously, the effect produced is similar to the effect the Bowleses produced upon others when they were encountered in life, whether in New York or Mexico or Tangier or Paris. Each seemed to sustain and magnify the other. Each threw the other into relief. And yet one could not say which was in the background and which was in the foreground.

Paul Bowles was born in New York in 1910 of New England parentage. An only child in a family that placed great emphasis on propriety and the containment of emotion, he took refuge from that restraint in his imagination. From a very early age, prohibited from playing with other children, he wrote stories and musical works. When he was sixteen, several of his poems were published in the French literary magazine *transition.* In 1929, without notice to anyone, he suddenly left the University of Virginia and set out for Europe. There he met many important artists, including Gertrude Stein. She was so "real," he would say later, she made him feel "real." Returning to the United States, he began to study musical composition with Aaron Copland. By the time he was in his twenties he had already traveled widely, not only in Europe but in North Africa, and was on his way to becoming a well-known composer of chamber music, songs, and theater pieces.

Jane Auer was born in 1917 in New York, her heritage German Jewish through her father, Hungarian Jewish through her mother. An only child, Jane lived in great part through her imagination, in play and playacting. When she was twelve her father died and Jane was left alone with her mother, a circumstance she later described to Paul as "the worst thing that could have happened" to her. At fourteen she became ill with tuberculosis of the right knee and was taken by her mother to a sanatorium in Leysin, Switzerland, for treatment. Much of the time she was in Leysin, from 1932 to 1934, she lay in bed in traction. On her return to New York, Jane was operated on and her right leg permanently stiffened. Breaking away from the constant worry of her overprotective and highly demonstrative mother, she became part of a young bohemian group that frequented Greenwich Village and the fashionable Askew salon. To her friends she said she wanted to be a writer and, in fact, she did write a novel in French—in imitation of a fashionable French style—and promptly lost the manuscript.

Paul Bowles and Jane Auer met in 1937. He was twenty-six years old, blond, strikingly handsome, impeccably dressed, formal, polite, reserved, witty, and charming, with a certain quality of detachment in that charm. She was twenty, dark-haired, wild, unpredictable, fey, gaminlike, intense and intensely interested in others, incapable of even the pretense of detachment. She was, by all accounts, hilariously funny in her words and actions. She had had affairs only with women. He had had affairs with men and women.

Many years later Jane wrote of her response to Paul at their first meeting. "He wrote music and was mysterious and sinister. The first time I saw him I said to a friend: He's my enemy."

But whatever "enemy" meant to Jane, it was she who actively pursued the relationship. The second time they met she invited herself to go along on a trip he was about to take to Mexico with friends. That trip ended for Jane in her running off from Mexico and Paul, back to the United States. But four months later she reinitiated contact, inviting Paul to spend the weekend at Deal Beach, where her mother had rented a house for the summer.

In 1938, the day before her twenty-first birthday, Paul and Jane were married and set off on a honeymoon to Central America. At Paul's instigation they soon left the cities behind and went farther and farther into the primitive places he loved and that she feared. From Central America they traveled to Paris. There, in a world whose language and civilization were familiar to her, she began to work on a novel, based on the Central American honeymoon.

The marriage of the Bowleses was one to which the word "conventional" could hardly apply. Still, at first, it aimed toward aspects of the conventional, sexually and in other ways. He supported her financially, she began to learn to cook, they shared a sexual relationship. But after their return to New York, where Paul was called to work on music for the theater, the marriage changed and they lived separate sexual lives. The marriage was to endure, however, lasting through journeys that would be taken together and separately, and through casual and not so casual affairs with others. It was to remain intense and intimate and devoted, sustained through the intermingling of their creative lives.

Shuttling with Paul from New York to Mexico, back to New York, to Staten Island, to Mexico again—all places where he went to compose his music—Jane continued to work erratically on the novel.

One day in Mexico in the fall of 1941 Jane brought Paul the disordered manuscript of her novel, tentatively titled "Three Serious Ladies." Paul went over the manuscript with great care, and with his impeccable sense of form suggested a number of changes, including one major one: that the sections dealing with the third serious lady—a Señorita Córdoba—be deleted. The result was *Two Serious Ladies*, a work in which the form seems now to have been predetermined.

At the beginning of the novel the two serious ladies, the anxious but pleasure-seeking Mrs. Copperfield and the alarmingly eccentric and wealthy Miss Goering, meet at a party. Shortly afterward Mrs. Copperfield and Mr. Copperfield (clearly a portrait of Paul) take a boat to Panama. There Mrs. Copperfield, desperate to "make a nest" in this "outlandish place," finds solace from her fear of strangeness in a relationship with a prostitute named Pacifica. Meanwhile, in a locale reminiscent of Staten Island (where the Bowleses lived briefly in 1939), Miss Goering sets out on little trips to seek her salvation, an end she aims to achieve through relationships with various men, one more menacing than the next. At the end of the novel the two women meet once again and Miss Goering observes that Mrs. Copperfield seems to be going to pieces. Mrs. Copperfield agrees; yes, she has gone to pieces, she admits, but it is "a thing I've wanted to do for years. I know I am as guilty as I can be, but I have my happiness, which I guard like a wolf. . . ." As for Miss Goering, left alone by Mrs. Copperfield and deserted by the menacing gangster Ben, she reflects on the results of her own search for salvation: "Certainly I am nearer to becoming a saint," she concludes, "but is it possible that a part of me hidden from my sight is piling sin upon sin as fast as Mrs. Copperfield?"

Mysterious, funny, and profound, resisting analysis at every turn, the novel was published in 1943. Fifty years ahead of its time, it had a reception that was a critical disaster. One critic said that to try to tell its plot was to risk one's sanity. Another said that the only thing surprising about this "supposedly surprising" book was that it ever found a publisher. The novel was cherished by only a few, who saw in it an amazing and original talent.

But to Jane, who never made any true distinction between her life and her work, the judgment upon the book was to come to be a judgment upon herself and upon her life. Nevertheless, she continued to try to lead her life as she had done, her one life with Paul and her other life with Helvetia Perkins, an older woman who was her lover. More undisciplined than ever, working only fitfully, Jane did manage to complete one story, "Plain Pleasures," a puppet play, "A Quarreling Pair," and the first act of her play *In the Summer House*. At Paul's instigation two excerpted sections from her novel were published in a magazine as "A Day in the Open" and "A Guatemalan Idyll." But, Jane insisted, she felt no connection either to the excerpted stories or to the novel. To her they were old works, over and done with.

To Paul, however, the impact of his involvement with *Two Serious Ladies* was not over. Having been so caught up in the shaping of the work, he began to wish, he has since said, that he could write a novel; to wish, indeed, that he could have written that novel. He found himself wanting once again to enter into the imaginative world of fiction, a world he thought he had long since abandoned.

In early 1945 Charles Henri Ford, the editor of *View*, asked him to edit the May issue of the magazine, which would focus on tropical America. Reading myths from the Arapesh and from the Tarahumara, Paul began to think about fiction totemically. "Little by little," he later wrote, "the desire came to me to invent my own myths, adopting the point of view of the primitive mind." His first invented myth, a story called "The Scorpion," was published in *View*. From then on, there began to flow from his pen, unimpeded, one "invented myth" after another, dark stories of betrayal and greed, all written with great natural facility and all receiving immediate praise upon publication. Highly disciplined as he was, he still continued to compose his own works as well as incidental music for the theater, and to write reviews as a music critic for the *New York Herald Tribune*.

In early 1947, offered a contract to write a novel, he left the United States for Tangier, which he had last visited in 1931. On the boat to Morocco, Paul wrote "Pages from Cold Point," a story of the struggle for power between a father and a son, which ends in the son's triumph over the father through an incestuous relationship with him. (Norman Mailer would later write of this story: "Paul Bowles opened the world of Hip. He let in the murder, the drugs, the incest, the death of the Square . . . the call of the orgy, the end of civilization.") Once in North Africa, Paul began to work on *The Sheltering Sky*, making rapid progress through a technique of abandoning conscious control of the narrative.

Meanwhile, Jane, who had chosen to stay in the United States to work on her novel, was making little headway. To Paul, in one of her many lengthy letters—she called them "agonizers"—she wrote of her predicament as a writer:

> I am serious but I am isolated and my experience is probably of no interest at this point to anyone; . . . you have always been a truly isolated person so that whatever you write will

> be good because it will be true which is not so in my case because my kind of isolation I think is an accident, and not inevitable. . . . Not only is your isolation a positive and true one but when you do write from it you immediately receive recognition because what you write is in true relation to yourself which is always recognizable to the world outside. With me who knows? When you are capable only of a serious and ponderous approach to writing as I am—I should say solemn perhaps—it is almost more than one can bear to be continually doubting one's sincerity. . . . As I move along into this writing I think the part I mind the most is this doubt about my entire experience. This is far more important than feeling "out" of it and "isolated," I suppose, but it also accentuates that guilt a thousand times. . . . I realize now . . . that really *Two Serious Ladies* never *was* a novel.

In 1948, after months of indecision as to when or whether to go to Morocco, still blocked in her novel, Jane finally joined Paul there. To her surprise she was immediately fascinated by Tangier, saying that she felt she had "dreamed this life" before she was born. In Fez, where the Bowleses traveled a few months later, Paul completed *The Sheltering Sky*, while in an adjoining room Jane completed her most powerful story, "Camp Cataract."

While in Fez, Jane read the finished manuscript of *The Sheltering Sky*. That novel, as many now know who have seen the Bertolucci film version, is the story of Port and Kit Moresby, married for ten years but no longer involved with each other sexually. Accompanied by a male friend, they set out into the North African desert to escape the aftereffects of World War II and the rush to progress of Western civilization. Port's journey ends in death, Kit's in madness. According to Paul, when Jane read the novel, she saw Port as Paul and identified herself with Kit. It is true that in the early sequences Paul had consciously used Jane as a model for Kit (just as she had used Paul as a model for Mr. Copperfield in *Two Serious Ladies*). But, Paul insists, by the time Kit began her mad flight into the desert, she had achieved her own individual existence as a character and had no connection to Jane. Jane, who as always was not one to make sharp distinctions between literature and life, would eventually come to believe that Kit's terrible descent into madness was an accurate prediction of her own life to come.

Upon its publication in England and in the United States, *The Sheltering Sky* was a great success. It was followed soon after by Paul's short story collection *The Delicate Prey*, which also received enormous critical praise. This was further confirmation to Jane that she had been correct in saying that he would receive instant recognition because his work was in "true relation" to himself. As for her own writing, she was still impeded by doubt about her own experience and its relevance to others. She kept working on her novel and on the last act of her play, but she was continuously being distracted by love affairs, by social engagements, by her responsibility to others—in short, by her ongoing life. In 1949 on a trip to the desert with Paul she wrote "A Stick of Green Candy." The story of a young girl who loses her capacity to live in her imagination, it was to be the last work of prose fiction she was ever to complete.

In the next few years, traveling from London to Ceylon to India, to Morocco, to Spain, and back to Morocco, Paul worked on his second novel, *Let It Come Down*. It is a terrifying work about a young American, Nelson Dyar, who comes to Tangier and is drawn irresistibly into a downward spiral of murder and self-destruction. Paul completed the manuscript in the Moroccan hill town of Xauen, experimenting with the use of drugs to reach the core of Dyar's dissolution.

The novel was published in February 1952 and was reviewed on the front page of *The New York Times Book Review*. The reviewer wrote: "It drives its central character relentlessly toward doom, toward the final orgiastic shudder, with the nightmare clarity, the hallucinative exoticism, of the best of Bowles's short stories. And, as in the short stories, artistic power and inhumanity go together."

Simultaneously, in Paris, in New York, and in Tangier (where she had fallen in love with one or two illiterate Moroccan peasant women), Jane struggled to complete her novel *Out in the World*. She had in mind, she said, a Balzacian novel full of realistic detail, centering on two main characters. The first, Emmy Moore, fat and in her mid-forties, goes to the Hotel Henry in a small town in New England to be alone and to try to write. Blocked in her work, she either writes letters to her husband, Paul Moore, agonizing about her procrastination, or drinks, or becomes involved with a series of women. The second protagonist, Andrew McLain, is a soldier in his early twenties, who falls in love with another soldier. But despite all of Jane's efforts the two protagonists refused to be confined within any predetermined plot. The subsidiary characters in the novel kept multiplying and the narrative wandered further and further from Jane's original intention. No longer willing to ask Paul's help with her work—whether because of her own increasing uncertainty or her sense that he was preoccupied with his own work and that of his protégé, the Moroccan painter Ahmed Yacoubi—she kept writing in fits and starts but could not fix the form of the novel. (Fragments of *Out in the World* are included here as "Emmy Moore's Journal," and "The Children's Party.")

Encouraged by Tennessee Williams and Oliver Smith, Jane did, however, manage to bring the second act of her play to completion. *In the Summer House* was produced in Ann Arbor, Michigan, in May 1953 with Miriam Hopkins in the starring role, and opened on Broadway that December with Judith Anderson. The incidental music for the play was composed by Paul. A work about mothers and daughters, about hatred and love and jealousy and possession, *In the Summer House* was, like *Two Serious Ladies*, far ahead of its time. The initial reviews were devastating; they included comments like "pointlessly morbid," "useless," "deranged," "provokes a feeling of revulsion and fear." Nevertheless, there were those who were staunch adherents of the play. Tennessee Williams wrote: "It is not only the most original play I have ever read, I think it is also the oddest and the funniest and one of the most touching. . . . It is one of those very rare plays which are not tested by the theatre but by which the theatre is tested."

The New York production closed after a run of less than two months. To an interviewer from *Vogue*, as she prepared to leave the United States and return to Morocco, Jane said, "There's no point in writing a play for your five hundred goony friends. You have to reach more people."

Back in Tangier, Jane threw herself into her life with Cherifa, the Moroccan peasant woman she was pursuing. Although she kept trying spasmodically to write, her daily life in Morocco became the drama that she could not give form to in her fiction. (Jane's letter of June 1954 to her friends Katharine Hamill and Natasha von Hoershelman, reproduced in this text, portrays that drama in all its humor and intensity.)

For all that Paul's life was one of almost continuous travel, for all that he was involved in relationships with others, he was never distracted from his primary aim as an artist: to continue creating objectified works out of his imagination—whether in prose or in musical form. In fact, the traveling and the relationships seemed to act as catalysts. During the early and mid-fifties he wrote stories and travel articles, composed "The Picnic Cantata," and set to work on his third novel, *The Spider's House.*

Having lived in Morocco for almost ten years, having observed the social mores carefully through friendships with a number of Moroccans, including his intimate one with Ahmed Yacoubi, Paul felt able in fictional form to enter the mind of a young Moroccan boy living in Fez, torn between his allegiance to the old Moslem ways and the allure of the contemporary world. He felt ready, as well, to interweave with the boy's personal story the national political struggle, the conflict between the drive for independence and the adherence to old colonial ways.

In *The Spider's House* he set the story of the young Moroccan boy Amar against that of Stenham, an expatriate American writer living in Fez. For Stenham, Paul used many of his own experiences, but framed them ironically to show how the outsider ultimately fails to comprehend the true nature of Moroccan society. There is, as well, in *The Spider's House*, a subsidiary plot of a rather chilling romance between Stenham and an American woman who is traveling in Morocco. But it is the story of Amar, his growing trust in Stenham, and his eventual disillusionment that is at the heart of the novel. Paul's treatment of Amar is highly compassionate, a reflection of his own sympathy with the religious and political and moral conflict within Morocco.

Published in 1955, *The Spider's House* was praised by the critics but it was not a commercial success. The subject matter, the Moslem world in ferment, was ahead of its time. Nor did the book have the particular combination of exoticism and violence that had infused much of Paul's earlier work. Undeterred by the commercial failure of the book, Paul immediately set to work on other projects. He began composing the opera *Yerma*, and wrote the text for *Yallah*, an elegiac account of the way of life in the desert and hill country of northwestern Africa, illustrated with photographs by Peter W. Haeberlin. On a boat to Colombo in early 1957, Paul wrote the short story "The Frozen Fields," the most directly autobiographical of his works. Centering on a childhood memory of a Christmas vacation on a New England farm, it is, of course, not a memory but memory objectified. In its evocation of the terror of childhood, it suggests the possibility of a new approach in his own work, an opening up to feeling freed from irony or detachment.

But if there was an opening up taking place in Paul's work, in Jane's work—and in her life—a closure was about to take place. At some point earlier in the fifties she had made an entry in a notebook which is a painful assessment of her own predicament in life and in writing: "There comes a moment when there is no possibility of escape, as if the spirit were a box hitting at the walls of the head. . . .

Is it writing I'm putting off, or was it always something else—a religious sacrifice? The only time I wrote well, when I passed through the inner door, I felt guilt. I must find that again. If I can't, maybe I shall find a way to give it up. I cannot go on this way." (That entry is included in full in the accompanying text as "Curls and a Quiet Country Face.")

By 1957, afflicted with very high blood pressure and taking medication indiscriminately, drinking to keep herself from being depressed, still trying to write and still finding it impossible to complete anything, feeling herself estranged from Paul, Jane began to suffer from severe depression and anxiety. In February of that year, while Paul was on a voyage to Asia with Ahmed Yacoubi, she suffered a stroke. (The expatriate community of Tangier was alive with the rumor that Jane's stroke had been caused by her having been poisoned by her Moroccan lover. In fact, given Jane's medical history and her indiscriminate use of medication and her heavy drinking, it does not seem that it was necessary for anyone else to administer poison to her.)

As a result of the stroke she suffered a severe visual impairment as well as an aphasia, a confusion in her use of language. She suffered as well a terrible alteration in her imaginative capability. Now her imagination was channeled into a single-minded obsessiveness about her oncoming doom. In conversation with Paul she was to come back and back again to her belief that the fate of Kit in *The Sheltering Sky* as Paul had written it was predictive of her own destiny. Her illness and her preoccupation with the progressive deterioration she foresaw was to become, Paul later wrote, "the principal leitmotif" of their lives. Looking for adequate medical care for her condition, Paul took Jane to England for treatment. There he himself became ill with a powerful virus. Yet even at this moment, ill and anxious, he wrote the story "Tapiama," thereby giving form and substance to his fever-induced imaginings.

After treatment in England, Jane returned to Morocco. But as the political conditions in Tangier grew more threatening to foreigners, her physical and emotional condition worsened. In New York, where she went next for treatment, she wrote several "compositions" for a speech therapist, each one a painful statement about the doom she foresaw for herself. In one of the pieces she told of her inability to write, connecting it to some "failure of the will" on her part. ". . . there is such a thing as a failure of the will which is agony for the person who suffers from it. I did not suffer a stroke for nothing at my age. . . ."

From New York, Jane returned to Tangier once again, and her own condition stabilized as the political situation in the city stabilized. She threw herself into the daily life she had created as if it would ward off the threat of the future. At intervals, despite her visual and linguistic impairment, she still tried to write but the results were dismaying. The lightning-quick connections that had existed between her words and her thoughts had slowed markedly.

Paul, working assiduously as ever, began a new project which involved a series of journeys throughout Morocco to record Moroccan music for the Library of Congress. He also set to work recording and translating the words of Larbi Layachi, an illiterate Moroccan workman with a great gift for storytelling. The book that resulted from this collaboration is *A Life Full of Holes*. He continued to write travel articles and in his "spare" time in the evenings began to write four stories about Moroccans in a synthetic style. "The pleasure consisted in inventing a new problem and finding a way to solve it," he recalls. "Let us say that I started with four disparate fragments—anecdotes, quotations, or simple clauses deprived of context—gleaned from separate sources and involving, if anything, entirely different sets of characters. The task was to invent a connecting narrative tissue which would make all four of the original elements equally supportive of the resulting construction. It seemed to me that the subject of kif smoking . . . would provide an effective cement with which to put together the various fragments." These four stories were published as *A Hundred Camels in the Courtyard*. (Two of the stories, "He of the Assembly" and "The Wind at Beni Madir," are included here.) In 1962 Paul also wrote "The Time of Friendship," an account of a friendship between an older Swiss woman who spends her summers in the Sahara and a young village boy. It is a compassionate story but, as in *The Spider's House*, the compassion is modified by the sense of the inevitable betrayal of the young Moslem boy by the Westerner.

In the winter of 1963, encouraged by Jane's seeming stability, he felt able to start on a sustained literary work, a new novel, *Up Above the World*. According to Paul, he entered upon the writing of this work as a "purely pleasurable pastime." But in fact, once he was caught up in it, he reentered the world of terror and of violence so pervasive in his previous work. The novel tells the story of the Slades, a husband and wife who set off on a second honeymoon to Central America. By chance, at the beginning of their voyage, they encounter an older woman, a Mrs. Rainmantle, whose son has secretly planned to murder her. After the son kills his mother, fearful that the Slades might be suspicious of the circumstances of her death, he entraps them and subjects them to an ordeal through drugs and "brainwashing." The Slades' second honeymoon ends in their death; in their destruction is the added horror that they never comprehend the reason for their doom.

By the late sixties Jane's physical and emotional condition had worsened dramatically. Paul took her to Málaga, Spain, where she was confined to a sanatorium. Though she returned several times to Tangier, in 1969 she was permanently institutionalized in Málaga. During her final illness Paul continued to work on travel articles, composed his autobiography, *Without Stopping*, and worked on translations of the tales of his new protégé, Mohammed Mrabet. Mrabet, like Larbi Layachi, "spoke" his stories to Paul. Eleven books resulted from this collaboration.

Jane died in May 1973, having been unable to speak or see or move since 1971. After her death Paul returned once again to writing stories. Included in the accompanying text are stories written by him up to 1980 as well as the haunting poem "Next to Nothing," which was written in 1975.

In this collection I have chosen to adhere to chronological sequence (with a few minor exceptions) in the presentation of Paul's works. With Jane's later work I have departed from chronology. (Much of her unpublished work is undated, in any case.) I have chosen to place the three pieces excerpted from what had once been "Three Serious Ladies"—and therefore written in the early 1940s—in the last section of the text.

When the works are read in this particular continuity, alternating one with the other, they reveal curious byplays, a series of questions and answers tossed from one to the other. Placed against his work, her work seems to ask: What are the obligations we—as characters or as beings—owe to our destinies? Placed against her work, his seems to answer that we have no choice in our destinies: One acts—one does what one does—and primarily what we do is done out of the basest of motives. Yes, but—she seems to counter—isn't it true that most often we live our lives putting off doing what we intend to do? Are we not always seeking absolution and justification? Justification to whom? his work asks in reply. What is the sense or meaning of justification in a universe of emptiness, empty of God or of any moral order? There may be no God, she—or her characters—answers, but we must not stop trying to find salvation.

The dialogue between them, about hope and despair, about will and the absence of will, is unending. Each seems to be addressing the other as the ideal reader. I am reminded of what the writer Alfred Chester once said: that meeting the Bowleses was like encountering two parts of the same being.

Millicent Dillon

PART ONE

from *TWO SERIOUS LADIES*

JANE BOWLES

1

THE FOLLOWING extended excerpt is composed of Part 1 and Part 2 of the three-part novel.

CHRISTINA GOERING'S FATHER was an American industrialist of German parentage and her mother was a New York lady of a very distinguished family. Christina spent the first half of her life in a very beautiful house (not more than an hour from the city) which she had inherited from her mother. It was in this house that she had been brought up as a child with her sister Sophie.

As a child Christina had been very much disliked by other children. She had never suffered particularly because of this, having led, even at a very early age, an active inner life that curtailed her observation of whatever went on around her, to such a degree that she never picked up the mannerisms then in vogue, and at the age of ten was called old-fashioned by other little girls. Even then she wore the look of certain fanatics who think of themselves as leaders without once having gained the respect of a single human being.

Christina was troubled horribly by ideas which never would have occurred to her companions, and at the same time took for granted a position in society which any other child would have found unbearable. Every now and then a schoolmate would take pity on her and try to spend some time with her, but far from being grateful for this, Christina would instead try her best to convert her new friend to the cult of whatever she believed in at the time.

Her sister Sophie, on the other hand, was very much admired by everyone in the school. She showed a marked talent for writing poetry and spent all her time with a quiet little girl called Mary, who was two years younger.

When Christina was thirteen years old her hair was very red

(when she grew up it remained almost as red), her cheeks were sloppy and pink, and her nose showed traces of nobility.

That year Sophie brought Mary home with her nearly every day for luncheon. After they had finished eating she would take Mary for a walk through the woods, having provided a basket for each of them in which to carry back flowers. Christina was not permitted by Sophie to come along on these walks.

"You must find something of your own to do," Sophie would say to her. But it was hard for Christina to think of anything to do by herself that she enjoyed. She was in the habit of going through many mental struggles—generally of a religious nature—and she preferred to be with other people and organize games. These games, as a rule, were very moral, and often involved God. However, no one else enjoyed them and she was obliged to spend a great part of the day alone. She tried going to the woods once or twice by herself and bringing back flowers, in imitation of Mary and Sophie, but each time, fearing that she would not return with enough flowers to make a beautiful bouquet, she so encumbered herself with baskets that the walk seemed more of a hardship than a pleasure.

It was Christina's desire to have Mary to herself of an afternoon. One very sunny afternoon Sophie went inside for her piano lesson, and Mary remained seated on the grass. Christina, who had seen this from not far away, ran into the house, her heart beating with excitement. She took off her shoes and stockings and remained in a short white underslip. This was not a very pleasant sight to behold, because Christina at this time was very heavy and her legs were quite fat. (It was impossible to foresee that she would turn out to be a tall and elegant lady.) She ran out on the lawn and told Mary to watch her dance.

"Now don't take your eyes off me," she said. "I'm going to do a dance of worship to the sun. Then I'm going to show that I'd rather have God and no sun than the sun and no God. Do you understand?"

"Yes," said Mary. "Are you going to do it now?"

"Yes, I'm going to do it right here." She began the dance abruptly. It was a clumsy dance and her gestures were all undecided. When Sophie came out of the house, Christina was in the act of running backwards and forwards with her hands joined in prayer.

"What is she doing?" Sophie asked Mary.

"A dance to the sun, I think," Mary said. "She told me to sit here and watch her."

Sophie walked over to where Christina was now twirling around and around and shaking her hands weakly in the air.

"Sneak!" she said and suddenly she pushed Christina down on the grass.

For a long time after that, Christina kept away from Sophie, and consequently from Mary. She had one more occasion to be with Mary, however, and this happened because Sophie developed a terrible toothache one morning, and her governess was obliged to take her to the dentist immediately. Mary, not having heard of this, came over in the afternoon, expecting to find Sophie at home. Christina was in the tower in which the children often gathered, and saw her coming up the walk.

"Mary," she screamed, "come on up here." When Mary arrived in the tower, Christina asked her if she would not like to play a very special game with her. "It's called 'I forgive you for all your sins,' " said Christina. "You'll have to take your dress off."

"Is it fun?" Mary asked.

"It's not for fun that we play it, but because it's necessary to play it."

"All right," said Mary, "I'll play with you." She took her dress off and Christina pulled an old burlap sack over Mary's head. She cut two holes in the burlap for Mary to see through and then she tied a cord around her waist.

"Come," said Christina, "and you will be absolved for your sins. Keep repeating to yourself: 'May the Lord forgive me for my sins.' "

She hurried down the stairs with Mary and then out across the lawn towards the woods. Christina wasn't yet sure what she was going to do, but she was very much excited. They came to a stream that skirted the woods. The banks of the stream were soft and muddy.

"Come to the water," said Christina; "I think that's how we'll wash away your sins. You'll have to stand in the mud."

"Near the mud?"

"*In* the mud. Does your sin taste bitter in your mouth? It must."

"Yes," said Mary hesitantly.

"Then you want to be clean and pure as a flower is, don't you?"

Mary did not answer.

"If you don't lie down in the mud and let me pack the mud over you and then wash you in the stream, you'll be forever condemned. Do you want to be forever condemned? This is your moment to decide."

Mary stood beneath her black hood without saying a word. Christina pushed her down on the ground and started to pack the burlap with mud.

"The mud's cold," said Mary.

"The hell fires are hot," said Christina. "If you let me do this, you won't go to hell."

"Don't take too long," said Mary.

Christina was very much agitated. Her eyes were shining. She packed more and more mud on Mary and then she said to her:

"Now you're ready to be purified in the stream."

"Oh, please no, not the water—I hate to go into the water. I'm afraid of the water."

"Forget what you are afraid of. God's watching you now and He has no sympathy for you yet."

She lifted Mary from the ground and walked into the stream, carrying her. She had forgotten to take off her own shoes and stockings. Her dress was completely covered with mud. Then she submerged Mary's body in the water. Mary was looking at her through the holes in the burlap. It did not occur to her to struggle.

"Three minutes will be enough," said Christina. "I'm going to say a little prayer for you."

"Oh, don't do that," Mary pleaded.

"Of course," said Christina, lifting her eyes to the sky.

"Dear God," she said, "make this girl Mary pure as Jesus Your Son. Wash her sins away as the water is now washing the mud away. This black burlap proves to you that she thinks she is a sinner."

"Oh, stop," whispered Mary. "He can hear you even if you just say it to yourself. You're shouting so."

"The three minutes are over, I believe," said Christina. "Come darling, now you can stand up."

"Let's run to the house," said Mary. "I'm freezing to death."

They ran to the house and up the back stairway that led to the tower. It was hot in the tower room because all the windows had been shut. Christina suddenly felt very ill.

"Go," she said to Mary, "go into the bath and clean yourself off. I'm going to draw." She was deeply troubled. "It's over," she said to herself, "the game is over. I'll tell Mary to go home after she's dried off. I'll give her some colored pencils to take home with her."

Mary returned from the bath wrapped in a towel. She was still shivering. Her hair was wet and straight. Her face looked smaller than it did ordinarily.

Christina looked away from her. "The game is over," she said, "it took only a few minutes—you should be dried off—I'm going out." She walked out of the room leaving Mary behind, pulling the towel closer around her shoulders.

• • •

As a grown woman Miss Goering was no better liked than she had been as a child. She was now living in her home outside New York, with her companion, Miss Gamelon.

Three months ago Miss Goering had been sitting in the parlor, looking out at the leafless trees, when her maid announced a caller.

"Is it a gentleman or a lady?" Miss Goering asked.

"A lady."

"Show her in immediately," said Miss Goering.

The maid returned followed by the caller. Miss Goering rose from her seat. "How do you do?" she said. "I don't believe I've ever laid eyes on you before this moment, but please sit down."

The lady visitor was small and stocky and appeared to be in her late thirties or early forties. She wore dark, unfashionable clothing and, but for her large gray eyes, her face might on all occasions have passed unnoticed.

"I'm your governess's cousin," she said to Miss Goering. "She was with you for many years. Do you remember her?"

"I do," said Miss Goering.

"Well, my name is Lucie Gamelon. My cousin used to talk about you and about your sister Sophie all the time. I've been meaning to call on you for years now, but one thing and another always got in the way. But then, we never know it to fail."

Miss Gamelon reddened. She had not yet been relieved of her hat and coat.

"You have a lovely home," she said. "I guess you know it and appreciate it a lot."

By this time Miss Goering was filled with curiosity concerning Miss Gamelon. "What's your business in life?" she asked her.

"Not very much, I'm afraid. I've been typing manuscripts for famous authors all my life, but there doesn't seem to be much demand for authors any more unless maybe they are doing their own typing."

Miss Goering, who was busy thinking, said nothing.

Miss Gamelon looked around helplessly.

"Do you stay here the greater portion of the time or do you travel mostly?" she asked Miss Goering unexpectedly.

"I never thought of traveling," said Miss Goering. "I don't require travel."

"Coming from the family you come from," said Miss Gamelon, "I guess you were born full of knowledge about everything. You wouldn't need to travel. I had opportunity to travel two or three times with my authors. They were willing to pay all my expenses and my full salary besides, but I never did go except once, and that was to Canada."

"You don't like to travel," said Miss Goering, staring at her.

"It doesn't agree with me. I tried it that once. My stomach was upset and I had nervous headaches all the time. That was enough. I had my warning."

"I understand perfectly," said Miss Goering.

"I always believe," continued Miss Gamelon, "that you get your warning. Some people don't heed their warnings. That's when they come into conflict. I think that anything you feel strange or nervous about, you weren't cut out to do."

"Go on," said Miss Goering.

"Well, I know, for instance, that I wasn't cut out to be an aviator. I've always had dreams of crashing down to the earth. There are quite a few things that I won't do, even if I am thought of as a stubborn mule. I won't cross a big body of water, for instance. I could have everything I wanted if I would just cross the ocean and go over to England, but I never will."

"Well," said Miss Goering, "let's have some tea and some sandwiches."

Miss Gamelon ate voraciously and complimented Miss Goering on her good food.

"I like good things to eat," she said; "I don't have so much good food any more. I did when I was working for the authors."

When they had finished tea, Miss Gamelon took leave of her hostess.

"I've had a very sociable time," she said. "I would like to stay longer, but tonight I have promised a niece of mine that I would watch over her children for her. She is going to attend a ball."

"You must be very depressed with the idea," said Miss Goering.

"Yes, you're right," Miss Gamelon replied.

"Do return soon," said Miss Goering.

The following afternoon the maid announced to Miss Goering that she had a caller. "It's the same lady that called here yesterday," said the maid.

"Well, well," thought Miss Goering, "that's good."

"How are you feeling today?" Miss Gamelon asked her, coming into the room. She spoke very naturally, not appearing to find it strange that she was returning so soon after her first visit. "I was thinking about you all last night," she said. "It's a funny thing. I always thought I should meet you. My cousin used to tell me how queer you were. I think, though, that you can make friends more quickly with queer people. Or else you don't make friends with them at all—one way or the other. Many of my authors were very queer. In that way I've had an advantage of association that most people don't have. I know something about what I call real honest-to-God maniacs, too."

Miss Goering invited Miss Gamelon to dine with her. She found her soothing and agreeable to be with. Miss Gamelon was very much impressed with the fact that Miss Goering was so nervous. Just as they were about to sit down, Miss Goering said that she couldn't face eating in the dining-room and she asked the servant to lay the table in the parlor instead. She spent a great deal of time switching the lights off and on.

"I know how you feel," Miss Gamelon said to her.

"I don't particularly enjoy it," said Miss Goering, "but I expect in the future to be under control."

Over wine at dinner Miss Gamelon told Miss Goering that it was only correct that she should be thus. "What do you expect, dear," she said, "coming from the kind of family you come from? You're all tuned high, all of you. You've got to allow yourself things that other people haven't any right to allow themselves."

Miss Goering began to feel a little tipsy. She looked dreamily at Miss Gamelon, who was eating her second helping of chicken cooked in wine. There was a little spot of grease in the corner of her mouth.

"I love to drink," said Miss Gamelon, "but there isn't much point to it when you have to work. It's fine enough when you have plenty of leisure time. I have a lot of leisure time now."

"Have you a guardian angel?" asked Miss Goering.

"Well, I have a dead aunt, maybe that's what you mean; she might be watching over me."

"That is not what I mean—I mean something quite different."

"Well, of course . . ." said Miss Gamelon.

"A guardian angel comes when you are very young, and gives you special dispensation."

"From what?"

"From the world. Yours might be luck; mine is money. Most people have a guardian angel; that's why they move slowly."

"That's an imaginative way of talking about guardian angels. I guess my guardian angel is what I told you about heeding my warnings. I think maybe she could warn me about both of us. In that way I could keep you out of trouble. Of course, with your consent," she added, looking a little confused.

Miss Goering had a definite feeling at that moment that Miss Gamelon was not in the least a nice woman, but she refused to face this because she got too much enjoyment from the sensation of being nursed and pampered. She told herself that it would do no harm for a little while.

"Miss Gamelon," said Miss Goering, "I think it would be a very fine idea if you were to make this your home—for the time being, at least. I don't think you have any pressing business that would oblige you to remain elsewhere, have you?"

"No, I haven't any business," said Miss Gamelon. "I don't see why I couldn't stay here—I'd have to get my things at my sister's house. Outside of that I don't know of anything else."

"What things?" asked Miss Goering impatiently. "Don't go back at all. We can get things at the stores." She got up and walked quickly up and down the room.

"Well," said Miss Gamelon, "I think I had better get my things."

"But not tonight," said Miss Goering, "tomorrow—tomorrow in the car."

"Tomorrow in the car," repeated Miss Gamelon after her.

Miss Goering made arrangements to give Miss Gamelon a room near her own, to which she led her shortly after dinner was over.

"This room," said Miss Goering, "has one of the finest views in the entire house." She drew the curtains apart. "You've got your moon and your stars tonight, Miss Gamelon, and a very nice silhouette of trees against the sky."

Miss Gamelon was standing in semi-darkness near the dressing-table. She was fingering the brooch on her blouse. She wished that Miss Goering would leave so that she could think about the house and Miss Goering's offer, in her own way.

There was a sudden scrambling in the bushes below the window. Miss Goering jumped.

"What's that?" Her face was very white and she put her hand to her forehead. "My heart hurts so for such a long time afterwards whenever I'm frightened," she said in a small voice.

"I think I'd better go to bed now and go to sleep," said Miss Gamelon. She was suddenly overcome by all the wine that she had drunk. Miss Goering took her leave reluctantly. She had been prepared to talk half the night. The following morning Miss Gamelon went home to collect her things and give her sister her new address.

Three months later Miss Goering knew little more about Miss Gamelon's ideas than she had on the first night that they had dined together. She had learned quite a lot about Miss Gamelon's personal characteristics, however, through careful observation. When Miss Gamelon had first arrived she had spoken a great deal about her love of luxury and beautiful objects, but Miss Goering had since then taken her on innumerable shopping trips; and she had never seemed interested in anything more than the simplest necessities.

She was quiet, even a little sullen, but she seemed to be fairly contented. She enjoyed dining out at large, expensive restaurants, particularly if dinner music accompanied the meal. She did not seem to like the theater. Very often Miss Goering would buy tickets for a play, and at the last moment Miss Gamelon would decline to go.

"I feel so lazy," she would say, "that bed seems to be the most beautiful thing in the world at this moment."

When she did go to the theater, she was easily bored. Whenever the action of the play was not swift, Miss Goering would catch her looking down into her lap and playing with her fingers.

She seemed now to feel more violently about Miss Goering's activities than she did about her own, although she did not listen so sympathetically to Miss Goering's explanations of herself as she had in the beginning.

On Wednesday afternoon Miss Gamelon and Miss Goering were sitting underneath the trees in front of the house. Miss Goering was drinking whisky and Miss Gamelon was reading. The maid came out and announced to Miss Goering that she was wanted on the telephone.

The call was from Miss Goering's old friend Anna, who invited her to a party the following night. Miss Goering came back out on the lawn, very excited.

"I'm going to a party tomorrow night," she said, "but I don't see how I can wait until then—I look forward to going to parties so much and I am invited to so few that I scarcely know how to behave about them. What will we do to make the hours pass until then?" She took both Miss Gamelon's hands in her own.

It was getting a little chilly. Miss Goering shivered and smiled. "Do you enjoy our little life?" she asked Miss Gamelon.

"I'm always content," said Miss Gamelon, "because I know what to take and what to leave, but you are always at the mercy."

Miss Goering arrived at Anna's looking flushed and a little overdressed. She was wearing velvet and Miss Gamelon had fastened some flowers in her hair.

The men, most of whom were middle-aged, were standing together in one corner of the room, smoking and listening to each other attentively. The ladies, freshly powdered, were seated around the room, talking very little. Anna seemed to be a little tense, although she was smiling. She wore a hostess gown adapted from a central European peasant costume.

"You will have drinks in a minute," she announced to her guests, and then, seeing Miss Goering, she went over to her and led her to a chair next to Mrs. Copperfield's without saying a word.

Mrs. Copperfield had a sharp little face and very dark hair. She was unusually small and thin. She was nervously rubbing her bare arms and looking around the room when Miss Goering seated herself in the chair beside her. They had met for many years at Anna's parties and they occasionally had tea with each other.

"Oh! Christina Goering," cried Mrs. Copperfield, startled to see her friend suddenly seated beside her, "I'm going away!"

"Do you mean," said Miss Goering, "that you are leaving this party?"

"No, I am going on a trip. Wait until I tell you about it. It's terrible."

Miss Goering noticed that Mrs. Copperfield's eyes were brighter than usual. "What is wrong, little Mrs. Copperfield?" she asked, rising from her seat and looking around the room with a bright smile on her face.

"Oh, I'm sure," said Mrs. Copperfield, "that you wouldn't want to hear about it. You can't possibly have any respect for me, but that doesn't make any difference because I have the utmost respect for you. I heard my husband say that you had a religious nature one day, and we almost had a very bad fight. Of course he is crazy to say that. You are gloriously unpredictable and you are afraid of no one but yourself. I hate religion in other people."

Miss Goering neglected to answer Mrs. Copperfield because for the last second or two she had been staring at a stout dark-haired man who was walking heavily across the room in their direction. As he came nearer, she saw that he had a pleasant face with wide jowls that protruded on either side but did not hang down as they do on most obese persons. He was dressed in a blue business suit.

"May I sit beside you?" he asked them. "I have met this young lady before," he said, shaking hands with Mrs. Copperfield, "but I am afraid that I have not yet met her friend." He turned and nodded to Miss Goering.

Mrs. Copperfield was so annoyed at the interruption that she neglected to introduce Miss Goering to the gentleman. He drew up a chair next to Miss Goering's and looked at her.

"I have just come from a most wonderful dinner," he said to her, "moderate in price, but served with care and excellently prepared. If it would interest you I can write down the name of the little restaurant for you."

He reached into his vest pocket and pulled out a leather billfold. He found only one slip of paper which was not already covered with addresses.

"I will write this down for you," he said to Miss Goering. "Undoubtedly you will be seeing Mrs. Copperfield and then you can pass the information on to her, or perhaps she can telephone to you."

Miss Goering took the slip of paper in her hand and looked carefully at the writing.

He had not written down the name of a restaurant at all; instead he had asked Miss Goering to consent to go home with him later to his apartment. This pleased her greatly as she was usually delighted to stay out as late as possible once she had left her home.

She looked up at the man, whose face was now inscrutable. He sipped his drink with calm, and looked around the room like someone who has finally brought a business conversation to a close. However, there were some sweat beads on his forehead.

Mrs. Copperfield stared at him with distaste, but Miss Goering's face suddenly brightened. "Let me tell you," she said to them, "about a strange experience I had this morning. Sit still, little Mrs. Copperfield, and listen to me." Mrs. Copperfield looked up at Miss Goering and took her friend's hand in her own.

"I stayed in town with my sister Sophie last night," said Miss Goering, "and this morning I was standing in front of the window drinking a cup of coffee. The building next to Sophie's house is being torn down. I believe that they are intending to put an apartment house in its place. It was not only extremely windy this morning, but it was raining intermittently. From my window I could see into the rooms of this building, as the wall opposite me had already been torn down. The rooms were still partially furnished, and I stood looking at them, watching the rain spatter the wallpaper. The wallpaper was flowered and already covered with dark spots, which were growing larger."

"How amusing," said Mrs. Copperfield, "or perhaps it was depressing."

"I finally felt rather sad watching this and I was about to go away when a man came into one of these rooms and, walking deliberately over to the bed, took up a coverlet which he folded under his arm. It was undoubtedly a personal possession which he had neglected to pack and had just now returned to fetch. Then he walked around the room aimlessly for a bit and finally he stood at the very edge of his room looking down into the yard with his arms akimbo. I could see him more clearly now, and I could easily tell that he was an artist. As he stood there, I was increasingly filled with horror, very much as though I were watching a scene in a nightmare."

At this point Miss Goering suddenly stood up.

"Did he jump, Miss Goering?" Mrs. Copperfield asked with feeling.

"No, he remained there for quite a while looking down into the courtyard with an expression of pleasant curiosity on his face."

"Amazing, Miss Goering," said Mrs. Copperfield. "I do think it's such an interesting story, really, but it has quite scared me out of my wits and I shouldn't enjoy hearing another one like it." She had scarcely finished her sentence when she heard her husband say:

"We will go to Panama and linger there awhile before we penetrate into the interior." Mrs. Copperfield pressed Miss Goering's hand.

"I don't think I can bear it," she said. "Really, Miss Goering, it frightens me so much to go."

"I would go anyway," said Miss Goering.

Mrs. Copperfield jumped off the arm of the chair and ran into the library. She locked the door behind her carefully and then she fell in a little heap on the sofa and sobbed bitterly. When she had stopped crying she powdered her nose, seated herself on the window-sill, and looked down into the dark garden below.

An hour or two later Arnold, the stout man in the blue suit, was still talking to Miss Goering. He suggested to her that they leave the party and go to his own house. "I think that we will have a much nicer time there," he said to her. "There will be less noise and we will be able to talk more freely."

As yet Miss Goering had no desire at all to leave, she enjoyed so much being in a room full of people, but she did not quite know how to get out of accepting his invitation.

"Certainly," she said, "let's be on our way." They rose and left the room together in silence.

"Don't say anything to Anna about our leaving," Arnold told Miss Goering. "It will only cause a commotion. I promise you I'll send some sweets to her tomorrow, or some flowers." He pressed Miss Goering's hand and smiled at her. She was not sure that she did not find him a bit too familiar.

• • •

After leaving Anna's party, Arnold walked awhile with Miss Goering and then hailed a cab. The road to his home led through many dark and deserted streets. Miss Goering was so nervous and hysterical about this that Arnold was alarmed.

"I always think," said Miss Goering, "that the driver is only waiting for the passengers to become absorbed in conversation in order to shoot down some street, to an inaccessible and lonely place where he will either torture or murder them. I am certain that most people feel the same way about it that I do, but they have the good taste not to mention it."

"Since you live so far out of town," said Arnold, "why don't you spend the night at my house? We have an extra bedroom."

"I probably shall," said Miss Goering, "although it is against my entire code, but then, I have never even begun to use my code, although I judge everything by it." Miss Goering looked a little morose after having said this and they drove on in silence until they reached their destination.

Arnold's flat was on the second floor. He opened the door and they walked into a room lined to the ceiling with bookshelves. The couch had been made up and Arnold's slippers were lying on the rug beside it. The furniture was heavy and some small Oriental rugs were scattered here and there.

"I sleep in here," said Arnold, "and my mother and father occupy the bedroom. We have a small kitchen, but generally we prefer to eat out. There is another tiny bedroom, originally intended for a maid's room, but I would rather sleep in here and let my eye wander from book to book; books are a great solace to me." He sighed heavily and laid both his hands on Miss Goering's shoulders. "You see, my dear lady," he said, "I'm not exactly doing the kind of thing that I would like to do. . . . I'm in the real-estate business."

"What is it that you would like to do?" asked Miss Goering, looking weary and indifferent.

"Something, naturally," said Arnold, "in the book line, or in the painting line."

"And you can't?"

"No," said Arnold, "my family doesn't believe that such an occupation is serious, and since I must earn my living and pay for my share of this flat, I have been obliged to accept a post in my uncle's office, where I must say I very quickly have become his prize salesman. In the evenings, however, I have plenty of time to move among people who have nothing to do with real estate. As a matter of fact, they think very little about earning money at all. Naturally, these people are interested in having enough to eat. Even though I am thirty-nine years old I still am hoping very seriously that I will be able to make a definite break with my family. I do not see life through the same pair of eyes that they do. And I feel more and more that my life here with them is becoming insupportable in spite of the fact that I am free to entertain whom I please since I pay for part of the upkeep of the flat."

He sat down on the couch and rubbed his eyes with his hands.

"You'll forgive me, Miss Goering, but I'm feeling very sleepy suddenly. I'm sure the feeling will go away."

Miss Goering's drinks were wearing off and she thought it high time that she got back to Miss Gamelon, but she had not the courage to ride all the way out to her home by herself.

"Well, I suppose this is a great disappointment to you," said Arnold, "but you see I have fallen in love with you. I wanted to bring you here and tell you about my whole life, but now I don't feel like talking about anything."

"Perhaps some other time you'll tell me about your life," said Miss Goering, beginning to walk up and down very quickly. She stopped and turned towards him. "What do you advise me to do?" she asked him. "Do you advise me to go home or stay here?"

Arnold studied his watch. "Stay here by all means," he said.

Just then Arnold's father came in, wearing a lounging-robe and carrying a cup of coffee in his hand. He was very slender and he wore a small pointed beard. He was a more distinguished figure than Arnold.

"Good evening, Arnold," said his father. "Will you introduce me, please, to this young lady?"

Arnold introduced them and then his father asked Miss Goering why she did not take off her cloak.

"As long as you are up so late at night," he said, "and not enjoying the comfort and the security of your own bed, you might as well be at ease. Arnold, my son, never thinks of things like this." He took Miss Goering's cloak off and complimented her on her lovely dress.

"Now tell me where you have been and what you have done. I myself don't go out in society, being content with the company of my wife and son."

Arnold shrugged his shoulders and pretended to look absently around the room. But any person even a little observant could have seen that his face was decidedly hostile.

"Now tell me about this party," said Arnold's father adjusting the scarf that he was wearing around his neck. "*You* tell me." He pointed at Miss Goering, who was beginning to feel much gayer already. She had instantly preferred Arnold's father to Arnold himself.

"I'll tell you about it," said Arnold. "There were many people there, the majority of whom were creative artists, some successful and rich, others rich simply because they had inherited money from some member of the family, and others with just barely enough to eat. None of these people, however, were interested in money as an objective but would have been content, all of them, with just enough to eat."

"Like wild animals," said his father, rising to his feet. "Like wolves! What separates a man from a wolf if it is not that a man wants to make a profit?"

Miss Goering laughed until the tears streamed down her face. Arnold took some magazines from the table and began looking through them very quickly.

Just then Arnold's mother came into the room carrying in one hand a plate heaped with cakes and in the other a cup of coffee.

She was dowdy and unimpressive and of very much the same build as Arnold. She was wearing a pink wrapper.

"Welcome," said Miss Goering to Arnold's mother. "May I have a piece of your cake?"

Arnold's mother, who was a very gauche woman, did not offer Miss Goering any of the cake; instead, hugging the platter close to her, she said to Miss Goering: "Have you known Arnold for long?"

"No, I met your son tonight, at a party."

"Well," said Arnold's mother, putting the tray down and sitting on the sofa, "I guess that isn't long, is it?"

Arnold's father was annoyed with his wife and showed it plainly in his face.

"I hate that pink wrapper," he said.

"Why do you talk about that now when there is company?"

"Because the company doesn't make the wrapper look any different." He winked broadly at Miss Goering and then burst out laughing. Miss Goering again laughed heartily at his remark. Arnold was even glummer than he had been a moment before.

"Miss Goering," said Arnold, "was afraid to go home alone, so I told her that she was welcome to sleep in the extra room. Although the bed isn't very comfortable in there, I think that she will at least have privacy."

"And *why*," said Arnold's father, "was Miss Goering afraid to go home alone?"

"Well," said Arnold, "it is not really very safe for a lady to wander about the streets or even to be in a taxi without an escort at so late an hour. Particularly if she has very far to go. Of course if she hadn't had so far to go I should naturally have accompanied her myself."

"You sound like a sissy, the way you talk," said his father. "I thought that you and your friends were not afraid of such things. I thought you were wild ones and that rape meant no more to you than flying a balloon."

"Oh, don't talk like that," said Arnold's mother, looking really horrified. "Why do you talk like that to them?"

"I wish you would go to bed," Arnold's father said. "As a matter of fact, I am going to order you to go to bed. You are getting a cold."

"Isn't he terrible?" said Arnold's mother, smiling at Miss Goering. "Even when there is company in the house he can't control his lion nature. He *has* a nature like a lion, roaring in the apartment all day long, and he gets so upset about Arnold and his friends."

Arnold's father stamped out of the room and they heard a door slam down the hall.

"Excuse me," said Arnold's mother to Miss Goering, "I didn't want to upset the party."

Miss Goering was very annoyed, for she found the old man quite exhilarating, and Arnold himself was depressing her more and more.

"I think I'll show you where you're going to sleep," said Arnold, getting up from the sofa and in so doing allowing some magazines to slide from his lap to the floor. "Oh, well," he said, "come this way. I'm pretty sleepy and disgusted with this whole affair."

Miss Goering followed Arnold reluctantly down the hall.

"Dear me," she said to Arnold, "I must confess that I am not sleepy. There is really nothing worse, is there?"

"No, it's dreadful," said Arnold. "I personally am ready to fall down on the carpet and lie there until tomorrow noon, I am so completely exhausted."

Miss Goering thought this remark a very inhospitable one and she began to feel a little frightened. Arnold was obliged to search for the key to the spare room, and Miss Goering was left standing alone in front of the door for some time.

"Control yourself," she whispered out loud, for her heart was beginning to beat very quickly. She wondered how she had ever allowed herself to come so far from her house and Miss Gamelon. Arnold returned finally with the key and opened the door to the room.

It was a very small room and much colder than the room in which they had been sitting. Miss Goering expected that Arnold would be extremely embarrassed about this, but although he shivered and rubbed his hands together, he said nothing. There were no curtains at the window, but there was a yellow shade, which had already been pulled down. Miss Goering threw herself down on the bed.

"Well, my dear," said Arnold, "good night. I'm going to bed. Maybe we'll go and see some paintings tomorrow, or if you like I'll come out to your house." He put his arms around her neck and kissed her very lightly on the lips and left the room.

She was so angry that there were tears in her eyes. Arnold stood outside of the door for a little while and then after a few minutes he walked away.

Miss Goering went over to the bureau and leaned her head on her hands. She remained in this position for a long time in spite of the fact that she was shivering with the cold. Finally there was a light tap on the door. She stopped crying as abruptly as she had begun and hurried to open the door. She saw Arnold's father standing outside in the badly lighted hall. He was wearing pink striped pajamas and he gave her a brief salute as a greeting. After that he stood very still, waiting apparently for Miss Goering to ask him in.

"Come in, come in," she said to him, "I'm delighted to see you. Heavens! I've had such a feeling of being deserted."

Arnold's father came in and balanced himself on the foot of Miss Goering's bed, where he sat swinging his legs. He lit his pipe in rather an affected manner and looked around him at the walls of the room.

"Well, lady," he said to her, "are you an artist too?"

"No," said Miss Goering. "I wanted to be a religious leader when I was young and now I just reside in my house and try not to be too unhappy. I have a friend living with me, which makes it easier."

"What do you think of my son?" he asked, winking at her.

"I have only just met him," said Miss Goering.

"You'll discover soon enough," said Arnold's father, "that he's a rather inferior person. He has no conception of what it is to fight. I shouldn't think women would like that very much. As a matter of fact, I don't think Arnold has had many women in his life. If you'll forgive me for passing this information on to you. I myself am used to fighting. I've fought my neighbors all my life instead of sitting down and having tea with them like Arnold. And my neighbors have fought me back like tigers too. Now that's not Arnold's kind of thing. My life's ambition always has been to be a notch higher on the tree than my neighbors and I was willing to admit complete disgrace too when I ended up perching a notch lower than anybody else I knew. I haven't been out in a good many years. Nobody comes to see me and I don't go to see anybody. Now, with Arnold and his friends nothing ever really begins or finishes. They're like fish in dirty water to me. If life don't please them one way and nobody likes them one place, then they go someplace else. They aim to please and be pleased; that's why it's so easy to come and bop them on the head from behind, because they've never done any serious hating in their lives."

"What a strange doctrine!" said Miss Goering.

"This is no doctrine," said Arnold's father. "These are my own ideas, taken from my own personal experience. I'm a great believer in personal experience, aren't you?"

"Oh, yes," said Miss Goering, "and I do think you're right about Arnold." She felt a curious delight in running down Arnold.

"Now Arnold," continued his father, and he seemed to grow gayer as he talked, "Arnold could never bear to have anyone catch him sitting on the lowest notch. Everyone knows how big your house is, and men who are willing to set their happiness by that are men of iron."

"Arnold is not an artist, anyway," put in Miss Goering.

"No, that is just it," said Arnold's father, getting more and more excited. "That's just it! He hasn't got the brawn nor the nerve nor the perseverance to be a good artist. An artist must have brawn and pluck and character. Arnold is like my wife," he continued. "I married her when she was twenty years old because of certain business interests. Every time I tell her that, she cries. She's another fool. She doesn't love me a bit, but it scares her to think of it, so that she cries. She's green-eyed with jealousy too and she's coiled around her family and her house like a python, although she doesn't have a good time here. Her life, as a matter of fact, is a wretched one, I must admit. Arnold's ashamed of her and I knock her around all day long. But in spite of the fact that she is a timid woman, she is capable of showing a certain amount of violence and brawn. Because she too, like myself, is faithful to one ideal, I suppose."

Just then there was a smart rap on the door. Arnold's father did not say a word, but Miss Goering called out in a clear voice: "Who is it?"

"It's me, Arnold's mother," came the answer. "Please let me in right away."

"Just one moment," said Miss Goering, "and I certainly shall."

"No," said Arnold's father. "Don't open the door. She has no right whatsoever to command anyone to open the door."

"You had better open it," said his wife. "Otherwise, I'll call the police, and I mean that very seriously. I have never threatened to call them before, you know."

"Yes, you did threaten to call them once before," said Arnold's father, looking very worried.

"The way I feel about my life," said Arnold's mother, "I'd just as soon open all the doors and let everyone come in the house and witness my disgrace."

"That's the last thing she'd ever do," said Arnold's father. "She talks like a fool when she's angry."

"I'll let her in," said Miss Goering, walking towards the door. She did not feel very frightened because Arnold's mother, judging from her voice, sounded more as though she was sad than angry. But when Miss Goering opened the door she was surprised to see that, on the contrary, her face was blanched with anger and her eyes were little narrow slits.

"Why do you pretend always to sleep so well?" said Arnold's father. This was the only remark he was able to think of, although he realized himself how inadequate it must have sounded to his wife.

"You're a harlot," said his wife to Miss Goering. Miss Goering was gravely shocked by this remark, and very much to her own amazement, for she had always thought that such things meant nothing to her.

"I am afraid you are entirely on the wrong track," said Miss Goering, "and I believe that some day we shall be great friends."

"I'll thank you to let me choose my own friends," Arnold's mother answered her. "I already have my friends, as a matter of fact, and I don't expect to add any more to my list, and least of all, you."

"Still, you can't tell," said Miss Goering rather weakly backing up a bit, and trying to lean in an easy manner against the bureau. Unfortunately, in calling Miss Goering a harlot Arnold's mother had suggested to her husband the stand that he would take to defend himself.

"How dare you!" he said. "How dare you call anyone that is staying in our house a harlot! You are violating the laws of hospitality to the hundredth degree and I am not going to stand for it."

"Don't bully me," said Arnold's mother. "She's got to go right away this minute or I will make a scandal and you'll be sorry."

"Look, my dear," said Arnold's father to Miss Goering. "Perhaps it would be better if you did go, for your own sake. It is beginning to grow light, so that you needn't be at all frightened."

Arnold's father looked around nervously and then hurried out of the room and down the hall, followed by his wife. Miss Goering heard a door slam and she imagined that they would continue their argument in private.

She herself ran headlong down the hall and out of the house. She found a taxicab after walking a little while and she hadn't been riding more than a few minutes before she fell asleep.

• • •

On the following day the sun was shining and both Miss Gamelon and Miss Goering were sitting on the lawn arguing. Miss Goering was stretched out on the grass. Miss Gamelon seemed the more discontented of the two. She was frowning and looking over her shoulder at the house, which was behind them. Miss Goering had her eyes shut and there was a faint smile on her face.

"Well," said Miss Gamelon turning around, "you know so little about what you're doing that it's a real crime against society that you have property in your hands. Property should be in the hands of people who like it."

"I think," said Miss Goering, "that I like it more than most people. It gives me a comfortable feeling of safety, as I have explained to you at least a dozen times. However, in order to work out my own little idea of salvation I really believe that it is necessary for me to live in some more tawdry place and particularly in some place where I was not born."

"In my opinion," said Miss Gamelon, "you could perfectly well work out your salvation during certain hours of the day without having to move everything."

"No," said Miss Goering, "that would not be in accordance with the spirit of the age."

Miss Gamelon shifted in her chair.

"The spirit of the age, whatever that is," she said, "I'm sure it can get along beautifully without you—probably would prefer it."

Miss Goering smiled and shook her head.

"The idea," said Miss Goering, "is to change first of our own volition and according to our own inner promptings before they impose completely arbitrary changes on us."

"I have no such promptings," said Miss Gamelon, "and I think you have a colossal nerve to identify yourself with anybody else at all. As a matter of fact, I think that if you leave this house, I shall give you up as a hopeless lunatic. After all, I am not the sort of person that is interested in living with a lunatic, nor is anyone else."

"When I have given you up," said Miss Goering, sitting up and throwing her head back in an exalted manner, "when I have given you up, I shall have given up more than my house, Lucy."

"That's one of your nastinesses," said Miss Gamelon. "It goes in one of my ears and then out the other."

Miss Goering shrugged her shoulders and went inside the house.

She stood for a while in the parlor rearranging some flowers in a bowl and she was just about to go to her room and sleep when Arnold appeared.

"Hello," said Arnold, "I meant to come and see you earlier, but I couldn't quite make it. We had one of those long family lunches. I think flowers look beautiful in this room."

"How is your father?" Miss Goering asked him.

"Oh," said Arnold, "he's all right, I guess. We have very little to do with each other." Miss Goering noticed that he was sweating again. He had evidently been terribly excited about arriving at her house, because he had forgotten to remove his straw hat.

"This is a really beautiful house," he told her. "It has a quality of past splendor about it that thrills me. You must hate to leave it ever. Well, Father seemed to be quite taken with you. Don't let him get too cocky. He thinks the girls are crazy about him."

"I'm devoted to him," said Miss Goering.

"Well, I hope that the fact that you're devoted to him," said Arnold, "won't interfere with our friendship, because I have decided to see quite a bit of you, providing of course that it is agreeable to you that I do."

"Of course," said Miss Goering, "whenever you like."

"I think that I shall like being here in your home, and you needn't feel that it's a strain. I'm quite happy to sit alone and think, because as you know I'm very anxious to establish myself in some other way than I am now established, which is not satisfactory to me. As you can well imagine, it is even impossible for me to give a dinner party for a few friends because neither Father nor Mother ever stirs from the house unless I do."

Arnold seated himself in a chair by a big bay window and stretched his legs out.

"Come here!" he said to Miss Goering, "and watch the wind rippling through the tops of the trees. There is nothing more lovely in the world." He looked up at her very seriously for a little while.

"Do you have some milk and some bread and marmalade?" he asked her. "I hope there is to be no ceremony between us."

Miss Goering was surprised that Arnold should ask for something to eat so shortly after his luncheon, and she decided that this was undoubtedly the reason why he was so fat.

"Certainly we have," she said sweetly, and she went away to give the servant the order.

Meanwhile Miss Gamelon had decided to come inside and if possible pursue Miss Goering with her argument. When Arnold saw her he realized that she was the companion about whom Miss Goering had spoken the night before.

He rose to his feet immediately, having decided that it was very important for him to make friends with Miss Gamelon.

Miss Gamelon herself was very pleased to see him, as they seldom had company and she enjoyed talking to almost anyone better than to Miss Goering.

They introduced themselves and Arnold pulled up a chair for Miss Gamelon near his own.

"You are Miss Goering's companion," he said to Miss Gamelon. "I think that's lovely."

"Do you think it's lovely?" asked Miss Gamelon. "That's very interesting indeed."

Arnold smiled happily at this remark of Miss Gamelon's and sat on without saying anything for a little while.

"This house is done in exquisite taste," he said finally, "and it is filled with rest and peace."

"It all depends on how you look at it," said Miss Gamelon quickly, jerking her head around and looking out of the window.

"There are certain people," she said, "who turn peace from the door as though it were a red dragon breathing fire out of its nostrils and there are certain people who won't leave God alone either."

Arnold leaned forward trying to appear deferential and interested at the same time.

"I think," he said gravely, "I think I understand what you mean to say."

Then they both looked out of the window at the same time and they saw Miss Goering in the distance wearing a cape over her shoulders and talking to a young man whom they were scarcely able to distinguish because he was directly against the sun.

"That's the agent," said Miss Gamelon. "I suppose there is nothing to look forward to from now on."

"What agent?" asked Arnold.

"The agent through whom she's going to sell her house," said Miss Gamelon. "Isn't it all too dreadful for words?"

"Oh, I'm sorry," said Arnold. "I think it's very foolish of her, but I suppose it's not my affair."

"We're going to live," added Miss Gamelon, "in a four-room frame house and do our own cooking. It's to be in the country surrounded by woods."

"That does sound gloomy, doesn't it?" said Arnold. "But why should Miss Goering have decided to do such a thing?"

"She says it is only a beginning in a tremendous scheme."

Arnold seemed to be very sad. He no longer spoke to Miss Gamelon but merely pursed his lips and looked at the ceiling.

"I suppose the most important thing in the world," he said at length, "is friendship and understanding." He looked at Miss Gamelon questioningly. He seemed to have given up something.

"Well, Miss Gamelon," he said again, "do you not agree with me that friendship and understanding are the most important things in the world?"

"Yes," said Miss Gamelon, "and keeping your head is, too."

Soon Miss Goering came in with a batch of papers under her arm.

"These," she said, "are the contracts. My, they are lengthy, but I think the agent is a sweet man. He said he thought this house was lovely." She held out the contracts first to Arnold and then to Miss Gamelon.

"I should think," said Miss Gamelon, "that you would be afraid to look in the mirror for fear of seeing something too wild and peculiar. I don't want to have to look at these contracts. Please take them off my lap right away. Jesus God Almighty!"

Miss Goering, as a matter of fact, did look a little wild, and Miss Gamelon with a wary eye had noticed immediately that the hand in which she held the contracts was trembling.

"Where is your little house, Miss Goering?" Arnold asked her, trying to introduce a more natural note into the conversation.

"It's on an island," said Miss Goering, "not far from the city by ferryboat. I remember having visited this island as a child and always having disliked it because one can smell the glue factories from the mainland even when walking through the woods or across the fields. One end of the island is very well populated, although you can only buy third-rate goods in any of the stores. Farther out the island is wilder and more old-fashioned; nevertheless there is a little train that meets the ferry frequently and carries you out to the other end. There you land in a little town that is quite lost and looks very tough, and you feel a bit frightened, I think, to find that the mainland opposite the point is as squalid as the island itself and offers you no protection at all."

"You seem to have looked the situation over very carefully and from every angle," said Miss Gamelon. "My compliments to you!" She waved at Miss Goering from her seat, but one could easily see that she was not feeling frivolous in the least.

Arnold shifted about uneasily in his chair. He coughed and then he spoke very gently to Miss Goering.

"I am sure that the island has certain advantages too, which you know about, but perhaps you prefer to surprise us with them rather than disappoint us."

"I know of none at the moment," said Miss Goering. "Why, are you coming with us?"

"I think that I would like to spend quite a bit of time with you out there; that is, if you will invite me."

Arnold was sad and uneasy, but he felt that he must at any cost remain close to Miss Goering in whatever world she chose to move.

"If you will invite me," he said again, "I will be glad to come out with you for a little while anyway and we will see how it goes. I could continue to keep up my end of the apartment that I share with my parents without having to spend all my time there. But I don't advise you to sell your beautiful house; rather rent it or board it up while you are away. Certainly you might have a change of heart and want to return to it."

Miss Gamelon flushed with pleasure.

"That would be too human a thing for her to consider doing," she said, but she looked a little more hopeful.

Miss Goering seemed to be dreaming and not listening to what either of them was saying.

"Well," said Miss Gamelon, "aren't you going to answer him? He said: why not board your house up or rent it and then if you have a change of heart you can return to it."

"Oh, no," said Miss Goering. "Thank you very much, but I couldn't do that. It wouldn't make much sense to do that."

Arnold coughed to hide his embarrassment at having suggested something so obviously displeasing to Miss Goering.

"I mustn't," he said to himself, "I mustn't align myself too much on the side of Miss Gamelon, or Miss Goering will begin to think that my mind is of the same caliber."

"Perhaps it is better after all," he said aloud, "to sell everything."

2

Mr. and Mrs. Copperfield stood on the foredeck of the boat as it sailed into the harbor at Panama. Mrs. Copperfield was very glad to see land at last.

"You must admit now," she said to Mr. Copperfield, "that the land is nicer than the sea." She herself had a great fear of drowning.

"It isn't only being afraid of the sea," she continued, "but it's boring. It's the same thing all the time. The colors are beautiful, of course."

Mr. Copperfield was studying the shore line.

"If you stand still and look between the buildings on the docks," he said, "you'll be able to catch a glimpse of some green trains loaded with bananas. They seem to go by every quarter of an hour."

His wife did not answer him; instead she put on the sun-helmet which she had been carrying in her hand.

"Aren't you beginning to feel the heat already? I am," she said to him at last. As she received no answer she moved along the rail and looked down at the water.

Presently a stout woman whose acquaintance she had made on the boat came up to talk with her. Mrs. Copperfield brightened.

"You've had your hair marcelled!" she said. The woman smiled.

"Now remember," she said to Mrs. Copperfield, "the minute you get to your hotel, stretch yourself out and rest. Don't let them drag you through the streets, no matter what kind of a wild time they promise you. Nothing but monkeys in the streets anyway. There isn't a fine-looking person in the whole town that isn't connected with the American Army, and the Americans stick pretty much in their own quarter. The American quarter is called Cristobal. It's separated from Colon. Colon is full of nothing but half-breeds and monkeys. Cristobal is nice. Everyone in Cristobal has got his own little screened-in porch. They'd never dream of screening themselves in, the monkeys in Colon. They don't know when a mosquito's biting them anyway, and even if they did know they wouldn't lift their arm up to shoo him off. Eat plenty of fruit and be careful of the stores. Most of them are owned by Hindus. They're just like Jews, you know. They'll gyp you right and left."

"I'm not interested in buying anything," said Mrs. Copperfield, "but may I come and visit you while I'm in Colon?"

"I love you, dear," answered the woman, "but I like to spend every minute with my boy while I'm here."

"That's all right," said Mrs. Copperfield.

"Of course it's all right. You've got that beautiful husband of yours."

"That doesn't help," said Mrs. Copperfield, but no sooner had she said this than she was horrified at herself.

"Well now, you've had a tussle?" said the woman.

"No."

"Then I think you're a terrible little woman talking that way about your husband," she said, walking away. Mrs. Copperfield hung her head and went back to stand beside Mr. Copperfield.

"Why do you speak to such dopes?" he asked.

She did not answer.

"Well," he said, "for Heaven's sake, look at the scenery now, will you?"

They got into a taxicab and Mr. Copperfield insisted on going to a hotel right in the center of town. Normally all tourists with even a small amount of money stayed at the Hotel Washington, overlooking the sea, a few miles out of Colon.

"I don't believe," Mr. Copperfield said to his wife, "I don't believe in spending money on a luxury that can only be mine for a week at the most. I think it's more fun to buy objects which will last me perhaps a lifetime. We can certainly find a hotel in the town that will be comfortable. Then we will be free to spend our money on more exciting things."

"The room in which I sleep is so important to me," Mrs. Copperfield said. She was nearly moaning.

"My dear, a room is really only a place in which to sleep and dress. If it is quiet and the bed is comfortable, nothing more is necessary. Don't you agree with me?"

"You know very well I don't agree with you."

"If you are going to be miserable, we'll go to the Hotel Washington," said Mr. Copperfield. Suddenly he lost his dignity. His eyes clouded over and he pouted. "But I'll be wretched there, I can assure you. It's going to be so God-damned dull." He was like a baby and Mrs. Copperfield was obliged to comfort him. He had a trick way of making her feel responsible.

"After all, it's mostly my money," she said to herself. "I'm footing the bulk of the expenditures for this trip." Nevertheless, she was unable to gain a sense of power by reminding herself of this. She was completely dominated by Mr. Copperfield, as she was by almost anyone with whom she came in contact. Still, certain people who knew her well affirmed that she was capable of suddenly making a very radical and independent move without a soul to back her up.

She looked out the window of the taxicab and she noticed that there was a terrific amount of activity going on around her in the streets. The people, for the most part Negroes and uniformed men from the fleets of all nations, were running in and out and making so much noise that Mrs. Copperfield wondered if it was not a holiday of some kind.

"It's like a city that is being constantly looted," said her husband.

The houses were painted in bright colors and they had wide porches on the upper floors, supported beneath by long wooden posts. Thus they formed a kind of arcade to shade the people walking in the street.

"This architecture is ingenious," remarked Mr. Copperfield. "The streets would be unbearable if one had to walk along them with nothing overhead."

"You could not stand that, mister," said the cab-driver, "to walk along with nothing over your head."

"Anyway," said Mrs. Copperfield, "do let's choose one of these hotels quickly and get into it."

They found one right in the heart of the red-light district and agreed to look at some rooms on the fifth floor. The manager had told them that these were sure to be the least noisy. Mrs. Copperfield, who was afraid of lifts, decided to go up the stairs on foot and wait for her husband to arrive with the luggage. Having climbed to the fifth floor, she was surprised to find that the main hall contained at least a hundred straight-backed dining-room chairs and nothing more. As she looked around, her anger mounted and she could barely wait for Mr. Copperfield to arrive on the lift in order to tell him what she thought of him. "I must get to the Hotel Washington," she said to herself.

Mr. Copperfield finally arrived, walking beside a boy with the luggage. She ran up to him.

"It's the ugliest thing I've ever seen," she said.

"Wait a second, please, and let me count the luggage; I want to make sure it's all here."

"As far as I'm concerned, it could be at the bottom of the sea—all of it."

"Where's my typewriter?" asked Mr. Copperfield.

"Talk to me this minute," said his wife, beside herself with anger.

"Do you care whether or not you have a private bath?" asked Mr. Copperfield.

"No, no. I don't care about that. It's not a question of comfort at all. It's something much more than that."

Mr. Copperfield chuckled. "You're so crazy," he said to her with indulgence. He was delighted to be in the tropics at last and he was more than pleased with himself that he had managed to dissuade his wife from stopping at a ridiculously expensive hotel where they would have been surrounded by tourists. He realized that this hotel was sinister, but that was what he loved.

They followed the bellhop to one of the rooms, and no sooner had they arrived there than Mrs. Copperfield began pushing the door backwards and forwards. It opened both ways and could only be locked by means of a little hook.

"Anyone could break into this room," said Mrs. Copperfield.

"I dare say they could, but I don't think they would be very likely to, do you?" Mr. Copperfield made a point of never reassuring his wife. He gave her fears their just due. However, he did not insist, and they decided upon another room, with a stronger door.

• • •

Mrs. Copperfield was amazed at her husband's vivacity. He had washed and gone out to buy a papaya.

She lay on the bed thinking.

"Now," she said to herself, "when people believed in God they carried Him from one place to another. They carried Him through the jungles and across the Arctic Circle. God watched over everybody, and all men were brothers. Now there is nothing to carry with you from one place to another, and as far as I'm concerned, these people might as well be kangaroos; yet somehow there must be someone here who will remind me of something . . . I must try to find a nest in this outlandish place."

Mrs. Copperfield's sole object in life was to be happy, although people who had observed her behavior over a period of years would have been surprised to discover that this was all.

She rose from her bed and pulled Miss Goering's present, a manicuring set, from her grip. "Memory," she whispered. "Memory of the things I have loved since I was a child. My husband is a man without memory." She felt intense pain at the thought of this man whom she liked above all other people, this man for whom each thing he had not yet known was a joy. For her, all that which was not already an old dream was an outrage. She got back on her bed and fell sound asleep.

When she awoke, Mr. Copperfield was standing near the foot of the bed eating a papaya.

"You must try some," he said. "It gives you lots of energy and besides it's delicious. Won't you have some?" He looked at her shyly.

"Where have you been?" she asked him.

"Oh, walking through the streets. As a matter of fact, I've walked for miles. You should come out, really. It's a madhouse. The streets are full of soldiers and sailors and whores. The women are all in long dresses . . . incredibly cheap dresses. They'll all talk to you. Come on out."

• • •

They were walking through the streets arm in arm. Mrs. Copperfield's forehead was burning hot and her hands were cold. She felt something trembling in the pit of her stomach. When she looked ahead of her the very end of the street seemed to bend and then straighten out again. She told this to Mr. Copperfield and he explained that it was a result of their having so recently come off the boat. Above their heads the children were jumping up and down on the wooden porches and making the houses shake. Someone bumped against Mrs. Copperfield's shoulder and she was almost knocked over. At the same time she was very much aware of the strong and fragrant odor of rose perfume. The person who had collided with her was a Negress in a pink silk evening dress.

"I can't tell you how sorry I am. I can't tell you," she said to them. Then she looked around her vaguely and began to hum.

"I told you it was a madhouse," Mr. Copperfield said to his wife.

"Listen," said the Negress, "go down the next street and you'll like it better. I've got to meet my beau over at that bar." She pointed it out to them. "That's a beautiful barroom. Everyone goes in there," she said. She moved up closer and addressed herself solely to Mrs. Copperfield. "You come along with me, darling, and you'll have the happiest time you've ever had before. I'll be your type. Come on."

She took Mrs. Copperfield's hand in her own and started to drag her away from Mr. Copperfield. She was bigger than either of them.

"I don't believe that she wants to go to a bar just now," said Mr. Copperfield. "We'd like to explore the town awhile first."

The Negress caressed Mrs. Copperfield's face with the palm of her hand. "Is that what you want to do, darling, or do you want to come along with me?" A policeman stopped and stood a few feet away from them. The Negress released Mrs. Copperfield's hand and bounded across the street laughing.

"Wasn't that the strangest thing you've ever seen?" said Mrs. Copperfield, breathlessly.

"You better mind your own business," said the policeman. "Why don't you go over and look at the stores? Everybody walks along the streets where the stores are. Buy something for your uncle or your cousin."

"No, that's not what I want to do," said Mrs. Copperfield.

"Well, then, go to a movie," said the policeman, walking away.

Mr. Copperfield was hysterical with laughter. He had his handkerchief up to his mouth. "This is the sort of thing I love," he managed to say. They walked along farther and turned down another street. The sun was setting and the air was still and hot. On this street there were no balconies, only little one-story houses. In front of every door at least one woman was seated. Mrs. Copperfield walked up to the window of one house and looked in. The room inside was almost entirely filled by a large double bed with an extremely bumpy mattress over which was spread a lace throw. An electric bulb under a lavender chiffon lamp shade threw a garish light over the bed, and there was a fan stamped *Panama City* spread open on the pillow.

The woman seated in front of this particular house was rather old. She sat on a stool with her elbows resting on her knees, and it seemed to Mrs. Copperfield, who had now turned to look at her, that she was probably a West Indian type. She was flat-chested and rawboned, with very muscular arms and shoulders. Her long disgruntled-looking face and part of her neck were carefully covered with a light-colored face powder, but her chest and arms remained dark. Mrs. Copperfield was amused to see that her dress was of lavender theatrical gauze. There was an attractive gray streak in her hair.

The Negress turned around, and when she saw that both Mr. and Mrs. Copperfield were watching her, she stood up and smoothed the folds of her dress. She was almost a giantess.

"Both of you for a dollar," she said.

"A dollar," Mrs. Copperfield repeated after her. Mr. Copperfield, who had been standing nearby at the curb, came closer to them.

"Frieda," he said, "let's walk down some more streets."

"Oh, please!" said Mrs. Copperfield. "Wait a minute."

"A dollar is the best price I can make," said the Negress.

"If you care to stay here," suggested Mr. Copperfield, "I'll walk around a bit and come back for you in a little while. Maybe you'd better have some money with you. Here is a dollar and thirty-five cents, just in case. . . ."

"I want to talk to her," said Mrs. Copperfield, looking fixedly into space.

"I'll see you, then, in a few minutes. I'm restless," he announced, and he walked away.

"I love to be free," Mrs. Copperfield said to the woman after he had left. "Shall we go into your little room? I've been admiring it through the window. . . ."

Before she had finished her phrase the woman was pushing her through the door with both hands and they were inside the room. There was no rug on the floor, and the walls were bare. The only adornments were those which had been visible from the street. They sat down on the bed.

"I had a little gramophone in that corner over there," said the woman. "Someone who came off a ship lent it to me. His friend came and took it back."

"Te-ta-ta-tee-ta-ta," she said and tapped her heels for a few seconds. She took both Mrs. Copperfield's hands in her own and pulled her off the bed. "Come on now, honey." She hugged Mrs. Copperfield to her. "You're awful little and very sweet. You *are* sweet, and maybe you are lonesome." Mrs. Copperfield put her cheek on the woman's breast. The smell of the theatrical gauze reminded her of her first part in a school play. She smiled up at the Negress, looking as tender and as gentle as she was able.

"What do you do in the afternoons?" she asked the woman.

"Play cards. Go to a movie. . . ."

Mrs. Copperfield stepped away from her. Her cheeks were flame-red. They both listened to the people walking by. They could now hear every word that was being said outside the window. The Negress was frowning. She wore a look of deep concern.

"Time is gold, honey," she said to Mrs. Copperfield, "but maybe you're too young to realize that."

Mrs. Copperfield shook her head. She felt sad, looking at the Negress. "I'm thirsty," she said. Suddenly they heard a man's voice saying:

"You didn't expect to see me back so soon, Podie?" Then several girls laughed hysterically. The Negress's eyes came to life.

"Give me one dollar! Give me one dollar!" she screamed excitedly at Mrs. Copperfield. "You have stayed your time here anyway." Mrs. Copperfield hurriedly gave her a dollar and the Negress rushed out into the street. Mrs. Copperfield followed her.

In front of the house several girls were hanging onto a heavy man who was wearing a crushed linen suit. When he saw Mrs. Copperfield's Negress in the lavender dress, he broke away from the others and put his arms around her. The Negress rolled her eyes joyously and led him into the house without so much as nodding good-by to Mrs. Copperfield. Very shortly the others ran down the street and Mrs. Copperfield was left alone. People passed by on either side of her, but none of them interested her yet. On the other hand, she herself was of great interest to everyone, particularly to those women who were seated in front of their doors. She was soon accosted by a girl with fuzzy hair.

"Buy me something, Momma," said the girl.

As Mrs. Copperfield did not answer but simply gave the girl a long sad look, the girl said:

"Momma, you can pick it out yourself. You can buy me even a feather, I don't care." Mrs. Copperfield shuddered. She thought she must be dreaming.

"What do you mean, a feather? What do you mean?"

The girl squirmed with delight.

"Oh, Momma," she said in a voice which broke in her throat. "Oh, Momma, you're funny! You're so funny. I don't know what is a feather, but anything you want with your heart, you know."

They walked down the street to a store and came out with a little box of face powder. The girl said good-by and disappeared round the corner with some friends. Once again Mrs. Copperfield was alone. The hacks went past filled with tourists. "Tourists, generally speaking," Mrs. Copperfield had written in her journal, "are human beings so impressed with the importance and immutability of their own manner of living that they are capable of traveling through the most fantastic places without experiencing anything more than a visual reaction. The hardier tourists find that one place resembles another."

Very soon Mr. Copperfield came back and joined her. "Did you have a wonderful time?" he asked her.

She shook her head and looked up at him. Suddenly she felt so tired that she began to cry.

"Cry-baby," said Mr. Copperfield.

Someone came up behind them. A low voice said: "She was lost?" They turned around to see an intelligent-looking girl with sharp features and curly hair standing right behind them. "I wouldn't leave her in the streets here if I were you," she said.

"She wasn't lost; she was just depressed," Mr. Copperfield explained.

"Would you think I was fresh if I asked you to come to a nice restaurant where we can all eat dinner?" asked the girl. She was really quite pretty.

"Let's go," said Mrs. Copperfield vehemently. "By all means." She was now excited; she had a feeling that this girl would be all right. Like most people, she never really believed that one terrible thing would happen after another.

The restaurant wasn't really nice. It was very dark and very long and there was no one in it at all.

"Wouldn't you rather eat somewhere else?" Mrs. Copperfield asked the girl.

"Oh no! I would never go anywhere else. I'll tell you if you are not angry. I can get a little bit of money here when I come and bring some people."

"Well, let me give you the money and we'll go somewhere else. I'll give you whatever he gives you," said Mrs. Copperfield.

"That's silly," said the girl. "That's very silly."

"I have heard there is a place in this city where we can order wonderful lobster. Couldn't we go there?" Mrs. Copperfield was pleading with the girl now.

"No—that's silly." She called a waiter who had just arrived with some newspapers under his arm.

"Adalberto, bring us some meat and some wine. Meat first." This she said in Spanish.

"How well you speak English!" said Mr. Copperfield.

"I always love to be with Americans when I can," said the girl.

"Do you think they're generous?" asked Mr. Copperfield.

"Oh, sure," said the girl. "Sure they're generous. They're generous when they have the money. They're even more generous when they've got their family with them. I once knew a man. He was an American man. A real one, and he was staying at the Hotel Washington. You know that's the most beautiful hotel in the world. In the afternoon every day his wife would take a siesta. He would come quickly in a taxicab to Colon and he was so excited and frightened that he would not get back to his wife on time that he would never take me into a room and so he would go with me instead to a store and he would say to me: 'Quick, quick—pick something—anything that you want, but be in a hurry about it.' "

"How terrifying!" said Mrs. Copperfield.

"It was terrible," said the Spanish girl. "I always went so crazy that once I was really crazy and I said to him: 'All right, I will buy this pipe for my uncle.' I don't like my uncle, but I had to give it to him."

Mr. Copperfield roared with laughter.

"Funny, isn't it?" said the girl. "I tell you if he ever comes back

I will never buy another pipe for my uncle when he takes me to the store. She's not a bad-looker."

"Who?" asked Mr. Copperfield.

"Your wife."

"I look terrible tonight," said Mrs. Copperfield.

"Anyway it does not matter because you are married. You have nothing to worry about."

"She'll be furious with you if you tell her that," said Mr. Copperfield.

"Why will she be furious? That is the most beautiful thing in the whole world, not to have something to worry about."

"That is not what beauty is made of," interposed Mrs. Copperfield. "What has the absence of worry to do with beauty?"

"That has everything to do with what is beautiful in the world. When you wake up in the morning and the first minute you open your eyes and you don't know who you are or what your life has been—that is beautiful. Then when you know who you are and what day in your life it is and you still think you are sailing in the air like a happy bird—that is beautiful. That is, when you don't have any worries. You can't tell me you like to worry."

Mr. Copperfield simpered. After dinner he suddenly felt very tired and he suggested that they go home, but Mrs. Copperfield was much too nervous, so she asked the Spanish girl if she would not consent to spend a little more time in her company. The girl said that she would if Mrs. Copperfield did not mind returning with her to the hotel where she lived.

They said good-by to Mr. Copperfield and started on their way.

The walls of the Hotel de las Palmas were wooden and painted a bright green. There were a good many bird-cages standing in the halls and hanging from the ceilings. Some of them were empty. The girl's room was on the second floor and had brightly painted wooden walls the same as the corridors.

"Those birds sing all day long," said the girl, motioning to Mrs. Copperfield to sit down on the bed beside her. "Sometimes I say to myself: 'Little fools, what are you singing about in your cages?' And then I think: 'Pacifica, you are just as much a fool as those birds. You are also in a cage because you don't have any money. Last night you were laughing for three hours with a German man because he had given you some drinks. And you thought he was stupid.' I laugh in my cage and they sing in their cage."

"Oh well," said Mrs. Copperfield, "there really is no rapport between ourselves and birds."

"You don't think it is true?" asked Pacifica with feeling. "I tell you it is true."

She pulled her dress over her head and stood before Mrs. Copperfield in her underslip.

"Tell me," she said, "What do you think of those beautiful silk kimonos that the Hindu men sell in their shops? If I were with such a rich husband I would tell him to buy me one of those kimonos. You don't know how lucky you are. I would go with him every day to the stores and make him buy me pretty things instead of standing around and crying like a little baby. Men don't like to see women cry. You think they like to see women cry?"

Mrs. Copperfield shrugged her shoulders. "I can't think," she said.

"You're right. They like to see women laugh. Women have got to laugh all night. You watch some pretty girl one time. When she laughs she is ten years older. That is because she does it so much. You are ten years older when you laugh."

"True," said Mrs. Copperfield.

"Don't feel bad," said Pacifica. "I like women very much. I like women sometimes better than men. I like my grandmother and my mother and my sisters. We always had a good time together, the women in my house. I was always the best one. I was the smartest one and the one who did the most work. Now I wish I was back there in my nice house, contented. But I still want too many things, you know. I am lazy but I have a terrible temper too. I like these men that I meet very much. Sometimes they tell me what they will do in their future life when they get off the boat. I always wish for them that it will happen very soon. The damn boats. When they tell me they just want to go around the world all their life on a boat I tell them: 'You don't know what you're missing. I'm through with you, boy.' I don't like them when they are like that. But now I am in love with this nice man who is here in business. Most of the time he can pay my rent for me. Not always every week. He is very happy to have me. Most of the men are very happy to have me. I don't hold my head too high for that. It's from God that it comes." Pacifica crossed herself.

"I once was in love with an older woman," said Mrs. Copperfield eagerly. "She was no longer beautiful, but in her face I found fragments of beauty which were much more exciting to me than any beauty that I have known at its height. But who hasn't loved an older person? Good Lord!"

"You like things which are not what other people like, don't you? I would like to have this experience of loving an older woman. I think that is sweet, but I really am always in love with some nice man. It is lucky for me, I think. Some of the girls, they can't fall in love any more. They only think of money, money, money. You don't think so much about money, do you?" She asked Mrs. Copperfield.

"No, I don't."

"Now we rest a little while, yes?" The girl lay down on the bed and motioned to Mrs. Copperfield to lie down beside her. She yawned, folded Mrs. Copperfield's hand in her own, and fell asleep almost instantly. Mrs. Copperfield thought that she might as well get some sleep too. At that moment she felt very peaceful.

They were awakened by a terrific knocking at the door. Mrs. Copperfield opened her eyes and in a second she was a prey to the most overwhelming terror. She looked at Pacifica, and her friend's face was not very much more reassuring than her own.

"Callate!" she whispered to Mrs. Copperfield reverting to her native tongue.

"What is it? What is it?" asked Mrs. Copperfield in a harsh voice. "I don't understand Spanish."

"Don't say a word," repeated Pacifica in English.

"I can't lie here without saying a word. I know I can't. What is it?"

"Drunken man. In love with me. I know him well. He hurt me very bad when I sleep with him. His boat has come in again."

The knocking grew more insistent and they heard a man's voice saying:

"I know you are there, Pacifica, so open the bloody door."

"Oh, open it, Pacifica!" pleaded Mrs. Copperfield, jumping up from the bed. "Nothing could be worse than this suspense."

"Don't be crazy. Maybe he is drunk enough and he will go away."

Mrs. Copperfield's eyes were glazed. She was becoming hysterical.

"No, no—I have always promised myself that I would open the door if someone was trying to break in. He will be less of an enemy then. The longer he stays out there, the angrier he will get. The first thing I will say to him when I open the door is: 'We are your friends,' and then perhaps he will be less angry."

"If you make me even more crazy than I am I don't know what to do," said Pacifica. "Now we just wait here and see if he goes away. We might move this bureau against the door. Will you help me move it against the door?"

"I can't push anything!" Mrs. Copperfield was so weak that she slid along the wall onto the floor.

"Have I got to break the God-damned door in?" the man was saying.

Mrs. Copperfield rose to her feet, staggered over to the door, and opened it.

The man who came in was hatchet-faced and very tall. He had obviously had a great deal to drink.

"Hello, Meyer," said Pacifica. "Can't you let me get some sleep?" She hesitated a minute, and as he did not answer her she said again: "I was trying to get some sleep."

"I was tight asleep," said Mrs. Copperfield. Her voice was higher than usual and her face was very bright. "I am sorry we did not hear you right away. We must have kept you waiting a long time."

"Nobody ever kept me waiting a long time," said Meyer, getting redder in the face. Pacifica's eyes were narrowing. She was beginning to lose her temper.

"Get out of my room," she said to Meyer.

In answer to this, Meyer fell diagonally across the bed, and the impact of his body was so great that it almost broke the slats.

"Let's get out of here quickly," said Mrs. Copperfield to Pacifica. She was no longer able to show any composure. For one moment she had hoped that the enemy would suddenly burst into tears as they do sometimes in dreams, but now she was convinced that this would not happen. Pacifica was growing more and more furious.

"Listen to me, Meyer," she was saying. "You go back into the street right away. Because I'm not going to do anything with you except hit you in the nose if you don't go away. If you were not such hot stuff we could sit downstairs together and drink a glass of rum. I have hundreds of boy friends who just like to talk to me and drink with me until they are stiffs under the table. But you always try to bother me. You are like an ape-man. I want to be quiet."

"Who the hell cares about your house!" Meyer bellowed at her. "I could put all your houses together in a row and shoot at them like they were ducks. A boat's better than a house any day! Any time! Come rain, come shine! Come the end of the world!"

"No one is talking about houses except you," said Pacifica, stamping her foot, "and I don't want to listen to your foolish talk."

"Why did you lock the door, then, if you weren't living in this house like you were duchesses having tea together, and praying that none of us were ever going to come on shore again. You were afraid I'd spoil the furniture and spill something on the floor. My mother had a house, but I always slept in the house next door to her house. That's how much I care about houses!"

"You misunderstand," said Mrs. Copperfield in a trembling voice. She wanted very much to remind him gently that this was not a house but a room in a hotel. However, she felt not only afraid but ashamed to make this remark.

"Jesus Christ, I'm disgusted," Pacifica said to Mrs. Copperfield without even bothering to lower her voice.

Meyer did not seem to hear this, but instead he leaned over the edge of the bed with a smile on his face and stretched one arm towards Pacifica. He managed to get hold of the hem of her slip and pull her towards him.

"Not as long as I live!" Pacifica screamed at him, but he had already wrapped his arms around her waist and he was kneeling on the bed, pulling her towards him.

"Housekeeper," he said, laughing, "I'll bet if I took you out to sea you'd vomit. You'd mess up the boat. Now lie down here and stop talking."

Pacifica looked darkly at Mrs. Copperfield for a moment. "Well then," she said, "give me first the money, because I don't trust you. I will sleep with you only for my rent."

He dealt her a terrific blow on the mouth and split her lip. The blood started to run down her chin.

Mrs. Copperfield rushed out of the room. "I'll get help, Pacifica," she yelled over her shoulder. She ran down the hall and down the stairs, hoping to find someone to whom she could report Pacifica's plight, but she knew she would not have the courage to approach any men. On the ground floor she caught sight of a middle-aged woman who was knitting in her room with the door ajar; Mrs. Copperfield rushed in to her.

"Do you know Pacifica?" she gasped.

"Certainly I know Pacifica," said the woman. She spoke like an Englishwoman who has lived for many years among Americans. "I know everybody that lives here for more than two nights. I'm the proprietor of this hotel."

"Well then, do something quickly. Mr. Meyer is in there and he's very drunk."

"I don't do anything with Meyer when he's drunk." The woman was silent for a moment and the idea of doing something with Meyer struck her sense of humor and she chuckled. "Just imagine it," she said, " 'Mr. Meyer, will you kindly leave the room? Pacifica is tired of you. Ha-ha-ha—*Pacifica* is tired of you.' Have a seat, lady, and calm down. There's some gin in that cut-glass decanter over there next to the avocados. Would you like some?"

"You know I'm not used to violence," Mrs. Copperfield said. She helped herself to some gin, and repeated that she was not used to violence. "I doubt that I shall ever get over this evening. The stubbornness of that man. He was like an insane person."

"Meyer isn't insane," said the proprietress. "Some of them are much worse. He told me he was very fond of Pacifica. I've always been decent to him and he's never given me any trouble."

They heard screams from the next floor. Mrs. Copperfield recognized Pacifica's voice.

"Oh, please, let's get the police," pleaded Mrs. Copperfield.

"Are you crazy?" said the woman. "Pacifica doesn't want to get mixed up with the police. She would rather have both legs chopped off. I can promise you that is true."

"Well then, let's go up there," said Mrs. Copperfield. "I'm ready to do anything."

"Keep seated, Mrs.—what's your name? My name is Mrs. Quill."

"I'm Mrs. Copperfield."

"Well, you see, Mrs. Copperfield, Pacifica can take care of herself better than we can take care of her. The fewer people that get involved in a thing, the better off everybody is. That's one law I have here in the hotel."

"All right," said Mrs. Copperfield, "but meanwhile she might be murdered."

"People don't murder as easy as that. They do a lot of hitting around but not so much murdering. I've had some murders here, but not many. I've discovered that most things turn out all right. Of course some of them turn out bad."

"I wish I could feel as relaxed as you about everything. I don't understand how you can sit here, and I don't understand how Pacifica can go through things like this without ending up in an insane asylum."

"Well, she's had a lot of experience with these men. I don't think she's scared really. She's much tougher than us. She's just bothered. She likes to be able to have her room and do what she likes. I think sometimes women don't know what they want. Do you think maybe she has a little yen for Meyer?"

"How could she possibly? I don't understand what you mean."

"Well now, that boy she says she's in love with; now, I don't really think she's in love with him at all. She's had one after another of them like that. All nice dopes. They worship the ground she walks on. I think she gets so jealous and nervous while Meyer's away that she likes to pretend to herself that she likes these other little men better.

When Meyer comes back she really believes she's mad at him for interfering. Now, maybe I'm right and maybe I'm wrong, but I think it goes a little something like that."

"I think it's impossible. She wouldn't allow him to hurt her, then, before she went to bed with him."

"Sure she would," said Mrs. Quill, "but I don't know anything about such things. Pacifica's a nice girl, though. She comes from a nice family too."

Mrs. Copperfield drank her gin and enjoyed it.

"She'll be coming down here soon to have a talk," said Mrs. Quill. "It's balmy here and they all enjoy themselves. They talk and they drink and they make love; they go on picnics; they go to the movies; they dance, sometimes all night long. . . . I need never be lonely unless I want to. . . . I can always go and dance with them if I feel like it. I have a fellow who takes me out to the dancing places whenever I want to go and I can always string along. I love it here. Wouldn't go back home for a load of monkeys. It's hot sometimes, but mostly balmy, and nobody's in a hurry. Sex doesn't interest me and I sleep like a baby. I am never bothered with dreams unless I eat something which sits on my stomach. You have to pay a price when you indulge yourself. I have a terrific yen for lobster à la Newburg, you see. I know exactly what I'm doing when I eat it. I go to Bill Grey's restaurant I should say about once every month with this fellow."

"Go on," said Mrs. Copperfield, who was enjoying this.

"Well, we order lobster à la Newburg. I tell you it's the most delicious thing in the world. . . ."

"How do you like frogs' legs?" asked Mrs. Copperfield.

"Lobster à la Newburg for me."

"You sound so happy I have a feeling I'm going to nestle right in here, in this hotel. How would you like that?"

"You do what you want to with your own life. That's my motto. For how long would you want to stay?"

"Oh, I don't know," said Mrs. Copperfield. "Do you think I'd have fun here?"

"Oh, no end of fun," said the proprietess. "Dancing, drinking . . . all the things that are pleasant in this world. You don't need much money, you know. The men come off the ships with their pockets bulging. I tell you this place is God's own town, or maybe the Devil's." She laughed heartily.

"No end of fun," she repeated. She got up from her chair with some difficulty and went over to a box-like phonograph which stood in the corner of the room. After winding it up she put on a cowboy song.

"You can always listen to this," she said to Mrs. Copperfield, "whenever your little heart pleases. There are the needles and the records and all you've got to do is wind it up. When I'm not here, you can sit in this rocker and listen. I've got famous people singing on those records like Sophie Tucker and Al Jolson from the United States, and I say that music is the ear's wine."

"And I suppose reading would be very pleasant in this room—at the same time that one listened to the gramophone," said Mrs. Copperfield.

"Reading—you can do all the reading you want."

They sat for some time listening to records and drinking gin. After an hour or so Mrs. Quill saw Pacifica coming down the hall. "Now," she said to Mrs. Copperfield, "here comes your friend."

Pacifica had on a little silk dress and bedroom slippers. She had made up her face very carefully and she had perfumed herself.

"Look what Meyer brought me," she said, coming towards them and showing them a very large wrist watch with a radium dial. She seemed to be in a very pleasant mood.

"You been talking here one to the other," she said, smiling at them kindly. "Now suppose we all three of us go and take a walk through the street and get some beer or whatever we want."

"That would be nice," said Mrs. Copperfield. She was beginning to worry a bit about Mr. Copperfield. He hated her to disappear this way for a long time because it gave him an unbalanced feeling and interfered very much with his sleep. She promised herself to drop by the room and let him know that she was still out, but the very idea of going near the hotel made her shudder.

"Hurry up, girls," said Pacifica.

They went back to the quiet restaurant where Pacifica had taken Mr. and Mrs. Copperfield to dinner. Opposite was a very large saloon all lighted up. There was a ten-piece band playing there, and it was so crowded that the people were dancing in the streets.

Mrs. Quill said: "Oh boy, Pacifica! There's the place where you could have the time of your life tonight. Look at the time *they're* having."

"No, Mrs. Quill," said Pacifica. "We can stay here fine. The light is not so bright and it is more quiet and then we will go to bed."

"Yes," said Mrs. Quill, her face falling. Mrs. Copperfield thought she saw in Mrs. Quill's eyes a terribly pained and thwarted look.

"I'll go there tomorrow night," said Mrs. Quill softly. "It doesn't mean a thing. Every night they have those dances. That's because the boats never stop coming in. The girls are never tired either," she said to Mrs. Copperfield. "That's because they sleep all they want in the daytime. They can sleep as well in the daytime as they do at night. They don't get tired. Why should they? It doesn't make you tired to dance. The music carries you along."

"Don't be a fool," said Pacifica. "They're always tired."

"Well, which is it?" asked Mrs. Copperfield.

"Oh," said Mrs. Quill, "Pacifica is always looking on the darkest side of life. She's the gloomiest thing I ever knew."

"I don't look at the dark side, I look at the truth. You're a little foolish sometimes, Mrs. Quill."

"Don't talk to me that way when you know how much I love you," said Mrs. Quill, her lips beginning to tremble.

"I'm sorry, Mrs. Quill," said Pacifica gravely.

"There is something very lovable about Pacifica," Mrs. Copperfield thought to herself. "I believe she takes everyone quite seriously."

She took Pacifica's hand in her own.

"In a minute we're going to have something nice to drink," she said, smiling up at Pacifica. "Aren't you glad?"

"Yes, it will be nice to have something to drink," said Pacifica politely; but Mrs. Quill understood the gaiety of it. She rubbed her hands together and said: "I'm with you."

Mrs. Copperfield looked out into the street and saw Meyer walking by. He was with two blondes and some sailors.

"There goes Meyer," she said. The other two women looked across the street and they all watched him disappear.

• • •

Mr. and Mrs. Copperfield had gone over to Panama City for two days. The first day after lunch Mr. Copperfield proposed a walk towards the outskirts of the city. It was the first thing he always did when he arrived in a new place. Mrs. Copperfield hated to know what was around her, because it always turned out to be even stranger than she had feared.

They walked for a long time. The streets began to look all alike. On one side they went gradually uphill, and on the other they descended abruptly to the muddy regions near the sea. The stone houses were completely colorless in the hot sun. All the windows were heavily grilled; there was very little sign of life anywhere. They came to three naked boys struggling with a football, and turned downhill towards the water. A woman dressed in black silk came their way slowly. When they had passed her she turned around and stared at them shamelessly. They looked over their shoulders several times and they could still see her standing there watching them.

The tide was out. They made their way along the muddy beach. Back of them there was a huge stone hotel built in front of a low cliff, so that it was already in the shade. The mud flats and the water were still in the sunlight. They walked along until Mr. Copperfield found a large, flat rock for them to sit on.

"It's so beautiful here," he said.

A crab ran along sideways in the mud at their feet.

"Oh, look!" said Mr. Copperfield. "Don't you love them?"

"Yes, I do love them," she answered, but she could not suppress a rising feeling of dread as she looked around her at the landscape. Someone had painted the words *Cerveza—Beer* in green letters on the façade of the hotel.

Mr. Copperfield rolled up his trousers and asked if she would care to go barefoot to the edge of the water with him.

"I think I've gone far enough," she said.

"Are you tired?" he asked her.

"Oh, no. I'm not tired." There was such a pained expression on her face as she answered him that he asked her what the trouble was.

"I'm unhappy," she said.

"Again?" asked Mr. Copperfield. "What is there to be unhappy about now?"

"I feel so lost and so far away and so frightened."

"What's frightening about this?"

"I don't know. It's all so strange and it has no connection with anything."

"It's connected with Panama," observed Mr. Copperfield acidly. "Won't you ever understand that?" He paused. "I don't think really that I'm going to try to make you understand any more. . . . But I'm going to walk to the water's edge. You spoil all my fun. There's absolutely nothing anyone can do with you." He was pouting.

"Yes, I know. I mean go to the water's edge. I guess I am tired after all." She watched him picking his way among the tiny stones, his arms held out for balance like a tight-rope walker's, and wished that she were able to join him because she was so fond of him. She began to feel a little exalted. There was a strong wind, and some lovely sailboats were passing by very swiftly not far from the shore. She threw her head back and closed her eyes, hoping that perhaps she might become exalted enough to run down and join her husband. But the wind did not blow quite hard enough, and behind her closed eyes she saw Pacifica and Mrs. Quill standing in front of the Hotel de las Palmas. She had said good-by to them from the old-fashioned hack that she had hired to drive her to the station. Mr. Copperfield had preferred to walk, and she had been alone with her two friends. Pacifica had been wearing the satin kimono which Mrs. Copperfield had bought her, and a pair of bedroom slippers decorated with pompons. She had stood near the wall of the hotel squinting, and complaining about being out in the street dressed only in a kimono, but Mrs. Copperfield had had only a minute to say good-by to them and she would not descend from the carriage.

"Pacifica and Mrs. Quill," she had said to them, leaning out of the victoria, "you can't imagine how I dread leaving you even for only two days. I honestly don't know how I'll be able to stand it."

"Listen, Copperfield," Mrs. Quill had answered, "you go and have the time of your life in Panama. Don't you think about us for one minute. Do you hear me? My, oh my, if I was young enough to be going to Panama City with my husband, I'd be wearing a different expression on my face than you are wearing now."

"That means nothing to be going to Panama City with your husband," Pacifica had insisted very firmly. "That does not mean that she is happy. Everyone likes to do different things. Maybe Copperfield likes better to go fishing or buy dresses." She had then smiled gratefully at Pacifica.

"Well," Mrs. Quill had retorted somewhat feebly, "I'm sure you would be happy, Pacifica, if you were going to Panama City with your husband. . . . It's beautiful over there."

"Anyway, she has been in Paris," Pacifica had answered.

"Well, promise me you will be here when I get back," Mrs. Copperfield had begged them. "I'm so terrified that you might suddenly vanish."

"Don't make up such stories to yourself, my dear; life is difficult enough. Where are we going away?" Pacifica had said to her, yawning and starting to go inside. Then she had blown a kiss to Mrs. Copperfield from the doorway and waved her hand.

"Such fun, to be with them," she said, audibly, opening her eyes. "They are a great comfort."

Mr. Copperfield was on his way back to the flat rock where she was sitting. He had a stone of strange texture and formation in his hand. He was smiling as he came towards her.

"Look," he said, "isn't this an amusing stone? It's really quite beautiful. I thought you would like to see it, so I brought it to you." Mrs. Copperfield examined the stone and said: "Oh, it is beautiful and very strange. Thanks ever so much." She looked at it lying in the palm of her hand. As she examined it Mr. Copperfield pressed her shoulder and said: "Look at the big steamer plowing through the water. Do you see it?" He twisted her neck slightly so that she might look in the right direction.

"Yes, I see it. It's wonderful too. . . . I think we had better be walking back home. It's going to be dark soon."

They left the beach and started walking through the streets again. It was getting dark, but there were more people standing around now. They commented openly on Mr. and Mrs. Copperfield as they passed by.

"It's really been the most wonderful day," Mr. Copperfield said. "You must have enjoyed some of it, because we've seen such incredible things." Mrs. Copperfield squeezed his hand harder and harder.

"I don't have wingèd feet like you," she said to him. "You must forgive me. I can't move about so easily. At thirty-three I have certain habits."

"That's bad," he answered. "Of course, I have certain habits too—habits of eating, habits of sleeping, habits of working—but I don't think that is what you meant, was it?"

"Let's not talk about it. That isn't what I meant, no."

• • •

The next day Mr. Copperfield said that they would go out and see some of the jungle. Mrs. Copperfield said they hadn't the proper equipment and he explained that he hadn't meant that they would go exploring into the jungle but only around the edges where there were paths.

"Don't let the word 'jungle' frighten you," he said. "After all it only means tropical forest."

"If I don't feel like going in I won't. It doesn't matter. Tonight we are going back to Colon, aren't we?"

"Well, maybe we'll be too tired and we'll have to stay here another night."

"But I told Pacifica and Mrs. Quill that we would be back tonight. They'll be so disappointed if we aren't."

"You aren't really considering *them*, are you? . . . After all, Frieda! Anyway, I don't think they'll mind. They'll understand."

"Oh, no, they won't," answered Mrs. Copperfield. "They'll be disappointed. I told them I would be back before midnight and that we would go out and celebrate. I'm positive that Mrs. Quill will be very disappointed. She loves to celebrate."

"Who on earth is Mrs. Quill?"

"Mrs. Quill . . . Mrs. Quill and Pacifica."

"Yes, I know, but it's so ridiculous. It seems to me you wouldn't care to see them for more than one evening. I should think it would be easy to know what they were like in a very short time."

"Oh, I know what they're like, but I do have so much fun with them." Mr. Copperfield did not answer.

They went out and walked through the streets until they came to a place where there were some buses. They inquired about schedules, and boarded a bus called *Shirley Temple.* On the insides of the doors were painted pictures of Mickey Mouse. The driver had pasted postcards of the saints and the holy virgin on the windshield above his head. He was drinking a Coca-Cola when they got in the bus.

"*¿En que barco vinieron?*" asked the driver.

"*Venimos de Colon,*" said Mr. Copperfield.

"What was that?" Mrs. Copperfield asked him.

"Just what boat did we come on, and I answered we have just arrived from Colon. You see, most people have just come off a boat. It corresponds to asking people where they live, in other places."

"*J'adore Colon, c'est tellement* . . ." began Mrs. Copperfield. Mr. Copperfield looked embarrassed. "Don't speak in French to him. It doesn't make any sense. Speak to him in English."

"I adore Colon."

The driver made a face. "Dirty wooden city. I am sure you have made a big mistake. You will see. You will like Panama City better. More stores, more hospitals, wonderful cinemas, big clean restaurants, wonderful houses in stone; Panama City is a big place. When we drive through Ancon I will show you how nice the lawns are and the trees and the sidewalks. You can't show me anything like that in Colon. You know who likes Colon?" He leaned way over the back of his seat, and as they were sitting behind him he was breathing right in their faces.

"You know who likes Colon?" He winked at Mr. Copperfield. "They're all over the streets. That is what it is there; nothing else much. We have that here too, but in a separate place. If you like that you can go. We have everything here."

"You mean the whores?" asked Mrs. Copperfield in a clear voice.

"*Las putas,*" Mr. Copperfield explained in Spanish to the driver.

He was delighted at the turn in the conversation and fearful lest the driver should not get the full savor of it.

The driver covered his mouth with his hand and laughed.

"She loves that," said Mr. Copperfield, giving his wife a push.

"No—no," said the driver, "she could not."

"They've all been very sweet to me."

"*Sweet!*" said the driver, almost screaming. "There is not this much sweet in them." He made a tiny little circle with his thumb and forefinger. "No, not sweet—someone has been fooling you. He knows." He put his hand on Mr. Copperfield's leg.

"I'm afraid I don't know anything about it," said Mr. Copperfield. The driver winked at him again, and then he said, "She thinks she knows *las*—I will not say the word, but she has never met one of them."

"But I have. I have even taken a siesta with one."

"*Siesta!*" the driver roared with laughter. "Don't make fun please, lady. That is not very nice, you know." He suddenly looked very sober. "No, no, no." He shook his head sadly.

By now the bus had filled up and the driver was obliged to start off. Every time they stopped he would turn around and wag a finger at Mrs. Copperfield. They went through Ancon and passed several long low buildings set up on some small hills.

"Hospitals," yelled the driver for the benefit of Mr. and Mrs. Copperfield. "They have doctors here for every kind of thing in the world. The Army can go there for nothing. They eat and they sleep and they get well all for nothing. Some of the old ones live there for the rest of their lives. I dream to be in the American Army and not driving this dirty bus."

"I should hate to be regimented," said Mr. Copperfield with feeling.

"They are always going to dinners and balls, balls and dinners," commented the driver. There was a murmuring from the back of the bus. The women were all eager to know what the driver had said. One of them who spoke English explained rapidly to the others in Spanish. They all giggled about it for fully five minutes afterwards. The driver started to sing *Over There*, and the laughter reached the pitch of hysteria. They were now almost in the country, driving alongside a river. Across the river was a very new road and behind that a tremendous thick forest.

"Oh, look," said Mr. Copperfield, pointing to the forest. "Do you see the difference? Do you see how enormous the trees are and how entangled the undergrowth is? You can tell that even from here. No northern forests ever look so rich."

"That's true, they don't," said Mrs. Copperfield.

The bus finally stopped at a tiny pier. Only three women and the Copperfields remained inside by now. Mrs. Copperfield looked at them hoping that they were going to the jungle, too.

Mr. Copperfield descended from the bus and she followed reluctantly. The driver was already in the street smoking. He was standing beside Mr. Copperfield, hoping that he would start another conversation. But Mr. Copperfield was much too excited at being so near the jungle to think of anything else. The three women did not get out. They remained in their seats talking. Mrs. Copperfield looked back into the bus and stared at them with a perplexed expression on her face. She seemed to be saying: "Please come out, won't you?" They were embarrassed and they started to giggle again.

Mrs. Copperfield went over to the driver and said to him: "Is this the last stop?"

"Yes," he said.

"And they?"

"Who?" he asked, looking dumb.

"Those three ladies in the back."

"They ride. They are very nice ladies. This is not the first time they are riding on my bus."

"Back and forth?"

"Sure," said the driver.

Mr. Copperfield took Mrs. Copperfield's hand and led her onto the pier. A little ferry was coming towards them. There seemed to be no one on the ferry at all.

Suddenly Mrs. Copperfield said to her husband: "I just don't want to go to the jungle. Yesterday was such a strange, terrible day. If I have another day like it I shall be in an awful state. Please let me go back on the bus."

"But," said Mr. Copperfield, "after you've come all the way here, it seems to me so silly and so senseless to go back. I can assure you that the jungle will be of some interest to you. I've been in them before. You see the strangest-shaped leaves and flowers. And I'm sure you would hear wonderful noises. Some of the birds in the tropics have voices like xylophones, others like bells."

"I thought maybe when I arrived here I would feel inspired; that I would feel the urge to set out. But I don't in the least. Please let's not discuss it."

"All right," said Mr. Copperfield. He looked sad and lonely. He enjoyed so much showing other people the things he liked best. He started to walk away towards the edge of the water and stared out across the river at the opposite shore. He was very slight and his head was beautifully shaped.

"Oh, please don't be sad!" said Mrs. Copperfield, hurrying over to him. "I refuse to allow you to be sad. I feel like an ox. Like a murderer. But I would be such a nuisance over on the other side of the river in the jungle. You'll love it once you're over there and you will be able to go much farther in without me."

"But my dear—I don't mind . . . I only hope you will be able to get home all right on the bus. Heaven knows when I'll get home. I might decide to just wander around and around . . . and you don't like to be alone in Panama."

"Well then," said Mrs. Copperfield, "suppose I take the train back to Colon. It's a simple trip, and I have only one grip with me. Then you can follow me tonight if you get back early from the jungle, and if you don't you can come along tomorrow morning. We had planned to go back tomorrow anyway. But you must give me your word of honor that you will come."

"It's all so complicated," said Mr. Copperfield. "I thought we were going to have a nice day in the jungle. I'll come back tomorrow. The luggage is there, so there is no danger of my not coming back. Good-by." He gave her his hand. The ferry was scraping against the dock.

"Listen," she said, "if you're not back by twelve tonight, I shall sleep at the Hotel de las Palmas. I'll phone our hotel at twelve and see if you're there, in case I'm out."

"I won't be there until tomorrow."

"I'm at the Hotel de las Palmas if I'm not home, then."

"All right, but be good and get some sleep."

"Yes, of course I will."

He got into the boat and it pulled out.

"I hope his day has not been spoiled," she said to herself. The tenderness that she was feeling for him now was almost overwhelming. She got back on the bus and stared fixedly out the window because she did not want anyone to see that she was crying.

• • •

Mrs. Copperfield went straight to the Hotel de las Palmas. As she descended from the carriage she saw Pacifica walking towards her alone. She paid the driver and rushed up to her.

"Pacifica! How glad I am to see you!"

Pacifica's forehead had broken out. She looked tired.

"Ah, Copperfield," she said, "Mrs. Quill and I did not think we would ever see you again and now you are back."

"But, Pacifica, how can you say a thing like that? I'm surprised at both of you. Didn't I promise you I would be back before midnight and that we would celebrate?"

"Yes, but people often say this. After all, nobody gets angry if they don't come back."

"Let's go and say hello to Mrs. Quill."

"All right, but she has been in a terrible humor all the day, crying a lot and not eating anything."

"What on earth is the matter?"

"She had some fight, I think, with her boy friend. He don't like her. I tell her this but she won't listen."

"But the first thing she told me was that sex didn't interest her."

"To go to bed she don't care so much, but she is terribly sentimental, like she was sixteen years old. I feel sorry to see an old woman making such a fool."

Pacifica was still wearing her bedroom slippers. They went past the bar, which was filled with men smoking cigars and drinking.

"My God! how in one minute they make a place stink," said Pacifica. "I wish I could go and have a nice little house with a garden somewhere."

"I'm going to live here, Pacifica, and we'll all have lots of fun."

"The time for fun is over," said Pacifica gloomily.

"You'll feel better after we've all had a drink," said Mrs. Copperfield.

They knocked on Mrs. Quill's door.

They heard her moving about in her room and rattling some papers. Then she came to the door and opened it. Mrs. Copperfield noticed that she looked weaker than usual.

"Do come in," she said to them, "although I have nothing to offer you. You can sit down for a while."

Pacifica nudged Mrs. Copperfield. Mrs. Quill went back to her chair and took up a handful of bills which had been lying on the table near her.

"I must look over these. You will excuse me, but they're terribly important."

Pacifica turned to Mrs. Copperfield and talked softly.

"She can't even see them, because she does not have her glasses on. She is behaving like a child. Now she will be mad at us because her boy friend, like she calls him, has left her alone. I will not be treated like a dog very long."

Mrs. Quill overheard what Pacifica was saying, and reddened. She turned to Mrs. Copperfield.

"Do you still intend to come and live in this hotel?" she asked her.

"Yes," said Mrs. Copperfield buoyantly, "I wouldn't live anywhere else for the world. Even if you do growl at me."

"You probably will not find it comfortable enough."

"Don't growl at Copperfield," put in Pacifica. "First, she's been away for two days, and second, she doesn't know, like I do, what you are like."

"I'll thank you to keep your common little mouth shut," retorted Mrs. Quill, shuffling the bills rapidly.

"I am sorry to have disturbed you, Mrs. Quill," said Pacifica, rising to her feet and going towards the door.

"I wasn't yelling at Copperfield, I just said that I didn't think she would be comfortable here." Mrs. Quill laid down the bills. "Do you think she would be comfortable here, Pacifica?"

"A common little thing does not know anything about these questions," answered Pacifica and she left the room, leaving Mrs. Copperfield behind with Mrs. Quill.

Mrs. Quill took some keys from the top of her dresser and motioned to Mrs. Copperfield to follow her. They walked through some halls and up a flight of stairs and Mrs. Quill opened the door of one of the rooms.

"Is it near Pacifica's?" asked Mrs. Copperfield.

Mrs. Quill without answering led her back through the halls and stopped near Pacifica's room.

"This is dearer," said Mrs. Quill, "but it's near Miss Pacifica's room if that's your pleasure and you can stand the noise."

"What noise?"

"She'll start yammering away and heaving things around the minute she wakes up in the morning. It don't affect her any. She's tough. She hasn't got a nerve in her body."

"Mrs. Quill—"

"Yes."

"Could you have someone bring me a bottle of gin to my room?"

"I think I can do that. . . . Well, I hope you are comfortable." Mrs. Quill walked away. "I'll have your bag sent up," she said, looking over her shoulder.

Mrs. Copperfield was appalled at the turn of events.

"I thought," she said to herself, "that they would go on the way they were forever. Now I must be patient and wait until everything is all right again. The longer I live, the less I can foresee anything." She lay down on the bed, put her knees up, and held onto her ankles with her hands.

"Be gay . . . be gay . . . be gay," she sang, rocking back and forth on the bed. There was a knock on the door and a man in a striped sweater entered the room without waiting for an answer to his knock.

"You ask for a bottle of gin?" he said.

"I certainly did—hooray!"

"And here's a suitcase. I'm putting it down here."

Mrs. Copperfield paid him and he left.

"Now," she said, jumping off the bed, "now for a little spot of gin to chase my troubles away. There just isn't any other way that's as good. At a certain point gin takes everything off your hands and you flop around like a little baby. Tonight I want to be a little baby." She took a hookerful, and shortly after that another. The third one she drank more slowly.

The brown shutters of her window were wide open and a small wind was bringing the smell of frying fat into the room. She went over to the window and looked down into the alleyway which separated the Hotel de las Palmas from a group of shacks.

There was an old lady seated in a chair in the alleyway, eating her dinner.

"Eat every bit of it!" Mrs. Copperfield said. The old lady looked up dreamily, but she did not answer.

Mrs. Copperfield put her hand over her heart. "*Le bonheur*," she whispered, "*le bonheur* . . . what an angel a happy moment is—and how nice not to have to struggle too much for inner peace! I know that I shall enjoy certain moments of gaiety, willy-nilly. No one among my friends speaks any longer of character—and what interests us most, certainly, is finding out what we are like."

"Copperfield!" Pacifica burst into the room. Her hair was messy and she seemed to be out of breath. "Come on downstairs and have some fun. Maybe they are not the kind of men you like to be with, but if you don't like them you just walk away. Put some rouge on your face. Can I have some of your gin, please?"

"But a moment ago you said the time for fun was over!"

"What the hell!"

"By all means what the hell," said Mrs. Copperfield. "That's music to anyone's ears. . . . If you could only stop me from thinking, always, Pacifica."

"You don't want to stop thinking. The more you can think, the more you are better than the other fellow. Thank your God that you can think."

Downstairs in the bar Mrs. Copperfield was introduced to three or four men.

"This man is Lou," said Pacifica, pulling out a stool from under the bar and making her sit next to him.

Lou was small and over forty. He wore a light-weight gray suit that was too tight for him, a blue shirt, and a straw hat.

"She wants to stop thinking," said Pacifica to Lou.

"Who wants to stop thinking?" asked Lou.

"Copperfield. The little girl who is sitting on a stool, you big boob."

"Boob yourself. You're gettin' just like one of them New York girls," said Lou.

"Take me to Nueva York, take me to Nueva York," said Pacifica, bouncing up and down on her stool.

Mrs. Copperfield was shocked to see Pacifica behaving in this kittenish manner.

"Remember the belly buttons," said Lou to Pacifica.

"The belly buttons! The belly buttons!" Pacifica threw up her arms and screeched with delight.

"What about the belly buttons?" asked Mrs. Copperfield.

"Don't you think those two are the funniest words in the whole world? Belly and button—belly and button—in Spanish it is only *ombligo*."

"I don't think anything's *that* funny. But you like to laugh, so go ahead and laugh," said Lou, who made no attempt to talk to Mrs. Copperfield at all.

Mrs. Copperfield pulled at his sleeve. "Where do you come from?" she asked him.

"Pittsburgh."

"I don't know anything about Pittsburgh," said Mrs. Copperfield. But Lou was already turning his eyes in Pacifica's direction.

"Belly button," he said suddenly without changing his expression. This time Pacifica did not laugh. She did not seem to have heard him. She was standing up on the rail of the bar waving her arms in an agitated and officious manner.

"Well, well," she said, "I see that nobody has yet bought for Copperfield a drink. Am I with grown men or little boys? No, no . . . Pacifica will find other friends." She started to climb down from the bar, commanding Mrs. Copperfield to follow her. In the meantime she knocked off the hat of the man who was seated next to her with her elbow.

"Toby," she said to him, "you ought to be ashamed." Toby had a sleepy fat face and a broken nose. He was dressed in a dark brown heavy-weight suit.

"What? Did you want a drink?"

"Of course I wanted a drink." Pacifica's eyes were flashing.

Everyone was served and she settled back on her stool. "Come on now," she said, "what are we going to sing?"

"I'm a monotone," said Lou.

"Singing ain't in my line," said Toby.

They were all surprised to see Mrs. Copperfield throw her head back as though filled with a sudden feeling of exaltation and start to sing.

"Who cares if the sky cares to fall into the sea
Who cares what banks fail in Yonkers
As long as you've got the kiss that conquers
Why should I care?
Life is one long jubilee
As long as I care for you
And you care for me."

"Good, fine . . . now another one," said Pacifica in a snappy voice.

"Did you ever sing in a club?" Lou asked Mrs. Copperfield. Her cheeks were very red.

"Actually, I didn't. But when I was in the mood, I used to sing very loudly at a table in a restaurant and attract a good bit of attention."

"You wasn't such good friends with Pacifica the last time I was in Colon."

"My dear man, I wasn't here. I was in Paris, I suppose."

"She didn't tell me you were in Paris. Are you a screwball or were you really in Paris?"

"I was in Paris. . . . After all, stranger things have happened."

"Then you're fancy?"

"What do you mean, fancy?"

"Fancy is what fancy does."

"Well, if you care to be mysterious it's your right, but the word 'fancy' doesn't mean a thing to me."

"Hey," said Lou to Pacifica, "is she tryin' to be highhat with me?"

"No, she's very intelligent. She's not like you."

For the first time Mrs. Copperfield sensed that Pacifica was proud of her. She realized that all this time Pacifica had been waiting to show her to her friends and she was not so sure that she was pleased. Lou turned to Mrs. Copperfield again.

"I'm sorry, Duchess. Pacifica says you got something on the ball and that I shouldn't address myself to you."

Mrs. Copperfield was bored with Lou, so she jumped down and went and stood between Toby and Pacifica. Toby was talking in a thick low voice with Pacifica.

"I'm tellin' you if she gets a singer in here and paints the place up a little she could make a lot of money on the joint. Everybody knows it's a good place to hit the hay in, but there ain't no music. You're here, you got a lot of friends, you got a way with you. . . ."

"Toby, I don't want to start with music and a lot of friends. I'm quiet. . . ."

"Yeah, you're quiet. This week you're quiet and maybe next week you won't want to be so quiet."

"I don't change my mind like that, Toby. I have a boy friend. I don't want to live in here much longer, you know."

"But you're livin' here now."

"Yes."

"Well, you want to make a little money. I'm tellin' you, with a little money we could fix up the joint."

"But why must I be here?"

"Because you got contacts."

"I never saw such a man. Talking all the time about business."

"You're not such a bad one for business yourself. I saw you hustlin' up a drink for that pal of yours. You get your cut, don't you?"

Pacifica kicked Toby with her heel.

"Listen, Pacifica, I like to have fun. But I can't see somethin' that could be coinin' the money takin' in petty cash."

"Stop being so busy." Pacifica pushed his hat off his head. He realized there was nothing to be done and sighed.

"How's Emma?" he asked her listlessly.

"Emma? I have not seen her since that night on the boat. She looked so gorgeous dressed up like a sailor."

"Women look fantastic dressed up in men's clothes," put in Mrs. Copperfield with enthusiasm.

"That's what you think," said Toby. "They look better to me in ruffles."

"She was only talking for a *minute* they look nice," said Pacifica.

"Not for me," said Toby.

"All right, Toby, maybe not for you, but for her they look nice that way."

"I still think I'm right. It ain't only a matter of opinion."

"Well, you can't prove it mathematically," said Mrs. Copperfield. Toby looked at her with no interest in his face.

"What about Emma?" said Pacifica. "You are really not interested finally in somebody?"

"You asked me to talk about somethin' besides business, so I asked you about Emma, just to show how sociable I am. We both know her. We were on a party together. Ain't that the right thing to do? How's Emma, how's your momma and poppa. That's the kind of talk you like. Next I tell you how my family is gettin' along and maybe I bring in another friend who we both forgot we knew, and then we say prices are goin' up and comes the revolution and we all eat strawberries. Prices are goin' up fast and that's why I wanted you to cash in on this joint."

"My God!" said Pacifica, "my life is hard enough and I am all alone, but I can still enjoy myself like a young girl. *You*, you are an old man."

"Your life don't have to be hard, Pacifica."

"Well, your life is still very hard and you are always trying to make it easy. That's the hardest part even of your life."

"I'm just waitin' to get a break. With my ideas and a break my life can be easy overnight."

"And then what will you do?"

"Keep it that way or maybe make it even easier. I'll be plenty busy."

"You will never have any time for anything."

"What's a guy like me want time for—plantin' tulips?"

"You don't enjoy to talk to me, Toby."

"Sure. You're friendly and cute and you got a good brain aside from a few phony ideas."

"And what about me? Am I friendly and cute too?" asked Mrs. Copperfield.

"Sure. You're all friendly and cute."

"Copperfield, I think we have just been insulted," said Pacifica, drawing herself up.

Mrs. Copperfield started to march out of the room in mock anger, but Pacifica was already thinking of something else and Mrs. Copperfield found herself to be in the ridiculous position of the performer who is suddenly without an audience. She came back to the bar.

"Listen," said Pacifica, "go upstairs and knock on Mrs. Quill's door. Tell her that Mr. Toby wants to meet her very much. Don't say Pacifica sent you. She will know this anyway and it will be easier for her if you don't say it. She will love to come down. That I know like if she was my mother."

"Oh, I'd love to, Pacifica," said Mrs. Copperfield, running out of the room.

When Mrs. Copperfield arrived in Mrs. Quill's room, Mrs. Quill was busy cleaning the top drawer of her dresser. It was very quiet in her room and very hot.

"I never have the heart to throw these things away," said Mrs. Quill, turning around and patting her hair. "I suppose you've met half of Colon," she said sadly, studying Mrs. Copperfield's flushed face.

"No, I haven't, but would you care to come down and meet Mr. Toby?"

"Who is Mr. Toby, dear?"

"Oh, please come, please come just for me."

"I will, dear, if you'll sit down and wait while I change into something better."

Mrs. Copperfield sat down. Her head was spinning. Mrs. Quill pulled out a long black silk dress from her closet. She drew it over her head and then selected some strings of black beads from her jewelbox, and a cameo pin. She powdered her face carefully and stuck several more hairpins into her hair.

"I'm not going to bother to take a bath," she said when she had finished. "Now, do you really think that I should meet this Mr. Toby, or do you think perhaps another night would be better?"

Mrs. Copperfield took Mrs. Quill's hand and pulled her out of the room. Mrs. Quill's entrance into the barroom was gracious and extremely formal. She was already using the hurt that her beau had caused her to good advantage.

"Now, dear," she said quietly to Mrs. Copperfield, "tell me which one is Mr. Toby."

"That one over there, sitting next to Pacifica," Mrs. Copperfield said hesitantly. She was fearful lest Mrs. Quill should find him completely unattractive and leave the room.

"I see. The stout gentleman."

"Do you hate fat people?"

"I don't judge people by their bodies. Even when I was a young girl I liked men for their minds. Now that I'm middle-aged I see how right I was."

"I've always been a body-worshipper," said Mrs. Copperfield, "but that doesn't mean that I fall in love with people who have beautiful bodies. Some of the bodies I've liked have been awful. Come, let's go over to Mr. Toby."

Toby stood up for Mrs. Quill and took off his hat.

"Come sit down with us and have a drink."

"Let me get my bearings, young man. Let me get my bearings."

"This bar belongs to you, don't it?" said Toby, looking worried.

"Yes, yes," said Mrs. Quill blandly. She was staring at the top of Pacifica's head. "Pacifica," she said, "don't you drink too much. I have to watch out for you."

"Don't you worry, Mrs. Quill. I have been taking care of myself for a long time." She turned to Lou and said solemnly: "Fifteen years." Pacifica was completely natural. She behaved as though nothing had occurred between her and Mrs. Quill. Mrs. Copperfield was enchanted. She put her arms around Mrs. Quill's waist and hugged her very tight.

"Oh," she said, "oh, you make me so happy!"

Toby smiled. "The girl's feelin' good, Mrs. Quill. Now don't you want a drink?"

"Yes, I'll have a glass of gin. It pains me the way these girls come away from their homes so young. I had my home and my mother and my sisters and my brothers until the age of twenty-six. Even so, when I got married I felt like a scared rabbit. As if I was going out into the world. Mr. Quill was like a family to me, though, and it wasn't until he died that I really got out into the world. I was in my thirties then, and more of a scared rabbit than ever. Pacifica's really been out in the world much longer than I have. You know, she is like an old sea captain. Sometimes I feel very silly when she tells me of some of her experiences. My eyes almost pop right out of my head. It isn't so much a question of age as it is a question of experience. The Lord has spared me more than he has spared Pacifica. She hasn't been spared a single thing. Still, she's not as nervous as I am."

"Well, she certainly don't know how to look out for herself for someone who's had so much experience," said Toby. "She don't know a good thing when she sees it."

"Yes, I expect you're right," said Mrs. Quill, warming up to Toby.

"Sure I'm right. But she's got lots of friends here in Panama, ain't she?"

"I dare say Pacifica has a great many friends," said Mrs. Quill.

"Come on, you know she's got lots of friends, don't you?"

As Mrs. Quill looked as though she had been somewhat startled by the pressing tone in his voice, Toby decided he was hurrying things too much.

"Who the hell cares, anyway?" he said, looking at her out of the corner of his eye. This seemed to have the right effect on Mrs. Quill, and Toby breathed a sigh of relief.

Mrs. Copperfield went over to a bench in the corner and lay down. She shut her eyes and smiled.

"That's the best thing for her," said Mrs. Quill to Toby. "She's a nice woman, a dear sweet woman, and she'd had a little too much to drink. Pacifica, she can really take care of herself like she says. I've seen her drink as much as a man, but with her it's different. As I said, she's had all the experience in the world. Now, Mrs. Copperfield and me, we have to watch ourselves more carefully or else have some nice man watching out for us."

"Yeah," said Toby, twisting around on his stool. "Bartender, another gin. You want one, don't you?" he asked Mrs. Quill.

"Yes, if you'll watch out for me."

"Sure I will. I'll even take you home in my arms if you fall down."

"Oh, no." Mrs. Quill giggled and flushed. "You wouldn't try that, young man. I'm heavy, you know."

"Yeah. . . . Say—"

"Yes?"

"Would you mind telling me something?"

"I'd be delighted to tell you anything you'd like to hear."

"How is it you ain't never bothered to fix this place up?"

"Oh, dear, isn't it awful? I've always promised myself I would and I never get around to it."

"No dough?" asked Toby. Mrs. Quill looked vague. "Haven't you got no money to fix it up with?" he repeated.

"Oh yes, certainly I have." Mrs. Quill looked around at the bar. "I even have some things upstairs that I always promised myself to hang up on the walls here. Everything is so dirty, isn't it? I feel ashamed."

"No, no," said Toby impatiently. He was now very animated. "That ain't what I mean at all."

Mrs. Quill smiled at him sweetly.

"Listen," said Toby, "I been handlin' restaurants and bars and clubs all my life, and I can make them go."

"I'm certain that you can."

"I'm tellin' you that I can. Listen, let's get out of here; let's go some place else where we can really talk. Any place in town you name

I'll take you to. It's worth it to me and it'll be worth it to you even more. You'll see. We can have more to drink or maybe a little bite to eat. Listen"—he grabbed hold of Mrs. Quill's upper arm—"would you like to go to the Hotel Washington?"

At first Mrs. Quill did not react, but when she realized what he had said, she answered that she would enjoy it very much, in a voice trembling with emotion. Toby jumped off the stool, pulled his hat down over his face, and started walking out of the bar, saying: "Come on, then," over his shoulder to Mrs. Quill. He looked annoyed but resolute.

Mrs. Quill took Pacifica's hand in her own and told her that she was going to the Hotel Washington.

"If there was any possible way I would take you with us, I would, Pacifica. I feel very badly to be going there without you, but I don't see how you can come, do you?"

"Now, don't you worry about that, Mrs. Quill. I'm having a very good time here," said Pacifica in a sincerely world-weary tone of voice.

"That's a hocus-pocus joint," said Lou.

"Oh no," said Pacifica, "it is very nice there, very beautiful. She will have a lovely time." Pacifica pinched Lou. "You don't know," she said to him.

Mrs. Quill walked out of the bar slowly and joined Toby on the sidewalk. They got into a hack and started for the hotel. Toby was silent. He sprawled way back in his seat and lighted a cigar.

"I regret that automobiles were ever invented," said Mrs. Quill.

"You'd go crazy tryin' to get from one place to another if they wasn't."

"Oh, no. I always take my time. There isn't anything that can't wait."

"That's what you think," said Toby in a surly tone of voice, sensing that this was just the thing that he would have to combat in Mrs. Quill. "It's just that extra second that makes Man O'War or any other horse come in first," he said.

"Well, life isn't a horse race."

"Nowadays that's just what life is."

"Well, not for me," said Mrs. Quill.

Toby was disgusted.

The walk which led up to the veranda of the Hotel Washington was lined with African date-palms. The hotel itself was very impressive. They descended from the carriage. Toby stood in the middle of the walk between the scraping palms and looked towards the hotel. It was all lighted up. Mrs. Quill stood beside Toby.

"I'll bet they soak you for drinks in there," said Toby. "I'll bet they make two hundred per cent profit."

"Oh, please," said Mrs. Quill, "if you don't feel you can afford it let's take a carriage and go back. The ride is so pleasant anyway." Her heart was beating very quickly.

"Don't be a God-damn fool!" Toby said to her, and they headed for the hotel.

The floor in the lobby was of imitation yellow marble. There was a magazine stand in one corner where the guests were able to buy chewing gum and picture postcards, maps, and souvenirs. Mrs. Quill felt as though she had just come off a ship. She wandered about in circles, but Toby went straight up to the man behind the magazine stand and asked him where he could get a drink. He suggested to Toby that they go out on the terrace.

"It's generally where everyone goes," he said.

They were seated at a table on the edge of the terrace, and they had a very nice view of a stretch of beach and the sea.

Between them on the table there was a little lamp with a rose-colored shade. Toby began at once to twirl the lamp shade. His cigar by now was very short and very wet.

Here and there on the terrace small groups of people were talking together in low voices.

"Dead!" said Toby.

"Oh, I think it's lovely," said Mrs. Quill. She was shivering a little, as the wind kept blowing over her shoulder, and it was a good deal cooler than in Colon.

A waiter was standing beside them with his pencil poised in the air waiting for an order.

"What do you want?" asked Toby.

"What would you suggest, young man, that's really delicious?" said Mrs. Quill, turning to the waiter.

"Fruit punch à la Washington Hotel," said the waiter abruptly.

"That *does* sound good."

"O.K.," said Toby, "bring one, and a straight rye for me."

When Mrs. Quill had sipped quite a bit of her drink Toby spoke to her. "So you got the dough, but you never bothered to fix it up."

"Mmmmmm!" said Mrs. Quill. "They've got every kind of fruit in the world in this drink. I'm afraid I'm behaving just like a baby, but there's no one who likes the good things in this world better than me. Of course, I've never had to do without them, you know."

"You don't call livin' the way you're livin' havin' the good things in life, do you?" said Toby.

"I live much better than you think. How do you know how I live?"

"Well, you could have more style," said Toby, "and you could have that easy. I mean the place could be better very easy."

"It probably would be easy, wouldn't it?"

"Yeah." Toby waited to see if she would say anything more by herself before he addressed her again.

"Take all these people here," said Mrs. Quill. "There aren't many of them, but you'd think they'd all get together instead of staying in twos and threes. As long as they're all living here in this gorgeous hotel, you'd think they'd have on their ball dresses and be having a wonderful time every minute, instead of looking out over the terrace or reading. You'd think they'd always be dressed up to the hilt and flirting together instead of wearing those plain clothes."

"They got on sport clothes," said Toby. "They don't want to be bothered dressin'. They probably come here for a rest. They're probably business people. Maybe some of them belong to society. They got to rest too. They got so many places they got to show up at when they're home."

"Well, I wouldn't pay out all that money just to rest. I'd stay in my own house."

"It don't make no difference. They got plenty."

"That's true enough. Isn't it sad?"

"I don't see nothin' sad about it. What looks sad to me," said Toby, leaning way over and crushing his cigar out in the ash-tray, "what looks sad to me is that you've got that bar and hotel set-up and you ain't makin' enough money on it."

"Yes, isn't it terrible?"

"I like you and I don't like to see you not gettin' what you could." He took hold of her hand with a certain amount of gentleness. "Now, I know what to do with your place. Like I told you before. Do you remember what I told you before?"

"Well, you've told me so many things."

"I'll tell you again. I've been working with restaurants and bars and hotels all my life and makin' them go. I said makin' them go. If I had the dough right now, if it wasn't that I'm short because I had to help my brother and his family out of a jam, I'd take my own dough before you could say Jack Robinson and sink it into your joint and fix it up. I know that I'd get it right back anyway, so it wouldn't be no act of charity."

"Certainly it wouldn't," said Mrs. Quill. Her head was swaying gently from side to side. She looked at Toby with luminous eyes.

"Well, I got to go easy now until next October, when I got a big contract comin'. A contract with a chain. I could use a little money now, but that ain't the point."

"Don't bother to explain, Toby," said Mrs. Quill.

"What do you mean, don't bother to explain? Ain't you interested in what I've got to tell you?"

"Toby, I'm interested in every word you have to say. But you must not worry about the drinks. Your friend Flora Quill tells you that you needn't worry. We're out to enjoy ourselves and Heaven knows we're going to, aren't we, Toby?"

"Yeah, but just let me explain this to you. I think the reason you ain't done nothin' about the place is because you didn't know where to begin, maybe. Understand? You don't know the ropes. Now, I know all about gettin' orchestras and carpenters and waiters, cheap. I know how to do all that. You got a name, and lots of people like to come there even now because they can go right from the bar upstairs. Pacifica is a big item because she knows every bloke in town and they like her and they trust her. The trouble is, you ain't got no atmosphere, no bright lights, no dancin'. It ain't pretty or big enough. People go to the other places and then they come to your place late. Just before they go to bed. If I was you, I'd turn over in my grave. It's the other guys that are gettin' the meat. You only get a little bit. What's left near the bone, see?"

"The meat nearest the bone is the sweetest," said Mrs. Quill.

"Hey, is there any use my talkin' to you or are you gonna be silly? I'm serious. Now, you got some money in the bank. You got money in the bank, ain't you?"

"Yes, I've got money in the bank," said Mrs. Quill.

"O.K. Well, you let me help you fix up the joint. I'll take everything off your hands. All you got to do is lie back and enjoy the haul."

"Nonsense," said Mrs. Quill.

"Now come on," said Toby, beginning to get angry. "I'm not askin' you for nothin' except maybe a little percentage in the place and a little cash to pay expenses for a while. I can do it all for you cheap and quick and I can manage the joint for you so that it won't cost you much more than it's costin' you now."

"But I think that's wonderful, Toby. I think it's so wonderful."

"You don't have to tell me it's wonderful. I know it's wonderful. It ain't wonderful, it's swell. It's marvelous. We ain't got no time to lose. Have another drink."

"Yes, yes."

"I'm spendin' my last cent on you," he said recklessly.

Mrs. Quill was drunk by now and she just nodded her head.

"It's worth it." He sat back in his chair and studied the horizon. He was very busy calculating in his head. "What percentage in the place do you think I ought to get? Don't forget I'm gonna manage the whole thing for you for a year."

"Oh, dear," said Mrs. Quill, "I'm sure I haven't got any idea." She smiled at him blissfully.

"O.K. How much advance will you give me just so I can stay on here until I get the place goin'?"

"I don't know."

"Well, we'll figure it this way," said Toby cautiously. He was not sure yet that he had taken the right move. "We'll figure it this way. I don't want you to do more than you can. I want to go in this deal with you. You tell me how much money you got in the bank. Then I'll figure out how much fixin' the place up will cost you and then how much I think is a minimum for me. If you ain't got much I'm not gonna let you go busted. You be honest with me and I'll be honest with you."

"Toby," said Mrs. Quill seriously, "don't you think I'm an honest woman?"

"What the hell," said Toby, "do you think I'd put a proposition like that to you if I didn't think you were?"

"No, I guess you wouldn't," said Mrs. Quill sadly.

"How much you got?" asked Toby, looking at her intently.

"What?" asked Mrs. Quill.

"How much money you got in the bank?"

"I'll show you, Toby. I'll show you right away." She started to fumble in her big black leather pocketbook.

Toby had his jaw locked and his eyes averted from the face of Mrs. Quill.

"Messy—messy—messy," Mrs. Quill was saying. "I have everything in this pocketbook but the kitchen stove."

There was a very still look in Toby's eyes as he stared first at the water and then at the palm trees. He considered that he had already won, and he was beginning to wonder whether or not it was really a good thing.

"Dear me," said Mrs. Quill, "I live just like a gypsy. Twenty-two fifty in the bank and I don't even care."

Toby snatched the book from her hands. When he saw that the balance was marked twenty-two dollars and fifty cents, he rose to his feet and, clutching his napkin in one hand and his hat in the other, he walked off the terrace.

After Toby had left the table so abruptly, Mrs. Quill felt deeply ashamed of herself.

"He's just so disgusted," she decided, "that he can't even look me in the face without feeling like throwing up. It's because he thinks I'm balmy to go around gay as a lark with only twenty-two fifty in the bank. Well, well, I expect I'd better start worrying a little more. When he comes back I'll tell him I'll turn over a new leaf."

Everyone had left the terrace by now with the exception of the waiter who had served Mrs. Quill. He stood with his hands behind his back and stared straight ahead of him.

"Sit down for a bit and talk to me," said Mrs. Quill to him. "I'm lonesome on this dark old terrace. It's really a beautiful terrace. You might tell me something about yourself. How much money have you got in the bank? I know you think I'm fresh to ask you, but I'd really like to know."

"Why not?" answered the waiter. "I've got about three hundred and fifty dollars in the bank." He did not sit down.

"Where did you get it?" asked Mrs. Quill.

"From my uncle."

"I guess you feel pretty secure."

"No."

Mrs. Quill began to wonder whether or not Toby would come back at all. She pressed her hands together and asked the young waiter if he knew where the gentleman who had been sitting next to her had gone.

"Home, I guess," said the waiter.

"Well, let's just have one look in the lobby," said Mrs. Quill nervously. She beckoned to the waiter to follow her.

They went into the lobby and together they searched the faces of the guests, who were either standing around in groups or sitting along the wall in armchairs. The hotel was much livelier now than it had been when Mrs. Quill first arrived with Toby. She was deeply troubled and hurt at not seeing Toby anywhere.

"I guess I'd better go home and let you get some sleep," she said absentmindedly to the waiter, "but not before I've bought something for Pacifica. . . ." She had been trembling a little, but the thought of Pacifica filled her with assurance.

"Such an awful, dreadful, mean thing to be alone in the world even for a minute," she said to the waiter. "Come with me and help me choose something, nothing important, just some remembrance of the hotel."

"They're all the same," said the waiter, following her reluctantly.

"Just a lot of junk. I don't know what your friend wants. You might get her a little pocketbook with *Panama* painted on it."

"No, I want it to be specially marked with the name of the hotel."

"Well," said the waiter, "most people don't go in for that."

"Oh my—oh my," said Mrs. Quill emphatically, "must I always be told what other people do? I've had just about enough of it." She marched up to the magazine stand and said to the young man behind the counter: "Now, I want something with *Hotel Washington* written on it. For a woman."

The man looked through his stock and pulled out a handkerchief on the corner of which were painted two palm trees and the words: *Souvenir of Panama.*

"Most people prefer this, though," he said, drawing a tremendous straw hat from under the counter and placing it on his own head.

"You see, it gives you as much shadow as an umbrella and it is very becoming." There was nothing written on the hat at all.

"That handkerchief," continued the young man, "most people consider it kind of, you know . . ."

"My dear young man," said Mrs. Quill, "I expressly told you that I wanted this gift to bear the words *Hotel Washington* and if possible also a picture of the hotel."

"But, lady, nobody wants that. People don't want pictures of hotels on their souvenirs. Palm trees, sunsets, sometimes even bridges, but not hotels."

"Do you or do you not have anything that bears the words *Hotel Washington*?" said Mrs. Quill, raising her voice.

The salesman was beginning to get angry. "I *do* have," he said, his eyes flashing, "if you will wait one minute please, madam." He opened a little gate and went out into the lobby. He was back in a short time carrying a heavy black ash-tray which he set on the counter in front of Mrs. Quill. The name of the hotel was stamped in the center of the ash-tray in yellow lettering.

"Is this the type of thing you wanted?" asked the salesman.

"Why, yes," said Mrs. Quill, "it is."

"All right, madam, that'll be fifty cents."

"That's not worth fifty cents," whispered the waiter to Mrs. Quill.

Mrs. Quill looked through her purse; she was able to find no more than a quarter in change and no bills at all.

"Look," she said to the young man, "I'm the proprietress of the Hotel de las Palmas. I will show you my bank book with my address written in the front of it. Are you going to trust me with this ash-tray just this once? You see, I came with a gentleman friend and we had a falling out and he went home ahead of me."

"I can't help that, madam," said the salesman.

Meanwhile one of the assistant managers who had been watching the group at the magazine stand from another corner of the lobby thought it time to intervene. He was exceedingly suspicious of Mrs. Quill, who did not appear to him to measure up to the standard of the other guests in any way, not even from a distance. He also wondered what could possibly be keeping the waiter standing in front of the magazine stand for such a long while. He walked over to them looking as serious and as thoughtful as he was able.

"Here's my bank book," Mrs. Quill was saying to the salesman.

The waiter, seeing the assistant manager approaching, was frightened and immediately presented Mrs. Quill with the check for the drinks she and Toby had consumed together.

"You owe six dollars on the terrace," he said to Mrs. Quill.

"Didn't he pay for them?" she said. "I guess he must have been in an awful state."

"Can I help you?" the assistant manager asked of Mrs. Quill.

"I'm sure you can," she said. "I'm the owner of the Hotel de las Palmas."

"I'm sorry," the manager said, "but I'm not familiar with the Hotel de las Palmas."

"Well," said Mrs. Quill, "I have no money with me. I came here with a gentleman, we had a falling out, but I have my bank book here with me which will prove to you that I will have the money as soon as I can run over to the bank tomorrow. I can't sign a check because it's in the savings bank."

"I'm sorry," said the assistant manager, "but we extend credit only to guests residing in the hotel."

"I do that too, in my hotel," said Mrs. Quill, "unless it is something out of the ordinary."

"We make a rule of never extending credit . . ."

"I wanted to take this ash-tray home to my girl friend. She admires your hotel."

"That ash-tray is the property of the Hotel Washington," said the assistant manager, frowning sternly at the salesman, who said quickly: "She wanted something with *Hotel Washington* written on it. I didn't have anything so I thought I'd sell her one of these—for fifty cents," he added, winking at the assistant manager, who was standing farther and farther back on his heels.

"These ash-trays," he repeated, "are the property of the Hotel Washington. We have only a limited number of them in stock and every available tray is in constant use."

The salesman, not caring to have anything more to do with the ash-tray lest he lose his job, carried it back to the table from which he had originally removed it and took up his position again behind the counter.

"Do you want either the handkerchief or the hat?" he asked of Mrs. Quill as though nothing had happened.

"She's got all the hats and the hankies she needs," said Mrs. Quill. "I suppose I'd better go home."

"Would you care to come to the desk with me and settle the bill?" asked the assistant manager.

"Well, if you'll just wait until tomorrow—"

"I'm afraid it is definitely against the rules of the hotel, madam. If you'll just step this way with me." He turned to the waiter, who was following the conversation intently. *"Te necesitan afuera,"* he said to him, "go on."

The waiter was about to say something, but he decided against it and walked slowly away towards the terrace. Mrs. Quill began to cry.

"Wait a minute," she said, taking a handkerchief from her bag. "Wait a minute—I would like to telephone to my friend Pacifica."

The assistant manager pointed in the direction of the telephone booths, and she hurried away, her face buried in her handkerchief. Fifteen minutes later she returned, crying more pitifully than before.

"Mrs. Copperfield is coming to get me—I told her all about it. I think I'll sit down somewhere and wait."

"Does Mrs. Copperfield have the necessary funds with which to cover your bill?"

"I don't know," said Mrs. Quill, walking away from him.

"You mean you don't know whether or not she will be able to pay your bill?"

"Yes, yes, she'll pay my bill. Please let me sit down over there."

The manager nodded. Mrs. Quill fell into an armchair that stood beside a tall palm tree. She covered her face with her hands and continued to cry.

Twenty minutes later Mrs. Copperfield arrived. In spite of the heat she was wearing a silver-fox cape which she had brought with her for use only in higher altitudes.

Although she was perspiring and badly made up, she felt assured of being treated with a certain amount of deference by the hotel employees because of the silver-fox cape.

She had awakened quite some time before and was again a little drunk. She rushed up to Mrs. Quill and kissed her on the top of her head.

"Where's the man who made you cry?" she asked.

Mrs. Quill looked around through her tear-veiled eyes and pointed to the assistant manager. Mrs. Copperfield beckoned to him with her index finger.

He came over to them and she asked him where she could get some flowers for Mrs. Quill.

"There's nothing like flowers when you're either sick at heart or physically ill," she said to him. "She's been under a terrible strain. Would you get some flowers?" she asked, taking a twenty-dollar bill from her purse.

"There is no florist in the hotel," said the assistant manager.

"That's not very luxurious," said Mrs. Copperfield.

He did not reply.

"Well then," she continued, "the next best thing to do is to buy her something nice to drink. I suggest that we all go to the bar."

The assistant manager declined.

"But," said Mrs. Copperfield, "I insist that you come along. I want to talk things over with you. I think you've been horrid."

The assistant manager stared at her.

"The most horrid thing about you," continued Mrs. Copperfield, "is that you're just as grouchy now that you know your bill will be paid as you were before. You were mean and worried then and you're mean and worried now. The expression on your face hasn't changed one bit. It's a dangerous man who reacts more or less in the same way to good news or bad news."

Since he still made no effort to speak, she continued: "You've not only made Mrs. Quill completely miserable for no reason at all, but you've spoiled my fun too. You don't even know how to please the rich." The assistant manager raised his eyebrows.

"You won't understand this but I shall tell it to you anyway. I came here for two reasons. The first reason, naturally, was in order to get my friend Mrs. Quill out of trouble; the second reason was in order to see your face when you realized that a bill which you never expected to be paid was to be paid after all. I expected to be able to watch the transition. You understand—enemy into friend—that's always terribly exciting. That's why in a good movie the hero often hates the heroine until the very end. But you, of course, wouldn't dream of lowering your standards. You think it would be cheap to turn into an affable human being because you discovered there was money where you had been sure there was no money to be forthcoming. Do you think the rich mind? They never get enough of it. They want to be liked for their money too, and not only for themselves. You're not even a good hotel manager. You're definitely a boor in every way."

The assistant manager looked down with loathing at Mrs. Copperfield's upturned face. He hated her sharp features and her high voice. He found her even more disgusting than Mrs. Quill. He was not fond of women anyway.

"You have no imagination," she said, "*none whatever*! You are missing everything. Where do I pay my bill?"

All the way home Mrs. Copperfield felt sad because Mrs. Quill was dignified and remote and did not give her the lavish thanks which she had been expecting.

• • •

Early the next morning Mrs. Copperfield and Pacifica were together in Pacifica's bedroom. The sky was beginning to grow light. Mrs. Copperfield had never seen Pacifica this drunk. Her hair was pushed up on her head. It looked now somewhat like a wig which is a little too small for the wearer. Her pupils were very large and slightly filmed. There was a large dark spot on the front of her checked skirt, and her breath smelled very strongly of whisky. She stumbled over to the window and looked out. It was quite dark in the room. Mrs. Copperfield could barely discern the red and purple squares in Pacifica's skirt. She could not see her legs at all, the shadows were so deep, but she knew the heavy yellow silk stockings and the white sneakers well.

"It's so lovely," said Mrs. Copperfield.

"Beautiful," said Pacifica, turning around, "beautiful." She moved unsteadily around the room. "Listen," she said, "the most wonderful thing to do now is to go to the beach and swim in the water. If you have enough money we can take a taxicab and go. Come on. Will you?"

Mrs. Copperfield was very startled indeed, but Pacifica was already pulling a blanket from the bed. "Please," she said. "You cannot know how much pleasure this would give me. You must take that towel over there."

The beach was not very far away. When they arrived, Pacifica told the cab-driver to come back in two hours.

The shore was strewn with rocks; this was a disappointment to Mrs. Copperfield. Although the wind was not very strong, she noticed that the top branches of the palm trees were shaking.

Pacifica took her clothes off and immediately walked into the water. She stood for a time with her legs wide apart, the water scarcely reaching to her shins, while Mrs. Copperfield sat on a rock trying to decide whether or not to remove her own clothes. There was a sudden splash and Pacifica started to swim. She swam first on her back and then on her stomach, and Mrs. Copperfield was certain that she could hear her singing. When at last Pacifica grew tired of splashing about in the water, she stood up and walked towards the beach. She took tremendous strides and her pubic hair hung between her legs sopping wet. Mrs. Copperfield looked a little embarrassed, but Pacifica plopped down beside her and asked her why she did not come in the water.

"I can't swim," said Mrs. Copperfield.

Pacifica looked up at the sky. She could see now that it was not going to be a completely fair day.

"Why do you sit on that terrible rock?" said Pacifica. "Come, take your clothes off and we go in the water. I will teach you to swim."

"I was never able to learn."

"I will teach you. If you cannot learn I will let you sink. No, this is only a joke. Don't take it serious."

Mrs. Copperfield undressed. She was very white and thin, and her spine was visible all the way along her back. Pacifica looked at her body without saying a word.

"I know I have an awful figure," said Mrs. Copperfield.

Pacifica did not answer. "Come," she said, getting up and putting her arm around Mrs. Copperfield's waist.

They stood with the water up to their thighs, facing the beach and the palm trees. The trees appeared to be moving behind a mist. The beach was colorless. Behind them the sky was growing lighter very rapidly, but the sea was still almost black. Mrs. Copperfield noticed a red fever sore on Pacifica's lip. Water was dripping from her hair onto her shoulders.

She turned away from the beach and pulled Mrs. Copperfield farther out into the water.

Mrs. Copperfield held onto Pacifica's hand very hard. Soon the water was up to her chin.

"Now lie on your back. I will hold you under your head," said Pacifica.

Mrs. Copperfield looked around wildly, but she obeyed, and floated on her back with only the support of Pacifica's open hand under her head to keep her from sinking. She could see her own narrow feet floating on top of the water. Pacifica started to swim, dragging Mrs. Copperfield along with her. As she had only the use of one arm, her task was an arduous one and she was soon breathing like a bull. The touch of her hand underneath the head of Mrs. Copperfield was very light—in fact, so light that Mrs. Copperfield feared that she would be left alone from one minute to the next. She looked up. The sky was packed with gray clouds. She wanted to say something to Pacifica, but she did not dare to turn her head.

Pacifica swam a little farther inland. Suddenly she stood up and placed both her hands firmly in the small of Mrs. Copperfield's back. Mrs. Copperfield felt happy and sick at once. She turned her face and in so doing she brushed Pacifica's heavy stomach with her cheek. She held on hard to Pacifica's thigh with the strength of years of sorrow and frustration in her hand.

"Don't leave me," she called out.

At this moment Mrs. Copperfield was strongly reminded of a dream that had recurred often during her life. She was being chased up a short hill by a dog. At the top of the hill there stood a few pine trees and a mannequin about eight feet high. She approached the mannequin and discovered her to be fashioned out of flesh, but without life. Her dress was of black velvet, and tapered to a very narrow width at the hem. Mrs. Copperfield wrapped one of the mannequin's arms tightly around her own waist. She was startled by the thickness of the arm and very pleased. The mannequin's other arm she bent upward from the elbow with her free hand. Then the mannequin began to sway backwards and forwards. Mrs. Copperfield clung all the more tightly to the mannequin and together they fell off the top of the hill and continued rolling for quite a distance until they landed on a little walk, where they remained locked in each other's arms. Mrs. Copperfield loved this part of the dream best; and the fact that all the way down the hill the mannequin acted as a buffer between herself and the broken bottles and little stones over which they fell gave her particular satisfaction.

Pacifica had resurrected the emotional content of her dream for a moment, which Mrs. Copperfield thought was certainly the reason for her own peculiar elation.

"Now," said Pacifica, "if you don't mind I will take one more swim by myself." But first she helped Mrs. Copperfield to her feet and led her back to the beach, where Mrs. Copperfield collapsed on the sand and hung her head like a wilted flower. She was trembling and exhausted as one is after a love experience. She looked up at Pacifica, who noticed that her eyes were more luminous and softer than she had ever seen them before.

"You should go in the water more," said Pacifica; "you stay in the house too much."

She ran back into the water and swam back and forth many times. The sea was now blue and much rougher than it had been earlier. Once during the course of her swimming Pacifica rested on a large flat rock which the outgoing tide had uncovered. She was directly in the line of the hazy sun's pale rays. Mrs. Copperfield had a difficult time being able to see her at all and soon she fell asleep.

• • •

Upon arriving back at the hotel, Pacifica announced to Mrs. Copperfield that she was going to sleep like a dead person. "I hope I don't wake up for ten days," she said.

Mrs. Copperfield watched her stumble down the bright green corridor, yawning and tossing her head.

"Two weeks I'll sleep," she said again, and then she went into her room and shut the door behind her. In her own room Mrs. Copperfield decided that she had better call on Mr. Copperfield. She went downstairs and walked out into the street, which seemed to be moving as it had on the first day of her arrival. There were a few people already seated on their balconies who were looking down at her. A very thin girl, wearing a red silk dress which hung down to her ankles, was crossing the street towards her. She looked surprisingly young and fresh. When Mrs. Copperfield was nearer to her she decided that she was a Malayan. She was rather startled when the girl stopped directly in front of her and addressed her in perfect English.

"Where have you been that you got your hair all wet?" she said.

"I've been taking a swim with a friend of mine. We—we went early to the beach." Mrs. Copperfield didn't feel much like talking.

"What beach?" asked the girl.

"I don't know," said Mrs. Copperfield.

"Well, did you walk there or did you ride?"

"We rode."

"There isn't any beach really near enough to walk to, I guess," said the girl.

"No, I guess there isn't," said Mrs. Copperfield, sighing and looking around her. The girl was walking along with her.

"Was the water cold?" asked the girl.

"Yes and no," said Mrs. Copperfield.

"Did you swim in the water naked with your friend?"

"Yes."

"Then there weren't any people around, I suppose."

"No, there wasn't a soul there. Do you swim?" Mrs. Copperfield asked the girl.

"No," she said, "I never go near the water." The girl had a shrill voice. She had light hair and brows. She could easily have been partly English. Mrs. Copperfield decided not to ask her. She turned to the girl.

"I'm going to make a telephone call. Where is the nearest place with a phone?"

"Come to Bill Grey's restaurant. They keep it very cool. I generally spend my mornings there drinking like a fish. By the time it's noon I'm cockeyed drunk. I shock the tourists. I'm half Irish and half Javanese. They make bets about what I am. Whoever wins has to buy me a drink. Guess how old I am."

"God knows," said Mrs. Copperfield.

"Well, I'm sixteen."

"Very possible," said Mrs. Copperfield. The girl seemed peeved. They walked in silence to Bill Grey's restaurant, where the girl pushed Mrs. Copperfield through the door and along the floor towards a table in the middle of the restaurant.

"Sit down and order whatever you like. It's on me," said the girl.

There was an electric fan whirling above their heads.

"Isn't it delicious in here?" she said to Mrs. Copperfield.

"Let me make my phone call," said Mrs. Copperfield, who was terrified lest Mr. Copperfield should have come in a few hours ago and be waiting impatiently for her call even at this very moment.

"Make all the phone calls you like," said the girl.

Mrs. Copperfield went into the booth and phoned her husband. He said that he had arrived a short time ago, and that he would have breakfast and join her afterwards at Bill Grey's. He sounded cold and tired.

The girl, while waiting anxiously for her return, had ordered two old-fashioneds. Mrs. Copperfield came back to the table and flopped into her seat.

"I never can sleep late in the mornings," said the girl. "I don't even like to sleep at night if I have anything better to do. My mother told me that I was as nervous as a cat, but very healthy. I went to dancing school but I was too lazy to learn the steps."

"Where do you live?" asked Mrs. Copperfield.

"I live alone in a hotel. I've got plenty of money. A man in the

Army is in love with me. He's married but I never go with anyone else. He gives me plenty of money. He's even got more money at home. I'll buy you what you want. Don't tell anyone around here, though, that I've got money to spend on other people. I never buy them anything. They give me a pain. They live such terrible lives. So cheap; so stupid; so very stupid! They don't have any privacy. I have two rooms. You can use one of them if you like."

Mrs. Copperfield said she wouldn't need to, very firmly. She wasn't fond of this girl in the least.

"What is your name?" the girl asked her.

"Frieda Copperfield."

"My name is Peggy—Peggy Gladys. You looked kind of adorable to me with your hair all wet and your little nose as shiny as it was. That's why I asked you to drink with me."

Mrs. Copperfield jumped. "Please don't embarrass me," she said.

"Oh, let me embarrass you, adorable. Now finish your drink and I'll get you some more. Maybe you're hungry and would like some steak."

The girl had the bright eyes of an insatiable nymphomaniac. She wore a ridiculous little watch on a black ribbon around her wrist.

"I live at the Hotel de las Palmas," said Mrs. Copperfield. "I am a friend of the manager there, Mrs. Quill, and one of her guests, Pacifica."

"That's no good, that hotel," said Peggy. "I went in there with some fellows for drinks one night and I said to them: 'If you don't turn right around and leave this hotel, I'll never allow you to take me out again.' It's a cheap place; awful place; it's filthy dirty besides. I'm surprised at you living there. My hotel is much nicer. Some Americans stay there when they come off the boat if they don't go to the Hotel Washington. It's the Hotel Granada."

"Yes, that is where we were staying originally," said Mrs. Copperfield. "My husband is there now. I think it is the most depressing place I have ever set foot in. I think the Hotel de las Palmas is a hundred million times nicer."

"But," said the girl, opening her mouth wide in dismay, "I think you have not looked very carefully. I've put all my own things around in my room of course, and that makes a lot of difference."

"How long have you been living there?" asked Mrs. Copperfield. She was completely puzzled by this girl and a little bit sorry for her.

"I have been living there for a year and a half. It seems like a lifetime. I moved in a little while after I met the man in the Army.

He's very nice to me. I think I'm smarter than he is. That's because I'm a girl. Mother told me that girls were never dumb like men, so I just go ahead and do whatever I think is right."

The girl's face was elfin and sweet. She had a cleft chin and a small snub-nose.

"Honestly," she said, "I've got lots of money. I can always get more. I'd love to get you anything you like, because I love the way you talk and look and the way you move; you're elegant." She giggled and put her own dry rough hand in Mrs. Copperfield's.

"Please," she said, "be friendly to me. I don't often see people I like. I never do the same thing twice, really I don't. I haven't asked anyone up to my rooms in the longest while because I'm not interested and because they get everything so dirty. I know you wouldn't get everything dirty because I can tell that you come from a nice class of people. I love people with a good education. I think it's wonderful."

"I have so much on my mind," said Mrs. Copperfield. "Generally I haven't."

"Well, forget it," said the young girl imperiously. "You're with Peggy Gladys and she's paying for your drinks. Because she wants to pay for your drinks with all her heart. It's such a beautiful morning. Cheer up!" She took Mrs. Copperfield by the sleeve and shook her.

Mrs. Copperfield was still deep in the magic of her dream and in thoughts of Pacifica. She was uneasy and the electric fan seemed to blow directly on her heart. She sat staring ahead of her, not listening to a word the girl was saying.

She could not tell how long she had been dreaming when she looked down and saw a lobster lying on a plate in front of her.

"Oh," she said, "I can't eat this. I can't possibly eat this."

"But I ordered it for you," said Peggy, "and there is some beer coming along. I had your old-fashioned taken away because you weren't touching it." She leaned across the table and tucked Mrs. Copperfield's napkin under her chin.

"Please eat, dearest," said Peggy, "you'll give me such great pleasure if you do."

"What do you think you're doing?" said Mrs. Copperfield fretfully. "Playing house?"

Peggy laughed.

"You know," said Mrs. Copperfield, "my husband is coming here to join us. He'll think we're both stark raving mad to be eating lobster in the morning. He doesn't understand such things."

"Well, let's eat it up quickly, then," said Peggy. She looked wistfully at Mrs. Copperfield. "I wish he wasn't coming," she said. "Couldn't you telephone him and tell him not to come?"

"No, my dear, that would be impossible. Besides, I don't have any reason to tell him not to come. I am very anxious to see him." Mrs. Copperfield could not resist being just a little bit sadistic with Peggy Gladys.

"Of course you want to see him," said Peggy, looking very shy and demure. "I'll be quiet while he's here, I'll promise you."

"That's just what I don't want you to do. Please continue to prattle when he's here."

"Of course, darling. Don't be so nervous."

Mr. Copperfield arrived as they were eating their lobster. He was wearing a dark green suit and looking extremely well. He came over to them smiling pleasantly.

"Hello," said Mrs. Copperfield. "I'm very glad to see you. You look very well. This is Peggy Gladys; we've just met."

He shook hands with her and seemed very pleased. "What on earth are you eating?" he asked them.

"Lobster," they answered. He frowned. "But," he said, "you'll have indigestion, and you're drinking beer too! Good God!" He sat down.

"I don't mean to interfere, of course," said Mr. Copperfield, "but it's very bad. Have you had breakfast?"

"I don't know," said Mrs. Copperfield purposely. Peggy Gladys laughed. Mr. Copperfield raised his brows.

"You must know," he murmured. "Don't be ridiculous."

He asked Peggy Gladys where she was from.

"I'm from Panama," she told him, "but I'm half Irish and half Javanese."

"I see," said Mr. Copperfield. He kept smiling at her.

"Pacifica's asleep," said Mrs. Copperfield suddenly.

Mr. Copperfield frowned. "Really," he said, "are you going back there?"

"What do you think I'm going to do?"

"There isn't any point in staying here much longer. I thought we'd pack. I've made arrangements in Panama. We can sail tomorrow. I have to phone them tonight. I've found out a lot about the various countries in Central America. It might be possible for us to stay on a kind of cattle ranch in Costa Rica. A man told me about it. It's completely isolated. You have to get there on a river boat."

Peggy Gladys looked bored.

Mrs. Copperfield put her head in her hands.

"Imagine red and blue guacamayos flying over the cattle," Mr. Copperfield laughed. "Latin Texas. It must be completely crazy."

"Red and blue guacamayos flying over the cattle," Peggy Gladys repeated after him. "What are guacamayos?" she asked.

"They're tremendous red and blue birds, more or less like parrots," said Mr. Copperfield. "As long as you are eating lobster I think I shall have ice cream with whipped cream on top."

"He's nice," said Peggy Gladys.

"Listen," said Mrs. Copperfield, "I feel sick. I don't think I can sit through the ice cream."

"I won't take long," said Mr. Copperfield. He looked at her. "It must be the lobster."

"Maybe I'd better take her to my Hotel Granada," said Peggy Gladys, jumping to her feet with alacrity. "She'll be very comfortable there. Then you can come after you've eaten your ice cream."

"That seems sensible, don't you think so, Frieda?"

"No," said Mrs. Copperfield vehemently, clutching at the chain she wore around her neck. "I think I'd better go right straight back to the Hotel de las Palmas. I *must* go. I must go immediately. . . ." She was so distraught that she rose from the table, forgetting her pocketbook and her scarf, and started to leave the restaurant.

"But you've left everything behind you," Mr. Copperfield called out after her.

"I'll take them," exclaimed Peggy Gladys. "You eat your ice cream and come later." She rushed after Mrs. Copperfield and together they ran down the suffocatingly hot street towards the Hotel de las Palmas.

Mrs. Quill was standing in the doorway drinking something out of a bottle.

"I'm on the cherry-pop wagon until dinner time," she said.

"Oh, Mrs. Quill, come up to my room with me!" said Mrs. Copperfield, putting her arms around Mrs. Quill and sighing deeply. "Mr. Copperfield is back."

"Why don't you come upstairs with *me*?" said Peggy Gladys. "I promised your husband I'd take care of you."

Mrs. Copperfield wheeled round. "Please be quiet," she shouted, looking fixedly at Peggy Gladys.

"Now, now," said Mrs. Quill, "don't upset the little girl. We'll have to be giving her a honey bun to quiet her. Of course it took more than a honey bun to quiet me at her age."

"I'm all right," said Peggy Gladys. "Will you kindly take us to her room? She's supposed to be flat on her back."

The young girl sat on the edge of Mrs. Copperfield's bed with her hand on Mrs. Copperfield's forehead.

"I'm sorry," she said. "You look very badly. I wish you wouldn't be so unhappy. Couldn't you possibly not think about it now and think about it some other day? Sometimes if you let things rest . . . I'm not sixteen, I'm seventeen. I feel like a child. I can't seem to say anything unless people think I'm very young. Maybe you don't like the fact that I'm so fresh. You're white and green. You don't look pretty. You looked much prettier before. After your husband has been here I'll take you for a ride in a carriage if you like. My mother's dead," she said softly.

"Listen," said Mrs. Copperfield. "If you don't mind going away now . . . I'd like to be by myself. You can come back later."

"What time can I come back?"

"I don't know; come back later; can't you see? I don't know."

"All right," said Peggy Gladys. "Maybe I should just go downstairs and talk to that fat woman, or drink. Then when you're ready you can come down. I have nothing to do for three days. You really want me to go?"

Mrs. Copperfield nodded.

The girl left the room reluctantly.

Mrs. Copperfield started to tremble after the girl had closed the door behind her. She trembled so violently that she shook the bed. She was suffering as much as she had ever suffered before, because she was going to do what she wanted to do. But it would not make her happy. She did not have the courage to stop from doing what she wanted to do. She knew that it would not make her happy, because only the dreams of crazy people come true. She thought that she was only interested in duplicating a dream, but in doing so she necessarily became the complete victim of a nightmare.

Mr. Copperfield came very quietly into her room. "How do you feel now?" he asked.

"I'm all right," she said.

"Who was that young girl? She was very pretty—from a sculptural point of view."

"Her name is Peggy Gladys."

"She spoke very well, didn't she? Or am I wrong?"

"She spoke beautifully."

"Have you been having a nice time?"

"I've had the most wonderful time in my whole life," said Mrs. Copperfield, almost weeping.

"I had a nice time too, exploring Panama City. But my room was so uncomfortable. There was too much noise. I couldn't sleep."

"Why didn't you take a nicer room in a better hotel?"

"You know me. I hate to spend money. I never think it's worth it. I guess I should have. I should have been drinking too. I'd have had a better time. But I didn't."

They were silent. Mr. Copperfield drummed on the bureau. "I guess we should be leaving tonight," he said, "instead of staying on here. It's terribly expensive here. There won't be another boat for quite a few days."

Mrs. Copperfield did not answer.

"Don't you think I'm correct?"

"I don't want to go," she said, twisting on the bed.

"I don't understand," said Mr. Copperfield.

"I can't go. I want to stay here."

"For how long?"

"I don't know."

"But you can't plan a trip that way. Perhaps you don't intend to plan a trip."

"Oh, I'll plan a trip," said Mrs. Copperfield vaguely.

"You will?"

"No, I won't."

"It's up to you," said Mr. Copperfield. "I just think you'll be missing a great deal by not seeing Central America. You're certain to get bored here unless you start to drink. You probably will start to drink."

"Why don't you go, and then come back when you've seen enough?" she suggested.

"I won't come back because I can't look at you," said Mr. Copperfield. "You're a horror." So saying, he took an empty pitcher from the bureau, threw it out of the window into the alley, and left the room.

An hour later Mrs. Copperfield went downstairs into the bar. She was surprised and glad to see Pacifica there. Although Pacifica had powdered her face very heavily, she looked tired. She was sitting at a little table holding her pocketbook in her hands.

"Pacifica," said Mrs. Copperfield, "I didn't know that you were awake. I was certain that you were asleep in your room. I'm so glad to see you."

"I could not close my eyes. I was sleeping for fifteen minutes and then after that I could not close my eyes. Someone came to see me."

Peggy Gladys walked over to Mrs. Copperfield. "Hello," she said, running her fingers through Mrs. Copperfield's hair. "Are you ready to take that ride yet?"

"What ride?" asked Mrs. Copperfield.

"The ride in the carriage with me."

"No, I'm not ready," said Mrs. Copperfield.

"When will you be?" asked Peggy Gladys.

"I'm going to buy some stockings," said Pacifica. "You want to come with me, Copperfield?"

"Yes. Let's go."

"Your husband looked upset when he left the hotel," said Peggy Gladys. "I hope you didn't have a fight."

Mrs. Copperfield was walking out of the door with Pacifica. "Excuse us," she called over her shoulder to Peggy Gladys. She was standing still and looking after them like a hurt animal!

It was so hot out that even the most conservative women tourists, their faces and chests flame-red, were pulling off their hats and drying their foreheads with their handkerchiefs. Most of them, to escape the heat, were dropping into the little Hindu stores where, if the shop wasn't too crowded, the salesman offered them a little chair so that they might view twenty or thirty kimonos without getting tired.

"*Qué calor!*" said Pacifica.

"To hell with stockings," said Mrs. Copperfield, who thought she was about to faint. "Let's get some beer."

"If you want, go and get yourself some beer. I must have stockings. I think bare legs on a woman is something terrible."

"No, I'll come with you." Mrs. Copperfield put her hand in Pacifica's.

"Ay!" cried Pacifica, releasing her hand. "We are both too wet, darling. *Qué barbaridad!*"

The store into which Pacifica took Mrs. Copperfield was very tiny. It was even hotter in there than on the street.

"You see you can buy many things here," said Pacifica. "I come here because he knows me and I can get my stockings for very little money."

While Pacifica was buying her stockings Mrs. Copperfield looked at all the other little articles in the store. Pacifica took such a long time that Mrs. Copperfield grew more and more bored. She stood first on one foot and then on the other. Pacifica argued and argued. There were dark perspiration stains under her arms, and the wings of her nose were streaming.

When it was all over and Mrs. Copperfield saw that the salesman was wrapping the package, she went over and paid the bill. The salesman wished her good luck and they left the store.

There was a letter for her at home. Mrs. Quill gave it to her.

"Mr. Copperfield left this for you," she said. "I tried to urge him to stay and have a cup of tea or some beer, but he was in a hurry. He's one handsome fellow."

Mrs. Copperfield took the letter and started towards the bar.

"Hello, sweet," said Peggy Gladys softly.

Mrs. Copperfield could see that Peggy was very drunk. Her hair was hanging over her face and her eyes were dead.

"Maybe you're not ready yet . . . but I can wait a long time. I love to wait. I don't mind being by myself."

"You'll excuse me a minute if I read a letter which I just received from my husband," said Mrs. Copperfield.

She sat down and tore open the envelope.

> Dear Frieda [*she read*],
>
> I do not mean to be cruel but I shall write to you exactly what I consider to be your faults and I hope sincerely that what I have written will influence you. Like most people, you are not able to face more than one fear during your lifetime. You also spend your life fleeing from your first fear towards your first hope. Be careful that you do not, through your own wiliness, end up always in the same position in which you began. I do not advise you to spend your life surrounding yourself with those things which you term necessary to your existence, regardless of whether or not they are objectively interesting in themselves or even to your own particular intellect. I believe sincerely that only those men who reach the stage where it is possible for them to combat a second tragedy within themselves, and not the first over again, are worthy of being called mature. When you think someone is going ahead, make sure that he is not really standing still. In order to go ahead, you must leave things behind which most people are unwilling to do. Your first pain, you carry it with you like a lodestone in your breast because all tenderness will come from there. You must carry it with you through your whole life but you must not circle around it. You must give up the search for those symbols which only serve to hide its face from you. You will have the illusion that they are disparate and manifold but they are always the same. If you are

> only interested in a bearable life, perhaps this letter does not concern you. For God's sake, a ship leaving port is still a wonderful thing to see.
>
> J.C.

Mrs. Copperfield's heart was beating very quickly. She crushed the letter in her hand and shook her head two or three times.

"I'll never bother you unless you ask me to bother you," Peggy Gladys was saying. She did not seem to be addressing anyone in particular. Her eyes wandered from the ceiling to the walls. She was smiling to herself.

"She is reading a letter from her husband," she said, letting her arm fall down heavily on the bar. "I myself don't want a husband—never—never—never. . . ."

Mrs. Copperfield rose to her feet.

"*Pacifica,*" she shouted, "*Pacifica!*"

"Who is Pacifica?" asked Peggy Gladys. "I want to meet her. Is she as beautiful as you are? Tell her to come here. . . ."

"Beautiful?" the bartender laughed. "Beautiful? Neither of them is beautiful. They're both old hens. You're beautiful even if you are blind drunk."

"Bring her in here, darling," said Peggy Gladys, letting her head fall down on the bar.

"Listen, your pal's been out of the room two whole minutes already. She's gone to look for Pacifica."

Taxco, 1942

CALL AT CORAZÓN

PAUL BOWLES

"BUT WHY WOULD YOU WANT a little horror like that to go along with us? It doesn't make sense. You know what they're like."

"I know what they're like," said her husband. "It's comforting to watch them. Whatever happens, if I had that to look at, I'd be reminded of how stupid I was ever to get upset."

He leaned further over the railing and looked intently down at the dock. There were baskets for sale, crude painted toys of hard natural rubber, reptile-hide wallets and belts, and a few whole snakeskins unrolled. And placed apart from these wares, out of the hot sunlight, in the shadow of a crate, sat a tiny furry monkey. The hands were folded, and the forehead was wrinkled in sad apprehensiveness.

"Isn't he wonderful?"

"I think you're impossible—and a little insulting," she replied.

He turned to look at her. "Are you serious?" He saw that she was.

She went on, studying her sandaled feet and the narrow deckboards beneath them: "You know I don't really mind all this nonsense, or your craziness. Just let me finish." He nodded his head in agreement, looking back at the hot dock and the wretched tin-roofed village beyond. "It goes without saying I don't mind all that, or we wouldn't be here together. You might be here alone. . . ."

"You don't take a honeymoon alone," he interrupted.

"*You* might." She laughed shortly.

He reached along the rail for her hand, but she pulled it away, saying, "I'm still talking to you. I expect you to be crazy, and I expect to give in to you all along. I'm crazy too, I know. But I wish there were some way I could just once feel that my giving in meant anything to you. I wish you knew how to be gracious about it."

"You think you humor me so much? I haven't noticed it." His voice was sullen.

"I don't *humor* you at all. I'm just trying to live with you on an extended trip in a lot of cramped little cabins on an endless series of stinking boats."

"What do you mean?" he cried excitedly. "You've always said you loved the boats. Have you changed your mind, or just lost it completely?"

She turned and walked toward the prow. "Don't talk to me," she said. "Go and buy your monkey."

An expression of solicitousness on his face, he was following her. "You know I won't buy it if it's going to make you miserable."

"I'll be more miserable if you don't, so please go and buy it." She stopped and turned. "I'd love to have it. I really would. I think it's sweet."

"I don't get you at all."

She smiled. "I know. Does it bother you very much?"

After he had bought the monkey and tied it to the metal post of the bunk in the cabin, he took a walk to explore the port. It was a town made of corrugated tin and barbed wire. The sun's heat was painful, even with the sky's low-lying cover of fog. It was the middle of the day and few people were in the streets. He came to the edge of the town almost immediately. Here between him and the forest lay a narrow, slow-moving stream, its water the color of black coffee. A few women were washing clothes; small children splashed. Gigantic gray crabs scuttled between the holes they had made in the mud along the bank. He sat down on some elaborately twisted roots at the foot of a tree and took out the notebook he always carried with him. The day before, in a bar at Pedernales, he had written: "Recipe for dissolving the impression of hideousness made by a thing: Fix the attention upon the given object or situation so that the various elements, all familiar, will regroup themselves. Frightfulness is never more than an unfamiliar pattern."

He lit a cigarette and watched the women's hopeless attempts to launder the ragged garments. Then he threw the burning stub at the nearest crab, and carefully wrote: "More than anything else, woman requires strict ritualistic observance of the traditions of sexual behavior. That is her definition of love." He thought of the derision that would be called forth should he make such a statement to the girl back on the ship. After looking at his watch, he wrote hurriedly: "Modern, that is, intellectual education, having been devised by males for males, inhibits and confuses her. She avenges. . . ."

Two naked children, coming up from their play in the river, ran screaming past him, scattering drops of water over the paper. He called out to them, but they continued their chase without noticing him. He put his pencil and notebook into his pocket, smiling, and watched them patter after one another through the dust.

When he arrived back at the ship, the thunder was rolling down from the mountains around the harbor. The storm reached the height of its hysteria just as they got under way.

She was sitting on her bunk, looking through the open porthole. The shrill crashes of thunder echoed from one side of the bay to the other as they streamed toward the open sea. He lay doubled up on his bunk opposite, reading.

"Don't lean your head against that metal wall," he advised. "It's a perfect conductor."

She jumped down to the floor and went to the washstand.

"Where are those two quarts of White Horse we got yesterday?"

He gestured. "In the rack on your side. Are you going to drink?"

"I'm going to *have* a drink, yes."

"In this heat? Why don't you wait until it clears, and have it on deck?"

"I want it now. When it clears I won't need it."

She poured the whisky and added water from the carafe in the wall bracket over the washbowl.

"You realize what you're doing, of course."

She glared at him. "What am I doing?"

He shrugged his shoulders. "Nothing, except just giving in to a passing emotional state. You could read, or lie down and doze."

Holding her glass in one hand, she pulled open the door into the passageway with the other, and went out. The noise of the slamming door startled the monkey, perched on a suitcase. It hesitated a second, and hurried under its master's bunk. He made a few kissing sounds to entice it out, and returned to his book. Soon he began to imagine her alone and unhappy on the deck, and the thought cut into the pleasure of his reading. He forced himself to lie still a few minutes, the open book face down across his chest. The boat was moving at full speed now, and the sound of the motors was louder than the storm in the sky.

Soon he rose and went on deck. The land behind was already hidden by the falling rain, and the air smelled of deep water. She was standing alone by the rail, looking down at the waves, with the empty glass in her hand. Pity seized him as he watched, but he could not walk across to her and put into consoling words the emotion he felt.

Back in the cabin he found the monkey on his bunk, slowly tearing the pages from the book he had been reading.

The next day was spent in leisurely preparation for disembarking and changing of boats: in Villalta they were to take a smaller vessel to the opposite side of the delta.

When she came in to pack after dinner, she stood a moment studying the cabin. "He's messed it up, all right," said her husband, "but I found your necklace behind my big valise, and we'd read all the magazines anyway."

"I suppose this represents Man's innate urge to destroy," she said, kicking a ball of crumpled paper across the floor. "And the next time he tries to bite you, it'll be Man's basic insecurity."

"You don't know what a bore you are when you try to be caustic. If you want me to get rid of him, I will. It's easy enough."

She bent to touch the animal, but it backed uneasily under the bunk. She stood up. "I don't mind him. What I mind is you. *He* can't help being a little horror, but he keeps reminding me that you could if you wanted."

Her husband's face assumed the impassivity that was characteristic of him when he was determined not to lose his temper. She knew he would wait to be angry until she was unprepared for his attack. He said nothing, tapping an insistent rhythm on the lid of a suitcase with his fingernails.

"Naturally I don't really mean you're a horror," she continued.

"Why not mean it?" he said, smiling pleasantly. "What's wrong with criticism? Probably I am, to you. I like monkeys because I see them as little model men. You think men are something else, something spiritual or God knows what. Whatever it is, I notice you're the one who's always being disillusioned and going around wondering how mankind can be so bestial. I think mankind is fine."

"Please don't go on," she said. "I know your theories. You'll never convince yourself of them."

When they had finished packing, they went to bed. As he snapped off the light behind his pillow, he said, "Tell me honestly. Do you want me to give him to the steward?"

She kicked off her sheet in the dark. Through the porthole, near the horizon, she could see stars, and the calm sea slipped by just below her. Without thinking she said, "Why don't you drop him overboard?"

In the silence that followed she realized she had spoken carelessly, but the tepid breeze moving with languor over her body was making it increasingly difficult for her to think or speak. As she fell asleep it seemed to her she heard her husband saying slowly, "I believe you would. I believe you would."

The next morning she slept late, and when she went up for breakfast her husband had already finished his and was leaning back, smoking.

"How are you?" he asked brightly. "The cabin steward's delighted with the monkey."

She felt a flush of pleasure. "Oh," she said, sitting down, "did you give it to him? You didn't have to do that." She glanced at the menu; it was the same as every other day. "But I suppose really it's better. A monkey doesn't go with a honeymoon."

"I think you're right," he agreed.

Villalta was stifling and dusty. On the other boat they had grown accustomed to having very few passengers around, and it was an unpleasant surprise to find the new one swarming with people. Their new boat was a two-decked ferry painted white, with an enormous paddle wheel at the stern. On the lower deck, which rested not more than two feet above the surface of the river, passengers and freight stood ready to travel, packed together indiscriminately. The upper deck had a salon and a dozen or so narrow staterooms. In the salon the first-class passengers undid their bundles of pillows and opened their paper bags of food. The orange light of the setting sun flooded the room.

They looked into several of the staterooms.

"They all seem to be empty," she said.

"I can see why. Still, the privacy would be a help."

"This one's double. And it has a screen in the window. This is the best one."

"I'll look for a steward or somebody. Go on in and take over." He pushed the bags out of the passageway where the *cargador* had left them, and went off in search of an employee. In every corner of the boat the people seemed to be multiplying. There were twice as many as there had been a few moments before. The salon was completely full, its floor space occupied by groups of travelers with small children and elderly women, who were already stretched out on blankets and newspapers.

"It looks like Salvation Army headquarters the night after a major disaster," he said as he came back into the stateroom. "I can't find anybody. Anyway, we'd better stay in here. The other cubicles are beginning to fill up."

"I'm not so sure I wouldn't rather be on deck," she announced. "There are hundreds of cockroaches."

"And probably worse," he added, looking at the bunks.

"The thing to do is take those filthy sheets off and just lie on the mattresses." She peered out into the corridor. Sweat was trickling down her neck. "Do you think it's safe?"

"What do you mean?"

"All those people. This old tub."

He shrugged his shoulders.

"It's just one night. Tomorrow we'll be at Cienaga. And it's almost night now."

She shut the door and leaned against it, smiling faintly.

"I think it's going to be fun," she said.

"The boat's moving!" he cried. "Let's go on deck. If we can get out there."

Slowly the old boat pushed across the bay toward the dark east shore. People were singing and playing guitars. On the bottom deck a cow lowed continuously. And louder than all the sounds was the rush of water made by the huge paddles.

They sat on the deck in the middle of a vociferous crowd, leaning against the bars of the railing, and watched the moon rise above the mangrove swamps ahead. As they approached the opposite side of the bay, it looked as if the boat might plow straight into the shore, but a narrow waterway presently appeared, and the boat slipped cautiously in. The people immediately moved back from the railing, crowding against the opposite wall. Branches from the trees on the bank began to rub against the boat, scraping along the side walls of the cabins, and then whipping violently across the deck.

They pushed their way through the throng and walked across the salon to the deck on the other side of the boat; the same thing was happening there.

"It's crazy," she declared. "It's like a nightmare. Whoever heard of going through a channel no wider than the boat! It makes me nervous. I'm going in and read."

Her husband let go of her arm. "You can never enter into the spirit of a thing, can you?"

"You tell me what the spirit is, and I'll see about entering into it," she said, turning away.

He followed her. "Don't you want to go down onto the lower deck? They seem to be going strong down there. Listen." He held up his hand. Repeated screams of laughter came up from below.

"I certainly don't!" she called, without looking around.

He went below. Groups of men were seated on bulging burlap sacks and wooden crates, matching coins. The women stood behind them, puffing on black cigarettes and shrieking with excitement. He watched them closely, reflecting that with fewer teeth missing they would be a handsome people. "Mineral deficiency in the soil," he commented to himself.

Standing on the other side of a circle of gamblers, facing him, was a muscular young native whose visòred cap and faint air of aloofness suggested official position of some sort aboard the boat. With difficulty the traveler made his way over to him, and spoke to him in Spanish.

"Are you an employee here?"

"Yes, sir."

"I am in cabin number eight. Can I pay the supplementary fare to you?"

"Yes, sir."

"Good."

He reached into his pocket for his wallet, at the same time remembering with annoyance that he had left it upstairs locked in a suitcase. The man looked expectant. His hand was out.

"My money is in my stateroom." Then he added, "My wife has it. But if you come up in half an hour I can pay you the fare."

"Yes, sir." The man lowered his hand and merely looked at him. Even though he gave an impression of purely animal force, his broad, somewhat simian face was handsome, the husband reflected. It was surprising when, a moment later, that face betrayed a boyish shyness as the man said, "I am going to spray the cabin for your señora."

"Thank you. Are there many mosquitoes?"

The man grunted and shook the fingers of one hand as if he had just burned them.

"Soon you will see how many." He moved away.

At that moment the boat jolted violently, and there was great merriment among the passengers. He pushed his way to the prow and saw that the pilot had run into the bank. The tangle of branches and roots was a few feet from his face, its complex forms vaguely lighted by the boat's lanterns. The boat backed laboriously and the channel's agitated water rose to deck level and lapped the outer edge. Slowly they nosed along the bank until the prow once more pointed to midstream, and they continued. Then almost immediately the passage curved so sharply that the same thing happened again, throwing him sideways against a sack of something unpleasantly soft and wet. A bell clanged below deck in the interior of the boat; the passengers' laughter was louder.

Eventually they pushed ahead, but now the movement became painfully slow as the sharpness of the curves in the passage increased.

Under the water the stumps groaned as the boat forced its sides against them. Branches cracked and broke, falling onto the forward and upper decks. The lantern at the prow was swept into the water.

"This isn't the regular channel," muttered a gambler, glancing up.

Several travelers exclaimed, "What?" almost in unison.

"There's a pile of passages through here. We're picking up cargo at Corazón."

The players retreated to a square inner arena which others were forming by shifting some of the crates. The husband followed them. Here they were comparatively safe from the intruding boughs. The deck was better lighted here, and this gave him the idea of making an entry in his notebook. Bending over a carton marked *Vermifugo Santa Rosalia,* he wrote: "November 18. We are moving through the blood stream of a giant. A very dark night." Here a fresh collision with the land knocked him over, knocked over everyone who was not propped between solid objects.

A few babies were crying, but most of them still slept. He slid down to the deck. Finding his position fairly comfortable, he fell into a dozing state which was broken irregularly by the shouting of the people and the jolting of the boat.

When he awoke later, the boat was quite stationary, the games had ceased, and the people were asleep, a few of the men continuing their conversation in small groups. He lay still, listening. The talk was all about places; they were comparing the unpleasant things to be found in various parts of the republic: insects, weather, reptiles, diseases, lack of food, high prices.

He looked at his watch. It was half past one. With difficulty he got to his feet, and found his way to the stairs. Above, in the salon, the kerosene lamps illumined a vast disorder of prostrate figures. He went into the corridor and knocked on the door marked with an eight. Without waiting for her to answer, he opened the door. It was dark inside. He heard a muffled cough nearby, and decided that she was awake.

"How are the mosquitoes? Did my monkey man come and fix you up?" he asked.

She did not answer, so he lit a match. She was not in the bunk on the left. The match burned his thumb. With the second one, he looked at the right-hand bunk. A tin insecticide sprayer lay there on the mattress; its leak had made a large circle of oil on the bare ticking. The cough was repeated. It was someone in the next cabin.

"Now what?" he said aloud, uncomfortable at finding himself upset to this degree. A suspicion seized him. Without lighting the hanging lamp, he rushed to open her valises, and in the dark felt hurriedly through the flimsy pieces of clothing and the toilet articles. The whisky bottles were not there.

This was not the first time she had gone on a solitary drinking bout, and it would be easy to find her among the passengers. However, being angry, he decided not to look for her. He took off his shirt and trousers and lay down on the left-hand bunk. His hand touched a bottle standing on the floor by the head of the bunk. He raised himself enough to smell it; it was beer and the bottle was half full. It was hot in the cabin, and he drank the remaining warm, bitter liquid with relish and rolled the bottle across the room.

The boat was not moving, but voices shouted out here and there. An occasional bump could be felt as a sack of something heavy was heaved aboard. He looked through the little square window with the screen in it. In the foreground, dimly illumined by the boat's lanterns, a few dark men, naked save for their ragged underdrawers, stood on a landing made in the mud and stared toward the boat. Through the endless intricacies of roots and trunks behind them he saw a bonfire blazing, but it was far back in the swamp. The air smelled of stagnant water and smoke.

Deciding to take advantage of the relative silence, he lay down and tried to sleep; he was not surprised, however, by the difficulty he found in relaxing. It was always hard to sleep when she was not there in the room. The comfort of her presence was lacking, and there was also the fear of being awakened by her return. When he allowed himself to, he would quickly begin to formulate ideas and translate them into sentences whose recording seemed the more urgent because he was lying comfortably in the dark. Sometimes he thought about her, but only as an unclear figure whose character lent flavor to a succession of backdrops. More often he reviewed the day just completed, seeking to convince himself that it had carried him a bit further away from his childhood. Often for months at a time the strangeness of his dreams persuaded him that at last he had turned the corner, that the dark place had finally been left behind, that he was out of hearing. Then, one evening as he fell asleep, before he had time to refuse, he would be staring closely at a long-forgotten object—a plate, a chair, a pin-cushion—and the accustomed feeling of infinite futility and sadness would recur.

The motor started up, and the great noise of the water in the paddle wheel recommenced. They pushed off from Corazón. He was pleased. "Now I shan't hear her when she comes in and bangs around," he thought, and fell into a light sleep.

He was scratching his arms and legs. The long-continued, vague malaise eventually became full consciousness, and he sat up angrily. Above the sounds made by the boat he could hear another sound, one which came through the window: an incredibly high and tiny tone, tiny but constant in pitch and intensity. He jumped down from the berth and went to the window. The channel was wider here, and the overhanging vegetation no longer touched the sides of the boat. In the air, nearby, far away, everywhere, was the thin wail of mosquito wings. He was aghast, and completely delighted by the novelty of the phenomenon. For a moment he watched the tangled black wilderness slip past. Then with the itching he remembered the mosquitoses inside the cabin. The screen did not reach quite to the top of the window; there was ample space for them to crawl in. Even there in the dark as he moved his fingers along the frame to find the handle he could feel them; there were that many.

Now that he was fully awake, he lighted a match and went to her bunk. Of course she was not there. He lifted the Flit gun and shook it. It was empty, and as the match went out, he saw that the spot on the mattress had spread even further.

"Son of a bitch!" he whispered, and going back to the window he tugged the screen vigorously upward to close the crack. As he let go of it, it fell out into the water, and almost immediately he became conscious of the soft caress of tiny wings all about his head. In his undershirt and trousers he rushed out into the corridor. Nothing had changed in the salon. Almost everyone was asleep. There were screen doors giving onto the deck. He inspected them: they appeared to be more firmly installed. A few mosquitoes brushed against his face, but it was not the horde. He edged in between two women who were sleeping sitting with their backs against the wall, and stayed there in acute discomfort until again he dozed. It was not long before he opened his eyes to find the dim light of dawn in the air. His neck ached. He arose and went out onto the deck, to which most of the people from the salon had already crowded.

The boat was moving through a wide estuary dotted with clumps of plants and trees that rose out of the shallow water. Along the edges of the small islands stood herons, so white in the early gray light that their brightness seemed to come from inside them.

It was half past five. At this moment the boat was due in Cienaga, where it was met on its weekly trip by the train that went into the interior. Already a thin spit of land ahead was being identified by eager watchers. Day was coming up swiftly; sky and water were the same color. The deck reeked of the greasy smell of mangoes as people began to breakfast.

And now at last he began to feel pangs of anxiety as to where she might be. He determined to make an immediate and thorough search of the boat. She would be instantly recognizable in any group. First, he looked methodically through the salon, then he exhausted the possibilities on the upper decks. Then he went downstairs, where the gambling had already begun again. Toward the stern, roped to two flimsy iron posts, stood the cow, no longer bellowing. Nearby was an improvised lean-to, probably the crew's quarters. As he passed the small door, he peered through the low transom above it, and saw her lying beside a man on the floor. Automatically he walked on; then he turned and went back. The two were asleep, and half-clothed. In the warm air that came through the screened transom there was the smell of whisky that had been drunk and whisky that had been spilled.

He went upstairs, his heart beating violently. In the cabin, he closed her two valises, packed his own, set them all together by the door and laid the raincoats on top of them. He put on his shirt, combed his hair carefully, and went on deck. Cienaga was there ahead, in the mountains' morning shadow: the dock, a line of huts against the jungle behind, and the railway station to the right beyond the village.

As they docked, he signaled the two urchins who were waving for his attention, screaming, "*Equipajes!*" They fought a bit with one another until he made them see his two fingers held aloft. Then to make them certain, he pointed at each of them in turn, and they grinned. Still grinning, they stood beside him with the bags and coats, and he was among the first of the upper-deck passengers to get on land. They went down the street to the station with the parrots screaming at them from each thatched gable along the way.

On the crowded, waiting train, with the luggage finally in the rack, his heart beat harder than ever, and he kept his eyes painfully on the long dusty street that led back to the dock. At the far end, as the whistle blew, he thought he saw a figure in white running among the dogs and children toward the station, but the train started up as he watched, and the street was lost to view. He took out his notebook, and sat with it on his lap, smiling at the shining green landscape that moved with increasing speed past the window.

New York, 1946

HOW MANY MIDNIGHTS

PAUL BOWLES

HOW MANY MIDNIGHTS, she wondered, had she raised the shade, opened the big window, and leaned out to gaze across the gently stirring city toward the highest towers? Over there behind a certain unmistakable group of them was his building, and at the very top of the building was his apartment, six flights up. In the summer she would look out over the rooftops at some length and sigh, and during the hottest weeks she moved her bed over, directly under the window. Then she would turn off all the lights and sit on the bed combing her hair in the glowing dimness of the city night, or sometimes even by moonlight, which of course was perfect. In the winter however she had to content herself with a moment of looking and a flash of imagining before she bounded across the room into bed.

It was winter now. She was walking crosstown, east, along one of the late Forties. This part of town always had seemed vaguely mysterious to her because of its specially constructed buildings that did not quite touch the pavement. All the buildings just north of the Grand Central were built that way, to absorb the shock, Van had told her; and there were long stretches of grillwork in the sidewalks through which, particularly at night, one could see another world beneath: railway tracks and sometimes a slowly moving train. When it snowed, as it was doing now, the snow filtered down through the grills and covered the ties; then they were even more apparent.

Van worked here in this neighborhood: he was manager of a large bookshop and lending library on Madison Avenue. And he lived in the neighborhood as well, only farther over east, between Third and Second Avenues. His place was not ideal, either as to actual physical comfort or as to locality (since the immediate district was clearly a slum), but with her help he had made it livable, and she used to tell him: "New York and Paris are like that: no clear demarcation of neighborhoods."

In any case, they already had signed a sublease for a place near Gramercy Park which was to be free the first of March. This was of prime importance because they planned to marry on Valentine's Day. They were by no means sentimental souls, either one of them, and for that very reason it seemed to June a little daring to announce to their friends during cocktails: "It's to be Valentine's Day."

Her father, who always was to be counted on to do the thoughtful thing, was staking them to two weeks in Bermuda. "God knows why," Van said. "He hates my guts."

"I don't know how you can say a thing like that about Dad," objected June. "He's never been anything but the essence of politeness with you."

"That's right," said Van, but impenitently.

She crossed Lexington Avenue. The entire sky looked as though it were being illumined from above by gray-violet neons. The tops of the buildings were lost in the cloud made by the falling snow. And the harbor sounds, instead of coming from the river ahead, came from above, as if the tugs were making their careful way around the tips of the towers. "This is the way New York was meant to be," she thought—not the crowded fire-escape, open-hydrant, sumac-leaved summer. Just this quiet, damp, neutral weather when the water seemed all around. She stood still a moment in the middle of the block, listening to the fog horns; there was a whole perspective of them. In the remotest background was a very faint, smothered one that said: "Mmmmm! Mmmmm!" "It must be on the Sound," she thought. She started to walk again.

In her coat pocket she had the keys, because this was to be a special night. Not that there had been any overt reference to that: there was no need for it. It had been implicit in their conversation yesterday afternoon when she had stopped in at the bookshop to see him. They had stood a few minutes talking in the back of the store among the desks, and then he had slipped her the keys. That was surely the most exciting single thing that ever had happened between them—the passage of the keys from his hand to hers. By the gesture he gave up what she knew was most dear to him: his privacy. She did not want him to think that she was in any way unaware of this, and she said in a low voice: "You can trust me with them, I think," laughing immediately afterward so that her remark should not sound ridiculous. He had kissed her and they had gone out for ten minutes to have coffee.

Sitting at the counter he had told how he had caught a man stealing books the night before. (The bookshop was open at night; because of the location it seemed they did almost as much business in the evening as they did during the day.) Van had just finished arranging a display of new books in one of the show windows, and was standing outside in the street looking in. He had noticed a man wearing a long overcoat, standing by the technical books. "I had my eye on him from the beginning. It's a type, you know. You get to spot them. He looked at me right through the window. I suppose he thought I was just another man in the street. I had on *my* overcoat, too." And the man had taken a quick glance around the store to be sure that no one was watching him, had reached up, snatched down a book and dropped it inside his coat. Van had gone quickly to the corner, tapped the traffic policeman on the shoulder and said: "Would you mind coming into my store for a minute? I want you to arrest a man." They had caught him, and when they had opened his coat they found he already had taken three books.

Van always said: "You see some funny things in a bookshop," and often they were really funny. But this story struck June as remotely sinister rather than amusing. Not because it had to do with a theft, certainly. It was not the first case of booklifting he had related to her. Perhaps it was because more than anything else she hated being watched behind her back, and involuntarily she put herself in the place of the thief, with whom she felt that Van had not been quite fair. It seemed to her that he might have gone in and said to him: "I've been watching you. I've seen everything you've been doing. Now, I give you one last chance. Put back whatever you've taken and get the hell out, and don't come back in here." To spring on the man out of the dark after spying on him did seem a little unfair. But she knew she was being absurd. Van could never be unfair with anyone; this was his way of handling the affair, and it was typical of him: he never would argue. She never knew even when he was angry with her until after it was all over, and he told her, smiling: "Gee, I was burned up last Friday."

She crossed Third Avenue. Up to now the snow had been melting as fast as it fell, but the air was getting colder, and the sidewalk began to show silver. The keys jingled in her coat pocket; she pulled off her glove and felt for them. They also were cold. When she had left her house, she had said to her parents: "I'm going out with Van. I'll probably be rather late." They had merely said: "Yes." But she thought she had intercepted a look of mutual understanding between them. It was all right: in ten more days they would be married. She had climbed up the six steep flights of stairs on a good many evenings during the past two years, just to spend an hour or so with him, but never, she reflected with an obscure sort of pride, had anything ever occurred between them which was not what her parents would call "honorable."

She had arrived at the apartment house; it had a gray-stone façade and a good deal of wrought iron around the entrance door. A woman who looked like a West Indian of some sort came out. Noticing that June was carrying a potted plant under her arm, she held the door partially open for her. June thanked her and went in. It was a rubber plant she had bought for Van's apartment. He was inclined to be indifferent about flowers, and, she feared, about decoration in general. She always had hoped to develop aesthetic appreciation in him, and she considered that she had made remarkable progress during the past year. Practically all the adornments in his apartment were objects either of her buying or her choosing.

She knew just how many steps there were to each flight of stairs: nineteen for the first and fifteen for the others. The halls were tiled in black and white, like a bathroom, and tonight, to add to that impression, the stairs and floors were thoroughly wet with the melting snow people had tracked in; the air smelled of wet doormats, wet rubbers, wet clothing. On the third floor a huge perambulator of black leatherette nearly blocked the passageway between the stairs. She frowned at it and thought of the fire regulations.

Because she did not want to be out of breath she mounted the stairs slowly. Not that Van would be there when she arrived—it was still too early—but being out of breath always created in her a false kind of excitement which she particularly wanted to avoid tonight. She turned the key in the lock and stepped inside. It gave her a strange sensation to push open the door all by herself and stand there in the hall alone, smelling the special odor of the place: an amalgam in which she imagined she detected furniture polish, shaving cream and woodsmoke. Woodsmoke there surely was, because he had a fireplace. It was she who had persuaded him to have it installed. And it had not been nearly so expensive to build as he had imagined it was going to be, because since this was the top floor the chimney had only to be built up through the roof. Many times he had said to her: "That was one sensible idea you had," as though the others had not been just as good! They had cut down the legs of all the living-room furniture so that it nestled nearer the floor and made the room seem spacious; they had painted each wall a different shade of gray, adding the occasional wall brackets of ivy; they had bought the big glass coffee table. All these things had made the place pleasanter, and they had all been her ideas.

She shut the door and went into the kitchen. It was a little chilly in the apartment; she lit the gas oven. Then she unwrapped the wet brown paper from around the rubber plant, and set the pot upright on the table. The plant leaned somewhat to one side. She tried to make it stand straight, but it would not. The icebox motor was purring. She took out two trays of ice and dumped the cubes into a bowl. Reaching up to the top shelf of the cabinet she brought down an almost full bottle of Johnny Walker, and set it, along with two highball glasses, onto the big lacquer tray. The room suddenly seemed terribly close; she turned off the oven. Then she scurried about looking for newspapers with which to lay a fire. There were only a few, but she found some old magazines in the kitchen. She rolled the newspapers into thin little logs and set them at various angles across the andirons. Underneath she pushed crumpled pages of the magazines, and on top she put what kindling wood there was. The logs she decided to leave until the kindling already was burning. When the fire was laid, but not lighted, she looked out the window. The snow was coming down thicker than it had been when she came in. She drew the heavy woolen curtains; they covered one entire wall, and they too had been her idea. Van had wanted to have Venetian blinds made. She had tried to make him see how hideous they would be, but although he had agreed that the black-and-white curtains were smart, he never would admit that Venetian blinds were ugly. "Maybe you're right, for this room," he said. "For every room in the world," she had wanted to declare, but she decided against it, since after all, he had given in.

It wasn't that Van had really bad taste. He had an innate sensitivity and a true intelligence which became manifest whenever he talked about the books he had read (and he read a good many during odd moments at the bookshop). But his aesthetic sense had never been fully awakened. Naturally she never mentioned it—she merely made small suggestions which he was free to take or to leave as he saw fit. And usually, if she let her little hints fall at strategic moments, he would take them.

On the mantel were two enormous plaster candelabra covered with angels; she had brought them herself all the way from Matamoros Izúcar in Mexico. Actually she had packed six of them, and all had broken except these two which did not quite match, one of them being somewhat taller than the other. (These were among the few things about which Van was still a bit recalcitrant: he could not be sure he liked them, even yet.) Each one held six candles. She went to a drawer in the desk and got out a dozen long yellow tapers. Often she brought him a dozen at a time. "Where am I supposed to put the damned things?" he would complain. She got a knife from the kitchen and began to scrape the bottoms of the candles to make them fit the holders. "In the middle of this operation he's going to arrive," she said to herself. She wanted the place to be perfect before he got there. Nervously she tossed the paraffin scrapings into the fireplace. She had a feeling that he would not just come up; it would be more like him to ring from the vestibule downstairs. At least, she hoped he would do that. The time it would take him to get up the six flights might make a great difference in the way the room would look. She fitted the last candle into the bright holder and sighed with relief. They were slow-burning ones; she decided to light them now before returning the candelabra to the mantel. Up there they looked beautiful. She stepped back to admire their splendor, and for a moment watched the slowly moving interplay of shadows on the wall. She switched off the electric lights in the room. With the fireplace aglow the effect would be breathtaking.

Impetuously she determined to do a very daring thing. It might possibly annoy Van when he first saw it, but she would do it anyway. She rushed to the other side of the room and feverishly began to push the divan across the floor toward the fireplace. It would be so snug to be right in front of the blaze, especially with the snow outside. The cushions fell off and a caster got entangled with the long wool of the goatskin rug she had given him for his birthday. She got the rug out of the way and continued to manipulate the divan. It looked absurd out there in the middle of the room, and she swung one end around so that it lay at right angles to the fireplace, against the wall. After she had piled the cushions back she stepped aside to observe it, and decided to leave it there. Then the other pieces had to be arranged. The whole room was in disorder at this point.

"I know he's going to open that door this minute," she thought. She turned the overhead light back on and quickly began to shift chairs, lamps and tables. The last piece to be moved was a small commode that she had once helped him sandpaper. As she carried it across the room its one little drawer slid out and fell on the floor. All the letters Van had received in the past months were there, lying in a fairly compact heap at her feet. "Damnation!" she said aloud, and as she said it, the hideous metallic sound of the buzzer in the kitchen echoed through the apartment. She let go of the commode and rushed out to press the button that opened the door downstairs onto the street. Then, without pressing it, she ran back into the living room and knelt on the floor, quickly gathering up the letters and dumping them into the drawer. But they had been piled carefully into that small space before the accident, and now they were not; as a result the drawer was overfull and would not close. Again she spoke aloud. "Oh, my God!" she said. And she said that because for no reason at all it had occurred to her that Van might think she had been reading his correspondence. The main thing now was to get the commode over into the corner; then she might be able to force the drawer shut. As she lifted it, the buzzer pealed again, with insistence. She ran into the kitchen, and this time pressed the answer button with all her might. Swiftly she hurried back and carried the commode into the corner. Then she tried to close the drawer and found it an impossibility. In a burst of inspiration she turned the little piece of furniture around so that the drawer opened toward the wall. She stepped to the fireplace and touched a match to the paper logs. By now he would got only about to the fourth floor; there were three more.

She turned off the lights once again, went into the hall and looked at herself briefly in the mirror, put out the light there, and moved toward the entrance door. With her hand on the knob, she held her breath, and found that her heart was beating much too fast. It was just what she had not wanted. She had hoped to have him step into a little world of absolute calm. And now because of that absurd drawer she was upset. Or perhaps it was the dragging around of all that furniture. She opened the door a crack and listened. A second later she stepped out into the hall, and again she listened. She walked to the stairs. "Van?" she called, and immediately she was furious with herself.

A man's voice answered from two floors below. "Riley?" he yelled.

"What?" she cried.

"I'm looking for Riley."

"You've rung the wrong bell," she shouted, enunciating the words very distinctly in spite of her raised voice.

She went in and shut the door, holding onto the knob and leaning her forehead against the panel for a moment. Now her heart was beating even more violently. She returned to the commode in the corner. "I might as well fix it once and for all right now," she thought. Otherwise her mind would be on it every instant. She turned it around, took out all the letters and carefully replaced them in four equal piles. Even then the drawer shut with difficulty, but it did close. When that was done, she went to the window and pulled back the curtain. It seemed to be growing much colder. The wind had risen; it was blowing from the east. The sky was no longer violet. It was black. She could see the snow swirling past the street lamp below. She wondered if it were going to turn into a blizzard. Tomorrow was Sunday; she simply would stay on. There would be a terrible moment in the morning, of course, when her parents arose and found she had not come in, but she would not be there to see it, and she could make it up with them later. And what an ideal little vacation it would make: a night and day up there in the snow, isolated from everything, shut away from everyone but Van. As she watched the street, she gradually became convinced that the storm would last all night. She looked back into the room. It gave her keen pleasure to contrast its glow with the hostile night outside. She let the curtain fall and went to the fireplace. The kindling was at the height of its blazing and there was no more; she piled two small logs on top of it. Soon they were crackling with such energy that she thought it wise to put the screen across in front of them. She sat on the divan looking at her legs in the blended firelight and candleglow. Smiling, she leaned back against the cushions. Her heart was no longer racing. She felt almost calm. The wind whined outside; to her it was inevitably a melancholy sound. Even tonight.

Suddenly she decided that it would be inexcusable not to let her parents know she was staying the night. She went into the bedroom and lay on the bed, resting the telephone on her stomach. It moved ridiculously while she dialed. Her mother, not her father, answered. "Thank God," she said to herself, and she let her head fall back upon the pillows. Her mother had been asleep; she did not sound too pleased to have been called to the telephone. "You're all right, I hope," she said. They spoke of the storm. "Yes, it's awful out," said June. "Oh, no, I'm at Van's. We have a fire. I'm going to stay. All night." There was a short silence. "Well, I think you're very foolish," she heard her mother say. And she went on. June let her talk a bit. Then she interrupted, letting a note of impatience sound in her voice. "I can't very well discuss it now. You understand." Her mother's voice was shrill. "No, I *don't* understand!" she cried. She was taking it more seriously than June had expected. "I can't talk now," said June. "I'll see you tomorrow." She said good night and hung up, lying perfectly still for a moment. Then she lifted the telephone and set it on the night table, but still she did not move. When she had heard herself say: "We have a fire," a feeling of dread had seized her. It was as if in giving voice to the pretense she thereby became conscious of it. Van had not yet arrived; why then had she taken care to speak as though he had? She could only have been trying to reassure herself. Again her heart had begun to beat heavily. And finally she did what she had been trying not to think of doing ever since she had arrived: she looked at her watch.

It was a little after midnight. There was absolutely no doubt about it; already he was quite late. He no longer could arrive without going into explanations. Something must have happened, and it only could be something bad. "Ridiculous!" she cried in anger, jumping up and going out into the kitchen. The ice cubes had melted a good deal; she poured the cold water into the sink between her spread fingers, and shook the cubes around the bowl petulantly, trying to stem the resentment she felt rising up inside her. "It will be interesting to know what his excuse will be," she said to herself. She decided that when he arrived her only possible behavior would be to pretend not to have noticed his lateness.

She dropped some of the ice cubes into one of the glasses, poured in some Scotch, stirred it, and went into the living room with it. The fire was burning triumphantly; the whole room danced in flamelight. She sat on the couch and downed her drink, a little too quickly for a young woman completely at her ease, which was what she was trying to be. When she had finished the last drop, she forced herself to sit without moving for ten minutes by her watch. Then she went out and made herself another drink, a little stronger. This one she drank walking thoughtfully around and around the center of the room. She was fighting against an absurd impulse to put on her coat and go into the street to look for him. "Old woman," she said to herself. Old people always had that reaction—they always expected tragedies. As she came to the end of her second drink she succeeded in convincing herself that the mathematical probabilities of Van's having met with his first serious accident on this particular evening were extremely slight. This moral certitude engendered a feeling of lightheartedness, which expressed itself in the desire for a third drink. She had only just begun this one when an even sharper anguish seized her. If it was not likely that he had had an accident, it was utterly unthinkable that he should have let some unforeseen work detain him until this late; he would have telephoned her anyway. It was even more inconceivable that their rendezvous should have slipped his mind. The final, remaining possibility therefore was that he had deliberately avoided it, which of course was absurd. She tossed another log onto the fire. Again she went to the window and peered between the curtains down into the empty street. The wind had become a gale. She felt each blast against her face through the closed window. Listening for sounds of traffic, she heard none; even the boats seemed to have been silenced. Only the rushing of the wind was left—that and the occasional faint hissing of the fine snow against the glass. She burst into tears; she did not know whether it was out of self-pity, anger and humiliation, loneliness, or just plain nervousness.

As she stood there in the window with the tears covering her sight, it occurred to her how ironic it would be if he should come and find her like this: slightly drunk, sobbing, with her make-up surely in a state of complete ruin. A sound behind her ended her weeping instantly. She let go of the curtain and turned to face the room: through her tears she could see nothing but quivering webs of light. She squeezed her lids tightly together: one of the logs had broken in two. The smaller half lay on the hearth smoking. She went over and kicked it into the fire. Then she tiptoed into the hall to the entrance door and slipped the chain on. As soon as she had done that she was terrified. It was nothing less than a symbol of fear—she realized it as she looked at the brass links stretching across from jamb to door. But once having put it up, she did not have the courage to take it down again.

Still on tiptoe, she returned to the living room and lay on the divan, burying her face in the cushions. She was not crying any longer—she felt too empty and frightened to do anything but lie quite still. But after a while she sat up and looked slowly about the room. The candles had burned down half way; she looked at them, at the ivy trailing down from the little pots on the wall, at the white goatskin by her feet, as the striped curtains. They were all hers. "Van, Van," she said under her breath. Unsteadily she rose and made her way to the bathroom. The glaring light hurt her eyes. Hanging on the inside of the door was Van's old flannel bathrobe. It was too big for her, but she got into it and rolled the sleeves back, turning up the collar and pulling the belt tightly about her waist. In the living room she lay down again on the divan among the cushions. From time to time she rubbed her cheek against the wool of the sleeve under her face. She stared into the fire.

Van was in the room. It was daylight out—a strange gray dawn. She sat up, feeling light-headed. "Van," she said. He was moving slowly across the floor toward the window. And the curtains had been drawn back. There was the rectangle of dim white sky, with Van going toward it. She called to him again. If he heard her he paid no attention. She sat back, watching. Now and then he shook his head slowly from side to side; the gesture made her feel like crying again, but not for herself this time. It was quite natural that he should be there, shuffling slowly across the room in the pale early light, shaking his head from one side to the other. Suddenly she said to herself that he was looking for something, that he might find it, and she began to shiver sitting up there in the cold. "He *has* found it," she thought, "but he's pretending he hasn't because he knows I'm watching him." And even as the idea formed itself in her mind she saw him reach up and swing himself through the window. She screamed, jumped down from the couch and ran across the room. When she got to the window there was nothing to see but the vast gray panorama of a city at dawn, spitefully clear in every tiniest detail. She stood there looking out, seeing for miles up and down the empty streets. Or were they canals? It was a foreign city.

The sputtering of a candle as it went out roused her. Several of them had already burned out. The shadows on the ceiling were wavering like bats. The room was cold and the curtains across the closed window moved inward with the force of the wind. She lay perfectly still. In the fireplace she heard the powdery, faintly metallic sound of a cooling ember as it fell. For a long time she remained unmoving. Then she sprang up, turned on all the lights, went into the bedroom and stood for a moment looking at the telephone. The sight of it calmed her a little. She took off the bathrobe and opened the closet door to hang it up. She knew his luggage by heart; his small overnight valise was missing. Slowly her mouth opened. She did not think to put her hand over it.

She slipped on her coat and unhooked the chain on the entrance door. The hall outside was full of scurrying draughts. Down the six flights she ran, one after the other, until she was at the front door. The snow had drifted high, completely covering the steps. She went out. It was bitter cold in the wind, but only a stray flake fell now and then. She stood there. The street did not tell her what to do. She began to wade through the deep snow, eastward. A taxi, moving cautiously down Second Avenue, its chains clanking rhythmically, met her at the corner. She hailed it, got in.

"Take me to the river," she said, pointing.

"What street?"

"Any street that goes down all the way."

Almost immediately they were there. She got out, paid the driver, walked slowly to the end of the pavement, and stood watching. The dawn was really breaking now, but it was very different from the one she had seen through the window. The wind took her breath away, the water out there was alive. Against the winter sky across the river there were factories. The lights of a small craft moved further down in midstream. She clenched her fists. A terrible anguish had taken possession of her. She was trembling, but she did not feel the cold. Abruptly she turned around. The driver was standing in the street blowing into his cupped hands. And he was looking at her intently.

"You're not waiting for me, are you?" she said. (Was that her voice?)

"Yes, *Ma'am*," he said with force.

"I didn't tell you to." (With her whole life falling to pieces before her, how was it that her voice rang with such asperity, such hard self-assurance?)

"That's right." He put his gloves back on. "Take your time," he said.

She turned her back on him and watched the changing water. Suddenly she felt ridiculous. She went over to the cab, got in, and gave her home address.

The doorman was asleep when she rang, and even after she was inside she had to wait nearly five minutes for the elevator boy to bring the car up from the basement. She tiptoed through the apartment to her room, shutting the door behind her. When she had undressed she opened the big window without looking out, and got into bed. The cold wind blew through the room.

Tangier, 1947

PLAIN PLEASURES

JANE BOWLES

ALVA PERRY WAS A DIGNIFIED and reserved woman of Scotch and Spanish descent, in her early forties. She was still handsome, although her cheeks were too thin. Her eyes particularly were of an extraordinary clarity and beauty. She lived in her uncle's house, which had been converted into apartments, or tenements, as they were still called in her section of the country. The house stood on the side of a steep, wooded hill overlooking the main highway. A long cement staircase climbed halfway up the hill and stopped some distance below the house. It had originally led to a power station, which had since been destroyed. Mrs. Perry had lived alone in her tenement since the death of her husband eleven years ago; however, she found small things to do all day long and she had somehow remained as industrious in her solitude as a woman who lives in the service of her family.

John Drake, an equally reserved person, occupied the tenement below hers. He owned a truck and engaged in free-lance work for lumber companies, as well as in the collection and delivery of milk cans for a dairy.

Mr. Drake and Mrs. Perry had never exchanged more than the simplest greeting in all the years that they had lived here in the hillside house.

One night Mr. Drake, who was standing in the hall, heard Mrs. Perry's heavy footsteps, which he had unconsciously learned to recognize. He looked up and saw her coming downstairs. She was dressed in a brown overcoat that had belonged to her dead husband, and she was hugging a paper bag to her bosom. Mr. Drake offered to help her with the bag and she faltered, undecided, on the landing.

"They are only potatoes," she said to him, "but thank you very much. I am going to bake them out in the back yard. I have been meaning to for a long time."

Mr. Drake took the potatoes and walked with a stiff-jointed gait through the back door and down the hill to a short stretch of level land in back of the house which served as a yard. Here he put the paper bag on the ground. There was a big new incinerator smoking near the back stoop and in the center of the yard Mrs. Perry's uncle had built a roofed-in pigpen faced in vivid artificial brick. Mrs. Perry followed.

She thanked Mr. Drake and began to gather twigs, scuttling rapidly between the edge of the woods and the pigpen, near which she was laying her fire. Mr. Drake, without any further conversation, helped her to gather the twigs, so that when the fire was laid, she quite naturally invited him to wait and share the potatoes with her. He accepted and they sat in front of the fire on an overturned box.

Mr. Drake kept his face averted from the fire and turned in the direction of the woods, hoping in this way to conceal somewhat his flaming-red cheeks from Mrs. Perry. He was a very shy person and though his skin was naturally red all the time it turned to such deep crimson when he was in the presence of a strange woman that the change was distinctly noticeable. Mrs. Perry wondered why he kept looking behind him, but she did not feel she knew him well enough to question him. She waited in vain for him to speak and then, realizing that he was not going to, she searched her own mind for something to say.

"Do you like plain ordinary pleasures?" she finally asked him gravely.

Mr. Drake felt very much relieved that she had spoken and his color subsided. "You had better first give me a clearer notion of what you mean by ordinary pleasures, and then I'll tell you how I feel about them," he answered soberly, halting after every few words, for he was as conscientious as he was shy.

Mrs. Perry hesitated. "Plain pleasures," she began, "like the ones that come without crowds or fancy food." She searched her brain for more examples. "Plain pleasures like this potato bake instead of dancing and whisky and bands. . . . Like a picnic but not the kind with a thousand extra things that get thrown out in a ditch because they don't get eaten up. I've seen grown people throw cakes away because they were too lazy to wrap them up and take them back home. Have you seen that go on?"

"No, I don't think so," said Mr. Drake.

"They waste a lot," she remarked.

"Well, I do like plain pleasures," put in Mr. Drake, anxious that she should not lose the thread of the conversation.

"Don't you think that plain pleasures are closer to the heart of God?" she asked him.

He was a little embarrassed at her mentioning anything so solemn and so intimate on such short acquaintance, and he could not bring himself to answer her. Mrs. Perry, who was ordinarily shut-mouthed, felt a stream of words swelling in her throat.

"My sister, Dorothy Alvarez," she began without further introduction, "goes to all gala affairs downtown. She has invited me to go and raise the dickens with her, but I won't go. She's the merriest one in her group and separated from her husband. They take her all the places with them. She can eat dinner in a restaurant every night if she wants to. She's crazy about fried fish and all kinds of things. I don't pay much mind to what I eat unless it's a potato bake like this. We each have only one single life which is our real life, starting at the cradle and ending at the grave. I warn Dorothy every time I see her that if she doesn't watch out her life is going to be left aching and starving on the side of the road and she's going to get to her grave without it. The farther a man follows the rainbow, the harder it is for him to get back to the life which he left starving like an old dog. Sometimes when a man gets older he has a revelation and wants awfully bad to get back to the place where he left his life, but he can't get to that place—not often. It's always better to stay alongside of your life. I told Dorothy that life was not a tree with a million different blossoms on it." She reflected upon this for a moment in silence and then continued. "She has a box that she puts pennies and nickels in when she thinks she's running around too much and she uses the money in the box to buy candles with for church. But that's all she'll do for her spirit, which is not enough for a grown woman."

Mr. Drake's face was strained because he was trying terribly hard to follow closely what she was saying, but he was so fearful lest she reveal some intimate secret of her sister's and later regret it that his mind was almost completely closed to everything else. He was fully prepared to stop her if she went too far.

The potatoes were done and Mrs. Perry offered him two of them.

"Have some potatoes?" she said to him. The wind was colder now than when they had first sat down, and it blew around the pigpen.

"How do you feel about these cold howling nights that we have? Do you mind them?" Mrs. Perry asked.

"I surely do," said John Drake.

She looked intently at his face. "He is as red as a cherry," she said to herself.

"I might have preferred to live in a warm climate maybe," Mr. Drake was saying very slowly with a dreamy look in his eye, "if I happened to believe in a lot of unnecessary changing around. A lot of going forth and back, I mean." He blushed because he was approaching a subject that was close to his heart.

"Yes, yes, yes," said Mrs. Perry. "A lot of switching around is no good."

"When I was a younger man I had a chance to go way down south to Florida," he continued. "I had an offer to join forces with an alligator-farm project, but there was no security in the alligators. It might not have been a successful farm; it was not the risk that I minded so much, because I have always yearned to see palm trees and coconuts and the like. But I also believed that a man has to have a pretty good reason for moving around. I think that is what finally stopped me from going down to Florida and raising alligators. It was not the money, because I was not raised to give money first place. It was just that I felt then the way I do now, that if a man leaves home he must leave for some very good reason—like the boys who went to construct the Panama Canal or for any other decent reason. Otherwise I think he ought to stay in his own home town, so that nobody can say about him, 'What does he think he can do here that we can't?' At least that is what I think people in a strange town would say about a man like myself if I landed there with some doubtful venture as my only excuse for leaving home. My brother don't feel that way. He never stays in one place more than three months." He ate his potato with a woeful look in his eye, shaking his head from side to side.

Mrs. Perry's mind was wandering, so that she was very much startled when he suddenly stood up and extended his hand to her.

"I'll leave now," he said, "but in return for the potatoes, will you come and have supper with me at a restaurant tomorrow night?"

She had not received an invitation of this kind in many years, having deliberately withdrawn from life in town, and she did not know how to answer him. "Do you think I should do that?" she asked.

Mr. Drake assured her that she should do it and she accepted his invitation. On the following afternoon, Mrs. Perry waited for the bus at the foot of the short cement bridge below the house. She needed help and advice from her sister about a lavender dress which no longer fitted her. She herself had never been able to sew well and she knew little about altering women's garments. She intended to wear her dress to the restaurant where she was to meet John Drake, and she was carrying it tucked under her arm.

Dorothy Alvarez lived on a side street in one half of a two-family house. She was seated in her parlor entertaining a man when Mrs. Perry rang the bell. The parlor was immaculate but difficult to rest in because of the many bright and complicated patterns of the window curtains and the furniture covers, not the least disquieting of which was an enormous orange and black flowerpot design repeated a dozen times on the linoleum floor covering.

Dorothy pulled the curtain aside and peeked out to see who was ringing her bell. She was a curly-headed little person, with thick, unequal cheeks that were painted bright pink.

She was very much startled when she looked out and saw her sister, as she had not been expecting to see her until the following week.

"Oh!" Dorothy exclaimed.

"Who is it?" her guest asked.

"It's my sister. You better get out of here, because she must have something serious to talk to me about. You better go out the back door. She don't like bumping up against strangers."

The man was vexed, and left without bidding Dorothy good-bye. She ran to the door and let Mrs. Perry in.

"Sit down," she said, pulling her into the parlor. "Sit down and tell me what's new." She poured some hard candy from a paper bag into a glass dish.

"I wish you would alter this dress for me or help me do it," said Mrs. Perry. "I want it for tonight. I'm meeting Mr. Drake, my neighbor, at the restaurant down the street, so I thought I could dress in your house and leave from here. If you did the alteration yourself. I'd pay you for it."

Dorothy's face fell. "Why do you offer to pay me for it when I'm your sister?"

Mrs. Perry looked at her in silence. She did not answer, because she did not know why herself. Dorothy tried the dress on her sister and pinned it here and there. "I'm glad you're going out at last," she said. "Don't you want some beads?"

"I'll take some beads if you've got a spare string."

"Well I hope this is the right guy for you," said Dorothy, with her customary lack of tact. "I would give anything for you to be in love, so you would quit living in that ugly house and come and live on some street nearby. Think how different everything would be for me. You'd be jollier too if you had a husband who was dear to you.

Not like the last one. . . . I suppose I'll never stop dreaming and hoping," she added nervously because she realized, but, as always, a little too late, that her sister hated to discuss such matters. "Don't think," she began weakly, "that I'm so happy here all the time. I'm not so serious and solemn as you, of course. . . ."

"I don't know what you've been talking about," said Alva Perry, twisting impatiently. "I'm going out to have a dinner."

"I wish you were closer to me," whined Dorothy. "I get blue in this parlor some nights."

"I don't think you get very blue," Mrs. Perry remarked briefly.

"Well, as long as you're going out, why don't you pep up?"

"I am pepped up," replied Mrs. Perry.

• • •

Mrs. Perry closed the restaurant door behind her and walked the full length of the room, peering into each booth in search of her escort. He had apparently not yet arrived, so she chose an empty booth and seated herself inside on the wooden bench. After fifteen minutes she decided that he was not coming and, repressing the deep hurt that this caused her, she focused her full attention on the menu and succeeded in shutting Mr. Drake from her mind. While she was reading the menu, she unhooked her string of beads and tucked them away in her purse. She had called the waitress and was ordering pork when Mr. Drake arrived. He greeted her with a timid smile.

"I see that you are ordering your dinner," he said, squeezing into his side of the booth. He looked with admiration at her lavender dress, which exposed her pale chest. He would have preferred that she be bareheaded because he loved women's hair. She had on an ungainly black felt hat which she always wore in every kind of weather. Mr. Drake remembered with intense pleasure the potato bake in front of the fire and he was much more excited than he had imagined he would be to see her once again.

Unfortunately she did not seem to have any impulse to communicate with him and his own tongue was silenced in a very short time. They ate the first half of their meal without saying anything at all to each other. Mr. Drake had ordered a bottle of sweet wine and after Mrs. Perry had finished her second glass she finally spoke. "I think they cheat you in restaurants."

He was pleased she had made any remark at all, even though it was of an ungracious nature.

"Well, it is usually to be among the crowd that we pay large prices for small portions," he said, much to his own surprise, for he had always considered himself a lone wolf, and his behavior had never belied this. He sensed this same quality in Mrs. Perry, but he was moved by a strange desire to mingle with her among the flock.

"Well, don't you think what I say is true?" he asked hesitantly. There appeared on his face a curious, dislocated smile and he held his head in an outlandishly erect position which betrayed his state of tension.

Mrs. Perry wiped her plate clean with a piece of bread. Since she was not in the habit of drinking more than once every few years, the wine was going very quickly to her head.

"What time does the bus go by the door here?" she asked in a voice that was getting remarkably loud.

"I can find out for you if you really want to know. Is there any reason why you want to know now?"

"I've got to get home some time so I can get up tomorrow morning."

"Well, naturally I will take you home in my truck when you want to go, but I hope you won't go yet." He leaned forward and studied her face anxiously.

"I can get home all right," she answered him glumly, "and it's just as good now as later."

"Well, no, it isn't," he said, deeply touched, because there was no longer any mistaking her distinctly inimical attitude. He felt that he must at any cost keep her with him and enlist her sympathies. The wine was contributing to this sudden aggressiveness, for it was not usually in his nature to make any effort to try to get what he wanted. He now began speaking to her earnestly and quickly.

"I want to share a full evening's entertainment with you, or even a week of entertainment," he said, twisting nervously on his bench. "I know where all the roadside restaurants and dance houses are situated all through the county. I am master of my truck, and no one can stop me from taking a vacation if I want to. It's a long time since I took a vacation—not since I was handed out my yearly summer vacation when I went to school. I never spent any real time in any of these roadside houses, but I know the proprietors, nearly all of them, because I have lived here all of my life. There is one dance hall that is built on a lake. I know the proprietor. If we went there, we could stray off and walk around the water, if that was agreeable to you." His face was a brighter red than ever and he appeared to be temporarily stripped of the reserved and cautious demeanor that had so characterized him the evening before. Some quality in Mrs. Perry's nature which he had only dimly perceived at first now sounded like a deep bell within himself because of her anger and he was flung backward into a forgotten and weaker state of being. His yearning for a word of kindness from her increased every minute.

Mrs. Perry sat drinking her wine more and more quickly and her resentment mounted with each new glass.

"I know all the proprietors of dance houses in the county also," she said. "My sister Dorothy Alvarez has them up to her house for beer when they take a holiday. I've got no need to meet anybody new or see any new places. I even know this place we are eating in from a long time ago. I had dinner here with my husband a few times." She looked around her. "I remember *him*," she said, pointing a long arm at the proprietor, who had just stepped out of the kitchen.

"How are you after these many years?" she called to him.

Mr. Drake was hesitant about what to do. He had not realized that Mrs. Perry was getting as drunk as she seemed to be now. Ordinarily he would have felt embarrassed and would have hastened to lead her out of the restaurant, but he thought that she might be more approachable drunk and nothing else mattered to him. "I'll stay with you for as long as you like," he said.

His words spun around in Mrs. Perry's mind. "What are you making a bid for, anyway?" she asked him, leaning back heavily against the bench.

"Nothing dishonorable," he said. "On the contrary, something extremely honorable if you will accept." Mr. Drake was so distraught that he did not know exactly what he was saying, but Mrs. Perry took his words to mean a proposal of marriage, which was unconsciously what he had hoped she would do. Mrs. Perry looked at even this exciting offer through the smoke of her resentment.

"I suppose," she said, smiling joylessly, "that you would like a lady to mash your potatoes for you three times a day. But I am not a mashed-potato masher and I never have been. I would prefer," she added, raising her voice, "I would prefer to have *him* mash my potatoes for *me* in a big restaurant kitchen." She nodded in the direction of the proprietor, who had remained standing in front of the kitchen door so that he could watch Mrs. Perry. This time he grinned and winked his eye.

Mrs. Perry fumbled through the contents of her purse in search of a handkerchief and, coming upon her sister's string of beads, she pulled them out and laid them in her gravy. "I am not a mashed-potato masher," she repeated, and then without warning she clambered out of the booth and lumbered down the aisle. She disappeared up a dark brown staircase at the back of the restaurant. Both Mr. Drake and the proprietor assumed that she was going to the ladies' toilet.

Actually Mrs. Perry was not specifically in search of the toilet, but rather for any place where she could be alone. She walked down the hall upstairs and jerked open a door on her left, closing it behind her. She stood in total darkness for a minute, and then, feeling a chain brush her forehead, she yanked at it brutally, lighting the room from a naked ceiling bulb, which she almost pulled down together with its fixtures.

She was standing at the foot of a double bed with a high Victorian headboard. She looked around her and, noticing a chair placed underneath a small window, she walked over to it and pushed the window open, securing it with a short stick; then she sat down.

"This is perfection," she said aloud, glaring at the ugly little room. "This is surely a gift from the Lord." She squeezed her hands together until her knuckles were white. "Oh, how I love it here! How I love it! How I love it!"

She flung one arm out over the window sill in a gesture of abandon, but she had not noticed that the rain was teeming down, and it soaked her lavender sleeve in a very short time.

"Mercy me!" she remarked, grinning. "It's raining here. The people at the dinner tables don't get the rain, but I do and I like it!" She smiled benignly at the rain. She sat there half awake and half asleep and then slowly she felt a growing certainty that she could reach her own room from where she was sitting without ever returning to the restaurant. "I have kept the pathway open all my life," she muttered in a thick voice, "so that I could get back."

A few moments later she said, "I am sitting there." An expression of malevolent triumph transformed her face and she made a slight effort to stiffen her back. She remained for a long while in the stronghold of this fantasy, but it gradually faded and in the end dissolved. When she drew her cold shaking arm in out of the rain, the tears were streaming down her cheeks. Without ceasing to cry she crept on to the big double bed and fell asleep, face downward, with her hat on.

Meanwhile the proprietor had come quietly upstairs, hoping that he would bump into her as she came out of the ladies' toilet. He had been flattered by her attention and he judged that in her present drunken state it would be easy to sneak a kiss from her and perhaps even more. When he saw the beam of light shining under his own bedroom door, he stuck his tongue out over his lower lip and smiled. Then he tiptoed down the stairs, plotting on the way what he would tell Mr. Drake.

Everyone had left the restaurant, and Mr. Drake was walking up and down the aisle when the proprietor reached the bottom of the staircase.

"I am worried about my lady friend," Mr. Drake said, hurrying up to him. "I am afraid that she may have passed out in the toilet."

"The truth is," the proprietor answered, "that she has passed out in an empty bedroom upstairs. Don't worry about it. My daughter will take care of her if she wakes up feeling sick. I used to know her husband. You can't do nothing about her now." He put his hands into his pockets and looked solemnly into Mr. Drake's eyes.

Mr. Drake, not being equal to such a delicate situation, paid his bill and left. Outside he crawled into his freshly painted red truck and sat listening desolately to the rain.

• • •

The next morning Mrs. Perry awakened a little after sunrise. Thanks to her excellent constitution she did not feel very sick, but she lay motionless on the bed looking around her at the walls for a long time. Slowly she remembered that this room she was lying in was above the restaurant, but she did not know how she had gotten there. She remembered the dinner with Mr. Drake, but not much of what she had said to him. It did not occur to her to blame him for her present circumstance. She was not hysterical at finding herself in a strange bed because, although she was a very tense and nervous woman, she possessed great depth of emotion and only certain things concerned her personally.

She felt very happy and she thought of her uncle who had passed out at a convention fifteen years ago. He had walked around the town all the morning without knowing where he was. She smiled.

After resting a little while longer, she got out of bed and clothed herself. She went into the hall and found the staircase and she descended with bated breath and a fast-beating heart, because she was so eager to get back down into the restaurant.

It was flooded with sunshine and still smelled of meat and sauce. She walked a little unsteadily down the aisle between the rows of wooden booths and tables. The tables were all bare and scrubbed clean. She looked anxiously from one to the other, hoping to select the booth they had sat in, but she was unable to choose among them. The tables were all identical. In a moment this anonymity served only to heighten her tenderness.

"John Drake," she whispered. "My sweet John Drake."

New York, 1945

PAGES FROM COLD POINT

PAUL BOWLES

OUR CIVILIZATION IS DOOMED to a short life: its component parts are too heterogeneous. I personally am content to see everything in the process of decay. The bigger the bombs, the quicker it will be done. Life is visually too hideous for one to make the attempt to preserve it. Let it go. Perhaps some day another form of life will come along. Either way, it is of no consequence. At the same time, I am still a part of life, and I am bound by this to protect myself to whatever extent I am able. And so I am here. Here in the Islands vegetation still has the upper hand, and man has to fight even to make his presence seen at all. It is beautiful here, the trade winds blow all year, and I suspect that bombs are extremely unlikely to be wasted on this unfrequented side of the island, if indeed on any part of it.

I was loath to give up the house after Hope's death. But it was the obvious move to make. My university career always having been an utter farce (since I believe no reason inducing a man to "teach" can possibly be a valid one), I was elated by the idea of resigning, and as soon as her affairs had been settled and the money properly invested, I lost no time in doing so.

I think that week was the first time since childhood that I had managed to recapture the feeling of there being a content in existence. I went from one pleasant house to the next, making my adieux to the English quacks, the Philosophy fakirs, and so on—even to those colleagues with whom I was merely on speaking terms. I watched the envy in their faces when I announced my departure by Pan American on Saturday morning; and the greatest pleasure I felt in all this was in being able to answer, "Nothing," when I was asked, as invariably I was, what I intended to do.

When I was a boy people used to refer to Charles as "Big Brother

C.," although he is only a scant year older than I. To me now he is merely "Fat Brother C.," a successful lawyer. His thick, red face and hands, his back-slapping joviality, and his fathomless hypocritical prudery, these are the qualities which make him truly repulsive to me. There is also the fact that he once looked not unlike the way Racky does now. And after all, he still is my big brother, and disapproves openly of everything I do. The loathing I feel for him is so strong that for years I have not been able to swallow a morsel of food or a drop of liquid in his presence without making a prodigious effort. No one knows this but me—certainly not Charles, who would be the last one I should tell about it. He came up on the late train two nights before I left. He got quickly to the point—as soon as he was settled with a highball.

"So you're off for the wilds," he said, sitting forward in his chair like a salesman.

"If you can call it the wilds," I replied. "Certainly it's not wild like Mitichi." (He has a lodge in northern Quebec.) "I consider it really civilized."

He drank and smacked his lips together stiffly, bringing the glass down hard on his knee.

"And Racky. You're taking him along?"

"Of course."

"Out of school. Away. So he'll see nobody but you. You think that's good."

I looked at him. "I do," I said.

"By God, if I could stop you legally, I would!" he cried, jumping up and putting his glass on the mantel. I was trembling inwardly with excitement, but I merely sat and watched him. He went on. "You're not fit to have custody of the kid!" he shouted. He shot a stern glance at me over his spectacles.

"You think not?" I said gently.

Again he looked at me sharply. "D'ye think I've forgotten?"

I was understandably eager to get him out of the house as soon as I could. As I piled and sorted letters and magazines on the desk, I said: "Is that all you came to tell me? I have a good deal to do tomorrow and I must get some sleep. I probably shan't see you at breakfast. Agnes'll see that you eat in time to make the early train."

All he said was: "God! Wake up! Get wise to yourself! You're not fooling anybody, you know."

That kind of talk is typical of Charles. His mind is slow and obtuse; he constantly imagines that everyone he meets is playing some private game of deception with him. He is so utterly incapable of following the functioning of even a moderately evolved intellect that he finds the will to secretiveness and duplicity everywhere.

"I haven't time to listen to that sort of nonsense," I said, preparing to leave the room.

But he shouted, "You don't want to listen! No! Of course not! You just want to do what you want to do. You just want to go on off down there and live as you've a mind to, and to hell with the consequences!" At this point I heard Racky coming downstairs. C. obviously heard nothing and he raved on. "But just remember, I've got your number all right, and if there's any trouble with the boy I'll know who's to blame."

I hurried across the room and opened the door so he could see that Racky was there in the hallway. That stopped his tirade. It was hard to know whether Racky had heard any of it or not. Although he is not a quiet young person, he is the soul of discretion, and it is almost never possible to know any more about what goes on inside his head than he intends one to know.

I was annoyed that C. should have been bellowing at me in my own house. To be sure, he is the only one from whom I would accept such behavior, but then, no father likes to have his son see him take criticism meekly. Racky simply stood there in his bathrobe, his angelic face quite devoid of expression, saying: "Tell Uncle Charley good night for me, will you? I forgot."

I said I would, and quickly shut the door. When I thought Racky was back upstairs in his room, I bade Charles good night. I have never been able to get out of his presence fast enough. The effect he has on me dates from an early period in our lives, from days I dislike to recall.

Racky is a wonderful boy. After we arrived, when we found it impossible to secure a proper house near any town where he might have the company of English boys and girls his own age, he showed no sign of chagrin, although he must have been disappointed. Instead, as we went out of the renting office into the glare of the street, he grinned and said: "Well, I guess we'll have to get bikes, that's all."

The few available houses near what Charles would have called "civilization" turned out to be so ugly and so impossibly confining in atmosphere that we decided immediately on Cold Point, even though it was across the island and quite isolated on its seaside cliff. It was beyond a doubt one of the most desirable properties on the island, and Racky was as enthusiastic about its splendors as I.

"You'll get tired of being alone out there, just with me," I said to him as we walked back to the hotel.

"Aw, I'll get along all right. When do we look for the bikes?"

At his insistence we bought two the next morning. I was sure I should not make much use of mine, but I reflected that an extra bicycle might be convenient to have around the house. It turned out that the servants all had their own bicycles, without which they would not have been able to get to and from the village of Orange Walk, eight miles down the shore. So for a while I was forced to get astride mine each morning before breakfast and pedal madly along beside Racky for a half hour. We would ride through the cool early air, under the towering silk-cotton trees near the house, and out to the great curve in the shoreline where the waving palms bend landward in the stiff breeze that always blows there. Then we would make a wide turn and race back to the house, loudly discussing the degrees of our desires for the various items of breakfast we knew were awaiting us there on the terrace. Back home we would eat in the wind, looking out over the Caribbean, and talk about the news in yesterday's local paper, brought to us by Isiah each morning from Orange Walk. Then Racky would disappear for the whole morning on his bicycle, riding furiously along the road in one direction or the other until he had discovered an unfamiliar strip of sand along the shore that he could consider a new beach. At lunch he would describe it in detail to me, along with a recounting of all the physical hazards involved in hiding the bicycle in among the trees, so that natives passing along the road on foot would not spot it, or in climbing down unscalable cliffs that turned out to be much higher than they had appeared at first sight, or in measuring the depth of the water preparatory to diving from the rocks, or in judging the efficacy of the reef in barring sharks and barracuda. There is never any element of bragadoccio in Racky's relating of his exploits—only the joyous excitement he derives from telling how he satisfies his inexhaustible curiosity. And his mind shows its alertness in all directions at once. I do not mean to say that I expect him to be an "intellectual." That is no affair of mine, nor do I have any particular interest in whether he turns out to be a thinking man or not. I know he will always have a certain boldness of manner and a great purity of spirit in judging values. The former will prevent his becoming what I call a "victim": he never will be brutalized by realities. And his unerring sense of balance in ethical considerations will shield him from the paralyzing effects of present-day materialism.

For a boy of sixteen Racky has an extraordinary innocence of vision. I do not say this as a doting father, although God knows I can never even think of the boy without that familiar overwhelming sensation of delight and gratitude for being vouchsafed the privilege of sharing my life with him. What he takes so completely as a matter of course, our daily life here together, is a source of never-ending wonder to me; and I reflect upon it a good part of each day, just sitting here being conscious of my great good fortune in having him all to myself, beyond the reach of prying eyes and malicious tongues. (I suppose I am really thinking of C. when I write that.) And I believe that a part of the charm of sharing Racky's life with him consists precisely in his taking it all so utterly for granted. I have never asked him whether he likes being here—it is so patent that he does, very much. I think if he were to turn to me one day and tell me how happy he is here, that somehow, perhaps, the spell might be broken. Yet if he were to be thoughtless and inconsiderate, or even unkind to me, I feel that I should be able only to love him the more for it.

I have reread that last sentence. What does it mean? And why should I even imagine it could mean anything more than it says?

Still, much as I may try, I can never believe in the gratuitous, isolated fact. What I must mean is that I feel that Racky already has been in some way inconsiderate. But in what way? Surely I cannot resent his bicycle treks; I cannot expect him to want to stay and sit talking with me all day. And I never worry about his being in danger; I know he is more capable than most adults of taking care of himself, and that he is no more likely than any native to come to harm crawling over the cliffs or swimming in the bays. At the same time there is no doubt in my mind that something about our existence annoys me. I must resent some detail in the pattern, whatever that pattern may be. Perhaps it is just his youth, and I am envious of the lithe body, the smooth skin, the animal energy and grace.

For a long time this morning I sat looking out to sea, trying to solve that small puzzle. Two white herons came and perched on a dead stump east of the garden. They stayed a long time there without stirring. I would turn my head away and accustom my eyes to the bright sea-horizon, then I would look suddenly at them to see if they had shifted position, but they would always be in the same attitude. I tried to imagine the black stump without them—a purely vegetable landscape—but it was impossible. All the while I was slowly forcing myself to accept a ridiculous explanation of my annoyance with Racky. It had made itself manifest to me only yesterday, when instead of appearing for lunch, he sent a young colored boy from Orange Walk to say that he would be lunching in the village. I could not help noticing that the boy was riding Racky's bicycle. I had been waiting lunch a good half hour for him, and I had Gloria serve immediately as the boy rode off, back to the village. I was curious to know in what sort of place and with whom Racky could be eating, since Orange Walk, as far as I know, is inhabited exclusively by Negroes, and I was sure Gloria would be able to shed some light on the matter, but I could scarcely ask her. However, as she brought on the dessert, I said: "Who was that boy that brought the message from Mister Racky?"

She shrugged her shoulders. "A young lad of Orange Walk. He's named Wilmot."

When Racky returned at dusk, flushed from his exertion (for he never rides casually), I watched him closely. His behavior struck my already suspicious eye as being one of false heartiness and a rather forced good humor. He went to his room early and read for quite a while before turning off his light. I took a long walk in the almost day-bright moonlight, listening to the songs of the night insects in the trees. And I sat for a while in the dark on the stone railing of the bridge across Black River. (It is really only a brook that rushes down over the rocks from the mountain a few miles inland, to the beach near the house.) In the night it always sounds louder and more important than it does in the daytime. The music of the water over the stones relaxed my nerves, although why I had need of such a thing I find it difficult to understand, unless I was really upset by Racky's not having come home for lunch. But if that were true it would be absurd, and moreover, dangerous—just the sort of the thing the parent of an adolescent has to beware of and fight against, unless he is indifferent to the prospect of losing the trust and affection of his offspring permanently. Racky must stay out whenever he likes, with whom he likes, and for as long as he likes, and I must not think twice about it, much less mention it to him, or in any way give the impression of prying. Lack of confidence on the part of a parent is the one unforgivable sin.

Although we still take our morning dip together on arising, it is three weeks since we have been for the early spin. One morning I found that Racky had jumped onto his bicycle in his wet trunks while I was still swimming, and gone by himself, and since then there has been an unspoken agreement between us that such is to be the procedure; he will go alone. Perhaps I held him back; he likes to ride so fast.

Young Peter, the smiling gardener from Saint Ives Cove, is Racky's special friend. It is amusing to see them together among the bushes, crouched over an ant-hill or rushing about trying to catch a lizard, almost of an age the two, yet so disparate—Racky with his tan skin looking almost white in contrast to the glistening black of the other. Today I know I shall be alone for lunch, since it is Peter's day off. On such days they usually go together on their bicycles into Saint Ives Cove, where Peter keeps a small rowboat. They fish along the coast there, but they have never returned with anything so far.

Meanwhile I am here alone, sitting on the rocks in the sun, from time to time climbing down to cool myself in the water, always conscious of the house behind me under the high palms, like a large glass boat filled with orchids and lilies. The servants are clean and quiet, and the work seems to be accomplished almost automatically. The good, black servants are another blessing of the islands; the British, born here in this paradise, have no conception of how fortunate they are. In fact, they do nothing but complain. One must have lived in the United States to appreciate the wonder of this place. Still, even here ideas are changing each day. Soon the people will decide that they want their land to be a part of today's monstrous world, and once that happens, it will be all over. As soon as you have that desire, you are infected with the deadly virus, and you begin to show the symptoms of the disease. You live in terms of time and money, and you think in terms of society and progress. Then all that is left for you is to kill the other people who think the same way, along with a good many of those who do not, since that is the final manifestation of the malady. Here for the moment at any rate, one has a feeling of staticity—existence ceases to be like those last few seconds in the hourglass when what is left of the sand suddenly begins to rush through to the bottom all at once. For the moment, it seems suspended. And if it seems, it is. Each wave at my feet, each bird-call in the forest at my back, does *not* carry me one step nearer the final disaster. The disaster is certain, but it will suddenly have happened, that is all. Until then, time stays still.

I am upset by a letter in this morning's mail: The Royal Bank of Canada requests that I call in person at its central office to sign the deposit slips and other papers for a sum that was cabled from the bank in Boston. Since the central office is on the other side of the island, fifty miles away, I shall have to spend the night over there and return the following day. There is no point in taking Racky along. The sight of "civilization" might awaken a longing for it in him; one never knows. I am sure it would have in me when I was his age. And if that should once start, he would merely be unhappy, since there is nothing for him but to stay here with me, at least for the next two years, when I hope to renew the lease, or, if things in New York pick up, buy the place. I am sending word by Isiah when he goes home into Orange Walk this evening, to have the McCoigh car call for me at seven-thirty tomorrow morning. It is an enormous old open Packard, and Isiah can save the ride out to work here by piling his bicycle into the back and riding with McCoigh.

The trip across the island was beautiful, and would have been highly enjoyable if my imagination had not played me a strange trick at the very outset. We stopped in Orange Walk for gasoline, and while that was being seen to, I got out and went to the corner store for some cigarettes. Since it was not yet eight o'clock, the store was still closed, and I hurried up the side street to the other little shop which I thought might be open. It was, and I bought my cigarettes. On the way back to the corner I noticed a large black woman leaning with her arms on the gate in front of her tiny house, staring into the street. As I passed by her, she looked straight into my face and said something with the strange accent of the island. It was said in what seemed an unfriendly tone, and ostensibly was directed at me, but I had no notion what it was. I got back into the car and the driver started it. The sound of the words had stayed in my head, however, as a bright shape outlined by darkness is likely to stay in the mind's eye, in such a way that when one shuts one's eyes one can see the exact contour of the shape. The car was already roaring up the hill toward the overland road when I suddenly reheard the very words. And they were: "Keep your boy at home, mahn." I sat perfectly rigid for a moment as the open countryside rushed past. Why should I think she had said that? Immediately I decided that I was giving an arbitrary sense to a phrase I could not have understood even if I had been paying strict attention. And then I wondered why my subconscious should have chosen that sense, since now that I whispered the words over to myself they failed to connect with any anxiety to which my mind might have been disposed. Actually I have never given a thought to Racky's wanderings about Orange Walk. I can find no such preoccupation no matter how I put the question to myself. Then, could she really have said those words? All the way through the mountains I pondered the question, even though it was obviously a waste of energy. And soon I could no longer hear the sound of her voice in my memory: I had played the record over too many times, and worn it out.

Here in the hotel a gala dance is in progress. The abominable orchestra, comprising two saxophones and one sour violin, is playing directly under my window in the garden, and the serious-looking couples slide about on the waxed concrete floor of the terrace, in the light of strings of paper lanterns. I suppose it is meant to look Japanese.

At this moment I wonder what Racky is doing there in the house with only Peter and Ernest the watchman to keep him company. I wonder if he is asleep. The house, which I am accustomed to think of as smiling and benevolent in its airiness, could just as well be in the most sinister and remote regions of the globe, now that I am here. Sitting here with the absurd orchestra bleating downstairs, I picture it to myself, and it strikes me as terribly vulnerable in its isolation. In my mind's eye I see the moonlit point with its tall palms waving restlessly in the wind, its dark cliffs licked by the waves below. Suddenly, although I struggle against the sensation, I am inexpressibly glad to be away from the house, helpless there, far on its point of land, in the silence of the night. Then I remember that the night is seldom silent. There is the loud sea at the base of the rocks, the droning of the thousands of insects, the occasional cries of the night birds—all the familiar noises that make sleep so sound. And Racky is there surrounded by them as usual, not even hearing them. But I feel profoundly guilty for having left him, unutterably tender and sad at the thought of him, lying there alone in the house with the two Negroes the only human beings within miles. If I keep thinking of Cold Point I shall be more and more nervous.

I am not going to bed yet. They are all screaming with laughter down there, the idiots; I could never sleep anyway. The bar is still open. Fortunately it is on the street side of the hotel. For once I need a few drinks.

Much later, but I feel no better; I may be a little drunk. The dance is over and it is quiet in the garden, but the room is too hot.

As I was falling asleep last night, all dressed, and with the overhead light shining sordidly in my face, I heard the black woman's voice again, more clearly even than I did in the car yesterday. For some reason this morning there is no doubt in my mind that the words I heard are the words she said. I accept that and go on from there. Suppose she did tell me to keep Racky home. It could only mean that she, or someone else in Orange Walk, has had a childish altercation with him; although I must say it is hard to conceive of Racky's entering into any sort of argument or feud with those people. To set my mind at rest (for I do seem to be taking the whole thing with great seriousness), I am going to stop in the village this afternoon before going home, and try to see the woman. I am extremely curious to know what she could have meant.

I had not been conscious until this evening when I came back to Cold Point how powerful they are, all those physical elements that go to make up its atmosphere: the sea and wind-sounds that isolate the house from the road, the brilliancy of the water, sky and sun, the bright colors and strong odors of the flowers, the feeling of space both outside and within the house. One naturally accepts these things when one is living here. This afternoon when I returned I was conscious of them all over again, of their existence and their strength. All of them together are like a powerful drug; coming back made me feel as though I had been disintoxicated and were returning to the scene of my former indulgences. Now at eleven it is as if I had never been absent an hour. Everything is the same as always, even to the dry palm branch that scrapes against the window screen by my night table. And indeed, it is only thirty-six hours since I was here; but I always expect my absence from a place to bring about irremediable changes.

Strangely enough, now that I think of it, I feel that something *has* changed since I left yesterday morning, and that is the general attitude of the servants—their collective aura, so to speak. I noticed that difference immediately upon arriving back, but was unable to define it. Now I see it clearly. The network of common understanding which slowly spreads itself through a well-run household has been destroyed. Each person is by himself now. No unfriendliness, however, that I can see. They all behave with the utmost courtesy, excepting possibly Peter, who struck me as looking unaccustomedly glum when I encountered him in the kitchen after dinner. I meant to ask Racky if he had noticed it, but I forgot and he went to bed early.

In Orange Walk I made a brief stop on the pretext to McCoigh that I wanted to see the seamstress in the side street. I walked up and back in front of the house where I had seen the woman, but there was no sign of anyone.

As for my absence, Racky seems to have been perfectly content, having spent most of the day swimming off the rocks below the terrace. The insect sounds are at their height now, the breeze is cooler than usual, and I shall take advantage of these favorable conditions to get a good long night's rest.

Today has been one of the most difficult days of my life. I arose early, we had breakfast at the regular time, and Racky went off in the direction of Saint Ives Cove. I lay in the sun on the terrace for a while, listening to the noises of the household's regime. Peter was all over the property, collecting dead leaves and fallen blossoms in a huge basket and carrying them off to the compost heap. He appeared to be in an even fouler humor than last night. When he came near to me at one point on his way to another part of the garden I called to him. He set the basket down and stood looking at me; then he walked across the grass toward me slowly—reluctantly, it seemed to me.

"Peter, is everything all right with you?"

"Yes, sir."

"No trouble at home?"

"Oh, no, sir."

"Good."

"Yes, sir."

He went back to his work. But his face belied his words. Not only did he seem to be in a decidedly unpleasant temper; out here in the sunlight he looked positively ill. However, it was not my concern, if he refused to admit it.

When the heavy heat of the sun reached the unbearable point for me, I got out of my chair and went down the side of the cliff along the series of steps cut there into the rock. A level platform is below, and a diving board, for the water is deep. At each side, the rocks spread out and the waves break over them, but by the platform the wall of rock is vertical and the water merely hits against it below the springboard. The place is a tiny amphitheatre, quite cut off in sound and sight from the house. There too I like to lie in the sun; when I climb out of the water I often remove my trunks and lie stark naked on the springboard. I regularly make fun of Racky because he is embarrassed to do the same. Occasionally he will do it, but never without being coaxed. I was spread out there without a stitch on, being lulled by the slapping of the water, when an unfamiliar voice very close to me said: "Mister Norton?"

I jumped with nervousness, nearly fell off the springboard, and sat up, reaching at the same time, but in vain, for my trunks, which were lying on the rock practically at the feet of a middle-aged mulatto gentleman. He was in a white duck suit, and wore a high collar with a black tie, and it seemed to me that he was eyeing me with a certain degree of horror.

My next reaction was one of anger at being trespassed upon in this way. I rose and got the trunks, however, donning them calmly and saying nothing more meaningful than: "I didn't hear you come down the steps."

"Shall we go up?" said my caller. As he led the way, I had a definite premonition that he was here on an unpleasant errand. On the terrace we sat down, and he offered me an American cigarette which I did not accept.

"This is a delightful spot," he said, glancing out to sea and then at the end of his cigarette, which was only partially aglow. He puffed at it.

I said, "Yes," waiting for him to go on; presently he did.

"I am from the constabulary of this parish. The police, you see." And seeing my face, "This is a friendly call. But still it must be taken as a warning, Mister Norton. It is very serious. If anyone else comes to you about this it will mean trouble for you, heavy trouble. That's why I want to see you privately this way and warn you personally. You see."

I could not believe I was hearing his words. At length I said faintly: "But what about?"

"This is not an official call. You must not be upset. I have taken it upon myself to speak to you because I want to save you deep trouble."

"But I *am* upset!" I cried, finding my voice at last. "How can I help being upset, when I don't know what you're talking about?"

He moved his chair close to mine, and spoke in a very low voice.

"I have waited until the young man was away from the house so we could talk in private. You see, it is about him."

Somehow that did not surprise me. I nodded.

"I will tell you very briefly. The people here are simple country folk. They make trouble easily. Right now they are all talking about the young man you have living here with you. He is your son, I hear." His inflection here was sceptical.

"Certainly he's my son."

His expression did not change, but his voice grew indignant. "Whoever he is, that is a bad young man."

"What do you mean?" I cried, but he cut in hotly: "He may be your son; he may not be. I don't care who he is. That is not my affair. But he is bad through and through. We don't have such things going on here, sir. The people in Orange Walk and Saint Ives Cove are very cross now. You don't know what these folk do when they are aroused."

I thought it my turn to interrupt. "Please tell me why you say my son is bad. What has he done?" Perhaps the earnestness in my voice reached him, for his face assumed a gentler aspect. He leaned still closer to me and almost whispered.

"He has no shame. He does what he pleases with all the young boys, and the men too, and gives them a shilling so they won't tell about it. But they talk. Of course they talk. Every man for twenty miles up and down the coast knows about it. And the women too, they know about it." There was a silence.

I had felt myself preparing to get to my feet for the last few seconds because I wanted to go into my room and be alone, to get away from that scandalized stage whisper. I think I mumbled "Good morning" or "Thank you," as I turned away and began walking toward the house. But he was still beside me, still whispering like an eager conspirator into my ear: "Keep him home, Mister Norton. Or send him away to school, if he is your son. But make him stay out of these towns. For his own sake."

I shook hands with him and went to lie on my bed. From there I heard his car door slam, heard him drive off. I was painfully trying to formulate an opening sentence to use in speaking to Racky about this, feeling that the opening sentence would define my stand. The attempt was merely a sort of therapeutic action, to avoid thinking about the thing itself. Every attitude seemed impossible. There was no way to broach the subject. I suddenly realized that I should never be able to speak to him directly about it. With the advent of this news he had become another person—an adult, mysterious and formidable. To be sure, it did occur to me that the mulatto's story might not be true, but automatically I rejected the doubt. It was as if I wanted to believe it, almost as if I had already known it, and he had merely confirmed it.

Racky returned at midday, panting and grinning. The inevitable comb appeared and was used on the sweaty, unruly locks. Sitting down to lunch, he exclaimed: "Gosh! Did I find a swell beach this morning! But what a job to get to it!" I tried to look unconcerned as I met his gaze; it was as if our positions had been reversed, and I were hoping to stem his rebuke. He prattled on about thorns and vines and his machete. Throughout the meal I kept telling myself: "Now is the moment. You must say something." But all I said was: "More salad? Or do you want dessert now?" So the lunch passed and nothing happened. After I had finished my coffee I went into my bedroom and looked at myself in the large mirror. I saw my eyes trying to give their reflected brothers a little courage. As I stood there I heard a commotion in the other wing of the house: voices, bumpings, the sound of a scuffle. Above the noise came Gloria's sharp voice, imperious and excited: "No, mahn! Don't strike him!" And louder: "Peter, mahn, no!"

I went quickly toward the kitchen, where the trouble seemed to be, but on the way I was run into by Racky, who staggered into the hallway with his hands in front of his face.

"What is it, Racky?" I cried.

He pushed past me into the living room without moving his hands away from his face; I turned and followed him. From there he went into his own room, leaving the door open behind him. I heard him in his bathroom running the water. I was undecided what to do. Suddenly Peter appeared in the hall doorway, his hat in his hand. When he raised his head, I was surprised to see that his cheek was bleeding. In his eyes was a strange, confused expression of transient fear and deep hostility. He looked down again.

"May I please talk with you, sir?"

"What was all the racket? What's been happening?"

"May I talk with you outside, sir?" He said it doggedly, still not looking up.

In view of the circumstances, I humored him. We walked slowly up the cinder road to the main highway, across the bridge, and through the forest while he told me his story. I said nothing.

At the end he said: "I never wanted to, sir, even the first time, but after the first time I was afraid, and Mister Racky was after me every day."

I stood still, and finally said: "If you had only told me this the first time it happened, it would have been much better for everyone."

He turned his hat in his hands, studying it intently. "Yes, sir. But I didn't know what everyone was saying about him in Orange Walk until today. You know I always go to the beach at Saint Ives Cove with Mister Racky on my free days. If I had known what they were all saying I wouldn't have been afraid, sir. And I wanted to keep on working here. I needed the money." Then he repeated what he had already said three times. "Mister Racky said you'd see about it that I was put in the jail. I'm a year older than Mister Racky, sir."

"I know, I know," I said impatiently; and deciding that severity was what Peter expected of me at this point I added: "You had better get your things together and go home. You can't work here any longer, you know."

The hostility in his face assumed terrifying proportions as he said: "If you killed me I would not work any more at Cold Point, sir."

I turned and walked briskly back to the house, leaving him standing there in the road. It seems he returned at dusk, a little while ago, and got his belongings.

In his room Racky was reading. He had stuck some adhesive tape on his chin and over his cheekbone.

"I've dismissed Peter," I announced. "He hit you, didn't he?"

He glanced up. His left eye was swollen, but not yet black.

"He sure did. But I landed him one, too. And I guess I deserved it anyway."

I rested against the table. "Why?" I asked nonchalantly.

"Oh, I had something on him from a long time back that he was afraid I'd tell you."

"And just now you threatened to tell me?"

"Oh, no! He said he was going to quit the job here, and I kidded him about being yellow."

"Why did he want to quit? I thought he liked the job."

"Well, he did, I guess, but he didn't like me." Racky's candid gaze betrayed a shade of pique. I still leaned against the table.

I persisted. "But I thought you two got on fine together. You seemed to."

"Nah. He was just scared of losing his job. I had something on him. He was a good guy, though; I liked him all right." He paused. "Has he gone yet?" A strange quaver crept into his voice as he said the last words, and I understood that for the first time Racky's heretofore impeccable histrionics were not quite equal to the occasion. He was very much upset at losing Peter.

"Yes, he's gone," I said shortly. "He's not coming back, either." And as Racky, hearing the unaccustomed inflection in my voice, looked up at me suddenly with faint astonishment in his young eyes, I realized that this was the moment to press on, to say: "What did you have on him?" But as if he had arrived at the same spot in my mind a fraction of a second earlier, he proceeded to snatch away my advantage by jumping up, bursting into loud song, and pulling off all his clothes simultaneously. As he stood before me naked, singing at the top of his lungs, and stepped into his swimming trunks, I was conscious that again I should be incapable of saying to him what I must say.

He was in and out of the house all afternoon: some of the time he read in his room, and most of the time he was down on the diving board. It is strange behavior for him; if I could only know what is in his mind. As evening approached, my problem took on a purely obsessive character. I walked to and fro in my room, always pausing at one end to look out the window over the sea, and at the other end to glance at my face in the mirror. As if that could help me! Then I took a drink. And another. I thought I might be able to do it at dinner, when I felt fortified by the whisky. But no. Soon he will have gone to bed. It is not that I expect to confront him with any accusations. That I know I never can do. But I must find a way to keep him from his wanderings, and I must offer a reason to give him, so that he will never suspect that I know.

We fear for the future of our offspring. It is ludicrous, but only a little more palpably so than anything else in life. A length of time has passed; days which I am content to have known, even if now they are over. I think that this period was what I had always been waiting for life to offer, the recompense I had unconsciously but firmly expected, in return for having been held so closely in the grip of existence all these years.

That evening seems long ago only because I have recalled its details so many times that they have taken on the color of legend. Actually my problem already had been solved for me then, but I did not know it. Because I could not perceive the pattern, I foolishly imagined that I must cudgel my brains to find the right words with which to approach Racky. But it was he who came to me. That same evening, as I was about to go out for a solitary stroll which I thought might help me hit upon a formula, he appeared at my door.

"Going for a walk?" he asked, seeing the stick in my hand.

The prospect of making an exit immediately after speaking with him made things seem simpler. "Yes," I said, "But I'd like to have a word with you first."

"Sure. What?" I did not look at him because I did not want to see the watchful light I was sure was playing in his eyes at this moment. As I spoke I tapped with my stick along the designs made by the tiles in the floor. "Racky, would you like to go back to school?"

"Are you kidding? You know I hate school."

I glanced up at him. "No, I'm not kidding. Don't look so horrified. You'd probably enjoy being with a bunch of fellows your own age." (That was not one of the arguments I had meant to use.)

"I might like to be with guys my own age, but I don't want to have to be in school to do it. I've had school enough."

I went to the door and said lamely: "I thought I'd get your reactions."

He laughed. "No, thanks."

"That doesn't mean you're not going," I said over my shoulder as I went out.

On my walk I pounded the highway's asphalt with my stick, stood on the bridge having dramatic visions which involved such eventualities as our moving back to the States, Racky's having a bad spill on his bicycle and being paralyzed for some months, and even the possibility of my letting events take their course, which would doubtless mean my having to visit him now and then in the governmental prison with gifts of food, if it meant nothing more tragic and violent. "But none of these things will happen," I said to myself, and I knew I was wasting precious time; he must not return to Orange Walk tomorrow.

I went back toward the point at a snail's pace. There was no moon and very little breeze. As I approached the house, trying to tread lightly on the cinders so as not to awaken the watchful Ernest and have to explain to him that it was only I, I saw that there were no lights in Racky's room. The house was dark save for the dim lamp on my night table. Instead of going in, I skirted the entire building, colliding with bushes and getting my face sticky with spider webs, and went to sit a while on the terrace where there seemed to be a breath of air. The sound of the sea was far out on the reef, where the breakers sighed. Here below, there were only slight watery chugs and gurgles now and then. It was unusually low tide. I smoked three cigarettes mechanically, having ceased even to think, and then, my mouth tasting bitter from the smoke, I went inside.

My room was airless. I flung my clothes onto a chair and looked at the night table to see if the carafe of water was there. Then my mouth opened. The top sheet of my bed had been stripped back to the foot. There on the far side of the bed, dark against the whiteness of the lower sheet, lay Racky asleep on his side, and naked.

I stood looking at him for a long time, probably holding my breath, for I remember feeling a little dizzy at one point. I was whispering to myself, as my eyes followed the curve of his arm, shoulder, back, thigh, leg: "A child. A child." Destiny, when one perceives it clearly from very near, has no qualities at all. The recognition of it and the consciousness of the vision's clarity leave no room on the mind's horizon. Finally I turned off the light and softly lay down. The night was absolutely black.

He lay perfectly quiet until dawn. I shall never know whether or not he was really asleep all that time. Of course he couldn't have been, and yet he lay so still. Warm and firm, but still as death. The darkness and silence were heavy around us. As the birds began to sing, I sank into a soft, enveloping slumber; when I awoke in the sunlight later, he was gone.

I found him down by the water, cavorting alone on the springboard; for the first time he had discarded his trunks without my suggesting it. All day we stayed together around the terrace and on the rocks, talking, swimming, reading, and just lying flat in the hot sun. Nor did he return to his room when night came. Instead after the servants were asleep, we brought three bottles of champagne in and set the pail on the night table.

Thus it came about that I was able to touch on the delicate subject that still preoccupied me, and profiting by the new understanding between us, I made my request in the easiest, most natural fashion.

"Racky, would you do me a tremendous favor if I asked you?"

He lay on his back, his hands beneath his head. It seemed to me his regard was circumspect, wanting in candor.

"I guess so," he said. "What is it?"

"Will you stay around the house for a few days—a week, say? Just to please me? We can take some rides together, as far as you like. Would you do that for me?"

"Sure thing," he said, smiling.

I was temporizing, but I was desperate.

Perhaps a week later—(it is only when one is not fully happy that one is meticulous about time, so that it may have been more or less) —we were having breakfast. Isiah stood by, in the shade, waiting to pour us more coffee.

"I noticed you had a letter from Uncle Charley the other day," said Racky. "Don't you think we ought to invite him down?"

My heart began to beat with great force.

"Here? He'd hate it here," I said casually. "Besides, there's no room. Where would he sleep?" Even as I heard myself saying the words, I knew that they were the wrong ones, that I was not really participating in the conversation. Again I felt the fascination of complete helplessness that comes when one is suddenly a conscious onlooker at the shaping of one's fate.

"In my room," said Racky. "It's empty."

I could see more of the pattern at that moment than I had ever suspected existed. "Nonsense," I said. "This is not the sort of place for Uncle Charley."

Racky appeared to be hitting on an excellent idea. "Maybe if I wrote and invited him," he suggested, motioning to Isiah for more coffee.

"Nonsense," I said again, watching still more of the pattern reveal itself, like a photographic print becoming constantly clearer in a tray of developing solution.

Isiah filled Racky's cup and returned to the shade. Racky drank slowly, pretending to be savoring the coffee.

"Well, it won't do any harm to try. He'd appreciate the invitation," he said speculatively.

For some reason, at this juncture I knew what to say, and as I said it, I knew what I was going to do.

"I thought we might fly over to Havana for a few days next week."

He looked guardedly interested, and then he broke into a wide grin. "Swell!" he cried. "Why wait till next week?"

The next morning the servants called "Good-bye" to us as we drove up the cinder road in the McCoigh car. We took off from the airport at six that evening. Racky was in high spirits; he kept the stewardess engaged in conversation all the way to Camagüey.

He was delighted also with Havana. Sitting in the bar at the Nacional, we continued to discuss the possibility of having C. pay us a visit at the island. It was not without difficulty that I eventually managed to persuade Racky that writing him would be inadvisable.

We decided to look for an apartment right there in Vedado for Racky. He did not seem to want to come back here to Cold Point. We also decided that living in Havana he would need a larger income than I. I am already having the greater part of Hope's estate transferred to his name in the form of a trust fund which I shall administer until he is of age. It was his mother's money, after all.

We bought a new convertible, and he drove me out to Rancho Boyeros in it when I took my plane. A Cuban named Claudio with very white teeth, whom Racky had met in the pool that morning, sat between us.

We were waiting in front of the landing field. An official finally unhooked the chain to let the passengers through. "If you get fed up, come to Havana," said Racky, pinching my arm.

The two of them stood together behind the rope, waving to me, their shirts flapping in the wind as the plane started to move.

The wind blows by my head; between each wave there are thousands of tiny licking and chopping sounds as the water hurries out of the crevices and holes; and a part-floating, part-submerged feeling of being in the water haunts my mind even as the hot sun burns my face. I sit here and I read, and I wait for the pleasant feeling of repletion that follows a good meal, to turn slowly, as the hours pass along, into the even more delightful, slightly stirring sensation deep within, which accompanies the awakening of the appetite.

I am perfectly happy here in reality, because I still believe that nothing very drastic is likely to befall this part of the island in the near future.

MS Ferncape
(New York–Casablanca),
1947

from *THE SHELTERING SKY*

PAUL BOWLES

THE SHELTERING SKY is the story of Port and Kit Moresby, a husband and wife, married for twelve years, who arrive in North Africa "fleeing the aftermath and memory" of World War II. Port is a traveler, not a tourist, "a man who moves slowly, over periods of years, from one part of the earth to another. . . . Before the war it had been Europe and the Near East, during the war the West Indies and South America. And [Kit] had accompanied him without reiterating her complaints too often or too bitterly."

With them on their trip is an astonishingly handsome young man, Tunner, whom Port has persuaded to come along. Tunner keeps trying to convince Kit to have an affair with him. Port and Kit have not had sexual relations for some time but Kit continues to hope that Port will return to her. He, for his part, thinks of the possibility of returning, but tells himself that it is not yet the right time.

Shortly after the three arrive in Africa, Port goes for a walk alone in the medina, where he sleeps with a beautiful young prostitute who tries to rob him. Soon after Port's return, the three travelers set out for the desert, Port in a car with the Lyles, an incestuous mother and son he has met at the hotel, and Kit and Tunner by train. On the train Kit is thrown into terror by the appearance and behavior of the other passengers, and for comfort she submits to Tunner's sexual advances.

The following selection, Chapter 13 of the novel, takes place in the desert town of Boussif, where Tunner and Kit have caught up with Port. Port has persuaded Kit to ride out with him into the countryside at sunset.

XIII

THEY RODE SLOWLY out the long street toward the cleft in the low mountain ridge south of the town. Where the houses ended the plain began, on either side of them, a sea of stones. The air was cool, the dry sunset wind blew against them. Port's bicycle squeaked slightly as he pedaled. They said nothing, Kit riding a little ahead. In the distance, behind them, a bugle was being blown; a firm, bright blade of sound in the air. Even now, when it would be setting in a half-hour or so, the sun burned. They came to a village, went through it. The dogs barked wildly and the women turned away, covering their mouths. Only the children remained as they were, looking, in a paralysis of surprise. Beyond the village, the road began to rise. They were aware of the grade only from their pedaling; to the eye it looked flat. Soon Kit was tired. They stopped, looked back across the seemingly level plain to Boussif, a pattern of brown blocks at the base of the mountains. The breeze blew harder.

"It's the freshest air you'll ever smell," said Port.

"It's wonderful," said Kit. She was in a dreamy, amiable state of mind, and she did not feel talkative.

"Shall we try and make the pass there?"

"In a minute. I just want to catch my breath."

Presently they started out again, pedaling determinedly, their eyes on the gap in the ridge ahead. As they approached it, already they could see the endless flat desert beyond, broken here and there by sharp crests of rock that rose above the surface like the dorsal fins of so many monstrous fish, all moving in the same direction. The road had been blasted through the top of the ridge, and the jagged boulders had slid down on both sides of the cut. They left the bicycles by the road and started to climb upward among the huge rocks, toward the top of the ridge. The sun was at the flat horizon; the air was suffused with redness. As they stepped around the side of a boulder they came all at once on a man, seated with his burnous pulled up about his neck—so that he was stark naked from the shoulders down—deeply immersed in the business of shaving his pubic hair with a long pointed knife. He glanced up at them with indifference as they passed before him, immediately lowering his head again to continue the careful operation.

Kit took Port's hand. They climbed in silence, happy to be together.

"Sunset is such a sad hour," she said, presently.

"If I watch the end of a day—any day—I always feel it's the end of a whole epoch. And the autumn! It might as well be the end of everything," he said. "That's why I hate cold countries, and love the warm ones, where there's no winter, and when night comes you feel an opening up of the life there, instead of a closing down. Don't you feel that?"

"Yes," said Kit, "but I'm not sure I prefer the warm countries. I don't know. I'm not sure I don't feel that it's wrong to try to escape the night and winter, and that if you do you'll have to pay for it somehow."

"Oh, Kit! You're really crazy." He helped her up the side of a low cliff. The desert was directly below them, much farther down than the plain from which they had just climbed.

She did not answer. It made her sad to realize that in spite of their so often having the same reactions, the same feelings, they never would reach the same conclusions, because their respective aims in life were almost diametrically opposed.

They sat down on the rocks side by side, facing the vastness below. She linked her arm through his and rested her head against his shoulder. He only stared straight before him, sighed, and finally shook his head slowly.

It was such places as this, such moments that he loved above all else in life; she knew that, and she also knew that he loved them more if she could be there to experience them with him. And although he was aware that the very silences and emptinesses that touched his soul terrified her, he could not bear to be reminded of that. It was as if always he held the fresh hope that she, too, would be touched in the same way as he by solitude and the proximity to infinite things. He had often told her: "It is your only hope," and she was never sure what he meant. Sometimes she thought he meant that it was *his* only hope, that only if she were able to become as he was, could he find his way back to love, since love for Port meant loving her—there was no question of anyone else. And now for so long there had been no love, no possibility of it. But in spite of her willingness to become whatever he wanted her to become, she could not change that much: the terror was always there inside her ready to take command. It was useless to pretend otherwise. And just as she was unable to shake off the dread that was always with her, he was unable to break out of the cage into which he had shut himself, the cage he had built long ago to save himself from love.

She pinched his arm. "Look there!" she whispered. Only a few paces from them, atop a rock, sitting so still that they had not noticed him, was a venerable Arab, his legs tucked under him, his eyes shut.

At first it seemed as though he might be asleep, in spite of his erect posture, since he made no sign of being conscious of their presence. But then they saw his lips moving ever so little, and they knew he was praying.

"Do you think we should watch like this?" she said, her voice hushed.

"It's all right. We'll just sit here quietly." He put his head in her lap and lay looking up at the clear sky. Over and over, very lightly, she stroked his hair. The wind from the regions below gathered force. Slowly the sky lost its intensity of light. She glanced up at the Arab; he had not moved. Suddenly she wanted to go back, but she sat perfectly still for a while looking tenderly down at the inert head beneath her hand.

"You know," said Port, and his voice sounded unreal, as voices are likely to do after a long pause in an utterly silent spot, "the sky here's very strange. I often have the sensation when I look at it that it's a solid thing up there, protecting us from what's behind."

Kit shuddered slightly as she said: "From what's behind?"

"Yes."

"But what *is* behind?" Her voice was very small.

"Nothing, I suppose. Just darkness. Absolute night."

"*Please* don't talk about it now." There was agony in her entreaty. "Everything you say frightens me, up here. It's getting dark, and the wind is blowing, and I can't stand it."

He sat up, put his arms about her neck, kissed her, drew back and looked at her, kissed her again, drew back again, and so on, several times. There were tears on her cheeks. She smiled forlornly as he rubbed them away with his forefingers.

"You know what?" he said with great earnestness. "I think we're both afraid of the same thing. And for the same reason. We've never managed, either one of us, to get all the way into life. We're hanging on to the outside for all we're worth, convinced we're going to fall off at the next bump. Isn't that true?"

She shut her eyes for a moment. His lips on her cheek had awakened the sense of guilt, and it swept over her now in a great wave that made her dizzy and ill. She had spent her siesta trying to wipe her conscience clean of the things that had happened the night before, but now she was clearly aware that she had not been able to do it, and that she never would be able to do it. She put her hand to her forehead, holding it there. At length she said: "But if we're not in, then we *are* more likely to—fall off."

She had hoped he would offer some argument to this, that he

would find his own analogy faulty, perhaps—that some consolation would be forthcoming. All he said was: "I don't know."

The light was growing palpably dimmer. Still the old Arab sat buried in his prayers, severe and statue-like in the advancing dusk. It seemed to Port that behind them, back on the plain, he could hear one long-drawn-out bugle note, but it went on and on. No man could hold his breath that long: it was his imagination. He took her hand and pressed it. "We must go back," he whispered. Quickly they rose and went leaping over the rocks down to the road. The bicycles were there where they had left them. They coasted silently back toward the town. The dogs in the village set up a clamor as they sped past. At the market place they left the bicycles, and walked slowly through the street that led to the hotel, head on into the parade of men and sheep that continued its steady advance into the town, even at night.

All the way back to town Kit had been turning an idea over and over in her head: "Somehow Port knows about Tunner and me." At the same time she did not believe he was conscious of knowing it. But with a deeper part of his intelligence she was certain he felt the truth, felt what had happened. As they walked along the dark street she was almost tempted to ask him how he knew. She was curious about the functioning of a purely animal sense like that, in a man as complex as Port. But it would have done no good; as soon as he had been made aware of his knowledge he would have decided to be furiously jealous, immediately there would have been a scene, and all the implicit tenderness between them would have vanished, perhaps never to be recovered. To have not even that tenuous communion with him would be unbearable.

Port did a curious thing when dinner was over. Alone he went out to the market, sat in the café for a few minutes watching the animals and men by the flickering carbide lamps, and on passing the open door of the shop where he had rented the bicycles, went in. There he asked for a bicycle equipped with a headlight, told the man to wait for him until he returned, and quickly rode off in the direction of the gap. Up there among the rocks it was cold, the night wind blew. There was no moon; he could not see the desert in front of him, down below—only the hard stars above that flared in the sky. He sat on the rock and let the wind chill him. Riding down to Boussif he realized he never could tell Kit that he had been back there. She would not understand his having wanted to return without her. Or perhaps, he reflected, she would understand it too well.

Fez, 1948

CAMP CATARACT

JANE BOWLES

"CAMP CATARACT" was completed in Fez in the spring of 1948, as Paul, in an adjoining room, was finishing The Sheltering Sky. *In 1966 Truman Capote wrote in his introduction to* The Collected Works of Jane Bowles *that "Camp Cataract" was "the most complete of Mrs. Bowles's stories and the one most representative of her work. [It] is a rending sample of controlled compassion: a comic tale of doom that has at its heart, and as its heart, the subtlest comprehension of eccentricity and human apartness. This story alone would require that we accord Jane Bowles high esteem."*

BERYL KNOCKED ON Harriet's cabin door and was given permission to enter. She found her friend seated near the window, an open letter in her hand.

"Good evening, Beryl," said Harriet. "I was just reading a letter from my sister." Her fragile, spinsterish face wore a canny yet slightly hysterical expression.

Beryl, a stocky blond waitress with stubborn eyes, had developed a dogged attachment to Harriet and sat in her cabin whenever she had a moment to spare. She rarely spoke in Harriet's presence, nor was she an attentive listener.

"I'll read you what she says; have a seat." Harriet indicated a straight chair and Beryl dragged it into a dark corner where she sat down. It creaked dangerously under the weight of her husky body.

"Hope I don't bust the chair," said Beryl, and she blushed furiously, digging her hands deep into the pockets of the checked plus-fours she habitually wore when she was not on duty.

" 'Dear Sister,' " Harriet read. " 'You are still at Camp Cataract visiting the falls and enjoying them. I always want you to have a good time. This is your fifth week away. I suppose you go on standing behind the falls with much enjoyment like you told me all the guests did. I think you said only the people who don't stay overnight have to pay to stand behind the waterfall . . . you stay ten weeks . . . have a nice time, dear. Here everything is exactly the same as when you left. The apartment doesn't change. I have something I want to tell you, but first let me say that if you get nervous, why don't you come home instead of waiting until you are no good for the train trip? Such a thing could happen. I wonder of course how you feel about the apartment once you are by the waterfall. Also, I want to put this to you. Knowing that you have an apartment and a loving family must make Camp Cataract quite a different place than it would be if it were all the home and loving you had. There must be wretches like that up there. If you see them, be sure to give them loving because they are the lost souls of the earth. I fear nomads. I am afraid of them and afraid for them too. I don't know what I would do if any of my dear ones were seized with the wanderlust. We are meant to cherish those who through God's will are given into our hands. First of all come the members of the family, and for this it is better to live as close as possible. Maybe you would say, "Sadie is old-fashioned; she doesn't want people to live on their own." I am not old-fashioned, but I don't want any of us to turn into nomads. You don't grow rich in spirit by widening your circle but by tending your own. When you are gone, I get afraid about you. I think that you might be seized with the wanderlust and that you are not remembering the apartment very much. Particularly this trip . . . but then I know this cannot be true and that only my nerves make me think such things. It's so hot out. This is a record-breaking summer. Remember, the apartment is not just a row of rooms. It is the material proof that our spirits are so wedded that we have but one blessed roof over our heads. There are only three of us in the apartment related by blood, but Bert Hoffer has joined the three through the normal channels of marriage, also sacred. I know that you feel this way too about it and that just nerves makes me think Camp Cataract can change anything. May I remind you also that if this family is a garland, you are the middle flower; for me you are anyway. Maybe Evy's love is now flowing more to Bert Hoffer because he's her husband, which is natural. I wish they didn't think you needed to go to Camp Cataract because of your spells. Haven't I always tended you when you had them? Bert's always taken Evy to the Hoffers and we've stayed together, just the two of us, with the door safely locked so you wouldn't in your excitement run to a neighbor's house at all hours of the morning. Evy liked going to the Hoffers because they always gave her chicken with dumplings or else goose with red cabbage. I hope you haven't got it in your head that just because you are an old maid you have to go somewhere and be by yourself. Remember, I am also an old maid. I must close now, but I am not satisfied with my letter because I have so much more to say. I know you love the apartment and feel the way I feel. You are simply getting a tourist's thrill out of being there in a cabin like all of us do. I count the days until your sweet return. Your loving sister, Sadie.' "

Harriet folded the letter. "Sister Sadie," she said to Beryl, "is a great lover of security."

"She sounds swell," said Beryl, as if Harriet were mentioning her for the first time, which was certainly not the case.

"I have no regard for it whatsoever," Harriet announced in a positive voice. "*None.* In fact, I am a great admirer of the nomad, vagabonds, gypsies, seafaring men. I tip my hat to them; the old prophets roamed the world for that matter too, and most of the visionaries." She folded her hands in her lap with an air of satisfaction. Then, clearing her throat as if for a public address, she continued. "I don't give a tinker's damn about feeling part of a community, I can assure you. . . . That's not why I stay on at the apartment . . . not for a minute, but it's a good reason why she does . . . I mean Sadie; she loves a community spirit and she loves us all to be in the apartment because the apartment is in the community. She can get an actual thrill out of knowing that. But of course I can't . . . I never could, never in a thousand years."

She tilted her head back and half-closed her eyes. In the true style of a person given to interminable monologues, she was barely conscious of her audience. "Now," she said, "we can come to whether I, on the other hand, get a thrill out of Camp Cataract." She paused for a moment as if to consider this. "Actually, I don't," she pronounced sententiously, "but if you like, I will clarify my statement by calling Camp Cataract my *tree house.* You remember tree houses from your younger days. . . . You climb into them when you're a child and plan to run away from home once you are safely hidden among the leaves. They're popular with children. Suppose I tell you point-blank that I'm an extremely original woman, but also a very shallow one . . . in a sense, a *very* shallow one. I am afraid of scandal." Harriet assumed a more erect position. "I despise anything that smacks of a bohemian dash for freedom; I know that this has nothing to do with the more serious things in life . . . I'm sure there are hundreds of serious people who kick over their traces and jump into the gutter; but I'm too shallow for anything like that . . . I know it and I enjoy knowing it. Sadie on the other hand cooks and cleans all day long and yet takes her life as seriously as she would a religion . . . myself and the apartment and the Hoffers. By the Hoffers, I mean my sister Evy and her big pig of a husband Bert." She made a wry face. "I'm the only one with taste in the family but I've never even suggested a lamp for the apartment. I wouldn't lower myself by becoming involved. I do however refuse to make an unseemly dash for freedom. I refuse to be known as 'Sadie's wild sister Harriet.' There is something intensively repulsive to me about unmarried women setting out on their own . . . also a very shallow attitude. You may wonder how a woman can be shallow and know it at the same time, but then, this is precisely the tragedy of any person, if he allows himself to be griped." She paused for a moment and looked into the darkness with a fierce light in her eyes. "Now let's get back to Camp Cataract," she said with renewed vigor. "The pine groves, the canoes, the sparkling purity of the brook water and cascade . . . the cabins . . . the marshmallows, the respectable clientele."

"Did you ever think of working in a garage?" Beryl suddenly blurted out, and then she blushed again at the sound of her own voice.

"No," Harriet answered sharply. "Why should I?"

Beryl shifted her position in her chair. "Well," she said, "I think I'd like that kind of work better than waiting on tables. Especially if I could be boss and own my garage. It's hard, though, for a woman."

Harriet stared at her in silence. "Do you think Camp Cataract smacks of the gutter?" she asked a minute later.

"No, sir. . . ." Beryl shook her head with a woeful air.

"Well then, there you have it. It is, of course, the farthest point from the gutter that one could reach. Any blockhead can see that. My plan is extremely complicated and from my point of view rather brilliant. First I will come here for several years . . . I don't know yet exactly how many, but long enough to imitate roots . . . I mean to imitate the natural family roots of childhood . . . long enough so that I myself will feel: "Camp Cataract is *habit*, Camp Cataract is life, Camp Cataract is not escape." Escape is unladylike, habit isn't. As I remove myself gradually from within my family circle and establish myself more and more solidly into Camp Cataract, then from here at some later date I can start making my sallies into the outside world almost unnoticed. None of it will seem to the onlooker like an ugly impetuous escape. I intend to rent the same cabin every year and to stay a little longer each time. Meanwhile I'm learning a great deal about trees and flowers and bushes . . . I am interested in nature." She was quiet for a moment. "It's rather lucky too," she added, "that the doctor has approved of my separating from the family for several months out of every year. He's a blockhead and doesn't remotely suspect the extent of my scheme nor how perfectly he fits into it . . . in fact, he has even sanctioned my request that no one visit me here at the camp. I'm afraid if Sadie did, and she's the only one who would dream of it, I wouldn't be able to avoid a wrangle and then I might have a fit. The fits are unpleasant; I get much more nervous than I usually am and there's a blank moment or two." Harriet glanced sideways at Beryl to see how she was reacting to this last bit of information, but Beryl's face was impassive.

"So you see my plan," she went on, in a relaxed, offhand manner, "complicated, a bit dotty and completely original . . . but then, I *am* original . . . not like my sisters . . . oddly enough I don't even seem to belong socially to the same class as my sisters do. I am somehow" —she hesitated for a second—"more fashionable."

Harriet glanced out of the window. Night had fallen during the course of her monologue and she could see a light burning in the next cabin. "Do you think I'm a coward?" she asked Beryl.

The waitress was startled out of her torpor. Fortunately her brain registered Harriet's question as well. "No, sir," she answered. "If you were, you wouldn't go out paddling canoes solo, with all the scary shoots you run into up and down these rivers. . . ."

Harriet twisted her body impatiently. She had a sudden and uncontrollable desire to be alone. "Good-bye," she said rudely. "I'm not coming to supper."

Beryl rose from her chair. "I'll save something for you in case you get hungry after the dining room's closed. I'll be hanging around the lodge like I always am till bedtime." Harriet nodded and the waitress stepped out of the cabin, shutting the door carefully behind her so that it would not make any noise.

• • •

Harriet's sister Sadie was a dark woman with loose features and sad eyes. She was turning slightly to fat in her middle years, and did not in any way resemble Harriet, who was only a few years her senior. Ever since she had written her last letter to Harriet about Camp Cataract and the nomads Sadie had suffered from a feeling of steadily mounting suspense—the suspense itself a curious mingling of apprehension and thrilling anticipation. Her appetite grew smaller each day and it was becoming increasingly difficult for her to accomplish her domestic tasks.

She was standing in the parlor gazing with blank eyes at her new furniture set—two enormous easy chairs with bulging arms and a sofa in the same style—when she said aloud: "I can talk to her better than I can put it in a letter." Her voice had been automatic and when she heard her own words a rush of unbounded joy flooded her heart. Thus she realized that she was going on a little journey to Camp Cataract. She often made important decisions this way, as if some prearranged plot were being suddenly revealed to her, a plot which had immediately to be concealed from the eyes of others, because for Sadie, if there was any problem implicit in making a decision, it lay, not in the difficulty of choosing, but in the concealment of her choice. To her, secrecy was the real absolution from guilt, so automatically she protected all of her deepest feelings and compulsions from the eyes of Evy, Bert Hoffer and the other members of the family, although she had no interest in understanding or examining these herself.

The floor shook; recognizing Bert Hoffer's footsteps, she made a violent effort to control the flux of her blood so that the power of her emotion would not be reflected in her cheeks. A moment later her brother-in-law walked across the room and settled in one of the easy chairs. He sat frowning at her for quite a little while without uttering a word in greeting, but Sadie had long ago grown accustomed to his unfriendly manner; even in the beginning it had not upset her too much because she was such an obsessive that she was not very concerned with outside details.

"God-damned velours," he said finally. "It's the hottest stuff I ever sat on."

"Next summer we'll get covers," Sadie reassured him, "with a flower pattern if you like. What's your favorite flower?" she asked, just to make conversation and to distract him from looking at her face.

Bert Hoffer stared at her as if she'd quite taken leave of her senses. He was a fat man with a red face and wavy hair. Instead of answering this question, which he considered idiotic, he mopped his brow with his handkerchief.

"I'll fix you a canned pineapple salad for supper," she said to him with glowing eyes. "It will taste better than heavy meat on a night like this."

"If you're going to dish up pineapple salad for supper," Bert Hoffer answered with a dark scowl, "you can telephone some other guy to come and eat it. You'll find me over at Martie's Tavern eating meat and potatoes, if there's any messages to deliver."

"I thought because you were hot," said Sadie.

"I was talking about the velvet, wasn't I? I didn't say anything about the meat."

He was a very trying man indeed, particularly in a small apartment, but Sadie never dwelled upon this fact at all. She was delighted to cook and clean for him and for her sister Evelyn so long as they consented to live under the same roof with her and Harriet.

Just then Evelyn walked briskly into the parlor. Like Sadie she was dark, but here the resemblance ceased, for she had a small and wiry build, with a flat chest, and her hair was as straight as an Indian's. She stared at her husband's shirt sleeves and at Sadie's apron with distaste. She was wearing a crisp summer dress with a very low neckline, an unfortunate selection for one as bony and fierce-looking as she.

"You both look ready for the dump heap, not for the dining room," she said to them. "Why do we bother to have a dining room . . . is it just a farce?"

"How was the office today?" Sadie asked her sister.

Evelyn looked at Sadie and narrowed her eyes in closer scrutiny. The muscles in her face tightened. There was a moment of dead silence, and Bert Hoffer, cocking a wary eye in his wife's direction, recognized the dangerous flush on her cheeks. Secretly he was pleased. He loved to look on when Evelyn blew up at Sadie, but he tried to conceal his enjoyment because he did not consider it a very masculine one.

"What's the matter with you?" Evelyn asked finally, drawing closer to Sadie. "There's something wrong besides your dirty apron."

Sadie colored slightly but said nothing.

"You look crazy," Evelyn yelled. "What's the matter with you? You look so crazy I'd be almost afraid to ask you to go to the store for something. Tell me what's happened!" Evelyn was very excitable; nonetheless hers was a strong and sane nature.

"I'm not crazy," Sadie mumbled. "I'll go get the dinner." She pushed slowly past Evelyn and with her heavy step she left the parlor.

The mahogany dining table was much too wide for the small oblong-shaped room, clearing the walls comfortably only at the two ends. When many guests were present some were seated first on one side of the room and were then obliged to draw the table toward themselves, until its edge pressed painfully into their diaphragms, before the remaining guests could slide into their seats on the opposite side.

Sadie served the food, but only Bert Hoffer ate with any appetite. Evelyn jabbed at her meat once or twice, tasted it, and dropped her fork, which fell with a clatter on to her plate.

Had the food been more savory she might not have pursued her attack on Sadie until later, or very likely she would have forgotten it altogether. Unfortunately, however, Sadie, although she insisted on fulfilling the role of housewife, and never allowed the others to acquit themselves of even the smallest domestic task, was a poor cook and a careless cleaner as well. Her lumpy gravies were tasteless, and she had once or twice boiled a good cut of steak out of indifference. She was lavish, too, in spite of being indifferent, and kept her cupboards so loaded with food that a certain quantity spoiled each week and there was often an unpleasant odor about the house. Harriet, in fact, was totally unaware of Sadie's true nature and had fallen into the trap her sister had instinctively prepared for her, because beyond wearing an apron and simulating the airs of other housewives, Sadie did not possess a community spirit at all, as Harriet had stated to Beryl the waitress. Sadie certainly yearned to live in the grown-up world that her parents had established for them when they were children, but in spite of the fact that she had wanted to live in that world with Harriet, and because of Harriet, she did not understand it properly. It remained mysterious to her even though she did all the housekeeping and managed the apartment entirely alone. She couldn't ever admit to herself that she lived in constant fear that Harriet would go away, but she brooded a great deal on outside dangers, and had she tried, she could not have remembered a time when this fear had not been her strongest emotion.

Sometimes an ecstatic and voracious look would come into her eyes, as if she would devour her very existence because she loved it so much. Such passionate moments of appreciation were perhaps her only reward for living a life which she knew in her heart was one of perpetual narrow escape. Although Sadie was neither sly nor tricky, but on the contrary profoundly sincere and ingenuous, she schemed unconsciously to keep the Hoffers in the apartment with them, because she did not want to reveal the true singleness of her interest either to Harriet or to herself. She sensed as well that Harriet would find it more difficult to break away from all three of them (because as a group they suggested a little society, which impressed her sister) than she would to escape from her alone. In spite of her mortal dread that Harriet might strike out on her own, she had never brooded on the possibility of her sister's marrying. Here, too, her instinct was correct: she knew that she was safe and referred often to the "normal channels of marriage," conscious all the while that such an intimate relationship with a man would be as uninteresting to Harriet as it would to herself.

From a financial point of view this communal living worked out more than satisfactorily. Each sister had inherited some real estate which yielded her a small monthly stipend; these stipends, combined with the extra money that the Hoffers contributed out of their salaries, covered their common living expenses. In return for the extra sum the Hoffers gave toward the household expenses, Sadie contributed her work, thus saving them the money they would have spent hiring a servant, had they lived alone. A fourth sister, whose marriage had proved financially more successful than Evy's, contributed generously toward Harriet's support at Camp Cataract, since Harriet's stipend certainly did not yield enough to cover her share of their living expenses at the apartment and pay for a long vacation as well.

Neither Sadie nor Bert Hoffer had looked up when Evy's fork clattered onto her plate. Sadie was truly absorbed in her own thoughts, whereas Bert Hoffer was merely pretending to be, while secretly he rejoiced at the unmistakable signal that his wife was about to blow up.

"When I find out why Sadie looks like that if she isn't going to be crazy, then I'll eat," Evelyn announced flatly, and she folded her arms across her chest.

"I'm not crazy," Sadie said indistinctly, glancing toward Bert Hoffer, not in order to enlist his sympathies, but to avoid her younger sister's sharp scrutiny.

"There's a big danger of your going crazy because of Grandma and Harriet," said Evelyn crossly. "That's why I get so nervous the minute you look a little out of the way, like you do tonight. It's not that you get Harriet's expression . . . but then you might be getting a different kind of craziness . . . maybe worse. She's all right if she can go away and there's not too much excitement . . . it's only in spells anyway. But you—you might get a worse kind. Maybe it would be steadier."

"I'm not going to be crazy," Sadie murmured apologetically.

Evelyn glowered in silence and picked up her fork, but then immediately she let it fall again and turned on her sister with renewed exasperation. "Why don't you ask me why *I'm* not going to be crazy?" she demanded. "Harriet's my sister and Grandma's my grandma just as much as she is yours, isn't she?"

Sadie's eyes had a faraway look.

"If you were normal," Evelyn pursued, "you'd give me an intelligent argument instead of not paying any attention. Do you agree, Hoffer?"

"Yes, I do," he answered soberly.

Evelyn stiffened her back. "I'm too much like everybody else to be crazy," she announced with pride. "At a picture show, I feel like the norm."

The technical difficulty of disappearing without announcing her plan to Evelyn suddenly occurred to Sadie, who glanced up quite by accident at her sister. She knew, of course, that Harriet was supposed to avoid contact with her family during those vacation months at the doctor's request and even at Harriet's own; but like some herd animal, who though threatened with the stick continues grazing, Sadie pursued her thoughts imperturbably. She did not really believe in Harriet's craziness nor in the necessity of her visits to Camp Cataract, but she was never in conscious opposition to the opinions of her sisters. Her attitude was rather like that of a child who is bored by the tedium of grown-up problems and listens to them with a vacant ear. As usual she was passionately concerned only with successfully dissimulating what she really felt, and had she been forced to admit openly that there existed such a remarkable split between her own opinions and those of her sisters, she would have suffered unbelievable torment. She was able to live among them, listening to their conferences with her dead outside ear (the more affluent sister was also present at these sessions, and her husband as well), and even to contribute a pittance toward Harriet's support at the camp, without questioning the validity either of their decisions or of her own totally divergent attitude. By a self-imposed taboo, awareness of this split was denied her, and she had never reflected upon it.

Harriet had gone to Camp Cataract for the first time a year ago, after a bad attack of nerves combined with a return of her pleurisy. It had been suggested by the doctor himself that she go with his own wife and child instead of traveling with one of her sisters. Harriet had been delighted with the suggestion and Sadie had accepted it without a murmur. It was never her habit to argue, and in fact she had thought nothing of Harriet's leaving at the time. It was only gradually that she had begun writing the letters to Harriet about Camp Cataract, the nomads and the wanderlust—for she had written others similar to her latest one, but never so eloquent or full of conviction. Previous letters had contained a hint or two here and there, but had been for the main part factual reports about her summer life in the apartment. Since writing this last letter she had not been able to forget her own wonderful and solemn words (for she was rarely eloquent), and even now at the dinner table they rose continually in her throat so that she was thrilled over and over again and could not bother her head about announcing her departure to Evelyn. "It will be easier to write a note," she said to herself. "I'll pack my valise and walk out tomorrow afternoon, while they're at business. They can get their own dinners for a few days. Maybe I'll leave a great big meat loaf." Her eyes were shining like stars.

"Take my plate and put it in the warmer, Hoffer," Evelyn was saying. "I won't eat another mouthful until Sadie tells us what we can expect. If she feels she's going off, she can at least warn us about it. I deserve to know how she feels . . . I tell every single thing I feel to her and Harriet . . . I don't sneak around the house like a thief. In the first place I don't have any time for sneaking, I'm at the office all day! Is this the latest vogue, this sneaking around and hiding everything you can from your sister? Is it?" She stared at Bert Hoffer, widening her eyes in fake astonishment. He shrugged his shoulders.

"I'm no sneak or hypocrite and neither are you, Hoffer, you're no hypocrite. You're just sore at the world, but you don't pretend you love the world, do you?"

Sadie was lightheaded with embarrassment. She had blanched at Evy's allusion to her going, which she mistook naturally for a reference to her intention of leaving for Camp Cataract.

"Only for a few days . . ." she mumbled in confusion, "and then I'll be right back here at the table."

Evelyn looked at her in consternation. "What do you mean by announcing calmly how many days it's going to be?" she shouted at her sister. "That's really sacrilegious! Did you ever hear of such a crusty sacrilegious remark in your life before?" She turned to Bert Hoffer, with a horror-stricken expression on her face. "How can I go to the office and look neat and clean and happy when this is what I hear at home . . . when my sister sits here and says she'll only go crazy for a few days? How *can* I go to the office after that? How can I look right?"

"I'm not going to be crazy," Sadie assured her again in a sorrowful tone, because although she felt relieved that Evelyn had not, after all, guessed the truth, hers was not a nature to indulge itself in trivial glee at having put someone off her track.

"You just said you were going to be crazy," Evelyn exclaimed heatedly. "Didn't she, Bert?"

"Yes," he answered, "she did say something like that. . . ."

The tendons of Evelyn's neck were stretched tight as she darted her eyes from her sister's face to her husband's. "Now, tell me this much," she demanded, "do I go to the office every day looking neat and clean or do I go looking like a bum?"

"You look O.K.," Bert said.

"Then why do my sisters spit in my eye? Why do they hide everything from me if I'm so decent? I'm wide open, I'm frank, there's nothing on my mind besides what I say. Why can't they be like other sisters all over the world? One of them is so crazy that she must live in a cabin for her nerves at *my* expense, and the other one is planning to go crazy deliberately and behind my back." She commenced to struggle out of her chair, which as usual proved to be a slow and laborious task. Exasperated, she shoved the table vehemently away from her toward the opposite wall. "Why don't we leave the space all on one side when there's no company?" she screamed at both of them, for she was now annoyed with Bert Hoffer as well as with Sadie. Fortunately they were seated at either end of the table and so did not suffer as a result of her violent gesture, but the table jammed into four chairs ranged on the opposite side, pinning three of them backward against the wall and knocking the fourth onto the floor.

"Leave it there," Evelyn shouted dramatically above the racket. "Leave it there till doomsday," and she rushed headlong out of the room.

They listened to her gallop down the hall.

"What about the dessert?" Bert Hoffer asked Sadie with a frown. He was displeased because Evelyn had spoken to him sharply.

"Leftover bread pudding without raisins." She had just gotten up to fetch the pudding when Evelyn summoned them from the parlor.

"Come in here, both of you," she hollered. "I have something to say."

They found Evelyn seated on the couch, her head tilted way back on a cushion, staring fixedly at the ceiling. They settled into easy chairs opposite her.

"I could be normal and light in any other family," she said, "I'm normally a gay light girl . . . not a morose one. I like all the material things."

"What do you want to do tonight?" Bert Hoffer interrupted, speaking with authority. "Do you want to be excited or do you want to go to the movies?" He was always bored by these self-appraising monologues which succeeded her explosions.

Evy looked as though she had not heard him, but after a moment or two of sitting with her eyes shut she got up and walked briskly out of the room; her husband followed her.

Neither of them had said good-bye to Sadie, who went over to the window as soon as they'd gone and looked down on the huge unsightly square below her. It was crisscrossed by trolley tracks going in every possible direction. Five pharmacies and seven cigar stores were visible from where she stood. She knew that modern industrial cities were considered ugly, but she liked them. "I'm glad Evy and Bert have gone to a picture show," Sadie remarked to herself after a while. "Evy gets high-strung from being at the office all day."

A little later she turned her back on the window and went to the dining room.

"Looks like the train went through here," she murmured, gazing quietly at the chairs tilted back against the wall and the table's unsightly angle; but the tumult in her breast had not subsided, even though she knew she was leaving for Camp Cataract. Beyond the first rush of joy she had experienced when her plan had revealed itself to her earlier, in the parlor, the feeling of suspense remained identical, a curious admixture of anxiety and anticipation, difficult to bear. Concerning the mechanics of the trip itself she was neither nervous nor foolishly excited. "I'll call up tomorrow," she said to herself, "and find out when the buses go, or maybe I'll take the train. In the morning I'll buy three different meats for the loaf, if I don't forget. It won't go rotten for a few days, and even if it does they can eat at Martie's or else Evy will make bologna and eggs . . . she knows how, and so does Bert." She was not really concentrating on these latter projects any more than she usually did on domestic details.

The lamp over the table was suspended on a heavy iron chain. She reached for the beaded string to extinguish the light. When she released it the massive lamp swung from side to side in the darkness.

"Would you like it so much by the waterfall if you didn't know the apartment was here?" she whispered into the dark, and she was thrilled again by the beauty of her own words. "How much more I'll be able to say when I'm sitting right next to her," she murmured almost with reverence. ". . . And then we'll come back here," she added simply, not in the least startled to discover that the idea of returning with Harriet had been at the root of her plan all along.

Without bothering to clear the plates from the table, she went into the kitchen and extinguished the light there. She was suddenly overcome with fatigue.

• • •

When Sadie arrived at Camp Cataract it was raining hard.

"This shingled building is the main lodge," the hack driver said to her. "The ceiling in there is three times higher than average, if you like that style. Go up on the porch and just walk in. You'll get a kick out of it."

Sadie reached into her pocketbook for some money.

"My wife and I come here to drink beer when we're in the mood," he continued, getting out his change. "If there's nobody much inside, don't get panicky; the whole camp goes to the movies on Thursday nights. The wagon takes them and brings them back. They'll be along soon."

After thanking him she got out of the cab and climbed the wooden steps on to the porch. Without hesitating she opened the door. The driver had not exaggerated; the room was indeed so enormous that it suggested a gymnasium. Wicker chairs and settees were scattered from one end of the floor to the other and numberless sawed-off tree stumps had been set down to serve as little tables.

Sadie glanced around her and then headed automatically for a giant fireplace, difficult to reach because of the accumulation of chairs and settees that surrounded it. She threaded her way between these and stepped across the hearth into the cold vault of the chimney, high enough to shelter a person of average stature. The andirons, which reached to her waist, had been wrought in the shape of witches. She fingered their pointed iron hats. "Novelties," she murmured to herself without enthusiasm. "They must have been especially made." Then, peering out of the fireplace, she noticed for the first time that she was not alone. Some fifty feet away a fat woman sat reading by the light of an electric bulb.

"She doesn't even know I'm in the fireplace," she said to herself. "Because the rain's so loud, she probably didn't hear me come in." She waited patiently for a while and then, suspecting that the woman might remain oblivious to her presence indefinitely, she called over to her. "Do you have anything to do with managing Camp Cataract?" she asked, speaking loudly so that she could be heard above the rain.

The woman ceased reading and switched her big light off at once, since the strong glare prevented her seeing beyond the radius of the bulb.

"No, I don't," she answered in a booming voice. "Why?"

Sadie, finding no answer to this question, remained silent.

"Do you think I look like a manager?" the woman pursued, and since Sadie had obviously no intention of answering, she continued the conversation by herself.

"I suppose you might think I was manager here, because I'm stout, and stout people have that look; also I'm about the right age for it. But I'm not the manager . . . I don't manage anything, anywhere. I have a domineering cranium all right, but I'm more the French type. I'd rather enjoy myself than give orders."

"French . . ." Sadie repeated hesitantly.

"Not French," the woman corrected her. "French *type*, with a little of the actual blood." Her voice was cold and severe.

For a while neither of them spoke, and Sadie hoped the conversation had drawn to a definite close.

"Individuality is my god," the woman announced abruptly, much to Sadie's disappointment. "That's partly why I didn't go to the picture show tonight. I don't like doing what the groups do, and I've seen the film." She dragged her chair forward so as to be heard more clearly. "The steadies here—we call the ones who stay more than a fortnight steadies—are all crazy to get into birds-of-a-feather-flock-together arrangements. If you look around, you can see for yourself how clubby the furniture is fixed. Well, they can go in for it, if they want, but I won't. I keep my chair out in the open here, and when I feel like it I take myself over to one circle or another . . . there's about ten or twelve circles. Don't you object to the confinement of a group?"

"We haven't got a group back home," Sadie answered briefly.

"I don't go in for group worship either," the woman continued, "any more than I do for the heavy social mixing. I don't even go in for individual worship, for that matter. Most likely I was born to such a vigorous happy nature I don't feel the need to worry about what's up there over my head. I get the full flavor out of all my days whether anyone's up there or not. The groups don't allow for that kind of zip . . . never. You know what rotten apples in a barrel can do to the healthy ones."

Sadie, who had never before met an agnostic, was profoundly shocked by the woman's blasphemous attitude. "I'll bet she slept with a lot of men she wasn't married to when she was younger," she said to herself.

"Most of the humanity you bump into is unhealthy and nervous," the woman concluded, looking at Sadie with a cold eye, and then without further remarks she struggled out of her chair and began to walk toward a side door at the other end of the room. Just as she approached it the door was flung open from the other side by Beryl, whom the woman immediately warned of the new arrival. Beryl, without ceasing to spoon some beans out of a can she was holding, walked over to Sadie and offered to be of some assistance. "I can show you rooms," she suggested. "Unless you'd rather wait till the manager comes back from the movies."

When she realized, however, after a short conversation with Sadie, that she was speaking to Harriet's sister, a malevolent scowl darkened her countenance, and she spooned her beans more slowly.

"Harriet didn't tell me you were coming," she said at length; her tone was unmistakably disagreeable.

Sadie's heart commenced to beat very fast as she in turn realized that this woman in plus-fours was the waitress, Beryl, of whom Harriet had often spoken in her letters and at home.

"It's a surprise," Sadie told her. "I meant to come here before. I've been promising Harriet I'd visit her in camp for a long time now, but I couldn't come until I got a neighbor in to cook for Evy and Bert. They're a husband and wife . . . my sister Evy and her husband Bert."

"I know about those two," Beryl remarked sullenly. "Harriet's told me all about them."

"Will you please take me to my sister's cabin?" Sadie asked, picking up her valise and stepping forward.

Beryl continued to stir her beans around without moving.

"I thought you folks had some kind of arrangement," she said. She had recorded in her mind entire passages of Harriet's monologues out of love for her friend, although she felt no curiosity concerning the material she had gathered. "I thought you folks were supposed to stay in the apartment while she was away at camp."

"Bert Hoffer and Evy have never visited Camp Cataract," Sadie answered in a tone that was innocent of any subterfuge.

"You bet they haven't," Beryl pronounced triumphantly. "That's part of the arrangement. They're supposed to stay in the apartment while she's here at camp; the doctor said so."

"They're not coming up," Sadie repeated, and she still wore, not the foxy look that Beryl expected would betray itself at any moment, but the look of a person who is attentive though being addressed in a foreign language. The waitress sensed that all her attempts at starting a scrap had been successfully blocked for the present and she whistled carefully, dragging some chairs into line with a rough hand. "I'll tell you what," she said, ceasing her activities as suddenly as she had begun them. "Instead of taking you down there to the Pine Cones—that's the name of the grove where her cabin is—I'll go myself and tell her to come up here to the lodge. She's got some nifty rain equipment so she won't get wet coming through the groves like you would . . . lots of pine trees out there."

Sadie nodded in silence and walked over to a fantasy chair, where she sat down.

"They get a lot of fun out of that chair. When they're drunk," said Beryl pointing to its back, made of a giant straw disc. "Well . . . so long. . . ." She strode away. "Dear Valley . . ." Sadie heard her sing as she went out the door.

Sadie lifted the top off the chair's left arm and pulled two books out of its woven hamper. The larger volume was entitled *The Growth and Development of the Texas Oil Companies*, and the smaller, *Stories from Other Climes*. Hastily she replaced them and closed the lid.

• • •

Harriet opened the door for Beryl and quickly shut it again, but even in that instant the wooden flooring of the threshold was thoroughly soaked with rain. She was wearing a lavender kimono with a deep ruffle at the neckline; above it her face shone pale with dismay at Beryl's late and unexpected visit. She feared that perhaps the waitress was drunk. "I'm certainly not hacking out a free place for myself in this world just in order to cope with drunks," she said to herself with bitter verve. Her loose hair was hanging to her shoulders and Beryl looked at it for a moment in mute admiration before making her announcement.

"Your sister Sadie's up at the lodge," she said, recovering herself; then, feeling embarrassed, she shuffled over to her usual seat in the darkest corner of the room.

"What are you saying?" Harriet questioned her sharply.

"Your sister Sadie's up at the lodge," she repeated, not daring to look at her. "Your sister Sadie who wrote you the letter about the apartment."

"But she can't be!" Harriet screeched. "She can't be! It was all arranged that no one was to visit me here."

"That's what I told her," Beryl put in.

Harriet began pacing up and down the floor. Her pupils were dilated and she looked as if she were about to lose all control of herself. Abruptly she flopped down on the edge of the bed and began gulping in great draughts of air. She was actually practicing a system which she believed had often saved her from complete hysteria, but Beryl, who knew nothing about her method, was horrified and utterly bewildered. "Take it easy," she implored Harriet. "Take it easy!"

"Dash some water in my face," said Harriet in a strange voice, but horror and astonishment anchored Beryl securely to her chair, so that Harriet was forced to stagger over to the basin and manage by herself. After five minutes of steady dousing she wiped her face and chest with a towel and resumed her pacing. At each instant the expression on her face was more indignant and a trifle less distraught. "It's the boorishness of it that I find so appalling," she complained, a suggestion of theatricality in her tone which a moment before had not been present. "If she's determined to wreck my schemes, why doesn't she do it with some style, a little slight bit of cunning? I can't picture anything more boorish than hauling oneself onto a train and simply chugging straight up here. She has no sense of scheming, of intrigue in the grand manner . . . none whatever. Anyone meeting only Sadie would think the family raised potatoes for a living. Evy doesn't make a much better impression, I must say. If they met her they'd decide we were all clerks! But at least she goes to business. . . . She doesn't sit around thinking about how to mess my life up all day. She thinks about Bert Hoffer. Ugh!" She made a wry face.

"When did you and Sadie start fighting?" Beryl asked her.

"I don't fight with Sadie," Harriet answered, lifting her head proudly. "I wouldn't dream of fighting like a common fishwife. Everything that goes on between us goes on undercover. It's always been that way. I've always hidden everything from her ever since I was a little girl. She's perfectly aware that I know she's trying to hold me a prisoner in the apartment out of plain jealousy and she knows too that I'm afraid of being considered a bum, and that makes matters simpler for her. She pretends to be worried that I might forget myself if I left the apartment and commit a folly with some man I wasn't married to, but actually she knows perfectly well that I'm as cold as ice. I haven't the slightest interest in men . . . nor in women either for that matter; still if I stormed out of the apartment dramatically the way some do, they might think I was a bum on my way to a man . . . and I won't give Sadie that satisfaction, ever. As for marriage, of course I admit I'm peculiar and there's a bit wrong with me, but even so I shouldn't want to marry: I think the whole system of going through life with a partner is repulsive in every way." She paused, but only for a second. "Don't you imagine, however," she added severely, looking directly at Beryl, "don't you imagine that just because I'm a bit peculiar and different from the others, that I'm not fussy about my life. I *am* fussy about it, and I *hate* a scandal."

"To hell with sisters!" Beryl exclaimed happily. "Give 'em all a good swift kick in the pants." She had regained her own composure watching the color return to Harriet's cheeks and she was just beginning to think with pleasure that perhaps Sadie's arrival would serve to strengthen the bond of intimacy between herself and Harriet, when this latter buried her head in her lap and burst into tears. Beryl's face fell and she blushed at her own frivolousness.

"I can't any more," Harriet sobbed in anguished tones. "I can't . . . I'm old . . . I'm much too old." Here she collapsed and sobbed so pitifully that Beryl, wringing her hands in grief, sprang to her side, for she was a most tenderhearted person toward those whom she loved. "You are not old . . . you are beautiful," she said, blushing again, and in her heart she was thankful that Providence had granted her the occasion to console her friend in a grief-stricken moment, and to compliment her at the same time.

After a bit, Harriet's sobbing subsided, and jumping up from the bed, she grabbed the waitress. "Beryl," she gasped, "you must run back to the lodge right away." There was a beam of cunning in her tear-filled eyes.

"Sure will," Beryl answered.

"Go back to the lodge and see if there's a room left up there, and if there is, take her grip into it so that there will be no question of her staying in my cabin. I can't have her staying in my cabin. It's the only place I have in the whole wide world." The beam of cunning disappeared again and she looked at Beryl with wide, frightened eyes. ". . . And if there's no room?" she asked.

"Then I'll put her in my place," Beryl reassured her. "I've got a neat little cabin all to myself that she can have and I'll go bunk in with some dopey waitress."

"Well, then," said Harriet, "go, and hurry! Take her grip to a room in the upper lodge annex or to your own cabin before she has a chance to say anything, and then come straight back here for me. I can't get through these pine groves alone . . . now . . . I know I can't." It did not occur to her to thank Beryl for the kind offer she had made.

"All right," said the waitress, "I'll be back in a jiffy and don't you worry about a thing." A second later she was lumbering through the drenched pine groves with shining eyes.

• • •

When Beryl came into the lodge and snatched Sadie's grip up without a word of explanation, Sadie did not protest. Opposite her there was an open staircase which led to a narrow gallery hanging halfway between the ceiling and the floor. She watched the waitress climbing the stairs, but once she had passed the landing Sadie did not trouble to look up and follow her progress around the wooden balcony overhead.

A deep chill had settled into her bones, and she was like a person benumbed. Exactly when this present state had succeeded the earlier one Sadie could not tell, nor did she think to ask herself such a question, but a feeling of dread now lay like a stone in her breast where before there had been stirring such powerful sensations of excitement and suspense. "I'm so low," she said to herself. "I feel like I was sitting at my own funeral." She did not say this in the spirit of hyperbolic gloom which some people nurture to work themselves out of a bad mood, but in all seriousness and with her customary attitude of passivity; in fact, she wore the humble look so often visible on the faces of sufferers who are being treated in a free clinic. It did not occur to her that a connection might exist between her present dismal state and the mission she had come to fulfill at Camp Cataract, nor did she take any notice of the fact that the words which were to enchant Harriet and accomplish her return were no longer welling up in her throat as they had done all the past week. She feared that something dreadful might happen, but whatever it was, this disaster was as remotely connected with her as a possible train wreck. "I hope nothing bad happens . . ." she thought, but she didn't have much hope in her.

Harriet slammed the front door and Sadie looked up. For the first second or two she did not recognize the woman who stood on the threshold in her dripping rubber coat and hood. Beryl was beside her; puddles were forming around the feet of the two women. Harriet had rouged her cheeks rather more highly than usual in order to hide all traces of her crying spell. Her eyes were bright and she wore a smile that was fixed and hard.

"Not a night fit for man or beast," she shouted across to Sadie, using a voice that she thought sounded hearty and yet fashionable at the same time; she did this, not in order to impress her sister, but to keep her at a safe distance.

Sadie, instead of rushing to the door, stared at her with an air of perplexity. To her Harriet appeared more robust and coarse-featured than she had five weeks ago at the apartment, and yet she knew that such a rapid change of physiognomy was scarcely possible. Recovering, she rose and went to embrace her sister. The embrace failed to reassure her because of Harriet's wet rubber coat, and her feeling of estrangement became more defined. She backed away.

Upon hearing her own voice ring out in such hearty and fashionable tones, Harriet had felt crazily confident that she might, by continuing to affect this manner, hold her sister at bay for the duration of her visit. To increase her chances of success she had determined right then not to ask Sadie why she had come, but to treat the visit in the most casual and natural way possible.

"Have you put on fat?" Sadie asked, at a loss for anything else to say.

"I'll never be fat," Harriet replied quickly. "I'm a fruit lover, not a lover of starches."

"Yes, you love fruit," Sadie said nervously. "Do you want some? I have an apple left from my lunch."

Harriet looked aghast. "Now!" she exclaimed. "Beryl can tell you that I never eat at night; in fact I never come up to the lodge at night, *never*. I stay in my cabin. I've written you all about how early I get up . . . I don't know anything about the lodge at night," she added almost angrily, as though her sister had accused her of being festive.

"You don't?" Sadie looked at her stupidly.

"No, I don't. Are you hungry, by the way?"

"If she's hungry," put in Beryl, "we can go into the Grotto Room and I'll bring her the food there. The tables in the main dining room are all set up for tomorrow morning's breakfast."

"I despise the Grotto," said Harriet with surprising bitterness. Her voice was getting quite an edge to it, and although it still sounded fashionable it was no longer hearty.

"I'm not hungry," Sadie assured them both. "I'm sleepy."

"Well, then," Harriet replied quickly, jumping at the opportunity, "we'll sit here for a few minutes and then you must go to bed."

The three of them settled in wicker chairs close to the cold hearth. Sadie was seated opposite the other two, who both remained in their rubber coats.

"I really do despise the Grotto," Harriet went on. "Actually I don't hang around the lodge at all. This is not the part of Camp Cataract that interests me. I'm interested in the pine groves, my cabin, the rocks, the streams, the bridge, and all the surrounding natural beauty . . . the sky also."

Although the rain still continued its drumming on the roof above them, to Sadie, Harriet's voice sounded intolerably loud, and she could not rid herself of the impression that her sister's face had grown fatter. "Now," she heard Harriet saying in her loud voice, "tell me about the apartment. . . . What's new, how are the dinners coming along, how are Evy and Bert?"

Fortunately, while Sadie was struggling to answer these questions, which unaccountably she found it difficult to do, the stout agnostic reappeared, and Harriet was immediately distracted.

"Rover," she called gaily across the room, "come and sit with us. My sister Sadie's here."

The woman joined them, seating herself beside Beryl, so that Sadie was now facing all three.

"It's a surprise to see you up at the lodge at night, Hermit," she remarked to Harriet without a spark of mischief in her voice.

"You see!" Harriet nodded at Sadie with immense satisfaction. "I was not fibbing, was I? How are Evy and Bert?" she asked again, her face twitching a bit. "Is the apartment hot?"

Sadie nodded.

"I don't know how long you plan to stay," Harriet rattled on, feeling increasingly powerful and therefore reckless, "but I'm going on a canoe trip the day after tomorrow for five days. We're going up the river to Pocahontas Falls. . . . I leave at four in the morning, too, which rather ruins tomorrow as well. I've been looking forward to this trip ever since last spring when I applied for my seat, back at the apartment. The canoes are limited, and the guides. . . . I'm devoted to canoe trips, as you know, and can fancy myself a red-skin all the way to the Falls and back, easily."

Sadie did not answer.

"There's nothing weird about it," Harriet argued. "It's in keeping with my hatred of industrialization. In any case, you can see what a chopped-up day tomorrow's going to be. I have to make my pack in the morning and I must be in bed by eight-thirty at night, the latest, so that I can get up at four. I'll have only one real meal, at two in the afternoon. I suggest we meet at two behind the souvenir booth; you'll notice it tomorrow." Harriet waited expectantly for Sadie to answer in agreement to this suggestion, but her sister remained silent.

"Speaking of the booth," said Rover, "I'm not taking home a single souvenir this year. They're expensive and they don't last."

"You can buy salt-water taffy at Gerald's Store in town," Beryl told her. "I saw some there last week. It's a little stale but very cheap."

"Why would they sell salt-water taffy in the mountains?" Rover asked irritably.

Sadie was half listening to the conversation; as she sat watching them, all three women were suddenly unrecognizable; it was as if she had flung open the door to some dentist's office and seen three strangers seated there. She sprang to her feet in terror.

Harriet was horrified. "What is it?" she yelled at her sister. "Why do you look like that? Are you mad?"

Sadie was pale and beads of sweat were forming under her felt hat, but the women opposite her had already regained their correct relation to herself and the present moment. Her face relaxed, and although her legs were trembling as a result of her brief but shocking experience, she felt immensely relieved that it was all over.

"Why did you jump up?" Harriet screeched at her. "Is it because you are at Camp Cataract and not at the apartment?"

"It must have been the long train trip and no food . . ." Sadie told herself, "only one sandwich."

"Is it because you are at Camp Cataract and not at the apartment?" Harriet insisted. She was really very frightened and wished to establish Sadie's fit as a purposeful one and not as an involuntary seizure similar to one of hers.

"It was a long and dirty train trip," Sadie said in a weary voice. "I had only one sandwich all day long, with no mustard or butter . . . just the processed meat. I didn't even eat my fruit."

"Beryl offered to serve you food in the Grotto!" Harriet ranted. "Do you want some now or not? For heaven's sake, speak up!"

"No . . . no." Sadie shook her head sorrowfully. "I think I'd best go to bed. Take me to your cabin . . . I've got my slippers and my kimono and my nightgown in my satchel," she added, looking around her vaguely, for the fact that Beryl had carried her grip off had never really impressed itself upon her consciousness.

Harriet glanced at Beryl with an air of complicity and managed to give her a quick pinch. "Beryl's got you fixed up in one of the upper lodge annex rooms," she told Sadie in a false, chatterbox voice. "You'll be much more comfortable up here than you would be down in my cabin. We all use oil lamps in the grove and you know how dependent you are on electricity."

Sadie didn't know whether she was dependent on electricity or not since she had never really lived without it, but she was so tired that she said nothing.

"I get up terribly early and my cabin's drafty, besides," Harriet went on. "You'll be much more comfortable here. You'd hate the Boulder Dam wigwams as well. Anyway, the wigwams are really for boys and they're always full. There's a covered bridge leading from this building to the annex on the upper floor, so that's an advantage."

"O.K., folks," Beryl cut in, judging that she could best help Harriet by spurring them on to action. "Let's get going."

"Yes," Harriet agreed, "if we don't get out of the lodge soon the crowd will come back from the movies and we certainly want to avoid them."

They bade good night to Rover and started up the stairs.

"This balustrade is made of young birch limbs," Harriet told Sadie as they walked along the narrow gallery overhead. "I think it's very much in keeping with the lodge, don't you?"

"Yes, I do," Sadie answered.

Beryl opened the door leading from the balcony onto a covered bridge and stepped through it, motioning to the others. "Here we go onto the bridge," she said, looking over her shoulder. "You've never visited the annex, have you?" she asked Harriet.

"I've never had any reason to," Harriet answered in a huffy tone. "You know how I feel about my cabin."

They walked along the imperfectly fitted boards in the darkness. Gusts of wind blew about their ankles and they were constantly spattered with rain in spite of the wooden roofing. They reached the door at the other end very quickly, however, where they descended two steps leading into a short, brightly lit hall. Beryl closed the door to the bridge behind them. The smell of fresh plaster and cement thickened the damp air.

"This is the annex," said Beryl. "We put old ladies here mostly, because they can get back and forth to the dining room without going outdoors . . . and they've got the toilet right here, too." She flung open the door and showed it to them. "Then also," she added, "we don't like the old ladies dealing with oil lamps and here they've got electricity." She led them into a little room just at their left and switched on the light. "Pretty smart, isn't it?" she remarked, looking around her with evident satisfaction, as if she herself had designed the room; then, sauntering over to a modernistic wardrobe-bureau combination, she polished a corner of it with her pocket handkerchief. This piece was made of shiny brown wood and fitted with a rimless circular mirror. "Strong and good-looking," Beryl said, rapping on the wood with her knuckles. "Every room's got one."

Sadie sank down on the edge of the bed without removing her outer garments. Here, too, the smell of plaster and cement permeated the air, and the wind still blew about their ankles, this time from under the badly constructed doorsill.

"The cabins are much draftier than this," Harriet assured Sadie once again. "You'll be more comfortable here in the annex." She felt confident that establishing her sister in the annex would facilitate her plan, which was still to prevent her from saying whatever she had come to say.

Sadie was terribly tired. Her hat, dampened by the rain, pressed uncomfortably against her temples, but she did not attempt to remove it. "I think I've got to go to sleep," she muttered. "I can't stay awake any more."

"All right," said Harriet, "but don't forget tomorrow at two by the souvenir booth . . . you can't miss it. I don't want to see anyone in the morning because I can make my canoe pack better by myself

. . . it's frightfully complicated. . . . But if I hurried I could meet you at one-thirty; would you prefer that?"

Sadie nodded.

"Then I'll do my best. . . . You see, in the morning I always practice imagination for an hour or two. It does me lots of good, but tomorrow I'll cut it short." She kissed Sadie lightly on the crown of her felt hat. "Good night," she said. "Is there anything I forgot to ask you about the apartment?"

"No," Sadie assured her. "You asked everything."

"Well, good night," said Harriet once again, and followed by Beryl, she left the room.

• • •

When Sadie awakened the next morning a feeling of dread still rested like a leaden weight on her chest. No sooner had she left the room than panic, like a small wing, started to beat under her heart. She was inordinately fearful that if she strayed any distance from the main lodge she would lose her way and so arrive late for her meeting with Harriet. This fear drove her to stand next to the souvenir booth fully an hour ahead of time. Fortunately the booth, situated on a small knoll, commanded an excellent view of the cataract, which spilled down from some high rock ledges above a deep chasm. A fancy bridge spanned this chasm only a few feet below her, so that she was able to watch the people crossing it as they walked back and forth between the camp site and the waterfall. An Indian chief in full war regalia was seated at the bridge entrance on a kitchen chair. His magnificent feather headdress curved gracefully in the breeze as he busied himself collecting the small toll that all the tourists paid on returning from the waterfall; he supplied them with change from a nickel-plated conductor's belt which he wore over his deer-hide jacket, embroidered with minute beads. He was an Irishman employed by the management, which supplied his costume. Lately he had grown careless, and often neglected to stain his freckled hands the deep brick color of his face. He divided his time between the bridge and the souvenir booth, clambering up the knoll whenever he sighted a customer.

A series of wooden arches, Gothic in conception, succeeded each other all the way across the bridge; bright banners fluttered from their rims, each one stamped with the initials of the camp, and some of them edged with a glossy fringe. Only a few feet away lay the dining terrace, a huge flagstone pavilion whose entire length skirted the chasm's edge.

Unfortunately, neither the holiday crowds, nor the festooned bridge, nor even the white waters of the cataract across the way could distract Sadie from her misery. She constantly glanced behind her at the dark pine groves wherein Harriet's cabin was concealed. She dreaded to see Harriet's shape define itself between the trees, but at the same time she feared that if her sister did not arrive shortly some terrible catastrophe would befall them both before she'd had a chance to speak. In truth all desire to convince her sister that she should leave Camp Cataract and return to the apartment had miraculously shriveled away, and with the desire, the words to express it had vanished too. This did not in any way alter her intention of accomplishing her mission; on the contrary, it seemed to her all the more desperately important now that she was almost certain, in her innermost heart, that her trip was already a failure. Her attitude was not an astonishing one, since like many others she conceived of her life as separate from herself; the road was laid out always a little ahead of her by sacred hands, and she walked down it without a question. This road, which was her life, would go on existing after her death, even as her death existed now while she still lived.

There were close to a hundred people dining on the terrace, and the water's roar so falsified the clamor of voices that one minute the guests seemed to be speaking from a great distance and the next right at her elbow. Every now and then she thought she heard someone pronounce her name in a dismal tone, and however much she told herself that this was merely the waterfall playing its tricks on her ears she shuddered each time at the sound of her name. Her very position next to the booth began to embarrass her. She tucked her hands into her coat sleeves so that they would not show, and tried to keep her eyes fixed on the foaming waters across the way, but she had noticed a disapproving look in the eyes of the diners nearest her, and she could not resist glancing back at the terrace every few minutes in the hope that she had been mistaken. Each time, however, she was more convinced that she had read their expressions correctly, and that these people believed, not only that she was standing there for no good reason, but that she was a genuine vagrant who could not afford the price of a dinner. She was therefore immensely relieved when she caught sight of Harriet advancing between the tables from the far end of the dining pavilion. As she drew nearer, Sadie noticed that she was wearing her black winter coat trimmed with red fur, and that her marceled hair remained neatly arranged in spite of the strong wind. Much to her relief Harriet had omitted to rouge her cheeks and her face therefore had regained its natural proportions. She saw Harriet wave at the sight of her and quicken her step. Sadie was pleased that the diners were to witness the impending meeting. "When they see us together," she thought, "they'll realize that I'm no vagrant, but a decent woman visiting her sister." She herself started down the knoll to hasten the meeting. "I thought you'd come out of the pine grove," she called out, as soon as they were within a few feet of one another. "I kept looking that way."

"I would have ordinarily," Harriet answered, reaching her side and kissing her lightly on the cheek, "but I went to the other end of the terrace first, to reserve a table for us from the waiter in charge there. That end is quieter, so it will be more suitable for a long talk."

"Good," thought Sadie as they climbed up the knoll together. "Her night's sleep has done her a world of good." She studied Harriet's face anxiously as they paused next to the souvenir booth, and discovered a sweet light reflected in her eyes. All at once she remembered their childhood together and the great tenderness Harriet had often shown towards her then.

"They have Turkish pilaff on the menu," said Harriet, "so I told the waiter to save some for you. It's such a favorite that it usually runs out at the very beginning. I know how much you love it."

Sadie, realizing that Harriet was actually eager for this dinner, the only one they would eat together at Camp Cataract, to be a success, felt the terrible leaden weight lifted from her heart; it disappeared so suddenly that for a moment or two she was like a balloon without its ballast; she could barely refrain from dancing about in delight. Harriet tugged on her arm.

"I think we'd better go now," she urged Sadie, "then after lunch we can come back here if you want to buy some souvenirs for Evy and Bert . . . and maybe for Flo and Carl and Bobby too. . . ."

Sadie bent down to adjust her cotton stockings, which were wrinkling badly at the ankles, and when she straightened up again her eyes lighted on three men dining very near the edge of the terrace; she had not noticed them before. They were all eating corn on the cob and big round hamburger sandwiches in absolute silence. To protect their clothing from spattering kernels, they had converted their napkins into bibs.

"Bert Hoffer's careful of his clothes too," Sadie reflected, and then she turned to her sister. "Don't you think men look different sitting all by themselves without women?" she asked her. She felt an extraordinary urge to chat—an urge which she could not remember ever having experienced before.

"I think," Harriet replied, as though she had not heard Sadie's comment, "that we'd better go to our table before the waiter gives it to someone else."

"I don't like men," Sadie announced without venom, and she was about to follow Harriet when her attention was arrested by the eyes of the man nearest her. Slowly lowering his corn cob to his plate, he stared across at her, his mouth twisted into a bitter smile. She stood as if rooted to the ground, and under his steady gaze all her newborn joy rapidly drained away. With desperation she realized that Harriet, darting in and out between the crowded tables, would soon be out of sight. After making what seemed to her a superhuman effort she tore herself away from the spot where she stood and lunged after Harriet shouting her name.

Harriet was at her side again almost instantly, looking up at her with a startled expression. Together they returned to the souvenir booth, where Sadie stopped and assumed a slightly bent position as if she were suffering from an abdominal pain.

"What's the trouble?" she heard Harriet asking with concern. "Are you feeling ill?"

Instead of answering Sadie laid her hand heavily on her sister's arm and stared at her with a hunted expression in her eyes.

"Please try not to look so much like a gorilla," said Harriet in a kind voice, but Sadie, although she recognized the accuracy of this observation (for she could feel very well that she was looking like a gorilla), was powerless to change her expression, at least for a moment or two. "Come with me," she said finally, grabbing Harriet's hand and pulling her along with almost brutal force. "I've got something to tell you."

She headed down a narrow path leading into a thickly planted section of the grove, where she thought they were less likely to be disturbed. Harriet followed with such a quick, light step that Sadie felt no pull behind her at all and her sister's hand, folded in her own thick palm, seemed as delicate as the body of a bird. Finally they entered a small clearing where they stopped. Harriet untied a handkerchief from around her neck and mopped her brow. "Gracious!" she said. "It's frightfully hot in here." She offered the kerchief to Sadie. "I suppose it's because we walked so fast and because the pine trees shut out all the wind. . . . First I'll sit down and then you must tell me what's wrong." She stepped over to a felled tree whose length blocked the clearing. Its torn roots were shockingly exposed, whereas the upper trunk and branches lay hidden in the surrounding grove. Harriet sat down; Sadie was about to sit next to her when she noticed a dense swarm of flies near the roots. Automatically she stepped toward them. "Why are they here?" she asked herself—then immediately she spotted the cause, an open can of beans some careless person had deposited inside a small hollow at the base of the trunk. She turned away in disgust and looked at Harriet. Her sister was seated on the fallen tree, her back gracefully erect and her head tilted in a listening attitude. The filtered light imparted to her face an incredibly fragile and youthful look, and Sadie gazed at her with tenderness and wonder. No sound reached them in the clearing, and she realized with a pounding heart that she could no longer postpone telling Harriet why she had come. She could not have wished for a moment more favorable to the accomplishment of her purpose. The stillness in the air, their isolation, the expectant and gentle light in Harriet's eye, all these elements should have combined to give her back her faith—faith in her own powers to persuade Harriet to come home with her and live among them once again, winter and summer alike, as she had always done before. She opened her mouth to speak and doubled over, clutching at her stomach as though an animal were devouring her. Sweat beaded her forehead and she planted her feet wide apart on the ground as if this animal would be born. Though her vision was barred with pain, she saw Harriet's tear-filled eyes, searching hers.

"Let's not go back to the apartment," Sadie said, hearing her own words as if they issued not from her mouth but from a pit in the ground. "Let's not go back there . . . let's you and me go out in the world . . . just the two of us." A second before covering her face to hide her shame Sadie glimpsed Harriet's eyes, impossibly close to her own, their pupils pointed with a hatred such as she had never seen before.

It seemed to Sadie that it was taking an eternity for her sister to leave. "Go away . . . go away . . . or I'll suffocate." She was moaning the words over and over again, her face buried deep in her hands. "Go away . . . please go away . . . I'll suffocate. . . ." She could not tell, however, whether she was thinking these words or speaking them aloud.

At last she heard Harriet's footstep on the dry branches, as she started out of the clearing. Sadie listened, but although one step followed another, the cracking sound of the dry branches did not grow any fainter as Harriet penetrated farther into the grove. Sadie knew then that this agony she was suffering was itself the dreaded voyage into the world—the very voyage she had always feared Harriet would make. That she herself was making it instead of Harriet did not affect her certainty that this was it.

• • •

Sadie stood at the souvenir booth looking at some birchbark canoes. The wind was blowing colder and stronger than it had a while ago, or perhaps it only seemed this way to her, so recently returned from the airless clearing. She did not recall her trip back through the grove; she was conscious only of her haste to buy some souvenirs and to leave. Some chains of paper tacked to the side of the booth as decoration kept flying into her face. The Indian chief was smiling at her from behind the counter of souvenirs.

"What can I do for you?" he asked.

"I'm leaving," said Sadie, "so I want souvenirs. . . ."

"Take your choice; you've got birchbark canoes with or without mailing cards attached, Mexican sombrero ashtrays, exhilarating therapeutic pine cushions filled with the regional needles . . . and banners for a boy's room."

"There's no boy home," Sadie said, having caught only these last words.

"How about cushions . . . or canoes?"

She nodded.

"Which do you want?"

"Both," she answered quickly.

"How many?"

Sadie closed her eyes. Try as she would she could not count up the members of the family. She could not even reach an approximate figure. "Eleven," she blurted out finally, in desperation.

"Eleven of each?" he asked raising his eyebrows.

"Yes . . . yes," she answered quickly, batting the paper chains out of her face, "eleven of each."

"You sure don't forget the old folks at home, do you?" he said, beginning to collect the canoes. He made an individual package of each souvenir and then wrapped them all together in coarse brown paper which he bound with thick twine.

Sadie had given him a note and he was punching his money belt for the correct change when her eyes fell on his light, freckled hand. Startled, she shifted her glance from his hand punching the nickel belt to his brick-colored face streaked with purple and vermilion paint. For the first time she noticed his Irish blue eyes. Slowly the hot flush of shame crept along the nape of her neck. It was the same unbearable mortification that she had experienced in the clearing; it spread upward from her neck to the roots of her hair, coloring her face a dark red. That she was ashamed for the Indian this time, and not of her own words, failed to lessen the intensity of her suffering; the boundaries of her pride had never been firmly fixed inside herself. She stared intently at his Irish blue eyes, so oddly light in his brick-colored face. What was it? She was tormented by the sight of an incongruity she couldn't name. All at once she remembered the pavilion and the people dining there; her heart started to pound. "They'll see it," she said to herself in a panic. "They'll see it and they'll know that I've seen it too." Somehow this latter possibility was the most perilous of all.

"They must never know I've seen it," she said, grinding her teeth, and she leaned over the counter, crushing some canoes under her chest. "Quickly," she whispered. "Go out your little door and meet me back of the booth. . . ."

A second later she found him there. "Listen!" She clutched his hand. "We must hurry . . . I didn't mean to see you . . . I'm sorry . . . I've been trying not to look at you for years . . . for years and years and years. . . ." She gaped at him in horror. "Why are you standing there? We've got to hurry. . . . They haven't caught me looking at you yet, but we've got to hurry." She headed for the bridge, leading the Indian behind her. He followed quickly without saying a word.

The water's roar increased in volume as they approached the opposite bank of the chasm, and Sadie found relief in the sound. Once off the bridge she ran as fast as she could along the path leading to the waterfall. The Indian followed close on her heels, his hand resting lightly in her own, as Harriet's had earlier when they'd sped together through the grove. Reaching the waterfall, she edged along the wall of rock until she stood directly behind the water's cascade. With a cry of delight she leaned back in the curve of the wall, insensible to its icy dampness, which penetrated even through the thickness of her woollen coat. She listened to the cataract's deafening roar and her heart almost burst for joy, because she had hidden the Indian safely behind the cascade where he could be neither seen nor heard. She turned around and smiled at him kindly. He too smiled, and she no longer saw in his face any trace of the incongruity that had shocked her so before.

The foaming waters were beautiful to see. Sadie stepped forward, holding her hand out to the Indian.

• • •

When Harriet awakened that morning all traces of her earlier victorious mood had vanished. She felt certain that disaster would overtake her before she could start out for Pocahontas Falls. Heavyhearted and with fumbling hands, she set about making her pack. Luncheon with Sadie was an impossible cliff which she did not have the necessary strength to scale. When she came to three round cushions that had to be snapped into their rainproof casings she gave up with a groan and rushed headlong out of her cabin in search of Beryl.

Fortunately Beryl waited table on the second shift and so she found her reading a magazine, with one leg flung over the arm of her chair.

"I can't make my pack," Harriet said hysterically, bursting into Beryl's cabin without even knocking at the door.

Beryl swung her leg around and got out of her chair, "I'll make your pack," she said in a calm voice, knocking some tobacco out of her pipe. "I would have come around this morning, but you said last night you wanted to make it alone."

"It's Sadie," Harriet complained. "It's that cursed lunch with Sadie. I can't go through with it. I know I can't. I shouldn't have to in the first place. She's not even supposed to be here. . . . I'm an ass. . . ."

"To hell with sisters," said Beryl. "Give 'em all a good swift kick in the pants."

"She's going to stop me from going on my canoe trip . . . I know she is. . . ." Harriet had adopted the whining tone of a little girl.

"No, she isn't," said Beryl, speaking with authority.

"Why not?" Harriet asked. She looked at Beryl almost wistfully.

"She'd better not try anything . . ." said Beryl. "Ever hear of jujitsu?" She grunted with satisfaction. "Come on, we'll go make your pack." She was so pleased with Harriet's new state of dependency that she was rapidly overcoming her original shyness. An hour later she had completed the pack, and Harriet was dressed and ready.

"Will you go with me to the souvenir booth?" she begged the waitress. "I don't want to meet her alone." She was in a worse state of nerves than ever.

"I'll go with you," said Beryl, "but let's stop at my cabin on the way so I can change into my uniform. I'm on duty soon."

They were nearly twenty minutes late arriving at the booth, and Harriet was therefore rather surprised not to see Sadie standing there. "Perhaps she's been here and gone back to the lodge for a minute," she said to Beryl. "I'll find out." She walked up to the souvenir counter and questioned the Indian, with whom she was slightly familiar. "Was there a woman waiting here a while ago, Timothy?" she asked.

"A dark middle-aged woman?"

"That's right."

"She was here for an hour or more," he said, "never budged from this stall until about fifteen minutes ago."

"She couldn't have been here an hour!" Harriet argued. "Not my sister. . . . I told her one-thirty and it's not yet two."

"Then it wasn't your sister. The woman who was here stayed more than an hour, without moving. I noticed her because it was such a queer-looking thing. I noticed her first from my chair at the bridge and then when I came up here she was still standing by the booth. She must have stood here over an hour."

"Then it was a different middle-aged woman."

"That may be," he agreed, "but anyway, this one left about fifteen minutes ago. After standing all that time she turned around all of a sudden and bought a whole bunch of souvenirs from me . . . then just when I was punching my belt for the change she said something I couldn't understand—it sounded like Polish—and then she lit out for the bridge before I could give her a penny. That woman's got impulses," he added with a broad grin. "If she's your sister, I'll give you her change, in case she don't stop here on her way back. . . . But she sounded to me like a Polak."

"Beryl," said Harriet, "run across the bridge and see if Sadie's behind the waterfall. I'm sure this Polish woman wasn't Sadie, but they might both be back there. . . . If she's not there, we'll look in the lodge."

• • •

When Beryl returned her face was dead white; she stared at Harriet in silence, and even when Harriet finally grabbed hold of her shoulders and shook her hard, she would not say anything.

Fez, 1948

YOU ARE NOT I

PAUL BOWLES

YOU ARE NOT I. No one but me could possibly be. I know that, and I know where I have been and what I have done ever since yesterday when I walked out the gate during the train wreck. Everyone was so excited that no one noticed me. I became completely unimportant as soon as it was a question of cut people and smashed cars down there on the tracks. We girls all went running down the bank when we heard the noise, and we landed against the cyclone fence like a lot of monkeys. Mrs. Werth was chewing on her crucifix and crying her eyes out. I suppose it hurt her lips. Or maybe she thought one of her daughters was on the train down there. It was really a bad accident; anyone could see that. The spring rains had dissolved the earth that kept the ties firm, and so the rails had spread a little and the train had gone into the ditch. But how everyone could get so excited I still fail to understand.

I always hated the trains, hated to see them go by down there, hated to see them disappear way off up the valley toward the next town. It made me angry to think of all those people moving from one town to another, without any right to. Whoever said to them: "You may go and buy your ticket and make the trip this morning to Reading. You will go past twenty-three stations, over forty bridges, through three tunnels, and still keep going, if you want to, even after you get to Reading"? No one. I know that. I know there is no chief who says things like that to people. But it makes it pleasanter for me when I imagine such a person does exist. Perhaps it would be only a tremendous voice speaking over a public-address system set up in all the main streets.

When I saw the train down there helpless on its side like an old worm knocked off a plant, I began to laugh. But I held on to the fence very hard when the people started to climb out the windows bleeding.

I was up in the courtyard, and there was the paper wrapper off a box of Cheese Tid Bits lying on the bench. Then I was at the main gate, and it was open. A black car was outside at the curb, and a man was sitting in front smoking. I thought of speaking to him and asking him if he knew who I was, but I decided not to. It was a sunny morning full of sweet air and birds, I followed the road around the hill, down to the tracks. Then I walked up the tracks feeling excited. The dining car looked strange lying on its side with the window glass all broken and some of the cloth shades drawn down. A robin kept whistling in a tree above. "Of course," I said to myself. "This is just in man's world. If something real should happen, they would stop singing." I walked up and down along the cinder bed beside the track, looking at the people lying in the bushes. Men were beginning to carry them up toward the front end of the train where the road crosses the tracks. There was a woman in a white uniform, and I tried to keep from passing close to her.

I decided to go down a wide path that led through the blackberry bushes, and in a small clearing I found an old stove with a lot of dirty bandages and handkerchiefs in the rubbish around the base of it. Underneath everything was a pile of stones. I found several round ones and some others. The earth here was very soft and moist. When I got back to the train there seemed to be a lot more people running around. I walked close to the ones who were lying side by side on the cinders, and looked at their faces. One was a girl and her mouth was open. I dropped one of the stones in and went on. A fat man also had his mouth open. I put in a sharp stone that looked like a piece of coal. It occurred to me that I might not have enough stones for them all, and the cinders were too small. There was one old woman walking up and down wiping her hands on her skirt very quickly, over and over again. She had on a long black silk dress with a design of blue mouths stamped all over it. Perhaps they were supposed to be leaves but they were formed like mouths. She looked crazy to me and I kept clear of her. Suddenly I noticed a hand with rings on the fingers sticking out from under a lot of bent pieces of metal. I tugged at the metal and saw a face. It was a woman and her mouth was closed. I tried to open it so I could get a stone in. A man grabbed me by the shoulder and pulled at me. He looked angry. "What are you doing?" he yelled. "Are you crazy?" I began to cry and said she was my sister. She did look a little like her, and I sobbed and kept saying: "She's dead. She's dead." The man stopped looking so angry and pushed me along toward the head of the train, holding my arm tightly with one hand. I tried to jerk away from him. At the same time I decided not to say anything more except "She's dead" once in a while. "That's all right," the man said. When we got to the front end of the train he made me sit down on the grass embankment alongside a lot of other people. Some of them were crying, so I stopped and watched them.

It seemed to me that life outside was like life inside. There was always somebody to stop people from doing what they wanted to do. I smiled when I thought that this was just the opposite of what I had felt when I was still inside. Perhaps what we want to do is wrong, but why should they always be the ones to decide? I began to consider this as I sat there pulling the little new blades of grass out of the ground. And I thought that for once *I* would decide what was right, and do it.

It was not very long before several ambulances drove up. They were for us, the row of people sitting on the bank, as well as for the ones lying around on stretchers and overcoats. I don't know why, since the people weren't in pain. Or perhaps they were. When a great many people are in pain together they aren't so likely to make a noise about it, probably because no one listens. Of course I was in no pain at all. I could have told anyone that if I had been asked. But no one asked me. What they did ask me was my address, and I gave my sister's address because it is only a half hour's drive. Besides, I stayed with her for quite a while before I went away, but that was years ago, I think. We all drove off together, some lying down inside the ambulances, and the rest of us sitting on an uncomfortable bench in one that had no bed. The woman next to me must have been a foreigner; she was moaning like a baby, and there was not a drop of blood on her that I could see, anywhere. I looked her all over very carefully on the way, but she seemed to resent it, and turned her face the other way, still crying. When we got to the hospital we were all taken in and examined. About me they just said: "Shock," and asked me again where I lived. I gave them the same address as before, and soon they took me out again and put me into the front seat of a sort of station wagon, between the driver and another man, an attendant, I suppose. They both spoke to me about the weather, but I knew enough not to let myself be trapped that easily. I know how the simplest subject can suddenly twist around and choke you when you think you're quite safe. "She's dead," I said once, when we were halfway between the two towns. "Maybe not, maybe not," said the driver, as if he were talking to a child. I kept my head down most of the time, but I managed to count the gas stations as we went along.

When we arrived at my sister's house the driver got out and rang the bell. I had forgotten that the street was so ugly. The houses were built one against the other, all alike, with only a narrow cement walk between. And each one was a few feet lower than the other, so that the long row of them looked like an enormous flight of stairs. The children were evidently allowed to run wild over all the front yards, and there was no grass anywhere in sight, only mud.

My sister came to the door. The driver and she spoke a few words, and then I saw her look very worried very suddenly. She came out to the car and leaned in. She had new glasses, thicker than the others. She did not seem to be looking at me. Instead she said to the driver: "Are you *sure* she's all right?"

"Absolutely," he answered. "I wouldn't be telling you if she wasn't. She's just been examined all over up at the hospital. It's just shock. A good rest will fix her up fine." The attendant got out, to help me out and up the steps, although I could have gone perfectly well by myself. I saw my sister looking at me out of the corner of her eye the same as she used to. When I was on the porch I heard her whisper to the attendant: "She don't look well yet to *me*." He patted her arm and said: "She'll be fine. Just don't let her get excited."

"That's what they always said," she complained, "but she just *does*."

The attendant got into the car. "She ain't hurt at *all*, lady." He slammed the door.

"Hurt!" exclaimed my sister, watching the car. It drove off and she stood following it with her eyes until it got to the top of the hill and turned. I was still looking down at the porch floor because I wasn't sure yet what was going to happen. I often feel that something is about to happen, and when I do, I stay perfectly still and let it go ahead. There's no use wondering about it or trying to stop it. At this time I had no particular feeling that a special event was about to come out, but I did feel that I would be more likely to do the right thing if I waited and let my sister act first. She stood where she was, in her apron, breaking off the tips of the pussywillow stems that stuck out of the bush beside her. She still refused to look at me. Finally she grunted: "Might as well go on inside. It's cold out here." I opened the door and walked in.

Right away I saw she had had the whole thing rebuilt, only backward. There was always a hall and a living room, except that the hall used to be on the left-hand side of the living room and now it was on the right. That made me wonder why I had failed to notice that the front door was now at the right end of the porch. She had even switched the stairs and fireplace around into each other's places. The furniture was the same, but each piece had been put into the position exactly opposite to the way it had been before. I decided to say nothing and let her do the explaining if she felt like it. It occurred to me that it must have cost her every cent she had in the bank, and still it looked exactly the same as it had when she began. I kept my mouth shut, but I could not help looking around with a good deal of curiosity to see if she had carried out the reversal in every detail.

I went into the living room. The three big chairs around the center table were still wrapped in old sheets, and the floor lamp by the pianola had the same torn cellophane cover on its shade. I began to laugh, everything looked so comical backward. I saw her grab the fringe of the portiere and look at me hard. I went on laughing.

The radio next door was playing an organ selection. Suddenly my sister said: "Sit down, Ethel. I've got something to do. I'll be right back." She went into the kitchen through the hall and I heard the back door open.

I knew already where she was going. She was afraid of me, and she wanted Mrs. Jelinek to come over. Sure enough, in a minute they both came in, and my sister walked right into the living room this time. She looked angry now, but she had nothing to say. Mrs. Jelinek is sloppy and fat. She shook hands with me and said: "Well, well, old-timer!" I decided not to talk to her either because I distrust her, so I turned around and lifted the lid of the pianola. I tried to push down some keys, but the catch was on and they were all stiff and wouldn't move. I closed the lid and went over to see out the window. A little girl was wheeling a doll carriage along the sidewalk down the hill; she kept looking back at the tracks the wheels made when they left a wet part of the pavement and went onto a dry patch. I was determined not to let Mrs. Jelinek gain any advantage over me, so I kept quiet. I sat down in the rocker by the window and began to hum.

Before long they started to talk to each other in low voices, but of course I heard everything they said. Mrs. Jelinek said: "I thought they was keeping her." My sister said: "I don't know. So did I. But the man kept telling me she was all right. Huh! She's just the same." "Why, sure," said Mrs. Jelinek. They were quiet a minute.

"Well, I'm not going to put up with it!" said my sister, suddenly. "I'm going to tell Dr. Dunn what I think of him."

"Call the Home," urged Mrs. Jelinek.

"I certainly am," my sister answered. "You stay here. I'll see if Kate's in." She meant Mrs. Schultz, who lives on the other side and has a telephone. I did not even look up when she went out. I had made a big decision, and that was to stay right in the house and under no condition let myself be taken back there. I knew it would be difficult, but I had a plan I knew would work if I used all my will power. I have great will power.

The first important thing to do was to go on keeping quiet, not to speak a word that might break the spell I was starting to work. I knew I would have to concentrate deeply, but that is easy for me. I knew it was going to be a battle between my sister and me, but I was confident that my force of character and superior education had fitted me for just such a battle, and that I could win it. All I had to do was to keep insisting inside myself, and things would happen the way I willed it. I said this to myself as I rocked. Mrs. Jelinek stood in the hall doorway with her arms folded, mostly looking out the front door. By now life seemed much clearer and more purposeful than it had in a long, long time. This way I would have what I wanted. "No one can stop you," I thought.

It was a quarter of an hour before my sister came back. When she walked in she had both Mrs. Schultz and Mrs. Schultz's brother with her, and all three of them looked a little frightened. I knew exactly what had happened even before she told Mrs. Jelinek. She had called the Home and complained to Dr. Dunn that I had been released, and he had been very much excited and told her to hold on to me by all means because I had not been discharged at all but had somehow *got out*. I was a little shocked to hear it put that way, but now that I thought of it, I had to admit to myself that that was just what I had done.

I got up when Mrs. Schultz's brother came in, and glared at him hard.

"Take it easy, now, Miss Ethel," he said, and his voice sounded nervous. I bowed low to him: at least he was polite.

"Lo, Steve," said Mrs. Jelinek.

I watched every move they made. I would have died rather than let the spell be broken. I felt I could hold it together only by a great effort. Mrs. Schultz's brother was scratching the side of his nose, and his other hand twitched in his pants pocket. I knew he would give me no trouble. Mrs. Schultz and Mrs. Jelinek would not go any further than my sister told them to. And she herself was terrified of me, for although I had never done her any harm, she had always been convinced that some day I would. It may be that she knew now what I was about to do to her, but I doubt it, or she would have run away from the house.

"When they coming?" asked Mrs. Jelinek.

"Soon's they can get here," said Mrs. Schultz.

They all stood in the doorway.

"I see they rescued the flood victims, you remember last night on the radio?" said Mrs. Schultz's brother. He lit a cigarette and leaned back against the banisters.

The house was very ugly, but I already was getting ideas for making it look better. I have excellent taste in decoration. I tried not to think of those things, and said over and over inside my head: "Make it work."

Mrs. Jelinek finally sat down on the couch by the door, pulled her skirt around her legs and coughed. She still looked red in the face and serious. I could have laughed out loud when I thought of what they were really waiting to see if they had only known it.

I heard a car door slam outside. I looked out. Two of the men from the Home were coming up the walk. Somebody else was sitting at the wheel, waiting. My sister went quickly to the front door and opened it. One of the men said: "Where is she?" They both came in and stood a second looking at me and grinning.

"Well, hel-*lo*!" said one. The other turned and said to my sister: "No trouble?" She shook her head. "It's a wonder you couldn't be more careful," she said angrily. "They get out like that, how do *you* know what they're going to do?"

The man grunted and came over to me. "Wanna come with us? I know somebody who's waiting to see you."

I got up and walked slowly across the room, looking at the rug all the way, with one of the men on each side of me. When I got to the doorway beside my sister I pulled my hand out of the pocket of my coat and looked at it. I had one of my stones in my hand. It was very easy. Before either of them could stop me I reached out and stuffed the stone into her mouth. She screamed just before I touched her, and just afterward her lips were bleeding. But the whole thing took a very long time. Everybody was standing perfectly still. Next, the two men had hold of my arms very tight and I was looking around the room at the walls. I felt that my front teeth were broken. I could taste blood on my lips. I thought I was going to faint. I wanted to put my hand to my mouth, but they held my arms. "This is the turning point," I thought.

I shut my eyes very hard. When I opened them everything was different and I knew I had won. For a moment I could not see very clearly, but even during that moment I saw myself sitting on the divan with my hands in front of my mouth. As my vision cleared, I saw that the men were holding my sister's arms, and that she was putting up a terrific struggle. I buried my face in my hands and did not look up again. While they were getting her out the front door, they managed to knock over the umbrella stand and smash it. It hurt her ankle and she kicked pieces of porcelain back into the hall. I was delighted. They dragged her along the walk to the car, and one man sat on each side of her in the back. She was yelling and showing her teeth, but as they left the city limits she stopped, and began to cry. All the same, she was really counting the service stations along the road on the way back to the Home, and she found there was one more of them than she had thought. When they came to the grade crossing near the spot where the train accident had happened, she looked out, but the car was over the track before she realized she was looking out the wrong side.

Driving in through the gate, she really broke down. They kept promising her ice cream for dinner, but she knew better than to believe them. As she walked through the main door between the two men she stopped on the threshold, took out one of the stones from her coat pocket and put it into her mouth. She tried to swallow it, but it choked her, and they rushed her down the hall into a little waiting room and made her give it up. The strange thing, now that I think about it, was that no one realized she was not I.

They put her to bed, and by morning she no longer felt like crying: she was too tired.

It's the middle of the afternoon and raining torrents. She is sitting on her bed (the very one I used to have) in the Home, writing all this down on paper. She never would have thought of doing that up until yesterday, but now she thinks she has become me, and so she does everything I used to do.

The house is very quiet. I am still in the living room, sitting on the divan. I could walk upstairs and look into her bedroom if I wanted to. But it is such a long time since I have been up there, and I no longer know how the rooms are arranged. So I prefer to stay down here. If I look up I can see the square window of colored glass over the stairs. Purple and orange, an hourglass design, only the light never comes in very much because the house next door is so close. Besides, the rain is coming down hard here, too.

New York, 1948

A STICK OF GREEN CANDY

JANE BOWLES

"A STICK OF GREEN CANDY" was written in 1949 in Taghit, in the desert, where Jane had traveled with Paul. The last work of fiction she was to complete, it remained unpublished until 1957, when it appeared in Vogue.

THE CLAY PIT had been dug in the side of a long hill. By leaning back against the lower part of its wall, Mary could see the curved highway above her and the cars speeding past. On the other side of the highway the hill continued rising, but at a steeper angle. If she tilted her head farther back, she could glimpse the square house on the hill's summit, with its flight of stone steps that led from the front door down to the curb, dividing the steep lawn in two.

She had been playing in the pit for a long time. Like many other children, she fancied herself at the head of a regiment; at the same time, she did not join in any neighborhood games, preferring to play all alone in the pit, which lay about a mile beyond the edge of town. She was a scrupulously clean child with a strong, immobile face and long, well-arranged curls. Sometimes when she went home toward evening there were traces of clay on her dark coat, even though she had worked diligently with the brush she carried along every afternoon. She despised untidiness, and she feared that the clay might betray her headquarters, which she suspected the other children of planning to invade.

One afternoon she stumbled and fell on the clay when it was still slippery and wet from a recent rainfall. She never failed to leave the pit before twilight, but this time she decided to wait until it was dark so that her sullied coat would attract less attention. Wisely she refrained from using her brush on the wet clay.

Having always left the pit at an earlier hour, she felt that an explanation was due to her soldiers; to announce simply that she had fallen down was out of the question. She knew that her men trusted her and would therefore accept in good faith any reason she chose to give them for this abrupt change in her day's routine, but convincing herself was a more difficult task. She never told them anything until she really believed what she was going to say. After concentrating a few minutes, she summoned them with a bugle call.

"Men," she began, once they were lined up at attention, "I'm staying an hour longer today than usual, so I can work on the mountain goat maneuvers. I explained mountain-goat fighting last week, but I'll tell you what it is again. It's a special technique used in the mountains around big cliffs. No machine can do mountain-goat fighting. We're going to specialize." She paused. "Even though I'm staying, I want you to go right ahead and have your recreation hour as usual, like you always do the minute I leave. I have total respect for your recreation, and I know you fight as hard as you play."

She dismissed them and walked up to her own headquarters in the deepest part of the pit. At the end of the day the color of the red pit deepened; then, after the sun had sunk behind the hill, the clay lost its color. She began to feel cold and a little uneasy. She was so accustomed to leaving her men each day at the same hour, just before they thronged into the gymnasium, that now lingering on made her feel like an intruder.

It was almost night when she climbed out of the pit. She glanced up at the hilltop house and then started down toward the deserted lower road. When she reached the outskirts of town she chose the darkest streets so that the coat would be less noticeable. She hated the thick pats of clay that were embedded in its wool; moreover she was suffering from a sense of inner untidiness as a result of the unexpected change in her daily routine. She walked along slowly, scuffing her heels, her face wearing the expression of a person surfeited with food. Far underneath her increasingly lethargic mood lurked a feeling of apprehension; she knew she would be reprimanded for returning home after dark, but she never would admit either the possibility of punishment or the fear of it. At this period she was rapidly perfecting a psychological mechanism which enabled her to forget, for long stretches of time, that her parents existed.

She found her father in the vestibule hanging his coat up on a peg. Her heart sank as he turned around to greet her. Without seeming to, he took in the pats of clay at a glance, but his shifting eyes never alighted candidly on any object.

"You've been playing in that pit below the Speed house again," he said to her. "From now on, I want you to play at the Kinsey Memorial Grounds." Since he appeared to have nothing to say, she started away, but immediately he continued. "Some day you may have to live in a town where the administration doesn't make any provision for children at all. Or it may provide you with a small plot of land and a couple of dinky swings. There's a very decent sum goes each year to the grounds here. They provide you with swings, seesaws and chin bars." He glanced furtively at her coat. "Tomorrow," he said, "I drive past that pit on my way out to Sam's. I'll draw up to the edge of the road and look down. See that you're over at the Memorial Grounds with the other children."

Mary never passed the playgrounds without quickening her step. This site, where the screams of several dozen children mingled with the high, grinding sound of the moving swings, she had always automatically hated. It was the antithesis of her clay pit and the well-ordered barracks inside it.

When she went to bed, she was in such a state of wild excitement that she was unable to sleep. It was the first time that her father's observations had not made her feel either humiliated or ill. The following day after school she set out for the pit. As she was climbing the long hill (she always approached her barracks from the lower road), she slackened her pace and stood still. All at once she had had the fear that by looking into her eyes the soldiers might divine her father's existence. To each one of them she was like himself—a man without a family. After a minute she resumed her climb. When she reached the edge of the pit, she put both feet together and jumped inside.

"Men," she said, once she had blown the bugle and made a few routine announcements, "I know you have hard muscles in your legs. But how would you like to have even harder ones?" It was a rhetorical question to which she did not expect an answer. "We're going to have hurdle races and plain running every day now for two hours."

Though in her mind she knew dimly that this intensified track training was preparatory to an imminent battle on the Memorial playgrounds, she did not dare discuss it with her men, or even think about it too precisely herself. She had to avoid coming face to face with an impossibility.

"As we all know," she continued, "we don't like to have teams because we've been through too much on the battlefield all together. Every day I'll divide you up fresh before the racing, so that the ones who are against each other today, for instance, will be running on the same side tomorrow. The men in our outfit are funny about taking sides against each other, even just in play and athletics. The other outfits in this country don't feel the same as we do."

She dug her hands into her pockets and hung her head sheepishly. She was fine now, and certain of victory. She could feel the men's hearts bursting with love for her and with pride in their regiment. She looked up—a car was rounding the bend, and as it came nearer she recognized it as her father's.

"Men," she said in a clear voice, "you can do what you want for thirty minutes while I make out the racing schedule and the team lists." She stared unflinchingly at the dark blue sedan and waited with perfect outward calm for her father to slow down; she was still waiting after the car had curved out of sight. When she realized that he was gone, she held her breath. She expected her heart to leap for joy, but it did not.

• • •

"Now I'll go to my headquarters," she announced in a flat voice. "I'll be back with the team lists in twenty-five minutes." She glanced up at the highway; she felt oddly disappointed and uneasy. A small figure was descending the stone steps on the other side of the highway. It was a boy. She watched in amazement; she had never seen anyone come down these steps before. Since the highway had replaced the old country road, the family living in the hilltop house came and went through the back door.

Watching the boy, she felt increasingly certain that he was on his way down to the pit. He stepped off the curb after looking prudently for cars in each direction; then he crossed the highway and clambered down the hill. Just as she had expected him to, when he reached the edge of the pit he seated himself on the ground and slid into it, smearing his coat—dark like her own—with clay.

"It's a big clay pit," he said, looking up at her. He was younger than she, but he looked straight into her eyes without a trace of shyness. She knew he was a stranger in town; she had never seen him before. This made him less detestable, nonetheless she had to be rid of him shortly because the men were expecting her back with the team lists.

"Where do you come from?" she asked him.

"From inside that house." He pointed at the hilltop.

"Where do you live when you're not visiting?"

"I live inside that house," he repeated, and he sat down on the floor of the pit.

"Sit on the orange crate," she ordered him severely. "You don't pay any attention to your coat."

He shook his head. She was exasperated with him because he was untidy, and he had lied to her. She knew perfectly well that he was merely a visitor in the hilltop house.

"Why did you come out this door?" she asked, looking at him sharply. "The people in that house go out the back. It's level there and they've got a drive."

"I don't know why," he answered simply.

"Where do you come from?" she asked again.

"That's my house." He pointed to it as if she were asking him for the first time. "The driveway in back's got gravel in it. I've got a whole box of it in my room. I can bring it down."

"No gravel's coming in here that belongs to a liar," she interrupted him. "Tell me where you come from and then you can go get it."

He stood up. "I live in that big house up there," he said calmly. "From my room I can see the river, the road down there and the road up here, and this pit and you."

"It's not your room!" she shouted angrily. "You're a visitor there. I was a visitor last year at my aunt's."

"Good-bye."

He was climbing out of the pit. Once outside he turned around and looked down at her. There was an expression of fulfillment on his face.

"I'll bring the gravel some time soon," he said.

She watched him crossing the highway. Then automatically she climbed out of the pit.

She was mounting the tedious stone steps behind him. Her jaw was clamped shut, and her face had gone white with anger. He had not turned around once to look at her. As they were nearing the top it occurred to her that he would rush into the house and slam the door in her face. Hurriedly she climbed three steps at once so as to be directly behind him. When he opened the door, she pushed across the threshold with him; he did not seem to notice her at all. Inside the dimly lit vestibule the smell of fresh paint was very strong. After a few seconds her eyes became more accustomed to the light, and she saw that the square room was packed solid with furniture. The boy was already pushing his way between two identical bureaus which stood back to back. The space between them was so narrow that she feared she would not be able to follow him. She looked around frantically for a wider artery, but seeing that there was none, she squeezed between the bureaus, pinching her flesh painfully, until she reached a free space at the other end. Here the furniture was less densely packed—in fact, three armchairs had been shoved together around an uncluttered area, wide enough to provide leg room for three people, providing they did not mind a tight squeeze. To her left a door opened on to total darkness. She expected him to rush headlong out of the room into the dark in a final attempt to escape her, but to her astonishment he threaded his way carefully in the opposite direction until he reached the circle of chairs. He entered it and sat down in one of them. After a second's hesitation, she followed his example.

The chair was deeper and softer than any she had ever sat in before. She tickled the thick velvet arms with her fingertips. Here and there, they grazed a stiff area where the nap had worn thin. The paint fumes were making her eyes smart, and she was beginning to feel apprehensive. She had forgotten to consider that grown people would probably be in the house, but now she gazed uneasily into the dark space through the open door opposite her. It was cold in the vestibule, and despite her woollen coat she began to shiver.

"If he would tell me now where he comes from," she said to herself, "then I could go away before anybody else came." Her anger had vanished, but she could not bring herself to speak aloud, or even to turn around and look at him. He sat so still that it was hard for her to believe he was actually beside her in his chair.

Without warning, the dark space opposite her was lighted up. Her heart sank as she stared at a green wall, still shiny with wet paint. It hurt her eyes. A woman stepped into the visible area, her heels sounding on the floorboards. She was wearing a print dress and over it a long brown sweater which obviously belonged to a man.

"Are you there, Franklin?" she called out, and she walked into the vestibule and switched on a second light. She stood still and looked at him.

"I thought I heard you come in," she said. Her voice was flat, and her posture at that moment did not inspire Mary with respect. "Come to visit Franklin?" she asked, as if suddenly aware that her son was not alone. "I think I'll visit for a while." She advanced toward them. When she reached the circle she squeezed in and sat opposite Mary.

"I hoped we'd get a visitor or two while we were here," she said to her. "That's why I arranged this little sitting place. All the rest of the rooms are being painted, or else they're still too smelly for visiting. Last time we were here we didn't see anyone for the whole two weeks. But he was a baby then. I thought maybe this time he'd contact when he went out. He goes out a lot of the day." She glanced at her son. "You've got some dirt on that chair," she remarked in a tone which did not express the slightest disapproval. She turned back to Mary. "I'd rather have a girl than a boy," she said. "There's nothing much I can discuss with a boy. A grown woman isn't interested in the same things a boy is interested in." She scratched a place below her shoulder blades. "My preference is discussing furnishings. Always has been. I like that better than I like discussing styles. I'll discuss styles if the company wants to, but I don't enjoy it nearly so well. The only thing about furnishings that leaves me cold is curtains. I never was interested in curtains, even when I was young. I like lamps about the best. Do you?"

Mary was huddling as far back into her chair as she could, but even so, without drawing her legs up and sitting on her feet, it was impossible to avoid physical contact with the woman, whose knees lightly touched hers every time she shifted a little in her chair. Inwardly, too, Mary shrank from her. She had never before been addressed so intimately by a grown person. She closed her eyes, seeking the dark gulf that always had separated her from the adult world. And she clutched the seat cushion hard, as if she were afraid of being wrenched from the chair.

"We came here six years ago," the woman continued, "when the Speeds had their house painted, and now they're having it painted again, so we're here again. They can't be in the house until it's good and dry because they've both got nose trouble—both the old man and the old lady—but we're not related. Only by marriage. I'm a kind of relative to them, but not enough to be really classed as a relative. Just enough so that they'd rather have me come and look after the house than a stranger. They gave me a present of money last time, but this time it'll be clothes for the boy. There's nothing to boys' clothes really. They don't mean anything."

She sighed and looked around her.

"Well," she said, "we would like them to ask us over here more often than they do. Our town is way smaller than this, way smaller, but you can get all the same stuff there that you can here, if you've got the money to pay. I mean groceries and clothing and appliances. We've got all that. As soon as the walls are dry we go back. Franklin doesn't want to. He don't like his home because he lives in an apartment; it's in the business section. He sits in a lot and don't go out and contact at all."

The light shone through Mary's tightly closed lids. In the chair next to her there was no sound of a body stirring. She opened her eyes and looked down. His ankles were crossed and his feet were absolutely still.

"Franklin," the woman said, "get some candy for me and the girl."

When he had gone she turned to Mary. "He's not a rough boy like the others," she said. "I don't know what I'd do if he was one of the real ones with all the trimmings. He's got some girl in him, thank the Lord. I couldn't handle one of the real ones."

He came out of the freshly painted room carrying a box.

"We keep our candy in tea boxes. We have for years," the woman said. "They're good conservers." She shrugged her shoulders. "What more can you expect? Such is life." She turned to her son. "Open it and pass it to the girl first. Then me."

The orange box was decorated with seated women and temples. Mary recognized it; her mother used the same tea at home. He slipped off the two rubber bands that held the cover on, and offered her the open box. With stiff fingers she took a stick of green candy from the top; she did not raise her eyes.

A few minutes later she was running alone down the stone steps. It was almost night, but the sky was faintly green near the horizon. She crossed the highway and stood on the hill only a few feet away from the pit. Far below her, lights were twinkling in the Polish section. Down there the shacks were stacked one against the other in a narrow strip of land between the lower road and the river.

After gazing down at the sparkling lights for a while, she began to breathe more easily. She had never experienced the need to look at things from a distance before, nor had she felt the relief that it can bring. All at once, the air stirring around her head seemed delightful; she drank in great draughts of it, her eyes fixed on the lights below.

"This isn't the regular air from up here that I'm breathing," she said to herself. "It's the air from down there. It's a trick I can do."

She felt her blood tingle as it always did whenever she scored a victory, and she needed to score several of them in the course of each day. This time she was defeating the older woman.

The following afternoon, even though it was raining hard, her mother could not stop her from going out, but she had promised to keep her hood buttoned and not to sit on the ground.

The stone steps were running with water. She sat down and

looked into the enveloping mist, a fierce light in her eyes. Her fingers twitched nervously, deep in the recess of her rubber pockets. It was unbelievable that they should not at any moment encounter something wonderful and new, unbelievable, too, that he should be ignorant of her love for him. Surely he knew that all the while his mother was talking, she in secret had been claiming him for her own. He would come out soon to join her on the steps, and they would go away together.

Hours later, stiff with cold, she stood up. Even had he remained all day at the window he could never have sighted her through the heavy mist. She knew this, but she could never climb the steps to fetch him; that was impossible. She ran headlong down the stone steps and across the highway. When she reached the pit she stopped dead and stood with her feet in the soft clay mud, panting for breath.

"Men," she said after a minute, "men, I told you we were going to specialize." She stopped abruptly, but it was too late. She had, for the first time in her life, spoken to her men before summoning them to order with a bugle call. She was shocked, and her heart beat hard against her ribs, but she went on. "We're going to be the only outfit in the world that can do real mountain-goat fighting." She closed her eyes, seeking the dark gulf again; this time she needed to hear the men's hearts beating, more clearly than her own. A car was sounding its horn on the highway. She looked up.

"We can't climb those stone steps up there." She was shouting and pointing at the house. "No outfit can, no outfit ever will. . . ." She was desperate. "It's not for outfits. It's a flight of steps that's not for outfits . . . because it's . . . because. . . ." The reason was not going to come to her. She had begun to cheat now, and she knew it would never come.

She turned her cold face away from the pit, and without dismissing her men, crept down the hill.

Taghit, 1949

PART TWO

from *LET IT COME DOWN*

PAUL BOWLES

The title of Paul's second novel comes from Act 3, scene 3, of Macbeth, *in which Banquo comes out of the castle with his son and says to the men outside, "It will be rain to-night." In response, the First Murderer calls out, "Let it come down!" and the men set upon Banquo and kill him.*

Let It Come Down *begins with the arrival of Nelson Dyar in Tangier several years after the end of World War II. Having spent the last ten years as a bank clerk in New York, where he felt "confined to a cage," he has chosen to break out of that cage by accepting the offer of a job from an old acquaintance, Jack Wilcox, who runs a travel agency in Tangier. Once in Tangier, Dyar continues to be tormented by the sense that nothing is happening, even as he becomes involved with a native prostitute, gets drawn into a fraudulent money-exchange scheme, and accepts money from a Russian, Madame Jouvenon, to act as a spy.*

Determined that for once he will make "something happen," he steals a large amount of money and arranges with Thami, the shady son of the well-to-do Beidaoui family, to hire a boat so he can escape from Tangier into the Spanish Zone of Morocco. Waiting out the time before his escape, Dyar goes to the house of Daisy, the Marquesa de Valverde, "a well-preserved woman of forty," who has invited him to dinner while her husband, Luis, is away.

The following selection begins with Dyar, carrying the briefcase filled with money, entering Daisy's bedroom as he is announced by the manservant Hugo. This extract consists of chapters 18 and 19 of Section 3, "The Age of Monsters," and all of Section 4, "Another Kind of Silence."

18

DAISY STRUGGLED TO a sitting position, a little resentful at having been caught unawares. Dyar held a briefcase in his hand; he looked more wide-awake than she remembered him. She wondered in passing why Hugo had not taken the briefcase from him along with his coat, and even more fleetingly she wondered why she had not heard the taxi arrive, but he was advancing toward the bed, and Hugo was going out and closing the door.

"Hi!" he said, shaking her hand vigorously. "I hope you're sicker than you look, because you look fine." He bent over and pushed the briefcase under the table beside the bed.

"I'm not really sick at all. It's just a twinge of sciatica that comes now and then. Nothing at all, darling. But I'm such a God-damned crybaby and I loathe pain so, that I simply pamper myself. And here I am. Sit down." She indicated the foot of the bed.

He obeyed, and she looked at him attentively. It seemed to her that his eyes were unusually bright, that his whole face shone with an unaccustomed physical glow. At the same time he struck her as being nervous and preoccupied. None of these things tallied with what she remembered about him; he had been restless at the Beidaoui party, but it was a restlessness that came from boredom or apathy, whereas at the moment he looked uneasy, intense, almost apprehensive. They talked a bit; his remarks were not the sort she would have expected from him; neither more intelligent nor more stupid, they nevertheless seemed to come from a different person. "But then, how do I know what he's like? I scarcely know him at all," she reflected.

"It feels good to get inside where it's warm," he said. "It's chilly out."

"I take it your taxi wasn't heated. Unless the car was delivered last week the heater would be broken by now. The Moroccans have an absolute genius for smashing things. If you want to get rid of anything, just let a Moroccan touch it, and it'll fall to pieces as he hands it back to you. They're fantastic! *What* destructive people! God! Drinks will be along any minute. Tell me about yourself in the meantime." She pushed herself further back into the mound of pillows behind her and peered out at him with the expression of one about to be told a long story.

Dyar glanced at her sharply. "About myself," he said, looking away again. "Nothing much to tell. More of the same. I think you know most of it." Now that everything was arranged, with Thami waiting in the mimosa scrub below the garden, and the Jilali dispatched to fetch the boat and bring it to the beach at Oued el Ihud at the foot of the cliffs, he was eager to be off, anxious lest some unforeseen event occur which could be a snag in his plans. The arrival of Wilcox, for instance, to pay an unexpected after-dinner call—that was one idea whose infinite possibilities of calamity paralyzed him; he forced himself to think of something else.

"Have you seen our silly Jack since night before last?" asked Daisy suddenly, as if she were inside Dyar's mind. He felt such acute alarm that he made a great effort to turn his head slowly and look at her with a carefully feigned expression of preoccupation turning to casual interest. "I'm worried about him," she was saying. "And I was certainly not reassured by your little description of his behavior."

But he thought: "Night before last? Why night before last? What happened then?" In his mind the party at the Beidaoui Palace had been weeks ago; it did not occur to him that she was referring to that. "No, I haven't seen him," he said, forgetting even that he had had breakfast with him that very morning. Hugo entered, wheeling a table covered with bottles and glasses. "I've learned one thing in my life, if nothing else," Daisy said. "And that is, that it's utterly useless to give anyone advice. Otherwise I'd ask Luis to talk with him. He might be able to worm something out of him. Because I have a distinct feeling he's up to something, and whatever it is, he won't get away with it. I'll wager you ten pounds he doesn't. Ten pounds! Why have you brought just these few pieces of ice? Bring a whole bowl of it," she called after Hugo as he closed the door behind him.

"I don't know," Dyar said. "Don't know what?" he thought, suppressing a tickling desire to laugh aloud. "Jack's pretty careful. He's nobody's fool, you know. I can't see him getting into any serious trouble, somehow." He felt that he must put a stop to this conversation or it would bring him bad luck. The mere fact that he was in a position for the moment to be offhand about the subject, even though his nonchalance was being forced upon him, seemed to indicate likely disaster. "Pride before a fall," he thought. It was a moment for humility, a moment to touch wood. The expression *get away with it* bothered him. "I don't know," he said again.

"Ten pounds!" Daisy reiterated, handing him a whiskey-soda. He sipped it slowly, telling himself that above all things he must not get drunk. At the end of ten minutes or so she noticed that he was not drinking.

"Something's wrong with your drink!" she exclaimed. "What have I done? Give it to me. What does it need?" She reached out for the glass.

"No, no, no!" he objected, hanging on to it. "It's fine. I just don't feel like drinking, somehow. I don't know why."

"Aha!" she cried, as though she had made a great discovery. "I see! Your system's hyperacid, darling. It's just the moment for a little majoun. I don't feel much like whiskey myself tonight." She made a place for her glass among the bottles and tubes on the night-table, opened the drawer and took out a small silver box which she handed him.

"Have a piece," she said. "Just don't tell anyone about it. All the little people in Tangier'd be scandalized, all but the Moroccans, of course. They eat it all the time. It's the only thing allowed the poor darlings, with alcohol forbidden. But a European, a Nazarene? Shocking! Unforgivable! Depths of depravity! Tangier, sink-hole of iniquity, as your American journalists say. 'Your correspondent has it on reliable authority that certain members of the English colony begin their evening meal with a dish of majoun, otherwise known as hashish.' Good God!"

He was looking with interest at the six cubes of greenish black candy which exactly filled the box. "What is it?" he said.

"Majoun, darling. Majoun." She reached out, took a square and bit it in half. "Have a piece. It's not very good, but it's the best in Tangier. My sweet old Ali gets it for me." She rang the bell.

The candy was gritty, its flavor a combination of figs, ginger, cinnamon and licorice; there was also a pungent herbal taste which he could not identify. "What's it supposed to do?" he asked with curiosity.

She put the box back onto its shelf. "The servants would be horrified. Isn't it ghastly, living in fear of one's own domestics? But I've never known a place like Tangier for wagging tongues. God! The place is incredible." She paused and looked at him. "What does it do?" she said. "It's miraculous. It's what we've all been waiting for all these years. If you've never had it, you can't possibly understand. But I call it the key to a forbidden way of thought." She leaned down and patted his arm. "I'm not going mystical on you, darling, although I easily could if I let myself go. *J'ai de quoi,* God knows. There's nothing mystical about majoun. It's all very down to earth and real." A maid knocked. Daisy spoke to her briefly in Spanish. "I've ordered tea," she explained, as the girl wheeled the table of drinks away.

"Tea!"

She laughed merrily. "It's absolutely essential."

To Dyar, who had pulled his left cuff up so he could glance surreptitiously now and then at his watch, the time was creeping by with incredible slowness. Daisy talked about black magic, about exhibitions of hatha-yoga she had seen in Travancore, about the impossibility of understanding Islamic legal procedure in Morocco unless one took for granted the everyday use of spells and incantations. At length the tea came, and they each had three cups. Dyar listened apathetically; it all sounded to him like decoration, like the Pekineses, incense-burners and Spanish shawls with which certain idle women filled their apartments, back in New York. He let her talk for a while. Then he said: "But what's the story about that candy? What is it? Some kind of dope, isn't it? I think you were cheated. I don't feel anything."

She smiled. "Yes, I know. Everyone says that. But it's very subtle. One must know which direction to look in for the effect. If you expect to feel drunk, you're looking the wrong way, it takes twice as long, and you miss half the pleasure."

"But what *is* the pleasure? Do *you* feel anything, right now?"

She closed her eyes and remained silent a moment, a slightly beatific expression coming to rest on her upturned face. "Yes," she answered at length. "Definitely."

"You do?" The incredulity in his voice made her open her eyes and look at him an instant reproachfully. "You don't believe me? I'm not just imagining things. But I've had it before and I know exactly what to expect. Darling, you're not comfortable there on the edge of the bed. Draw up that big chair and relax."

When he was sprawled in the chair facing the bed, he said to her: "Well, then, suppose you try and tell me what it feels like. I might as well get some benefit out of the stuff, even if it comes second-hand."

"Oh, at the moment it's nothing very exciting. Just a slight buzzing in my ears and an accelerated pulse."

"Sounds like fun," he scoffed. For a few minutes he had forgotten that this evening he was waiting above all for time to pass. Now he turned his arm a bit, to see the face of his watch; it was eight-twenty. He had set the meeting with Thami for no definite hour, not knowing exactly when he would be able to get away, but he had assured him it would not be after midnight. The understanding was that the Jilali would go back to town to the port, and would bring the boat to a small beach just west of Oued el Ihud, also not later than twelve o'clock. In the meantime Thami was to sit and wait, a little below the far end of the garden, so that when Dyar left the house he could lead him down across the face of the mountain, directly to the beach. Thami had insisted he would not be bored by waiting so long: he had his supper and his kif pipe with him.

"Yes," Daisy was saying. "If I let too much time go by, I shan't be able to tell you anything at all. One becomes fantastically inarticulate at a certain point. Not always, but it can happen. One thinks one's making sense, and so one is, I daresay, but in a completely different world of thought."

It seemed to him that the wind outside was rising a little, or else a window had opened a minute ago to let the sound in. He turned his head; the drawn curtains did not move. "What are you looking at?" she asked. He did not answer. At the same time he had a senseless desire to turn his head in the other direction and look at the other wall, because he thought he had seen a slight movement on that side of the room. Instead, he pulled out a pack of cigarettes and offered her one.

"No thanks, darling. I couldn't. You have a house. You see?"

"What?" He stared at her.

"I'm explaining, darling, or at least trying to. You have a house. In the middle of some modest grounds, where you're used to walking about." She waited, apparently to be certain he was following her argument. Since he said nothing, she went on. "You can always see the house. At least, from most parts of the property, but in any case, you know it's there. It's the center of your domain. Call it your objective idea about yourself."

He toyed with the pack of cigarettes, extracted one and lighted it, frowning.

"Say it's the idea of yourself by which you measure what's real. You have to keep it straight in your mind, keep it in working order. Like a compass."

He was making an effort to go along with the sense of what she was saying, but all he could follow was the words. "Like a compass," he repeated, as if he thought that might help.

"And so. You know every path, every plant, every stone on the grounds. But one day while you're out walking you suddenly catch sight of what looks like a path in a spot where you've never noticed, nor even suspected one before." Slowly her voice was taking on dramatic fervor. "The entrance is perhaps half hidden by a bush. You go over and look, and find there actually is a path there. You pull the bush aside, take a few steps down the path, and see ahead of you a grove of trees you never before knew existed. You're dumbfounded! You go through the grove touching the tree trunks to be sure they're really there, because you can't believe it. . . ."

This time he jerked his head quickly to the left, to catch whatever was over there by the windows, staring at the blank expanse of unmoving white curtain with disbelief. "Just relax," he said to himself, as he turned back to see if she had noticed him; she seemed not to have. "Relax, and be careful. Be careful." Why he was adding the second admonition he did not know, save that he was conscious of an overwhelming sense of uneasiness, as if a gigantic hostile figure towered above him, leaning over his shoulder, and he believed the only way to combat the feeling was to remain quite calm so that he could control his movements.

". . . Then through the trees you see that the path leads up a hill. 'But there *is* no hill!' you exclaim, probably aloud by this time, you're so excited and muddled. So you hurry on, climb the hill, which is rather high, and when you get to the top you see the countryside, perfectly familiar on all sides. You can identify every detail. And there's your house below, just where it should be. Nothing is wrong. It's not a dream and you've not gone mad. If you hadn't seen the house, of course, you'd know you'd gone mad. But it's there. Everything is all right." She sighed deeply, as if in relief. "It's just upsetting to find that grove of trees and that strange hill in the middle of your land. Because it can't be there, and yet it is. You're forced to accept it. But it's how you think once you've accepted it that makes what I call the forbidden way of thought. Forbidden, of course, by your own mind, until the moment you accept the fact of the hill. That's majoun for you. You find absolutely new places inside yourself, places you feel simply couldn't be a part of you, and yet there they are. Does what I said mean anything at all to you, or have I been ranting like a maniac?"

"Oh, no. Not at all." All his effort was going to giving a sincere ring to the words. An intense silence followed, which he felt he was also making, as he had uttered the words, only it went on for an endless length of time, like telegraph wires across miles of waste land. A pole, a pole, a pole, a pole, the wires strung between, the flat horizon lying beyond the eyes' reach. Then someone said: "Not at all" again, and it was he who had said it.

"What the hell is this?" he asked himself in a sudden rage. He had promised himself not to get drunk; it was the most important thing to remember while he was at the Villa Hesperides this evening. "I'm not drunk," he thought triumphantly, and he found himself on his feet, stretching. "It's stuffy in here," he remarked, wondering if she would think he was being rude.

She laughed. "Come, now, darling. Admit you're feeling the majoun at last."

"Why? Because I say it's stuffy? Nope. I'm damned if I feel anything." He was not being obstinate; already he had forgotten the little side-trip his mind had made a moment ago. Now that he was standing up the air in the room did not seem close. He walked over to a window, pulled the heavy curtain aside, and peered out into the dark.

"You don't mind being alone here at night?" he said.

"Sometimes," she answered vaguely, wondering if his question would be followed by others. "Stop thinking like that," she told herself with annoyance.

He still stood by the window. "You're pretty high up here."

"About six hundred feet."

"Have you ever been down to the bottom?"

"Over those rocks? God, no! Do you think I'm a chamois?"

He began to walk around the room slowly, his hands behind him, stepping from one zebra skin to the next as if they were rocks in a stream. There was no doubt that he felt strange, but it was not any way he had expected to feel, and so he laid it to his own perturbation. The evening was going to be agonizingly long. "I'd like to be saying good night right now," he thought. Everything he took the trouble to look at carefully seemed to be bristling with an intense but undecipherable meaning: Daisy's face with its halo of white pillows, the light pouring over the array of bottles on the table, the glistening black floor and the irregular black and white stripes on the skins at his feet, the darker and more distant parts of the room by the windows where the motionless curtains almost touched the floor. Each thing was uttering a wordless but vital message which was a key; a symbol, but which there was no hope of seizing or understanding. And inside himself, now that he became conscious of it, in his chest more than anywhere else, there was a tremendous trembling pressure, as though he were about to explode. He breathed in various ways to see if he could change it, and then he realized that his heart was beating too fast. "Ah, hell," he said aloud, because he was suddenly frightened.

"Come and sit down, darling. What's the matter with you? You're as restless as a cat. Are you hungry? Or has the majoun got you?"

"No," he said shortly. "Nothing's got me." He thought that sounded absurd. "If I go and sit down," he thought, "I'll get up again, and she'll know something's the matter." He felt he must make every effort to prevent Daisy from knowing what was going on inside him. The objects in the room, its walls and furniture, the air around his head, the idea that he was in the room, that he was going to eat dinner, that the cliffs, and the sea were below, all these things were playing a huge, inaudible music that was rising each second toward a climax which he knew would be unbearable when it was reached. "It's going to get worse."

He swallowed with difficulty. "Something's got to happen in a minute. Something's got to happen." He reached the chair and stood behind it, his hands on the back. Daisy looked at him distraughtly. She was thinking: "Why have I never dared tell Luis about majoun?" She knew he would disapprove, if only because it was a native concoction. But that was not why she had kept silent. She had never told *anyone* about it; the taking of it was a supremely private ritual. The experience was such a personal one that she had never wanted to share it with another. And here she was, undergoing it with someone she scarcely knew. All at once she wanted to tell him, so that he might know he was the first to be invited into this inner chamber of her life. She took a deep breath, and instead, said petulantly: "For God's sake, sit down. You look like a Calvinist rector telling his flock about Hell."

He laughed and sat in the chair. Under the table in the shadow he saw his briefcase. The tremulous feeling inside him suddenly expressed a great elation; it was still the same sensation, but it had changed color. The relief made him laugh again.

"Really!" exclaimed Daisy. "You may as well admit you're feeling the majoun. Because I know damned well you are. At least admit it to yourself. You'll have more fun with it. You've been fighting it for the past ten minutes. That's not the way to treat it. Just sit back and let it take its course. It's in you, and you can't get rid of it, so you may as well enjoy it."

"How about you?" He would not admit it.

"I told you long ago I was feeling it. At the moment I'm about to take off on a non-stop flight to Arcturus."

"You are, are you?" His voice was unfriendly. "Personally, I think the stuff is a fake. I'm not saying it has no effect at all, but I don't call feeling jumpy and having my heart beat twice too fast, I don't call that a kick, myself."

She laughed commiseratingly. "You should have drunk your whiskey, darling. You'd have felt more at home with it. *Mais enfin. . . .*" She sat up and rang the bell. "I expect the kitchen is in a turmoil because we're taking so long with our tea."

19

All during the dinner Daisy talked unceasingly; often Dyar found himself replying in monosyllables, not because he was uninterested, although occasionally he had very little idea what she was saying, but because half the time he was off somewhere else in a world of his own.

He did not know what he was thinking about, but his brain was swarming with beginnings of thoughts fastened on to beginnings of other thoughts. To receive so many took all his attention; even had they not been incommunicable he would have had no desire to impart them to Daisy. It was as if his mind withdrew to a remote, dark corner of his being. Then it would come out into the light again, and he would find himself actually believing that he sat having dinner at a small table in a quiet room while a woman lay in bed nearby eating the same food from a tray.

"You're awfully untalkative," Daisy said presently. "I'd never have given the majoun to you if I'd known it was going to make a statue out of you."

Her words made him uncomfortable. "Oh," he said. And what seemed to him a long time later: "I'm all right."

"Yes, I daresay you are. But you make a God-damned unsatisfactory dinner partner."

Now he became fully present, began to stammer apologies more florid than the occasion warranted. "I couldn't feel worse," he said finally, "if I'd kicked you. I don't know what was the matter with me. It must be that stuff that did something crazy to me."

"It's all my fault. Don't give it another thought, poor darling."

He would not have it that way. "No, no, no," he said. "There's no excuse." And in an excess of contrition he rose and sat down heavily on the bed beside her. The tray tipped perilously.

"Be careful, darling!" she exclaimed. "I shall have peas and wine all over me in another moment." But he had already seized her hand and was covering it with quick kisses. He was floating in the air, impelled by a hot, dry wind which enveloped him, voluptuously caressed him. For the space of two long breaths she was silent, and he heard his own breathing, and confused it with the sound of the wind that was blowing him along, above the vast, bare, sunlit valley. The skin of her arm was smooth, the flesh was soft. He pulled her further toward him, over the balancing tray.

"Be careful!" she cried again in alarm, as the tray tilted in his direction. "No, no!"

The wine glass went over first; the icy stain on his thigh made him jump convulsively. Then, very slowly it seemed to him, plates slid and tumbled toward him as the tray overturned and buried the lower part of his body in a confusion of china, glassware and warm food. "Oh!" she cried. But he held her more tightly with one arm, sweeping the tray and some of the dishes onto the floor with the other. And he scrambled up to be completely near her, so that there were only a few thicknesses of wet cloth, a fork and a spoon or two between them, and presently, after a short struggle with pieces of clinging clothing, nothing but a few creamed mushrooms.

"For God's sake, no! Not like this!" she was on the point of shouting, but as if she sensed how tenuous was the impulse that moved him, she thought: "At this very moment you're hoping desperately that nothing will happen to stop this. So you did want it to happen. Why wouldn't you admit it? Why can't you be frank? You wanted it; let it happen, even this way. Even this way." And so she said nothing, reaching out and turning off the light beside the bed. A word, she told herself, could have broken the thread by which he hung suspended from the sky; he would have fallen with a crash into the room, a furiously embarrassed young man with no excuse for his behavior, no escape from his predicament, no balm for his injured pride. "He's very sweet. And a little mad. So compact. Not at all like Luis. But could I really love any man I don't respect? I don't respect him at all. How can one respect an impersonal thing? He's scarcely human. He's not conscious of me as me. As another natural force, perhaps, yes. But that's not enough. I could never love him. But he's sweet. God knows, he's sweet."

The soft endless earth spread out beneath him, glowing with sunlight, untouched by time, uninhabited, belonging wholly to him. How far below it lay, he could not have said, gliding soundlessly through the pure luminous air that admitted no possibility of distance or dimension. Yet he could touch its smooth resilient contours, smell its odor of sun, and even taste the salt left in its pores by the sea in some unremembered age. And this flight—he had always known it was to be made, and that he would make it. This was a corner of existence he had known was there, but until now had not been able to reach; at present, having discovered it, he also knew he would be able to find his way back another time. Something was being completed; there would be less room for fear. The thought filled him with an ineffable happiness. "Ah, God," he murmured aloud, not knowing that he did so.

Beyond the windows the rising wind blew through the cypresses, bringing with it occasionally the deeper sound of the sea below. Regularly the drawn white curtains on one side of the room glowed white as the lighthouse's beam flashed across it. Daisy coughed.

"You're a slut," she said to herself. "How could you ever have allowed this to happen? But it's ghastly! The door's not locked. One of the servants may knock at any minute. Just collect yourself and do something. Do something!"

She coughed again.

"Darling, this is dreadful," she said softly, smiling in the dark, trying to keep her voice free of reproach. He did not answer; he might have been dead. "Darling," she said again hesitantly. Still he gave no sign of having heard her. For a moment she drifted back into her thoughts. If one could only let go, even for a few seconds, if only one could cease caring about everything, but really everything, what a wonderful thing it would be. But that would probably be death. Life means caring, is one long struggle to keep from going to pieces. If you let yourself have a really good time, your health goes to pieces, and if your health goes, your looks go. The awful part is that in the end, no matter what you have done, no matter how careful you may have been, everything falls apart anyway. The disintegration merely comes sooner, or later, depending on you. Going to pieces is inevitable, and you haven't even any pieces to show when you're finished. "Why should that be a depressing thought?" she wondered. "It's the most obvious and fundamental one there is. *Mann muss nur sterben.* But that means something quite different. That means we are supposed to have free will. . . ."

Far in the distance, out over the Atlantic, she heard the faint hum of a plane as the dark mountain and the Villa Hesperides were included briefly within the radius of its sound. Northward to Lisbon, southward to Casablanca. In another hour Luis might be hearing that same motor as it circled above the airport.

"Darling, *please!*" She struggled a little to free herself from his embrace. Since he still held her, she squirmed violently and managed to sit up, bathed in sweat, wine and grease. The air of the room suddenly seemed bitter cold. She ran her hand tentatively over her stomach and drew it back, disgusted. Quickly she jumped out of bed, locked the door into the corridor, drew her peignoir around her, and disappeared into the bathroom without turning on any light.

She stayed in the shower rather longer than was necessary, hoping that by the time she came out he would have got up, dressed, and perhaps cleared away some of the mess around the bed. Then she could ring, say: "I've had a little accident," and have coffee served. When she opened the bathroom door the room was still in darkness. She went over to the night table and switched on the light. He lay asleep, partially covered by the sheet.

"But this is the *end!*" she told herself. And with an edge of annoyance in her voice: "Darling, I'm sorry. You absolutely *must* get dressed immediately." He did not stir; she seized his shoulder and shook it with impatience. "Come along! Up with you! This little orgy has gone on long enough. . . ."

He heard her words with perfect clarity, and he understood what they meant, but they were like a design painted on a wall, utterly without relation to him. He lay still. The most important thing in the world was to prolong the moment of soothing emptiness in the midst of which he was living.

Taking hold of the sheet, she jerked it back over the foot of the bed. Then she bent over and shouted in his ear: "You're stark naked!" Immediately he sat upright, fumbling ineffectively around his feet for the missing cover. She turned and went back into the bathroom, calling over her shoulder: "Get dressed immediately, darling." Looking into the mirror, arranging her hair, she said to herself: "Well, are you pleased or displeased with the episode?" and she found herself unable to answer, dwelling rather on the miraculous fact that Hugo had not walked in on them; the possibility of his having done so seemed now more dreadful each minute. "I must have been quite out of my senses." She closed her eyes for an instant and shuddered.

Dyar had pulled on his clothing mechanically, without being fully conscious of what he was doing. However, by the time he came to putting on his tie, his mind was functioning. He too stood before a mirror, smiling a little triumphantly as he made the staccato gestures with the strip of silk. He combed his hair and knelt by the bed, where he began to scrape up bits of food from the floor and put them on the tray. Daisy came out of the bathroom. "You're an angel!" she cried. "I was just going to ask if you'd mind trying to make a little order out of this chaos." She lay down on a chaise longue in the center of the room and pulled a fur coverlet around her, and she was about to say: "I'm sorry there was no opportunity for you to have a shower, too," when she thought: "Above all, I must not embarrass him." She decided to make no reference to what had occurred. "Be a darling and ring the bell, will you, and we'll have coffee. I'm exhausted."

But apparently he was in no way ill at ease; he did as she suggested, and then went to sit cross-legged on the floor at her side. "I've got to get going," he said to himself, and he was not even preoccupied with the idea of how he would broach the subject of his departure; after the coffee he would simply get up, say good-bye, and leave. It had been an adventure, but Daisy had had very little to do with it, beyond being the detonating factor; almost all of it had taken place inside him. Still, since the fact remained that he had had his way with her, he was bound to behave in a manner which was a little more intimate, a shade on the side of condescension.

"You warm enough?" He touched her arm.

"No. It's glacial in this room. Glacial. God! I can't think why I didn't have a fireplace installed when they were building the house."

Hugo knocked on the door. For ten minutes or so the room was full of activity: Inez and another girl changing the sheets, Mario cleaning up the food from the floor, Paco removing grease spots from the rug beside the bed, Hugo serving coffee. Daisy sat studying Dyar's face as she sipped her coffee, noting with a certain slight resentment that, far from being embarrassed, on the contrary he showed signs of feeling more at ease with her than earlier in the evening. "But what do I expect?" she thought, whereupon she had to admit to herself that she would have liked him to be a little more impressed by what had passed between them. He had come through untouched; she had the uneasy impression that even his passion had been objectless, automatic.

"What goes on in your head?" he said when the servants had all gone out and the room had fallen back into its quiet.

Even that annoyed her. She considered the question insolent. It assumed an intimacy which ought to have existed between them, but which for some reason did not. "But *why* not?" she wondered, looking closely at his satisfied, serious expression. The answer came up ready-made and absurd from her subconscious; it sounded like doggerel. "It doesn't exist because he doesn't exist." This was ridiculous, certainly, but it struck a chord somewhere in the vicinity of the truth. "Unreal. What does it mean for a person to be unreal? And why should I feel he is unreal?" Then she laughed and said: "My God! Of course! You want to feel you're alive!"

He set his cup and saucer on the floor, saying: "Huh?"

"Isn't that what you said to me the first night you came here, when I asked what you wanted most in life?"

"Did I?"

"You most assuredly did. You said those very words. And of course, you know, you're so right. Because you're *not* really alive, in some strange way. You're dead." With the last two words, it seemed to her she heard her voice turning a shade bitter.

He glanced at her swiftly; she thought he looked hurt.

"Why am I trying to bait the poor man?" she thought. "He's done no harm." It was reasonless, idiotic, yet the desire was there, very strong.

"Why dead?" His voice was even; she imagined its inflection was hostile.

"Oh, not dead!" she said impatiently. "Just not alive. Not really.

But we're all like that, these days, I suppose. Not quite so blatantly as you, perhaps, but still . . ."

"Ah." He was thinking: "I've got to get out of here. I've got to get going."

"We're all monsters," said Daisy with enthusiasm. "It's the *Age* of Monsters. Why is the story of the woman and the wolves so terrible? You know the story, where she has a sled full of children, crossing the tundra, and the wolves are following her, and she tosses out one child after another to placate the beasts. Everyone thought it ghastly a hundred years ago. But today it's much more terrible. Much. Because then it was remote and unlikely, and now it's entered into the realm of the possible. It's a terrible story not because the woman is a monster. Not at all. But because what she did to save herself is exactly what we'd all do. It's terrible because it's so desperately true. I'd do it, you'd do it, everyone we know would do it. Isn't that so?"

Across the shining stretches of floor, at the bottom of a well of yellow light, he saw his briefcase waiting. The sight of it lying there reinforced his urge to be gone. But it was imperative that the leave-taking be casual. If he mentioned it vaguely now, the suggestion would be easier to act upon in another five minutes. By then it would be eleven-thirty.

"Well," he began, breathing in deeply and stretching, as if to rise.

"Do you know anyone who wouldn't?" He suddenly realized that she was serious about whatever it was she was saying. There was something wrong with her; she ought to have been lying there contentedly, perhaps holding his hand or ruffling his hair and saying a quiet word now and then. Instead she was tense and restless, talking anxiously about wolves and monsters, seeking either to put something into his mind or to take something out of it; he did not know which.

"*Do* you?" she insisted, the words a despairing challenge. It was as if, had he been able to answer "Yes," the sound of the word might have given her a little peace. He might have said: "Yes, I do know someone," or even: "Yes, such a person exists," and she would perhaps have been comforted. The world, that faraway place, would have become inhabitable and possible once again. But he said nothing. Now she took his hand, turned her face down to him coquettishly.

"Speaking of monsters, now that I recall your first evening here, I remember. God! You're the greatest monster of all. Of course! With that great emptiness in your hand. But my God! Don't you remember? Don't you remember what I told you?"

"Not very much of it," he said, annoyed to see his chance of escape being pulled further away from him. "I don't take much stock in that sort of stuff, you know."

"Stock, indeed!" she snorted. "Tveryone knows it's perfectly true and quite scientific. But in any case, whether you take stock or not—what an expression!—just remember, you can do what you want. If you know what you want!" she added, a little harshly. "You have an empty hand, and vacuums have a tendency to fill up. Be careful what goes into your life."

"I'll be careful," he said, standing up. "I'm afraid I've got to be going. It's getting late."

"It's not late, darling," she said, but she made no effort to persuade him to stay on. "Call a cab." She pointed to the telephone. "It's 24–80."

He had not thought of that complication. "I'll walk," he said. "I need the exercise."

"Nonsense! It's five miles. You can't."

"Sure I can," he said smiling.

"You'll get lost. You're mad." She was thinking: "He probably wants to save the money. Shall I tell him to have it put on our bill?" She decided against it. "Do as you like," she said, shrugging.

As he took up his briefcase, she said: "I shall see you down to the door," and despite his protestations she walked ahead of him down the stairs into the hall where a few candles still burned. The house was very still.

"The servants are all in bed, I guess," he said.

"Certainly not! I haven't dismissed Hugo yet." She opened the door. The wind blew in, rippling her peignoir.

"You'd better go up to bed. You'll catch cold."

He took the hand she held forth. "It was a wonderful evening," he declared.

"Luis will be back in a few days. You must come to dinner then. I'll call you, darling."

"Right." He backed away a few steps along the gravel walk.

"Turn to your left there by that clump of bamboo. The gate's open."

"Good night."

"Good night."

Stepping behind the bamboo thicket, he waited to hear her close the door. Instead, he heard her say: "Ah, Hugo. There you are! You may lock the gate after Mr. Dyar."

"Got to do something about *that,*" he thought, walking quickly to the right, around the side of the house to the terrace where the swimming pool reflected the stars in its black water. It was a chance to take, because she would probably have been watching, to see him go out through the gate. But she might think he already had slipped out when she was not looking; otherwise it would be very bad. The idea of just how bad it could be struck him with full force as he hesitated there by the pool, and as he hurried ahead down the steps into the lower garden he understood that he had committed an important tactical error. "But I'd have been locked out of the garden, God damn it," he thought. "There was nothing else I could do."

He had now come out from behind the shadow of the house into the open moonlight. Ahead of him something which had looked like part of the vegetation along the path slowly rose and walked toward him. "Let's go," said Thami.

"Shut up," Dyar whispered furiously. At the moment they were in full view of the house.

And as she strained to identify the second person, even to the point of opening one of the doors and silently stepping out onto the terrace to peer down through the deforming moonlight, the two men hurried along the path that led to the top of the cliff, and soon were hidden from her sight.

20

Dyar lay on his back across the seat in the stern of the boat, his hands beneath his head, looking up at the stars, vaguely wishing that at some time or another he had learned a little about astronomy. The rowboat they had brought along to get aboard and ashore in scudded on top of the dark waves a few feet behind him, tied to a frayed towing rope that was too short. He had started out by arguing about the rope; back at Oued el Ihud when they were bobbing around out there a hundred feet or so from the cliffs, trying to attach the two craft together, but then he had decided to save his words for other, more important, things. And in any case, now that the Jilali was away from the land, he paid no attention to what was said to him, feeling, no doubt, that he was master of the immediate situation, and could afford to disregard suggestions made by two such obvious landlubbers as Thami and the crazy Christian gentleman with him. The moment of greatest danger from the police had been passed when the Jilali was rounding the breakwater, before the others had ever got into the boat. Now they were a good mile and a half from shore; there was little likelihood of their being seen.

From time to time the launch passed through choppy waters where the warmer Mediterranean current disagreed with the waves moving in from the Atlantic. Small whitecaps broke and hissed in the dark alongside, and the boat, heaving upward, would remain poised an instant, shuddering as its propeller left the water, and then plunging ahead like a happy dolphin. To the right, cut out by a razor blade, the black mountains of Africa loomed against the bright sky behind them. "This lousy motor's going to give us trouble yet," thought Dyar: the smell of gasoline was too strong. An hour ago the main thing had been to get aboard; now it was to get ashore. When he felt the land of the Spanish Zone under his feet he supposed he would know what the next step was to be; there was no point in planning unless you knew what the possibilities were. He relaxed his body as much as he could without risking being pitched to the floor. "Smoke?" called Thami.

"I told you no!" Dyar yelled, sitting up in fury, gesturing. "No cigarettes, no matches in the boat. What's the matter with you?"

"He wants one," Thami explained, even as the Jilali, who was steering, struck a match and tried to shelter the flame from the wind. The attempt was unsuccessful, and Thami managed to dissuade him from lighting another. "Tell him he's a God-damned fool," called Dyar, hoping thus to enlist Thami on his side. But Thami said nothing, remaining hunched up on the floor near the motor.

There was no question of sleeping; he was much too alert for that, but as he lay there in a state of enforced inactivity, thinking of nothing at all, he found himself entering a region of his memory which, now that he saw it again, he thought had been lost forever. It began with a song, brought back to him, perhaps, by the motion of the boat, and it was the only song that had ever made him feel really happy. "Go. To sleep. My little pickaninny. Mammy's goin' to slap you if you don't. Hushabye. Rockabye. Mammy's little baby. Mammy's little Alabama coon." Those could not have been the words, but they were the words he remembered now. He was covered by a patchwork quilt which was being tucked in securely on both sides—with his fingers he could feel the cross-stitching where the pieces were joined—and his head was lying on the eiderdown pillow his grandmother had made for him, the softest pillow he had ever felt. And like the sky, his mother was spread above him; not her face, for he did not want to see her eyes at such moments because she was only a person like anyone else, and he kept his eyes shut so that she could become something much more powerful. If he opened his eyes, there were her eyes looking at him, and that terrified him. With his eyes closed there was nothing but his bed and her presence. Her voice was above, and she was all around; that way there was no possible danger in the world.

"How the hell did I think of that?" he wondered, looking behind him as he sat up, to see if the lights of Tangier had yet been hidden by Cape Malabata. They were still there, but the black ragged rocks were cutting across them slowly, covering them with the darkness of the deserted coast. Atop the cliff the lighthouse flashed again and again, automatically, becoming presently a thing he no longer noticed. He rubbed his fingers together with annoyance: somehow they had got resin on them, and it would not come off.

And as the small boat passed more certainly into a region of shadowed safety, farther from lights and the possibility of discovery, he found himself thinking of the water as a place of solitude. The boat seemed to be making less noise now. His mind turned to wondering what kind of man it was who sat near him on the floor, saying nothing. He had talked with Thami, sat and drunk with him, but during all the moments they had been in one another's company it never had occurred to him to ask himself what thoughts went on behind those inexpressive features. He looked at Thami: his arms were folded around his tightly drawn-up knees, and his head, thrown back, rested against the gunwale. He seemed to be looking upward at the sky, but Dyar felt certain that his eyes were closed. He might even be asleep. "Why not?" he thought, a little bitterly. "He's got nothing to lose. He's risking nothing." Easy money for Thami—probably the easiest he ever would make with the little boat. "He doesn't give a damn whether I get there or not. Of course he can sleep. I ought to have come alone." So he fumed silently, without understanding that the only reason why he resented this hypothetical sleep was that he would have no one to talk to, would feel more solitary out there under the winter sky.

The Jilali, standing in the bow, began to sing, a ridiculous song which to Dyar's ears sounded like a prolonged and strident moaning. The noise it made had no relation to anything—not to the night, the boat, not to Dyar's mood. Suddenly he had a sickeningly lucid glimpse of the whole unlikely situation, and he chuckled nervously. To be tossing about in a ramshackle old launch at three in the morning in the Strait of Gibraltar with a couple of idiotic barbarians, on his way God only knew where, with a briefcase crammed with money—it made no sense. That is to say, he could not find a way of believing it. And since he could not believe it, he did not really have any part in it; thus he could not be very deeply concerned in any outcome the situation might present. It was the same old sensation of not being involved, of being left out, of being beside reality rather than in it. He stood up, and almost fell forward onto the floor. "Shut up!" he roared; the Jilali stopped singing and called something in a questioning voice. Then he resumed his song. But as Dyar sat down again he realized that the dangerous moment had passed: the vision of the senselessness of his predicament had faded, and he could not recall exactly why it had seemed absurd. "*I* wanted to do this," he told himself. It had been his choice. He was responsible for the fact that at the moment he was where he was and could not be elsewhere. There was even a savage pleasure to be had in reflecting that he could do nothing else but go on and see what would happen, and that this impossibility of finding any other solution was a direct result of his own decision. He sniffed the wet air, and said to himself that at last he was living, that whatever the reason for his doubt a moment ago, the spasm which had shaken him had been only an instant's return of his old state of mind, when he had been anonymous, a victim. He told himself, although not in so many words, that his new and veritable condition was one which permitted him to believe easily in the reality of the things his senses perceived—to take part in their existences, that is, since belief is participation. And he expected now to lead the procession of his life, as the locomotive heads the train, no longer to be a helpless incidental object somewhere in the middle of the line of events, drawn one way and another, without the possibility or even the need of knowing the direction in which he was heading.

These certainties he pondered explain the fact that an hour or so later, when he could no longer bear the idea that Thami had not once shifted his position, Dyar lurched to his feet, stepped over, and kicked him lightly in the ribs. Thami groaned and murmured something in Arabic.

"What's the idea? You can sleep later."

Thami groaned again, said: "What you want?" but the words were covered by the steady stream of explosions made by the motor. Dyar leaned down, and yelled. "It's going to be light soon, for God's sake! Sit up and keep an eye open. Where the hell are we?"

Thami pointed lazily toward the Jilali. "He knows. Don't worry." But he rose and went to sit in the bow, and Dyar squatted down between the motor and the gunwale, more or less where Thami had been sitting. It was warmer here, out of the wind, but the smell of the gasoline was too strong. He felt a sharp emptiness in his stomach; he could not tell whether it was hunger or nausea, because it wavered between the two sensations. After a few minutes he rose and walked uncertainly to join Thami. The Jilali motioned to them both to go and sit in the stern. When Dyar objected, because the air was fresh here by the wheel, Thami said: "Too heavy. It won't go fast this way," and they stumbled aft to sit side by side back there on the wet canvas cushions. Long ago the moon had fallen behind a bank of towering, thick clouds in the west. Above were the stars, and ahead the sky presently assumed a colorless aspect, the water beneath melting smokelike, rising to merge momentarily with the pallid air. The Jilali's turbaned head took on shape, became sharp and black against the beginning eastern light.

"You sure you know where we're going?" Dyar said finally.

Thami laughed. "Yes. I'm sure."

"I may be wanting to stay up there quite a while, you know."

Thami did not speak for a moment. "You can stay all your life if you want," he said somberly, making it clear that he did not relish the idea of staying at all.

"What about you? How do you feel about it?"

"Me? Feel about what?"

"Staying."

"I have to go to Tangier with him." Thami indicated the Jilali.

Dyar turned to face him furiously. "The hell you do. You're going to stay with me. How the hell d'you think I'm going to eat up there all by myself?"

It was not yet light enough to see the contours of Thami's face, but Dyar had the feeling he was genuinely surprised. "Stay with you?" he repeated slowly. "But how long? Stay up there?" Then, with more assurance: "I can't do that. I have to work. I'll lose money. You're paying me for the boat and to go with you and show you the house, that's all."

"He knows I've got money here," Dyar thought savagely. "Damn his soul."

"You don't think I'm giving you enough?" He heard his own voice tremble.

Thami was stubborn. "You said only the boat. If I don't work I lose money." Then he added brightly: "Why you think I bought this boat? Not to make money? If I stay with you at Agla I make nothing. He takes the boat to Tangier, everything is in Tangier. My boat, my house, my family. I sit in Agla and talk to you. It's very good, but I make no money."

Dyar thought: "Why doesn't he ask me why I want to stay up there? Because he knows. Plain, ordinary blackmail. A war of nerves. I'm God damned if I give in to him." But even as he formed the words in his mind, he knew that what Thami was saying had logic.

"So what d'you expect me to do?" he said slowly, proceeding with caution. "Pay you so much a day to stay up there?"

Thami shrugged his shoulders. "It's no use to stay at Agla anyway. It's no good there. What do you want to do there? It's cold and with mud all over. I have to go back."

"So I have to make you an offer," he thought grimly. "Why don't you ask me how much I've got here in the briefcase?" Aloud he said: "Well, you can stay a few days at least. I'll see you don't lose anything by it." Thami seemed satisfied. But Dyar was ill at ease. It was impossible to tell how much he knew, even how much he was interested in knowing, or to form any idea of what he thought about the whole enterprise. If he would only ask an explicit question, the way he phrased it might help determine how much he knew, and the reply could be formed accordingly. Since he said nothing, he remained a mystery. At one point, when they had been silent for some minutes, Dyar said to him suddenly: "What are you thinking about?" and in the white light of dawn his smooth face looked childishly innocent as he answered: "Me? Thinking? Why should I think? I'm happy. I don't need to think." All the same, to Dyar the reply seemed devious and false, and he said to himself: "The bastard's planning something or other."

With the arrival of daylight, the air and water had become calmer. On the Spanish side of the strait they saw a large freighter moving slowly westward, statuelike, imperturbable. The progress of the launch was so noisy and agitated in its motion that it seemed to Dyar the freighter must be gliding forward in absolute silence. He looked in all directions uneasily, scanning the African coast with particular attention. The mountains tumbled precipitately down into the froth-edged sea, but in a few spots he thought he could see a small stretch of sand in a cove.

"What's this Spanish Zone like?" he asked presently.

Thami yawned. "Like every place. Like America."

Dyar was impatient. "What d'you mean, like America? Do the houses have electric lights? Do they have telephones?"

"Some."

"They do?" said Dyar incredulously. In Tangier he had heard vaguely that the Spanish Zone was a primitive place, and he pictured it as a wilderness whose few inhabitants lived in caves and talked in grunts or sign language. "But in the country," he pursued. "They don't have telephones out there, do they?"

Thami looked at him, as if mildly surprised at his insistence upon continuing so childish a conversation. "Sure they do. What do you think? How they going to run the government without telephones? You think it's like the Senegal?" The Senegal was Thami's idea of a really uncivilized country.

"You're full of crap," said Dyar shortly. He would not believe it. Nevertheless he examined the nearby coastline more anxiously, telling himself even as he did so that he was foolish to worry. The telephoning might begin during the day; it certainly had not already begun. Who was there to give the alarm? Wilcox could not—at least, not through the police. As for the American Legation, it would be likely to wait several days before instigating a search for him, if it did anything at all. Once it was thought he had left the International Zone, the Legation would in all probability shelve the entire Jouvenon affair, to await a possible return, even assuming that was why they had telephoned him. Then who was there to worry about? Obviously only Wilcox, but a Wilcox hampered by his inability to enlist official aid. Relieved in his mind for a moment, he stole a glance at Thami, who was looking at him fixedly like a man watching a film, as if he had been following the whole panorama of thoughts as they filed past in Dyar's mind. "I can't even think in front of him," he told himself. He was the one to look out for, not Wilcox or anybody Wilcox might hire. Dyar looked back at him defiantly. "*You're* the one," he made his eyes say, like a challenge. "I'm onto you," he thought they were saying. "I just want you to know it." But Thami returned his gaze blandly, blinked like a cat, looked up at the gray sky, and said with satisfaction: "No rain today."

He was wrong; within less than half an hour a wind came whipping around the corner of the coast out of the Mediterranean, past the rocky flanks of Djebel Musa, bringing with it a fine cold rain.

Dyar put on his overcoat, holding the briefcase in his lap so that it was shielded from the rain. Thami huddled in the bow beside the Jilali, who covered his head with the hood of his djellaba. The launch began to make a wide curve over the waves, soon turning back almost in the direction from which it had come. They were on the windward side of a long rocky point which stretched into the sea from the base of a mountain. The sheer cliffs rose upward and were lost in the low-hanging cloudbank. There was no sign of other craft, but it was impossible to see very far through the curtain of rain. Dyar sat up straight. The motor's sound seemed louder than ever; anyone within two miles could surely hear it. He wished there were some way of turning it off and rowing in to shore. Thami and the Jilali were talking with animation at the wheel. The rain came down harder, and now and then the wind shook the air, petulantly. Dyar sat for a while looking downward at his coat, watching rivulets form in valleys of gabardine. Soon the boat rested on water that was smoother. He supposed they had entered an inlet of some sort, but when he raised his head, still only the rocks on the right were visible. Now that these were nearer and he could see the dark water washing and swirling around them, he was disagreeably conscious of their great size and sharpness. "The quicker we get past, the better," he thought, glad he had not called to the Jilali and made a scene about shutting off the motor. As he glanced backward he had the impression that at any moment another boat would emerge from the grayness there and silently overtake them. What might happen as a result did not preoccupy him; it was merely the idea of being followed and caught while in flight which was disturbing. He sat there, straining to see farther than it was possible to see, and he felt that the motor's monotonous racket was the one thin rope which might haul him to safety. But at any instant it could break, and there would be only the soft sound of the waves touching the boat. When he felt a cold drop of water moving down his neck he was not sure whether it was rain or sweat. "What's all the excitement about?" he asked himself in disgust.

The Jilali stepped swiftly to the motor and turned it off; it died with a choked sneeze, as if it could never be started again. He returned to the wheel, which Thami held. The launch still slid forward. Dyar stood up. "Are we there?" Neither one answered. Then the Jilali moved again to the center of the boat and began desperately to force downward the heavy black disk which was the flywheel. With each tug there was another sneeze, but the motor did not start. Raging inwardly, Dyar sat down again. For a full five minutes the Jilali continued his efforts, as the boat drifted indolently toward the rocks. In the end the motor responded, the Jilali cut it down to half speed, and they moved slowly ahead through the rain.

21

There was a small sloping beach in the cove, ringed by great half-destroyed rocks. The walls of the mountain started directly behind, rose and disappeared in the rain-filled sky. They leaped from the rowboat and stood a moment on the deserted strip of sand without speaking. The launch danced nearby on the deep water.

"Let's go," Dyar said. This also was a dangerous moment. "Tell him you'll write him when you want him to come and get you."

Thami and the Jilali entered into a long conversation which soon degenerated from discussion into argument. As Dyar stood waiting he saw that the two were reaching no understanding, and he became inpatient. "Get him out of here, will you?" he cried. "Have you got his address?"

"Just a minute," Thami said, and he resumed the altercation. But remembering what he considered Dyar's outstanding eccentricity—his peculiar inability to wait while things took their natural course—he turned presently and said: "He wants money," which, while it was true, was by no means the principal topic of the conversation. Thami was loath to see his boat, already paid for, go back to Tangier in the hands of its former owner, and he was feverishly trying to devise some protective measure whereby he could be reasonably sure that both the Jilali and the boat would not disappear.

"How much?" said Dyar, reaching under his overcoat into his pocket, holding his briefcase between his knees meanwhile. His collar was soaked; the rain ran down his back.

Thami had arranged a price of four hundred pesetas with the Jilali for his services; he had intended to tell Dyar it was eight hundred, and pay the Jilali out of that. Now, feeling that things were turning against him from all sides, he exclaimed: "He wants too much! In Dradeb he said seven fifty. Now he says a thousand." Then, as Dyar pulled a note from his pocket, he realized he had made a grievous error. "Don't give it to him!" he cried in entreaty, stretching out a hand as if to cover the sight of the bill. "He's a thief! Don't give it to him!"

Dyar pushed him aside roughly. "Just keep out of this," he said. He handed the thousand-peseta note to the expectant Jilali. "D'you think I want to stand around here all day?" Turning to the Jilali, who stood holding the note in his hand, looking confused, he demanded: "Are you satisfied?"

Thami, determined not to let any opportunity slip by, immediately translated this last sentence into Arabic as a request for change. The Jilali shook his head slowly, announced that he had none, and held the bill out for Dyar to take back. "He says it's not enough," said Thami. But Dyar did not react as he had hoped. "He knows God-damned well it's enough," he muttered, turning away. "Have you got his address?" Thami stood unmoving, tortured by indecision. And he did the wrong thing. He reached out and tried to snatch the note from the Jilali's hand. The latter, having decided that the Christian gentleman was being exceptionally generous, behaved in a natural fashion, spinning around to make a running dash for the boat, pushing it afloat as he jumped in. Thami hopped with rage at the water's edge as the other rowed himself out of reach laughing.

"My boat!" he screamed, turning an imploring face to Dyar. "You see what a robber he is! He's taking my boat!"

Dyar tooked at him with antipathy. "I've got to put up with this for how many days?" he thought. "The guy's not even a half-wit." The Jilali kept rowing away, toward the launch. Now he shouted various reassurances and waved. Thami shook his fist and yelled back threats and curses in a sobbing voice, watching the departing Jilali get aboard the launch, tie the rowboat to the stern, and finally manage to start the motor. Then, inconsolable, he turned to Dyar. "He's gone. My boat's gone. Everything."

"Shut up," Dyar said, not looking at him. He felt physically disgusted, and he wanted to get away from the beach as quickly as possible, particularly now that the motor's noise had started up again.

Listlessly Thami led the way along the beach to its western end, where they walked among the tall rocks that stood upright. Skirting the base of the mountain, they followed an almost invisible path upward across a great bank of red mud dotted with occasional boulders. It was a climb that became increasingly steeper. The rain fell more intensely, in larger drops. There were no trees, no bushes, not even any small plants. Now cliffs rose on both sides, and the path turned into a gully with a stream of rust-colored water running against them. At one point Dyar slipped and fell on his back into the mud. It made a sucking sound as Thami helped him up out of it; he did not thank him. They were both panting, and in too disagreeable a humor to speak. But neither one expected the other to say anything, in any case. It was a question of watching where you put each foot as you climbed, nothing more. The walls of rock on either side were like blinders, keeping the eye from straying, and ahead there were more stones, more mud, and more pools and trickles of red-brown water. With the advance of the morning the sky grew darker. Dyar looked occasionally at his watch. "At half-past nine I'm going to sit down, no matter where we are," he thought. When the moment came, however, he waited a while until he found a comfortable boulder before seating himself and lighting a cigarette which, in spite of his precautions, the rain managed to extinguish after a few puffs. Thami pretended not to have noticed him, and continued to plod ahead. Dyar let him walk on, did not call to him to wait. He had only a half-pack of cigarettes, and he had forgotten to buy any. "No more cigarettes, for how long?" The landscape did not surprise him; it was exactly what he had expected, but for some reason he had failed to imagine that it might be raining, seeing it always in his mind's eye as windswept, desolate and baking in a brilliant sunlight.

Those of his garments which had not already been wet by the rain were soaked with sweat, for the steady climbing was arduous and he was hot. But he would not take off his overcoat, because under his arm, covered by the coat, was the briefcase, and he determined to keep it there, as much out of the rain as possible.

He kept thinking that Thami, when he had got to a distance he considered dignified, would stop and wait for him, but he had mistaken the cause of his companion's depression, imagining that it was largely pique connected with his defeat at the hands of the Jilali, whereas it was a genuine belief that all was lost, that for the time being his soul lay in darkness, without the blessing of Allah. This meant that everything having to do with the trip was doomed beforehand to turn out badly for him. He was not angry with Dyar, whom he considered a mere envoy of ill-luck; his emotion was the more general one of despondency.

Thami did not stop; he went on his way until a slight change in the direction of the gully took him out of Dyar's view. "The son of a bitch!" Dyar cried, jumping up suddenly and starting to run up the canyon, still holding his sodden cigarette in his hand. When he came to the place where the passage turned, Thami was still far ahead, trudging along mechanically, his head down. "He wants me to yell to him to wait," Dyar thought. "I'll see him in Hell first."

It was another half-hour before he arrived within speaking distance of Thami's back, but he did not speak, being content to walk at the other's pace behind him. As far as he could tell, Thami had never noticed his short disappearance. Thami climbed and that was all.

And so they continued. By midday they were inland, no longer within reach of the sea's sound or smell. Still Dyar felt that had it not been for the miles of rainy air behind them the sea would be somewhere there spread out below them, visible even now. The sky continued gray and thick, the rain went on falling, the wind still came from the east, and they kept climbing slowly, through a vast world of rocks, water and mud.

A ham sandwich, Dyar found himself thinking. He could have bought all he wanted the day before while he waited to get into Ramlal's. Instead he had gone and lain on the beach. The sunbaked hour or so seemed impossibly distant now, a fleeting vista from a dream, or the memory of a time when he had been another person. It was only when he considered that he could not conceivably have bought food then for this excursion since he had not in any way suspected he was going to make it, that he understood how truly remote yesterday was, how greatly the world had changed since he had gone into Chocron's stuffy little office and begun to watch the counting of the money.

Looming suddenly out of the rain, coming toward them down the ravine, a figure appeared. It was a small gray donkey moving along slowly, his panniers empty, drops of rain hanging to the fuzz along his legs and ears. Thami stood aside to let the animal pass, his face showing no expression of surprise. "We must be getting near," said Dyar. He had meant to keep quiet, let Thami break the silence between them, but he spoke without thinking.

"A little more," said Thami impassively. An old man dressed in a tattered woolen garment came into view around a bend, carrying a stick and making occasional guttural sounds at the donkey ahead. "A little more," Dyar thought, beginning to feel light-headed. "How much more?" he demanded. But Thami, with the imprecise notions of his kind about space and time, could not say. The question meant nothing to him. "Not much," he replied.

The way became noticeably steeper; it required all their attention and effort to continue, to keep from sliding back on loose stones. The wind had increased, and was blowing what looked like an endless thick coil of cloud from the crags above downward into their path. Presently they were in its midst. The world was darker. "This isn't funny," Dyar found himself thinking, and then he laughed because it was absurd that a mere sudden change in lighting should affect his mood so deeply. "Lack of food," he said to himself. He bumped against Thami purposely now and then as he climbed. If they should get too far apart they would not be able to see each other. "I hope you've got something to eat up in this cabin of yours," he said.

"Don't worry." Thami's voice was a little unpleasant. "You'll eat tonight. I'll get you food. I'll bring it to you. Don't worry."

"You mean there's no food in the house? Where the hell are you going to get it?"

"They got nothing to eat at the house because no one is living there since a long time. But not very far is the house of my wife's family. I'll get you whatever you want there. They won't talk about it. They're good people."

"He thinks he's going to keep me cooped up," Dyar said to himself. "He's got another think coming." Then as he climbed in silence: "But why? Why does he want to keep me hidden?" And so the question was reduced once more to its basic form: "What does he know?" He resolved to ask him tonight, point-blank, when they were sitting quietly face to face and he could observe whatever changes might come into Thami's expression: "What did you mean when you said your wife's family wouldn't talk about it?"

As the gradient increased, their climb became an exhausting scramble to keep from sliding backward. The heavy fog was like wind-driven smoke; every few seconds they were revealed briefly to each other, and even a sidewall of rock beyond might appear. Then with a swoop the substance of the air changed, became white and visible, and wrapped itself around their faces and bodies, blotting out everything. They went on and on. It was afternoon; to Dyar it seemed to have been afternoon forever. All at once, a little above him Thami grunted with satisfaction, emitted a long: "Aaah!" He had sat down. Dyar struggled ahead for a moment and saw him. He had pulled out his kif pipe and was filling it from the long leather mottoui that was unrolled across his knees. "Now it's easy," he said, moving a little along the rock to make room for Dyar. "Now we go down. The town is there." He pointed straight downward. "The house is there." He pointed slightly downward, but to the left. Dyar seated himself, accepting the pipe. Between puffs he sniffed the air, which had come alive, smelled now faintly like pine trees and farmyards. When he had finished the pipe he handed it back. The kif was strong; he felt pleasantly dizzy. Thami refilled the pipe, looking down at it lovingly. The stem was covered with tiny colored designs of fish, water-jars, birds and swords. "I bought this sebsi three years ago. In Marrakech," he said.

They sat alone in the whiteness. Dyar waited for him to smoke; the kif was burned in three long vigorous puffs. Thami blew the ball of glowing ash from the little bowl, wound the leather thongs around the mottoui, and gravely put the objects into his pocket.

They got up and went on. The way was level for only an instant, almost immediately becoming a steep descent. They had been sitting at the top of the pass. After the long hours of breathing in air that smelled only of rain, it was pleasantly disturbing to be able to distinguish signs of vegetable and animal life in the mist that came up from the invisible valley below. Now their progress was quicker; they hurried with drunken movements from one boulder to another, sometimes landing against them with more force than was comfortable. It had stopped raining; Dyar had pulled the briefcase out from under his coat and was carrying it in his left hand, using his free right arm for balance and as a bumper when it was feasible.

Soon they were below the cloud level, and in the sad fading light Dyar stood a moment looking at the gray panorama of mountains, clouds and shadowy depths. Almost simultaneously too, they were out of reach of the wind. The only sound that came up from down there was the soft unvaried one made by a stream following its course over many rocks. Nor could he distinguish any signs of human habitation. "Where's the house?" he said gruffly. That was the most important detail.

"Come on," Thami replied. They continued the downward plunge, and presently they came to a fork in the trail. "This way," said Thami, choosing the path that led along the side of the mountain, a sheer drop on its right, and on the left above, a succession of cliffs and steep ravines filled with the debris of landslides.

Then Thami stood still, one eyebrow arched, his hand to his ear. He seized Dyar's wrist, pulled him back a few paces to a huge slab of rock slightly off the path, pushed him to a squatting position behind it, and bent down himself, peering around every few seconds. "Look," he said. Half a hundred brown and gray goats came along the path, their hooves making a cluttered sound among the stones. The first ones stopped near the rock, their amber eyes questioning. Then the pressure of those following behind pushed them ahead, and they went on past in disorder, the occasional stones they dislodged bouncing from rock to rock with a curious metallic ring. A youth with a staff, wearing a single woolen cape slung over his shoulders, followed the flock. When he had passed, Thami whispered: "If he sees you, my friend, it would be very bad. Everybody in Agla would know tomorrow."

"What difference would that make?" Dyar demanded, not so much because he believed it did not matter, as because he was curious to know exactly what his situation was up here.

"The Spaniards. They would come to the house."

"Well, let 'em come. What difference would it make?" He was determined to see the thing through, and it was a good opportunity. "I haven't done anything. Why should they take the trouble to come looking for me?" He watched Thami's face closely.

"Maybe they wouldn't hurt you when you show them you got an American passport." Thami spoke aloud now. "Me, I'd be in the jail right away. You have to have a visa to get here, my friend. And then they'd say: How did you get in? Don't you worry. They'd know you were coming in by a boat. And then they'd say: Where is the boat? And whose boat? And worst: Why did you come by boat? Why didn't you come by the *frontera* like everybody else? Then they talk on the telephone to Tangier and try to know why from the police there. . . ." He paused, looking questioningly at Dyar, who said: "So what?" still studying Thami's eyes intently.

"So what?" said Thami weakly, smiling. "How do I know so

what? I know you said you will give me five thousand pesetas to take you here, and so I do it because I know Americans keep their word. And so you want to get here very much. How do I know why?" He smiled again, a smile he doubtless felt to be disarming, but which to Dyar's way of thinking was the very essence of Oriental deviousness and cunning.

Dyar grunted, got up, thinking: "From now on I'm going to watch every move you make." As Thami rose to his feet he was still explaining about the Spanish police and their insistence upon getting all possible information about foreigners who visited the Protectorate. His words included a warning never to stand outside the house in the daytime, and never—it went without saying—to set foot inside the village at any hour of the day or night. As they went along he embroidered on the probable consequences to Dyar of allowing himself to be seen by anyone at all, in the end making everything sound so absurdly dangerous that a wave of fear swept over his listener—not fear that what Thami said might be true, for he did not believe all these variations on catastrophe for an instant, but a fear born of having asked himself only once: "Why is he saying all this? Why is he so excited about nobody's seeing me?" For him the answer was to be found, of course, at the limits of Thami's infamy. It was merely a question of knowing how far the man was prepared to go, or rather, since he was a Moroccan, how far he would be able to go. And the answer at this point was, thought Dyar: he will go as far as I let him go. So I give him no chance. Vigilance was easy enough; the difficulty lay in disguising it. The other must not suspect that he suspected. Thami was already playing the idiot; he too would be guileless, he would encourage Thami to think himself the cleverer, so that his actions might be less cautious, his decisions less hidden. One excellent protective measure, it seemed to him, would be to go to the village and then tell Thami about it. That would let him know that he was not afraid of being seen, thus depriving Thami of one advantage he seemed to feel he had over him. "And then he'd think twice before pulling anything too rough if he realized people knew I had been up here with him," he reasoned.

"Well," he said reluctantly, "I'm going to have a fine time up here. I can see that. You down in the town all the time and me sitting on my ass up here on the side of a mountain."

"What you mean, all the time? How many days do you want to stay? I have to go to Tangier. My boat. That Jilali's no good. I know him. He's going to sell it to somebody else. You don't care. It's not your boat—"

"Don't start in again," said Dyar. But Thami launched into a lengthy monologue which ended where it had been meant to end, on the subject of how many pesetas a day Dyar was willing to pay him for his presence at Agla.

"Maybe I want him here and maybe I don't," he thought. It would depend on what he found and learned in the town. Plans had to be made carefully, and they might easily include the necessity of having Thami take him somewhere else. "But the quicker I can get rid of him the better." That much was certain.

Was this haggling, genuine enough in appearance, merely a part of Thami's game, intended to dull whatever suspicion he might have, replacing it with a sense of security which would make him careless? He did not know; he thought so. In any case, he must seem to take it very seriously.

"D'you think I'm made of money?" he said with simulated ill-humor, but in such a tone that Thami might feel that the money eventually would be forthcoming. The other did not answer.

There was an olive grove covering the steep side hill that had to be gone through, a rushing stream to cross, and a slight rise to climb before one reached the house. It was built out on a flat shelf of rock whose base curved downward to rest against the mountainside astonishingly far below.

"There's the house," said Thami.

It's a fort, thought Dyar, seeing the little structure crouching there atop its crazy pillar. Its thick earthen walls once had been partially whitewashed, and its steep roof, thatched in terraces, looked like a flounced petticoat of straw. The path led up, around, and out onto the promontory where the ground was bare save for a few overgrown bushes. There were no windows, but there was a patchwork door with a homemade lock, to fit which Thami now pulled from his pocket a heavy key as long as his hand.

"This is the jumping-off place all right," said Dyar, stepping to the edge and peering down. Below, the valley had prepared itself for night. He had the feeling that no light could pierce the profound gloom in which the lower mountainside was buried, no sound change the distant, impassive murmur of water, which, although scarcely audible, somehow managed to fill the entire air. After struggling a moment with the lock Thami succeeded in getting the door open. As Dyar walked toward the house he noticed the deep troughs dug in the earth by the rain that had run from the overhanging eaves; it still dripped here and there, an intimate sound in the middle of the encompassing solitude—almost with an overtone of welcome, as if the mere existence of the house offered a possibility of relief from the vast melancholy grayness of the dying afternoon.

At least, he thought, as he stepped inside into the dark room that smelled like a hayloft, this will give me a chance to catch my breath. It might be only for a day or two, but it provided a place to lie down.

Thami opened a door on the other side of the room and the daylight came in from a tiny patio filled with broken crates and refuse. "There's another room there," he said with an air of satisfaction. "And a kitchen, too."

Surprisingly, the earth floor was dry. There was no furniture, but a clean straw mat covered almost half the floor space. Dyar threw himself down and lay with his head propped against the wall. "Don't say kitchen to me unless you've got something in it. When are we going to eat? That's all I want to know."

Thami laughed. "You want to sleep? I'm going now to the house of my wife's family and get candles and food. You sleep."

"The hell with the candles, chum. You get that food."

Thami looked slightly scandalized. "Oh, no," he said with great seriousness and an air of faint reproof. "You can't eat without candles. That's no good."

"Bring whatever you like." He could feel himself falling asleep even as he said it. "Just bring food too." He slipped his fingers through the handle of the briefcase and laid it over his chest. Thami stepped out, closed the door and locked it behind him. There was the sound of his footsteps, and then only the occasional falling of a drop of water from the roof outside. Then there was nothing.

22

Even when he was fully conscious of the fact that Thami had returned and was moving about the room making a certain amount of noise, that a candle had been lighted and was shining into this face, his awakening seemed incomplete. He rose from the mat, said: "Hi!" and stretched, but the heaviness of sleep weighed him down. He did not even remember that he was hungry; although the emptiness was there in him, more marked than before he had slept, it seemed to have transformed itself into a simple inability to think or feel. He took a few steps out into the center of the room, grunting and yawning violently, and immediately wanted to lie down again. With the sensation of being half-dead, he staggered back and forth across the floor, stumbling over a large blanket which Thami had apparently brought from the other house, and from which he was extracting food and dishes. Then he went back to the mat and sat down. Triumphantly Thami held up a battered teapot. "I got everything," he announced. "Even mint to put in the tea. You want to sleep again? Go on. Go to sleep." There was a crackle and sputter from the patio as the charcoal in the brazier took fire. Dyar still said nothing; it would have cost him too great an effort.

As he watched Thami busying himself with the preparations he was conscious of an element of absurdity in the situation. If it had been Hadija preparing his dinner, perhaps he would have found it more natural. Now he thought he should offer to help. But he said to himself: "I'm paying the bastard," did not stir, and followed Thami's comings and goings, feeling nothing but his consuming emptiness inside, which, now that at last he was slowly waking, made itself felt unequivocally as hunger.

"God, let's eat!" he exclaimed presently.

Thami laughed. "Wait. Wait." he said. "You have to wait a long time still." He pulled out his kif pipe, filled and lit it, handed it to Dyar, who drew on it deeply, filling his lungs with the burning smoke, as if he might thereby acquire at least a little of the nourishment he so intensely wanted at the moment. At the end of the second pipeful his ears rang, he felt dizzy, and an extraordinary idea had taken possession of him: the certainty that somewhere, subtly blended with the food Thami was going to hand him, poison would be hidden. He saw himself awakening in the dark of the night, an ever-increasing pain spreading through his body, he saw Thami lighting a match, and then a candle, his face and lips expressing sympathy and consternation, he saw himself crawling to the door and opening it, being confronted with the utter impossibility of reaching help, but going out anyway, to get away from the house. The detailed clarity of the visions, their momentary cogency, electrified him; he felt a great need to confide them immediately. Instead, he handed the pipe back to Thami, his gestures a little uncertain, and shutting his eyes, leaned back against the wall, from which position he was roused only when Thami kicked the sole of his shoe several times, saying: "You want to eat?"

He did eat, and in great quantity—not only of the vermicelli soup and the sliced tomatoes and onions, but also of the chopped meat and egg swimming in boiling bright green olive oil, which, in imitation of Thami, he sopped up with ends of bread. Then they each drank two glasses of sweet mint tea.

"Well, that's that," he finally said, settling back. "Thami, I take my hat off to you."

"Your hat?" Thami did not understand.

"The hat I don't own." He was feeling expansive at the moment. Thami, looking politely confused, offered him his pipe which he had just lighted, but Dyar refused. "I'm going to turn in," he said. If possible he wanted to package the present feeling of being at ease, and carry it with him to sleep, so that it might stay with him all night. A pipe of kif and he could easily be stuck with nightmares.

Surreptitiously he glanced at his briefcase lying on the mat in the corner near him. In spite of the fact that he had carried it inside his coat whenever it rained, thus drawing at least some attention to it, he thought this could be accounted for in Thami's mind by its newness; he would understand his not wanting to spot the light-colored cowhide and the shining nickel lock and buckles. Thus now he decided to pay no attention to the case, to leave it nonchalantly nearby once he had tossed his toothbrush back into it, near enough on the floor so that if he stretched his arm out he could reach it. Putting it under his head or holding it in his hand would certainly arouse Thami's curiosity, he argued. Once the light was out, he could reach over and pull it closer to his mat.

Thami took out an old djellaba from the blanket in which he had brought the food, put it on, and handed the blanket to Dyar. Then he dragged a half-unraveled mat from the room across the patio and spread it along the opposite wall, where he lay continuing to smoke his pipe. Several times Dyar drifted into sleep, but because he knew the other was there wide awake, with the candle burning, the alarm he had set inside himself brought him back, and he opened his eyes wide and suddenly, and saw the dim ceiling of reeds and the myriad gently fluttering cobwebs above. Finally he turned his head and looked over at the other side of the room. Thami had laid his pipe on the floor and ostensibly was asleep. The candle had burned down very low; in another five minutes it would be gone. He watched the flame for what seemed to him a half-hour. On the roof there were occasional spatters of rain, and when a squall of wind went past, the door rattled slightly, but in a peremptory fashion, as if someone were trying hurriedly to get in. Even so, he did not witness the candle's end; when he opened his eyes again it was profoundly dark, and he had the impression that it had been so for a long time. He lay still, displeased with the sudden realization that he was not at all sleepy. The indistinct call of water came up from below, from a place impossibly faraway. In the fitful wind the door tapped discreetly, then shook with loud impatience. Silently he cursed it, resolving to make it secure for tomorrow night. Quite awake, he nevertheless let himself dream a little, finding himself walking (or driving a car—he could not tell which) along a narrow mountain road with a sheer drop on the right. The earth was so far below that there was nothing to see but sky when he glanced over the precipice. The road grew narrower. "I've got to go on," he thought. Of course, but it was not enough simply to go on. The road could go on, time could go on, but he was neither time nor the road. He was an extra element between the two, his precarious existence mattering only to him, known only to him, but more important than everything else. The problem was to keep himself there, to seize firmly with his consciousness the entire structure of the reality around him, and engineer his progress accordingly. The structure and the consciousness were there, and so was the knowledge of what he must do. But the effort required to leap across the gap from knowing to doing, that he could not make. "Take hold. Take hold," he told himself, feeling his muscles twitch even as he lay there in his revery. Then the door roused him a little, and he smiled in the dark at his own nonsense. He had already gone over the mountain road, he said to himself, insisting on taking his fantasy literally; that was past, and now he was here in the cottage. This was the total reality of the moment, and it was all he needed to consider. He stretched out his arm in the dark toward the center of the room, and met Thami's hand lying warm and relaxed, directly on top of the briefcase.

If he had felt the hairy joints of a tarantula under his fingers he could scarcely have drawn back more precipitately, or opened his eyes wider against the darkness. "I've caught him at it," he thought with a certain desperate satisfaction, feeling his whole body become tense as if of its own accord it were preparing for a struggle of which he had not yet thought. Then he considered how the hand had felt. Thami had rolled over in his sleep, and his hand had fallen there, that was all. But Dyar was not sure. It was a long way to roll, and it seemed a little too fortuitous that the briefcase should happen to be exactly under the spot where his hand had dropped. The question now was whether to do something about it or not. He lay still a while in the dark, conscious of the strong smell of mildewed straw in the room, and decided that unless he took the initiative and changed the situation he would get no more sleep; he must move the briefcase out from under Thami's hand. He coughed, pretended to sniffle a bit, squirmed around for a moment as if he were searching for a handkerchief, reached out and pulled the briefcase by the handle. Partially sitting up, he lit a match to set the combination of the lock, and before the flame went out he glanced over toward the middle of the room. Thami was lying on his mat, but at some point he had pulled it out, away from the wall; his hand still lay facing upward, the fingers curled in the touching helplessness of sleep. Dyar snuffed the match out, took a handkerchief from the case, and blew his nose with energy. Then he felt inside the briefcase; the notes were there. One by one he removed the packets and stuffed them inside his undershirt. Without his overcoat he might look a little plumper around the waist, but he doubted Thami could be that observant. He lay back and listened to the caprices of the wind, playing on the door, hating each sound not so much because it kept him from sleeping as because in his mind the loose door was equivalent to an open door. A little piece of wood, a hammer and one nail could arrange everything: the barrier between himself and the world outside would be much more real. He slept badly.

When it first grew light, Thami got up and built a charcoal fire in the brazier. "I'm going to my wife's family's house," he said as Dyar surveyed him blinking, from his mat. There was tea and there was a little bread left, but that was all. As he drank the hot green tea which Thami had brought to his mat, he noticed that the other had pushed his own mat back to the opposite wall where it had been at the beginning of the night. "Well, that's that," he thought. "No explanation offered. Nothing."

"I'll come back later," Thami said, gathering up the blanket from Dyar's feet. "I got to take this to carry things. You stay in the house. Don't go out. Remember."

"Yes, yes," said Dyar, annoyed at being left alone, at not having slept well, at having the blanket removed in case he wanted to try to sleep now, and most of all at the situation of complete dependence upon Thami in which he found himself at the moment.

When Thami had gone out, the feeling of solitude which replaced his presence in the house, contrary to his expectations, proved to be an agreeable one. First Dyar got up and looked at the door. As he thought, a small chip of wood nailed to the jamb would do the trick. When the door was shut you would simply pull the piece of wood down tight like a bolt. Then he set out on an exploratory tour of the cottage, to search for a hammer and a nail. The terrain was quickly exhausted, because the place was empty. There was nothing, not even the traditional half candle, empty sardine tin and ancient newspapers left by tramps in abandoned houses in America. Here everything had to be bought, he reminded himself; nothing was discarded, which meant that nothing was left around. An old tin can, a broken cup, an empty pill bottle, these things were put on sale. He remembered walking through the Joteya in Tangier and seeing the thousands of things on display, hopelessly useless articles, but for which the people must have managed to find a use. His only interesting discovery was made in the corner between Thami's mat and the door leading into the patio, where behind a pile of straw matting partially consumed by dry-rot he found a small fireplace, a vestige of the days when the house had been someone's home. "We'll damned well have a fire tonight," he thought. He went back to the entrance door, opened it, and stood bathing in the fresh air and the sensation of freedom that lay in the vast space before him. Then he realized that the sky was clear and blue. The sun had not risen high enough behind the mountains to touch the valley, but the day danced with light. Immediately an extraordinary happiness took possession of him. As if some part of him already had suspected the arrival of the idea which was presently to occur to him, and which was to make the day such a long one to live through, he said to himself: "Thank God" when he saw the blueness above. And far below, on a ridge here, in a ravine there, a minute figure moved, clothed in garments the color of the pinkish earth itself. It even seemed to him that in the tremendous stillness he could hear now and then the faint frail sound of a human voice, calling from one distant point to another, but it was like the crying of tiny insects, and the confused backdrop of falling water blurred the thin lines of sound, making him wonder a second later if his ears had not played him false.

He sat down on the doorstep. It was nonsense, this being dependent on an idiot, and an idiot who had given every sign, moreover, of being untrustworthy. For instance, he had said he was going to his relatives' house. But what was to prevent him from going instead to the town and arranging with a group of cutthroats down there to come up after dark? Or even in the daytime, for that matter? What Thami did not quite dare do himself, he could get others to do for him; then he would act his part, looking terrified, indignant, letting them hit him once or twice and tie him up. . . . The scenes Dyar invented here were absurdly reminiscent of all the Western films he had seen as a child. He was conscious of distorting probability, and yet, goaded by an overwhelming desire to make something definite out of what was now equivocal (to assume complete control himself, in other words), he allowed his imagination full play in forming its exaggerated versions of what the day might bring forth. "Why did I let him out of my sight?" he thought, but he knew quite well it had been inevitable. His sojourn up here was predicated on Thami's making frequent trips, if not to the village, at least to the family's abode. "Like a rat in a trap," he told himself, looking longingly out at the furthest peaks, which the sun was now flooding with its early light. But now he knew it would not be like that, because he was going to get out of the trap. It was a morning whose very air, on being breathed, gave life, and there was the path, its stones still clean and shadowless because they lay in the greater shadow of the cliffs above. He had only to rise and begin to walk. There was no problem, unless he asked himself "Where?" and he took care not to allow this question to cross his mind; he wanted to believe he must not hesitate. Yet to make sure that he would act, and not think, he got up and went inside to where he knew Thami had left his two little leather cases—one containing the sections of the dismantled kif-pipe, and the other with the kif itself in it. He picked them both up and put them in his pocket. Since he had decided to leave the house, it now seemed a hostile place, one to get out of quickly. And so, seizing his briefcase, talking a final disapproving sniff of the moldy air in the room, he stepped outside into the open.

Once before, two days ago, he had become intoxicated upon emerging into a world of sun and air. This morning the air was even stranger. When he felt it in his lungs he had the impression that flying would be easy, merely a matter of technique. Two days ago he had been moved to feel the trunks of the palms outside the Hotel de la Playa, to raise his head doglike into the breeze that came across the harbor, to rejoice at the fact of being alive on a fine morning. But then, he remembered, he had still been in his cage of cause and effect, the cage to which others held the keys. Wilcox had been there, hurrying him on, standing between him and the sun in the sky. Now at this moment there was no one. It was possible he was still in the cage—that he could not know—but at least no one else had the keys. If there were any keys, he himself had them. It was a question of starting to walk and continuing to walk. Slowly the contours of the valleys beneath shifted as he went along. He paid no attention to the path, save to note that it was no longer the one by which he had come yesterday. He met no one, nothing. After an hour or so he sat down and had two pipes of kif. The sun still had not climbed high enough to strike this side of the mountain, but there were eminences not far below which already caught its rays. The bottoms of the valleys down there were green snakes of vegetation; they lay warming themselves in the bright morning sun, their heads pointing downward toward the outer country, their tails curling back into the deep-cut recesses of rock.

He continued with less energy, because the smoke had cut his wind somewhat, and his heartbeat had accelerated a little. In compensation, however, he felt a steadily increasing sense of well-being. Soon he no longer noticed his shortness of breath. Walking became a marvelously contrived series of harmonious movements, the execution of whose every detail was in perfect concordance with the vast, beautiful machine of which the air and the mountainside were parts. By the time the sun had reached a point in the sky where he could see it, he was not conscious of taking steps at all; the landscape merely unrolled silently before his eyes. The triumphant thought kept occurring to him that once again he had escaped becoming a victim. And presently, without his knowing how he had got there, he found himself in a new kind of countryside. At some point he had wandered over a small crest and begun going imperceptibly downward, to be now on this upland, sloping plain, so different from the region he had left. Long ago he had ceased paying attention to where he was going. The sun was high overhead; it was so warm that he took off his coat. Then he folded it and sat down on it. His watch said half-past twelve. "I'm hungry," he let himself think, but only once. Determinedly he pulled out the sections of the pipe, fitted them together, and buried the little terra cotta bowl in the mass of fragrant, moist kif that filled the mottoui. And he drew violently on the pipe, holding the smoke inside him until his head spun and his eyes found themselves unable to move from the contemplation of a small crooked bush that grew in front of him. "With this you don't need food," he said. Soon enough he had forgotten his hunger; there were only the multiple details of the bright landscape around him. He studied them attentively; it was as though each hill, stone, gully and tree held a particular secret for him to discover. Even more—the configuration of the land seemed to be the expression of a hidden dramatic situation whose enigma it was imperative that he understand. It was like a photograph of a scene from some play in which the attitudes and countenances of the players, while normal enough at first glance, struck one as equivocal a moment later. And the longer he considered the mysterious ensemble, the more undecipherable the meaning of the whole became. He continued to smoke and stare. "I've got to get this straight," he thought. If he could catch the significance of what he saw before him at the moment, he would have understood a great deal more than what was denoted by these few bushes and stones. His head was clear; all the same, he felt peculiarly uneasy. It was the old fear of not being sure he was really there. He seized a stone and from where he sat threw it as far as he was able. "All right," he told himself, "you're here or you're not here. It doesn't matter a good God damn. Forget about it. It doesn't matter. Keep going from there. Where do you get?" He rose suddenly, took up his coat and began to walk. Perhaps the answer lay in continuing to move. Certainly the natural objects around him went on acting out their silent pantomime, posing their ominous riddle; he was aware of that as he went along. But, he reflected, if he felt strange and unreal at this instant he had good reason to: he was full of kif. "High as a kite," he chuckled. That was a consolation, and if it were not enough, there was the further possibility that he was right, that it was completely unimportant whether you were here or not. But unimportant to whom? He began to whistle as he walked, became engrossed in the sounds he made, ceased his game of mental solitaire.

Little by little the uncertain trail led downward across regions of rough pastureland and stony heaths. It was with astonishment that he saw on a hillside a group of cows grazing. During the morning he had grown used to thinking of himself as the only living creature under this particular sky. If he were coming to a village, so much the worse; he would continue anyway. His hunger, which long ago had reached mammoth proportions, no longer expressed itself as such, but rather as a sensation of general nervous voraciousness which he felt could be relieved only by more kif. And so he sat down and smoked some more, feeling his throat turn a little more inevitably to the iron it was on its way to becoming. If the cows surprised him, the sight now of a dozen or more natives working in a remote field did not. Only their minuteness amazed him; the landscape was so much larger than it looked. He sat on a rock and stared upward. The sky seemed to have reached a paroxysm of brilliancy. He had never known it was possible to take such profound delight in sheer brightness. The pleasure consisted simply in letting his gaze wander over the pure depths of the heavens, which he did until the extreme light forced him to look away.

Here the terrain was a chorus of naked red-gray valleys descending gently from the high horizon. The clumps of spiny palmetto, green nearby, became black in the distance. But it was hard to tell how far away anything was in this deceptive landscape. What looked nearby was far off; the tiny dots which were the cattle in the foreground proved that—and if his eye followed the earth's contours to the farthest point, the formation of the land there was so crude and on such a grand scale that it seemed only a stone's throw away.

He let his head drop, and feeling the sun's heat on the back of his neck, watched a small black beetle moving laboriously on its way among the pebbles. An ant, hurrying in the opposite direction, came up against it; apparently the meeting was an undesirable one, for the ant changed its course and dashed distractedly off with even greater haste. "To see infinity in a grain of sand." The line came to him across the empty years, from a classroom. Outside was the winter dusk, dirty snow lay in the empty lots; beyond, the traffic moved. And in the stifling room, overheated to bursting, everyone was waiting for the bell to ring, precisely to escape from the premonition of infinity that hung so ominously there in the air. The feeling he associated with the word *infinity* was one of physical horror. If only existence could be cut down to the pinpoint of here and now, with no echoes reverberating from the past, no tinglings of expectation from time not yet arrived! He stared harder at the ground, losing his focus so that all he saw was a bright blur. But then, would not the moment, the flick of the eyelid, like the grain of sand, still be imponderably weighted down with the same paralyzing element? Everything was part of the same thing. There was no part of him which had not come out of the earth, nothing which would not go back into it. He was an animated extension of the sunbaked earth itself. But this was not quite true. He raised his head, fumbled, lit another pipe. There was one difference, he told himself as he blew the smoke out in a long white column that straightway broke and dissolved. It was a small difference, self-evident and absurd, and yet because it was the only difference that came to him then, it was also the only suggestion of meaning he could find in being alive. The earth did not know it was there; it merely was. Therefore living meant first of all knowing one was alive, and life without that certainty was equal to no life at all. Which was surely why he kept asking himself: am I really here? It was only natural to want such reassurance, to need it desperately. The touchstone of any life was to be able at all times to answer unhesitatingly: "Yes." There must never be an iota of doubt. A life must have all the qualities of the earth from which it springs, plus the consiousness of having them. This he saw with perfect clarity in a wordless exposition—a series of ideas which unrolled inside his mind with the effortlessness of music, the precision of geometry. In some remote inner chamber of himself he was staring through the wrong end of a telescope at his life, seeing it there in intimate detail, far away but with awful clarity, and as he looked, it seemed to him that now each circumstance was being seen in its final perspective. Always before, he had believed that, although childhood had been left far behind, there would still somehow, some day, come the opportunity to finish it in the midst of its own anguished delights. He had awakened one day to find childhood gone—it had come to an end when he was not looking, and its elements remained undefinable, its design nebulous, its harmonies all unresolved. Yet he had felt still connected to every part of it by ten thousand invisible threads; he thought he had the power to recall it and change it merely by touching these hidden filaments of memory.

The sun's light filtered through his closed eyelids, making a blind world of burning orange warmth; with it came a corresponding ray of understanding which, like a spotlight thrown suddenly from an unexpected direction, bathed the familiar panorama in a transforming glow of finality. The years he had spent in the bank, standing in the teller's cage, had been real, after all; he could not call them an accident or a stop-gap. They had gone by and they were finished, and now he saw them as an unalterable part of the pattern. Now all the distant indecisions, the postponements and unsolved questions were beyond his reach. It was too late, only until now he had not known it. His life had not been the trial life he had vaguely felt it to be—it had been the only one possible, the only conceivable one.

And so everything turned out to have been already complete, its form decided and irrevocable. A feeling of profound contentment spread through him. The succession of ideas evaporated, leaving him with only the glow of well-being attendant upon their passage. He looked among the pebbles for the beetle; it had disappeared along the path. But now he heard voices, nearby. A group of turbaned Berbers came past, and looking at him without surprise went on, still conversing. Their appearance served to bring him back from the interior place where he had been. He took the pipe to pieces, put it away. Feeling drunk and light-headed, he rose and followed behind them at a discreet distance. The path they presently chose led over a hill and down—down across a wilderness of cactus, through shady olive groves (the decayed trunks were often no more than wide gnarled shells), over cascades of smooth rocks, through meadows dotted with oleander bushes, becoming finally a narrow lane bordered on either side by high holly. Here it twisted so frequently that he lost sight of the men several times, and eventually they disappeared completely. Almost at the moment he realized they were gone, he came unexpectedly out onto a belvedere strewn with boulders, directly above the rooftops, terraces and minarets of the town.

23

Sometimes on Friday mornings, Hadj Mohammed Beidaoui would send one of his older sons to fetch the last-born, Thami, where he was playing in the garden, and the little boy would be carried in, squirming to prevent his brother from covering his cheeks with noisy kisses all the way. Then he would be placed on his father's knee, his face would momentarily be buried in the hard white beard, and he would hold his breath until his father's face was raised again, and the old man began to pinch his infant cheeks and smooth his hair. He remembered clearly his father's ivory-colored skin, and how beautiful and majestic the smooth ancient face had seemed to him framed in its white silk djellaba. When he thought of it now, perhaps he was referring in memory to one particular morning, a day radiant as only a day in spring in childhood can be, when his father, after sprinkling him with orange flower water until he was quite wet and almost sick from the sweet smell, had taken him by the hand and led him through the streets and parks of sunlight and flowers to the mosque of the Marshan, through the streets openly, where everyone they met, the men who kissed the hem of Hadj Mohammed's sleeve, and those who did not, could see that Thami was his son. And Abdelftah and Abdelmalek and Hassan and Abdallah had all been left home! That was the most important part. The conscious campaign to seek to gain more than his share of his father's favor dated from that morning; he had waged it unceasingly from then until the old man's death. Then, of course, it was all over. The others were older than he, and by that time disliked him, and he returned their antipathy. He began to bribe the servants to let him out of the house, and this got several of them into trouble with Abdelftah, master of the household then, who was short-tempered and flew into a rage each time he learned that Thami had escaped into the street. But it was the street with its forbidden delights that tempted the boy more than anything else, once the world had ceased being a place where the greatest good was to climb into his father's lap and listen to the flow of legends and proverbs and songs and poems that he wished would never come to an end. There was one song he still recalled in its entirety. It went: *Ya ouled al harrata, Al mallem Bouzekri. . . .* His father had told him all the boys of Fez ran through the streets singing it when rain was needed. And there was one proverb which he associated intimately with the memory of his father's face and with the sensation of being held by him, surrounded by the mountains of brocade-covered cushions, with the great lanterns and high looped draperies above, and no matter how often his father acceded to his pleas to repeat it, always it was fresh with a mysterious, magical truth when he heard it.

"Tell about the day."

"The day?" Old Hadj Mohammed would repeat, looking deliberately, cunningly vague, and pulling at his lower lip while he rolled his eyes upward with a vacant expression. "The day? What day?"

"The day," Thami would insist.

"Aaah!" And the old man would begin, and begin at the same time the dovening motion which accompanied the utterance of any words that were not extemporaneous. "The morning is a little boy." He made his eyes large and round. "Noon is a man." He sat up very straight and looked fierce. "Twilight is an old man." He relaxed and looked into Thami's face with tenderness. "What do I do?" Thami knew, but he remained silent, waiting breathless, spellbound for the moment when he would take part in the ritual, his eyes unwaveringly fixed on the ivory face.

"I smile at the first. I admire the second. I venerate the last." And as he finished saying the words, Thami would seize the frail white hand, bend his head forward, and with passion press his lips against the back of the fingers. Then, renewed love in his eyes, the old man would sit back and look at his son. Abdallah once had spied on this game (of the brothers he was the nearest Thami's age, being only a year older), and later when he got him alone, he had subjected Thami to a series of tortures which the boy had borne silently, scarcely offering resistence. It seemed to him a small enough price to pay for his father's favor. "And if you tell Father I'll tell Abdelftah," Abdallah had warned him. Abdelftah would devise something infinitely worse —of that they were both certain—but Thami had laughed scornfully through his tears. He had no intention of telling; to bring to his father's attention the fact that the others could be jealous of his participation in this sacred game would have meant to risk losing his privilege of playing it.

Later it was the streets, the hidden cafés at Sidi Bouknadel that closed their doors leaving the boys inside sitting on mats playing ronda and smoking kif and drinking cognac until morning; it was the beach where they played football and, pooling their money, would rent a caseta for the season, which they used for drinking competitions and the holding of small private orgies whose etiquette demanded that the younger boys be at the entire disposal of the older ones. And above all it was the bordels. By the time Thami was eighteen he had had all the girls in all the establishments, and a good many more off the street. He took to staying away from home for several days at a time, and when he returned it would be in a state of dishevelment which infuriated his brothers. After his sixth arrest for drunkenness Abdelmalek, who was now the head of the family, Abdelftah having moved to Casablanca, gave orders to the guards of the house to refuse him entrance unless he was in a state of complete sobriety and properly dressed. This meant, more than anything else, that he would no longer receive his daily spending money. "This will change him," he said confidently to Hassan. "You'll see the difference very soon." But Thami was more headstrong and resourceful than they had suspected. He found ways of living—what ways they never knew—without needing to return home, without having to forego the independence so necessary to him. And since then he never had gone back, save now and then for a moment of conversation with his brothers at the entrance door, usually to ask a favor which they seldom granted. There was nothing basically anti-social about Thami; hostility was alien to him. He merely had expended almost all his capacities for respect and devotion upon his father, so that he could not give the traditional amount of either to his brothers. Also he would not agree to pretend. He did not respect them and he had had too much contact with European culture to believe he was committing a sin in refusing to feign a respect which custom demanded but which he did not feel.

It was at the annual moussem of Moulay Abdeslam, where serious men go for the good of their souls, that Thami had met Kinza, among the tents and donkeys and fanatical pilgrims. The situation was one with which Moslem tradition is totally unprepared to deal. Young men and women cannot know each other, and if by some disgraceful chance they happen to have managed to see each other alone for a minute, the idea is so shameful that everyone forgets it immediately. But to follow it up, to see the girl again, to suggest marrying her—it would be hard to conceive of more outrageous conduct. Thami did all these things. He went back to Agla at the same time as she did, got to know the family, who were naturally much impressed with his city ways and his erudition, and wrote to Abdelmalek saying that he was about to be married and thought it time he received his inheritance. His brother's reply was a telegram bidding him return to Tangier at once to discuss the matter. It was then that the two had their serious falling-out, since Abdelmalek refused outright to let him touch his money or his property. "I'll go to the Qadi," threatened Thami. Abdelmalek merely laughed. "Go," he said, "if you think there is anything about you he doesn't already know." In the end, after lengthy discussions with Hassan, who thought marriage, even with a shamefully low peasant girl, might possibly be a means of changing Thami's ways, Abdelmalek gave him a few thousand pesetas. He fetched the whole family from Agla and they had a wedding in Emsallah, the humblest quarter of Tangier, all of which nevertheless seemed magnificent to Kinza and her tribe. In due time all but the bride returned to the farmhouse on the mountain above Agla, where they lived working their fields, gathering the fruit from their trees and sending the children to tend the goats on the heights above.

To them Thami was a glamorous, important figure, and they had been overjoyed to see him come knocking at the door the previous evening. They were not so pleased, however, to learn that he had a Nazarene with him, up in the other house, and although he had managed last night to slide over it by talking of other things and then leaving suddenly, he could see that his father-in-law had not finished expressing his views on the subject.

At the house they told him that the men were down in the orchard. He followed the high cactus fence until he came to a gate made of sheet tin. Where he knocked, the sound was very loud, and it was with a certain amount of mild apprehension that he waited for someone to come. One of the sons let him in. An artificial stream ran through the orchard, part of the system which irrigated the entire valley with the spring water that came out of the rocks above the town. Kinza's father was watering the rose-bushes. He hurried back and forth, his baggy trousers hitched above his knees, stooping by the edge of the channel to fill an ancient oil can that spouted water from all corners, running with it each time, to arrive before it was empty. When he saw Thami he ceased his labors, and together they sat down in the shade of a huge fig tree. Almost immediately he brought up the subject of the Nazarene. Having him in the house would make trouble, he predicted. No one had ever heard of a Spaniard living in the same house with a Moslem, and besides, what was the purpose, what was the reason for such a thing? "Why doesn't he stay at the fonda at Agla like all the others?" he demanded. Thami tried to explain. "He's not a Spaniard," he began, but already he foresaw the difficulties he was going to meet, trying to make the other understand. "He's an American." "Melikan?" cried Kinza's father. "And where is Melika? Where? In Spain! Ah! You see?" The oldest son timidly suggested that perhaps the Nazarene was a Frenchman. Frenchmen were not Spaniards, he said. "Not Spaniards?" cried his father. "And where do you think France is, if it's not in Spain? Call him Melikan, call him French, call him English, call him whatever you like. He's still a Spaniard, he's still a Nazarene, and it's bad to have him in the house." "You're right," said Thami, deciding that acquiescence was the easiest way out of the conversation, because his only argument at that point would have been to tell them that Dyar was paying him for the privilege of staying in the house, and that was a detail he did not want them to know. The old man was mollified; then, "Why doesn't he stay at the fonda, anyway? Tell me that," he said suspiciously. Thami shrugged his shoulders, said he did not know. "Ah! You see?" the old man cried in triumph. "He has a reason, and it's a bad reason. And only bad things can happen when Nazarenes and Moslems come together."

There was a halfwit son who sat with them; he nodded his head endlessly, overcome by the wisdom of his father's utterances. The other sons looked at Thami, slightly embarrassed at hearing these ideas, which they supposed he must consider ridiculously old-fashioned. Then they talked of other things, and presently the old man returned to watering his flowers. Thami and the sons retired to a secluded part of the orchard where they could not be seen by him, and smoked, Thami feeling that under the circumstances he could not very well insult the family by returning to the house on the mountain solely to take food to the Christian. They passed the day eating, sleeping and playing cards, and it was twilight when he took his leave, not having dared to suggest that they give him food again, nor even finding the courage to ask for the use of the blanket. But he could not go back up to the house without food, for Dyar would be ravenous by now, and this meant that he must go into Agla and buy supplies for dinner. "*Yah latif, yah latif,*" he said under his breath as he followed the path that led downward to the village.

• • •

There was little doubt in Dyar's mind, as he stumbled along the cobbled road that led through the town gate, that the place was Agla. He had merely come down by a very wide detour, by going around to the back of the mountain, and then returning to the steep side once again. Thus there was a real possibility of his running into Thami, who, it now occurred to him, would be convinced he had run away in order to avoid having to pay him what he owed him. Or no, he thought, not at all. If Thami were after everything, such a detail would naturally be of no importance. In that case the meeting would bring matters to a head very quickly. The men he had chosen to help him would be nearby; by some casual gesture as they walked along the street together, he and Thami, in full view of the populace, the signal would be given. Or they might even be with him. The only hope would be to defend the briefcase as though his whole life were locked inside. Then, when they got it open and found it empty, he might possibly be far enough away to escape.

The tiny streets and houses were smothered with whitewash, which glowed as if all during the day it had been absorbing the sunlight and now, at dusk, were slowly giving it off into the fading air. It all looked, he thought, as though it had been made by a pastry-cook, but probably that was only because at the moment he did not need much imagination for things to look edible. With infallible intuition he chose the streets that led to the center of town, and there he saw a small native restaurant where the cooking was being done in the entrance. The cook lifted the covers of the various copper cauldrons for him; he looked down into them and ordered soup, chickpeas stewed with pieces of lamb, and skewered liver. There was a small dim room behind the kitchen with two tables in it, and beyond that a raised niche covered with matting where several rustics squatted with enormous loaves of bread which they tore into pieces and put into the soup. For Dyar the assuaging of his appetite was a voluptuous act; it went on and on. What he had ordered at first proved to be completely inadequate. Thami had told him that the desire for food after smoking kif was like no other appetite. He sighed apprehensively. Thami and his kif. How would he feel when he realized his prisoner had escaped, taking with him even Thami's own pipe and mottoui? He wondered if perhaps that might not be considered a supreme injury, an unforgivable act. He had no idea; he knew nothing about this country, save that all its inhabitants behaved like maniacs. Maybe it was not Thami himself of whose reactions he was afraid, he reflected—it might be only that Thami was part of the place and therefore had everything in the place behind him so to speak. Thami in New York—he almost laughed at the image the idea evoked—he was the sort no one would even take the trouble to look at in the street when he asked for a dime. Here it was another matter. He was a spokesman for the place; like Antaeus, whatever strength he had came out of the earth, and his feet were planted squarely upon it. "So you're afraid of him," he remarked to himself in disgust. He looked through the bright kitchen out into the black street beyond. "Afraid he might walk in that door." He sat perfectly still, somehow expecting the idea to conjure up the reality. Instead, an oversized Berber appeared in the doorway, his djellaba slung loosely over one shoulder, and ordered a glass of tea. While he waited the five minutes it always took to prepare the tea, (because the water, while hot, was never boiling, and the mint leaves had to be stripped one by one from the stalk) he stood staring at Dyar in a manner which the other at first found disconcerting, then disturbing, and finally, because he had begun to ask himself the possible reason for this insolent scrutiny, downright frightening. "Why does he block the door like that?" he thought, his heart beginning to beat too fast in a sudden wave of desperate conjecture. For the moment there was only one answer: one of Thami's henchmen had arrived to keep watch, to prevent his escape. They were probably posted in every café and eating-place in the town. For the first time it occurred to him that they might do their work on him in Thami's absence, with Thami conveniently seated in some respectable home, laughing, drinking tea, strumming on an oud. And this possibility seemed in a way worse, perhaps because he had never been able to see Thami in the role of a brutal torturer, the tacit understanding with his own imagination having been that things would somehow be done with comparative gentleness, painlessly. He looked up once again at the Neanderthal head, the deep furrows in the slanting forehead and the brows that formed a single ragged line across the face, and knew that for such a man there were no halfway measures. Yet he could not see any baseness in the face, nor even any particular cunning—merely a primal, ancient blindness, the ineffable, unfocused melancholy of the great apes as they stare between the cage bars.

"I don't want any of this," he told himself. You didn't try to outwit such beings; you simply got out if you could. He rose and walked over to the stove. "How much?" he said in English. The man understood, held up his two hands, the fingers outspread, then raised one lone forefinger. Turning his back on the giant in the doorway, so as to hide as well as possible the fistful of bills he pulled out of his pocket, he handed the cook a hundred-peseta note. The man looked startled, indicated he had no change. Dyar searched further, found twenty-five pesetas. Dubiously the cook accepted it, and pushing aside the Berber in the entrance, went out into the street to get change. "But good God," Dyar thought, seeing the prospect of a whole new horizon of difficulties spreading itself before him. No change for a hundred pesetas. Then a thousand pesetas would be just ten times as hard to get rid of. He moved his shoulder a little, to feel the twelve hundred and sixty thousand-peseta notes against his skin, around his middle. He stood there, conscious of the huge Berber's gaze, but not for an instant returning it, until the cook came back and handed him fourteen pesetas. When he went out into the street he turned to the right, where there seemed to be the greater number of passers-by, and walked quickly away, looking back only once just before he forced himself through the middle of an ambling group, and being not at all surprised to see the Berber step out of the restaurant and start slowly in the same direction. But Dyar was going rapidly; the next time he turned around to look, he was satisfied that he had lost him.

The whitewashed cobbled street was full of strollers in djellabas moving in both directions; the groups saluted each other constantly as they passed. Dyar threaded his way among them as unostentatiously as he could for a man in a hurry. Sometimes the street would turn into a long, wide flight of stairs with a shop no bigger than a stall on each step, and he would run lightly all the way down, gauging his distances with care to be sure of not plunging into a group of walkers, not daring to look up to see what effect his passage was having on the populace. When he came out into an open space lined on one side with new one-story European buildings he stopped short, not certain whether to continue or go back. There was a café over there with tables and chairs set out along a narrow strip of sidewalk, and at the tables sat Spaniards, some of whom wore the white uniforms of officers in the Moroccan army. His instinct told him to stay in the shade, to go back into the Moroccan town. The question was: where would he be safer? There was no doubt that the greater danger was the possibility of being stopped and questioned by the Spanish. Yet the fear he felt was not of them, but of what could happen back in the streets he had just come from. And now as he stood there clutching his briefcase, the people pushing past him on both sides, his mind still muzzy from the kif, he saw with terror that he was hopelessly confused. He had imagined the town would be something else, that somewhere there would be a place he could go into and ask for information; he had counted on the town to help him as a troubled man counts on a friend to give him advice, knowing beforehand that he will follow whatever advice he gets, because the important thing is to do *something*, to move in any direction, out of his impasse. Once he had been to Agla, he had thought, he would know more about his situation. But he had not understood until now how heavily he was counting on it, partly perhaps because all day he had been thinking only of escaping from Thami. However, at this moment he was conscious that the props that held up his future were in the act of crumbling: he never had had any plan of action, he could not imagine now what he had ever intended to "find out" here in the town, what sort of people he had thought he would be able to see in order to get his information, or even what kind of information he had meant to get. For an instant he looked upward into the sky. The stars were there; they did not tell him what to do. He had turned, he had started to walk, back through the town's entrance gate into the crooked street, but his legs were trembling, and he was only indistinctly aware of what went on around him. This time, since a part of the mechanism that held his being together seemed to have given way, he somehow got turned off the principal street which led steeply upward, and let his legs lead him along a smaller flat one that had fewer lights and people in it, and no shops at all.

24

Sometimes there was the dribbling of fountains into their basins, sometimes only the sound of the fast-running spring water under the stones, behind the walls. Occasionally a single large night-bird dipped toward the ground near a lamp, its crazy shadow running swiftly over the white walls; each time, Dyar started with nervousness, cursing himself silently for not being able to dislodge the fear in him. He walked slowly now, overtaking no one. Ahead, when the way was straight enough, he sometimes caught sight of two men in dark robes, walking hand in hand. They were singing a song with a short vigorous refrain which kept recurring at brief intervals; in between was a lazy variation on the refrain which followed like a weak, uncertain answer to the other. This in itself Dyar surely would not have noticed, had it not been for the fact that each time the meandering section began, just for the first few notes, he had the distinct impression that the sound came from somewhere behind him. By the time he had stopped to listen (his interest aroused not by the music, but by his own fear) the two ahead had always started in again. Finally, in order to be sure, he stood quite still for the space of several choruses, while little by little the voices of the two ahead grew fainter. There was no longer any doubt in his mind; a querulous falsetto voice was singing the same song, coming along behind him. He could hear it more plainly now, like a mocking shadow of the music that went on ahead. But from the strategic spaces that were left in the design of the melody and rhythm by the two men for the single voice in the rear to fill in, he knew immediately that they were conscious of the other's participation in the song. He stepped back into a recess between the houses, where there was a small square tank with water pouring into it, and waited for the owner of the single voice to go by. From in here he could hear nothing but the hollow falling of the water into the cistern beside him, and he strained, listening, to see if the other, on noticing his disappearance, would stop singing, change the sound of his voice, or in some other manner send a signal to those who went ahead. If only he had a good-sized flashlight, he thought, or a monkey-wrench, he could hit him on the back of the head as he went past, drag him into the dark here, and go back quickly in the other direction. But when the lone vocalist appeared, he turned out to be accompanied by a friend. Both were youths in their teens, and they stumbled along with the air of not having a thought in their heads, beyond that of not losing the thread of the song that floated back through the street to them. He waited until they had gone past, counted to twenty, and peered around the corner of the house: they were still going along with the same careless, unsteady gait. When they had disappeared he turned and went back, still by no means convinced that when they noticed his absence ahead of them, they would not hurry to confer with the other couple and set out with them to look for him.

Because fear is without any true relationship to reality each time he left a lighted patch of street and entered the dark, he now expected the singers and their friends to be somewhere there waiting, having taken a short cut and got there before him. An iron arm would reach out of an invisible doorway and yank him inside before he knew what was happening, a terrific blow from behind would fell him, and he would come to in some deserted alley, lying in a pile of garbage, his money gone, his passport gone, his watch and clothes gone, with no one to help him either here or in Tangier or anywhere else. No one to cover his nakedness or to provide him with even tomorrow morning's meal. From the jail where they would lodge him they would telephone the American Legation, and he would soon see Tangier again, a thousand times more a victim than ever.

Going by each side street and passageway he opened his eyes wider and stared, as if that might help him to see through the darkness. Back on the main street, climbing the long stairs, where the light from the stalls spilled across the steps, he felt a little better, even though his legs were hollow and seemed not to want to go where he tried to direct them. There was some comfort in being back among people; all he had to do here was walk along his head down and not look up into their faces. When he had got almost back up to the place where he had eaten, he heard drums beating out a peculiar, breathless rhythm. Here the street made several abrupt turns, becoming a series of passageways that led through the buildings. He glanced up at the second-story window overlooking the entrance to one of these tunnels, and saw, through the iron grillework, the back of a row of turbaned heads. At the same instant a peremptory voice in the street behind him called out, "*Hola, señor! Oiga!*" He turned his head quickly and saw, fifty feet back, a native in what looked like a policeman's uniform and helmet, and there was no doubt that the man was trying to attract his attention. He plunged ahead into the darkness, made the first turn with the street, and seeing a partially open door on his right, pushed against it.

The light came from above. A steep stairway led up. The drums were there, and also a faint, wheezing music. He stood behind the door at the foot of the stairs, not having pushed it any further shut than it had been. He waited; nothing happened. Then a man appeared at the top of the stairs, was about to come down, saw him, motioned to another, who presently also came into view. Together they beckoned to him. "*Tlah. Tlah. Agi,*" they said. Because their faces were unmistakably friendly, he slowly started to mount the steps.

It was a small, very crowded café with benches along the walls.

The dim light came from a bulb hung above a high copper samovar which stood on a shelf in a corner. All the men wore white turbans, and they looked up with interest as Dyar entered, making room for him at the end of a bench by the drummers, who sat in a circle on the floor at the far end of the room. Over here it was very dark indeed, and he had the impression that something inexplicable was taking place on the floor almost at his feet. The men were looking downward through the smoke at a formless mass that quaked, jerked, shuddered and heaved, and although the room shook with the pounding of the drums, it was as if another kind of silence were there in the air, an imperious silence that stretched from the eyes of the men watching to the object moving at their feet. As his own eyes grew accustomed to the confused light, Dyar saw that it was a man, his hands locked firmly together behind him as if they were chained there. Until this moment he had been writhing and twisting on the floor, but now slowly he was rising to his knees, turning his head desperately from side to side, an expression of agony on his tortured face. Even when, five minutes later, he had finally got to his feet, he did not alter the position of his hands, and always the spasms that forced his body this way and that, in perfect rhythm with the increasing hysteria of the drums and the low cracked voice of the flute, seemed to come from some secret center far inside him. Dyar watched impassively. He was completely hidden by the ranks of the men who stood near him looking at the spectacle, and more of whom kept crowding up; from the door he was invisible, and the consciousness of that gave him momentary relief. Someone passed him a glass of tea from the other end of the long table. As he held it under his nose, the sharp fumes of hot spearmint cleared his head, and he became aware of another odor in the air, a spicy resinous smell which he traced to a brazier behind one of the drummers; a heavy smudge of sweet smoke rose constantly. The man had begun to cry out, softly at first, and then savagely; his cries were answered by rhythmical calls of "*Al-lah!*" from the drummers. Dyar stole a glance around at the faces of the spectators. The expression he saw was the same on all sides: utter absorption in the dance, almost adoration of the man performing it. A lighted kif pipe was thrust in front of him. He took it and smoked it without looking to see who had offered it to him. His heart, which had been beating violently when he came in, had ceased its pounding; he felt calmer now.

After a day passed largely in the contemplation of that far-off and unlikely place which was the interior of himself, he did not find it difficult now to reject flatly the reality of what he was seeing. He merely sat and watched, content in the conviction that the thing he was looking at was not taking place in the world that really existed. It was too far beyond the pale of the possible. The kif pipe was refilled several times for him, and the smoke, rising to his head, helped him to sit there and watch a thing he did not believe.

According to Dyar's eyes, the man now at last moved his hands, reached inside his garments and pulled out a large knife, which he flourished with wide gestures. It gleamed feebly in the faint light. Without glancing behind him, one of the drummers threw a handful of something over his shoulder and resumed beating, coming in on the complex rhythm perfectly: the smoke rose in thicker clouds from the censer. The chanted strophes were now antiphonal, with "*Al-lah!*" being thrown back and forth like a red-hot stone from one side of the circle to the other. At the same time it was as if the sound had become two high walls between which the dancer whirled and leapt, striking against their invisible surfaces with his head in a vain effort to escape beyond them.

The man held up his bare arm. The blade glinted, struck at it on a down beat of the drum pattern. And again. And again and again, until the arm and hand were shining and black. Then the other arm was slashed, the tempo increasing as the drummers' bodies bent further forward toward the center of the circle. In the sudden flare of a match nearby, Dyar saw the glistening black of the arms and hands change briefly to red, as if the man had dipped his arms in bright red paint; he saw, too, the ecstatic face as an arm was raised to the mouth and the swift tongue began to lick the blood in rhythm. With the shortening of the phrases, the music had become an enormous panting. It had kept every detail of syncopation intact, even at its present great rate of speed, thus succeeding in destroying the listeners' sense of time, forcing their minds to accept the arbitrary one it imposed in its place. With this hypnotic device it had gained complete domination. But as to the dancer, it was hard to say whether they were commanding him or he them. He bent over, and with a great sweep of his arm began a thorough hacking of his legs; the music's volume swelled in accompaniment.

Dyar was there, scarcely breathing. It could not be said that he watched now, because in his mind he had moved forward from looking on to a kind of participation. With each gesture the man made at this point, he felt a sympathetic desire to cry out in triumph. The mutilation was being done for him, to him; it was his own blood that spattered onto the drums and made the floor slippery. In a world which had not yet been muddied by the discovery of thought, there was this certainty, as solid as a boulder, as real as the beating of his heart, that the man was dancing to purify all who watched. When the dancer threw himself to the floor with a despairing cry, Dyar knew that in reality it was a cry of victory, that spirit had triumphed; the expressions of satisfaction on the faces around him confirmed this. The musicians hesitated momentarily, but at a signal from the men who bent solicitously over the dancer's twitching body they resumed playing the same piece, slowly as at the beginning. Dyar sat perfectly still, thinking of nothing, savoring the unaccustomed sensations which had been freed within him. Conversation had started up; since no one passed him a pipe, he took out Thami's and smoked it. Soon the dancer rose from where he lay on the floor, stood up a little unsteadily, and going to each musician in turn, took each head between his hands from which the blood still dripped, and planted a solemn kiss on the forehead. Then he pushed his way through the crowd, paid for his tea, and went out.

Dyar stayed on a few minutes, and after drinking what remained of his tea, which had long ago grown cold, gave the qaouaji the peseta it cost, and slowly went down the steps. Inside the door he hesitated; it seemed to him he was making a grave decision in venturing out into the street again. But whatever awaited him out there had to be faced, he told himself, and it might as well be now as a few minutes or hours later. He opened the door. The covered street was deserted and black, but beyond the farthest arch, where it led into the open, the walls and paving stones glowed as the moonlight poured over them. He walked out into a wide plaza dominated by a high minaret, feeling only acute surprise to find that none of his fear was left. It had all been liberated by the past hour in the café; how, he would never understand, nor did he care. But now, whatever circumstance presented itself, he would find a way to deal with it. The confidence of his mood was augmented by the several pipes of kif he presently smoked sitting on the ledge of the fountain in the center of the plaza.

A hundred feet away, in a café overlooking the same plaza, Thami was lamenting having left his pipe and mottoui behind in the house. He had to accept the qaouaji's generosity, and it was embarrassing to him. With the number of parcels he had, he was understandably loath to set off up the mountain, and besides, he had just eaten heavily. He had wanted very much to buy a bottle of good Terry cognac to drink that night, but his money had proved insufficient for such a luxury. Instead, he had got a large mass of majoun, at the same time making a firm resolution to demand his five thousand pesetas as soon as he got back up to the house. The extra money he had been promised could wait, but not that initial sum. Dyar would be in no mood to give it to him, he knew, but after all, he had the upper hand: he would simply threaten to leave tomorrow. That would bring him around.

Dyar sat, watching the strong moonlight flood the white surface of the plaza, letting his mind grow lucid and hard like the objects and their shadows around him. (At noon the kif had had a diffusing effect, softening and melting his thought, spreading it within him, but now it had tightened him; he felt alert and fully in touch with the world.) Since the situation was worse than he had imagined, because of the patent impossibility of his getting change for the notes anywhere in Agla, the only thing to do was to spend a little money improving that situation. It would mean taking Thami into his confidence, but it was simple, and if he could instil into him the idea that once a man has agreed to be an accomplice he is as guilty as his companion, he thought the risk would not be too great. The fact that he had already dismissed as childish and neurotic the fear which had driven him out of the house and along the mountainside all day, did not strike him as suspect or worthy of any particular scrutiny. The important thing, he thought, was to get over the border into French Morocco, which was many times larger than the Spanish Zone, where he would be less conspicuous (because, while he might be taken for French, he could never pass for a Spaniard), and where the police were less on the lookout for strangers. But before that they would have to have change for the banknotes. Feeling the need to walk as he made his plans, he rose and went across to the dark side of the plaza, where small trees lined the walk. Without paying attention to where he was going, he turned off into a side street.

Every day for the next week he would send Thami down here to Agla for provisions, and each time he would give him a thousand peseta note with which to purchase them. He was confident Thami could get change. That way at the end of the week they would at least have enough to start south. He would also give Thami five hundred pesetas a day until they were across the border, with a promised bonus of an extra five thousand when they were in French territory, and a hundred on each thousand-peseta note Thami could change into francs for him once there were there. Assuming he were able to get it all changed, this project would cost him over two thousand dollars, but that was a small price to pay for being in the clear.

From ahead came the noise of voices raised in angry dispute. Although the plaza out there was empty, the town was by no means entirely asleep. Turning a bend in the street he came out upon a small square darkened by a trellis of vines overhead. A group of excited men had gathered around two small boys who apparently had been fighting; they had started by being onlookers, and then, inevitably, had entered into the altercation with all the passion of the original participants. The rectangles of yellow light that lay on the pavement came from the shops that were open; in contrast the mottles of moonlight in dark corners were blue. He did not stop to watch the argument: walking along the white street in the moon's precise light was conducive to the unfolding of plans. The commotion was such that no one noticed him as he passed through the shady square. The shops, which seemed to belong primarily to tailors and carpenters, were empty at the moment, having been deserted at the first indication of a diversion in the street. The way twisted a little; there was one more stall open here, and beyond, only the moonlight. It was a carpenter's shop, and the man had been working in the doorway, building a high wooden chest shaped like a steamer trunk. The hammer lay where he had left it. Dyar saw it without seeing it; then he looked at it hard, looked involuntarily for the nails. They too were there, a bit long, but straight and new, lying on a little square stool nearby. Only when he had passed the shouting group again and had got so far beyond that he could no longer hear the hoarse cries, the hammer and one big nail in his coat pocket, did he realize that for all his great clarity of mind sitting by the fountain smoking his kif, he had been unbelievably stupid. What were the hammer and nail for? To fix the door. What door? The door to the cottage, the rattling door that kept him from sleeping. And where was the cottage, how was he going to get there?

He stood still, more appalled by the revelation of this incredible lapse in his mental processes than by the fact itself that he could not get to the house, that he had nowhere to sleep. This kif is treacherous stuff, he thought, starting ahead slowly.

Back in the deserted plaza he seated himself once again on the edge of the fountain and pulled out the pipe. Treacherous or not, like alcohol it at least made the present moment bearable. As he smoked he saw a figure emerge from the shadows on the dark side of the plaza and come sauntering over in his direction. When it was still fairly far away, but near enough for him to see it was a man carrying a large basket, it said: "*Salam.*" Dyar grunted.

"Andek es sebsi?"

He looked up unbelieving. It was impossible. The stuff was treacherous, so he did not move, but waited.

The man came nearer, exclaimed. Then Dyar jumped up. "You son of a bitch!" he cried, laughing with pleasure, clapping Thami's shoulder several times.

Thami was delighted, too. Dyar had eaten, was in a good humor.

The return to the house with its attendant furious reproaches no longer had to be dreaded. He could broach the subject of the money. And there was his own kif-pipe, whose absence he had been so lately regretting, right in Dyar's hand. But he was nervous about being here in the plaza.

"You're going to have trouble here," he said. "It's very bad. I told you not to come. If one moqqaddem sees you, '*Oiga, señor,* come on to the comisaría, we look at your papers, my friend.' Let's go."

The moonlight was very bright when they had left the town behind and were among the olive trees. Halfway up the mountain, among the ragged rocks, they sat down, and Thami took out the majoun.

"You know what this is?" he asked.

"Sure I know. I've had it before."

"This won't make you drunk for an hour yet. Or more. When we get to the house I'll make tea. Then you'll see how drunk."

"I know. I've had it before, I said."

Thami looked at him with disbelief, and divided the cake into two unequal pieces, handing the larger to Dyar.

"It's soft," Dyar remarked in some surprise. "The kind I had was hard."

"Same thing," Thami said with indifference. "This is better." Dyar was inclined to agree with him, as regarded the flavor. They sat, quietly eating, each one conscious in his own fashion that as he swallowed the magical substance he was irrevocably delivering himself over to unseen forces which would take charge of his life for the hours to come.

They did not speak, but sat hearing the water moving downward in the gulf of moonlight and shadows that lay open at their feet.

25

"Home again!" Dyar said jovially as he went inside the house, greeted by the close mildewed smell he had said good-bye to so long ago. "Let's make that fire before we blow our respective tops." He tossed the briefcase into a corner, glad to be rid of it.

Thami shut the door, locked it, and stared at him, not understanding. "You're already m'hashish," he said. "I know when I look at you. What are you talking about?"

"The fire. The fire. Get some wood. Quick!"

"Plenty of wood," said Thami imperturbably, pointing to the

patio with its crates. Dyar stepped out and began to throw them wildly into the center of the room. "Break 'em up!" he shouted. "Smash 'em! It's going to be God-damned cold in here without any blanket. We've got to keep the fire going as long as we can."

Thami obeyed, wondering at the surprising transformation a little majoun could work in a Christian. He had never before seen Dyar in good spirits. When he had an enormous pile of slats, he pushed it to one side and spread the two mats, one on top of the other, in front of the fireplace. Then he went out into the kitchen and busied himself building a charcoal fire in the earthen brazier, in order to prepare the tea.

"Ah!" he heard Dyar cry in triumph from the patio. "Just what we wanted!" He had unearthed several small logs in one corner, which he carried in and dumped beside the fireplace. He joined Thami in the kitchen. "Give me a match," he said. "My candle's gone out." Thami was squatting over the brazier, and he looked up smiling. "How do you feel now?" he asked.

"I feel great. Why? How do you feel?"

Thami handed him his box of matches. "I feel good," he answered. He was not sure how to begin. Perhaps it would be better to wait until they were lying in front of the fire. But by then Dyar's mood might have changed. "I wanted to buy a big bottle of cognac tonight, you know." He paused.

"Well, why didn't you? I could do with a drink right now."

Thami rubbed his forefinger against his thumb, back and forth, expressively.

"Oh," said Dyar soberly. "I see." He went back into the other room, stuffed some paper into the fireplace, put some crate wood on top, and lighted it. Then he walked over to the darkest corner of the room and keeping his eye on the door into the patio, pulled out five notes from the inside of his shirt. "This'll show him I'm playing straight with him," he said to himself. He returned to the kitchen and handed the money to Thami, saying: "Here."

"Thank you," Thami said. He stood up and patted him on the back lightly, three pats.

"When you come in I'll talk to you about the rest of it." He went out into the patio and stood looking up at the huge globe of the full moon; never had he seen it so near or so strong. A night bird screamed briefly in the air overhead—a peculiar, chilly sound, not quite like anything he had heard before. He stood, hearing the sound again and again in his head, a long string of interior echoes that traced an invisible ladder across the black sky. The crackling of the fire inside roused him. He went in and threw on a log. He crouched down, looking into the fire, following the forms of the flames with his eyes. The fireplace drew well; no smoke came out into the room.

They were putting their feet carefully on the square gray flagstones that led through the grass across the garden, having to step off them at one point onto the soaked turf to avoid the hose with the sprinkler attachment. It went around and around, unevenly. Mrs. Shields had pulled down all the shades in the big room, because the sun shone in and faded the "drapes," she said. Once the windows were shut, the thunderstorm could come whenever it liked; it had been threatening all afternoon. Across the river it looked very dark. It was probably raining there already, but the rolling of the thunder was more distant. Far up the valley toward the gap it groaned. There was wild country up there, and the people did not have the same friendliness they had here where the land was good. Mrs. Shields had let the hose spot her dress. It was a shame, he thought, looking closely at the paisley design.

He did not want to be in the house when they left. Turning to the empty rooms where the air still moved with the currents set up by their last-minute hurryings, feeling the seat of a chair in which one of them had sat, because of that a little warmer than the others, but the warmth still palpable after they had gone, seeing the cord of a window-shade still swinging almost imperceptibly—he could not bear any of those things. It was better to stay in the garden, say goodbye to them there, and wait to go in until the house was completely dead. And the storm would either break or it would growl around the countryside until evening. The grapes are getting ripe, she said as they passed under the arbor. And the sailboats will be making for the harbor. He stood against a cherry tree and watched the ants running up and down across the rough brown bark of the trunk, very near his face. That summer was in a lost region, and all roads to it had been cut.

Thami came in, carrying the burning brazier. He set it down in the middle of the room, went and got the teapot and the glasses. While he waited for the water to boil, blowing from time to time on the glowing coals, Dyar told him of his plans. But when he came to the point of mentioning the sum he had, he found he could not do it. Thami listened, shook his head skeptically when Dyar had finished. "Pesetas are no good in the French Zone," he said. "You can't change them. You'd have to take them to the Jews if you did that."

"Well, we'll take 'em to the Jews, then. Why not?"

Thami looked at him pityingly. "The Jews?" he cried. "They won't give you *anything* for them. They'll give you five francs for one peseta. Maybe six." Dyar knew the current rate was a little over eight. He sighed. "I don't know. We'll have to wait and see." But secretly he was determined to do it that way, even if he got only five.

Thami poured the boiling tea into the glasses. "No mint this time," he said.

"It doesn't matter. It's the heat that does it."

"Yes." He blew out the candle and they sat by the light of the flames. Dyar settled back, leaning against the wall, but immediately Thami objected. "You'll get sick," he explained. "That wall is very wet. Last night I moved my bed, it was so wet there."

"Ah." Dyar sat up, drew his legs under him, and continued to drink his tea. Was the hand on the briefcase explained away for all time? Why not, he asked himself. Believing or doubting is a matter of wanting to believe or doubt; at the moment he felt like believing because it suited his mood.

"So, are you with me?" he said.

"What?"

"We stay a week, and you go every day and change a thousand pesetas?"

"Whatever you say," said Thami, reaching for his glass to pour him more tea."

The room was getting taut and watchful around him; Dyar remembered the sensation from the night at the Villa Hesperides. But it was not the same this time because he himself felt very different. The bird outside cried again. Thami looked surprised. "I don't know how you call that bird in English. We call it *youca*."

Dyar shut his eyes. A terrible motor had started to throb at the back of his head. It was not painful; it frightened him. With his eyes shut he had the impression that he was lying on his back, that if he opened them he would see the ceiling. It was not necessary to open them—he could see it anyway, because his lids had become transparent. It was a gigantic screen against which images were beginning to be projected—tiny swarms of colored glass beads arranged themselves obligingly into patterns, swimming together and apart, forming mosaics that dissolved as soon as they were made. Feathers, snow-crystals, lace and church windows crowded consecutively onto the screen, and the projecting light grew increasingly powerful. Soon the edges of the screen would begin to burn, and the fire would be on each side of his head. "God, this is going to blind me," he said suddenly; he opened his eyes and realized he had said nothing.

"Do you know what they look like?" Thami asked.

"What what look like?"

"*Youcas.*"

"I don't know what anything looks like. I don't know what you're talking about!"

Thami looked slightly aggrieved. "You're m'hashish, my friend. M'hashish *bezef!*"

Each time Thami spoke to him, he raised his head and shook it slightly, opened his eyes, and made a senseless reply. Thami began to sing in a small, faraway voice. It was a sound you could walk on, a soft carpet that stretched before him across the flat blinding desert. *Ijbed selkha men rasou. . . .* But he came up against the stone walls of an empty house beside a mountain. The fire was raging behind it, burning wildly and silently, the door was open and it was dark inside. Cobwebs hung to the walls, soldiers had been there, and there were women's silk underclothes strewn about the empty rooms. He knew that a certain day, at a certain moment, the house would crumble and nothing would be left but dust and rubble, indistinguishable from the talus of gravel that lay below the cliffs. It would be absolutely silent, the falling of the house, like a film that goes on running after the sound apparatus has broken. *Bache idaoui sebbatou. . . .* The carpet had caught on fire, too. Someone would blame him.

"I'm God damned if I'll pay for it," he said. Regular hours, always superiors to give you orders, no security, no freedom, no freedom, no freedom.

Thami said: "*Hak.* Take your tea."

Dyar reached forward and swam against the current toward the outstretched glass shining with reflected firelight. "I've got it. *Muchas gracias, amigo.*" He paused, seemed to be listening, then with exaggerated care he set the glass down on the mat beside him. "I put it there because it's hot, see?" (But Thami was not paying attention; already he was back in his own pleasure pavilion overlooking his miles of verdant gardens, and the water ran clear in blue enamel channels. *Chta! Chta! Sebbatou aând al qadi!*)

"Thami, I'm in another world. Do you understand? Can you hear me?"

Thami, his eyes shut, his body weaving slowly back and forth as he sang, did not answer. The perspective from his tower grew vaster, the water bubbled up out of the earth on all sides. He had ordered it all to be, many years ago. (The night is a woman clothed in a robe of burning stars. . . .) *Ya, Leïla, Lia. . . .*

"I can see you sitting there," Dyar insisted, "but I'm in another world." He began to laugh softly with delight.

"I don't know," he said reflectively. "Sometimes I think the other way around. I think. . . ." He spoke more slowly. "We. . . . would be better. . . . . . . I think. . . . if you can get through. . . . if you can get through. . . . Why can't anyone get through?" His voice became so loud and sharp here that Thami opened his eyes and stopped singing.

"*Chkoun entina*?" he said. "My friend, I'm m'hashish as much as you."

"You get here, you float away again, you come to that *crazy* place! Oh, my *God*!" He was talking very fast, and he went into a little spasm of laughter, then checked himself. "*I've* got nothing to laugh about. It's not funny." With a whoop he rolled over onto the floor and abandoned himself to a long fit of merriment. Thami listened without moving.

After a long time the laughter stopped as suddenly as it had begun; he lay quite still. The other's little voice crept out again: "*Ijbed selkha men rasou* . . ." and went on and on. From time to time the fire stirred, as an ember shifted its position. Every small sound was razor-sharp, but inside there was a solid silence. He was trying not to breathe, he wanted to be absolutely motionless, because he felt that the air which fitted so perfectly around him was a gelatinous substance which had been moulded to match with infinite exactitude every contour of his person. If he moved ever so slightly he would feel it pushing against him, and that would be unbearable. The monstrous swelling and deflating of himself which each breath occasioned was a real peril. But that wave broke, receded, and he was left stranded for a moment in a landscape of liquid glassy light, greengold and shimmering. Burnished, rich and oily, then swift like flaming water. Look at it! Look at it! Drink it with your eyes. It's the only water you'll ever see. Another wave would roll up soon; they were coming more often.

Ya Leïla, Lia. . . . For a moment he was quite in his senses. He lay there comfortably and listened to the long, melancholy melodic line of the song, thinking: "How long ago was it that I was laughing?" Perhaps the whole night had gone by, and the effect had already worn off.

"Thami?" he said. Then he realized it had been almost impossible to get the word out, because his mouth was of cardboard. He gasped a little, and thought of moving. (I must remember to tell myself to move my left hand so I can raise myself onto my elbow. It must move back further before I can begin to pull my knees up. But I don't want to move my knees. Only my hand. So I can raise myself onto my elbow. If I move my knees I can sit up . . .)

He was sitting up.

(I'm sitting up.) *Is this what I wanted? Why did I want to sit up?*

He waited.

(I didn't. I only wanted to raise myself onto my elbow.) *Why*? (I wanted to lie facing the other way. It's going to be more comfortable that way.)

He was lying down.

(. . . from the gulf of the infinite, Allah looks across with an eye of gold. . . .) *Alef leïlat ou leïla, ya leïla, lia!*

Before the wind had arrived, he heard it coming, stirring stealthily around the sharp pinnacles of rock up there, rolling down through the ravines, whispering as it moved along the surface of the cliffs, coming to wrap itself around the house. He lay a year, dead, listening to it coming.

There was an explosion in the room. Thami had thrown another log onto the fire. "That gave me designs. Red, purple," said Dyar without speaking, sitting up again. The room was a red grotto, a theatre, a vast stable with a balcony that hung in the shadows. Up there was a city of little rooms, a city inside a pocket of darkness, but there were windows in the walls you could not see, and beyond these the sun shone down on an outer city built of ice.

"My God, Thami, water!" he cried thickly. Thami was standing above him.

"Good-bye," said Thami. Heavily he sat down and rolled over onto his side, sang no more.

"Water," he tried to say again in a very soft voice, and tremblingly he made a supreme effort to get to his feet. "My God, I've got to have water," he whispered to himself; it was easier to whisper. Because he was looking down at his feet from ten thousand feet up, he had to take exquisite care in walking, but he stepped over Thami and got out into the patio to the pail. Sighing with the effort of kneeling down, he put his face into the fire of the cold water and drew it into his throat.

When it was finished he rose, threw his head up, and looked at the moon. The wind had come, but it had been here before. Now it was necessary to get back into the room, to get all the way across the room to the door. But he must not breathe so heavily. To open the door and go out. Out there the wind would be cold, but he must go anyway.

The expedition through the magic room was hazardous. There was a fragile silence there which must not be shattered. The fire, shedding its redness on Thami's masklike face, must not know he was stealing past. At each step he lifted his feet far off the floor into the air, like someone walking through a field of high wet grass. He saw the door ahead of him, but suddenly between him and it a tortuous corridor made of pure time interposed itself. It was going to take endless hours to get down to the end. And a host of invisible people was lined up along its walls, but on the other side of the walls, mutely waiting for him to go by—an impassive chorus, silent and without pity. "Waiting for me," he thought. The sides of his mind, indistinguishable from the walls of the corridor, were lined with messages in Arabic script. All the time, directly before his eyes was the knobless door sending out its ominous message. It was not sure, it could not be trusted. If it opened when he did not want it to open, by itself, all the horror of existence could crowd in upon him. He stretched his hand out and touched the large cold key. The key explained the heaviness in his overcoat pocket. He put his left hand into the pocket and felt the hammer, and the head and point of the nail. That was work to be done, but later, when he came in. He turned the key, pulled open the door, felt the bewildered wind touch his face. "Keep away from the cliff," he whispered as he stepped outside. Around him stretched the night's formless smile. The moon was far out over the empty regions now. Relieving himself against the wall of the house, he heard the wind up here trying to cover the long single note of the water down in the valley. Inside, by the fire, time was slowly dissolving, falling to pieces. But even at the end of the night there would still be an ember of time left, of a subtle, bitter flavor, soft to the touch, glowing from its recess of ashes, before it paled and died, and the heart of the ancient night stopped beating.

He turned toward the door, his steps short and halting like those of an old man. It was going to require a tremendous effort to get back to the mat, but because the only thing he could conceive of at this instant was to sink down on it and lie out flat by the fire, he felt certain he could make the effort. As he shut the door behind him he murmured to it: "You know I'm here, don't you?" The idea was hateful to him, but there was something he could do about it. What that thing was he could not recall, yet he knew the situation was not hopeless; he could remedy it later.

Thami had not stirred. As he looked down from his remote height at the relaxed body, a familiar uneasiness stole over him, only he could connect it with no cause. Partly he knew that what he saw before him was Thami, Thami's head, trunk, arms and legs. Partly he knew it was an unidentifiable object lying there, immeasurably heavy with its own meaninglessness, a vast imponderable weight that nothing could lighten. As he stood lost in static contemplation of the thing, the wind pushed the door feebly, making a faint rattling. But *could* nothing lighten it? If the air were let in, the weight might escape of its own accord, into the shadows of the room and the darkness of the night. He looked slowly behind him. The door was silent, staring, baleful. "You know I'm here, all right," he thought, "but you won't know long." He had willed the hammer and nail into existence, and they were there in his pocket. Thinking of their heaviness, he felt his body lean to one side. He had to shift the position of his foot to retain his balance, to keep from being pulled down by their weight. The rattle came again, a series of slight knockings, knowing and insinuating. But now, did they come from the mat below him? "If it opens," he thought, looking at the solid, inert mass in front of him in the fire's dying light, his eyes staring, gathering fear from within him. "If it opens." There was that thing he had to do, he must do it, and he knew what it was but he could not think what it was.

A mass of words had begun to ferment inside him, and now they bubbled forth. "Many Mabel damn. Molly Daddy lamb. Lolly dibble up-man. Dolly little Dan," he whispered, and then he giggled. The hammer was in his right hand, the nail in his left. He bent over, swayed, and fell heavily to his knees on the mat, beside the outstretched door. It did not move. The mountain wind rushed through his head, his head that was a single seashell full of grottoes; its infinitely smooth pink walls, delicate, paper-thin, caught the light of the embers as he moved along the galleries. "Melly diddle din," he said, quite loud, putting the point of the nail as far into Thami's ear as he could. He raised his right arm and hit the head of the nail with all his might. The object relaxed imperceptibly, as if someone had said to it: "It's all right." He laid the hammer down, and felt of the nail-head, level with the soft lobe of the ear. It had two little ridges on it; he rubbed his thumbnail across the imperfections in the steel. The nail was as firmly embedded as if it had been driven into a coconut. "Merry Mabel dune." The children were going to make a noise when they came out at recess-time. The fire rattled, the same insistent music that could not be stilled, the same skyrockets that would not hurry to explode. And the floor had fallen over onto him. His hand was bent under him, he could feel it, he wanted to move. "I must remember that I exist," he told himself; that was clear, like a great rock rising out of the sea around it. "I must remember that I am alive."

He did not know whether he was lying still or whether his hands and feet were shaking painfully with the effort of making himself believe he was there and wanted to move his hand. He knew his skin was more tender than the skin of an overripe plum; no matter how softly he touched it, it would break and smear him with the stickiness beneath. Someone had shut the bureau drawer he was lying in and gone away, forgotten him. The great languor. The great slowness. The night had sections filled with repose, and there were places in time to be visited, faces to forget, words to understand, silences to be studied.

The fire was out; the inhuman night had come into the room. Once again he wanted water. "I've come back," he thought; his mouth, gullet, stomach ached with dryness. "Thami has stayed behind. I'm the only survivor. That's the way I wanted it." That warm, humid, dangerous breeding-place for ideas had been destroyed. "Thank God he hasn't come back with me," he told himself. "I never wanted him to know I was alive." He slipped away again; the water was too distant.

A maniacal light had fallen into the room and was hopping about. He sat up and frowned. The ear in the head beside him. The little steel disc with the irregular grooves in it. He had known it would be there. He sighed, crept on his hands and knees around the ends of the drawn-up legs, arrived in the cold, blinding patio, and immersed his face in the pail. He was not real, but he knew he was alive. When he lifted his head, he let it fall all the way back against the wall, and he stayed there a long time, the mountains' morning light pressing brutally into his eyelids.

Later he rose, went into the room, dragged Thami by his legs through the patio into the kitchen and shut the door. Overpowered by weakness, he lay down on the mat, and still trembling fell into a bottomless sleep. As the day advanced the wind increased, the blue sky grew white, then gray. The door rattled unceasingly, but he heard nothing.

26

The pounding on the door had been going on for a long time before, becoming aware of it, he began to scramble up the slippery sides of the basin of sleep where he found himself, in a frantic attempt to escape into consciousness. When finally he opened his eyes and was back in the room, a strange languor remained, like a great, soft cushion beneath him; he did not want to move. Still the fist went on hitting the door insistently, stopping now and then so that when it began again it was louder after the silence that had come in between.

There were cushions under him and cushions on top of him; he would not move. But he called out: "Who is it?" several times, each time managing to put a little more force into his unruly voice. The knocking ceased. Soon he felt a faint curiosity to know who it was out there. He sat up, then got up and went to the door, saying again, his mouth close to the wood: "Who is it?" Outside there was only the sound of the casual dripping of water from the eaves onto the bare earth. "So it's been raining again," he thought with unreasoning anger. "Who is it?" he said, louder, at the same time being startled as he put his hand to his face and felt the three-day beard there.

He unlocked the door, opened it and looked out. It was a dark day, and as he had expected, there was no one in sight. Nor was he still any more than vaguely interested in knowing who had been knocking. It was not indifference; he knew it concerned him vitally—he knew that he should care very much who had stood outside the door a moment ago. But now there was not enough of him left to feel strongly about anything; everything had been spent last night. Today was like an old, worn-out film being run off—dim, jerky, flickering, full of cuts, and with a plot he could not seize. It was hard to pay attention to it.

As he turned to go back in, for he felt like sleeping again, a voice called: "Hola!" from the direction of the stream. And although he was having difficulty focusing (the valley was a murky gray jumble), he saw a man who a second before had been standing still looking back at the house turn and start walking up toward it. Dyar did not move; he watched; on the top of his head now and then he felt the cold drops that fell singly, unhurriedly, from the sky.

The man was a Berber in country clothes. As he drew near the house he began to walk more slowly and to look back down the path. Soon he stopped altogether, and stood, obviously waiting for someone behind him. From between the rocks two figures presently emerged and climbed up across the stream, around the curve in the path. Dyar, remaining in the doorway, observing this unannounced arrival, feeling sure that it meant something of great importance to him, was unable to summon the energy necessary for conjecture; he watched. When the two figures had reached the spot where the lone one stood, they stopped and conferred with him; he waved his arm toward the house, and then sat down, while they continued along the path. But now Dyar had begun to stare, for one man was wearing a uniform with jodhpurs and boots, while the other, who seemed to need assistance in climbing, was in a raincoat and a brilliant purple turban. When the two had got about halfway between the seated Berber and the house, he realized with a shock that the second person was a woman in slacks. And an instant later his mouth opened slightly because he had recognized Daisy. Under his breath he said: "Good God!"

As she came nearer and saw him staring at her she waved, but said nothing. Dyar, behaving like a small child, stood watching her approach, did not even acknowledge her greeting.

"Oh!" she exclaimed, gasping a little as she came on to the level piece of ground where the house stood. She walked toward the door and put her hand out. He took it, still looking at her, unbelieving. "Hello," he said.

"Look. Will you please not think I'm a busybody. How are you?" She let go of his hand and directed a piercing glance at his face; unthinkingly he put his hand to his chin. "All right?" Without waiting for an answer she turned to the man in the chauffeur's uniform. *"Me puedes esparar ahí abajo."* She pointed to the native waiting below. The man made a listless salute and walked away.

"Oh!" said Daisy again, looking about for a place to sit, and seeing nothing but the wet earth. "I must sit down. Do you think we could go in where it's dry?"

"Oh, sure." Dyar came to life. "I'm just surprised to see you. Go on in." She crossed the room and sat down on the mat in front of the dead fireplace. "What are you doing here?" he said, his voice expressionless.

She had her knees together out to one side, and she had folded her hands over them. "Obviously, I've come to see you." She looked up at him. "But you want to know *why,* of course. If you'll be patient while I catch my breath, I'll tell you." She paused, and sighed. "I'll lay my case before you and you can do as you like." Now she reached up and seized his arm. "Darling" (the sound of her voice had changed, grown more intense), "you must go back. Sit down. No, here, beside me. You've got to go back to Tangier. That's why I'm here. To help you get back in."

She felt his body stiffen as he turned his head quickly to look at her. "Don't talk," she said. "Let me say my little piece. It's late, and it's going to rain, and we must leave Agla while there's still daylight. There are twenty-seven kilometers of trail before one gets to the *carretera.* You don't know anything about the roads because you didn't come that way."

"How do you know how I came?"

"You *do* think I'm an utter fool, don't you?" She offered him a cigarette from her case and they smoked a moment in silence. "I saw the little business in the garden the other night, and I thought I recognized that drunken brother of the Beidaoui's. And I had no reason to doubt his wife's word. According to her he brought you here. So that's that. But all that's of no importance."

He was thinking: "How can I find out how much she knows?" The best idea seemed to be simply to ask her; thus he cut her short, saying: "What have they told you?"

"Who?" she said drily. "Jack Wilcox and Ronny Ashcombe-Danvers?"

He did not reply.

"If you mean them," she pursued, "they told me everything, naturally. You're all bloody fools, all three of you, but you're the biggest bloody fool. What in *God's* name did you think you were doing? Of course, I don't know what Jack was thinking of in the first place to let you fetch Ronny's money, and he's so secretive I couldn't make anything out of his silly tale. It wasn't until I met Ronny yesterday at the airport that I got any sort of story that hung together at all. Ronny's an old friend of mine, you know, and I can tell you he's more than displeased about the whole thing, as well he may be."

"Yes," he said, completely at a loss for anything else to say.

"I've argued with him until I'm hoarse, trying to persuade him to let me come up here. Of course he was all for coming himself with a band of ruffians from the port and taking his chances on getting the money back by force. Because obviously he can't do it by legal means. But I think now he understands how childish that idea is. I made him see how much better it would be if I could get you to come back of your own accord."

Dyar thought: So Ashcombe-Danvers is an old friend of hers. He's promised her a percentage of everything she can get back for him. And he remembered Mme. Werth's reservation at the hotel in Marrakech; Daisy might as well have been saying to him: "Do come back and be a victim again for my sake."

"It's out of the question," he said shortly.

"Oh, is it?" she cried, her eyes blazing. "Because little Mr. Dyar says it is, I suppose?"

He flushed. "You're God-damned right."

She leaned toward him. "Why do you think I came up here, you bloody, bloody fool, you conceited idiot? God!"

"I don't know. I'm wondering, myself," he said, tossing his cigarette into the fireplace.

"I came," she paused. "Because I'm the biggest fool of all, because through some ghastly defect in my character, I—because I've somehow—let myself become fond of you. God knows why! *God* knows why! Do you think I'd come all the way here *only* to help Ronny get his money back?" ("Yes, you would," he thought.) "He's better equipped for a manhunt than I am, with his gang of cutthroats from the Marsa." ("She doesn't believe any of that. She thinks she can do the job better," he told himself.) "I'm here because Ronny's a friend of mine, yes, and because I should like to help him get back what belongs to him, what you've stolen from him." (Her voice trembled a little on the word *stolen.*) "Yes, of course. All of that. And I'm here also because what will help him happens to be the only thing that'll help you."

"Do my soul good. I know. Walk in and make a clean breast of it."

"Your soul!" she snapped. "Bugger your soul! I said help you. You're in a mess. You know damned well what a mess you're in. And you're not going to get out of it without some help. I want very much to see you through this. And if I must be quite frank, I don't think anyone else can or will."

"Oh, I know," he said. "I don't expect anybody to take up a collection for me. Nobody can help me. Fine. So how can you?"

"Don't you think Luis knows a few people in Tangier? It's a question of getting you and the money across the frontier. In any case, I've borrowed a diplomatic car. With the CD plates one goes right through, usually. Even if we don't it's all seen to. You run no risk."

"No risk!" he repeated, with a brief laugh. "And in Tangier?"

"Ronny? What can he do? I assure you he'll be so delighted to see his money, he'll—"

He cut her short. "Not that," he said. "I'm not worried about that. I'm just thinking."

She looked puzzled an instant. "You don't mean the check you accepted from that hideous little Russian woman?"

"Oh, Jesus," he groaned. "Is there anything you don't know?"

"In the way of Tangier gossip, no, darling. But everyone knows about that. She's been ordered to leave the International Zone. Day before yesterday. She's probably already gone. The only useful thing Uncle Goode's done since she arrived in Tangier. I don't know what the official American attitude would be toward your sort of stupid behavior. But that's a chance you'll have to take. I think we've talked about enough, don't you?"

"I guess we have," he said. It was a solution, he thought, but it was not the right one, because it would undo everything he had done. It had to be his way, he said to himself. He knew what the other way was like.

"Do you think we could have some tea before we leave?" Daisy inquired suddenly. "It would help." ("She doesn't understand," he thought.)

"I'm not going," he said.

"Oh, darling, don't be difficult." He had never seen her eyes so large and serious. "It's late. You know God-damned well you're going. There's nothing else you can do. The trouble is you just can't make up your mind to face Jack and Ronny. But you've *got* to face them, that's all."

"I tell you I'm not going."

"Rot! Rubbish! Now come! Don't disgust me with your fear. There's nothing more revolting than a man who's afraid."

He laughed unpleasantly.

"Come along, now," she said in a comfortable voice, as though each sentence she had uttered until then had succeeded in persuading him a little. "Make some good hot tea and we'll each have a cup. Then we'll go back. It's that simple." As a new idea occurred to her, she looked around the room for the first time. "Where's the Beidaoui boy? Not that I can take him; he'll have to get back by himself, but I daresay that offers no particular problem."

Because what had been going on for the past half-hour had been in a world so absolutely alien to the one he had been living in (where the mountain wind blew and rattled the door), that world of up here, like something of his own invention, had receded, become unlikely, momentarily effaced itself. He caught his breath, said nothing. At the same time he glanced swiftly over her shoulder toward the kitchen door, and felt his heart make a painful movement in his chest. For an instant his eyes opened very wide. Then he looked into her face, frowning and not letting his eyelids resume their natural position too quickly. "I don't know," he said, hoping that his expression could be interpreted as one of no more than normal concern. With the wind, the door had swung outward a little, and a helpless hand showed through the opening. "I haven't seen him all day. He was gone when I woke up."

Now his heart was pounding violently, and the inside of his head pushed against his skull as if it would break through the fragile wall. He tried to play the old game with himself. "It's not true. He's not lying there." It would not work. He knew positively, even without looking again; games were finished. He sat in the room, he was the center of a situation of whose every detail he was aware; the very presence of the hand gave him his unshakable certainty, his conviction that his existence, along with everything in it, was real, solid, undeniable. Later he would be able to look straight at this knowledge without the unbearable, bursting anguish, but now, at the beginning, sitting beside Daisy in the room where the knowledge had been born, it was too much. He jumped to his feet.

"Tea?" he cried crazily. "Yeah, sure. Of course." He stepped to the front door and looked out: the chauffeur and the guide were still sitting down there in the gathering gloom, on opposite sides of the path. "I don't know where he is," he said. "He's been gone all day." It was still raining a little, but in a moment it would fall harder. A dense cloud was drifting down from the invisible peaks above. In the wet gray twilight everything was colorless. He heard a sound behind him, turned and stood frozen as he watched Daisy rise slowly, deliberately, walk into the patio, her eyes fixed on the bottom of the kitchen door. She pulled it all the way open, and bent down, her back to him. He was not sure, but he thought he heard, a second later, a slight, almost inaudible cry. And she stayed crouching there a long time. Little by little the dead, flat sound of the falling rain spread, increased. He started to walk across the room toward the patio, thinking: "This is the moment to show her I'm not afraid. Not afraid of what she thinks." Because of the rain splattering from the eaves into the patio, she did not hear him coming until he was almost in the doorway. She looked up swiftly; there were tears in her eyes, and the sight of them was a sharp pain inside him.

He stood still.

"Did—?" She did not try to say anything more. He knew the reason: she had looked at his face and did not need to finish her question. She stood only a second now in front of him, yet even in that flash many things must have crossed her mind, because as he stared into her eyes he was conscious of the instantaneous raising of a great barrier that had not been there a moment before, and now suddenly was there, impenetrable and merciless. Quickly she walked in front of him into the room and across to the door. Only when she had stepped outside into the rain did she turn and say in a smothered voice: "I shall tell Ronny I couldn't find you." Then she moved out of his vision; where she had paused there was only the rectangle of grayness.

He stood there in the patio a moment, the cold rain wetting him. (A place in the world, a definite status, a precise relationship with the rest of men. Even if it had to be one of open hostility, it was his, created by him.) Suddenly he pushed the kitchen door shut and went into the room. He was tired, he wanted to sit down, but there was only one mat, and so he remained standing in the middle of the room. Soon it would be dark; stuck onto the floor was the little piece of candle the other had blown out last night when the fire was going. He did not know whether there was another candle in the kitchen, nor would he look to see. More to have something to do than because he wanted light, he knelt down to set the stub burning, felt in his pocket, in all his pockets, for a match. Finding none, he stood up again and walked to the door. Out in the murk there was no valley, there were no mountains. The rain fell heavily and the wind had begun to blow again. He sat down in the doorway and began to wait. It was not yet completely dark.

Amrah, Tangier, 1951

EMMY MOORE'S JOURNAL

JANE BOWLES

A FRAGMENT OF *Emmy Moore's story from the uncompleted novel* Out in the World.

ON CERTAIN DAYS I forget why I'm here. Today once again I wrote my husband all my reasons for coming. He encouraged me to come each time I was in doubt. He said that the worst danger for me was a state of vagueness, so I wrote telling him why I had come to the Hotel Henry—my eighth letter on this subject—but with each new letter I strengthen my position. I am reproducing the letter here. Let there be no mistake. My journal is intended for publication. I want to publish for glory, but also in order to aid other women. This is the letter to my husband, Paul Moore, to whom I have been married sixteen years. (I am childless.) He is of North Irish descent, and a very serious lawyer. Also a solitary and lover of the country. He knows all mushrooms, bushes and trees, and he is interested in geology. But these interests do not exclude me. He is sympathetic towards me, and kindly. He wants very much for me to be happy, and worries because I am not. He knows everything about me, including how much I deplore being the feminine kind of woman that I am. In fact, I am unusually feminine for an American of Anglo stock. (Born in Boston.) I am almost a "Turkish" type. Not physically, at least not entirely, because though fat I have ruddy Scotch cheeks and my eyes are round and not slanted or almond-shaped. But sometimes I feel certain that I exude an atmosphere very similar to theirs (the Turkish women's) and then I despise myself. I find the women in my country so extraordinarily manly and independent, capable of leading regiments, or of fending for themselves on desert islands if necessary. (These are poor examples, but I am getting my point across.) For me it is an experience simply to have come here alone to the Hotel Henry and to eat my dinner and lunch by myself. If possible before I die, I should like to become a little more independent, and a little less Turkish than I am now. Before I go any further, I had better say immediately that I mean no offense to Turkish women. They are probably busy combating the very same Turkish quality in themselves that I am controlling in me. I understand, too (though this is irrelevant), that many Turkish women are beautiful, and I think that they have discarded their veils. Any other American woman would be sure of this. She would know one way or the other whether the veils had been discarded, whereas I am afraid to come out with a definite statement. I have a feeling that they really have got rid of their veils, but I won't swear to it. Also, if they have done so, I have no idea when they did. Was it many years ago or recently?

Here is my letter to Paul Moore, my husband, in which there is more about Turkish women. Since I am writing this journal with a view to publication, I do not want to ramble on as though I had all the space in the world. No pubiisher will attempt printing an *enormous* journal written by an unknown woman. It would be too much of a financial risk. Even I, with my ignorance of all matters pertaining to business, know this much. But they may print a small one.

My letter (written yesterday, the morrow of my drunken evening in the Blue Bonnet Room when I accosted the society salesman):

> Dearest Paul:
>
> I cannot simply live out my experiment here at the Hotel Henry without trying to justify or at least explain in letters my reasons for being here, and with fair regularity. You encouraged me to write whenever I felt I needed to clarify my thoughts. But you did tell me that I must not feel the need to *justify* my actions. However, I *do* feel the need to justify my actions, and I am certain that until the prayed-for metamorphosis has occurred I shall go on feeling just this need. Oh, how well I know that you would interrupt me at this point and warn me against expecting too much. So I shall say in lieu of metamorphosis, the prayed-for *improvement*. But until then I must justify myself every day. Perhaps you will get a letter every day. On some days the need to write lodges itself in my throat like a cry that must be uttered.
>
> As for the Turkish problem, I am coming to it. You must understand that I am an admirer of Western civilization; that

is, of the women who are members of this group. I feel myself that I fall short of being a member, that by some curious accident I was not born in Turkey but should have been. Because of my usual imprecision I cannot even tell how many countries belong to what we call Western Civilization, but I believe Turkey is the place where East meets West, isn't it? I can just about imagine the women there, from what I have heard about the country and the pictures I have seen of it. As for being troubled or obsessed by real Oriental women, I am not. (I refer to the Chinese, Japanese, Hindus, and so on.) Naturally I am less concerned with the Far Eastern women because there is no danger of my being like them. (The Turkish women are just near enough.) The Far Eastern ones are so very far away, at the opposite end of the earth, that they could easily be just as independent and masculine as the women of the Western world. The ones living in-between the two masculine areas would be soft and feminine. Naturally I don't believe this for a minute, but still, the real Orientals are so far away and such a mystery to me that it might as well be true. Whatever they are, it couldn't affect me. They look too different from the way I look. Whereas Turkish women don't. (Their figures are exactly like mine, alas!)

Now I shall come to the point. I know full well that you will consider the above discourse a kind of joke. Or if you don't, you will be irritated with me for making statements of such a sweeping and inaccurate nature. For surely you will consider the picture of the world that I present as inaccurate. I myself know that this concept of the women (all three sets—Western, Middle and Eastern) is a puerile one. It could even be called downright idiotic. Yet I assure you that I see things this way, if I relax even a little and look through my own eyes into what is really inside my head. (Though because of my talent for mimicry I am able to simulate looking through the eyes of an educated person when I wish to.) Since I am giving you such a frank picture of myself, I may as well go the whole hog and admit to you that my secret picture of the world is grossly inaccurate. I have completely forgotten to include in it any of the Latin countries. (France, Italy, Spain.) For instance, I have jumped from the Anglo world to the semi-Oriental as if there were no countries in between at all. I know that these exist. (I have even lived in two of them.)

But they do not fit into my scheme. I just don't think about the Latins very much, and this is less understandable than my not thinking about the Chinese or Javanese or Japanese women. You can see why without my having to explain it to you. I do know that the French women are more interested in sports than they used to be, and for all I know they may be indistinguishable from Anglo women by now. I haven't been to France recently so I can't be sure. But in any case the women of those countries don't enter into my picture of the world. Or shall I say that the fact of having forgotten utterly to consider them has not altered the way I visualize the division of the world's women? Incredible though it may seem to you, it hasn't altered anything. (My having forgotten all Latin countries, South America included.) I want you to know the whole truth about me. But don't imagine that I wouldn't be capable of concealing my ignorance from you if I wanted to. I am so wily and feminine that I could live by your side for a lifetime and deceive you afresh each day. But I will have no truck with feminine wiles. I know how they can absorb the hours of the day. Many women are delighted to sit around spinning their webs. It is an absorbing occupation, and the women feel they are getting somewhere. And so they are, but only for as long as the man is there to be deceived. And a wily woman alone is a pitiful sight to behold. Naturally.

I shall try to be honest with you so that I can live with you and yet won't be pitiful. Even if tossing my feminine tricks out the window means being left no better than an illiterate backwoodsman, or the bottom fish scraping along the ocean bed, I prefer to have it this way. Now I am too tired to write more. Though I don't feel that I have clarified enough or justified enough.

I shall write you soon about the effect the war has had upon me. I have spoken to you about it, but you have never seemed to take it very seriously. Perhaps seeing in black and white what I feel will affect your opinion of me. Perhaps you will leave me. I accept the challenge. My Hotel Henry experience includes this risk. I got drunk two nights ago. It's hard to believe that I am forty-seven, isn't it?

My love,
Emmy

Now that I have copied this letter into my journal (I had forgotten to make a carbon), I shall take my walk. My scheme included a few weeks of solitude at the Hotel Henry before attempting anything. I did not even intend to write in my journal as soon as I started to, but simply to sit about collecting my thoughts, waiting for the knots of habit to undo themselves. But after only a week here—two nights ago—I felt amazingly alone and disconnected from my past life, so I began my journal.

My first interesting contact was the salesman in the Blue Bonnet Room. I had heard about this eccentric through my in-laws, the Moores, before I ever came up here. My husband's cousin Laurence Moore told me about him when he heard I was coming. He said: "Take a walk through Grey and Bottle's Department Store, and you'll see a man with a lean red face and reddish hair selling materials by the bolt. That man has an income and is related to Hewitt Molain. He doesn't need to work. He was in my fraternity. Then he disappeared. The next I heard of him he was working there at Grey and Bottle's. I stopped by and said hello to him. For a nut he seemed like a very decent chap. You might even have a drink with him. I think he's quite up to general conversation."

I did not mention Laurence Moore to the society salesman because I thought it might irritate him. I lied and pretended to have been here for months, when actually this is still only my second week at the Hotel Henry. I want everyone to think I have been here a long time. Surely it is not to impress them. Is there anything impressive about a lengthy stay at the Hotel Henry? Any sane person would be alarmed that I should even ask such a question. I ask it because deep in my heart I *do* think a lengthy stay at the Hotel Henry is impressive. Very easy to see that I would, and even sane of me to think it impressive, but not sane of me to expect anyone else to think so, particularly a stranger. Perhaps I simply like to hear myself telling it. I hope so. I shall write some more tomorrow, but now I must go out. I am going to buy a supply of cocoa. When I'm not drunk I like to have a cup of cocoa before going to sleep. My husband likes it too.

• • •

She could not stand the overheated room a second longer. With some difficulty she raised the window, and the cold wind blew in. Some loose sheets of paper went skimming off the top of the desk and flattened themselves against the bookcase. She shut the window and they fell to the floor. The cold air had changed her mood. She looked down at the sheets of paper. They were part of the letter she had just copied. She picked them up: "*I don't feel that I have clarified enough or justified enough,*" she read. She closed her eyes and shook her head. She had been so happy copying this letter into her journal, but now her heart was faint as she scanned its scattered pages. "I have said nothing," she muttered to herself in alarm. "I have said nothing at all. I have not clarified my reasons for being at the Hotel Henry. I have not justified myself."

Automatically she looked around the room. A bottle of whiskey stood on the floor beside one of the legs of the bureau. She stepped forward, picked it up by the neck, and settled with it into her favorite wicker chair.

1948–1950 (?)

THE CHILDREN'S PARTY

JANE BOWLES

A FRAGMENT OF *Andrew McLain's story from the uncompleted novel* Out in the World. *It is a memory of Andrew's childhood.*

FROM *OUT IN THE WORLD* (ANDREW'S STORY)

[HE WAS WEARING] a green sleeveless tunic that buttoned below his knees, and a yellow paper ruff that scratched his chin . . . real corn sprouted out of the cardboard hat . . . He was the only vegetable in the room. He had felt ashamed of his costume and the weight of the corn on his head; but of all the costumes in the room his was the only one that seemed sweet and natural to him. The others were alarming. He wanted to stare at each one forever and at the same time he wanted to hide his face and look away.

His arm grazed the peculiarly dry flank of a papier-maché cow. The painted eye came close to his. Through a hole in the stiff pupil he saw another eye moving: his stomach wobbled and he hurried away, embarrassed and excited, the smell of glue in his nostrils. From a distance he watched the cow. He could still feel the touch of its dry powdery flank on his arm. It was the most important costume in the room. Other costumes clustered near it, one a policeman's suit with a club.

The cow moved backward and forward at the same pace. It stayed near the middle of the room. There were children inside it. He knew that. He gazed at it with a feeling of deep longing and admiration. It had a serene face, whether it walked backward or forward—and everyone was paying attention to it, talking and laughing with it and with the children inside. He longed for the cow and was dreaming a plan of how they would meet, and prayed that it would not come near him.

The cow was millions and millions of miles away from him, across the ocean, across several oceans and another ocean, where instead of land a whole new ocean began . . . When he reached the middle waters of the second ocean he would be able to see the cow's land, where it lived. But that would not be for many many weeks or months or years. When he reached the middle waters of the second ocean, the cow would tell the children that he was coming. Then the children and the cow would go to the water's edge each day and look out to sea . . . they would have a place ready for him inside the cow . . .

While he was deeply absorbed in his long dream a paper costume smashed into his face and chest. When he opened his eyes, everything was pink. He commenced to thrash at the paper but it backed away of itself. A little fat girl stood blinking at him. She was dressed as a big rose. Her face was beet red and her spectacles were gold-rimmed. She pointed her fat finger at his hat and started screaming. It was a happy scream. He watched her jump heavily from one foot to the other and listened to the faint paper crash of her petals . . .

"Corn for the cow—corn for the cow—corn for the cow—" she sang out.

They were coming toward him singing and clapping. He had seen the cow turn around slowly in the middle of the room. It was moving toward him with its serene face and its stiff painted eyes. When the cow was so near that he could smell the cardboard and the glue, he wanted to run from the room. He would have done so had not the paper hat been strapped firmly under his chin and the corn wired to its crown.

They were praising his costume, admiring the lettuce green ruff at his throat and the way the corn sprouted out of his hat. The cow's large and weightless head prodded the corn in a mild simulacrum of a cow eating.

He had his eyes shut when the corn wobbled ever so lightly on his head. He tried not to feel it. He was not ashamed of his costume, but it was not sweet and familiar to him any more. He would have run away but he stood there stiffly waiting because his costume was not his own any more. It belonged to the children inside the cow. . . .

1948–1950 (?)

EAST SIDE: NORTH AFRICA

JANE BOWLES

"East Side: North Africa" was published in April 1951 in Mademoiselle *as an account of Jane's experiences in Tangier. It was republished in the sixties as the story "Everything Is Nice," after a number of changes were made in order to convert it to a fictional piece. It is presented here in its original form as Jane's one nonfiction piece.*

THE HIGHEST STREET in this blue Arab town skirted the edge of a cliff. I walked over to the thick protecting wall and looked down. The tide was out and the flat scummy rocks below were swarming with skinny boys. All of them were wearing pleated bloomer-shaped knickers and little skullcaps as bright as colored candies. An Arab woman came up to the blue wall and stood next to me, grazing my hip with her basket. I pretended not to notice and kept my eyes fixed on a white dog that had just slipped down the side of a rock and was plunged up to his belly in a crater filled with sea water. The sound of his bark reverberating against the high cliff was earsplitting. The woman next to me jabbed the basket firmly into my ribs, and I looked down. It was stuffed full with a big dead porcupine; a pair of new yellow socks were folded on top of its pretty quills.

"That one is a porcupine," she said, pointing a finger stained with red henna into the basket.

I looked at her. She was dressed in a haik and the white cloth covering the lower half of her face was loose, about to fall down.

"I am Zodelia," she announced in a high voice, "and you are a friend of Cherifa and Betzoule." She spoke in Arabic. "You sit in their house and you eat in their house and you sleep in their house." The loose cloth slipped down below her chin and hung there like a bib. She did not pull it up.

Her information was correct. With the help of frequent gifts and a smattering of Arabic, I had made friends with two unmarried sisters who worked in the market. It was unheard of for any of these women whose lives were led almost entirely within a large circle of female relatives to associate with someone who was not only a stranger but a Nazarene. Nazarene is the popular term in Morocco for all non-Moslems of Western origin (out of Nazareth). Their association with me was a profitable one and so they were actually not deviating too far from the conventional relationship of any Arab market woman to any Nazarene, resident in the town or tourist.

Despite the fact that no other Nazarene woman had ever sat about with them before or for that matter with anyone they had ever known, these sisters and the other women in the family very soon took me for granted. They told me over and over again how much I missed my husband and my relatives and how much I enjoyed Moslem food and being with Moslems. They must have considered that this was sufficient reason for my extraordinary behavior, if they considered the situation from my point of view at all, which it is very possible they did not. They were perpetually weaving little plots to outwit me but this never dampened the spontaneity of their moods; they were conniving, generous and hospitable. Sometimes I played the part of a Nazarene fool being outwitted by two shrewd market women and it seemed to me that they were playing the parts of two shrewd market women outwitting a Nazarene fool.

There was considerable speculation about us in the market place and many of the women claimed that when the rest of the family was asleep the three of us sat smoking in the dark. Smoking is strictly forbidden to Moslem women though some of it goes on behind closed doors, even among decent married women and virgins. Cherifa and Betzoule had learned to smoke from a corrupt cousin who was little better than a whore. I did supply them with cigarettes occasionally, but the room which they shared alone (the other sisters who were married slept with their husbands and children) was, more often than not, filled with visiting female relatives and any such scandalous behavior was impossible. These visits often lasted for months.

"You sit in their house and you sleep in their house and you eat in their house," the woman went on, and I nodded in agreement. "Your name is Jeanie and you live in a hotel with other Nazarenes. How much does the hotel cost you?"

Fortunately a round loaf of bread dropped on the ground from inside the folds of her haik and I did not have to answer her question. She picked the bread up and stuffed it between the quills of the porcupine and the basket handle with some difficulty; then she set the basket down on top of the blue wall and turned to me with bright eyes.

"I am the people in the hotel," she said. "Watch me."

I was pleased because I knew she was about to present me with a little sketch. It would be delightful to watch, since almost every Arab speaks and gestures as if he had studied at a Moslem equivalent of the Comédie Française. At times it would seem to me that they were, all of them, acting in some continuous pageant all about life in a Moslem country.

"The people in the hotel," she announced, formally beginning her sketch. "I am the people in the hotel.

"Good-by, Jeanie, good-by. Where are you going?

"I am going to a Moslem house to visit my Moslem friends, Cherifa and Betzoule. I will sit in a Moslem room and eat Moslem food and sleep on a Moslem bed.

"Jeanie, Jeanie, when will you come back to us in the hotel and sleep in your own room?

"I will come back to you in three days. I will come back and sit in a Nazarene room and eat Nazarene food and sleep on a Nazarene bed. I will spend half the week with Moslem friends and half with—Nazarenes."

Her voice had a triumphant ring as she finished her sentence, dividing my time equally between the Moslems and the Nazarenes; then, without formally announcing the end of the sketch, she walked over to the wall and put one arm around her porcupine basket.

I knew that she did not actually believe that I spent exactly half of my life with Moslem friends and the other half with the Christians in the hotel. A story or a sketch about happiness must not be about what actually happens.

I moved along the wall and stood next to her. Down below, just at the edge of the cliff's shadow, an Arab woman was seated on a rock, washing her legs in one of the craters filled with sea water. The folds of her voluminous white haik were piled in her lap and she was huddled over them.

"She is looking at the ocean," Zodelia said to me.

She was not looking at the ocean. Huddled over the piles of cloth in her lap she could not possibly have seen it without straightening up and turning around.

"She is *not* looking at the ocean," I said.

"She is looking at the ocean," Zodelia repeated, as if I had not spoken. I decided to change the subject.

"Why do you have a porcupine with you?" I asked her, though I knew that some of the Arabs, particularly the country people, enjoyed eating them.

"It is a present for my aunt," she told me. "Do you like it?"

"Yes," I said, "I like porcupines. I like big porcupines and little ones too."

She seemed bewildered and then bored. I had somehow ruined the conversation by mentioning little porcupines. I could tell this by her expression.

"Where is your mother?" she asked me.

"My mother is in my country in her own house," I said automatically; I had answered this question a hundred times.

"Why don't you write her a letter and tell her to come here? You can take her on a promenade and show her the ocean. After that she can go back to her own country and sit in her house." She picked up her basket and adjusted the cloth over her mouth. "Would you like to go to a wedding?" she asked me.

I said that I would love to go to a wedding, and we started off down the wavy blue street, heading into the wind.

When we came to a little store, built like a booth, she stopped.

"Stand here," she said, "I want to buy something."

After studying the counter for a minute or two, she poked me and pointed to some cakes inside a square box with glass sides. "Nice," she asked me, "or not nice?"

These cakes were actually not very nice. They were dusty looking and coated with thin, ugly-colored icing. They were called *galletas Ortiz* and they were made in Spain.

"They are very nice," I said to her and bought her a dozen cakes which I gave her as a gift. She thanked me briefly and we walked on.

After a while we turned off the street into a blind alley and started downhill. When we had nearly reached the end of this alley, she stopped at a heavy studded door on our right and lifted the knocker wrought in the shape of Fatima's hand.

"The wedding is here?" I said to her.

"There is no wedding here," she corrected me, shaking her head and looking grave.

A child opened the door for us and quickly hid behind it, covering her face. I followed Zodelia across the black and white tiles of a closed patio. The walls like those outside were washed in blue and a cold light shone through the broken glass panes far above our heads. Zodelia stopped at one of three doors giving onto this patio where a row of pointed slippers barred the threshold. She stepped out of her own slippers and set them down near the others. I followed her example, which took me quite a little time because there was a knot in my laces.

When I was ready, Zodelia took my hand and pulled me with her into a dimly lit room, where she led me over to a mattress against the wall.

"Sit," she told me, and I obeyed her; then without further comment she walked off, heading for the far end of the room, which was shaped like a trolley car.

At first, because my eyes were blinded by daylight, it seemed to me that Zodelia was disappearing down a long corridor, but after a minute or two I made out the short end wall and the brass bars of a bed glowing weakly in the darkness. Satisfied that she would not vanish entirely, I looked around me.

Only a few feet away an old lady was seated in the middle of the carpet directly underneath the only light bulb in the room, which hung on a long wire from the unbelievably high ceiling. She was wearing a sumptuous green and purple dress made of a heavy material suitable for draperies. It was solidly embroidered with dark, glossy flowers. Through the many vents and holes in the material I could see the printed cotton dress and the tan sweater she was wearing underneath.

On the mattress opposite mine several women were seated under a life-size photograph of the sultan, and farther along on this same mattress, which like mine ran almost the full length of the room, three babies were sleeping in a row. Each one of them lay close to the wall with his head resting on a fancy cushion.

"Is it nice here?" It was Zodelia, returning. She had removed her haik, and I was horrified to see that she was wearing a black crepe afternoon dress of modern European design. It hung unbelted all the way down to her ankles, almost grazing her bare feet. The hem was lopsided. More and more Moroccan women (in the larger cities) are beginning to wear European-made dresses or approximations of these. In the street they are fortunately still concealed by Moorish haiks or jellabas.

"Is it nice here?" Zodelia asked again, crouching on her haunches opposite the old lady and pointing at her. "That one is Tetum," she said to me. The old lady plunged both hands into a bowl on her lap that was filled with raw meat and began shaping the meat into little balls.

"Tetum," echoed the ladies on the mattress. Each one of these women seemed to be wearing several dresses at once and all of them had bound their heads in a variety of different-colored materials. Their clothes did not show any Western influence.

"This Nazarene," said Zodelia, gesturing in my direction, "spends half her time in a Moslem house with Moslem friends and the other half in a Nazarene hotel with other Nazarenes."

"That's nice," said the women opposite. "Half with Moslem friends and half with Nazarenes." The old lady looked very stern and I noticed that her bony cheeks were tattooed with tiny blue crosses. "Why?" she asked abruptly in a deep voice. "*Why* does she spend half her time with Moslem friends and half with Nazarenes?" She fixed her eyes on Zodelia never ceasing to shape the meat with swift and accurate fingers. Her knuckles, like her cheekbones, were tattooed with blue crosses.

Zodelia stared back at her with a stupid look on her face. "I don't know why," she answered, shrugging one fat shoulder. It was obvious that the picture she had been painting of my life had suddenly lost all its charm for her.

"Is she crazy?" the old lady asked.

"No," Zodelia answered listlessly. "She is not crazy."

There were shrieks of laughter from the mattress.

The old lady fixed her sharp eyes on me. They were heavily outlined in black. "Where is your husband?" she asked.

"He's traveling in the desert."

"Selling things," Zodelia put in.

Among the Arab women this had become the most popular explanation for my husband's trips. I had not tried to contradict it.

"Where is your mother?" the old lady asked.

"My mother is in our country in her own house."

"Why don't you go and sit with your mother in her own house?" she scolded. "The hotel costs lots of money."

I felt a sudden foolish urge, despite my limited vocabulary, to tell these women about New York City; doubly foolish because, even had I been able to speak fluent Arabic, they might have listened to what I told them with polite smiles but all the while, in their hearts, they would have pictured New York as a walled Moslem town with a predominantly Arab population. Nonetheless I was determined to say something about it and so I decided to tell them about the traffic. This was the simplest subject I could have chosen since even the Arabs use either Spanish or French words for all recent mechanical inventions such as automobiles.

"In the city where I was born," I began, "there are many, many automobiles and many, many trucks."

The women on the mattress were smiling pleasantly. "Is that true?" the center one remarked in a social tone.

"I hate trucks," I told them with feeling.

"She hates trucks," Zodelia explained.

The old lady lifted the bowl of meat off her lap and set it down on the carpet. "Trucks are nice," she said severely.

"That's true . . ." the women agreed, after only a moment's hesitation. "Trucks are very nice."

"Do you like trucks?" I asked Zodelia; I thought that perhaps because of our greater intimacy she might agree with me.

"Yes," she said, "they are nice. Trucks are very nice." She seemed lost in meditation but only for a moment. "Everything is nice," she announced with a look of triumph.

"It's the truth," the women joined in from their mattress. "Everything is nice."

They all looked happy with the exception of the old lady who was still frowning. "Aeshcha!" she hollered, twisting her neck so that her voice could be heard in the patio. "Bring the tea!"

In a minute several little girls came into the room carrying the tea things and a low round table.

"Pass the cakes to the Nazarene," the old lady told the smallest child, who was carrying a cut-glass dish. It was filled with the dry Spanish cakes I had bought for Zodelia. I did not want any of them. I wanted to leave.

"Eat," the women called out from their mattress. "Eat the cakes."

The child pushed the glass dish forward.

I knew that it would be rude of me to leave now without drinking any tea or eating any of the cakes I had myself bought for Zodelia, but it would be equally rude of me to stay just a little while longer and drink only one glass of tea. I would have to stay at least another hour and drink the minimum three glasses, and even after that the women would protest just as loudly when I finally stood up to leave as I knew they were about to now after this brief visit. Moroccan etiquette demands that a host make every effort to keep his guest from leaving, even when the guest has been sitting around for ten or eleven hours, which is very often the case. One is sometimes detained physically but it is a formality. I searched my mind for some excuse, any excuse, for my abrupt departure; though none would be acceptable to them, I knew that it was expected of me to make one.

"The dinner at the hotel is ready," I said, standing up. Since these women do not concern themselves with fixed meal hours this was the most ineffectual apology I could have made. They do not expect the truth, of course, but they expect an excuse to sound like one.

"Drink tea," said the old woman scornfully. "Later you will sit with the other Nazarenes and eat their food."

"The Nazarenes will be furious if I'm late," I lied more and more stupidly. "They will hit me." I tried to look wild and fearful.

"Drink tea. They will not hit you," the old woman said briefly. "Sit down and drink tea."

The child offered the glass dish once more, but I backed away toward the door.

At last, after a long and tiresome exchange of apologies on my part and shrieks of protest on theirs, I walked out of the room backward, raving to them about the delights of my visit.

Outside I sat down on the black and white tiles to lace my shoes. Only Zodelia followed me into the patio.

"Come back," they were calling, "come back into the room."

I noticed that the porcupine basket was standing only a few feet away from me against a wall. "Is that old lady in the room your aunt—the one you were bringing the porcupine to?" I asked her.

"No," she answered, "she is not my aunt."

"Where is your aunt?"

"My aunt is in her own house."

"When will you take the porcupine to her?" I wanted to keep talking so that she would be distracted and forget to fuss about my departure.

"The porcupine sits here," she said firmly, "in my own house."

There are certain Arab fabrications that seem to be utterly without motive, at least none that any Western mind can possibly fathom. Europeans living in Morocco often speak of something they call the "Oriental wall." I decided not to ask her about the wedding.

When we reached the heavy studded door she opened it just enough to let me through. "Good-by," she said. "I shall see you tomorrow, if Allah wills it."

"When?"

"At four o'clock."

It was obvious that she was choosing this hour at random. There was no way of determining whether or not she would actually turn up and if so at what time. One is not safe in assuming that they will be late.

Before closing the door behind me, she pressed two of the dry Spanish cakes into the palm of my hand.

"Eat them," she urged me graciously. "Eat them at the hotel with the other Nazarenes."

I started up the steep alley, headed once again for the walk along the cliff. The houses on either side of me were so close I could smell the dampness of the walls and feel it on my cheeks like thicker air.

When I reached the place where I had met Zodelia I went over to the wall and leaned on it. Although the sun had sunk behind the houses in back of me, the sky was still luminous and the color of the blue wall had deepened. I rubbed my fingers along it; the wash was fresh and a little of the powdery stuff came off; but no matter how often I walked through these streets reaching out to touch the chalky blue wash on the houses . . . on the walls, I could never satisfy my longing for the town.

I remember that once I reached out to touch the beautiful and powdery face of a clown because his face had awakened some longing; it happened at a little circus but not when I was a child.

New York, 1951

A MAN MUST NOT BE VERY MOSLEM

PAUL BOWLES

THE AUTHOR OF a large number of travel pieces, Paul collected a selection of them (including "A Man Must Not Be Very Moslem") in the volume Their Heads Are Green and Their Hands Are Blue.

ABOARD M/S TARSUS,
TURKISH MARITIME LINES
SEPTEMBER 25, 1953

WHEN I ANNOUNCED my intention of bringing Abdeslam along to Istanbul, the general opinion of my friends was that there were a good many more intelligent things to do in the world than to carry a Moroccan Moslem along with one to Turkey. I don't know. He may end up as a dead weight, but my hope is that he will turn out instead to be a kind of passkey to the place. He knows how to deal with Moslems, and he has the Moslem sense of seemliness and protocol. He has also an intuitive gift for the immediate understanding of a situation and at the same time is completely lacking in reticence or inhibitions. He can lie so well that he convinces himself straightway, and he is a master at bargaining; it is a black day for him when he has to pay the asking price for anything. He never knows what is printed on a sign because he is totally illiterate; besides, even if he did know he would pay no attention, for he is wholly deficient in respect for law. If you mention that this or that thing is forbidden, he is contemptuous: "Agh! a decree for the wind!" Obviously he is far better equipped than I to squeeze the last drop of adventure out of any occasion. I, unfortunately, *can* read signs but can't lie or bargain effectively, and will forgo any joy rather than risk unpleasantness or reprimand from whatever quarter. At all events, the die is cast: Abdeslam is here on the ship.

My first intimation of Turkey came during tea this afternoon, as the ship was leaving the Bay of Naples. The orchestra was playing a tango which finally established its identity, after several reprises, as the "Indian Love Call," and the cliffs of Capri were getting in the way of the sunset. I glanced at a biscuit that I was about to put into my mouth, then stopped the operation to examine it more closely. It was an ordinary little arrowroot tea-biscuit, and on it were embossed the words HAYD PARK. Contemplating this edible tidbit, I recalled what friends had told me of the amusing havoc that results when the Turks phoneticize words borrowed from other languages. These metamorphosed words have a way of looking like gibberish until you say them aloud, and then more likely than not they resolve themselves into perfectly comprehensible English or French or, even occasionally, Arabic. SKOÇ TUID looks like nothing; suddenly it becomes Scotch Tweed. TUALET, TRENÇKOT, OTOTEKNIK and SEKSOLOJI likewise reveal their messages as one stares at them. Synthetic orthography is a constantly visible reminder of Turkey's determination to be "modern." The country has turned its back on the East and Eastern concepts, not with the simple yearning of other Islamic countries to be European or to acquire American techniques, but with a conscious will to transform itself from the core outward—even to destroy itself culturally, if need be.

TARABYA, BOSPORUS

This afternoon it was blustery and very cold. The water in the tiny Sea of Marmara was choppy and dark, laced with froth; the ship rolled more heavily than it had at any time during its three days out on the open Mediterranean. If the first sight of Istanbul was impressive, it was because the perfect hoop of a rainbow painted across the lead-colored sky ahead kept one from looking at the depressing array of factory smokestacks along the western shore. After an hour's moving backward and forward in the harbor, we were close enough to see the needles of the minarets (and how many of them!) in black against the final flare-up of the sunset. It was a poetic introduction, and like the introductions to most books, it had very little to do with what followed. "Poetic" is not among the adjectives you would use to describe the disembarkation. The pier was festive; it looked like an elegant waterside restaurant or one of the larger Latin-American airports—brilliantly illumined, awnings flapping, its decks mobbed with screaming people.

The customs house was the epitome of confusion for a half-hour or so; when eventually an inspector was assigned us, we were fortunate enough to be let through without having to open anything. The taxis were parked in the dark on the far side of a vast puddle of water, for it had been raining. I had determined on a hotel in Istanbul proper, rather than one of those in Beyoğlu, across the Golden Horn, but the taxi driver and his front-seat companion were loath to take me there. "All hotels in Beyoğlu," they insisted. I knew better and did some insisting of my own. We shot into the stream of traffic, across the Galata Bridge, to the hotel of my choosing. Unhappily I had neglected, on the advice of various friends back in Italy, to reserve a room. There was none to be had. And so on, from hotel to hotel there in Istanbul, back across the bridge and up the hill to every establishment in Beyoğlu. Nothing, nothing. There are three international conventions in progress here, and besides, it is vacation time in Turkey; everything is full. Even the m/s *Tarsus*, from which we just emerged, as well as another ship in the harbor, has been called into service tonight to be used as a hotel. By half past ten I accepted the suggestion of being driven twenty-five kilometers up the Bosporus to a place, where they had assured me by telephone that they had space.

"Do you want a room with bath?" they asked.

I said I did.

"We haven't any," they told me.

"Then I want a room without bath."

"We have one." That was that.

Once we had left the city behind and were driving along the dark road, there was nothing for Abdeslam to do but catechize the two Turks in front. Obviously they did not impress him as being up-to-the-mark Moslems, and he started by testing their knowledge of the Koran. I thought they were replying fairly well, but he was contemptuous. "They don't know anything," he declared in Moghrebi. Going into English, he asked them: "How many times one day you pray?"

They laughed.

"People can sleep in mosque?" he pursued. The driver was busy navigating the curves in the narrow road, but his companion, who spoke a special brand of English all his own, spoke for him. "Not slep in mosque many people every got hoss," he explained.

"You make sins?" continued Abdeslam, intent on unearthing the hidden flaws in the behavior of these foreigners. "Pork, wine?"

The other shrugged his shoulders. "Muslim people every not eat pork not drink wine but maybe one hundred year ago like that. Now different."

"*Never* different!" shouted Abdeslam sternly. "You not good Moslems here. People not happy. You have bad government. Not like Egypt. Egypt have good government. Egypt one-hundred-percent Moslem."

The other was indignant. "Everybody happy," he protested. "Happy with Egypt too for religion. But the Egypts sometimes fight with Egypts. Arab fight Arabs. Why? I no like Egypt. I in Egypt. I ask my way. They put me say bakhshish. If you ask in Istanbul, you say I must go my way, he can bring you, but he no say give *bakhshish*. Before, few people up, plenty people down. Now, you make your business, I make my business. You take your money, I take my money. Before, *you* take *my* money. You rich with *my* money. Before, Turkey like Egypt with Farouk." He stopped to let all this sink in, but Abdeslam was not interested.

"Egypt very good country," he retorted, and there was no more conversation until we arrived. At the hotel the driver's comrade was describing a fascinating new ideology known as democracy. From the beginning of the colloquy I had my notebook out, scribbling his words in the dark as fast as he spoke them. They express the average uneducated Turk's reaction to the new concept. It was only in 1950 that the first completely democratic elections were held. (Have there been any since?) To Abdeslam, who is a traditionally-minded Moslem, the very idea of democracy is meaningless. It is impossible to explain it to him; he will not listen. If an idea is not explicitly formulated in the Koran, it is wrong; it came either directly from Satan or via the Jews, and there is no need to discuss it further.

This hotel, built at the edge of the lapping Bosporus, is like a huge wooden box. At the base of the balustrade of the grand staircase leading up from the lobby, one on each side, are two life-sized ladies made of lead and painted with white enamel in the hope of making them look like marble. The dining room's decorations are of a more recent period—the early 'twenties. There are high murals that look as though the artist had made a study of Boutet de Monvel's fashion drawings of the era; long-necked, low-waisted females in cloches and thigh-length skirts, presumably picnicking on the shores of the Bosporus.

At dinner we were the only people eating, since it was nearly midnight. Abdeslam took advantage of this excellent opportunity by delivering an impassioned harangue (partly in a mixture of Moghrebi and Standard Arabic and partly in English), with the result that by the end of the meal we had fourteen waiters and bus boys crowded around the table listening. Then someone thought of fetching the chef. He arrived glistening with sweat and beaming; he had been brought because he spoke more Arabic than the others, which was still not very much. "Old-fashioned Moslem," explained the head-waiter. Abdeslam immediately put him through the *chehade,* and he came off with flying colors, reciting it word for word along with Abdeslam: "*Achhad-douanlaillahainallah. . . .*" The faces of the younger men expressed unmistakable admiration, as well as pleasure at the approval of the esteemed foreigner, but none of them could perform the chef's feat. Presently the manager of the hotel came in, presumably to see what was going on in the dining room at this late hour. Abdeslam asked for the check, and objected when he saw that it was written with Roman characters. "Arabic!" he demanded. "You Moslem? Then bring check in Arabic." Apologetically the manager explained that writing in Arabic was "dangerous," and had been known on occasion to put the man who did it into jail. To this he added, just to make things quite clear, that any man who veiled his wife also went to jail. "A man must not be *very* Moslem," he said. But Abdeslam had had enough. "I *very very* Moslem," he announced. We left the room.

The big beds stand high off the floor and haven't enough covers on them. I have spread my topcoat over me; it is cold and I should like to leave the windows shut, but the mingled stenches coming from the combined shower-lavatory behind a low partition in the corner are so powerful that such a course is out of the question. The winds moving down from the Black Sea will blow over me all night. Sometime after we had gone to bed, following a long silence during which I thought he had fallen asleep, Abdeslam called over to me: "That Mustapha Kemal was carrion! He ruined his country. The son of a dog!" Because I was writing, and also because I am not sure exactly where I stand in this philosophical dispute, I said: "You're right. *Allah imsik bekhir.*"

SIRKECI, SEPTEMBER 29

We are installed at Sirkeci on the Istanbul side, in the hotel I had first wanted. Outside the window is a taxi stand. From early morning onward there is the continuous racket of men shouting and horns being blown in a struggle to keep recently arrived taxis from edging in ahead of those that have been waiting in line. The general prohibition of horn-blowing, which is in effect everywhere in the city, doesn't seem to apply here. The altercations are bitter, and everyone gets involved in them. Taxi drivers in Istanbul are something of a race apart. They are the only social group who systematically try to take advantage of the foreign visitor. In the ships, restaurants, cafés, the prices asked of the newcomer are the same as those paid by the inhabitants. (In the bazaars buying is automatically a matter of wrangling; that is understood.) The cab drivers, however, are more actively acquisitive. For form's sake, their vehicles are equipped with meters, but their method of using them is such that they might better do without them. You get into a cab whose meter registers seventeen liras thirty kuruş, ask the man to turn it back to zero and start again, and he laughs and does nothing. When you get out it registers eighteen liras eighty kuruş. You give him the difference—one lira and a half. Never! He may want two and a half or three and a half or a good deal more, but he will not settle for what seems equitable according to the meter. Since most tourists pay what they are asked and go on their way, he is not prepared for an argument, and he is likely to let his temper run away with him if you are recalcitrant. There is also the pre-arranged-price system of taking a cab. Here the driver goes as slowly and by as circuitous a route as possible, calling out the general neighborhood of his destination for all in the streets to hear, so that he can pick up extra fares en route. He will, unless you assert yourself, allow several people to pile in on top of you until there is literally no room left for you to breathe.

The streets are narrow, crooked and often precipitous; traffic is very heavy, and there are many tramcars and buses. The result is that the taxis go like the wind whenever there is a space of a few yards ahead, rushing to the extreme left to get around obstacles before oncoming traffic reaches them. I am used to Paris and Mexico, both cities of evil repute where taxis are concerned, but I think Istanbul might possibly win first prize for thrill-giving.

One day our driver had picked up two extra men and mercifully put them in front with him, when he spied a girl standing on the curb and slowed down to take her in, too. A policeman saw his maneuver and did not approve: one girl with five men seemed too likely to cause a disturbance. He blew his whistle menacingly. The driver, rattled, swerved sharply to the left, to pretend he had never thought of such a thing as stopping to pick up a young lady. There was a crash and we were thrown forward off the seat. We got out; the last we saw of the driver, he was standing in the middle of the street by his battered car, screaming at the man he had hit, and holding up all traffic. Abdeslam took down his license number in the hope of persuading me to instigate a lawsuit.

Since the use of the horn is proscribed, taxi drivers can make their presence known only by reaching out the window and pounding violently on the outside of the door. The scraping of the tramcars and the din of the enormous horse-drawn carts thundering over the cobbled pavements make it difficult to judge just how much the horn interdiction reduces noise. The drivers also have a pretty custom of offering cigarettes at the beginning of the journey; this is to soften up the victim for the subsequent kill. On occasion they sing for you. One morning I was entertained all the way from Sulemaniye to Taksim with "Jezebel" and "Come On-a My House." In such cases the traffic warnings on the side of the car are done in strict rhythm.

Istanbul is a jolly place; it's hard to find any sinister element in it, notwithstanding all the spy novels for which it provides such a handsome setting. A few of the older buildings are of stone; but many more of them are built of wood which looks as though it had never been painted. The cupolas and minarets rise above the disorder of the city like huge gray fungi growing out of a vast pile of ashes. For disorder is the visual keynote of Istanbul. It is not slovenly—only untidy; not dirty—merely dingy and drab. And just as you cannot claim it to be a beautiful city, neither can you accuse it of being uninteresting. Its steep hills and harbor views remind you a little of San Francisco; its overcrowded streets recall Bombay; its transportation facilities evoke Venice, for you can go many places by boats which are continually making stops. (It costs threepence to get across to Üsküdar in Asia.) Yet the streets are strangely reminiscent of an America that has almost disappeared. Again and again I have been reminded of some New England mill town in the time of my childhood. Or a row of little houses will suggest a back street in Stapleton, on Staten Island. It is a city whose esthetic is that of the unlikely and incongruous, a photographer's paradise. There is no native quarter, or, if you like, it is all native quarter. Beyoğlu, the site of the so-called better establishments, concerns itself as little with appearances as do the humbler regions on the other side of the bridges.

You wander down the hill toward Karaköy. Above the harbor with its thousands of caïques, rowboats, tugs, freighters and ferries, lies a pall of smoke and haze through which you can see the vague outline of the domes and towers of Aya Sofia, Sultan Ahmet, Süleyimaniye; but to the left and far above all that there is a pure region next to the sky where the mountains in Asia glisten with snow. As you descend the alleys of steps that lead to the water's level, there are more and more people around you. In Karaköy itself just to make progress along the sidewalk requires the best part of your attention. You would think that all of the city's million and a quarter inhabitants were in the streets on their way to or from Galata Bridge. By Western European standards it is not a well-dressed crowd. The chaotic sartorial effect achieved by the populace in Istanbul is not necessarily due to poverty, but rather to a divergent conception of the uses to which European garments should be put. The mass is not an ethnically homogeneous one. The types of faces range from Levantine through Slavic to Mongoloid, the last belonging principally to the soldiers from eastern Anatolia. Apart from language there seems to be no one common element, not even shabbiness, since there are usually a few men and women who do understand how to wear their clothing.

Galata Bridge has two levels, the lower of which is a great dock whence the boats leave to go up the Golden Horn and the Bosporus, across to the Asiatic suburbs, and down to the islands in the Sea of Marmara. The ferries are there, of all sizes and shapes, clinging to the edge like water beetles to the side of a floating stick. When you get across to the other side of the bridge there are just as many people and just as much traffic, but the buildings are older and the streets narrower, and you begin to realize that you are, after all, in an oriental city. And if you expect to see anything more than the "points of interest," you are going to have to wander for miles on foot. The character of Istanbul derives from a thousand disparate, nonevident details; only by observing the variations and repetitions of such details can you begin to get an idea of the patterns they form. Thus the importance of wandering. The dust is bad. After a few hours of it I usually have a sore throat. I try to get off the main arteries, where the horses and drays clatter by, and stay in the alleyways, which are too narrow for anything but foot traffic. These lanes occasionally open up into little squares with rugs hanging on the walls and chairs placed in the shade of the grapevines overhead. A few Turks will be sitting about drinking coffee; the *narghilehs* bubble. Invariably, if I stop and gaze a moment, someone asks me to have some coffee, eat a few green walnuts and share his pipe. An irrational disinclination to become involved keeps me from accepting, but today Abdeslam did accept, only to find to his chagrin that the narghileh contained tobacco, and not kif or hashish as he had expected.

Cannabis sativa and its derivatives are strictly prohibited in Turkey, and the natural correlative of this proscription is that alcohol, far from being frowned upon as it is in other Moslem lands, is freely drunk; being a government monopoly it can be bought at any cigarette counter. This fact is no mere detail; it is of primary social importance, since the psychological effects of the two substances are diametrically opposed to each other. Alcohol blurs the personality by loosening inhibitions. The drinker feels, temporarily at least, a sense of participation. Kif abolishes no inhibitions; on the contrary it reinforces them, pushes the individual further back into the recesses of his own isolated personality, pledging him to contemplation and inaction. It is to be expected that there should be a close relationship between the culture of a given society and the means used by its members to achieve release and euphoria. For Judaism and Christianity the means has always been alcohol; for Islam it has been hashish. The first is dynamic in its effects, the other static. If a nation wishes, however mistakenly, to Westernize itself, first let it give up hashish. The rest will follow, more or less as a matter of course. Conversely, in a Western country, if a whole segment of the population desires, for reasons of protest (as has happened in the United States), to isolate itself in a radical fashion from the society around it, the quickest and surest way is for it to replace alcohol by cannabis.

OCTOBER 2

Today in our wanderings we came upon the old fire tower at the top of the hill behind Süleymaniye, and since there was no sign at the door forbidding entry, we stepped in and began to climb the one hundred and eighty rickety wooden steps of the spiral staircase leading to the top. (Abdeslam counted them.) When we were almost at the top, we heard strains of Indian music; a radio up there was tuned in to New Delhi. At the same moment a good deal of water came pouring down upon us through the cracks above. We decided to beat a retreat, but then the boy washing the stairs saw us and insisted that we continue to the top and sit awhile. The view up there was magnificent; there is no better place from which to see the city. A charcoal fire was burning in a brazier, and we had tea and listened to some Anatolian songs which presently came over the air. Outside the many windows the wind blew, and the city below, made quiet by distance, spread itself across the rolling landscape on every side, its roof tiles pink in the autumn sun.

Later we sought out Pandeli's, a restaurant I had heard about but not yet found. This time we managed to discover it, a dilapidated little building squeezed in among harness shops and wholesale fruit stores, unprepossessing but cozy, and with the best food we have found in Istanbul. We had *pirinççorba, beyendeli kebap, barbunya fasulya* and other good things. In the middle of the meal, probably while chewing on the *taze makarna,* I bit my lip. My annoyance with the pain was not mitigated by hearing Abdeslam remark unsympathetically, "If you'd keep your mouth open when you chew, like everybody else, you wouldn't have accidents like this." Pandeli's is the only native restaurant I have seen which doesn't sport a huge refrigerated showcase packed with food. You are usually led to this and told to choose what you want to eat. In the glare of the fluorescent lighting the food looks pallid and untempting, particularly the meat, which has been hacked into unfamiliar-looking cuts. During your meal there is usually a radio playing ancient jazz; occasionally a Turkish or Syrian number comes up. Although the tea is good, it is not good enough to warrant its being served as though it were nectar, in infinitesimal glasses that can be drained at one gulp. I often order several at once, and this makes for confusion. When you ask for water, you are brought a tiny bottle capped with tinfoil. Since it is free of charge, I suspect it of being simple tap water; perhaps I am unjust.

In the evening we went to the very drab red-light district in Beyoğlu, just behind the British Consulate General. The street was mobbed with men and boys. In the entrance door of each house was a small square opening, rather like those through which one used to be denied access to American speak-easies, and framed in each opening, against the dull yellow light within, was a girl's head.

The Turks are the only Moslems I have seen who seem to have got rid of that curious sentiment (apparently held by all followers of the True Faith), that there is an inevitable and hopeless difference between themselves and non-Moslems. Subjectively, at least, they have managed to bridge the gulf created by their religion, that abyss which isolates Islam from the rest of the world. As a result the visitor feels a specific connection with them which is not the mere one-sided sympathy the well-disposed traveler has for the more basic members of other cultures, but is something desired and felt by them as well. They are touchingly eager to understand and please—so eager, indeed, that they often neglect to listen carefully and consequently get things all wrong. Their good will, however, seldom flags, and in the long run this more than compensates for being given the breakfast you did not order, or being sent in the opposite direction from the one you in which you wanted to go. Of course, there is the linguistic barrier. One really needs to know Turkish to live in Istanbul and because my ignorance of all Altaic languages is total, I suffer. The chances are nineteen in twenty that when I give an order things will go wrong, even when I get hold of the housekeeper who speaks French and who assures me calmly that all the other employees are idiots. The hotel is considered by my guidebook to be a "de luxe" establishment—the highest category. Directly after the "de luxe" listings come the "first class" places, which it describes in its own mysterious rhetoric: "These hotels have somewhat luxury, but are still comfortable with every convenience." Having seen the lobbies of several of the hostelries thus pigeonholed, complete with disemboweled divans and abandoned perambulators, I am very thankful to be here in my de-luxe suite, where the telephone is white so that I can see the cockroaches on the instrument before I lift it to my lips. At least the insects are discreet and die obligingly under a mild blast of DDT. It is fortunate I came here: my two insecticide bombs would never have lasted out a sojourn in a first-class hotel.

OCTOBER 6

Santa Sophia? Aya Sofya now, not a living mosque but a dead one, like those of Kairouan which can no longer be used because they have been profaned by the feet of infidels. Greek newspapers have carried on propaganda campaigns designed to turn the clock back, reinstate Aya Sofya as a tabernacle of the Orthodox Church. The move was obviously foredoomed to failure; after having used it as a mosque for five centuries the Moslems would scarcely relish seeing it put back into the hands of the Christians. And so now it is a museum which contains nothing but its own architecture. Sultan Ahmet, the mosque just across the park, is more to my own taste; but then, a corpse does not bear comparison to a living organism. Sultan Ahmet is still a place of worship, the *imam* is allowed to wear the classical headgear, the heavy final syllable of Allah's name reverberates in the air under the high dome, boys *dahven* in distant corners as they memorize surat from the Koran. When the tourists stumble over the prostrate forms of men in prayer, or blatantly make use of their light meters and Rolleiflexes, no one pays any attention. To Abdeslam this incredible invasion of privacy was tantamount to lack of respect for Islam; it fanned the coals of his resentment into flame. (In his country no unbeliever can put even one foot into a mosque.) As he wandered about, his exclamations of indignation became increasingly audible. He started out with the boys by suggesting to them that it was their great misfortune to be living in a country of widespread sin. They looked at him blankly and went on with their litanies. Then in a louder voice he began to criticize the raiment of the worshipers, because they wore socks and slippers on their feet and on their heads berets or caps with the visors at the back. He knows that the wearing of the *tarboosh* is forbidden by law, but his hatred of Kemal Ataturk, which has been growing hourly ever since his arrival, had become too intense, I suppose, for him to be able to repress it any longer. His big moment came when the imam entered. He approached the venerable gentleman with elaborate salaams which were enthusiastically reciprocated. Then the two retired into a private room, where they remained for ten minutes or so. When Abdeslam came out there were tears in his eyes and he wore an expression of triumph. "Ah, you see?" he cried, as we emerged into the street. "That poor man is very, *very* unhappy. They have only one day of Ramadan in the year." Even I was a little shocked to hear that the traditional month had been whittled down to a day. "This is an accursed land," he went on. "When we get power we'll soak it in petrol and set it afire and burn everyone in it. May it forever be damned! And all these dogs living in it, I pray Allah they may be thrown into the fires of Gehennem. Ah, if we only had our power back for one day, we Moslems! May Allah speed that day when we shall ride into Turkey and smash their government and all their works of Satan!" The imam, it seems, had been delighted beyond measure to see a young man who still had the proper respect for religion; he had complained bitterly that the youth of Turkey was spiritually lost.

Today I had lunch with a woman who has lived here a good many years. As a Westerner, she felt that the important thing to notice about Turkey is the fact that from having been in the grip of a ruthless dictatorship it has slowly evolved into a modern democracy, rather than having followed the more usual reverse process. Even Ataturk was restrained by his associates from going all the way in his iconoclasm, for what he wanted was a Turkish adaptation of what he had seen happen in Russia. Religion was to him just as much of an opiate in one country as in another. He managed to deal it a critical blow here, one which may yet prove to have been fatal. Last year an American, a member of Jehovah's Witnesses, arrived, and as is the custom with members of that sect, stood on the street handing out brochures. But not for long. The police came, arrested him, put him in jail, and eventually effected his expulsion from the country. This action, insisted my lunch partner, was not taken because the American was distributing Christian propaganda; had he been distributing leaflets advocating the reading of the Koran, it's likely that his punishment would have been more severe.

OCTOBER 10

At the beginning of the sixteenth century, Selim the Grim captured from the Shah of Persia one of the most fantastic pieces of furniture I have ever seen. The trophy was the poor Shah's throne, a simple but massive thing made of chiseled gold, decorated with hundreds of enormous emeralds. I went to see it today at the Topkapi Palace. There was a bed to match, also of emerald-studded gold. After a moment of looking, Abdeslam ran out of the room where these incredible objects stood into the courtyard, and could not be coaxed back in. "Too many riches are bad for the eyes," he explained. I could not agree; I thought them beautiful. I tried to make him tell me the exact reason for his sudden flight, but he found it difficult to give me a rational explanation of his behavior. "You know that gold and jewels are sinful," he began. To get him to go on, I said I knew. "And if you look at sinful things for very long you can go crazy; you know that. And I don't want to go crazy." I was willing to take the chance, I replied, and I went back in to see more.

OCTOBER 16

These last few days I have spent entirely at the covered souks. I discovered the place purely by accident, since I follow no plan in my wanderings about the city. You climb an endless hill; whichever street you take swarms with buyers and sellers who take up all the room between the shops on either side. It isn't good form to step on the merchandise, but now and then one can't avoid it.

The souks are all in one vast ant hill of a building, a city within a city whose avenues and streets, some wide, some narrow, are like the twisting hallways of a dream. There are more than five thousand shops under its roof, so they assure me; I have not wondered whether it seems a likely number or not, nor have I passed through all its forty-two entrance portals or explored more than a small number of its tunneled galleries. Visually the individual shops lack the color and life of the *kissarias* of Fez and Marrakech, and there are no painted Carthaginian columns like those which decorate the souks in Tunis. The charm of the edifice lies in its vastness and, in part, precisely from its dimness and clutter. In the middle of one open space where two large corridors meet, there is an outlandish construction, in shape and size not unlike one of the old traffic towers on New York's Fifth Avenue in the 'twenties. On the ground floor is a minute kitchen. If you climb the crooked outside staircase, you find yourself in a tiny restaurant with four miniature tables. Here you sit and eat, looking out along the tunnels over the heads of the passers-by. It is a place out of Kafka's *Amerika*.

The antique shops here in the souks are famous. As one might expect, tourists are considered to be a feeble-minded and nearly defenseless species of prey, and there are never enough of them to go around. Along the sides of the galleries stand whole tribes of merchants waiting for them to appear. These men have brothers, fathers, uncles and cousins, each of whom operates his own shop, and the tourist is passed along from one member of the family to the next with no visible regret on anyone's part. In one shop I heard the bearded proprietor solemnly assuring a credulous American woman that the amber perfume she had just bought was obtained by pressing beads of amber like those in the necklace she was examining. Not that it would have been much more truthful of him had he told her that it was made of ambergris; the amber I have smelled here never saw a whale, and consists almost entirely of benzoin.

If you stop to look into an antiquary's window you are lost. Suddenly you are aware that hands are clutching your clothing, pulling you gently toward the door, and honeyed voices are experimenting with greetings in all the more common European languages, one after the other. Unless you offer physical resistance you find yourself being propelled forcibly within. Then as you face your captors over arrays of old silver and silk, they begin to work on you in earnest, using all the classic clichés of Eastern sales-patter. "You have such a fine face that I want my merchandise to go with you." "We need money today; you are the first customer to come in all day long." A fat hand taps the ashes from a cigarette. "Unless I do business with you, I won't sleep tonight. I am an old man. Will you ruin my health?" "Just buy one thing, no matter what. Buy the cheapest thing in the store, if you like, but buy something. . . ." If you get out of the place without making a purchase, you are entitled to add ten to your score. A knowledge of Turkish is not necessary here in the bazaars. If you prefer not to speak English or French or German, you find that the Moslems love to be spoken to in Arabic, while the Jews speak a corrupt Andalucían version of Spanish.

Today I went out of the covered souks by a back street that I had not found before. It led downward toward the Rustempaşa Mosque. The shops gave the street a strange air: they all looked alike from the outside. On closer inspection I saw that they were all selling the same wildly varied assortment of unlikely objects. I wanted to examine the merchandise, and since Abdeslam had been talking about buying some rubber-soled shoes, we chose a place at random and went into it. While he tried on sneakers and sandals I made a partial inventory of the objects in the big, gloomy room. The shelves and counters exhibited footballs, Moslem rosaries, military belts, reed mouthpieces for native oboes, doorhooks, dice of many sizes and colors, narghilehs, watch-straps of false cobraskin, garden shears, slippers of untanned leather—hard as stone, brass taps for kitchen sinks, imitation ivory cigarette holders—ten inches long, suitcases made of pressed paper, tambourines, saddles, assorted medals for the military and plastic game counters. Hanging from the ceiling were revolver holsters, lutes, and zipper fasteners that looked like strips of flypaper. Ladders were stacked upright against the wall, and on the floor were striped canvas deck chairs, huge tin trunks with scenes of Mecca stamped on their sides, and a great pile of wood shavings among whose comfortable hills nestled six very bourgeois cats. Abdeslam bought no shoes, and the proprietor began to stare at me and my notebook with unconcealed suspicion, having decided, perhaps, that I was a member of the secret police looking for stolen goods.

OCTOBER 19

Material benefits may be accrued in this worldwide game of refusing to be oneself. Are these benefits worth the inevitable void produced by such destruction? The question is apposite in every case where the traditional beliefs of a people have been systematically modified by its government. Rationalizing words like "progress," "modernization," or "democracy" mean nothing because, even if they are used sincerely, the imposition of such concepts by force from above cancels whatever value they might otherwise have. There is little doubt that by having been made indifferent Moslems the younger generation in Turkey has become more like our idea of what people living in the twentieth century should be. The old helplessness in the face of *mektoub* (it is written) is gone, and in its place is a passionate belief in man's ability to alter his destiny. That is the greatest step of all; once it has been made, anything, unfortunately, can happen.

Abdeslam is not a happy person. He sees his world, which he knows is a good world, being assailed from all sides, slowly crumbling before his eyes. He has no means of understanding me should I try to explain to him that in this age what he considers to be religion is called superstition, and that religion today has come to be a desperate attempt to integrate metaphysics with science. Something will have to be found to replace the basic wisdom which has been destroyed, but the discovery will not be soon; neither Abdeslam nor I will ever know of it.

Istanbul, 1953

CURLS AND A QUIET COUNTRY FACE

JANE BOWLES

THIS FRAGMENT FROM a notebook is the one autobiographical entry Jane ever made. It was written sometime in the early fifties.

CURLS AND A QUIET COUNTRY FACE.

Jennifer-Madeleine. She seems to move in an afternoon light. A brilliantly lighted cold afternoon just before sunset. The melancholy gold color of hayfields from another time, an earlier time, but seen in our day, part of our time. The hay, but not the light. The double heart. Not a drama, but both families. The final painful experience. There must be no more pain like this. Death is better than a long murder.

Might bring into sharper focus what is surrounding and seeming to be outside when the inside is dying. There can be a new joy, a joy so false that one can be shaken with mirth, as one never is, can never be, when the joy is a true one and the inside is not dying.

A play. There comes a moment when there is no possibility of escape, as if the spirit were a box hitting at the walls of the head. Looking at the ocean is the only relief. I have trained my eye to look away from the beach where they are going to build the new docks. I cannot look at that part of the beach unless I think of my own end, curtail my own sense of time, as Paul says that we must all do now. I can do it, but it's like: "You too can live with cancer." When I was little I had to imagine that there was some limit to physical pain in order to enjoy the day. I have never yet enjoyed a day, but I have never stopped trying to arrange for happiness. My present plan to get Tetum into my house is as good as any other. It is at a very pleasant stage of development—still like a daydream. Nothing has changed. My father predicted everything when he said I would procrastinate until I died. I knew then it was true. In America it was terribly painful to know this as a child. Now that I am nearly forty and in North Africa it is still painful.

A play. Is it writing I'm putting off, or was it always something else—a religious sacrifice? The only time I wrote well, when I passed through the inner door, I felt guilt. I must find that again. If I can't, maybe I shall find a way to give it up. I cannot go on this way.

I love Tangier, but like a dying person. When Tetum and Cherifa die I might leave. But we are all three of us the same age, more or less. Tetum older, Cherifa a bit younger. I'd like to buy them meat and fish and oil so that they will stay alive longer. I don't know which one I like best, or how long I can go on this way, at the point of expectation, yet knowing at the same time that it is all hopeless. Does it matter? It is more the coming home to them that I want than it is they themselves. But I do want them to belong to me, which is of course impossible. I must try to stop thinking of them. Best to spend a month or two at Madame de Marquette's. The hardest time is now.

Tangier, early fifties

LETTER 58

JANE BOWLES

ADDRESSED TO JANE'S FRIENDS, Katharine Hamill and Natasha von Hoershelman, who had visited her in Tangier two months earlier, this letter was written in June 1954. Jane writes of the dramas of her daily life and, in particular, of the outcome of her pursuit of Cherifa and Tetum, two Moroccan peasant women. (The remark Jane refers to as having been published in Vogue *is quoted on page xiv of the Introduction.)*

58

Jane Bowles to Natasha von Hoershelman and Katharine Hamill

Darling Natasha and Katharine,

I never stop thinking about you but too much happened. Please forgive me if this is not an amusing letter. I tried last night to write you in detail but I had filled two pages just with Ellie* and some clothes that the ladies and babies were wearing down in M'sallah, the day you left. I think I had better simply write you a gross factual résumé of what has happened. Then if I have any sense I shall keep notes. Because what is happening is interesting and funny in itself. I am a fool to have lost two whole months of it. I have no memory—only a subconscious memory which I am afraid translates everything into something else,

* Pseudonym.

and so I shall have to take notes. I have a very pretty leather book for that purpose.

The day you left I was terribly terribly sad. I still miss you—in the sense that I keep thinking through it all that you should be here and how sorry I am that you left before I could truly take you into some of the life that I love. I turned sour on Ellie about half way up the pier. I could still see the boat. I worried about having exposed Katharine to all those tedious stories—touching in a way but tedious. Ice cream, herring, and the Chico Tax scandal with the brother. Of course it could only happen here on a trip for *Fortune*. I went down that long street, way down in, and landed in a room filled with eighteen women and a dozen or two little babies wearing knitted capes and hoods. One lady had on a peach satin evening dress and over it the jacket of a man's business suit. (A Spanish business suit.) I had been searching for Cherifa, and having been to about three houses all belonging to her family, I finally landed there. I thought I was in a bordello. The room was very plush, filled with hideous blue and white chenille cushions made in Manchester, England. Cherifa wore a pale blue sateen skirt down to the ground and a grayish Spanish sweater, a kind of school sweater but not sporty. She seemed to be constantly flirting with a woman in a pale blue kaftan (our hostess), and finally she sat next to her and encircled her waist. C. looked like a child. The woman weighed about 160 pounds and was loaded with rouge and eye makeup. Now I know her. An alcoholic named Fat Zohra, and one of two wives. She is married to a kind of criminal who I believe knifed his own brother over a card game and spent five years in jail. The other wife lives in a different house and does all the child bearing. Fat Zohra is barren. There was one pale-looking girl (very light green), who I thought was surely the richest and the most distinguished of the lot. She wore a wonderful embroidered kaftan, a rich spinach green with a leaf design. Her face was rather sour: thin compressed lips and a long mean-looking nose. I was sad while they played drums and did their lewd belly dances because I thought: My God if you had only stayed a day longer. But of course if you had, perhaps they wouldn't have asked you in (Cherifa I mean); they are so leery of strangers. In any case at the end of the afternoon (and part of my sadness was an aching jealousy of the woman in the blue kaftan), Cherifa took me to the doorway and into the blue courtyard where two boring pigeons were squatting, and asked me whether or not I was going to live in my house. The drums were still beating and I had sticky cakes in my hand—those I couldn't eat. (I stuffed down as many as I could. I loathe them.) But I was really too jealous and also sad because you had left to get down very many. I said I would of course but not before I found a maid. She told me to wait and a minute later came out with the distinguished pale green one. "Here's your maid," she said. "A very poor girl."

Anyway, a month and a half later she became my maid. I call her Sour Pickle, and she has stolen roughly about one thousand four hundred pesetas from me. I told C. about it who advised me not to keep any money in the house. She is a wonderful maid, an excellent cook, and sleeps with me here. I will go on about this later but I cannot remotely begin to get everything into this letter. You will want to know what happened about Paul, Ellie, Xauen.

Paul went to Xauen for one night, having sworn that he would not spend more than one or two nights at the Massilia. He came back disgusted with Xauen and then started a hopeless series of plans—plans for three of us in one house, and, as I wrote Lyn, I even planned to live in the bottom half of a policeman's house in Tangier Balia (the place with the corrugated tin roofs) while Paul and Ahmed lived in the little house in the Casbah. I felt Cherifa was a hopeless proposition, and had no particular desire to be in my house unless there was some hope of luring her into it. (Maid or no maid.) In the hotel I did try to work a little. But it is always impossible the first month and the wind and the rain continued. The rooms were very damp and cold and one could scarcely sit down in them. I became very attached to the French family who ran the hotel. We stayed on and on in an unsettled way. In the beginning Ellie would come by every day with her loud insensitive battering on the door, and her poor breezy efficient manner and I would try desperately not to smack her. I felt I could not simply drop her and so would make some half-hearted date with her always before lunch so that we could go to Georgette's. Ellie filled me with such a feeling of revulsion that I almost fell in love with Georgette. I never allowed Ellie within a foot of my bed from the moment you stepped on the boat. I have never in my life had such an experience. Nor will I quite understand what possessed me. Some devil but not my usual one. Someone else's devil. In any case she started taking trips. The first time she came back, when I heard the rapping, I said, "Who?" and she said, "The family!" That was it. From then on I could barely stand to be in the same room with her and I hated myself for it. All this revulsion and violence was on a far greater scale than the incident deserved but it must have touched something inside me—something in my childhood. I have never been quite such a horror. Some of it showed outwardly but thank God only a bit of what I was really feeling. She always asked after you. Every time I saw her, "Any letter today?" Also madly irritating for some reason. Finally she got the message and in any case she was away so much that I managed to sneak up here into the Casbah—and I don't believe she knows where I live, though surely she could find out. I hope by now that she is off on a new adventure. Sonie (a pal who takes in the cash at a whorehouse behind the Socco Chico), sees her occasionally and reported that she had left Chico Tax and was driving her own car.

Paul had typhoid in the hotel and that was a frightening mess for two weeks. We were both about to move into our houses. He had found one on a street called Sidi Bouknadel (overlooking the sea) and I was coming here. Then he had typhoid, and then Tennessee came for two whole weeks. I moved in here while Paul was still in the hotel. For a while Ahmed and I were living together while Paul lingered on at the hotel in a weakish state. He is all right now. Ahmed stayed here during the whole month of Ramadan (the month when they eat at night) and I was with him during the last two weeks. Not very interesting except that every night I woke up choking with charcoal smoke, and then he would insist that I eat with him. Liver or steak or whatever the hell it was. At first I minded terribly. Then I began to expect it, and one night he didn't buy really enough for the two of us, and I was grieved. Meanwhile in the daytime I was in the hotel preparing special food for Paul, to bring his appetite back. There were always four or five of us cooking at once in the long narrow hotel kitchen, the only room that looked out on the sea. Meeting Tennessee for dinner and Frankie (they were at the Rembrandt) was complicated too. Synchronizing took up most of the time. We were all in different places.

I have kept out of the David life very successfully except on occasion. I could not possibly manage from here nor do I want to very much though I love him and would hate never to see him. I couldn't go it. The ex-Marchioness of Bath is here for the moment (married her lover, Mister Fielding, a charming man). I went to a dinner party for her in slacks—a thing that I did not do on purpose. They gave a party on the beach which I wiggled out of but Tuesday I must go to a big ball. However if one only turns up once every two weeks or so it's nice. Or occasionally one goes out twice in a row. They are all constantly at it. David suggested a pool of money so that I might have a telephone. Only Jaime seemed to understand that I didn't want one. The Fieldings are enchanting people and are off to write about pirates in the old days. They have some kind of little car they are going to live in. They will be gone six or eight months. By then Enid Bagnold should be back. Her play was the end or wasn't it? Please write me what you think, now that some time has passed. I scarcely ever go to the Parade. Too depressing. Then came the ghastly Indo-China Oppenheimer period which dovetailed with Tennessee's last days here and also a pitch black boy called George Broadfield who called himself "The New American Negro," and attached himself to me and Paul. I liked him but almost went mad because he was determined to stay in Tangier, and thought nothing of talking for seven or eight hours in a row. I told him he should go and live where there were other artists because there were so few of them here. (He himself is a young writer, or is going to be??) He said that Paul and I were enough for him and I was horrified. It was all my fault. The night I got *Vogue* in the mail, which quoted the remark you might have since seen about writing for one's five hundred goony friends etc., I went out and got drunk. I was terribly upset about it. Though I knew what I had meant I had certainly not made the remark expecting it to be quoted or I would have elaborated. I hate being interviewed and something wrong always does pop out, everytime. I meant "intellectual" which Walter Kerr in the Trib seems to have understood, but at the time I was worried about my friends—the real supporters of the play and the contributors to whatever chance it had financial and otherwise. Anyway I was sick at my stomach. I did go to the Parade and did get very drunk. This pitch black boy seemed charming so I latched on to him as one does occasionally. He was a kind of God-sent antidote to the quotation which I was ashamed of. Paul tried to console me saying that nobody much read *Vogue* and that it would be forgotten. Of course later Walter Kerr devoted a column to it in New York and it appeared in Paris as well where there is no other paper for Americans, so if anyone missed it in New York they have seen it in Paris or Rome. I now think of it as a kind of joke. Every letter I receive has the article (Kerr's article) enclosed, with its title "Writing Plays for Goons." They come in from all over Europe and the United States. I keep teasing Paul about the scarcely read copy of Vogue lying on the floor of the beauty parlor. So much for that. But I did inherit George Broadfield for a while and because it was my doing had to see him constantly for a week. I was a wreck—nervously, because he talked so much. Then he shifted on to Paul, finally ran out of money and moved on to Casablanca.

One day before Ramadan and before Paul had paratyphoid, I went to the market and sat in a gloom about Indo-China and the Moroccan situation and every other thing in the world that was a situation outside my own. Soon I cheered up a little. I was in the part where Tetum sits in among the coal and the mules and the chickens. Two little boy musicians came by. I gave them some money and Tetum ordered songs. Soon we had a big crowd around us, one of those Marrakech circles. Everybody stopped working (working?) and we had one half hour of music, myself and everybody else, in that part of the market (you know). And people gathered from round about. Just like Tiflis. Tetum was in good spirits. She told me that Cherifa had a girl friend who was fat and white. I recognized Fat Zohra, though I shall never know whether I put the fat white picture in her mind or not. I might have said "Is she fat and white?" I don't know. Then she asked me if I wouldn't drive her out to Sidi Menari, one of the sacred groves around here where Sidi Menari (a saint) is buried. They like to visit as many saints as possible, of course, because it gives them extra gold stars for heaven. I thought: "Natasha and Katharine will be angry. They told me to stick to Cherifa but then, they didn't know about fat Zohra." After saying this in my head I felt free to offer Tetum a trip to the grove without making you angry.

Of course it turned out that she wanted to take not only one, but two neighbors and their children. We were to leave at eight thirty A.M., she insisted. The next day when I got to Tetum's house on the Marshan with Temsamany (nearly an hour late) Tetum came to the door in a grey bathrobe. I was very surprised. Underneath she was dressed in a long Zigdoun and under that she wore other things. I can't describe a Zigdoun but it is quite enough to wear without adding on a bathrobe. But when they wear our night clothes they wear them over or under their own (which are simply the underpeelings or first three layers of their day clothes. Like in Tiflis). She yanked me into her house, tickled my palm, shouted to her neighbor (asleep on the other side of a thin curtain) and in general pranced about the room. She dressed me up in a hideous half-Arab, half-Spanish cotton dress which came to my ankles and had no shape at all. Just a little round neck. She belted it and said "Now go back to the hotel and show your husband how pretty you look." I said I would some other day, and what about our trip to the saint's tomb. She said yes, yes, but she had to go and fetch the other two women who both lived in a different part of the town. I said would they be ready, and she said something like: "Bacai shouay." Which means just nothing. Finally I arranged to come back for her at three. Rather infuriated because I had gotten Temsamany up at the crack. But I was not surprised, nor was he. Tetum took me to her gate. "If you are not here at three," she said in sudden anger, "I shall walk to the grove myself on my own legs." (Five hours, roughly.) We went back at three and the laundry bags were ready, and the children, and Tetum.

"We are going to two saints," Tetum said. "First Sidi Menari and then we'll stop at the other saint's on the way back. He's buried on the edge of town and we've got to take the children to him and cut their throats because they have whooping cough." She poked one of the laundry bundles, who showed me a knife. I was getting rather nervous because Paul of course was expecting us back roughly around seven, and I know how long those things can take. We drove along the awful road (the one that frightened you) toward the grove, only we went on and on, much further out, and the road began to bother me a little after a while. You would have hated it. The knife of course served for the symbolic cutting of the children's throat, though at first I had thought they were going to draw some blood, if not a great deal. I didn't think they were actually going to kill the children or I wouldn't have taken them on the ride.

We reached the sacred grove which is not far from the lighthouse one can see coming into the harbor. Unfortunately they have built some ugly restaurants around and about the lighthouse, and not far from the sacred grove so that sedans are now constantly passing on the highway. The grove itself is very beautiful, and if one goes far enough inside it, far away from the road, one does not see the cars passing. We didn't penetrate very far into the grove because being a Christian (Oy!) I can't sit within the vicinity of the saint's tomb. Temsamany spread the tarpaulin on the ground and the endless tea equipment they had brought with them, and they were off to the saint's leaving Temsamany and myself behind. He said: "I shall make a fire, and then when they come back the water will be boiling." They came back. God knows when. The water was boiling. We had used up a lot of dead olive branches. They sat down and lowered their veils so that they hung under their chins like ugly bibs. They had bought an excellent sponge cake. As usual something sweet. I thought: "Romance here is impossible." Tetum's neighbors were ugly. One in particular. "Like a turtle," Temsamany said. She kept looking down into her lap. Tetum, the captain of the group, said to the turtle: "Look at the world, look at the world." "I am looking at the world," the other woman said, but she kept looking down into her lap. They cut up all the sponge cake. I said: "Stop! Leave it. We'll never eat it all." Temsamany said: "I'm going to roller skate." He went off and we could see him through the trees. After a while the conversation stopped. Even Tetum was at a loss. There was a little excitement when they spotted the woman who runs the toilets under the grain market, seated not far off with a group, somewhat larger than ours but nothing else happened.

I went to look for Temsamany on the highway. He had roller skated out of sight. I felt that all my pursuits here were hopeless. I looked back over my shoulder into the grove. Tetum was swinging upside down from an olive tree her knees hooked over a branch, and she is, after all, forty-five and veiled and a miser.

There is more to this day but I see now that I have done exactly what I did not want to do. I have gone into great detail about one incident, which is probably of no interest.

But as a result of that day Cherifa and I have been much closer. In fact she spends two or three nights here a week in dungarees and Haymaker shirts. She asked for five thousand pesetas (about one hundred and fifteen dollars) so that she could fill her grain stall to the brim. I have given her, so far, fifteen hundred pesetas. She sleeps in dungarees and several things underneath. I shall have to write you a whole other letter about this. In fact I waited and waited before writing because foolishly I hoped that I could write you: "I have or have not —Cherifa." The awful thing is that I don't even know. I don't know what they do. I don't know how much they feel. Sometimes I think that I am just up against that awful hard to get virgin block. Sometimes I think they just don't know. I—it is difficult to explain. So hard to know what is clever manoeuvering on her part, what is a lack of passion, and what is fear—just plain fear of losing all her marketable value and that I won't care once I've had her. She is terribly affectionate at times and kissing is heaven. However I don't know quite how soon or if I should clamp down. I simply don't know. All the rules for the playing the game are given me by Paul or else Temsamany. Both are men. T. says if you don't get them the first two times you never will. A frightening thought. But then he is a man. I told Paul one couldn't buy desire, and he said desire can come but only with habit. And never does it mean what it means to us—rather less than holding hands supposedly. Everything is very preliminary and pleasant like the beginning of a love affair between a virgin and her boy friend in some automobile. Then when we are finally in bed she says: "Now sleep." Then comes either "Goodbye" or a little Arabic blessing which I repeat after her. There we lie like two logs—one log with open eyes. I take sleeping pill after sleeping pill. Yet I'm afraid to strike the bargain. "If you do this, I will give you all of the money, if not—" It is very difficult for me. Particularly as her affection and tenderness seem so terribly real. I'm not even sure that this isn't the most romantic experience in a sense that I have ever had—and it is all so miraculous compared to what little went on before. I hesitate to rush it, to be brutal in my own eyes, even if she would understand it perfectly. I think love and *sex*, that is tenderness and sex, beyond kissing and les caresses, may be forever separate in their minds, so that one might be going toward something less rather than more than what one had in the beginning. According to the few people I have spoken to—among them P.M. (the Englishman who wrote the book)—I hate mentioning names—they have absolutely no aftermath. Lying back, relaxing, all that which is more pleasant than the thing itself, if one is in love (and only then) is non-existent. Just quickly "O.K. Now we sleep," or a rush for six water bowls to wash the sin away. I'm not even sure I haven't in a way slept with C. Because I did get "Safinaasu." ("O.K. Now we sleep.") But it does not mean always the same thing. I am up too many trees and cannot write you all obviously. Since I cannot seem to bring myself to the point of striking a verbal bargain (cowardice? delicacy? love?) I don't know—but I simply can't—not yet. I shall have to wait until I find the situation more impossible than pleasant, until my nerves are shot and I am screaming with exasperation. It will come. But I don't believe I can say anything before I feel that way. It would only sound fake. My hunch is she would go away saying "Never." Then eventually come back. At the moment, no matter what, I am so much happier than I was. She seems to be getting a habit of the house. Last night she said, "It's strange that I can't eat eggs in my own house. But here I eat them." Later she said that her bed at home was not as good as mine. Mine by the way is *something*. Lumpy with no springs. Just on straw. A thin wool mattress, on straw. At home she sleeps in a room with her great aunt. The great aunt on the floor, Cherifa on the bed, natch. She's that kind. I find her completely beautiful. A little smaller than myself but with strong shoulders, strong legs with a good deal of hair on them. At the same time soft soft skin—and twenty-eight years old. Last night we went up on the topmost terrace and looked at all of Tangier. The boats and the stars and the long curved line of lights along the beach. There was a cold wind blowing and Cherifa was shivering. I kissed her just a little. Later downstairs she said the roof was very beautiful, and she wondered whether or not God had seen us. I wonder. I could go on about this, dear Katharine and Natasha, and I will some other time. I wish to Christ you were here. I can talk to Paul and he is interested but not that interested because we are all women. We see each other almost daily. His house is not far from here. And it is a lovely walk. Outside the walls of the Casbah, overlooking the beach and the ocean. Most of my time is taken up with him or Cherifa or the house and now work. I am beginning again to work. Before she came I was such a nervous wreck I couldn't do anything. Also I was in despair about all the world news and as I told you Paul's illness. Everything was a mess. Now I am in a panic about money and though I will write a play, I must write other things too for immediate cash. Not that I don't have any for a while but I must not use it all up before I have completed at least enough of a play for an advance. Thank God I am in a house and not in a hotel. Although the house has cost me a good deal until now, it won't henceforth because I've bought most everything I needed except a new bed for upstairs. I shall fill the house with beds—traps for a virgin. I feel happier now that I've written you. All the time I have been saying: I should write about *this* to N. and K. But it seemed impossible, utterly impossible to make a résumé of all that happened before. And as you see, it was impossible. I have not even found it possible to write in this letter why Tetum swinging from an olive tree in her cloak and hood should have precipitated all this but it did. I think Cherifa got worried about losing me to Tetum. She was so worried she asked me for a kaftan right off. Then started a conversation, a bargaining conversation, which resulted in her coming here after Ramadan to spend the night. But I can't go into that now. I always let Fatima (Sour Pickle) decide what we are to eat. It is all so terribly simple—all in one dish. Either lamb with olives or with raisins, and onions, or chicken with the same or ground meat on skewers or beef or lamb on skewers. (You remember how wonderful they taste). Or a fried potato omelet with onions, or boiled noodles with butter or eggs fried in oil, and always lots of black bread and wine at five pesetas a quart (excellent). I've had guests once, Tennessee in fact. White beans in oil and with salt pork like the ones I cooked for you. Lots of salad: cucumber, tomato and onion, all chopped up, almost daily. Fresh figs, bananas, cherries. Whatever fruit is in season. Wonderful bowls of Turkish coffee in the morning which are brought to our bed (when she is here as she happens to be now for a kind of weekend) or to me alone and piles of toast soaked in butter. At noon we eat very little. Usually, if Cherifa isn't here (she supposedly comes twice a week but that can include two afternoons) I go over to Paul's for lunch. Except that he never eats until three thirty—sometimes four. I get up at seven and by then I am so hungry I don't even care. But I like seeing him. We eat soup and bread and butter and cheese and tuna fish. For me tuna fish is the main diet.

I love this life and I'm terrified of the day when my money runs out. The sex thing aside, it is as if I had dreamed this life before I was born. Perhaps I will work hard to keep it. I cannot keep Cherifa without money, or even myself, after all. Paul told Cherifa that without working I would never have any money so she is constantly sending me up into my little work room. A good thing. Naturally I think of her in terms of a long long time. How one can do this and at the same time fully realize the fact that money is of paramount importance to one's friend and etc., etc.—that if there is to be much sleeping it will most likely be against their will or something they will do to please one, I simply don't know. Possibly, if it came to that, I might lose interest in the sleeping part, possibly why I keep putting off the bargaining—but the money I know is paramount. Yet they are not like we are. Someone behaving in the same way who was not an Arab I couldn't bear. All this will have to wait for some other letter. Perhaps it is all a bore, if so tell me. But I thought since you have seen her and Tangier that it would interest you. Please do me a great favor and save this letter. I cannot write more than one letter on this subject. If you think Lyn would be interested in bits and snatches of the letter read them to her because I can't, as I said write about it more than once. Not having seen Tangier or Cherifa, perhaps it would mean nothing to her. But we are on an intimate enough basis—she and Polly and myself—and they went through Marty with me a bit. I shall simply write her about my work and my health and I will tell her that you have a letter about "more stuff," if she wants to see it. And I shall tell her to call you, at the office. Perhaps you can meet some day for a drink if you all want to. I long to know Oliver's address. Lyn wrote me that he was in Calif. That's all. No address. Please write. I shall worry now about this messy letter.

All my love, always,

J. Bowles.

P.S. This letter I shall now correct. I am sure it is unreadable but I'll do the best I can. Received your copy of "Confessions of an Honest Playwright" today. Thank you. In Paris it has the other title, "Writing Plays for Goons." It's the end.

Tangier, June 1954

from *THE SPIDER'S HOUSE*

PAUL BOWLES

THE SPIDER'S HOUSE *is set in Fez at the time the Moroccan struggle for independence from the French was reaching a crisis point. The story of the uprising in the city is told through two protagonists: Amar, a Moroccan boy, and John Stenham, an American writer who has been self-exiled in Morocco for some years. Stenham looks upon the political struggle as an outsider; he is paralyzed by the violence and yet he does not want to leave Fez. Amar, driven into a state of excitement by the uprising, is caught between adherence to the old Moslem ways and the appeal of the new revolutionary fervor. The two stories intersect and merge in Chapter 23, when Stenham (in the company of Lee Veyron, an American visiting Morocco) and Amar meet in a café while outside in the street a violent confrontation is taking place between the police and the demonstrators.*

The title of the book is taken from the Koran: "The likeness of those who choose other patrons than Allah is as the likeness of the spider when she taketh unto herself a house, and lo! the frailest of all houses is the spider's house, if they but knew."

The following excerpt includes chapters 23 and 24 of the novel.

CHAPTER 23

THERE WERE FOUR CAFÉS on the square, and each one had a large space in front of it which was ordinarily full of tables and chairs. Today, these had prudently not been set out, so that the sides of the square presented a deserted aspect which was emphasized by the fact that the center also was empty, for no one was walking in it. True, it was hot, and there would have been few strollers at this hour in any case, but the absence of people was so complete that the scene—even if the line of police could have been disregarded—had no element of the casualness which ordinarily gave the place its character.

"*Very* strange," Stenham muttered.

"Am I wrong," she said, "or does this look sort of sinister?"

"Come on." He took her arm and they hurried across to the café nearest the waiting buses. One of the *mokhaznia* standing by the footbridge across the stream looked at them dubiously, but did not stop them from passing. In the café, a group of thirty or forty men sat and stood quietly near the windows, peering out through the hanging fronds of the pepper trees at the emptiness of the sunny square. More than by the unusual tenseness of these faces, Stenham was at once struck by the silence of the place, by the realization that no one was talking, or, if someone did speak, it was in a low voice scarcely pitched above a whisper. Of course, without the radio there was no need to shout as they ordinarily had to do, but he felt that even had the radio been playing, together with all its extra amplifiers for the smaller rooms, they still would only have murmured. And he did not like the expressions on their faces when they looked up and saw him. It was the first time in many years that he had read enmity in Moroccan faces. Once more than twenty years ago he had ventured alone inside the *horm* of Moulay Idriss—not the sanctuary itself, but the streets surrounding it—and then he had seen hatred on a few faces; he had never forgotten the feeling it had given him. It was a physical thing that those fierce faces had confronted him with, and his reaction to it had likewise been purely physical; he had felt his spine stiffen and the hair at the back of his neck bristle.

He began to speak with Lee in a loud voice, not paying much attention to what he was saying, but using what he thought would be an unmistakably American intonation. He saw her glance at him once with surprise.

"There are a lot of little rooms out in the back," he went on. "Let's get one that's not so crowded." She was annoyed; he could see that. He could also see that the only result his bit of play-acting had brought him was that a good many more of the bearded, turbaned and *tarbouched* individuals had looked away from the window and were staring at them with equally hostile countenances.

"Let's just sit anywhere and stop being so conspicuous," she said nervously; at the same time she took several steps toward an unoccupied table by the wall opposite the entrance. But Stenham wanted, if it were possible, to get out of the range of these unfriendly faces. In the next room they found a party of elderly men from the country sprawled out, smoking kif and eating. A boy stood in the doorway to a further room. Behind him the room appeared to be empty. Stenham stepped across and peered in; the boy did not move. There was no one in there at all. Through a back window he caught sight of a sheet of water shining in the sun.

"Lee!" he called. She slipped through the doorway and they sat down.

"Are you yelling so they'll think you're an American? Is that it?" she demanded.

"It's very important they shouldn't think we're French, at least."

"But you sounded so funny!" She began to laugh. "It would have been so much more effective if you'd just roared: 'O.K., give money, twenty dollar, very good, yes, no, get outa here, god damned son of a bitch!' Perhaps they'd have gotten the point then. The way you did it, I don't think you got it across to them for a minute."

"Well, I did my best." Now that he was in the inner room out of sight of the inimical faces, he felt better.

Presently the waiter came in with a glass of tea for the boy at the other table. Stenham ordered tea and pastries.

"Damnation!" he said. "I forgot to leave a note for Moss."

"It's my fault," she declared.

"Very sweet of you, but completely untrue."

"You could phone him."

"No. There's no phone here. I don't know. Sometimes I wonder what's wrong with me. I know just how to behave, but only before or after the fact. When the moment's there in front of me, I don't seem to function."

"You're no different from anybody else," she said.

He suspected that she was waiting for an adverse reaction to this statement, so he said nothing. They were both silent for a minute. The Arab boy was sipping his tea with the customary Moslem noisiness. Stenham, in good spirits, did not mind his presence; he was a bit of native decoration. He would not have objected even if the boy had begun to make the loud belches that polite Moroccans make when they wish to show their appreciation of what they have eaten or drunk. The boy however did not belch; instead he rose from his table and taking up a good-sized stone from the floor, started to pound on the bolt of the door that led to the little garden outside. Stenham leaned across the table and took Lee's hand. He had never noticed the wedding ring until this minute—a simple gold band. "It's good to see you," he told her, and then immediately wished he had sat still and said nothing, for at the contact of his hand her face had clouded. "It's always good to see you," he added with less buoyancy, watching her closely. For a time she seemed to be trying to decide whether or not to speak. Then she said: "Why do you do that?"

"Why shouldn't I?" He spoke quietly because he wanted to avoid stirring up another argument.

Her expression was one of utter candor. "Because it puts me in a false position," she told him. "It makes me so uncomfortable. I can't help feeling that something's expected of me. I feel I should either go coquettish or prudish on you, and I don't want to be either one."

"Why don't you just be natural?" he suggested gently.

"I'm *trying* to be natural now," she said with impatience, "but you don't seem to understand. You put me in a position where it's next to impossible to be natural."

"Is it that bad?" he said, smiling sadly.

"They say you can't tell any man that you don't find him sexually attractive, that a woman's whole success in life is based on the principle of making every man feel that given the right circumstances she'd rush to bed with him. But I think there must be a few men bright enough to hear the news without going into a fit of depression. Don't you think so?" She smiled provocatively.

He said slowly: "I think you know that isn't true. What's being bright got to do with it? You might as well say an intelligent man won't mind being hungry as much as a slow-witted one will."

"Well, maybe that's true," she said gaily. "Who knows?"

He was hurt; to keep her from knowing it he held her hand tighter. "I'm not that easy to discourage," he assured her lightly. She shrugged and looked down at the table. "I was just being friendly," she pouted. "Because I really like you. I like just being with you. If that isn't enough—" she shrugged again— "well, then, the hell with it."

"Fine, fine. Maybe you'll change."

"Maybe I will. I like to think I have an open mind."

He did not answer, but sat back and looked out the window. The boy had taken off his shoes and was wading in the pool, a sight which, because of his state of mind, did not at once strike him as peculiar. When he saw him bend over and fish a large, bedraggled insect out of the water, he became interested. Now the boy held his hand very close to his face, studying his prey, smiling at it; he even moved his lips a few times, as though he were talking to it.

"What is it? What are you staring at?" she asked.

"Trying to make out what that kid's doing out there, standing in the middle of the water."

Suddenly the insect had flown away. The boy stood looking after it, his face expressing satisfaction rather than the disappointment Stenham had expected to see. He climbed out of the pool and sat down at its edge where he had been before.

Stenham shook his head. "Now, that was a strange bit of behavior. The boy made a special trip into the water just to pull out some kind of insect."

"Well, he's kind-hearted."

"I know, but they're not. That's the whole point. In all my time here I've never seen anyone do a thing like that."

He looked at the boy's round face, heavy, regular features, and curly black hair.

"He could be a Sicilian, or a Greek," he said as if to himself. "If he's not a Moroccan, there's nothing surprising about his deed. But if he is, then I give up. Moroccans just don't do things like that."

Lee stood up briefly and looked out the window; then she sat down again. "He looks like the model for all the worst paintings foreigners did in Italy a hundred years ago. *Boy at Fountain, Gipsy Carrying Water Jar*; you know?"

"You want another tea?"

"No!" she said. "One's plenty. It's so sweet. But anyway, I don't believe you can make such hard and fast general rules about people."

"You can in this case. I've watched them for years. I know what they're like."

"That doesn't mean you know what each one is like individually, after all."

"But the whole point is, they're not individuals in the sense you mean," he said.

"You're on dangerous ground," she warned him.

For fear that she might take exception to his words, he was quiet, did not attempt to explain to her how living among a less evolved people enabled him to see his own culture from the outside, and thus to understand it better. It was her express desire that all races and all individuals be "equal," and she would accept no demonstration which did not make use of that axiom. In truth, he decided, it was impossible to discuss anything at all with her, because instead of seeing each part of total reality as a complement to the other parts, with dogged insistence she forged ahead seeing only those things which she could twist into the semblance of an illustration for her beliefs.

From somewhere outside there came a faint sound which, if he had not known it was being made by human voices, he might have imagined sounded like the wind soughing through pine branches. The boy, who sat by the pool as though he were the express reason for the sun's existence at that moment, seemed to hear the sound, too. Stenham glanced at Lee: apparently she heard nothing. There were only two bits of stage business, he reflected, of which she was capable. One was to pull out her compact and occupy herself by looking into its mirror, and the other was to light a cigarette. On this occasion she used the compact.

He watched her. For her the Moroccans were backward onlookers standing on the sidelines of the parade of progress; they must be exhorted to join, if necessary pulled by force into the march. Hers was the attitude of the missionary, but whereas the missionary offered a complete if unusable code of thought and behavior, the modernizer offered nothing at all, save a place in the ranks. And the Moslems, who with their blind intuitive wisdom had triumphantly withstood the missionaries' cajoleries, now were going to be duped into joining the senseless march of universal brotherhood; for the privilege each man would have to give up only a small part of himself—just enough to make him incomplete, so that instead of looking into his own heart, to Allah, for reassurance, he would have to look to the others. The new world would be a triumph of frustration, where all humanity would be lifting itself by its own bootstraps—the equality of the damned. No wonder the religious leaders of Islam identified Western culture with the works of Satan: they had seen the truth and were expressing it in the simplest terms.

The sound of shouting suddenly increased in volume; it was obviously coming from a moving column of men. How many thousand throats did it take, he wondered, to make a sound like that?

"Listen," said Lee.

The progress through the streets was slow, and the acoustics, changing from moment to moment, brought the sound nearer, then removed it to a more distant plane. But it was clear that the crowd was on its way up toward Bou Jeloud.

"Here comes your trouble," he said to her.

She bit her upper lip for a second, and looked at him distraughtly. "What do you think we ought to do? Get out?"

"Sure, if you like."

The boy came through the door, glanced shyly at them, and turned to sit down at his table. Stenham called out to him: "*Qu'est-ce qui se passe dehors?*" The boy stared at him, uncomprehending. So he was a Moroccan, after all. "*Smahli,*" Stenham said. "*Chnou hadek el haraj?*"

The other looked at him with wide eyes, clearly wondering how anyone could be so stupid. "That's people yelling," he said.

"Are they happy or angry?" Stenham wanted to know.

The boy struggled to keep his sudden suspiciousness from becoming visible in his face. He smiled, and said: "Maybe some are happy, some are angry. Each man knows what is in his own heart."

"A philosopher," Stenham laughed in an aside to Lee.

"What does he say? What is it?" she asked impatiently.

"He's being cagey. *Egless.*" He indicated the third chair at their table, and the boy sat down carefully, never taking his eyes from Stenham's face. "I'd better offer him a cigarette," Stenham said, and did so. The boy refused, smiling. "Tea?" asked Stenham. "I've drunk it. Thank you," said the boy.

"Ask him what he thinks about staying here," Lee said nervously.

"You can't hurry these people," he told her. "You get nothing out of them if you do."

"I know, but if we're going to go we should go, don't you think?"

"Well, yes, if we are. But I'm not sure it's such a good idea to go out there running around looking for a cab now, do you think?"

"You're the expert. How should I know? But for God's sake try and make sense at this point. I don't feel like being massacred."

He laughed, then turned his head to face her completely. "Lee, if I thought there were any serious danger you don't think I'd have suggested coming here, do you?"

"How do I know what you'd have suggested? I'm just telling you that if there's any question of a mob smashing into this café I want to get out now, and not wait until it's too late."

"What's this sudden hysteria?" he demanded. "I don't understand."

"Hysteria!" She laughed scornfully. "I don't think you've ever seen a hysterical woman in your life."

"Listen. If you want to go, we'll go now."

"That's just what I *didn't* say. I merely asked you to be serious and realize that you've got the responsibility for us both, and act accordingly. That's all."

What a schoolmarm, he thought angrily. "All right," he said. "Let's sit right here. This is an Arab café. There are about fifty police outside and there's a *poste de garde* right across the square. I don't know where we could be safer, except in the Ville Nouvelle. Certainly not in the hotel."

She did not answer. The noise of the crowd had become much

louder; it sounded now like prolonged cheering. He turned to the boy again.

"The people are coming this way."

"Yes," said the boy; it was evident that he did not want to discuss the subject. Another tack, a different approach, thought Stenham, but not a personal one, either. "Do you like this café?" he said after a moment, remembering too late that statements were better than questions in the task of trying to establish contact with the Moroccans.

The boy hesitated. "I like it," he said grudgingly, "but it's not a good café."

"I thought it was a good café. I like it. It has water on both sides."

"Yes," the boy admitted. "I like to come and sit. But it's not a good café." He lowered his voice. "The owner has buried something outside the door. That's not good."

Stenham, bewildered, said: "I see."

The noise now could not be disregarded; its rhythmical chanting had grown into a gigantic roar, unmistakably of anger, and it was at last possible to hear details in its pattern. It had ceased being a unified wall of sound, and become instead a great, turbulent mass of innumerable separate human cries.

"*Smahli,*" said the boy. "I'm going to look." Quickly he rose and went out of the room.

"Are you nervous?" Stenham asked her.

"Well, I'm not exactly relaxed. Give me a cigarette. I've run out."

While he was lighting her cigarette there came the sound of one lone shot—a small dull pop which nevertheless carried above the roar of voices. They both froze; the roar subsided for a second or two, then rose to a chaos of frenzy. Their wide eyes met, but only by accident. Then from what they would have said was the front of the café there was a phrase of machine-gun fire, a short sequence of rapidly repeated, shattering explosions.

They both jumped up and ran to the door. The other room was empty now, Stenham noticed as they went through it, save for one old man sitting on the floor in the corner, holding a kif pipe in his hand. They went only as far as the doorway of the large front room. There men were still falling over each other in their haste to get to the windows. Two waiters were sliding enormous bolts across the closed entrance door. When they had finished doing that they hurriedly pushed a large chest in front of the door, and wedged tables between it and a pillar near by. They did the work automatically, as though it were the only reaction conceivable in such a situation. Then they went behind a wall of bottle cases and peered worriedly out a small window there. From where they stood in the inner doorway Lee and Stenham could see, through the florid designs of the grillwork in the windows, only a series of senseless vignettes which had as their background the hard earth of the square. Occasionally part of a running figure passed through one of the frames. The noise at the moment was largely one of screaming; there was also the tinkle of shattering glass at intervals. Suddenly, like so many huge motors starting up, machine-guns fired from all around the square. When they had finished, there was relative silence, broken by a few single revolver shots from further away. A police whistle sounded, and it was even possible to hear individual voices shouting commands in French. A man standing in one of the windows in front of them began to beat on the grillwork like a caged animal, shrieking imprecations; hands reached out from beside him and pulled him back, and a brief struggle ensued as he was forced to the floor by his companions. Stenham seized Lee by the wrist and wheeled her around, saying: "Come on." They returned to their little room.

"Sit down," said Stenham. Then he stepped out into the sunlight, looked up at the walls around the patio, sighed, and went back in. "No way out there," he said. "We'll just have to sit here."

Lee did not reply; she sat looking down at the table, her chin cupped in her hands. He observed her: he could not be certain, but it seemed to him that she was shivering. He put his hand on her shoulder, felt it tremble.

"Wouldn't you like some hot tea, without the sugar?" he asked her.

"It's all right," she said after a pause, without glancing up. "I'm all right."

He stood there helplessly, looking down at her. "Maybe—"

"Please sit down."

Automatically he obeyed. Then he lighted a cigarette. Presently she raised her head. "Give me one," she said. Her teeth were chattering. "I might as well smoke. I can't do anything else."

Someone was standing in the doorway. Swiftly Stenham turned his head. It was the boy, staring at them. Stenham rose and went over, pulling him with him out into the next room. The old man still sprawled in the corner in a cloud of kif smoke.

"Try and get a glass of tea for the *mra*," he told the boy, who did not appear to understand. "The lady wants some tea." He's looking at me as though I were a talking tree, thought Stenham. He took the boy's arm and squeezed it, but there was no reaction. The eyes were wide, and there was nothing in them. He looked back into the room and saw Lee hunched over the table, sobbing. Pulling the boy by the arm, he led him to the chair beside her and made him sit down. Then he went out to the main room to the alcove where the fire was, and ordered three teas from the *qaouaji*; he too seemed to be in a state bordering on catalepsy. "Three teas, three teas," Stenham repeated. "One with only a little sugar." It'll give him something to do, he thought.

The feeble chaos outside was now almost covered by the voices of the onlookers within the café. They were not talking loud, but they spoke with frantic intensity, and all together, so that no one was listening to anyone else. Happily, this occupied them; they paid him no attention. He felt that if he left the *qaouaji* to prepare the tea and bring it by himself, he would be likely to fall back into his lethargy; he determined to remain with him until it was ready. From where he stood, through the small window in front of him, he could see only a part of the center of the square. Usually it was empty, but when a figure appeared, moving across the space made by the window's frame, it was always a policeman or a *mokhazni*. What had happened was fairly clear: the crowd had attempted to pass out of the Medina through Bab Bou Jeloud, and had been stopped at the gate itself. Now there were small skirmishes taking place well within the gate as the marchers retreated. When he heard a cavalcade of trucks begin to arrive, he knew it would be safe to go and look out the window, and so he squeezed himself into the narrow corridor between the piles of cases of empty bottles and the wall, and went to peer out. There were four big army trucks and they had drawn up in a line behind the two abandoned buses. Berber soldiers in uniform, their rifles in their hands, were still leaping out of the backs of the trucks, running toward the gate. There must be about two hundred of them, he calculated.

Now a slow massacre would begin, inside the walls, in the streets and alleys, until every city-dweller who was able had reached some sort of shelter and no one was left outside but the soldiers. Even as he was thinking this, the pattern of the shooting changed from single, desultory shots to whole volleys of them, like strings of fire-crackers exploding. He stood there watching tensely, although there was nothing to see; it was like seeing a newsreel of the event, where what is presented is the cast of characters and the situation before and afterward, but never the action itself. Even the gunfire might as well have been a sound-track; it was hard to believe that the rifles he had seen two minutes before were at this moment being used to kill people; were firing the shots that he was hearing. If you had had no previous contact with this sort of violence, he reflected, even when it was happening where you were, it remained unreal.

He went back to the alcove where the fire was, and was pleasantly surprised to see that the *qaouaji* had nearly finished making the tea. When it was done, he followed the man as unobtrusively as he could to the back room. When he looked at the table he did not know whether he was annoyed or delighted to find Lee and the boy engaged in a mysterious bilingual dialogue.

"Have some hot tea," he told her.

She looked up; there was no sign on her face that she had been crying. "Oh, that's sweet of you," she said, lifting the glass, finding it too hot, and putting it down again. "These people are really amazing. It took this child about two minutes to get me over feeling sorry for myself. The first thing I knew he was tugging at my sleeve and turning on the most irresistible smile and saying things in his funny language, but with such gentleness and sweetness that there I was, feeling better, that's all."

"That *is* strange," Stenham said, thinking of the state the boy himself had been in when he had left him. He turned to him and said: "*O deba labè enta?* You feel better? You were a little sick."

"No, I wasn't sick," the boy said firmly, but his face showed three consecutive expressions: shame, resentment, and finally a certain trusting humility, as if by the last he meant that he threw himself upon Stenham's mercy not to tell Lee of his weakness.

"When can we get out of here? We want to go home," Stenham said to him.

The boy shook his head. "This isn't the time to go into the street."

"But the lady wants to go to the hotel."

"Of course." The boy laughed, as though Lee's desires were those of an unreasoning animal, and were to be taken no more seriously. "This café is a very good place for her. The soldiers won't know she's in here."

"The soldiers won't know?" echoed Stenham sharply, his intuition warning him that there was more import to the words than his mind had yet grasped. "What do you mean? *Chnou bghitsi ts'qoulli?*"

"Didn't you see the soldiers? I heard them come when you were getting the tea. If they know she's in here they'll break the door and come in."

"But why?" demanded Stenham idiotically.

The boy replied succinctly and in unequivocal terms.

"No, no." Stenham was incredulous. "They couldn't. The French."

"What French?" said the boy bitterly. "The French aren't with them. They send them out alone, so they can break the houses and kill the men and take the girls and steal what they want. The Berbers don't fight for the French just for those few francs a day they give them. You didn't know that? This way the French don't have to spend any money, and the city people are kept poor, and the Berbers are happy in their heads, and the people hate the Berbers more than they hate the French. Because if everybody hated the French they couldn't stay here. They'd have to go back to France."

"I see. And how do you know all that?" Stenham asked, impressed by the clarity of the boy's simple analysis.

"I know it because everybody knows it. Even the donkeys and mules know that. And the birds," he added with complete seriousness.

"If you know all that, maybe you know what's going to happen next," Stenham suggested, half in earnest.

"There will be more and more poison in the hearts of the Moslems, and more and more and more"—his face screwed itself up into a painful grimace—"until they all burst, just from hating. They'll set everything on fire and kill each other."

"I mean today. What's going to happen now? Because we want to go home."

"You must look out the window and wait until the only men there are French and *mokhaznia*—no partisans at all. Then you make the man open the door and let you out, and go to a policeman, and he'll take you home."

"But we don't like the French," objected Stenham, thinking this was as good a moment as any to reassure the boy as to where their sympathies lay; he did not want him to regret his candor when the excitement of the instant had passed.

A cynical smile appeared on the young face. "*Binatzkoum.* That's between you and them," he said impassively. "How did you get to Fez?"

"On the train."

"And where do you live?"

"At the Mérinides Palace."

"*Binatzkoum, binatzkoum.* You came with the French and you live with the French. What difference does it make whether you like them or not? If they weren't here you couldn't be here. Go to a French policeman. But don't tell him you don't like him."

"Look!" said Lee suddenly. "I don't feel like sitting here while you take an Arab lesson. I want to get out of here. Has he given you any information at all?"

"If you'll just have a little patience," said Stenham, nettled, "I'll get all the details. You can't hurry these people; I've told you that."

"I'm sorry. But it *is* going to be dark soon and we *have* got to get all the way back to the hotel. What I meant was, I hope you're not just having an ordinary conversation."

"We're not," Stenham assured her. He looked at his watch. "It's only four-twenty," he said. "It won't be dark for a long time. The boy doesn't think we ought to go outside quite yet. I'm inclined to think he's right."

"He probably doesn't know as much about it as you do, if you come down to that," she said. "But go ahead and talk."

The sounds of shooting had retreated into the distance. "Why don't you go and look out the window?" Stenham suggested to the boy, "and see what's happening."

Obediently the boy rose and went out.

"He's a good kid," said Stenham. "Bright as they come."

"Oh, he's a darling. I think we should each give him something when we go."

It was a long while before he returned, and when he came in they saw immediately that he was in a completely different state of mind. He walked slowly to his chair and sat down, looking ready to burst into tears.

"*Chnou?* What is it?" Stenham demanded impatiently.

The boy looked straight ahead of him, a picture of despair.

"Now *you* be patient," Lee said.

"You can go," the boy said finally in a toneless voice. "The man will open the door for you. There's nothing to be afraid of."

Stenham waited a moment for the boy to say more, but he merely sat there, his hands in his lap, his head bent forward, looking at the air. "What is it?" he finally asked him, conscious that both his experience and his Arabic were inadequate for dealing with a situation which demanded tact and delicacy. The boy shook his head very slowly without moving his eyes. "Did you see something bad?"

The boy heaved a deep sigh. "The city is closed," he said. "All the gates are closed. No one can go in. No one can come out."

Stenham relayed the information to Lee, adding: "I suppose that means going through hell to get into the hotel. Officially it's inside the walls."

She clicked her tongue with annoyance. "We'll get in. But what about him? Where does he live?"

Stenham talked with the boy for a bit, drawing only the briefest answers from him. At the end of a minute or so, he said to Lee: "He doesn't know where he's going to eat or sleep. That's the trouble. His family lives way down in the Medina. It's a mess, isn't it? And of course he has no money. They never have any. I think I'll give him a thousand. That ought to help some."

Lee shook her head. "Money's not what the poor kid needs. What good's money going to be to him?"

"What good is it!" exclaimed Stenham. "What else can you give him?"

Lee reached over and tapped the boy's shoulder. "Look!" she said, pointing at him. "You. Come." She waggled her fingers like two legs. "Him." She indicated Stenham. "Me." She pointed her thumb at herself. "Hotel." She described a wide arc with her hand. "Yes? *Oui?*"

"You're crazy," Stenham told her. A flicker of hope had appeared in the boy's eyes. Warming to her game, Lee bent forward and went on with her dumb-show. Stenham rose, saying: "Why get him all worked up? It's cruel." She paid him no attention.

"I'm going to take a look into the other room," he said, and he left them there, leaning toward each other intently, Lee gesticulating and uttering single words with exaggeratedly clear enunciation—like a schoolteacher, he thought again.

"What does she want? Gratitude?" He knew how it would end: the boy would disappear, and afterward it would be discovered that something was missing—a camera, a watch, a fountain pen. She would be indignant, and he would patiently explain that it had been inevitable from the start, that such behavior was merely an integral part of "their" ethical code.

The other room was quiet. Only a few men stood in the windows looking out. Of the rest, some talked and the others merely sat. He went to the little window where he had gone before, and peered out. In the square there was activity: the soldiers were piling sandbags in a curved line across the lower end, just outside the gate. A large calendar hung on the wall beside the window; its text written in Arabic characters, it showed an unmistakably American girl lifting a bottle of Coca-Cola to her lips. As he went back across the room two or three men turned angry faces toward him, and he heard the word *mericani,* as well as a few unflattering epithets. He was relieved: at least they all knew he was not French. It was unlikely that there would be any trouble.

In the middle room the old man had slumped to one side and closed his eyes: so many pipes of kif in one afternoon had proven more than he could manage. When Stenham stepped through the further doorway Lee stood up, smoothed her skirt, and said: "Well, it's all settled. Amar's coming with us. They can find somewhere for him to sleep, and if they won't, I'll simply take a room for him tonight."

Stenham smiled pityingly. "Well, your intentions are good, anyway. Is that his name? Amar?"

"Ask him. That's what he told me. He can say my name, but he pronounces it Bali. It's rather nice—certainly prettier than Polly."

"I see," said Stenham. "It means old, applied to objects. If you want to lug him along it's all right with me."

The boy was still seated, looking up at them anxiously, from her face to his and back again.

"Suppose he hadn't happened to meet us," Stenham suggested. "What would he have done then?"

"He'd probably have gone back into the town before the trouble started and gotten home somehow. Don't forget it was you who spoke to him and asked him to sit down with us."

"You're sure you wouldn't just like to give him some money and let it go at that?"

"Yes, I'm sure," she said flatly.

"All right. Then I guess we'd better go."

He handed the boy five hundred francs. "*Chouf*. Pay for the tea and *cabrhozels,* and ask the *qaouaji* to open the door for us." Amar went out. It was perfectly possible, thought Stenham, that the proprietor of the café would refuse to run the risk of opening the door; they had no one's word but the boy's to the contrary. He stepped to the back door and looked out once again at the pool. The sun had gone behind the walls; in the afternoon shade the patio had taken on an austere charm. The surface of the water was smooth, but the plants along the edges, trembling regularly, betrayed the current beneath. A swallow came careening down from the ramparts toward the pool, obviously with the intention of touching the water. Seeing Stenham, it changed its direction violently, and went off in blind haste toward the sky. He listened: the shooting was not audible at the moment, there were no street-vendors' shouts, no water-sellers' bells jangling, and the high murmur of human voices that formed the city's usual backdrop of sound was missing. What he heard was the sharp confusion of bird-cries. It was the hour of the swallows. Each evening at this time they set to wheeling and darting by the tens of thousands, in swift, wide circles above the walls and gardens and alleys and bridges, their shrill screams presaging the advent of twilight.

So, he thought, it's happened. They've done it. Whatever came to pass now, the city would never be the same again. That much he knew. He heard Lee's voice behind him.

"Amar says they've unlocked the door for us. Shall we go?"

CHAPTER 24

The man and the woman stood there for a moment while the *qaouaji* closed and bolted the door behind them. A pall of dust lay over the square, raised by the boots of the soldiers as they hurried back and forth from the trucks to the barricade they were building at the foot of the gate. In his head Amar was thinking: "Allah is all-powerful." Once more He had intervened in his favor. Now that he reviewed the events of the past two or three hours, it seemed to him that at the first moment when the man had come into the café he remembered having noticed a strange light around his head. A second later he had seen that it was only the glint in his blond hair. But now that their two fates were indissolubly linked, he recalled the brightness that had moved in the air where the man's head was, and preferred to interpret it as a sign given him by Allah to indicate the course he must follow. It was his own secret power, he told himself, which had made it possible for him to recognize the sign and behave accordingly. From the moment he had seen the man's grave face looking out the window at him as he sat by the pool he had known that he could, if he wanted, count on his protection. It was even possible that in addition he might be able to add enough to his savings to buy a pair of shoes. But that was a secondary consideration of which he was ashamed as soon as it occurred to him. "I don't want the shoes," he told Allah, while they were crossing the square. "All I want is to stay with the Nesrani and obey his commands until I can go home again."

The fact that it was the woman who had made the actual suggestion of taking him to the hotel counted for nothing: the pattern of life was such that women were on earth only to carry out the bidding of men, and however it might look as though a woman were imposing her desires, it was always the will of men that was done, since Allah worked only through men. And how rightly, he thought, gazing with distaste at this woman's scanty clothing and her shameless way of walking along jauntily beside the man, as though she thought it perfectly proper for her to be out in the street dressed in such a fashion.

They had come to a row of policemen who stood in the way of the exit from the square. The man was talking to them. One of them designated Amar. He supposed the man was explaining that this was his servant, for presently whatever difficulties had existed appeared to have been smoothed out, and the Frenchmen seemed satisfied. Two of the uniformed men began to walk with them, so that they were now a party of five, going up the long avenue between the walls toward the sunset.

There were soldiers everywhere; they walked in the public gardens under the orange trees, leaned against the wall along the river, strutted among the overturned deck-chairs of the cafés in the park, and stood glowering at attention on either side of the high portal that led into the old Sultan's palace. A few were French, but most of them were grim-faced Berbers with shaved heads and narrow slanting eyes. They had helped the French in Indochina, and now they were helping them once more in their own land, and against their own countrymen. Amar felt his heart swell with hatred as he walked past them, but then he tried to think of something else, for fear the Frenchmen going along beside him would feel the force of his hatred. The man and the woman were talking together in a lively fashion as they turned into the long street of Fez-Djedid, and occasionally they even laughed, as though it had not occurred to them that death was everywhere around them, behind the walls of the houses and in the twilit alleys to their left, to their right. Perhaps they did not even know what was happening: they belonged to another world, and the French had respect for them.

About halfway to Bab Semmarine the street took on a somewhat more usual aspect. Here the large Algerian cafés were full, the flames of the lamps flickered on the tea-drinkers' faces, certain clothing shops were open, throngs of men and boys walked back and forth talking excitedly, being prevented from stopping by the police who constantly prodded them, saying gruffly: "*Allez! Zid! Zid! Vas-y!*" It was along here that Amar suddenly became aware of someone walking behind him, softly saying his name: "*Amar! Yah, Amar!*" The voice was deep, mellow, resonant; it was Benani. But remembering Benani's warning of the night before, that he must not step outside the walls of the Medina, he decided to pretend to hear nothing, and walked along as close to the Christian man as he was able. Still the voice continued to call his name discreetly, perhaps two meters behind him, through the hubbub and chaos of the crowd, never increasing in volume or changing its inflection.

"So that's what they're like," he thought cynically. Amar was supposed to stay inside the Medina and wait for the French to shoot him or carry him off to jail, while the members of the Party, once they had made the trouble, took care to remain outside, so that they might enjoy complete freedom.

In a café on their right several Algerians were singing, grouped around a young man playing an *oud*. The two tourists wanted to stand still a moment and listen, but the police would not let them, and instead hurried them along toward Bab Semmarine. It was only when they had gone beneath the first arch, and were holding their breaths against the onslaught of the urinal's stench inside, that the insistent voice became more pressing. "Amar!" it said. "Don't turn around. It's all right; I know you hear me." (Amar glanced slyly first at the policeman on his left, then at the other. Apparently neither one of them understood Arabic, and even if they had, it was unlikely that they would have been able to notice and single out that one voice in the tumult around them.) "Amar! Remember you have no tongue. We—" The echoing sound of a carriage passing through the vaulted tunnel covered the rest of the message. When they had come beneath the further arch out into the open once more, the voice was gone. The bad dream had been dispersed by the admonition to keep silence; Benani imagined that he and the two foreigners were under arrest.

The Rue Bou Khessissate was virtually deserted, the shopfronts had been battened down, and the windows of the apartments in the upper stories, where the more fortunate Jewish families lived, were hidden behind their shutters. Here and there, as they went briskly down the long, curving street, Amar saw, in back of a blind partly ajar, a stout matron in her fringed headdress, holding a lamp and peering anxiously out, doubtless asking herself vaguely if the thing which every Jew feared in times of stress might come to pass—if the infuriated Moslems, frustrated by their powerlessness to retaliate against the Christians, might not vent at least a part of their rage in a traditional attack upon the Mellah. For there was certainly nothing to stop them, if the desire came to them: a token detachment of police, most of them Jewish themselves, and one little radio patrol car, stationed just inside Bab Chorfa, which the mob could have turned over with one hand if it had felt like it. He wondered whether the young Arabs would be coming tonight to kill the men and violate the girls (for although it was not a very great triumph to have a Jewish girl, still it was a fact that a good many of them were actually virgins, and this was an undeniable attraction in itself); his intuition told him that this time would not be like the other times, that the Istiqlal would issue special directives forbidding such useless excesses. For the moment he felt magnificently superior: he was walking with four Nazarenes, and he could count on their protection. Then he thought of the old adage: "You can share the meal of a Jew, but not his bed. You can share the bed of a Christian, but not his meal," and he wondered if he would have to share the man's bed. It was well known that many Christians liked young Arab boys. If the Christian attacked him, he would fight; of that he was certain. But he did not really believe in the likelihood of such a thing.

When they came to the Place du Commerce, he saw that the fair which had filled the square the night before was now almost entirely dismantled. Even in the dark, with the aid of flashlights and carbide flares, workmen were hastily folding the flimsy partitions, crating the mechanical apparatuses, and piling everything into the trucks that had been standing behind the booths. There were several taxis at the far end of the square. The policemen led them to the first car, and when Amar and the two tourists were inside, one of them got in front beside the driver. The other stepped back, saluted, and told the man at the wheel to go to the Mérinides Palace. Amar was elated. He had never before been in a taxi, nor, indeed, in any ordinary automobile—only in buses and trucks, and there was no denying that these small vehicles went much faster. The little suburban villas sped past, then the stadium and the railway crossing, and then there were, on one side, the long unbroken ramparts enclosing the Sultan's orchards, and the open desolate plain on the other.

So far, the man had studiously avoided speaking at all to Amar, and Amar guessed that he did not want the police to know he understood Arabic. Occasionally the woman flung an encouraging smile at him, as if she thought he might be afraid to be with strangers. Each time she did this he smiled back politely. They were talking about him now, he knew, but it was in their own language, and that was all right.

Outside Bab Segma there was great activity. In the dust raised by moving vehicles the beams of several powerful searchlights crossed each other, making a design that was complicated by the headlights of trucks and camionettes. As the taxi approached the gate, Amar saw a row of small tanks lined up against the wall. A sudden, enormous doubt surged within him. It was perfectly useless, this absurd flight he was making from his own people into a foreign precinct, with foreigners. Even if the police did not pull him out of the car here at Bab Segma, or further along the road, or at Bab Jamaï, they would surely take him from the hotel. And even if the kind lady and gentleman managed to protect him for a certain length of time, sooner or later there would come an hour when he would be alone momentarily, and that was all the French needed. Certainly in their eyes he would be more suspect for having been with these two outsiders.

The taxi swerved to the left, climbed the hill that led past the entrance to the Casbah Cherarda where the Senegalese troops were quartered. There were tanks there, too, and it was evident that tonight the guards were not the customary tall black men with their faces decorated by knife-scar designs, stiffly holding their bayonets at their sides; in their place stood red-faced Frenchmen with tommy-guns. At the top of the hill the car turned right, and went along the barren stretch where the cattle market was held on Thursdays. The policeman lolled beside the driver, one arm over the back of the seat, smoking a cigarette. Now that they were out in the country, and Amar's fear had subsided somewhat, he was again able to view things rationally, and to be ashamed of his emotions of a minute ago. Allah had provided him with a means of escape from the café, without which he would no doubt have remained in there indefinitely, for no one else would have stirred outside, with all those soldiers in the square. And it was probable that he would eat tonight, and sleep quietly until morning. No man could righteously ask for more than that. When morning came, it would be a new day with new problems and possibilities, but of course it was sinful to think about a day that had not yet arrived. Man was meant to consider only the present; to be preoccupied with the future, either pleasantly or with anxiety, implied a lack of humility in the face of Providence, and was unforgivable.

All at once the car was filled with a sweet smell, like flowers, as the lady opened a small bag she carried with her, and pulled out a pack of cigarettes. Fez lay far below, wrapped in darkness, its presence betrayed only here and there by a feeble reddish gleam—a lamp in some window or a fire in a courtyard, visible for the fraction of a second as the taxi moved ahead, following the sinuous course of the road along the edge of the cliffs.

They came to the summit, where the ruined tombs of the Mérinide royal family looked down across the olive groves and the eastern end of the city. The broken domes stood out black and jagged against the limpid night sky. Amar recalled the last time he had come down these slopes and rounded these curves: he had been on his way home to a beating. He smiled as he remembered how the boy steering the bicycle had misunderstood his query about the brakes, had imagined Amar was afraid it might go off the road, when actually he had been hoping that it would do just that, catapulting them both into a ravine. And he smiled again when he thought of how very seriously he had taken the prospect of that beating, whereas now, he decided, it would mean nothing to him, save the sadness he would feel at being the object of his father's displeasure, for he had grown up a good deal since then. But had he grown up entirely? For an instant he was sufficiently detached to be able to pose the question. In his pocket was a paper of kif, part of a long-term project of vengeance against Mustapha, in retaliation for that very beating. Would it not be pleasing to Allah if he should suddenly toss it out the window at this moment? But Bab Jamaï then appeared below in a confusion of moving lights, and the thought slipped out of his head to be replaced by the more real preoccupation with what might happen if the police should insist on pulling him from the taxi. This was the most dangerous spot, because it was here that they had to go into the Medina. They had arrived at the gate. The driver came to a halt and shut off the motor. A flashlight was played into their faces and then around the interior of the taxi, and a French soldier poked his head through the back window, exchanging a few words with the man and the woman. "*Et cet arabe-là,*" he said, indicating Amar with the faintly contemptuous familiarity of proprietorship, "he is your personal servant?" And although Amar did not understand the words, he knew perfectly well what the soldier had said. Both the foreigners replied yes, that was the case. "*Vous pouvez continuer à l' hôtel,*" he told them, and the car started up and went ahead the hundred yards to the hotel gateway.

And then began for Amar a strange series of confused impressions. Led by his new friends, he passed through two small courtyards and up two flights of carpeted stairs to an endless corridor, also carpeted, so that their footsteps made no sound. And there was expensive reed matting covering the walls all along the way, and lanterns overhead such as were found only in the Karouine Mosque or the Zaouia of Moulay Idriss. And then they opened two great doors of glass and went down a few steps into a room which was like nothing he had ever seen, but which, he decided, could not have been made for anyone but a sultan. The intricacies of the high domed ceiling were only faintly illumined by the many-colored rays of light that streamed from the colossal lanterns overhead; it was like being in a vast and perfect cave. He had only a short moment to look around as they crossed the room, and then they were out in another corridor climbing another flight of stairs, this time very old ones of mosaic, and without carpeting—rather like the stairs in his own house, except that the edges of the steps were of white marble instead of wood. The man and woman spoke in low voices as they climbed, Amar behind them. At the top of the stairs there was another corridor, less beautiful than the one below.

Then the man opened a door and they were in the room. "Go in," he said to Amar, breaking the long silence that had been between them. He spoke to the woman, urging her to enter, too. After some hesitation she finally agreed, and she and the man sat down in two large chairs. Amar remained standing by the door, looking at the magnificent room. "Sit down," the man said to him. He obeyed, seating himself on the floor at the spot where he had been standing, and continued his careful examination of the carvings on the beams overhead and the fancy painted plaster frieze of geometric designs. The rugs were thick, the heavy curtains hid the windows, and on the bed the covers had been pulled back to reveal the whiteness of clean sheets.

Now the man looked at him closely for the first time, took out a pack of cigarettes, and after offering the woman one, tossed the pack to Amar. "What's the matter with your nose and eyes?" he asked him. "Have you had a fight?" Amar laughed and said: "Yes." He was embarrassed, and he longed to get up and look into the mirror over the washstand, but he sat still and smoked. The man's manner of casual familiarity with him was assuredly designed to put him at his ease, and he was grateful to him for it; however, the presence of the woman made him nervous. She kept looking at him and smiling in a way that he found disconcerting. It was the way a mother smiles at her small child in a public place when many people are watching and she hopes that it will continue to behave properly. He supposed she meant it to be friendly and reassuring, perhaps even an encouragement, a promise of future intimacy if ever they should find themselves alone. But to him it was a shameless and indecent way for her to behave in front of the man, now that they were all three seated in his bedroom, and he felt that out of deference to his host he should pretend to ignore her smiles. Unfortunately she would have none of this; the less attention he paid her, the more determinedly she kept at him, grimacing, wrinkling her nose at him like a rabbit, blowing smoke toward him as she laughed at things the man said, and generally behaving in an increasingly shocking fashion. And the man went on talking, as if he were completely unaware of what she was doing—not pretending, not indifferent, either, but truly unaware.

Amar was embarrassed for them all, but particularly for the man. He disapproved likewise of the fact that the man and the woman presently embarked on a long and occasionally stormy conversation regarding him; he knew he was the subject by the glances they gave him while they were talking. Being with them was going to be difficult, he could see that, but he was determined to show a maximum of patience. It was the least he could do in return for having been offered protection, shelter and food in this time of hardship. The discussion appeared to be one concerning food, for suddenly without any pause or transition the man said to him: "Would you mind eating alone in this room?" He answered that he would not mind at all—that, indeed, he thought it the best idea. The man seemed relieved upon hearing his reply, but the woman began to make silly gestures meaning that he ought to go downstairs and eat with them. While she did this the man glowered. Amar had no intention of accompanying them to any public room where he would be on view to the French and the Moroccans who worked in the hotel. He smiled amiably and said: "This is a good room for eating." For a while the conversation between the two became more animated; then the woman got up petulantly and walked to the door, where she turned and waved coyly at Amar before she went out. The man stepped into the corridor with her for a moment, came back in, and shut the door. His expression was one of annoyance as he took up the telephone and spoke briefly into it.

Amar had been studying the patterns in the rug beside him; he had decided it was the most beautiful object in the room.

When he had hung up the receiver, the man sat down again, heaved a deep sigh, and lit another cigarette. Amar looked up at him.

"Why do you talk so much with that woman?" he said, the expression of his voice a mixture of shyness and curiosity. "Words are for people, not for women."

The man laughed. "Aren't women people?" he asked.

"People are people," Amar said stolidly. "Women are women. It's not the same thing."

The man looked very surprised, and laughed more loudly. Then his face became serious; he leaned forward in the chair. "If women aren't people," he said slowly, "how does it happen they can go to Paradise?"

Amar looked at him suspiciously: the man could scarcely be that ignorant. But he could discern no mockery in his face. "*El hassil,*" he began, "they have their own place in Heaven. They don't go inside where the men are."

"I see," the man said gravely. "It's like the mosques, is that it?"

"That's it," said Amar, still wondering if the man might not be making fun of him.

"You must know a lot about your religion," the man said dreamily. "I wish you'd tell me something about it."

Now Amar was convinced that he was being baited. He gave a short, bitter laugh. "I don't know anything," he said. "I'm like an animal."

The man raised his eyebrows. "Nothing at all? But you should. It's a very good religion."

Amar was displeased. He studied the face of this patronizing infidel for a moment. "It's the *only* one," he said evenly. Then he smiled.

"But now we are all like animals. Just look in the streets, see what's happening here. Don't you think it's the Moslems' fault?"

The man's swift glance told him that he was awakening some sort of respect. "The Moslems have some blame," he said quietly, "but I think the great blame goes to the French. You don't judge a man too harshly for what he does to an intruder he finds in his house, do you?"

Now Amar was about to reply: "Allah sees everything," but a voice in his head was whispering to him that it was not the sort of remark the Nazarene would really hear. If he wanted to keep alive the spark of respect he felt he had kindled, he must work hard inside himself. "The French are thieves in our house, you're right," he agreed. "We invited them in because we wanted to take lessons from them. We thought they'd teach us. They haven't taught us anything—not even how to be good thieves. So we want to put them out. But now they think the house is theirs, and that we're only servants in it. What can we do except fight? It is written."

"Do you hate them?" the man asked; he was leaning forward, looking at Amar with intensity. There was no one there but the two of them; if the man turned out to be a spy he would at least have no witnesses. But that was an extreme consideration: Amar was positive he was only an onlooker. "Yes, I hate them," he said simply. "That's written, too."

"You have to hate them, you mean? You can't decide: I will or I won't hate them?"

Amar did not completely understand. "But I hate them *now*," he explained. "The day Allah wants me to stop hating them, He'll change my heart."

The man was smiling, as if to himself. "If the world's really like that, it's very easy to be in it," he said.

"It will never be easy to be in the world," Amar said firmly. "*Er rabi mabrhach*. God doesn't want it easy."

The man did not answer. Soon he rose, went to the open window, and stood looking down at the dark Medina below. When he turned back into the room, he began to speak as though there had been no break in the conversation. "So you hate them," he mused. "Would you like to kill them?"

This immediately put Amar on his guard. "Why do you ask me all these questions?" he said aggrievedly. "Why do you want to know about me? That's not good at a time like now." He tried to keep his face empty of expression, so that it would not look as though he were indignant, but apparently his effort was not completely successful, for the man sat back and launched into a long apology, making a good many errors in Arabic, so that Amar often was not certain what it was he was trying to tell him. The recurrent motif of this speech, however, was that the Nazarene was not attempting to pry into Amar's life in any way, but only to learn about what was happening in the city. To Amar this was a most implausible explanation; if it were the truth, why did the man keep asking him for his personal opinion?

"What I think about the trouble is less than the wind," he finally said with a certain bitterness. "I can't even read or write my own name. What good could I be to anybody?" But even this confession, with all it cost him to make it, seemed not to convince the man, who, rather than accepting it and letting the matter drop, seemed positively delighted to learn of Amar's shame. "Aha!" he cried. "I see! I see! Very good! Then you have nothing to fear from anyone."

This remark Amar found particularly disturbing, for it must mean that he was going to send him away. The Nazarene had understood nothing at all; Amar's spirits sank as he perceived the gap that lay between them. If a Nazarene with so much good will and such a knowledge of Arabic was unable to grasp even the basic facts of such a simple state of affairs, then was there any hope that any Nazarene would ever aid any Moslem? And yet a part of his mind kept repeating to him that the man could be counted on, that he could be a true friend and protector if only he would let himself be shown how.

They continued to talk, but the conversation was now like a game in which the players, through fatigue or lack of interest, have ceased to keep the score, or even to pay attention to the sequence of plays. The point of contact was gone; they seemed to be looking in different directions, trying to say separate things, giving different meanings to words. Mercifully, a knock came at the door, and the man sprang to open it. The woman stood there, dressed in a more seemly manner this time, and looking very pleased with herself. In she came, down she sat, and then on and on she talked, while Amar's boredom and hunger grew. When there was another knock at the door, he rose, swiftly crossed the room, and managed to be at the window, leaning over the balcony, when the servant came in carrying his tray, and he remained there until he had heard him go out and shut the door behind him. His eyes having grown used to the dark as he stood there, he was able to find, among the thousands of cubes which were the houses in the dimness below, the mosque that stood on the hill at the back of his house. And off in the east, behind the barren mountains, there was a glow in the clear sky which meant that the moon would shortly be arriving.

In the room the man and the woman made clinking sounds with

their glasses, and talked, and went on talking. He wondered how the man found the patience to go on making conversation with her. After all, he reflected, if Allah had meant women to talk to men, He would have made them men, and given them intelligence and discernment. But in His infinite wisdom He had created them to serve men and be commanded by them. The man who, forgetting this, allowed one of them to addle his brain to such an extent that he was willing to meet her on equal terms, sooner or later would bitterly regret his weakness. For women, no matter how delightful they might seem, were basically evil, savage creatures who desired nothing better than to pull men down to their own low state, merely to watch them suffer. In Fez it was often said, half jokingly, that if the Moroccans had been really civilized men, they would have devised cages in which to keep their women. As it was, the women enjoyed far too much freedom of movement; and yet the Nationalists actually wanted to give them more, wanted to allow them to walk alone in the street, go to the cinema, sit in cafés, even swim in public places. And most unthinkable of all, they hoped to induce them to discard the *litham,* and show their faces openly, like Jewesses or Christians. Of course this could never really happen; even the prostitutes wore veils when they went out to shop, but it was characteristic of the times that some Nationalists dared speak openly of such things.

Soon the man called: "*Fik ej jeuhor?* Hungry?" Amar turned. On the tray there was a plate with pieces of white bread on it. "These are for you," the man said. "That's your dinner."

Determined not to show his disappointment at finding that the man held him in such low esteem as to offer him nothing but these few mouthfuls of bread, he smiled, went over to the table, and took a piece. Then he discovered that each one was two pieces, and that they had butter and chicken inside. This was partly consoling. The tray also held a bottle of Coca-Cola. He sipped a little, but it was too cold. "We're going down and eat," the man said. "This is enough for you?"

Amar said it would be. He was now terrified that someone might come to the room while he was in it alone. "Please lock the door," he said.

"Lock the door?"

"Lock the door, please, and take the key with you."

The man repeated this to the woman; he seemed to think it an amusing request. When she heard the words her face assumed a bewildered expression, as though it were an unheard-of idea to lock anyone into a room. Then the man, in passing him, tousled his hair, saying: "*Nchoufou menbad.*" Amar's mouth was full of bread and chicken, but he nodded his head vigorously. After the man had shut the door, he went over and tried the knob, just to be sure. Then he set the tray on the floor, sat down beside it, and began to eat in earnest.

Taprobane, Weligama, 1955

THE IRON TABLE

JANE BOWLES

This fragment appears in a notebook of Jane's; it was probably written in the early fifties.

THEY SAT IN THE SUN, looking out over a big new boulevard. The waiter had dragged an old iron table around from the other side of the hotel and set it down on the cement near a half-empty flower bed. A string stretched between stakes separated the hotel grounds from the sidewalk. Few of the guests staying at the hotel sat in the sun. The town was not a tourist center, and not many Anglo-Saxons came. Most of the guests were Spanish.

"The whole civilization is going to pieces," he said.

Her voice was sorrowful. "I know it." Her answers to his ceaseless complaining about the West's contamination of Moslem culture had become increasingly unpredictable. Today, because she felt that he was in a very irritable mood and in need of an argument, she automatically agreed with him. "It's going to pieces so quickly, too," she said, and her tone was sepulchral.

He looked at her without any light in his blue eyes. "There are places where the culture has remained untouched," he announced as if for the first time. "If we went into the desert you wouldn't have to face all this. Wouldn't you love that?" He was punishing her for her swift agreement with him a moment earlier. He knew she had no desire to go to the desert, and that she believed it was not possible to continue trying to escape from the Industrial Revolution. Without realizing he was doing it he had provoked the argument he wanted.

"Why do you ask me if I wouldn't love to go into the desert, when you know as well as I do I wouldn't. We've talked about it over and over. Every few days we talk about it." Although the sun was beating down on her chest, making it feel on fire, deep inside she could still feel the cold current that seemed to run near her heart.

"Well," he said. "You change. Sometimes you say you *would* like to go."

It was true. She did change. Sometimes she would run to him with bright eyes. "Let's go," she would say. "Let's go into the desert." But she never did this if she was sober.

There was something wistful in his voice, and she had to remind herself that she wanted to feel cranky rather than heartbroken. In order to go on talking she said: "Sometimes I feel like going, but it's always when I've had something to drink. When I've had nothing to drink I'm afraid." She turned to face him, and he saw that she was beginning to have her hunted expression.

"Do you think I *ought* to go?" she asked him.

"Go where?"

"To the desert. To live in an oasis." She was pronouncing her words slowly. "Maybe that's what I should do, since I'm your wife."

"You must do what you really want to do," he said. He had been trying to teach her this for twelve years.

"What I really want. . . . Well, if you'd be happy in an oasis, maybe I'd really want to do that." She spoke hesitantly, and there was a note of doubt in her voice.

"What?" He shook his head as if he had run into a spiderweb. "What is it?"

"I meant that maybe if you were happy in an oasis I would be, too. Wives get pleasure out of making their husbands happy. They really do, quite aside from its being moral."

He did not smile. He was in too bad a humor. "You'd go to an oasis because you wanted to escape from Western civilization."

"My friends and I don't feel there's any *way* of escaping it. It's not interesting to sit around talking about industrialization."

"What friends?" He liked her to feel isolated.

"Our friends." Most of them she had not seen in many years. She turned to him with a certain violence. "I think you come to these countries so you can complain. I'm tired of hearing the word *civilization.* It has no meaning. Or I've forgotten what it meant, anyway."

The moment when they might have felt tenderness had passed, and secretly they both rejoiced. Since he did not answer her, she went on. "I think it's uninteresting. To sit and watch costumes disappear, one by one. It's uninteresting even to mention it."

"They are not costumes," he said distinctly. "They're simply the clothes people wear."

She was as bitter as he about the changes, but she felt it would be indelicate for them both to reflect the same sorrow. It would happen some day, surely. A serious grief would silence their argument. They would share it and not be able to look into each other's eyes. But as long as she could she would hold off that moment.

Early fifties?

PART THREE

THE FROZEN FIELDS

PAUL BOWLES

THE TRAIN WAS LATE because the hot-box under one of the coaches had caught fire in the middle of a great flat field covered with snow. They had stayed there about an hour. After the noise and rushing of the train, the sudden silence and the embarrassed stirring of people in their seats induced a general restlessness. At one point another train had shot by on the next track with a roar worse than thunder; in the wake of that, the nervousness of the passengers increased, and they began to talk fretfully in low voices.

Donald had started to scratch pictures with his fingernail in the ice that covered the lower part of the windowpane by his seat. His father had said: "Stop that." He knew better than to ask "Why?" but he thought it; he could not see what harm it would do, and he felt a little resentful toward his mother for not intervening. He could have arranged for her to object to the senseless prohibition, but experience had taught him that she could be counted on to come to his defense only a limited number of times during any given day, and it was imprudent to squander her reserve of good will.

The snow had been cleared from the station platform when they got out. It was bitter cold; a fat plume of steam trailed downward from the locomotive, partially enveloping the first coach. Donald's feet ached with the cold.

"There's Uncle Greg and Uncle Willis!" he cried, and he jumped up and down several times.

"You don't have to shout," said his father. "We see them. And stand still. Pick up your bag."

Uncle Willis wore a black bearskin coat that almost touched the ground. He put his hands under Donald's arms and lifted him up so that his head was at a level with his own, and kissed him hard on the mouth. Then he swung him over into Uncle Greg's arms, and Uncle Greg did the same thing. "How's the man, hey?" cried Uncle Greg, as he set him down.

"Fine," said Donald, conscious of a feeling of triumph, because his father did not like to see boys being kissed. "Men shake hands," he had told him. "They don't kiss each other."

The sky was crystal clear, and although it was already turning lavender with the passing of afternoon, it still shone with an intense light, like the sky in one scene at the Russian Ballet. His mother had taken him a few weeks earlier because she wanted to see Pavlova; it was not the dancing that had excited him, but the sudden direct contact with the world of magic. This was a magic sky above him now, nothing like the one he was used to seeing above the streets of New York. Everything connected with the farm was imbued with magic. The house was the nucleus of an enchanted world more real than the world that other people knew about. During the long green summers he had spent there with his mother and the members of her family he had discovered that world and explored it, and none of them had ever noticed that he was living in it. But his father's presence here would constitute a grave danger, because it was next to impossible to conceal anything from him, and once aware of the existence of the other world he would spare no pains to destroy it. Donald was not yet sure whether all the entrances were safely guarded or effectively camouflaged.

They sat in the back of the sleigh with a brown buffalo robe tucked around them. The two big gray horses were breathing out steam through their wide nostrils. Silently the white countryside moved past, its frozen trees pink in the late light. Uncle Greg held the reins, and Uncle Willis, sitting beside him, was turned sideways in his seat, talking to Donald's mother.

"My feet hurt," said Donald.

"Well, God Almighty, boy!" cried Uncle Willis. "Haven't you got 'em on the bricks? There are five hot bricks down there. That's what they're there for." He bent over and lifted up part of the heavy lap-robe. The bricks were wrapped in newspaper.

"*My* feet are like blocks of ice, too," said Donald's mother. "Here, take your shoes off and put your feet on these." She pushed two of the bricks toward Donald.

"He just wants attention," said Donald's father. But he did not forbid him to have the bricks.

"Is that better?" Uncle Willis asked a moment later.

"It feels good. How many miles is it to the farm?"

"Seven miles to The Corner, and a mile and a half from there."

"Oh, I know it's a mile and a half from The Corner," said Donald. He had walked it many times in the summer, and he knew the names of the farms along the road. "First you come to the Elders, then the Landons, then the Madisons—"

His father pushed him hard in the ribs with his elbow. "Just keep quiet for a while."

Uncle Willis pretended not to have heard this. "Well, well. You certainly have a good memory. How old are you now?"

Donald's throat had constricted; it was a familiar occurrence which did not at all mean that he was going to cry—merely that he felt like crying. He coughed and said in a stifled voice: "Six." Then he coughed again; ashamed, and fearful that Uncle Willis might have noticed something amiss, he added: "But I'll be seven the day after New Year's."

They were all silent after that; there were only the muffled rhythm of the horses' trot and the soft, sliding sound of the runners on the packed snow. The sky was now a little darker than the white meadows, and the woods on the hillside beyond, with their millions of bare branches, began to look frightening. Donald was glad to be sitting in the middle. He knew there were no wolves out there, and yet, could anybody be really certain? There had been wolves at one time—and bears as well—and simply because nobody had seen one in many years, they now said there weren't any. But that was no proof.

They came to The Corner, where the road to the farm turned off from the main road. Seven rusty mail-boxes stood there in a crooked row, one for each house on the road.

"R.F.D. Number One," said Uncle Willis facetiously. This had always been a kind of joke among them, ever since they had bought the farm, because they were townspeople and thought the real farmers were very funny.

Now Donald felt he was on home ground, and it gave him the confidence to say: "Rural Free Delivery." He said the words carefully, since the first one sometimes gave him difficulty. But he pronounced it all right, and Uncle Greg, without turning round, shouted: "That's right! You go to school now?"

"Yes." He did not feel like saying more, because he was following the curves in the road, which he knew by heart. But everything looked so different from the way he remembered it that he found it hard to believe it was the same place. The land had lost its intimacy, become bare and unprotected. Even in the oncoming night he could see right through the leafless bushes that should have hidden the empty fields beyond. His feet were all right now, but his hands in their woolen mittens under the buffalo skin were numb with cold.

The farm came into view; in each downstairs window there was a lighted candle and a holly wreath. He bent over and put his shoes on. It was hard because his fingers ached. When he sat up again the sleigh had stopped. The kitchen door had opened; someone was coming out. Everyone was shouting "Hello!" and "Merry Christmas!" Between the sleigh and the kitchen he was aware only of being kissed and patted, lifted up and set down, and told that he had grown. His grandfather helped him take off his shoes again and removed a lid from the top of the stove so he could warm his hands over the flames. The kitchen smelled, as in summer, of woodsmoke, sour milk and kerosene.

It was always very exciting to be in the midst of many people. Each one was an added protection against the constant watchfulness of his mother and father. At home there were only he and they, so that mealtimes were periods of torture. Tonight there were eight at the supper table. They put an enormous old leather-bound dictionary in a chair so he would be high enough, and he sat between his grandmother and Aunt Emilie. She had dark brown eyes and was very pretty. Uncle Greg had married her a year ago, and Donald knew from many overheard conversations that none of the others really liked her.

Gramma was saying: "Louisa and Ivor couldn't get down till tomorrow. Mr. Gordon's driving them down as far as Portersville in his car. They'll all stay in the hotel tonight, and we've got to go in first thing in the morning and bring them out."

"Mr. Gordon, too, I suppose," said his mother.

"Oh, probably," Uncle Greg said. "He won't want to stay alone Christmas Day."

His mother looked annoyed. "It seems sort of unnecessary," she said. "Christmas is a *family* day, after all."

"Well, he's part of the family now," said Uncle Willis with a crooked smile.

His mother replied with great feeling: "I think it's terrible."

"He's pretty bad these days," put in Grampa, shaking his head.

"Still on the old fire-water?" asked his father.

Uncle Greg raised his eyebrows. "That and worse. You know. . . . And Ivor too."

Donald knew they were being mysterious because of him. He pretended not to be listening, and busied himself making marks on the tablecloth with his napkin ring.

His father's mouth had fallen open with astonishment. "Where do they get it?" he demanded.

"Prescription," said Uncle Willis lightly. "Some crooked Polack doctor up there."

"Oh, honestly," cried his mother. "I don't see how Louisa *stands* it."

Aunt Emilie, who had been quiet until now, suddenly spoke. "Oh, I don't know," she said speculatively. "They're both very good to her. I think Mr. Gordon's very generous. *He* pays the rent on her apartment, you know, and gives her the use of the car and chauffeur most afternoons."

"You don't know anything about it," said Uncle Greg in a gruff, unpleasant voice which was meant to stop her from talking. But she went on, a bit shrilly, and even Donald could hear that they were in the habit of arguing.

"I *do* happen to know that Ivor's perfectly willing to give her a divorce any time she wants it, because she told me so herself."

There was silence at the table; Donald was certain that if he had not been there they would all have begun to talk at that point. Aunt Emilie had said something he was not supposed to hear.

"Well," said Uncle Willis heartily, "how about another piece of cake, Donald, old man?"

"How about bed, you mean," said his father. "It's time he went to bed."

His mother said nothing, helped him from his chair and took him upstairs.

The little panes of his bedroom window were completely covered with ice. Opening his mouth, he breathed on one pane until a round hole had been melted through and he could see blackness outside. "Don't do that, dear," said his mother. "Gramma'll have to clean the window. Now come on; into bed with you. There's a nice hot brick under the covers so your feet won't get cold." She tucked the blankets around him, kissed him, and took the lamp from the table. His father's voice, annoyed, came up from the foot of the stairs. "Hey, Laura! What's going on up there? Come on."

"Won't there be any light in my room at all?" Donald asked her.

"I'm coming," she called. She looked down at Donald. "You never have a light at home."

"I know, but home I can turn it on if I need it."

"Well, you're not going to need it tonight. Your father would have a fit if I left the lamp. You know that. Now just go to sleep."

"But I won't be able to sleep," he said miserably.

"Laura!" shouted his father.

"Just a *minute!*" she cried, vexed.

"Please, Mother . . . ?"

Her voice was adamant. "This cold air will put you to sleep in two shakes of a lamb's tail. Now go to sleep." She went to the doorway, the lamp in her hand, and disappeared through it, closing the door behind her.

There was a little china clock on the table that ticked very loud and fast. At infrequent intervals from below came a muffled burst of laughter which immediately subsided. His mother had said: "I'll open this window about an inch; that'll be enough." The room was growing colder by the minute. He pushed the sole of one foot against the heated brick in the middle of the bed, and heard the crackle of the newspaper that enfolded it. There was nothing left to do but go to sleep. On his way through the borderlands of consciousness he had a fantasy. From the mountain behind the farm, running silently over the icy crust of the snow, leaping over the rocks and bushes, came a wolf. He was running toward the farm. When he got there he would look through the windows until he found the dining-room where the grownups were sitting around the big table. Donald shuddered when he saw his eyes in the dark through the glass. And now, calculating every movement perfectly, the wolf sprang, smashing the panes, and seized Donald's father by the throat. In an instant, before anyone could move or cry out, he was gone again with his prey still between his jaws, his head turned sideways as he dragged the limp form swiftly over the surface of the snow.

The white light of dawn was in the room when he opened his eyes. Already there were bumpings in the bowels of the house: people were stirring. He heard a window slammed shut, and then the regular sound of someone splitting wood with a hatchet. Presently there were nearer noises, and he knew that his parents in the next room had gotten up. Then his door was flung open and his mother came in, wearing a thick brown flannel bathrobe, and with her hair falling loose down her back. "Merry Christmas!" she cried, holding up a gigantic red mesh stocking crammed with fruit and small packages. "Look what I found hanging by the fireplace!" He was disappointed because he had hoped to go and get his stocking himself. "I brought it up to you because the house is as cold as a barn," she told him. "You stay put right here in bed till it's warmed up a little."

"When'll we have the tree?" The important ritual was the tree: the most interesting presents were piled under it.

"You just hold your horses," she told him. "You've got your

stocking. We can't have the tree till Aunt Louisa gets here. You wouldn't want her to miss it, would you?"

"Where's my present for Aunt Louisa and Uncle Ivor? Uncle Ivor's coming, too, isn't he?"

"Of course he's coming," she replied, with that faintly different way of speaking she used when she mentioned Uncle Ivor. "I've already put it under the tree with the other things. Now you just stay where you are, all covered up, and look at your stocking. I'm going to get dressed." She shivered and hurried back into her room.

The only person he had to thank at breakfast was his grandfather, for a box of colored pencils which had been jammed into the foot of the stocking. The other gifts had been tagged: "For Donald from Santa." Uncle Willis and Uncle Greg had eaten an early breakfast and gone in the sleigh to the hotel in Portersville to fetch Aunt Louisa and Uncle Ivor. When they got back, Donald ran to the window and saw that Mr. Gordon had come. Everyone had talked so mysteriously about Mr. Gordon that he was very eager to see him. But at that moment his mother called him upstairs to help her make the beds. "We all have to do as much as we can for Gramma," she told him. "Lord knows she's got all she can manage with the kitchen work."

But eventually he heard Aunt Louisa calling up the staircase. They went down: he was smothered in kisses, and Aunt Louisa asked him: "How's my boy? You're *my* boy, aren't you?" Then Uncle Ivor kissed him, and he shook hands with Mr. Gordon, who was already sitting in Grampa's armchair, where nobody else ever sat. He was plump and pale, and he wore two big diamond rings on one hand and an even bigger sapphire on the other. As he breathed he wheezed slightly; now and then he pulled an enormous yellow silk handkerchief out of his breast pocket and wiped his forehead with it. Donald sat down on the other side of the room and turned the pages of a magazine, from time to time looking up to observe him. He had called Donald "my lad," which sounded very strange, like someone talking in a book. At one point he noticed Donald's attention, and beckoned to him. Donald went and stood beside the armchair while Mr. Gordon reached into his pocket and pulled out a fat watch with a little button, and tiny chimes struck inside the watch. A few minutes later he signaled to him afresh; Donald bounded over to him and pressed the button again. The next time, his mother told him to stop bothering Mr. Gordon.

"But he *asked* me to," objected Donald.

"Sit down right there. We're all going in and have our tree in a little while. Uncle Ivor's going to be Santa Claus."

Presently Uncle Willis came into the room. "Well, everybody," he said, rubbing his hands together, "I think the parlor's warm enough now. How about our tree?"

"It's about time," said Aunt Emilie. She was wearing a red taffeta dress which Donald had heard his mother discussing with his father earlier. "*Most* inappropriate," she had said. "The girl doesn't seem to realize she's living on a farm." Aunt Emilie reached down and took Donald's hand. "Would you care to accompany me, sir?" she said. They walked into the parlor holding hands. The fire in the fireplace roared and crackled.

"Where's Ivor?" said Uncle Greg. "Has everybody got a seat?"

"Here he is," said Uncle Ivor, coming in from the hallway. He had put on an old red knitted skull-cap and a red dressing gown, and he had a wreath of green fluted paper around his neck. "This is all Santa Claus could find," he announced.

Aunt Louisa began to laugh. "Look at your Uncle Ivor," she told Donald. "I am," said Donald. But he was really looking at the tree. It was a tall hemlock that reached to the ceiling, and underneath it was piled the most enormous assortment of packages he had ever seen. "Look at that!" they all cried.

"What *do* you suppose is in them all?" said Aunt Louisa.

"I don't know," he replied.

Uncle Ivor sat down on the floor as near the tree as he could get, and lifting up a large crate he passed it to Uncle Greg, who stood in the middle of the room. "Let's get this out of the way first," he said. Then Uncle Greg intoned: "To Donald from the Folks at Rutland."

While Uncle Ivor went on passing out packages, Donald struggled with his box. He was vaguely aware of the little cries that were being uttered around him: "How lovely! But it's too much!" "Oh, you shouldn't have!" "Why did you do it?" as the others opened their gifts, but he was too preoccupied to notice that most of the exclamations were being addressed to Mr. Gordon, who sat in the window looking very pleased.

It was too good to believe: a fire engine three feet long, with rubber tires and a bell and a siren and three ladders that shot upward automatically when it stopped. Donald looked at it, and for a moment was almost frightened by the power he knew it had to change his world.

"Oh . . . isn't . . . that . . . lovely!" said his mother, her annoyance giving a sharp edge to each word. "Louisa, why did you do it?" Donald glanced up quickly and saw Aunt Louisa indicate Mr. Gordon with a jerk of her head, as if she were saying: "Everything is his fault."

His mother moved along the floor toward the crate and fished out the greeting card. "I want you to keep each card in with the present it came with," she told Donald, "because you'll have a lot of thank-you notes to write tomorrow, and you don't want to get them mixed up. But you can thank Aunt Louisa and Uncle Ivor right now."

He hated to be told to thank a person in that person's presence, as though he were a baby. But he said the words bravely, facing Mr. Gordon: "Thank you so much for the beautiful fire engine."

"There's more there, my lad," beamed Mr. Gordon; the diamonds flashed in the sunlight.

Aunt Emilie was holding out her arm in front of her, looking at her new wrist-watch. Grampa had put on a black silk dressing gown and was smoking a cigar. He looked perfectly content as he turned to Mr. Gordon and said: "Well, you've spoiled us all." But Donald's mother interpreted his phrase as a reproach, and added in explanation: "We're not used to getting such *elaborate* gifts, Mr. Gordon."

Mr. Gordon laughed, and turning to Donald, told him: "You've barely started, my lad. Tell your Uncle Ivor to get on with it."

Now it seemed as though nearly every package was for Donald. He opened them as fast as he could, and was freshly bewildered by the apparition of each new marvel. There were, of course, the handkerchiefs and books and mufflers from the family, but there was also a Swiss music box with little metal records that could be changed; there were roller skates, a large set of lead soldiers, a real accordion, and a toy village with a streetcar system that ran on a battery. As Donald opened each package, the little cries of admiration made by his parents came closer to sounding like groans. Finally his father said, in a voice loud enough for Mr. Gordon to hear him above the general conversation: "It's bad business for one kid to get so much."

Mr. Gordon had heard him. "You were young once yourself," he said airily.

Aunt Emilie was trying on a fur jacket that Uncle Greg had given her. Her face was flushed with excitement; she had just planted a big kiss on Uncle Greg's cheek.

"The little Astor baby got five thousand dollars' worth of toys on its last birthday," she said to Donald's father, running her hand back and forth along the fur.

Donald's father looked at her with narrowed eyes. "That," he said, enunciating very clearly, "is what might be called an *asinine* remark."

Save for the crackling of the fire there was silence for a moment in the room. Those who had not heard knew that something had happened. Uncle Greg looked quickly at Donald's father, and then at Aunt

Emilie. Maybe there would be a quarrel, thought Donald, with everyone against his father. The idea delighted him; at the same time he felt guilty, as though it were his doing.

Uncle Ivor was handing him a package. Automatically he untied the ribbon, and pulled out a tan cashmere sweater. "That's Mother's and Daddy's present to you," his mother said quietly. "It's a little big for you now, but I got it big purposely so you could grow into it." The small crisis had passed; they all began to talk again. Donald was relieved and disappointed. "How about christening that bottle of brandy?" cried Uncle Willis.

"You menfolk sit here," Gramma told them. "We've got to get out into the kitchen."

"I'll bring yours out to you," said Uncle Ivor to Aunt Louisa as she got up.

On her way out of the room Donald's mother bent over and touched his shoulder. "I want you to put every present back into its box just the way it was. After that you carry them all up into our room and stack them carefully in the corner under the window. You hear me?"

She went out. Donald sat a moment; then he jumped up and ran after her to ask if he might save out just one thing—the fire engine, perhaps. She was saying to Gramma: ". . . quite uncalled for. Besides, I don't know how we're *ever* going to get it all back to New York. Owen can take the big things at least with him tomorrow, I suppose."

He stopped running, and felt peace descend upon him. His father was leaving the farm. Then let him take everything with him, fire engine and all; it would not matter. He turned and went back into the parlor, where he meticulously packed the toys into their boxes, put the covers on, and tied them up with lengths of ribbon and string.

"What's all this?" exclaimed Mr. Gordon suddenly, noticing him. "What are you doing?"

"I have to take everything upstairs," said Donald.

His father joined the conversation. "I don't want to find those boxes lying all over the place up there, either. See that you pile 'em neatly. Understand?"

Donald continued to work without looking up.

After a moment Mr. Gordon said under his breath: "Well, I'll be damned." Then to Donald's father: "I've seen some well-behaved kids in my time, but I don't mind telling you I never saw one like *that*. Never."

"Discipline begins in the cradle," said his father shortly.

"It's sinister," murmured Mr. Gordon to himself.

Donald glanced up and saw his father looking at Mr. Gordon with hatred.

In the kitchen his grandmother, his aunts and his mother were busy preparing dinner. Donald sat by the window mashing potatoes. The blue of the sky had disappeared behind one curtain of cloud, uniformly white. "We'll have more snow before night," said Gramma, looking out of the window above the sink.

"Want to smell something good?" Donald's mother asked him. He ran across to the stove and she opened the oven door: the aroma of onions mingled with that of the roasting turkey. "He's coming along beautifully," she announced. She shut the oven door with a bang and hung the potholders on their hooks. Then she went into the pantry. Donald followed her. It was very cold in here, and it smelled of pickles and spices. His mother was searching for something along the shelves, among the jars and tin boxes.

"Mother," he said.

"Hmm?" she replied distraughtly, without looking down at him.

"Why does Mr. Gordon live at Uncle Ivor's?"

Now she did look at him, and with an intensity that startled him. "What was that?" she demanded sharply. Then, before he could repeat his question, she went on in a suddenly matter-of-fact voice: "Dear, don't you know that Uncle Ivor's what they call a male nurse? Like Miss Oliver, you remember, who took care of you when you had influenza? Only a man. A man nurse."

"Is Mr. Gordon sick?"

"Yes, he is," she said, lowering her voice to little more than a whisper. "He's a very sick man, but we don't talk about it."

"What's he got?" He was conscious of being purposely childish at the moment, in the hope of learning more. But his mother was already saying: "I don't know, dear. You go back into the kitchen now. It's too cold for you in here. Scoot! Out with you!" He giggled, ran back into the kitchen, satisfied for having definitely established the existence of a mystery.

During dinner his father looked across at him with the particular kind of sternness he reserved for remarks which he knew were unwelcome, said: "You haven't been outside yet today, young man. We'll take a walk down the road later."

Aunt Louisa had brought a large glass of brandy to the table with her, and was sipping it along with her food. "It's too cold, Owen," she objected. "He'll catch his death o'cold." Donald knew she was trying to help him, but he wished she had kept quiet. If it became an issue, his father would certainly not forget about the walk.

"Too cold!" scoffed his father. "We have a few basic rules in *our* little family, and one of them is that he has to get some fresh air every day."

"Couldn't you make an exception for Christmas? Just for one day?" demanded Aunt Louisa.

Donald did not dare look up, for fear of seeing the expression on his father's face.

"Listen, Louisa," he said acidly. "I suggest you just stay on your side of the fence, and I'll stay on mine. We'll get along a lot better." Then as an afterthought he snapped: "That all right with you?"

Aunt Louisa leaned across Grampa's plate toward Donald's father and spoke very loud, so that everyone stopped eating. "No, it's not all right with me!" she cried. "All you do is pick on the child from morning till night. It's shameful! I won't sit by and watch my own flesh and blood plagued that way!"

Both Gramma and Donald's father began to speak at once. Gramma was saying, "Louisa," trying to soothe her. Donald's father shouted: "You've never *had* a kid. You don't know the first thing *about* raising kids."

"I know when a man's selfish and plain cussed," Aunt Louisa declared.

"Louisa!" cried Gramma in a tone of surprise and mild reproof. Donald continued to look at his plate.

"Have I ever come up to Rutland and stuck my nose in your affairs and criticized? Have I?" demanded Donald's father.

"Now come on," said Uncle Willis quickly. "Let's not spoil a beautiful Christmas."

"That's right," Grampa said. "We're all happy. Let's not say anything we'll be sorry for later."

But Aunt Louisa would not retreat. She took a fast gulp of brandy and almost choked on it. Then, still leaning toward Donald's father, she went on: "What do you mean, come to Rutland and criticize? What've you got to criticize in Rutland? Something wrong there?"

For an instant Donald's father did not reply. During that instant it was as though everyone felt the need to say something without being able to say it. The one who broke the short silence was Donald's father, using a peculiar, soft voice which Donald recognized immediately as a vicious imitation of Uncle Ivor. "Oh, *no!* There's nothing wrong in *Rut*land!"

Suddenly, with two simultaneous motions, Donald's mother slapped her napkin into her place and pushed her chair back violently. She rose and ran out of the room, slamming the door. No one said anything. Donald sat frozen, unable to look up, unable even to breathe. Then he realized that his father had got up, too, and was on his way out.

"Leave her alone, Owen," said Gramma.

"You keep out of this," his father said. His footsteps made the stairs creak as he went up. No one said anything until Gramma made as if to rise. "I'm going up," she declared.

"For God's sake, Abbie, sit still," Grampa told her. Gramma cleared her throat, but did not get up.

Aunt Louisa looked very red, and the muscles of her face were twitching. "Hateful," she said in a choked voice. "Just hateful."

"I felt like slapping his face," confided Aunt Emilie. "Did you hear what he said to me when we were having our presents?"

At a glance from Uncle Greg, Aunt Emilie stopped. "Why, Donald!" she exclaimed brightly, "you've scarcely touched your dinner! Aren't you hungry?"

In his mind's eye he was seeing the bedroom upstairs, where his father was twisting his mother's arm and shaking her to make her look at him. When she wouldn't, he punched her, knocking her down, and kicked her as hard as he could, all over her body. Donald looked up. "Not very," he said.

Without warning Mr. Gordon began to talk, holding his glass in front of him and examining it as he turned it this way and that. "Family quarrels," he sighed. "Same old thing. Reminds me of my boyhood. When I look back on it, it seems to me we never got through a meal without a fight, but I suppose we must have once in a while." He set the glass down. "Well, they're all dead now, thank God."

Donald looked quickly across at Mr. Gordon as if he were seeing him for the first time.

"It's snowing!" cried Gramma triumphantly. "Look, it's snowing again. I knew we'd have more snow before dark." She did not want Mr. Gordon to go on talking.

Aunt Louisa sobbed once, got up, and went out into the kitchen. Uncle Ivor followed her.

"Why, Donald! You've got the wishbone!" cried Aunt Emilie. "Eat the meat off it and we'll hang it up over the stove to dry, and tomorrow we'll wish on it. Wouldn't that be fun?"

He picked it up in his fingers and began to chew on the strips of white meat that clung to it. When he had carefully cleaned it, he got down and went out into the kitchen with it.

The room was very quiet; the tea-kettle simmered on the stove. Outside the window the falling snowflakes looked dark against the whiteness beyond. Aunt Louisa was sitting on the high stool, doubled over, with a crumpled handkerchief in her hand, and Uncle Ivor was bending over her talking in a very low voice. Donald laid the wishbone on the sink shelf and started to tiptoe out, but Uncle Ivor saw him. "How'd you like to go up to the henhouse with me, Donald?" he said. "I've got to find us a dozen eggs to take back to Rutland."

"I'll get my coat," Donald told him, eager to go out before his father came back downstairs.

The path up the hill to the henhouse had been made not by clearing the snow away, but by tramping it down. The new snow was drifting over the track; in some places it already had covered it. When Uncle Ivor went into the henhouse Donald stood still, bending his head back to catch some snowflakes in his mouth. "Come on in and shut the door. You'll let all the heat out," Uncle Ivor told him.

"I'm coming," said Donald. He stepped through the doorway and closed the door. The smell inside was very strong. As Uncle Ivor approached the hens, they set up a low, distrustful murmur.

"Tell me, Donald," said Uncle Ivor as he explored the straw with his hands.

"What?" said Donald.

"Does your mother often run to her room and shut the door, the way she did just now?"

"Sometimes."

"Why? Is your father mean to her?"

"Oh," said Donald vaguely, "they have fights." He felt uncomfortable.

"Yes. Well, it's a great pity your father ever got married. It would have been better for everybody if he'd stayed single."

"But then I wouldn't have been born at all," cried Donald, uncertain whether Uncle Ivor was serious or not.

"At least, we *hope* not!" said Uncle Ivor, rolling his eyes and looking silly. Now Donald knew it was a kind of joke, and he laughed. The door was flung open. "Donald!" roared his father.

"What is it?" he said, his voice very feeble.

"Come out here!"

He stumbled toward the door; his father was peering inside uncertainly. "What are you doing in there?" he demanded.

"Helping Uncle Ivor look for eggs."

"Hmmph!" Donald stepped out and his father shut the door.

They started to walk along the road in the direction of the Smithson farm. Presently his father fell in behind him and prodded him in the back, saying: "Keep your head up. Chest out! D'you want to get round-shouldered? Before you know it you'll have curvature of the spine."

When they had got out of sight of the house, in a place where the tangle of small trees came to the edge of the road on both sides, his father stopped walking. He looked around, reached down, picked up a handful of the new snow, and rolled it into a hard ball. Then he threw it at a fairly large tree, some distance from the road. It broke, leaving a white mark on the dark trunk. "Let's see you hit it," he told Donald.

A wolf could be waiting here, somewhere back in the still gloom of the woods. It was very important not to make him angry. If his father wanted to take a chance and throw snowballs into the woods, he could, but Donald would not. Then perhaps the wolf would understand that he, at least, was his friend.

"Go on," said his father.

"No. I don't want to."

With mock astonishment his father said: "Oh, you don't?" Then his face became dangerous and his voice cracked like a whip. "Are you going to do what I told you?"

"No." It was the first time he had openly defied him. His father turned very red.

"Listen here, you young whippersnapper!" he cried, his voice tight with anger. "You think you're going to get away with this?" Before Donald knew what was happening, his father had seized him with one hand while he bent over and with the other scooped up as much snow as he could. "We'll settle this little matter right now," he said through his teeth. Suddenly he was rubbing the snow violently over Donald's face, and at the same time that Donald gasped and squirmed, he pushed what was left of it down his neck. As he felt the wet, icy mass sliding down his back, he doubled over. His eyes were squeezed shut; he was certain his father was trying to kill him. With a desperate lunge he bounded free and fell face-downward into the snow.

"Get up," his father said disgustedly. He did not move. If he held his breath long enough he might die.

His father yanked him to his feet. "I've had just about enough of your monkeyshines," he said. Clutching him tightly with both hands, he forced him to hobble ahead of him, back through the twilight to the house.

Donald moved forward, looking at the white road in front of him, his mind empty of thoughts. An unfamiliar feeling had come to him: he was not sorry for himself for being wet and cold, or even resentful at having been mistreated. He felt detached; it was an agreeable, almost voluptuous sensation which he accepted without understanding or questioning it.

As they advanced down the long alley of maple trees in the dusk his father said: "Now you can go and cry in your mother's lap."

"I'm not crying," said Donald loudly, without expression. His father did not answer.

Fortunately the kitchen was empty. He could tell from the sound of the voices in the parlor that Aunt Louisa, Uncle Ivor and Mr. Gordon were getting ready to leave. He ran upstairs to his room and changed his clothes completely. The hole he had breathed in the ice on the windowpane had frozen over thickly again, but the round mark was still visible. As he finished dressing his mother called him. It was completely dark outside. He went downstairs. She was standing in the hallway.

"Oh, you've changed your clothes," she said. "Come out and say good-by to Aunt Louisa and Uncle Ivor. They're in the kitchen." He looked quickly at her face to see if there were signs of her recent tears: her eyes were slightly bloodshot.

Together they went into the kitchen. "Donald wants to say good-by to you" she told Mr. Gordon, steering Donald to Aunt Louisa. "You've given him a wonderful Christmas"—her voice became reproachful—"but it was *much* too much."

The thick beaver collar of Mr. Gordon's overcoat was turned up over his ears, and he had on enormous fur gloves. He smiled and clapped his hands together expectantly; it made a cushioned sound. "Oh, it was a lot of fun," he said. "He reminds me a little of myself, you know, when I was his age. I was a sort of shy and quiet lad, too." Donald felt his mother's hand tighten on his shoulder as she pushed him toward Aunt Louisa. "Mm," she said. "Well, Auntie Louisa, here's somebody who wants to say good-by to you."

Even in the excitement of watching Uncle Willis and Uncle Greg drive the others off in the sleigh, Donald did not miss the fact that his father had not appeared in the kitchen at all. When the sleigh had moved out of sight down the dark road, everyone went into the parlor and Grampa put another log on the fire.

"Where's Owen?" Gramma said in a low voice to Donald's mother.

"He must be upstairs. To tell the truth, I don't care very much where he is."

"Poor child," said Gramma. "Headache a little better?"

"A little." She sighed. "He certainly managed to take all the pleasure out of *my* Christmas."

"A mean shame," said Gramma.

"It was all I could do to look Ivor in the face just now. I meant it."

"I'm sure they all understood," said Gramma soothingly. "Just don't you fret about it. Anyway, Owen'll be gone tomorrow, and you can rest up."

Shortly after Uncle Willis and Uncle Greg got back, Donald's father came downstairs. Supper was eaten in almost complete silence; at no time did his father speak to him or pay him any attention. As soon as the meal was over his mother took him upstairs to bed.

When she had left him, he lay in the dark listening to the sound of the fine snow as the wind drove it against the panes. The wolf was out there in the night, running along paths that no one had ever seen, down the hill and across the meadow, stopping to drink at a deep place in the brook where the ice had not formed. The stiff hairs of his coat had caught the snow; he shook himself and climbed up the bank to where Donald sat waiting for him. Then he lay down beside him, putting his heavy head in Donald's lap. Donald leaned over and buried his face in the shaggy fur of his scruff. After a while they both got up and began to run together, faster and faster, across the fields.

MS Chakdara
(London–Colombo),
January 1957

TAPIAMA

PAUL BOWLES

JUST BEHIND THE HOTEL was the river. If it had come from very far inland it would have been wide and silent, but because it was really only a creek swollen by the rains, and its bed was full of boulders, it made a roaring noise which the photographer briefly mistook for more rain. The heat and the trip had tired him out; he had eaten the cold fried fish and the leathery omelet that oozed grease, the brown bean paste with rice and burned bananas, and had been overtaken suddenly by a sleepiness powerful as the effect of a drug. Staggering to his bed, he had ripped off his shirt and trousers, lifted the stiff mosquito-net that reeked of dust, and dropped like a stone onto the mattress, only distantly noticing its hardness before he lost himself in sleep.

But in the night when he awoke he realized he had been in the false sleep of indigestion; staring into the blackness over his head he told himself that it was going to be hard to find the way back into oblivion. It was then that he had become aware of the night's changeless backdrop of sound, and had taken it for rain. Now and then, far above his head (how could the ceiling be that high?) a firefly's nervous little light flashed its indecipherable code for an instant or two. He was lying on his back; something small was crawling down his chest. He put his hand there; it was a slowly moving drop of sweat. The rough sheet under him was wet. He wanted to move, but if he did there would be no end to the shifting, and each new position would be more uncomfortable than the last. In the anonymous darkness of a nearby room someone coughed from time to time; he could not tell whether it was a man or a woman. The meal he had eaten lay like ten meals in his stomach. Slowly the memory of it was suffused with a nebulous horror—particularly the heavy cold omelet shining with grease.

Lying there smelling the dust from the netting was like being tied up inside a burlap bag. To get out into the street and walk—that was what he wanted, but there were difficulties. The electricity went off at midnight; the old man who ran the hotel had told him that. Instead of putting the matches under his pillow he had left them in his trouser-pocket, and the idea of stepping out on to the floor barefoot without a light did not appeal to him. Besides, he reminded himself, listening again to the wide, strangely distant clamor out there, it was raining. But to move along the dead streets even under the invisible rain would be a pleasure. . . . If he lay quite still, sleep might return. Finally, in desperation he yanked the net aside and sprang out of bed, across the room in the direction of the chair over which he had thrown his clothes.

He managed to get into his shirt and trousers in the space of three matches; his shoes he pounded on the concrete floor in the dark, to tumble out a possible centipede or scorpion. Then he struck a fourth match and opened the door into the *patio*. Here it was no longer pitch-black. The huge potted plants were visible in the night's lead-colored light, but the sky, stifled by a cloud that no starlight could pierce, seemed not to be there at all. It was not raining. "The river must be very close," he thought.

He walked along the covered *corredor*, grazing the tentacles of orchids that hung in baskets and jars from the eaves, bumping into the pieces of wicker furniture, and found the entrance door, closed and doubly bolted. Carefully he slid back the metal bars and opened the door, pulling it shut after him. The gloom of the street was as profound as that of the *patio* and the air as still as it had been under the mosquito-net. But it had an indefinite vegetable scent—a sweet odor of both fulfillment and exhaustion.

He turned to the left: the long empty main street, lined with one-story buildings, led straight down to the *paseo* along the sea. As he walked, the unmoving hot-house air became veined with the fresher smell of seaweed on the beach. At each intersecting street he had to go down six steps to the road level, cross, and climb up again to the sidewalk. In the rainy season, the *propietario* of the hotel had told him, there was a rowboat at each corner to ferry the pedestrians across. Like the intermingling of the land and sea odors that he breathed, two opposing but entwined sensations took possession of him: a relief amounting almost to delight, and a faint feeling of nausea which he decided to combat because he felt that not to have been able to leave all suggestion of illness behind showed a lack of strength. He tried to put more springiness into his walk, but discovered almost immediately that it was too hot to make any more than a minimum of effort. He was sweating even more now than he had been in his bed. He lighted an Ovalado. The taste of the sweet tobacco was a part of the night.

The *paseo* bordering the sea-front was about half a mile long. He had imagined there would be some slight stirring of the air here, but he could detect no difference. Still, now and then there was the soft intimate sound of a small wave breaking gently on the sand just below. He sat down on the balustrade and rested, in the hope of cooling off a little. The sea was invisible. He could have been sitting on the peak of a cloud-covered mountain—the gloom in front of him would have been that formless and all-embracing. Yet the sea's casual noises had no element of distance in them, as sea sounds have. It was as though they were taking place in a vast, closed courtyard. The concrete slabs on which he sat were damp, and a little cooler than his flesh. He smoked two cigarettes and strained his ears to hear some sound, made even indirectly, by human agency. But there was nothing more than the desultory slipping and sucking of the lazy water on the beach below. He glanced up and down the empty *paseo*. Far out along the shore to the west there was a light. It was orange, it flickered: a bonfire? He resumed walking, more slowly than before, ahead of him the distant blaze, the one point of light in the landscape.

A wide flight of steps led down onto the beach. Just beyond, he could see the flimsy structure of a pier that had been built out over the water. He stood still and listened. The fitful licking of small waves around the piles sounded as though it were happening in an echo-chamber.

He ran lightly down the steps and passed underneath the pier. It was definitely cooler walking along on the sand than it had been up on the *paseo*. He felt wide-awake now, and decided to see how much nearer to the light down the shore fifteen minutes would put him. Night-colored crabs hurried along the sand just ahead of his moving feet, completely soundless and almost invisible. A little beyond the end of the *paseo* the sand gave place to a hard coral surface which was easier to walk on. Out of prudence he kept as near to the water's edge as possible.

There was a difference between this walk and innumerable other midnight jaunts he had made, and he was inclined to wonder what made it so pleasant. Perhaps he was enjoying it simply because the fabric here was of pure freedom. He was not looking for anything; all the cameras were back in the hotel room.

Occasionally he lifted his eyes from the dim brainlike configurations of coral beneath his feet and looked inland, to see whether he could make out any signs of habitation. It seemed to him that there might be sand dunes a few hundred feet back, but in the absence of light it was impossible to be certain of even that much. The sweat trickled down his spine and over his coccyx, sliding in between his buttocks. Maybe the best idea would be to undress completely. But then there would be the bother of carrying his clothing, and he wanted his hands free, even at the risk of chafing.

The question of freedom was governed by the law of diminishing returns, he said to himself, walking faster. If you went beyond a certain point of intensity in your consciousness of desiring it, you furnished yourself with a guarantee of not achieving it. In any case, he thought, what is freedom in the last analysis, other than the state of being totally, instead of only partially, subject to the tyranny of chance?

There was no doubt that this walk was dispelling the miasma of indigestion that had lain within him. Three minutes to go, said the bright minute-hand of his watch; the orange light ahead seemed smaller than it had from the town. Why an arbitrary fifteen minutes? He smiled at the precise urban pattern in which his mind had automatically moved. If he lifted his arm he could touch the sky, and it would be moist, tepid and voluptuously soft.

And now in the distance ahead, on the landward side, he heard sounds which he quickly identified as the voices of hundreds of young frogs. The light, now that he studied it, was moving in a strange fashion: slightly up and down, and sideways as well, but without appearing to alter its position. All at once it became a huge flame belching upward, an instant later scattering cascades of red sparks, and he understood that he had arrived. The bonfire burned on the floor of a gently swaying craft not a hundred feet ahead of him. A naked man stood above it, tossing it palm branches. The photographer stopped walking and listened for the sound of human voices, but the happy chorus of frogs filled the air.

He stepped ahead several paces and decided to call out. "*Hola!*" The man wheeled about, jumped over the nearer side of the boat (the water was extremely shallow) and came running up to him.

Without greeting him, taking him perhaps for someone else, the man said: "*Tapiama? Vas a Tapiama?*" The photographer, never having heard of Tapiama, stuttered a bit and finally said, "*Sí,*" whereupon the other seized his arm and pulled him along to the edge of the water. "The tide's all the way out. We'll start in a minute."

He could see two other people in the craft, lying flat on the floor, one on each side of the fire, as far from its heat as possible. The photographer squatted down and removed his shoes and socks, then waded to the boat. When he stood in the center of it (the fire was still crackling brightly) he turned and watched the naked man loosening the rope that held the craft in place.

"The whole thing is absurd." He could only distrust the very naturalness with which all this was coming about—the indifference to his unexpected arrival on the part of the two passengers, and perhaps even more, the highly suspect readiness of the boatmen to take off the moment he had appeared. He told himself, "Things don't happen this way," but since beyond a doubt they were doing so, any questioning of the process could lead only in the direction of paranoia. He dropped to the floor of the boat and pulled out his packet of Ovalados. The naked boatman, the coil of dripping rope around his black forearm like a bracelet, sprang aboard, and with his big toe nudged one of the supine passengers who stirred, rose to his knees, and glanced about with annoyance. "Where is it?" he demanded. Without replying, the boatman handed him the shorter of two poles that had lain along the gunwale. Together they began to propel the punt along the invisible surface of the water. The frogs' canticle and the fire's flare filled the night.

Having answered "*Sí*," to the Tapiama question, the photographer felt he could scarcely take the retrogressive step of asking "What is Tapiama?" or "Where is Tapiama?" And so, much as he would have liked to know, he decided to wait. This shallow body of water beneath them—estuary, lagoon? River more likely, since the boatman had said the tide was out. But not the stream whose troubled passage among the boulders he had heard from his bed.

They pushed on, now and then passing beneath clumps of high vegetation where the frogs' song was briefly covered by another sound, inexplicable and brutal, like the sudden tearing of a vast sheet of strong linen. From time to time something solid and heavy splashed nearby, as if a man had fallen into the water. And occasionally the other passenger raised himself on one elbow and without too much effort managed to revive the dying fire with another dry palm-leaf.

Probably it was less than an hour before they came to a landing in the mud. The two passengers leapt out and hurried away into the darkness. The boatman, after carefully donning a pair of short underpants, tapped the photographer on the arm and asked him for sixty centavos. He gave him seventy-five and clambered out into the soft mud, his shoes in his hand.

"Wait a minute," said the man. "I'll go with you." The photographer was pleased. When the boatman, looking blacker now in his white shorts, had secured the punt to an upright log driven into the mud, he led the way upward through a tangle of undergrowth, saying casually at one point: "Are you going across tomorrow?"

"Across? No."

"Aren't you here for the company?" The voice implied that to be here otherwise than for the company laid one open to unnameable suspicion.

The time had come to be truthful, he feared, although he did not relish the position he knew it would put him in. "I never heard of the company," he said. "I just arrived in Rio Martillo tonight. What sort of company?"

"Sugar," said the other. Then he stood still in the dark and spoke slowly: "*Entonces*—why have you come to Tapiama? They don't like *millonarios* here, you know." Understanding that this was the contemptuous coastal term for Americans, the photographer quickly lied. "I'm Danish," he said, but feeling that his voice lacked conviction he immediately added: "Do we go through any more mud, or can I put my shoes on?"

The man had started up again. "Wash your feet at the *cantina,* if you like," he told him over his shoulder. In another minute they were there: all in the dimness an open space, a dozen or so palm-leaf huts at one end of it, at the other a platform which must be a loading dock, the empty night and openness of water behind it; and half-way between the dock and the cluster of dwellings, the *cantina,* itself only a very large hut without a front wall.

A faint light came from within; there was no sound but the frogs on all sides, and the occasional tearing rasp in the branches high overhead. "Why is the place open at this hour?" demanded the photographer. The boatman stopped in the middle of the clearing and adjusted his shorts briefly. "Don Octavio runs it from six in the morning until six at night. His brother runs it from six at night until six in the morning. The company lets the men off from work at different hours. They come here with their *pago* and spend it. They like it better here than at home. Not so many mosquitoes." It could have been the photographer's imagination that made the man's voice sound bitter as he spoke the last words. They continued across the clearing and stepped into the *cantina*.

There was no floor; the ground was covered with white sand. A counter of boards had been built diagonally across a far corner. Here an oil lamp smoldered and two men stood drinking. Wooden packing-cases were scattered here and there, some standing on end with empty beer bottles on them, and others on their sides, to be used as seats.

"*Muy triste,*" commented the boatman, glancing around. Then he went behind the bar and disappeared through a small door in the wall there. Apart from the two at the bar, who had ceased their conversation and now stood staring at the photographer, there was no one else in the place. "When in doubt, speak," he told himself, advancing toward them, although it occurred to him that he might just as well have made it, "When in doubt, keep quiet," even as he opened his mouth to say, "*Buenas noches,*" for their expressions did not alter in any manner that he could detect. For a full three seconds they continued to gaze at him before they replied, which they then did more or less simultaneously. These two had nothing in common, he noted: one was a soldier in uniform, an Indian boy of perhaps eighteen, the other a tired-looking mulatto civilian of indeterminate age. Or perhaps—the idea came to him as he put his elbow on the bar with a show of casualness—they did have at least a common antagonism, now that he had entered the *cantina.* "Oh, well, I'm barefoot and my shoes are covered with mud," he thought.

"*Hay alguien?*" he said aloud to the palm-leaf wall behind the bar. The two neither resumed their conversation nor spoke further with him, and he did not turn his head again toward them. Presently the small door opened and a fat man pushed through. He stood with his hands outspread on the bar, his eyebrows raised in anticipation. "I'll have a *cumbiamba,*" said the photographer, remembering the name of the coastal region's favorite drink, a herbal concoction famous for its treacherous effects.

It was foul-tasting but strong. The second one seemed less objectionable. He walked across to the open side of the *cantina* and sat down on a packing-case, looking out at the formless night. The two at the bar were talking again in low tones. It was not long before five men appeared from the platform end of the clearing; they straggled in and stood at the bar, laughing as they waited for their drinks. All of them were black, and wore only underpants, like the boatman. Now a mulatto girl with gold teeth came through the little door behind the bar and joined them. Almost immediately, however, she became aware of the photographer sitting by himself, and with her hands on her hips, half dancing, she made her way across the open space toward him. When she arrived, she squatted down beside him grinning and with one thin yellow hand reached out to unfasten his fly. His reaction was instantaneous and automatic: he drew back his leg and kicked her full in the breast, so that she toppled over backward in silence onto the sand. The noise of the resulting laughter at the bar was not sufficient to cover her thin voice, made sharp by rage: "*Qué bruto, tú! Pendejo!*"

Hands on hips again, she retreated to the bar and was given a beer by one of the workmen. Although the photographer had not meant to kick her, he felt no regret at the turn the incident had taken. The *cumbiambas* seemed to be having their effect; he was beginning to feel very well. He sat still a while, tapping rhythms on the side of his empty glass. Soon more Negro workmen came in and joined the others at the bar. One carried a guitar on which he set to work strumming a syncopated chordal accompaniment for a melody which failed to appear. However, it was music of a sort, and everyone was pleased with it. Perhaps awakened by the sound, the dogs of the village had now started an angry chorus of barking; this was particularly audible to the photographer who sat at the entrance, and it bothered him. He rose and moved over to an empty crate alongside the opposite wall, resting his head against a rough-hewn pole that was one of the supports of the roof. A foot or so above his head there was a strange object dangling from a nail. Now and then he rolled his eyes upward and studied it.

All at once he jumped up and began violently to brush the back of his neck and head. The pole behind him was swarming with tiny ants, thousands upon thousands of them: someone had hung a small crushed coral snake over the nail, and they had come to eat the flesh. It took him a good while not to feel any more of the insects running over his back; during that time two other individuals had come into the *cantina* (whether from the outside or through the door behind the counter, he had not noticed), and now sat between him and the bar in such a fashion that both of them faced him. The old man looked Nordic, the innocent-looking one-legged boy with him could be Spanish; the old man was telling the boy a humorous story, leaning toward him with great interest, occasionally poking his arm with a forefinger to drive home a point, but the boy was distraughtly making designs in the sand with the tip of his crutch.

The photographer stood up; he had never before had such an effect from two drinks. "A very peculiar sensation," he said to himself. "Very peculiar," he repeated aloud under his breath as he started toward the bar to order another. It was not that he felt drunk so much as that he had become someone who was not he, someone for whom the act of living was a thing so different from what he had imagined it could be, that he was left stranded in a region of sensation far from any he had heretofore known. It was not unpleasant: it was merely indefinable. "*Dispénseme,*" he said to a tall Negro in pink and white striped BVD's and he handed his empty glass to the fat man. He wanted to see what went into a *cumbiamba,* but the barman did everything quickly beneath the counter and handed him back the glass, brimming with the slightly frothy mixture. He took a good swallow of it and set it down, turning a little to his right as he did so. Standing beside him was the Indian soldier, his cap at an angle atop a pre-Colombian face. "Why does the army put such big visors on them?" he wondered.

He saw that the soldier was about to speak. "Whatever he says is going to turn out to be an insult," he warned himself, in the hope that this would help him to avoid possible anger later.

"Do you like this place?" the soldier said; his voice was silken.

"*Es simpático*. Yes, I like it."

"Why?" The dogs outside had come nearer; he could hear their yapping now above the laughter.

"Can you tell me why they hung that dead snake on the wall there?" he found himself asking, and supposed it was to change the subject. But the soldier was going to be even more boring than he had feared. "I asked you why you like this *cantina*," he insisted.

"And I told you it was *simpático*. Isn't that enough?"

The soldier tilted his head back and looked down his nose.

"Far from being enough," he replied, his manner pedantic, his expression infuriating.

The photographer returned to his drink, picked it up, slowly finished it off. Then he pulled out his cigarettes and offered one to the other. With exaggerated deliberateness the soldier reached for the cigarette, took it, and began to tap it on the counter. The man playing the guitar at last had started to sing in a small falsetto voice along with it, but most of the words were in a dialect the photographer could not understand. When the cigarettes were lighted, he found himself wondering who had lighted them—he or the soldier.

"Just where did you come from?" asked the soldier.

He was not bothering to answer, but the soldier misunderstood even this. "I can see you're inventing something," he said, "and I don't want to hear it."

The photographer, disgusted, exclaimed, "Aaah!" and ordered another *cumbiamba*. This most recent one had done something extraordinary to him: he felt that he had become very precise, thin and hard, an object made of enamel or some similar material, something other than a living being, but intensely conscious all the same. "Four ought to do the trick," he thought.

The empty glass was in his hand, the fat barman was staring at him, and at that point he had not the slightest idea whether he had already drunk the fourth one or whether it was still the moment just after he had ordered it. He felt himself laughing, but he could not hear whether any sound was coming out or not. The mangled snake, seething with ants, had upset him a little; recognizing it, he had then been made aware of its smell, which he was not sure he had escaped even now. Here at the bar the kerosene lamp smoked heavily; its strong fumes choked him. "*Gracias a Dios,*" he confided to the barman, handing him the glass.

The old man who had been sitting on the crate behind them rose and came vaguely toward the bar. "Where did this come from?" said the photographer, laughing apologetically, looking at the full glass in his hand. The frenzied dogs out in the clearing yapped and howled, an exasperating sound. "*Qué tienen esos perros?*" he demanded of the soldier.

The old man had stopped beside them. "Say, Jack, I don't mean to butt in or anything," he began. He was bald, sunburned; he wore a fishnet shirt. The furrows between his ribs showed as parallel shadows, and irregular tufts of gray hair waved out from his chest between the meshes of the shirt. He stretched his lips in a smile, showing naked white gums. The soldier's stance became over-nonchalant; he stared at the newcomer, open hatred suddenly in his eyes, and gently blew the smoke from his cigarette into the old man's face.

"You from Milwaukee? Siddown."

"In a little while, thanks," said the photographer.

"A little while?" the old man echoed incredulously, running his hand over the top of his head. Then he called out in Spanish to the one-legged boy. The photographer was thinking: "This is not going to work out right, at all. It's just not going to work out." He wished the Negro would stop singing and the dogs would stop barking. He looked at the glass in his hand, full of what looked like soapsuds. Someone tapped him on the shoulder. "Say, bud, lemme give you a little advice." The old man again. "There's money in this country if you know where to look. But the guy that finds it is the guy that sticks to his own kind, if you know what I mean." He put his face nearer and lowered his voice. Three skeletal fingers touched the photographer's arm. "You take it from me, from one white man to another. I'm tellin' you!" The three fingers, dark with tobacco stain, lifted themselves, trembled, and dropped back. "These guys all mean trouble from the word go."

The boy having both gathered up his crutch and managed to rise from where he had been sitting, had now arrived at the bar. "Take a look at this, Jack," the old man said. "Show him," he told the boy in Spanish, and the boy, leaning on his crutch, bent over and rolled up the right leg of his ragged khaki shorts until he had exposed the stump of his amputated leg. It was not far below the groin; the scar tissue had puckered and wrinkled curiously in countless tiny convolutions. "See?" cried the old man. "Two hundred and sixty tons of bananas went over that. Feel it."

"You feel it," said the photographer, wondering how it was possible for him to go on standing and talking exactly as if he were a person like the rest of them. (Could it be that what had happened to him did not show?) He turned his head and looked towards the entrance. The mulatto girl was vomiting just outside. With a cry the barman rushed across and furiously pushed her farther away, out into the clearing. When he came back in he was theatrically holding his nose. "That prostitute ape!" he yelled. "In another minute we'd have had the dogs inside here."

The boy was still looking expectantly at the old man, to see if it was time to lower his trouser leg. "You think he got a centavo from them?" said the old man sadly. "Hah!"

The photographer had begun to suspect that something had gone very wrong inside him. He felt sick, but since he was no longer a living creature he could not conceive it in those terms. He had shut his eyes and put his hand over his face. "It's going around backward," he said. The undrunk *cumbiamba* was in his other hand.

Saying the sentence had made it more true. It was definitely going around backward. The important thing was to remember that he was alone here and that this was a real place with real people in it. He could feel how dangerously easy it would be to go along with the messages given him by his senses, and dismiss the whole thing as a nightmare in the secret belief that when the breaking-point came he could somehow manage to escape by waking himself up. A little unsteadily he set his drink down on the counter. An argument which had arisen a while ago between the Indian soldier and his sad companion had now reached its noisy stage, with the companion attempting to drag the soldier away from the bar against his will, and the soldier, his two booted legs firmly apart, breathing rapidly, noisily in his resistance. Suddenly there was a small, shining knife in his right hand, and his face assumed the look of a little boy about to burst into tears. The old man quickly moved around to the photographer's other side. "That guy's bad news in any language," he muttered, gesturing nervously to the boy with the crutch as he bade him move out of the way.

The photographer was saying to himself: "If I can hold out. If I can only hold out." The whole place was slipping away from him, downward and outward; the guitar strummed and the dogs barked, the soldier flashed his knife and pouted, the old American talked about caves with buried emeralds only six days up the Tupurú, the lamp grew redder and more smoke came out of it. He understood nothing except that he must stay there and suffer; to try to escape would be fatal. The soldier's face was very near his own now, breathing black tobacco smoke at him. Languorously, with an insane natural coquetry, he made his long lashes tremble as he asked: "Why have you not offered me a *copita?* All night I have been waiting for you to invite me." The hand holding the knife hung listlessly at his side; the photographer thought of a sleeping baby still clutching its rattle.

"*Sí quieres. . . . Qué tomas?*" he murmured, reflecting that his shoes should be in his hand and were not; then where were they? Someone had brought a large spider monkey into the *cantina* and was forcing it to dance to the guitar's syncopations, making it stand upright by holding its two front paws. With an air of distraught gravity it stepped about, peering this way and that, grimacing nervously at the loud peals of laughter that came from those at the bar watching its antics. The dogs, having noticed its arrival, had rushed to the very entrance of the *cantina,* where they braced themselves to shriek and snap with determined fury.

The soldier's drink had been bought and paid for, but he was not drinking it. He was leaning far back against the bar, reclining on his elbow almost as though he were in bed, his eyes simple black slits, whispering: "You don't like it here. You want to go, *verdad?* But you are afraid to go."

In spite of the constant sliding away, everything had remained just as it was. It would have been better if he could have sat down. "Oh, God," he asked himself. "Am I going to be able to stand this?"

"Why are you afraid to go?" pursued the other tenderly, smiling so that the photographer could admire his small, perfect teeth. The photographer laughed silently, did not reply.

The face of the soldier, ovoid, honey-colored, so near to his, moved now with consummate smoothness into another face, that of a general. ("*Sí, mi general,*" with stiff *bigotes* sprouting from beneath the nostrils, almond eyes, black, deadly with a delicate lust, the uniform svelte, plaited steel riding crop in hand, sharpened spurs shining by the anklebone. "*Bien, mi general.*" Lying on the hot barrack mattress, *tarde tras tarde,* the soldier had dreamed of being the general. Which mountain village had he said he was from? How long had he been talking?)

". . . and that day alone they killed forty-one pigs before my eyes. There in the corral. *Me hizo algo; no sé. . . .*" His smile was apologetic, intimate; he lowered his eyes imperceptibly, made the effort and raised them again to look at the photographer in such a way that, since they were wider than before, they glistened. "I never forgot it; I don't know why."

Between them the gold-toothed girl came sliding, her hands wriggling over her head, her hips circling, her thin voice shouting: "*Ahii! Ahii! El fandango de la Guajira.*" The soldier must have pushed her, for all at once she slapped him. But it was happening very slowly. How could it take the soldier so long to bring up his knife, and as he raised his hand, how could the stupid girl wait that way before screaming and ducking aside? Even so, the blade caught her only on the arm; she was in the middle of the floor, kneeling on the sand, moaning: "He cut me! Oh God! He cut me!" And because the man who had been dancing with the spider monkey let go of it to get as quickly as all the others to the bar, the beast toddled over to the girl and distractedly wrapped one long hairy arm around her neck. But then the photographer was being roughly jostled, his bare feet were being stepped on as everyone tried to get at the soldier and disarm him. (A demon mask shiny with venom, a voice of barbed wire that rasped: "*Os mato a todos! A todos!*")

It was exactly nineteen steps from the place where he had stood to the trunk of a small papaya tree in front of the entrance. The tree was not very strong; it swayed slightly as he leaned against it. The dogs were yelping now from inside the *cantina*. Here the air was sweet and almost cool; the faintest glimmer of morning was in the sky and water behind the landing. "I must start to walk," he told himself; it seemed important to believe it. The shouts and screams inside the *cantina* were growing in volume, and people were beginning to call to one another from the doors of their huts. The landing platform was empty—just boards and no railing. Shuffling along with great care because he was not used to going barefoot, he followed what he thought was the path he had taken earlier, through the undergrowth back down to the river's edge, and there was the punt, mud-beached in the mangroves.

It was easy to get in, easy to untie the rope, and easy (for the level of the water had risen considerably since the craft had been left) to pry it loose from the shelf of mud where it rested. But once he was floating among the now nearly visible trunks and branches, bumping against them and being spun to face first the dark chaotic riverbank and then the wide whitening emptiness of open sky and water, he understood dimly that it was not going to be possible to pole his way back to the beach whence he had come, since the tide was still coming in. It was a comforting thought, he decided, because it meant that everything was going ahead instead of backward. A minute later he was floating quietly by the base of the landing: people were running around the clearing. Quickly he lay down flat on the bottom of the punt, and there he stayed, looking straight up at the gray sky, hoping in this way to remain invisible until he had been carried out of sight, beyond Tapiama.

It was going to be one of those stillborn tropical days, when there would be no sun, no wind, no clouds—because the entire sky was enfolded in one vast suffocating blanket of cloud—when nothing at all would happen save that hourly it would grow hotter until an approximate dusk came along. Already the eastern side of the sky was the hot side, arching above the flatness of the swampland. The punt scarcely moved now, the channel having broadened into this wide marshy lake. The photographer lay still and groaned. Little by little the fear that someone might see him gave way to the hope that what current there was would propel the craft in the direction of the shore rather than out toward the wilderness of water and tiny islands; sometimes, even though suffering be implicit in it, contact with others is preferable to the terror of solitude and the unknown. He laid an arm over his eyes to shield them from the corrosive gray light that beat down upon him from the spaces above. The other hand lay in the ashes of last night's fire. And he floated in utter silence on the calm bosom of the lagoon, not stirring as the morning hours moved along, but growing increasingly conscious of the infernal seething of the *cumbiambas* in his brain, a seething which expressed itself as a senseless nightmare imposed from without, in the face of which he could only be totally passive. It was an invisible spectacle whose painful logic he followed with the entire fiber of his being, without, however, once being given a clear vision of what agonizing destinies were at stake.

Some time toward mid-morning the punt grazed a submerged root and was swung into an eddyless pool in the shelter of the vegetation near the shore. Here fierce flies stung him, and from among the leaves high above, a talking bird remarked casually, over and over again: "*Idigaraga. Idigaraga. Idigaraga.*"

It was no particular consolation to him, so intent was he on the obscure drama being enacted within him, to hear human voices presently, or to feel the craft seized by the hands of someone splashing in the water alongside. Only when several people had climbed in and crouched chattering around him did he move his arm and squint up at them. Five young men, all of whom looked remarkably alike, surrounded him. Water dripped down upon him from their naked bodies.

He shut his eyes again: it was too unlikely a scene. During this time one of them dived overboard, was gone a short while, and returned with a green coconut whose top he had sliced off. He began to let the water dribble into the photographer's face, whereupon the photographer partially sat up and drank the rest of it. In minute he looked around at them again, and said: "Are you brothers?"

"*Sí sí*" they chorused. This was for some reason a consolation. "*Hermanos,*" he sighed, sliding down into the ashes again. Then he added desperately, hoping they could still hear him: "Please take me to Rio Martillo."

It had been a brief interlude of clarity. Now they poled the punt back out under the hot sky, letting him lie there and moan as he liked. At one point he felt he must try to explain that he would give them each seventy-five centavos for their trouble, but they giggled and pushed him back down.

"My shoes!" he cried. "There are no shoes," they told him. "Lie still."

"And when we get to the beach," he panted, seizing a brown ankle beside his face, "how will you get me to Rio Martillo?" "We are not going to any beach," they replied. "We go through the swamp and the canal."

He lay still a while, trying to disassociate himself from the irrational ideas boiling up in his head. "Is this the way to Rio Martillo?" he demanded, thrusting himself up a little and gasping, trying to see beyond the enclosing thicket of brown legs and arms, and feeling a deep unreasoned shame at having once again accepted defeat. They laughed, pushed him gently down to the floor, and went on rhythmically poling the craft eastward. "The factory chimney," they said to one another, pointing into the distance. His mind took him back to the quiet region by the riverbank where the small bird had spoken, high up in the trees, and he heard again the conversational tone. "*Idigaraga,*" he said aloud, imitating perfectly its voice and intonation. There was an explosion of mirth around him. One of the youths took his arm, shook it lightly. "You know that bird?" he said. "It is a very comic bird. It goes to the nests of other birds and wants to sit there, and when the other birds fight with it and drive it away, it sits down in the same tree there and says: '*Idigaraga.*' That means: '*Iri garagua, nadie me quiere,* nobody likes me.' And it says it over and over, until they make it go farther away so they can't hear it any more. You said it just right. Say it again." "*Sí, sí*" the others agreed, "*otra vez!*"

The photographer had no intention of saying it again. His shame at having accepted defeat already troubled him less. It was hard in his present condition to fit the bird correctly into the pattern, but he knew it had to be done.

When the Compañia Azucarera Riomartillense blew a long blast on its whistle to announce the advent of noon, the sound hovered for an instant over the empty swampland like an invisible trail of smoke. "*Las doce,*" said one of the brothers. A great black and gold dragonfly came skimming across the water and lighted on the photographer's bare foot. After raising and lowering its wings twice, it was again on its crooked course, curving and swooping over the lagoon toward Tapiama. "Say it again," the brothers begged him.

London, October 1957

THE HYENA

PAUL BOWLES

A STORK WAS PASSING OVER desert country on his way north. He was thirsty, and he began to look for water. When he came to the mountains of Khang el Ghar, he saw a pool at the bottom of a ravine. He flew down between the rocks and lighted at the edge of the water. Then he walked in and drank.

At that moment a hyena limped up and, seeing the stork standing in the water, said: "Have you come a long way?" The stork had never seen a hyena before. "So this is what a hyena is like," he thought. And he stood looking at the hyena because he had been told that if the hyena can put a little of his urine on someone, that one will have to walk after the hyena to whatever place the hyena wants him to go.

"It will be summer soon," said the stork. "I am on my way north." At the same time, he walked further out into the pool, so as not to be so near the hyena. The water here was deeper, and he almost lost his balance and had to flap his wings to keep upright. The hyena walked to the other side of the pool and looked at him from there.

"I know what is in your head," said the hyena. "You believe the story about me. You think I have that power? Perhaps long ago hyenas were like that. But now they are the same as everyone else. I could wet you from here with my urine if I wanted to. But what for? If you want to be unfriendly, go to the middle of the pool and stay there."

The stork looked around at the pool and saw that there was no spot in it where he could stand and be out of reach of the hyena.

"I have finished drinking," said the stork. He spread his wings and flapped out of the pool. At the edge he ran quickly ahead and rose into the air. He circled above the pool, looking down at the hyena.

"So you are the one they call the ogre," he said. "The world is full of strange things."

The hyena looked up. His eyes were narrow and crooked. "Allah brought us all here," he said. "You know that. You are the one who knows about Allah."

The stork flew a little lower. "That is true," he said. "But I am surprised to hear you say it. You have a very bad name, as you yourself just said. Magic is against the will of Allah."

The hyena tilted his head. "So you still believe the lies!" he cried.

"I have not seen the inside of your bladder," said the stork. "But why does everyone say you can make magic with it?"

"Why did Allah give you a head, I wonder? You have not learned how to use it." But the hyena spoke in so low a voice that the stork could not hear him.

"Your words got lost," said the stork, and he let himself drop lower.

The hyena looked up again. "I said: 'Don't come too near me. I might lift my leg and cover you with magic!' " He laughed, and the stork was near enough to see that his teeth were brown.

"Still, there must be some reason," the stork began. Then he looked for a rock high above the hyena, and settled himself on it. The hyena sat and stared up at him. "Why do they call you an ogre? What have you done?"

The hyena squinted. "You are lucky," he told the stork. "Men never try to kill you, because they think you are holy. They call you a saint and a sage. And yet you seem like neither a saint nor a sage."

"What do you mean?" said the stork quickly.

"If you really understood, you would know that magic is a grain of dust in the wind, and that Allah has power over everything. You would not be afraid."

The stork stood for a long time, thinking. He lifted one leg and held it bent in front of him. The ravine grew red as the sun went lower. And the hyena sat quietly looking up at the stork, waiting for him to speak.

Finally the stork put his leg down, opened his bill, and said: "You mean that if there is no magic, the one who sins is the one who believes there is."

The hyena laughed. "I said nothing about sin. But you did, and you are the sage. I am not in the world to tell anyone what is right or wrong. Living from night to night is enough. Everyone hopes to see me dead."

The stork lifted his leg again and stood thinking. The last daylight rose into the sky and was gone. The cliffs at the sides of the ravine were lost in the darkness.

At length the stork said: "You have given me something to think about. That is good. But now night has come. I must go on my way." He raised his wings and started to fly straight out from the boulder where he had stood. The hyena listened. He heard the stork's wings beating the air slowly, and then he heard the sound of the stork's body as it hit the cliff on the other side of the ravine. He climbed up over the rocks and found the stork. "Your wing is broken," he said. "It would have been better for you to go while there was still daylight."

"Yes," said the stork. He was unhappy and afraid.

"Come home with me," the hyena told him. "Can you walk?"

"Yes," said the stork. Together they made their way down the valley. Soon they came to a cave in the side of the mountain. The hyena went in first and called out: "Bend your head." When they were well inside, he said: "Now you can put your head up. The cave is high here."

There was only darkness inside. The stork stood still. "Where are you?" he said.

"I am here," the hyena answered, and he laughed.

"Why are you laughing?" asked the stork.

"I was thinking that the world is strange," the hyena told him. "The saint has come into my cave because he believed in magic."

"I don't understand," said the stork.

"You are confused. But at least now you can believe that I have no magic. I am like anyone else in the world."

The stork did not answer right away. He smelled the stench of the hyena very near him. Then he said, with a sigh: "You are right, of course. There is no power beyond the power of Allah."

"I am happy," said the hyena, breathing into his face. "At last you understand." Quickly he seized the stork's neck and tore it open. The stork flapped and fell on his side.

"Allah gave me something better than magic," the hyena said under his breath. "He gave me a brain."

The stork lay still. He tried to say once more: "There is no power beyond the power of Allah." But his bill merely opened very wide in the dark.

The hyena turned away. "You will be dead in a minute," he said over his shoulder. "In ten days I shall come back. By then you will be ready."

Ten days later the hyena went to cave and found the stork where he had left him. The ants had not been there. "Good," he said. He devoured what he wanted and went outside to a large flat rock above the entrance to the cave. There in the moonlight he stood a while, vomiting.

He ate some of his vomit and rolled for a long time in the rest of it, rubbing it deep into his coat. Then he thanked Allah for eyes that could see the valley in the moonlight, and for a nose that could smell carrion on the wind. He rolled some more and licked the rock under him. For a while he lay there panting. Soon he got up and limped on his way.

Tangier, 1960

THE WIND AT BENI MIDAR

PAUL BOWLES

AT BENI MIDAR there is a barracks. It has many rows of small buildings, whitewashed, and everything is in the middle of big rocks, on the side of the mountain behind the town. A quiet place when the wind is not blowing. A few Spanish still live in the houses along the road. They run the shops. But now the people in the streets are Moslems, mountain men with goats and sheep, or soldiers from the *cuartel* looking for wine. The Spanish sell wine to men they know. One Jew sells it to almost anybody. But there never is enough wine in the town for everybody who wants it. Beni Midar has only one street, that comes down out of the mountains, curves back and forth like a snake between the houses for a while, and goes on, back into the mountains. Sunday is a bad day, the one free time the soldiers have, when they can walk back and forth all day between the shops and houses. A few Spaniards in black clothes go into the church at the hour when the Rhmara ride their donkeys out of the *souk*. Later the Spaniards come out of the church and go home. Nothing else happens because all the shops are shut. There is nothing the soldiers can buy.

Driss had been stationed for eight months in Beni Midar. Because the cabran in charge of his unit had been a neighbor of his in Tetuan, he was not unhappy. The cabran had a friend with a motorcycle. Together they went each month to Tetuan. There the cabran always saw Driss's sister, who made a big bundle of food to send back to the barracks for him. She sent him chickens and cakes, cigarettes and figs, and always many hard-boiled eggs. He shared the eggs with two or three friends, and did not complain about being in Beni Midar.

Not even the brothels were open on Sunday. It was the day when everyone walked from one end of the town to the other, back and forth, many times. Sometimes Driss walked like this with his friends.

Usually he took his gun and went down into the valley to hunt for hares. When he came back at twilight he stopped in a small café at the edge of town and had a glass of tea and a few pipes of kif. If it had not been the only café he would never have gone into it. Shameful things happened there. Several times he had seen men from the mountains get up from the mat and do dances that left blood on the floor. These men were Jilala, and no one thought of stopping them, not even Driss. They did not dance because they wanted to dance, and it was this that made him angry and ashamed. It seemed to him that the world should be made in such a way that a man is free to dance or not as he feels. A Jilali can do only what the music tells him to do. When the musicians, who are Jilala too, play the music that has the power, his eyes shut and he falls on the floor. And until the man has shown the proof and drunk his own blood, the musicians do not begin the music that will bring him back to the world. They should do something about it, Driss said to the other soldiers who went with him to the café, and they agreed.

He had talked about it with his cabran in the public garden. The cabran said that when all the children in the land were going to school every day there would be no more *djenoun.* Women would no longer be able to put spells on their husbands. And the Jilala and the Hamatcha and all the others would stop cutting their legs and arms and chests. Driss thought about this for a long time. He was glad to hear that the government knew about these bad things. "But if they know," he thought, "why don't they do something now? The day they get every one of the children in school I'll be lying beside Sidi Ali el Mandri." He was thinking of the cemetery at Bab Sebta in Tetuan. When he saw the cabran again he said: "If they can do something about it, they ought to do it now." The cabran did not seem interested. "Yes," he said.

When Driss got his permission and went home he told his father what the cabran had said. "You mean the government thinks it can kill all evil spirits?" his father cried.

"That's right. It can," said Driss. "It's going to."

His father was old and had no confidence in the young men who now ran the government. "It's impossible," he said. "They should let them alone. Leave them under their stones. Children have gone to school before, and how many were hurt by *djenoun?* But if the government begins to make trouble for them, you'll see what will happen. They'll go after the children first."

Driss had expected his father to speak this way, but when he heard the words he was ashamed. He did not answer. Some of his friends were without respect for God. They ate during Ramadan and argued with their fathers. He was glad not to be like them. But he felt his father was wrong.

One hot summer Sunday when the sky was very blue Driss lay in bed late. The men who slept in his room at the barracks had gone out. He listened to the radio. "It would be good down in the valley on a day like this," he thought. He saw himself swimming in one of the big pools, and he thought of the hot sun on his back afterward. He got up and unlocked the cupboard to look for his gun. Even before he took it out he said, "*Yah latif!*" because he remembered that he had only one cartridge left, and it was Sunday. He slammed the cupboard door shut and got back into bed. The radio began to give the news. He sat up, spat as far out as he could from the bed, and turned it off. In the silence he heard many birds singing in the *safsaf* tree outside the window. He scratched his head. Then he got up and dressed. In the courtyard he saw Mehdi going toward the stairs. Mehdi was on his way to do sentry duty in the box outside the main gate.

"*Khaï!* Does four rials sound good to you?"

Medhi looked at him. "Is this number sixty, three, fifty-one?" This was the name of an Egyptian song that came over the radio nearly every day. The song ended with the word nothing. Nothing, nothing, sung over and over again.

Why not? As they walked along together, Driss moved closer, so that his thigh rubbed against Mehdi's.

"The price is ten, *khoya*."

"With all its cartridges?"

"You want me to open it up and show you here?" Mehdi's voice was angry. The words came out of the side of his mouth.

Driss said nothing. They came to the top of the stairs. Mehdi was walking fast. "You'll have to have it back here by seven," he said. "Do you want it?"

In his head Driss saw the long day in the empty town. "Yes," he said. "Stay there." He hurried back to the room, unlocked his cupboard, and took out his gun. From the shelf he pulled down his pipe, his kif, and a loaf of bread. He put his head outside the door. There was no one in the courtyard but Mehdi sitting on the wall at the other end. Then with the old gun in his hands he ran all the way to Mehdi. Mehdi took it and went down the stairs, leaving his own gun lying on the wall. Driss took up the gun, waited a moment, and followed him. When he went past the sentry box he heard Mehdi's voice say softly: "I need the ten at seven, *khoya*."

Driss grunted. He knew how dark it was in there. No officer ever stuck his head inside the door on Sundays. Ten rials, he thought, and he's running no risk. He looked around at the goats among the rocks. The sun was hot, but the air smelled sweet, and he was happy to be walking down the side of the mountain. He pulled the visor of his cap further down over his eyes and began to whistle. Soon he came out in front of the town, below it on the other side of the valley. He could see the people on the benches in the park at the top of the cliff, small but clear and black. They were Spaniards and they were waiting for the bell of their church to begin to ring.

He got to the highest pool about the time the sun was overhead. When he lay on the rocks afterward eating his bread, the sun burned him. No animals will move before three, he thought. He put his trousers on and crawled into the shade of the oleander bushes to sleep. When he awoke the air was cooler. He smoked all the kif he had, and went walking through the valley. Sometimes he sang. He found no hares, and so he put small stones on the tops of the rocks and fired at them. Then he climbed back up the other side of the valley and followed the highway into the town.

He came to the café and went in. The musicians were playing and singing. The tea drinkers clapped their hands with the music. A soldier cried: "Driss! Sit down!" He sat with his friends and smoked some of their kif. Then he bought four rials' worth from the cutter who sat on the platform with the musicians, and went on smoking. "Nothing was moving in the valley today," he told them. "It was dead down there."

A man with a yellow turban on his head who sat nearby closed his eyes and fell against the man next to him. The others around him moved to a further part of the mat. The man toppled over and lay on the floor.

"Another one?" cried Driss. "They should stay in Djebel Habib. I can't look at him."

The man took a long time to get to his feet. His arms and legs had been captured by the drums, but his body was fighting, and he groaned. Driss tried to pay no attention to him. He smoked his pipe and looked at his friends, pretending that no Jilali was in front of him. When the man pulled out his knife he could not pretend any longer. He watched the blood running into the man's eyes. It made a blank red curtain over each hole. The man opened his eyes wider, as if he wanted to see through the blood. The drums were loud.

Driss got up and paid the *qahouaji* for his tea. He said good-by to the others and went out. The sun would soon go below the top of the mountains. Its light made him want to shut his eyes, because he had a lot of kif in his head. He walked through the town to the higher end and turned into a lane that led up into another valley. In this place there was no one. Cactuses grew high on each side of the lane, and the spiders had built a world of webs between their thorns. Because he walked fast, the kif began to boil in his head. Soon he was very hungry, but all the fruit had been picked from the cactuses along the lane. He came to a small farmhouse with a thatched roof. Behind it on the empty mountainside there were more cactuses still pink with hundreds of *hindiyats*. A dog in a shed beside the house began to bark. There was no sign of people. He stood still for a while and listened to the dog. Then he walked toward the cactus patch. He was sure no one was in the house. Many years ago his sister had shown him how to pick *hindiyats* without letting the needles get into the flesh of his hands. He laid his gun on the ground behind a low stone wall and began to gather the fruit. As he picked he saw in his head the two blind red holes of the Jilali's eyes, and under his breath he cursed all Jilala. When he had a great pile of fruit on the ground he sat down and began to eat, throwing the peels over his shoulder. As he ate he grew hungrier, and so he picked more. The picture he had in his head of the man's face shiny with blood slowly faded. He thought only of the *hindiyats* he was eating. It was almost dark there on the mountainside. He looked at his watch and jumped up, because he remembered that Mehdi had to have his gun at seven o'clock. In the dim light he could not see the gun anywhere. He searched behind the wall, where he thought he had laid it, but he saw only stones and bushes.

"It's gone, *Allah istir,*" he said. His heart pounded. He ran back to the lane and stood there a while. The dog barked without stopping.

It was dark before he reached the gate of the barracks. Another man was in the sentry box. The cabran was waiting for him in the room. The old gun Driss's father had given him lay on his bed.

"Do you know where Mehdi is?" the cabran asked him.

"No," said Driss.

"He's in the dark house, the son of a whore. And do you know why?"

Driss sat down on the bed. The cabran is my friend, he was thinking. "It's gone," he said, and told him how he had laid the gun on the ground, and a dog had been barking, and no one had come by, and still it had disappeared. "Maybe the dog was a *djinn,*" he said when he had finished. He did not really believe the dog had anything to do with it, but he could not think of anything else to say then.

The cabran looked at him a long time and said nothing. He shook his head. "I thought you had some brains," he said at last. Then his face grew very angry, and he pulled Driss out into the courtyard and told a soldier to lock him up.

At ten o'clock that night he went to see Driss. He found him smoking his *sebsi* in the dark. The cell was full of kif smoke. "Garbage!" cried the cabran, and he took the pipe and the kif away from him. "Tell the truth," he said to Driss. "You sold the gun, didn't you?"

"On my mother's head, it's just as I told you! There was only the dog."

The cabran could not make him say anything different. He slammed the door and went to the café in the town to have a glass of tea. He sat listening to the music, and he began to smoke the kif he had taken from Driss. If Driss was telling the truth, then it was only the kif in Driss's head that had made him lose the gun, and in that case there was a chance that it could be found.

The cabran had not smoked in a long time. As the kif filled his head he began to be hungry, and he remembered the times when he had been a boy smoking kif with his friends. Always they had gone to look for *hindiyats* afterward, because they tasted better than anything else and cost nothing. They always knew where there were some growing. "A *kouffa* full of good *hindiyats*," he thought. He shut his eyes and went on thinking.

The next morning early the cabran went out and stood on a high rock behind the barracks, looking carefully all around the valley and the bare mountainside. Not far away he saw a lane with cactuses along it, and farther up there was a whole forest of cactus. "There," he said to himself.

He walked among the rocks until he came to the lane, and he followed the lane to the farmhouse. The dog began to bark. A woman came to the doorway and looked at him. He paid no attention to her, but went straight to the high cactuses on the hillside behind the house. There were many *hindiyats* still to be eaten, but the cabran did not eat any of them. He had no kif in his head and he was thinking only of the gun. Beside a stone wall there was a big pile of *hindiya* peelings. Someone had eaten a great many. Then he saw the sun shining on part of the gun's barrel under the peelings. "Hah!" he shouted, and he seized the gun and wiped it all over with his handkerchief. On his way back to the barracks he felt so happy that he decided to play a joke on Driss.

He hid the gun under his bed. With a glass of tea and a piece of bread in his hand he went to see Driss. He found him asleep on the floor in the dark.

"Daylight is here!" he shouted. He laughed and kicked Driss's foot to wake him up. Driss sat on the floor drinking the tea and the cabran stood in the doorway scratching his chin. He looked down at the floor, but not at Driss. After a time he said: "Last night you told me a dog was barking?"

Driss was certain the cabran was going to make fun of him. He was sorry he had mentioned the dog. "Yes," he said, not sounding sure.

"If it was the dog," the cabran went on, "I know how to get it back. You have to help me."

Driss looked up at him. He could not believe the cabran was being serious. Finally he said in a low voice: "I was joking when I said that. I had kif in my head."

The cabran was angry. "You think it's a joke to lose a gun that belongs to the Sultan? You did sell it! You haven't got kif in your head now. Maybe you can tell the truth." He stepped toward Driss, and Driss thought he was going to hit him. He stood up quickly. "I told you the truth," he said. "It was gone."

The cabran rubbed his chin and looked down at the floor again for a minute. "The next time a Jilali begins to dance in the café, we'll do it," he told him. He shut the door and left Driss alone.

Two days later the cabran came again to the dark house. He had another soldier with him. "Quick!" he told Driss. "There's one dancing now."

They went out into the courtyard and Driss blinked his eyes. "Listen," said the cabran. "When the Jilali is drinking his own blood he has power. What you have to do is ask him to make the *djinn* bring me the gun. I'm going to sit in my room and burn *djaoui.* That may help."

"I'll do it," said Driss. "But it won't do any good."

The other soldier took Driss to the café. The Jilali was a tall man from the mountains. He had already taken out his knife, and he was waving it in the air. The soldier made Driss sit down near the musicians, and then he waited until the man began to lick the blood from his arms. Then, because he thought he might be sick if he watched any longer, Driss raised his right arm toward the Jilali and said in a low voice: "In the name of Allah, *khoya,* make the *djinn* that stole Mehdi's gun take it now to Aziz the cabran." The Jilali seemed to be staring at him, but Driss could not be sure whether he had heard his words or not.

The soldier took him back to the barracks. The cabran was sitting under a plum tree beside the kitchen door. He told the soldier to go away and jumped up. "Come," he said, and he led Driss to the room. The air was blue with the smoke of the *djaoui* he had been burning. He pointed to the middle of the floor. "Look!" he cried. A gun was lying there. Driss ran and picked it up. After he had looked at it carefully, he said: "It's the gun." And his voice was full of fear. The cabran could see that Driss had not been sure the thing was possible, but that now he no longer had any doubt.

The cabran was happy to have fooled him so easily. He laughed. "You see, it worked," he said. "It's lucky for you Mehdi's going to be in the dark house for another week."

Driss did not answer. He felt even worse than when he had been watching the Jilali slicing the flesh of his arms.

That night he lay in bed worrying. It was the first time he had had anything to do with a *djinn* or an *affrit*. Now he had entered into their world. It was a dangerous world and he did not trust the cabran any longer. "What am I going to do?" he thought. The men all around him were sleeping, but he could not close his eyes. Soon he got up and stepped outside. The leaves of the *safsaf* tree were hissing in the wind. On the other side of the courtyard there was light in one of the windows. Some of the officers were talking there. He walked slowly around the garden in the middle and looked up at the sky, thinking of how different his life was going to be now. As he came near the lighted window he heard a great burst of laughter. The cabran was telling a story. Driss stopped walking and listened.

"And he said to the Jilali: 'Please, sidi, would you ask the dog that stole my gun—' "

The men laughed again, and the sound covered the cabran's voice.

He went quickly back and got into bed. If they knew he had heard the cabran's story they would laugh even more. He lay in the bed thinking, and he felt poison come into his heart. It was the cabran's fault that the *djinn* had been called, and now in front of his superior officers he was pretending that he had had nothing to do with it. Later the cabran came in and went to bed, and it was quiet in the courtyard, but Driss lay thinking for a long time before he went to sleep.

In the days that came after that, the cabran was friendly again, but Driss did not want to see him smile. He thought with hatred: "In his head I'm afraid of him now because he knows how to call a *djinn*. He jokes with me now because he has power."

He could not laugh or be happy when the cabran was nearby. Each night he lay awake for a long time after the others had gone to sleep. He listened to the wind moving the hard leaves of the *safsaf* tree, and he thought only of how he could break the cabran's power.

When Mehdi came out of the dark house he spoke against the cabran. Driss paid him his ten rials. "A lot of money for ten days in the dark house," Mehdi grumbled, and he looked at the bill in his hand. Driss pretended not to understand. "He's a son of a whore," he said.

Mehdi snorted. "And you have the head of a needle," he said. "It all came from you. The wind blows the kif out your ears!"

"You think I wasn't in the dark house too?" cried Driss. But he could not tell Mehdi about the Jilali and the dog. "He's a son of a whore," he said again.

Mehdi's eyes grew narrow and stiff. "I'll do his work for him. He'll think he's in the dark house himself when I finish."

Mehdi went on his way. Driss stood watching him go.

The next Sunday Driss got up early and walked into Beni Midar. The *souk* was full of rows of mountain people in white clothes. He walked in among the donkeys and climbed the steps to the stalls. There he went to see an old man who sold incense and herbs. People called him El Fqih. He sat down in front of El Fqih and said: "I want something for a son of a whore."

El Fqih looked at him angrily. "A sin!" He raised his forefinger and shook it back and forth. "Sins are not my work." Driss did not say anything. El Fqih spoke more quietly now. "To balance that, it is said that each trouble in the world has its remedy. There are cheap remedies and remedies that cost a lot of money." He stopped.

Driss waited. "How much is this one?" he asked him. The old man was not pleased because he wanted to talk longer. But he said: "I'll give you a name for five rials." He looked sternly at Driss, leaned forward and whispered a name in his ear. "In the alley behind the sawmill," he said aloud. "The blue tin shack with the canebrake in back of it." Driss paid him and ran down the steps.

He found the house. The old woman stood in the doorway with a checkered tablecloth over her head. Her eyes had turned white like milk. They looked to Driss like the eyes of an old dog. He said: "You're Anisa?"

"Come into the house," she told him. It was almost dark inside. He told her he wanted something to break the power of a son of a whore. "Give me ten rials now," she said. "Come back at sunset with another ten. It will be ready."

After the midday meal he went out into the courtyard. He met Mehdi and asked him to go with him to the café in Beni Midar. They walked through the town in the hot afternoon sun. It was still early when they got to the café, and there was plenty of space on the mats.

They sat in a dark corner. Driss took out his kif and his *sebsi* and they smoked. When the musicians began to play, Mehdi said: "The circus is back!" But Driss did not want to talk about the Jilala. He talked about the cabran. He gave the pipe many times to Mehdi, and he watched Mehdi growing more angry with the cabran as he smoked. He was not surprised when Mehdi cried: "I'll finish it tonight!"

"No, *khoya,*" said Driss. "You don't know. He's gone way up. He's a friend of all the officers now. They bring him bottles of wine."

"He'll come down," Mehdi said. "Before dinner tonight. In the courtyard. You be there and watch it."

Driss handed him the pipe and paid for the tea. He left Mehdi there and went into the street to walk up and down because he did not want to sit still any longer. When the sky was red behind the mountain he went to the alley by the sawmill. The old woman was in the doorway.

"Come in," she said as before. When they were inside the room she handed him a paper packet. "He has to take all of it," she said. She took the money and pulled at his sleeve. "I never saw you," she said. "Good-by."

Driss went to his room and listened to the radio. When dinner time came he stood inside the doorway looking out into the courtyard. In the shadows at the other end he thought he could see Mehdi, but he was not sure. There were many soldiers walking around in the courtyard, waiting for dinner. Soon there was shouting near the top of the steps. The soldiers began to run toward the other end of the courtyard. Driss looked from the doorway and saw only the running soldiers. He called to the men in the room. "Something's happening!" They all ran out. Then with the paper of powder in his hand he went back into the room to the cabran's bed and lifted up the bottle of wine one of the officers had given the cabran the day before. It was almost full. He pulled out the cork and let the powder slide into the bottle. He shook the bottle and put the cork back. There was still shouting in the courtyard. He ran out. When he got near the crowd, he saw Mehdi being dragged along the ground by three soldiers. He was kicking. The cabran sat on the wall with his head down, holding his arm. There was blood all over his face and shirt.

It was almost a half hour before the cabran came to eat his dinner. His face was covered with bruises and his arm was bandaged and hung in a sling. Mehdi had cut it with his knife at the last minute when the soldiers had begun to pull them apart. The cabran did not speak much, and the men did not try to talk with him. He sat on his bed and ate. While he was eating he drank all the wine in the bottle.

That night the cabran moaned in his sleep. A dry wind blew between the mountains. It made a great noise in the *safsaf* tree outside the window. The air roared and the leaves rattled, but Driss still heard the cabran's voice crying. In the morning the doctor came to look at him. The cabran's eyes were open but he could not see. And his mouth was open but he could not speak. They carried him out of the room where the soldiers lived and put him somewhere else. "Maybe the power is broken now," thought Driss.

A few days later a truck came to the barracks, and he saw two men carrying the cabran on a stretcher to the truck. Then he was sure that the cabran's soul had been torn out of his body and that the power was truly broken. In his head he made a prayer of thanks to Allah. He stood with some other soldiers on a rock above the barracks watching the truck grow smaller as it moved down the mountain.

"It's bad for me," he told a man who stood nearby. "He always brought me food from home." The soldier shook his head.

Tangier, 1962

HE OF THE ASSEMBLY

PAUL BOWLES

He salutes all parts of the sky and the earth where it is bright. He thinks the color of the amethysts of Aguelmous will be dark if it has rained in the valley of Zerekten. The eye wants to sleep, he says, but the head is no mattress. When it rained for three days and water covered the flatlands outside the ramparts, he slept by the bamboo fence at the Café of the Two Bridges.

IT SEEMS THERE WAS A MAN named Ben Tajah who went to Fez to visit his cousin. The day he came back he was walking in the Djemaa el Fna, and he saw a letter lying on the pavement. He picked it up and found that his name was written on the envelope. He went to the Café of the Two Bridges with the letter in his hand, sat down on a mat and opened the envelope. Inside was a paper which read: "The sky trembles and the earth is afraid, and the two eyes are not brothers." Ben Tajah did not understand, and he was very unhappy because his name was on the envelope. It made him think that Satan was nearby. He of the Assembly was sitting in the same part of the café. He was listening to the wind in the telephone wires. The sky was almost empty of daytime light. "The eye wants to sleep," he thought, "but the head is no mattress. I know what that is, but I have forgotten it." Three days is a long time for rain to keep falling on flat bare ground. "If I got up and ran down the street," he thought, "a policeman would follow me and call to me to stop. I would run faster, and he would run after me. When he shot at me, I'd duck around the corners of houses." He felt the rough dried mud of the wall under his fingertips. "And I'd be running through the streets looking for a place to hide, but no door would be open, until finally I came to one door that was open, and I'd go in through the rooms and courtyards until finally I came to the kitchen. The old woman would be there." He stopped and wondered for a moment why an old woman should be there alone in the kitchen at that hour. She was stirring a big kettle of soup on the stove. "And I'd look for a place to hide there in the kitchen, and there'd be no place. And I'd be waiting to hear the policeman's footsteps, because he wouldn't miss the open door. And I'd look in the dark corner of the room where she kept the charcoal, but it wouldn't be dark enough. And the old woman would turn and look at me and say: 'If you're trying to get away, my boy, I can help you. Jump into the soup-kettle.' " The wind sighed in the telephone wires. Men came into the Café of the Two Bridges with their garments flapping. Ben Tajah sat on his mat. He had put the letter away, but first he had stared at it a long time. He of the Assembly leaned back and looked at the sky. "The old woman," he said to himself. "What is she trying to do? The soup is hot. It may be a trap. I may find there's no way out, once I get down there." He wanted a pipe of kif, but he was afraid the policeman would run into the kitchen before he was able to smoke it. He said to the old woman: "How can I get in? Tell me." And it seemed to him that he heard footsteps in the street, or perhaps even in one of the rooms of the house. He leaned over the stove and looked down into the kettle. It was dark and very hot down in there. Steam was coming up in clouds, and there was a thick smell in the air that made it hard to breathe. "Quick!" said the old woman, and she unrolled a rope ladder and hung it over the edge of the kettle. He began to climb down, and she leaned over and looked after him. "Until the other world!" he shouted. And he climbed all the way down. There was a rowboat below. When he was in it he tugged on the ladder and the old woman began to pull it up. And at that instant the policeman ran in, and two more were with him, and the old woman had just the time to throw the ladder down into the soup. "Now they are going to take her to the commissariat," he thought, "and the poor woman only did me a favor." He rowed around in the dark for a few minutes, and it was very hot. Soon he took off his clothes. For a while he could see the round top of the kettle up above, like a porthole in the side of a ship, with the heads of the policemen looking down in, but then it grew smaller as he rowed, until it was only a light. Sometimes he could find it and sometimes he lost it, and finally it was gone. He was worried about the old woman, and he thought he must find a way to help her. No policeman can go into the Café of the Two Bridges because it belongs to the Sultan's sister. This is why there is so much kif smoke inside that a *berrada* can't fall over even if it is pushed, and why most customers like to sit outside, and even there keep one hand on their money. As long as the thieves stay inside and their friends bring them food and kif, they are all right. One day police headquarters will forget to send a man to watch the café, or one man will leave five minutes before the other gets there to take his place. Outside everyone smokes kif too, but only for an hour or two—not all day and night like the ones inside. He of the Assembly had forgotten to light his *sebsi.* He was in a café where no policeman could come, and he wanted to go away to a kif world where the police were chasing him. "This is the way we are now," he thought. "We work backwards. If we have something good, we look for something bad instead." He lighted the *sebsi* and smoked it. Then he blew the hard ash out of the *chqaf*. It landed in the brook beside the second bridge. "The world is too good. We can only work forward if we make it bad again first." This made him sad, so he stopped thinking, and filled his *sebsi.* While he was smoking it, Ben Tajah looked in his direction, and although they were facing each other, He of the Assembly did not notice Ben Tajah until he got up and paid for his tea. Then he looked at him because he took such a long time getting up off the floor. He saw his face and he thought: "That man has no one in the world." The idea made him feel cold. He filled his *sebsi* again and lighted it. He saw the man as he was going to go out of the café and walk alone down the long road outside the ramparts. In a little while he himself would have to go out to the *souks* to try to borrow money for dinner. When he smoked a lot of kif he did not like his aunt to see him, and he did not want to see her. "Soup and bread. No one can want more than that. Will thirty francs be enough the fourth time? The *qahouaji* wasn't satisfied last night. But he took it. And he went away and let me sleep. A Moslem, even in the city, can't refuse his brother shelter." He was not convinced, because he had been born in the mountains, and so he kept thinking back and forth in this way. He smoked many *chqofa,* and when he got up to go out into the street he found that the world had changed.

Ben Tajah was not a rich man. He lived alone in a room near Bab Doukkala, and he had a stall in the bazaars where he sold coathangers and chests. Often he did not open the shop because he was in bed with a liver attack. At such times he pounded on the floor from his bed, using a brass pestle, and the postman who lived downstairs brought him up some food. Sometimes he stayed in bed for a week at a time. Each morning and night the postman came in with a tray. The food was not very good because the postman's wife did not understand much about cooking. But he was glad to have it. Twice he had brought the postman a new chest to keep clothes and blankets in. One of the postman's wives a few years before had taken a chest with her when she had left him and gone back to her family in Kasba Tadla. Ben Tajah himself had tried having a wife for a while because he needed someone to get him regular meals and to wash his clothes, but the girl was from the mountains, and was wild. No matter how much he beat her she would not be tamed. Everything in the room got broken, and finally he had to put her out into the street. "No more women will get into my house," he told his friends in the bazaars, and they laughed. He took home many women, and one day he found that he had *en noua*. He knew that was a bad disease, because it stays in the blood and eats the nose from inside. "A man loses his nose only long after he has already lost his head." He asked a doctor for medicine. The doctor gave him a paper and told him to take it to the Pharmacie de l'Etoile. There he bought six vials of penicillin in a box. He took them home and tied each little bottle with a silk thread, stringing them so that they made a necklace. He wore this always around his neck, taking care that the glass vials touched his skin. He thought it likely that by now he was cured, but his cousin in Fez had just told him that he must go on wearing the medicine for another three months, or at least until the beginning of the moon of Chouwal. He had thought about this now and then on the way home, sitting in the bus for two days, and he had decided that his cousin was too cautious. He stood in the Djemaa el Fna a minute watching the trained monkeys, but the crowd pushed too much, so he walked on. When he got home he shut the door and put his hand in his pocket to pull out the envelope, because he wanted to look at it again inside his own room, and be sure that the name written on it was beyond a doubt his. But the letter was gone. He remembered the jostling in the Djemaa el Fna. Someone had reached into his pocket and imagined his hand was feeling money, and taken it. Yet Ben Tajah did not truly believe this. He was convinced that he would have known such a theft was happening. There had been a letter in his pocket. He was not even sure of that. He sat down on the cushions. "Two days in the bus," he thought. "Probably I'm tired. I found no letter." He searched in his pocket again, and it seemed to him he could still remember how the fold of the envelope had felt. "Why would it have my name on it? I never found any letter at all." Then he wondered if anyone had seen him in the café with the envelope in one hand and the sheet of paper in the other, looking at them both for such a long time. He stood up. He wanted to go back to the Café of the Two Bridges and ask the *qahouaji:* "Did you see me an hour ago? Was I looking at a letter?" If the *qahouaji* said, "Yes," then the letter was real. He repeated the words aloud: "The sky trembles and the earth is afraid, and the two eyes are not brothers." In the silence afterwards the memory of the sound of the words frightened him. "If there was no letter, where are these words from?" And he shivered because the answer to that was: "From Satan." He was about to open the door when a new fear stopped him. The *qah-*

ouaji might say, "No," and this would be still worse, because it would mean that the words had been put directly into his head by Satan, that Satan had chosen him to reveal Himself to. In that case He might appear at any moment. "*Ach haddou laillaha ill' Allah . . .* ," he prayed, holding his two forefingers up, one on each side of him. He sat down again and did not move. In the street the children were crying. He did not want to hear the *qahouaji* say: "No. You had no letter." If he knew that Satan was coming to tempt him, he would have that much less power to keep Him away with his prayers, because he would be more afraid.

He of the Assembly stood. Behind him was a wall. In his hand was the *sebsi.* Over his head was the sky, which he felt was about to burst into light. He was leaning back looking at it. It was dark on the earth, but there was still light up there behind the stars. Ahead of him was the pissoir of the Carpenters' Souk which the French had put there. People said only Jews used it. It was made of tin, and there was a puddle in front of it that reflected the sky and the top of the pissoir. It looked like a boat in the water. Or like a pier where boats land. Without moving from where he stood, He of the Assembly saw it approaching slowly. He was going toward it. And he remembered he was naked, and put his hand over his sex. In a minute the rowboat would be bumping against the pier. He steadied himself on his legs and waited. But at that moment a large cat ran out of the shadow of the wall and stopped in the middle of the street to turn and look at him with an evil face. He saw its two eyes and for a while could not take his own eyes away. Then the cat ran across the street and was gone. He was not sure what had happened, and he stood very still looking at the ground. He looked back at the pissoir reflected in the puddle and thought: "It was a cat on the shore, nothing else." But the cat's eyes had frightened him. Instead of being like cats' eyes, they had looked like the eyes of a person who was interested in him. He made himself forget he had had this thought. He was still waiting for the rowboat to touch the landing pier, but nothing had happened. It was going to stay where it was, that near the shore but not near enough to touch. He stood still a long time, waiting for something to happen. Then he began to walk very fast down the street toward the bazaars. He had just remembered that the old woman was in the police station. He wanted to help her, but first he had to find out where they had taken her. "I'll have to go to every police station in the Medina," he thought, and he was not hungry any more. It was one thing to promise himself he would help her when he was far from land, and another when he was a few doors from a commissariat. He walked by the entrance. Two policemen stood in the doorway. He kept walking. The street curved and he was alone. "This night is going to be a jewel in my crown," he said, and he turned quickly to the left and went along a dark passageway. At the end he saw flames, and he knew that Mustapha would be there tending the fire of the bakery. He crawled into the mud hut where the oven was. "Ah, the jackal has come back from the forest!" said Mustapha. He of the Assembly shook his head. "This is a bad world," he told Mustapha. "I've got no money," Mustapha said. He of the Assembly did not understand. "Everything goes backwards," he said. "It's bad now, and we have to make it still worse if we want to go forwards." Mustapha saw that He of the Assembly was *mkiyif ma rassou* and was not interested in money. He looked at him in a more friendly way and said: "Secrets are not between friends. Talk." He of the Assembly told him that an old woman had done him a great favor, and because of that three policemen had arrested her and taken her to the police station. "You must go for me to the commissariat and ask them if they have an old woman there." He pulled out his *sebsi* and took a very long time filling it. When he finished it he smoked it himself and did not offer any to Mustapha, because Mustapha never offered him any of his. "You see how full of kif my head is," he said laughing. "I can't go." Mustapha laughed too and said it would not be a good idea, and that he would go for him.

"I was there, and I heard him going away for a long time, so long that he had to be gone, and yet he was still there, and his footsteps were still going away. He went away and there was nobody. There was the fire and I moved away from it. I wanted to hear a sound like a muezzin crying *Allah akbar!* or a French plane from the Pilot Base flying over the Medina, or news on the radio. It wasn't there. And when the wind came in the door it was made of dust high as a man. A night to be chased by dogs in the Mellah. I looked in the fire and I saw an eye in there, like the eye that's left when you burn *chibb* and you know there was a *djinn* in the house. I got up and stood. The fire was making a noise like a voice. I think it was talking. I went out and walked along the street. I walked a long time and I came to Bab el Khemiss. It was dark there and the wind was cold. I went to the wall where the camels were lying and stood there. Sometimes the men have fires and play songs on their *aouadas*. But they were asleep. All snoring. I walked again and went to the gate and looked out. The big trucks went by full of vegetables and I thought I would like to be on a truck and ride all night. Then in another city I would be a soldier and go to Algeria. Everything would be good if we had a war. I thought a long time. Then I was so cold I turned around and walked again. It was as cold as the belly of the oldest goat of Ijoukak. I thought I heard a muezzin and I stopped and listened. The only thing I heard was the water running in the *seguia* that carries the water out to the gardens. It was near the *mçid* of Moulay Boujemaa. I heard the water running by and I felt cold. Then I knew I was cold because I was afraid. In my head I was thinking: 'If something should happen that never happened before, what would I do?' You want to laugh? Hashish in your heart and wind in your head. You think it's like your grandmother's prayer-mat. This is the truth. This isn't a dream brought back from another world past the customs like a teapot from Mecca. I heard the water and I was afraid. There were some trees by the path ahead of me. You know at night sometimes it's good to pull out the *sebsi* and smoke. I smoked and I started to walk. And then I heard something. Not a muezzin. Something that sounded like my name. But it came up from below, from the *seguia, Allah istir!* And I walked with my head down. I heard it again saying my name, a voice like water, like the wind moving the leaves in the trees, a woman. It was a woman calling me. The wind was in the trees and the water was running, but there was a woman too. You think it's kif. No, she was calling my name. Now and then, not very loud. When I was under the trees it was louder, and I heard that the voice was my mother's. I heard that the way I can hear you. Then I knew the cat was not a cat, and I knew that Aïcha Qandicha wanted me. I thought of other nights when perhaps she had been watching me from the eyes of a cat or a donkey. I knew she was not going to catch me. Nothing in the seven skies could make me turn around. But I was cold and afraid and when I licked my lips my tongue had no spit on it. I was under the *safsaf* trees and I thought: 'She's going to reach down and try to touch me. But she can't touch me from the front and I won't turn around, not even if I hear a pistol.' I remembered how the policeman had fired at me and how I'd found only one door open. I began to yell: 'You threw me the ladder and told me to climb down. You brought me here! The filthiest whore in the Mellah, with the pus coming out of her, is a thousand times cleaner than you, daughter of all the padronas and dogs in seven worlds.' I got past the trees and I began to run. I called up to the sky so she could hear my voice behind: 'I hope the police put a hose in your mouth and pump you full of salt water until you crack open!' I thought: 'Tomorrow I'm going to buy *fasoukh* and *tib* and *nidd* and *hasalouba* and *mska* and all the *bakhour* in the Djemaa, and put them in the *mijmah* and burn them, and walk back and forth over the *mijmah* ten times slowly, so the smoke can clean out all my clothes. Then I'll see if there's an eye in the ashes afterwards.

If there is, I'll do it all over again right away. And every Thursday I'll buy the *bakhour* and every Friday I'll burn it. That will be strong enough to keep her away.' If I could find a window and look through and see what they're doing to the old woman! If only they could kill her! I kept running. There were a few people in the streets. I didn't look to see where I was going, but I went to the street near Mustapha's oven where the commissariat was. I stopped running before I got to the door. The one standing there saw me before that. He stepped out and raised his arm. He said to me: 'Come here.' "

He of the Assembly ran. He felt as though he were on horseback. He did not feel his legs moving. He saw the road coming toward him and the doors going by. The policeman had not shot at him yet, but it was worse than the other time because he was very close behind and he was blowing his whistle. "The policeman is old. At least thirty-five. I can run faster." But from any street others could come. It was dangerous and he did not want to think about danger. He of the Assembly let songs come into his head. When it rains in the valley of Zerekten the amethysts are darker in Aguelmous. The eye wants to sleep but the head is no mattress. It was a song. Ah, my brother, the ink on the paper is like smoke in the air. What words are there to tell how long a night can be? Drunk with love, I wander in the dark. He was running through the dye-souk, and he splashed into a puddle. The whistle blew again behind him, like a crazy bird screaming. The sound made him feel like laughing, but that did not mean he was not afraid. He thought: "If I'm seventeen I can run faster. That has to be true." It was very dark ahead. He had to slow his running. There was no time for his eyes to get used to the dark. He nearly ran into the wall of the shop at the end of the street. He turned to the right and saw the narrow alley ahead of him. The police had tied the old woman naked to a table with her thin legs wide apart and were sliding electrodes up inside her. He ran ahead. He could see the course of the alley now even in the dark. Then he stopped dead, moved to the wall, and stood still. He heard the footsteps slowing down. "He's going to turn to the left." And he whispered aloud: "It ends that way." The footsteps stopped and there was silence. The policeman was looking into the silence and listening into the dark to the left and to the right. He of the Assembly could not see him or hear him, but he knew that was what he was doing. He did not move. When it rains in the valley of Zerekten. A hand seized his shoulder. He opened his mouth and swiftly turned, but the man had moved and was pushing him from the side. He felt the wool of the man's *djellaba* against the back of his hand. He had gone through a door and the man had shut it without making any noise. Now they both stood still in the dark, listening to the policeman walking quickly by outside the door. Then the man struck a match. He was facing the other way, and there was a flight of stairs ahead. The man did not turn around, but he said, "Come up," and they both climbed the stairs. At the top the man took out a key and opened a door. He of the Assembly stood in the doorway while the man lit a candle. He liked the room because it had many mattresses and cushions and a white sheepskin under the tea-tray in the corner of the floor. The man turned around and said: "Sit down." His face looked serious and kind and unhappy. He of the Assembly had never seen it before, but he knew it was not the face of a policeman. He of the Assembly pulled out his *sebsi.*

Ben Tajah looked at the boy and asked him: "What did you mean when you said down there: 'It ends that way?' I heard you say it." The boy was embarrassed. He smiled and looked at the floor. Ben Tajah felt happy to have him there. He had been standing outside the door downstairs in the dark for a long time, trying to make himself go to the Café of the Two Bridges and talk to the *qahouaji.* In his mind it was almost as though he had already been there and spoken with him. He had heard the *qahouaji* telling him that he had seen no letter, and he had felt his own dismay. He had not wanted to believe that, but he would be willing to say yes, I made a mistake and there was no letter, if only he could find out where the words had come from. For the words were certainly in his head: ". . . and the two eyes are not brothers." That was like a footprint found in the garden the morning after a bad dream, the proof that there had been a reason for the dream, that something had been there after all. Ben Tajah had not been able to go or to stay. He had started and stopped so many times that now, although he did not know it, he was very tired. When a man is tired he mistakes the hopes of children for the knowledge of men. It seemed to him that He of the Assembly's words had a meaning all for him. Even though the boy might not know it, he could have been sent by Allah to help him at that minute. In a nearby street a police whistle blew. The boy looked at him. Ben Tajah did not care very much what the answer would be, but he said: "Why are they looking for you?" The boy held out his lighted *sebsi* and his *mottoui* fat with kif. He did not want to talk because he was listening. Ben Tajah smoked kif only when a friend offered it to him, but he understood that the police had begun once more to try to enforce their law against kif. Each year they arrested people for a few weeks, and then stopped arresting them. He looked at the boy, and decided that probably he smoked too much. With the *sebsi* in his hand he was sitting very still listening to the voices of some passers-by in the street below. "I know who he is," one said. "I've got his name from Mustapha." "The baker?" "That's the one." They walked on. The boy's expression was so intense that Ben Tajah said to him: "It's nobody. Just people." He was feeling happy because he was certain that Satan would not appear before him as long as the boy was with him. He said quietly: "Still you haven't told me why you said: 'It ends that way.' " The boy filled his *sebsi* slowly and smoked all the kif in it. "I meant," he said, "thanks to Allah. Praise the sky and the earth where it is bright. What else can you mean when something ends?" Ben Tajah nodded his head. Pious thoughts can be of as much use for keeping Satan at a distance as camphor or *bakhour* dropped onto hot coals. Each holy word is worth a high column of smoke, and the eyelids do not smart afterward. "He has a good heart," thought Ben Tajah, "even though he is probably a guide for the Nazarenes." And he asked himself why it would not be possible for the boy to have been sent to protect him from Satan. "Probably not. But it could be." The boy offered him the *sebsi*. He took it and smoked it. After that Ben Tajah began to think that he would like to go to the Café of the Two Bridges and speak to the *qahouaji* about the letter. He felt that if the boy went with him the *qahouaji* might say there had been a letter, and that even if the man could not remember, he would not mind so much because he would be less afraid. He waited until he thought the boy was not nervous about going into the street, and then he said: "Let's go out and get some tea." "Good," said the boy. He was not afraid of the police if he was with Ben Tajah. They went through the empty streets, crossed the Djemaa el Fna and the garden beyond. When they were near the café, Ben Tajah said to the boy: "Do you know the Café of the Two Bridges?" The boy said he always sat there, and Ben Tajah was not surprised. It seemed to him that perhaps he had even seen him there. He seized the boy's arm. "Were you there today?" he asked him. The boy said, "Yes," and turned to look at him. He let go of the arm. "Nothing," he said. "Did you ever see me there?" They came to the gate of the café and Ben Tajah stopped walking. "No," the boy said. They went across the first bridge and then the second bridge, and sat down in a corner. Not many people were left outside. Those inside were making a great noise. The *qahouaji* brought the tea and went away again. Ben Tajah did not say anything to him about the letter. He wanted to drink the tea quietly and leave trouble until later.

When the muezzin called from the minaret of the Koutoubia, He of the Assembly thought of being in the Agdal. The great mountains were ahead of him and the olive trees stood in rows on each side of him. Then he heard the trickle of water and he remembered the *seguia* that is there in the Agdal, and he swiftly came back to the Café of the Two Bridges. Aïcha Qandicha can be only where there are trees by running water. "She comes only for single men by trees and fresh moving water. Her arms are gold and she calls in the voice of the most cherished one." Ben Tajah gave him the *sebsi*. He filled it and smoked it. "When a man sees her face he will never see another woman's face. He will make love with her all the night, and every night, and in the sunlight by the walls, before the eyes of children. Soon he will be an empty pod and he will leave this world for his home in Jehennem." The last carriage went by, taking the last tourists down the road beside the ramparts to their rooms in the Mamounia. He of the Assembly thought: "The eye wants to sleep. But this man is alone in the world. He wants to talk all night. He wants to tell me about his wife and how he beat her and how she broke everything. Why do I want to know all those things? He is a good man but he has no head." Ben Tajah was sad. He said: "What have I done? Why does Satan choose me?" Then at last he told the boy about the letter, about how he wondered if it had had his name on the envelope and how he was not even sure there had been a letter. When he finished he looked sadly at the boy. "And you didn't see me." He of the Assembly shut his eyes and kept them shut for a while. When he opened them again he said: "Are you alone in the world?" Ben Tajah stared at him and did not speak. The boy laughed. "I did see you," he said, "but you had no letter. I saw you when you were getting up and I thought you were old. Then I saw you were not old. That's all I saw." "No, it isn't," Ben Tajah said. "You saw I was alone." He of the Assembly shrugged. "Who knows?" He filled the *sebsi* and handed it to Ben Tajah. The kif was in Ben Tajah's head. His eyes were small. He of the Assembly listened to the wind in the telephone wires, took back the *sebsi* and filled it again. Then he said: "You think Satan is coming to make trouble for you because you're alone in the world. I see that. Get a wife or somebody to be with you always, and you won't think about it any more. That's true. Because Satan doesn't come to men like you." He of the Assembly did not believe this himself. He knew that Father Satan can come for anyone in the world, but he hoped to live with Ben Tajah, so he would not have to borrow money in the *souks* to buy food. Ben Tajah drank some tea. He did not want the boy to see that his face was happy. He felt that the boy was right, and that there never had been a letter. "Two days on a bus is a long time. A man can get very tired," he said. Then he called the *qahouaji* and told him to bring two more glasses of tea. He of the Assembly gave him the *sebsi.* He knew that Ben Tajah wanted to stay as long as possible in the Café of the Two Bridges. He put his finger into the *mottoui.* The kif was almost gone. "We can talk," he said. "Not much kif is in the *mottoui.*" The *qahouaji* brought the tea. They talked for an hour or more. The *qahouaji* slept and snored. They talked about Satan and the bad thing it is to live alone, to wake up in the dark and know that there is no one else nearby. Many times He of the Assembly told Ben Tajah that he must not worry. The kif was all gone. He held his empty *mottoui* in his hand. He did not understand how he had got back to the town without climbing up out of the soup kettle. Once he said to Ben Tajah: "I never climbed back up." Ben Tajah looked at him and said he did not understand. He of the Assembly told him the story. Ben Tajah laughed. He said: "You smoke too much kif, brother." He of the Assembly put his *sebsi* into his pocket. "And you don't smoke and you're afraid of Satan," he told Ben Tajah. "No!" Ben Tajah shouted. "By Allah! No more! But one thing is in my head, and I can't put it out. The sky trembles and the earth is afraid, and the two eyes are not brothers. Did you ever hear those words? Where did they come from?" Ben Tajah looked hard at the boy. He of the Assembly understood that these had been the words on the paper, and he felt cold in the middle of his back because he had never heard them before and they sounded evil. He knew, too, that he must not let Ben Tajah know this. He began to laugh. Ben Tajah took hold of his knee and shook it. His face was troubled. "Did you ever hear them?" He of the Assembly went on laughing. Ben Tajah shook his leg so hard that he stopped and said: "Yes!" When Ben Tajah waited and he said nothing more, he saw the man's face growing angry, and so he said: "Yes, I've heard them. But will you tell me what happened to me and how I got out of the soup-kettle if I tell you about those words?" Ben Tajah understood that the kif was going away from the boy's head. But he saw that it had not all gone, or he would not have been asking that question. And he said: "Wait a while for the answer to that question." He of the Assembly woke the *qahouaji* and Ben Tajah paid him, and they went out of the café. They did not talk while they walked. When they got to the Mouassine mosque, Ben Tajah held out his hand to say goodnight, but He of the Assembly said: "I'm looking in my head for the place I heard your words. I'll walk to your door with you. Maybe I'll remember." Ben Tajah said: "May Allah help you find it." And he took his arm and they walked to Ben Tajah's door while He of the Assembly said nothing. They stood outside the door in the dark. "Have you found it?" said Ben Tajah. "Almost," said He of the Assembly. Ben Tajah thought that perhaps when the kif had gone out of the boy's head he might be able to tell him about the words. He wanted to know how the boy's head was, and so he said: "Do you still want to know how you got out of the soup-kettle?" He of the Assembly laughed. "You said you would tell me later," he told Ben Tajah. "I will," said Ben Tajah. "Come upstairs. Since we have to wait, we can sit down." Ben Tajah opened the door and they went upstairs. This time He of the Assembly sat down on Ben Tajah's bed. He yawned and stretched. It was a good bed. He was glad it was not the mat by the bamboo fence at the Café of the Two Bridges. "And so, tell me how I got out of the soup-kettle," he said laughing. Ben Tajah said: "You're still asking me that? Have you thought of the words?" "I know the words," the boy said. "The sky trembles. . . ." Ben Tajah did not want him to say them again. "Where did you hear them? What are they? That's what I want to know." The boy shook his head. Then he sat up very straight and looked beyond Ben Tajah, beyond the wall of the room, beyond the streets of the Medina, beyond the gardens, toward the mountains where the people speak Tachelhait. He remembered being a little boy. "This night is a jewel in my crown," he thought. "It went this way." And he began to sing, making up a melody for the words Ben Tajah had told him. When he had finished ". . . and the two eyes are not brothers," he added a few more words of his own and stopped singing. "That's all I remember of the song," he said. Ben Tajah clapped his hands together hard. "A song!" he cried. "I must have heard it on the radio." He of the Assembly shrugged. "They play it sometimes," he said. "I've made him happy," he thought. "But I won't ever tell him another lie. That's the only one. What I'm going to do now is not the same as lying." He got up off the bed and went to the window. The muezzins were calling the *fjer*. "It's almost morning," he said to Ben Tajah. "I still have kif in my head." "Sit down," said Ben Tajah. He was sure now there had been no letter. He of the Assembly took off his *djellaba* and got into bed. Ben Tajah looked at him in surprise. Then he undressed and got into bed beside him. He left the candle burning on the floor beside the bed. He meant to stay awake, but he went to sleep because he was not used to smoking kif and the kif was in his head. He of the Assembly did not believe he was asleep. He lay for a long time without moving. He listened to the voices of the muezzins, and he thought that the man beside him would speak or move. When he saw that Ben Tajah was surely asleep, he was angry. "This is how he treats a friend who has made him happy. He forgets his trouble and his friend too." He thought about it more and he was angrier. The muezzins were still calling the *fjer*. "Before they stop, or he will hear." Very slowly he got out of the bed. He put on his *djellaba* and opened the door. Then he went back and took all the money out of Ben Tajah's pockets. In with the banknotes was an envelope that was folded. It had Ben Tajah's name written across it. He pulled out the piece of paper inside and held it near the candle, and then he looked at it as he would have looked at a snake. The words were written there. Ben Tajah's face was turned toward the wall and he was snoring. He of the Assembly held the paper above the flame and burned it, and then he burned the envelope. He blew the black paper-ashes across the floor. Without making any noise he ran downstairs and let himself out into the street. He shut the door. The money was in his pocket and he walked fast to his aunt's house. His aunt awoke and was angry for a while. Finally he said: "It was raining. How could I come home? Let me sleep." He had a little kif hidden under his pillow. He smoked a pipe. Then he looked across his sleep to the morning and thought: "A pipe of kif before breakfast gives a man the strength of a hundred camels in the courtyard."

Tangier, 1961

LOOKING FOR LANE

JANE BOWLES

A FRAGMENT SELECTED FROM a notebook, probably from the early fifties, "Looking for Lane" was first published in 1984.

THE TOWN OF X— was built on six or seven different levels. Right behind it there rose a heavily wooded mountain range, while below it stretched a swampy valley divided in the middle by a dark green river. Big wooden steps with iron handrails served as short cuts between one level of the town and the next. On the bottom level were the main streets, the shops, and the largest houses. On the third level at the end of the street there was a swift little waterfall near which Miss Dora Sitwell lived in a log house with her sister Lane. Lane was the younger but both sisters were in their middle years. Dora was a tall bony woman with bold black hair which she wore straight and pointing in toward her cheeks on either side. Her eye was bright and her nose long. Her sister was the opposite type—rather chunky and a blonde.

One morning in the fall of the year Dora was mending a pair of antique bellows and her sister lay in bed with a light case of grippe. She called in to Dora:

"Winter is coming and the damp is starting to seep in here already from that mountain. It's too near the house. As a matter of fact the whole town should be leveled. What's the point of living built into the side of a mountain? Why don't we go to Florida?"

"I like the change of seasons," Dora said pleasantly. "I love to watch each season come in—"

"We're too old for that winter summer spring stuff," Lane objected. "We should go to Florida and rest."

"I have as much zip as ever," Dora answered, "and I love the different seasons. So do you."

"I don't at all," said Lane.

Dora hung the bellows on their hook and walked into a dark and crowded corner of the room where she picked up a yellow crock designed to imitate a squash. She uncorked it and poured herself some sherry.

She drank sherry very often during the day but never so much that she lost interest in sewing or household work. Actually, she was more industrious and swifter than Lane, who did not drink but sat still dreaming for long periods of time. Dora returned to the couch which she herself had upholstered with two Indian blankets of different designs. There were a number of Indian and Russian objects in the room.

After a long period of silence, Lane called again.

"You can't tell me you enjoy November."

"I have nothing against November," said Dora. "In fact it's likely to make me feel zippy." Lane's feet thrashed angrily under the covers.

"It's not even natural to be as good-tempered as you are," she complained. "Every woman's got to have her humors."

"But I have nothing that makes me sad."

"Your husband died, didn't he?"

"Yes," Dora answered. "But he's so fortunate to be where he is. It's lovely up there."

"Well," Lane continued crossly. "You won't ever get there from this cluttered-up stupid little log house, I can tell you that."

"You don't have any knack for religion, Lane," Dora said. "You don't get what it's about—you never have."

Lane's face darkened. In referring to her religious inclination her sister had touched on a very sore spot. Lane did not have the fear of God.

She felt ashamed of this, and pretended to fear Him and to think about Him. She was free as well from any fear of the night or of wandering among the hills alone, and from any fear of strangers. This lack too she guarded from her sister's knowledge. It is impossible to foretell what a person will be ashamed of when finally grown up. Lane had no admiration at all for the type of woman so often described as "a dauntless woman" or even sometimes as a "she-devil". It had not even occurred to her that such a woman could be attractive, since moral character rather than personality concerned her, even though at a very underdeveloped level.

She also lived in fear that her sister would discover one day that she had never really formed any attachments. She felt attachment neither for her house, for her sister, nor for the town where she had been born. This secret, bitter but small in the beginning when she had first become conscious of it, had slowly come to contain her whole life. Not an hour passed that found her oblivious of the falsity of her position in the world. As a child believes that in five minutes he will have wings and be able to fly, so Lane hoped that she would awaken one day with a feeling of attachment and love for her sister and for the house, and with the fear of God in her heart.

She picked on her sister night and day, but concerning this behavior she felt no remorse.

Now Lane looked over her shoulder out of the window, and saw the wooded hill rising straight up behind the house. The trees were bare. A white dog ran along beneath the trees, with the dry deep autumn leaves almost covering his back each time his paws touched the ground.

"I wonder," Lane said, "if that dog's going to be out all night."

"What dog, dear?"

"There's a white dog running through the forest."

"I guess he's after chipmunks," said Dora, "or just taking the air. Dogs like air, you know."

"I don't believe they care about air," Lane frowned. "They like food and smells . . ."

". . . and their masters," Dora added. "Don't forget their loyalty—their admirable attachment to their masters. I wish we had a dog."

"He might be taking a short cut through the woods and striking out for the next town," Lane said, her heart sinking.

"With nothing but his tail as luggage, instead of a lot of satchels," Dora added. "Human beings don't know it all. Animals have things more conveniently. Think of the fuss a human being makes when he goes on a journey."

The word "journey" struck deep into Lane's heart, and she closed her eyes for a minute, overcome with shame and anxiety. "You are like that dog," a voice inside of her said. She turned away from the window so that the light would be in back of her and her face could not be seen.

Even though Dora had walked to the far corner of the room again and was lifting the yellow crock, she knew that her sister had "passed into darkness"—a phrase she used to describe certain of Lane's moods, but only to herself. A curious reticence had prevented her from ever wondering why her sister did "pass into darkness"—nor had she ever shown by word or expression that she knew anything was amiss with her sister at these moments.

Lane's moods lent a certain dignity to Dora which she would not otherwise have possessed. Dora loved the existence she led with Lane so passionately that she had actually to sit still on the sofa during certain moments of complete awareness of it, the impact of her joy acting upon her like a blow.

She had been pleased at the death of both her parents and her older sister because this left her free to sell the Sitwell homestead and to construct with the proceeds a log house, which she had been planning to do all her life. She had always longed as well to live in a house built on one floor only and to roll her meals into the parlor on a tea-table. This she did with Lane every day, and with unfailing delight. She lived for pleasure alone, which she thought was the way of an artist—it being natural for certain women to love even the word artist. And not all of them feel this way for snobbish motives. Sometimes when she was in particularly high spirits she referred to herself as an artist. At other times she merely mentioned that she lived like one. One afternoon when she was really tipsy in the hotel barroom she had referred to herself many times as "the artist in the little log house." Because of the wild and joyous look in her black eyes, her neighbors could not believe that her pleasures were simple ones.

Dora had started to love Lane one night when Lane was five years old and she herself was eleven. Her mother and father had told her to bathe Lane because they were going to a party. She prepared the tin tub with warm water and told Lane to wait in the kitchen while she went to fetch some soap. When she returned Lane was no longer in the kitchen. She searched throughout the house for nearly three hours, but she could not find Lane anywhere. Finally, bewildered and tired, she sat on the floor in the hall, planning to wait for her parents' return. While she sat there, it suddenly came to her that she loved Lane more than anything else in the world. "Lane," she said aloud. "You angel pie—you're better than Baby Jesus." She began feeling in her heart that Lane's flight from the kitchen was in the nature of a declaration of love and secret pact, and her own search through the dark cold rooms—some of them empty of everything but dust and unfamiliar to her—had caused her to feel that in Lane were centered the light and the warm colors of the universe. "Lane is a beautiful rose," she thought, thinking of Lane's curls on her short fat neck.

Later with the help of her parents she searched the barn and they found Lane curled up in the sleigh under some filthy horse blankets.

Dora leaned over and picked Lane up in her arms. Lane, groggy with sleep, bit Dora on the chin and made it bleed. Their mother started to scold, but Dora kissed Lane passionately for a long time, squeezing Lane's head against her own skinny chest. Mrs. Sitwell wrenched them apart in a sudden fury and pulled Dora's hair.

"Why do you kiss her, you little maniac? She just bit you!" Dora smiled but she did not answer.

"Why do you kiss her when she just bit you?" Mrs. Sitwell repeated. "Are you a maniac?"

Dora nodded.

"I won't have it," said Mrs. Sitwell, now cold with fury. "You tell her you're mad she bit you." Dora refused. Mrs. Sitwell twisted her arm. "Tell her you're mad she bit you."

"Lane and me are maniacs," said Dora, in a very quiet voice, still smiling. Mrs. Sitwell slapped her hard on the face.

"No one is a maniac," she said, "and you can't speak to Lane for two days." Then she burst into tears. They all went across the grass to the house. Mrs. Sitwell was sobbing freely. She was a very nervous woman and she had drunk a bit too much at the party. This had made her very gay at first, but later she had grown increasingly belligerent. They all went into the parlor, where Mrs. Sitwell sank into a chair and began staring at Lane through her tear-dimmed eyes.

"They should go to bed," her husband said.

"Lane doesn't look like anybody in the family on either side," said Mrs. Sitwell. "Why does she have such a short neck?"

"One of her antecedents most likely had a short neck," Mr. Sitwell suggested. "An aunt or an uncle."

"I don't feel like going on," said Mrs. Sitwell. "Everything is beyond me." She buried her face in her hands. Dora and Lane left the room.

After that Dora organized a game called "Looking for Lane" which she played with her sister. It was the usual hide-and-seek game that children play but it gave Dora a much keener pleasure than any ordinary game. Finally the search extended over the countryside and Dora allowed her imagination to run wild. For example, she imagined once that she would find Lane's body dismembered on the railroad tracks. Her feelings about this were mixed. The important thing was that the land became a magic one the moment the search began. Sometimes Lane didn't hide at all, and Dora would discover her in the nursery after searching for nearly a whole afternoon. On such occasions she would become so depressed that she wouldn't eat.

Lane never explained anything. She was a quiet child with round eyes and a fat face.

This game stopped abruptly when Dora was fourteen, and she never again thought about it.

Each time that Lane "passed into darkness" Dora had a curious reaction that was not unlike that of a person who remembers a sexual gratification when he does not expect to. She was never alarmed, nor did she feel lonely. To live with a person who is something of a lunatic is certainly a lonely experience even if it is not an alarming one, but Dora had never felt loneliness. Sometimes, although she knew Lane was having a spell, she continued talking.

"Suppose," she said on this particular day, "that we plan our itinerary for next spring. There are several mountains that I'd like to visit. As one grows older one has access to many more pleasures than one ever had as a young person. It's as if at a certain age a thick black curtain were wrenched aside, disclosing row upon row of goodies ready to be snatched. We're put on this earth for us to enjoy—although certain others get their thrill out of abstinence and devotion. That's just doing it the other way around. Not that I care at all what others do—too much contact spoils the essence of things. You'll agree to that, because you're a first-class hermit, anyway. Do you want to have dinner at the hotel?"

Lane did not answer, but looked again out of the window.

"If you're looking for that white dog, Lane, he's certainly deep into the woods by this time."

Early fifties (?)

GOING TO MASSACHUSETTS

JANE BOWLES

A FRAGMENT SELECTED FROM a notebook, probably from the mid-fifties, "Going to Massachusetts" was first published in 1977.

BOZOE RUBBED AWAY some tears with a closed fist.

"Come on, Bozoe," said Janet. "You're not going to the North Pole."

Bozoe tugged at the woolly fur, and pulled a little of it out.

"Leave your coat alone," said Janet.

"I don't remember why I'm going to Massachusetts," Bozoe moaned. "I knew it would be like this, once I got to the station."

"If you don't want to go to Massachusetts," said Janet, "then come on back to the apartment. We'll stop at Fanny's on the way. I want to buy those tumblers made out of knobby glass. I want brown ones."

Bozoe started to cry in earnest. This caused Janet considerable embarrassment. She was conscious of herself as a public figure because the fact that she owned and ran a garage had given her a good deal of publicity not only in East Clinton but in the neighboring counties. This scene, she said to herself, makes us look like two Italians saying goodbye. Everybody'll think we're Italians. She did not feel true sympathy for Bozoe. Her sense of responsibility was overdeveloped, but she was totally lacking in real tenderness.

"There's no reason for you to cry over a set of whiskey tumblers," said Janet. "I told you ten days ago that I was going to buy them."

"Passengers boarding Bus Number Twenty-seven, north-bound. . . ."

"I'm not crying about whiskey tumblers." Bozoe managed with

difficulty to get the words out. "I'm crying about Massachusetts. I can't remember my reasons."

"Rockport, Rayville, Muriel. . . ."

"Why don't you listen to the loudspeaker, Bozoe? It's giving you information. If you paid attention to what's going on around you you'd be a lot better off. You concentrate too much on your own private affairs. Try more to be a part of the world."

• • •

"*. . . The truth is that I am only twenty-five miles away from the apartment, as you have probably guessed. In fact, you could not help but guess it, since you are perfectly familiar with Larry's Bar and Grill. I could not go to Massachusetts. I cried the whole way up to Muriel and it was as if someone else were getting off the bus, not myself. But someone who was in a desperate hurry to reach the next stop. I was in mortal terror that the bus would not stop at Muriel but continue on to some further destination where I would not know any familiar face. My terror was so great that I actually stopped crying. I kept from crying all the way. That is a lie. Not an actual lie because I never lie as you know. Small solace to either one of us, isn't it? I am sure that you would prefer me to lie, rather than be so intent on explaining my dilemma to you night and day. I am convinced that you would prefer me to lie. It would give you more time for the garage.*"

"So?" queried Sis McEvoy, an unkind note in her voice. To Janet she did not sound noticeably unkind, since Sis McEvoy was habitually sharp-sounding, and like her had very little sympathy for other human beings. She was sure that Sis McEvoy was bad, and she was determined to save her. She was going to save her quietly without letting Sis suspect her determination. Janet did everything secretly; in fact, secrecy was the essence of her nature, and from it she derived her pleasure and her sense of being an important member of society.

"What's it all about?" Sis asked irritably. "Why doesn't she raise kids or else go to a psychologist or a psychoanalyst or whatever? My ovaries are crooked or I'd raise kids myself. That's what God's after, isn't it? Space ships or no space ships. What's the problem, anyway? How are her ovaries and the rest of the mess?"

Janet smiled mysteriously. "Bozoe has never wanted a child," she said. "She told me she was too scared."

"Don't you despise cowards?" said Sis. "Jesus Christ, they turn my stomach."

Janet frowned. "Bozoe says she despises cowards, too. She worries herself sick about it. She's got it all linked up together with Heaven and Hell. She thinks so much about Heaven and Hell that she's useless. I've told her for years to occupy herself. I've told her that God would like her better if she was occupied. But she says God isn't interested. That's a kind of slam at me, I suppose. At me and the garage. She's got it in for the garage. It doesn't bother me, but it makes me a little sore when she tries to convince me that I wouldn't be interested in the garage unless she talked to me day and night about her troubles. As if I was interested in the garage just out of spite. I'm a normal woman and I'm interested in my work, like all women are in modern times. I'm a little stockier than most, I guess, and not fussy or feminine. That's because my father was my ideal and my mother was an alcoholic. I'm stocky and I don't like pretty dresses and I'm interested in my work. My work is like God to me. I don't mean I put it above Him, but the next thing to Him. I have a feeling that he approves of my working. That he approves of my working in a garage. Maybe that's cheeky of me, but I can't help it. I've made a name for myself in the garage and I'm decent. I'm normal." She paused for a moment to fill the two whiskey tumblers.

"Do you like my whiskey tumblers?" She was being unusually spry and talkative. "I don't usually have much time to buy stuff. But I had to, of course. Bozoe never bought anything in her life. She's what you'd call a dead weight. She's getting fatter, too, all the time."

"They're good tumblers," said Sis McEvoy. "They hold a lot of whiskey."

Janet flushed slightly at the compliment. She attributed the unaccustomed excitement she felt to her freedom from the presence of Bozoe Flanner.

"Bozoe was very thin when I first knew her," she told Sis. "And she didn't show any signs that she was going to sit night and day making up problems and worrying about God and asking me questions. There wasn't any of that in the beginning. Mainly she was meek, I guess, and she had soft-looking eyes, like a doe or a calf. Maybe she had the problems the whole time and was just planning to spring them on me later. I don't know. I never thought she was going to get so tied up in knots, or so fat either. Naturally if she were heavy and happy too it would be better."

"I have no flesh on my bones at all," said Sis McEvoy, as if she had not even heard the rest of the conversation. "The whole family's thin, and every last one of us has a rotten lousy temper inherited from both sides. My father and my mother had rotten tempers."

"I don't mind if you have a temper display in my apartment," said Janet. "Go to it. I believe in people expressing themselves. If you've inherited a temper there isn't much you can do about it except express it. I think it's much better for you to break this crockery pumpkin, for instance, than to hold your temper in and become unnatural. For instance, I could buy another pumpkin and you'd feel relieved. I'd gather that, at any rate. I don't know much about people, really. I never dabbled in people. They were never my specialty. But surely if you've inherited a temper from both sides it would seem to me that you would have to express it. It isn't your fault, is it, after all?" Janet seemed determined to show admiration for Sis McEvoy.

"I'm having fun," she continued unexpectedly. "It's a long time since I've had any fun. I've been too busy getting the garage into shape. Then there's Bozoe trouble. I've kept to the routine. Late Sunday breakfast with popovers and home-made jam. She eats maybe six of them, but with the same solemn expression on her face. I'm husky but a small eater. We have record players and television. But nothing takes her mind off herself. There's no point in my getting any more machines. I've got the cash and the good will, but there's absolutely no point."

"You seem to be very well set up," said Sis McEvoy, narrowing her eyes. "Here's to you." She tipped her glass and drained it.

Janet filled Sister's glass at once. "I'm having a whale of a good time," she said. "I hope you are. Of course I don't want to butt into your business. Bozoe always thought I pored over my account books for such a long time on purpose. She thought I was purposely trying to get away from her. What do you think, Sis McEvoy?" She asked this almost in a playful tone that bordered on a yet unexpressed flirtatiousness.

"I'm not interested in women's arguments with each other," said Sis at once. "I'm interested in women's arguments with men. What else is there? The rest doesn't amount to a row of monkeys."

"Oh, I agree," Janet said, as if she were delighted by this statement which might supply her with the stimulus she was after. "I agree one thousand percent. Remember I spend more time in the garage with the men than I do with Bozoe Flanner."

"I'm not actually living with my husband because of my temper," said Sis. "I don't like long-standing relationships. They disagree with me. I get the blues. I don't want anyone staying in my life for a long time. It gives me the creeps. Men are crazy about me. I like the cocktails and the compliments. Then after a while they turn my stomach."

"You're a very interesting woman," Janet Murphy announced, throwing caution to the winds and finding it pleasant.

"I know I'm interesting," said Sis. "But I'm not so sure life is interesting."

"Are you interested in money?" Janet asked her. "I don't mean money for the sake of money, but for buying things."

Sis did not answer, and Janet feared that she had been rude. "I didn't mean to hurt your feelings," she said. "After all, money comes up in everybody's life. Even duchesses have to talk about money. But I won't, any more. Come on. Let's shake." She held out her hand to Sis McEvoy, but Sis allowed it to stay there foolishly, without accepting the warm grip Janet had intended for her.

"I'm really sorry," she went on, "if you think I was trying to be insulting and personal. I honestly was not. The fact is that I have been so busy building up a reputation for the garage that I behave like a savage. I'll never mention money again." In her heart she felt that Sis was somehow pleased that the subject had been brought up, but was not yet ready to admit it. Sis's tedious work at the combination tea-room and soda fountain where they had met could scarcely make her feel secure.

Bozoe doesn't play one single feminine trick, she told herself, and after all, after struggling nearly ten years to build up a successful and unusual business I'm entitled to some returns. I'm in a rut with Bozoe and this Sis is going to get me out of it. (By now she was actually furious with Bozoe.) I'm entitled to some fun. The men working for me have more fun than I have.

"I feel grateful to you, Sis," she said without explaining her remark. "You've done me a service. May I tell you that I admire your frankness, without offending you?"

Sis McEvoy was beginning to wonder if Janet were another nut like Bozoe Flanner. This worried her a little, but she was too drunk by now for clear thinking. She was enjoying the compliments, although it was disturbing that they should be coming from a woman. She was very proud of never having been depraved or abnormal, and pleased to be merely mean and discontented to the extent of not having been able to stay with any man for longer than the three months she had spent with her husband.

"I'll read you more of Bozoe's letter," Janet suggested.

"I can't wait," said Sis. "I can't wait to hear a lunatic's mind at work first-hand. Her letter's so cheerful and elevating. And so constructive. Go to it. But fill my glass first so I can concentrate. I'd hate to miss a word. It would kill me."

Janet realized that it was unkind of her to be reading her friend's letter to someone who so obviously had only contempt for it. But she felt no loyalty—only eagerness to make Sis see how hard her life had been. She felt that in this way the bond between them might be strengthened.

"Well, here it comes," she said. "Stop me when you can't stand it any more. *I know that you expected me to come back. You did not feel I had the courage to carry out my scheme. I still expect to work it out. But not yet. I am more than ever convinced that my salvation lies in solitude, and coming back to the garage before I have even reached Massachusetts would be a major defeat for me, as I'm sure you must realize, even though you pretend not to know what I'm talking about most of the time. I am convinced that you do know what I'm talking about and if you pretend ignorance of my dilemma so you can increase efficiency at the garage you are going to defeat yourself. I can't actually save you, but I can point little things out to you constantly. I refer to your soul, naturally, and not to any success you've had or to your determination. In any case it came to me on the bus that it was not time for me to leave you, and that although going to Massachusetts required more courage and strength than I seemed able to muster, I was at the same time being very selfish in going. Selfish because I was thinking in terms of my salvation and not yours. I'm glad I thought of this. It is why I stopped crying and got off the bus. Naturally you would disapprove, because I had paid for my ticket which is now wasted, if for no other reason. That's the kind of thing you like me to think about, isn't it? It makes you feel that I'm more human. I have never admired being human, I must say. I want to be like God. But I haven't begun yet. First I have to go to Massachusetts and be alone. But I got off the bus. And I've wasted the fare. I can hear you stressing that above all else, as I say. But I want you to understand that it was not cowardice alone that stopped me from going to Massachusetts. I don't feel that I can allow you to sink into the mire of contentment and happy ambitious enterprise. It is my duty to prevent you from it as much as I do for myself. It is not fair of me to go away until you completely understand how I feel about God and my destiny. Surely we have been brought together for some purpose, even if that purpose ends by our being separate again. But not until the time is ripe. Naturally, the psychiatrists would at once declare that I was laboring under a compulsion. I am violently against psychiatry, and, in fact, against happiness. Though of course I love it. I love happiness, I mean. Of course you would not believe this. Naturally darling I love you, and I'm afraid that if you don't start suffering soon God will take some terrible vengeance. It is better for you to offer yourself. Don't accept social or financial security as your final aim. Or fame in the garage. Fame is unworthy of you; that is, the desire for it. Janet, my beloved, I do not expect you to be gloomy or fanatical as I am. I do not believe that God intended you for quite as harrowing a destiny as He did for me. I don't mean this as an insult. I believe you should actually thank your stars. I would really like to be fulfilling humble daily chores myself and listening to a concert at night or television or playing a card game. But I can find no rest, and I don't think you should either. At least not until you have fully understood my dilemma on earth. That means that you must no longer turn a deaf ear to me and pretend that your preoccupation with the garage is in a sense a holier absorption than trying to understand and fully realize the importance and meaning of my dilemma. I think that you hear more than you admit, too. There is a stubborn streak in your nature working against you, most likely unknown to yourself. An insistence on being shallow rather than profound. I repeat: I do not expect you to be as profound as I am. But to insist on exploiting the most shallow side of one's nature, out of stubbornness and merely because it is more pleasant to be shallow, is certainly a sin. Sis McEvoy will help you to express the shallow side of your nature, by the way. Like a toboggan slide."*

Janet stopped abruptly, appalled at having read this last part aloud. She had not expected Bozoe to mention Sis at all. "Gee," she said. "Gosh! She's messing everything up together. I'm awfully sorry."

Sis McEvoy stood up and walked unsteadily to the television set. Some of her drink slopped onto the rug as she went. She faced Janet with fierce eyes. "There's nobody in the world who can talk to me like that, and there's not going to be. Never!" She was leaning on the set and steadying herself against it with both hands. "I'll keep on building double-decker sandwiches all my life first. It's five flights to the top of the building where I live. It's an insurance building, life insurance, and I'm the only woman who lives there. I have boy friends come when they want to. I don't have to worry, either. I'm crooked so I don't have to bother with abortions or any other kind of mess. The hell with television anyway."

She likes the set, Janet said to herself. She felt more secure. "Bozoe and I don't have the same opinions at all," she said. "We don't agree on anything."

"Who cares? You live in the same apartment, don't you? You've lived in the same apartment for ten years. Isn't that all anybody's got to know?" She rapped with her fist on the wood panelling of the television set. "Whose is it, anyhow?" She was growing increasingly aggressive.

"It's mine," Janet said. "It's my television set." She spoke loud so that Sis would be sure to catch her words.

"What the hell do I care?" cried Sis. "I live on top of a life-insurance building and I work in a combination soda-fountain lunch-room. Now read me the rest of the letter."

"I don't think you really want to hear any more of Bozoe's nonsense," Janet said smoothly. "She's spoiling our evening together. There's no reason for us to put up with it all. Why should we? Why don't I make something to eat? Not a sandwich. You must be sick of sandwiches."

"What I eat is my own business," Sis snapped.

"Naturally," said Janet. "I thought you might like something hot like bacon and eggs. Nice crisp bacon and eggs." She hoped to persuade her so that she might forget about the letter.

"I don't like food," said Sis. "I don't even like millionaires' food, so don't waste your time."

"I'm a small eater myself." She had to put off reading Bozoe's letter until Sis had forgotten about it. "My work at the garage requires some sustenance, of course. But it's brainwork now more than manual labor. Being a manager's hard on the brain."

Sis looked at Janet and said: "Your brain doesn't impress me. Or that garage. I like newspaper men. Men who are champions. Like champion boxers. I've known lots of champions. They take to me. Champions all fall for me, but I'd never want any of them to find out that I knew someone like your Bozoe. They'd lose their respect."

"I wouldn't introduce Bozoe to a boxer either, or anybody else who was interested in sports. I know they'd be bored. I know." She waited. "You're very nice. Very intelligent. You *know* people. That's an asset."

"Stay with Bozoe and her television set," Sis growled.

"It's not her television set. It's mine, Sis. Why don't you sit down? Sit on the couch over there."

"The apartment belongs to both of you, and so does the set. I know what kind of a couple you are. The whole world knows it. I could put you in jail if I wanted to. I could put you and Bozoe both in jail."

In spite of these words she stumbled over to the couch and sat down. "Whiskey," she demanded. "The world loves drunks but it despises perverts. Athletes and boxers drink when they're not in training. All the time."

Janet went over to her and served her a glass of whiskey with very little ice. Let's hope she'll pass out, she said to herself. She couldn't see Sis managing the steps up to her room in the insurance building, and in any case she didn't want her to leave. She's such a relief after Bozoe, she thought. Alive and full of fighting spirit. She's much more my type, coming down to facts. She thought it unwise to go near Sis, and was careful to pour the fresh drink quickly and return to her own seat. She would have preferred to sit next to Sis, in spite of her mention of jail, but she did not relish being punched or smacked in the face. It's all Bozoe's fault, she said to herself. That's what she gets for thinking she's God. Her holy words can fill a happy peaceful room with poison from twenty-five miles away.

"I love my country," said Sis, for no apparent reason. "I love it to death!"

"Sure you do, Hon," said Janet. "I could murder Bozoe for upsetting you with her loony talk. You were so peaceful until she came in."

"Read that letter," said Sister. After a moment she repeated, as if from a distance: "Read the letter."

Janet was perplexed. Obviously food was not going to distract Sis, and she had nothing left to suggest, in any case, but some Gorton's Codfish made into cakes, and she did not dare to offer her these.

What a rumpus that would raise, she said to herself. And if I suggest turning on the television she'll raise the roof. Stay off television and codfish cakes until she's normal again. Working at a lunch counter is no joke.

There was nothing she could do but do as Sis told her and hope that she might fall asleep while she was reading her the letter. "Damn Bozoe anyway," she muttered audibly.

"Don't put on any acts," said Sis, clearly awake. "I hate liars and I always smell an act. Even though I didn't go to college. I have no respect for college."

"I didn't go to college," Janet began, hoping Sis might be led on to a new discussion. "I went to commercial school."

"Shut up, God damn you! Nobody ever tried to make a commercial school sound like an interesting topic except you. Nobody! You're out of your mind. Read the letter."

"Just a second," said Janet, knowing there was no hope for her. "Let me put my glasses on and find my place. Doing accounts at the garage year in and year out has ruined my eyes. My eyes used to be perfect." She added this last weakly, without hope of arousing either sympathy or interest.

Sis did not deign to answer.

"Well, here it is again," she began apologetically. "Here it is in all its glory." She poured a neat drink to give herself courage. "*As I believe I just wrote you, I have been down to the bar and brought a drink back with me. (One more defeat for me, a defeat which is of course a daily occurrence, and I daresay I should not bother to mention it in this letter.) In any case I could certainly not face being without one after the strain of actually boarding the bus, even if I did get off without having the courage to stick on it until I got where I was going. However, please keep in mind the second reason I had for stopping short of my destination. Please read it over carefully so that you will not have only contempt for me. The part about the responsibility I feel toward you. The room here over Larry's Bar and Grill is dismal. It is one of several rented out by Larry's sister whom we met a year ago when we stopped here for a meal. You remember. It was the day we took Stretch for a ride and let him out of the car to run in the woods, that scanty patch of woods you found just as the sun was setting, and you kept picking up branches that were stuck together with wet leaves and dirt. . . .*"

Mid-fifties (?)

LAURA AND SALLY

JANE BOWLES

A FRAGMENT SELECTED FROM *a notebook, probably from the late forties to early fifties, "Laura and Sally" was first published in 1987.*

LAURA SEABROOK was lying in her bed at four in the afternoon. She lived with Sam Brewster, a mechanic trained as an engineer who helped in many different ways around Camp Cataract. He often drove the truck into town for provisions, or the bus that fetched those people who had no cars from the railroad station. He ran the wood-chopping machine and tended all the roofs and defective screens. He was very happy at his different tasks and did not seem to regret his engineering studies. He regretted having disappointed his mother, but he was usually satisfied with what he was doing, as long as his life was among friendly people and out of doors. He could not bear to live in cities but he did not out of this dislike make a cult of nature.

Laura's hair hung to her shoulders and fell over half of her brooding face. No sunlight penetrated through the thick black pine trees into her cabin, but a blue bulb simulating daylight hung over her head. She was a very great beauty.

Sally McBridge was standing on the door sill smiling at Laura. Hers was a delicate pink face with round but fanatical blue eyes. She came every summer to Camp Cataract and the staff considered her to be somewhat of a lunatic and a fool. She dressed in a provincial out-of-date manner and altogether seemed to belong to either another country or another time. At this moment she was wearing a black coat with an orange full collar and a bonnet-shaped hat. She could not have been much more than thirty-nine or forty.

"How are you?" she asked Laura. "I thought you'd be dressed and ready to have your dinner."

"I can't dress," said Laura without looking at her.

"Do you have your melancholia?" Sally questioned her with a smile. Laura refused to answer.

"I'll tell you one thing," Sally continued. "You have to live in peace whether you have it or not. You can beat life if you want to." Sally's expression at that moment was almost wicked and even calculating. Laura looked at her for the first time.

"And then what's left to you after you've beaten life?" she asked sullenly.

"Happiness is left," Sally said. "Life is chaos and happiness is system—as if in a very delicately wrought but strong cage, while the life chaos remains outside. But remember I said cage and not room. The distinction is tremendous."

"What distinction?"

"Between room and cage. Do you know what I'm implying?"

Laura shrugged her shoulders. "Don't tell me," she said. For she was very aware that Sally's explanation would be wordy and very boring to her. Sally continued, however, ignoring her remark.

"If your happiness system is like a very delicate cage, you can see out and others can see in, even though your protections are as strong as the silver wires of a cage," she said. "But in a room you're really shut off."

Laura covered her face with her hands. "I hate Camp Cataract," she said. "That's all I know."

"I love it," Sally replied in a simple tone. "Perhaps because an evergreen is my favorite tree. It's modest and always there, like a friend or a loyal dog, winter and summer alike. And when its branches are heavy with snow, there is no tree more beautiful in the universe. Do you like evergreens?"

Laura did not answer. Her eyes were brooding.

"I'm certain you would like some place like Hawaii," Sally said to her. "You're such an impatient restless type of person. A palm tree is more your emblem than a pine. Isn't that so?"

"I have never thought of it," Laura replied. "I don't think of any of the things you think of. I don't believe I've ever looked at a tree, much less thought of one. I don't have a light enough heart to sit and think about things like that."

"My heart is not light, Laura," Sally said. "I have to spend many hours in my cabin alone. I'm going there now—I had a fit of nervous irritability this afternoon, and I want to think about it."

"Anyone who can speak of a happiness system is lighthearted," Laura said flatly.

"Don't talk nonsense, Laura. The finest brains have been occupied with such systems since the beginning of time . . . orientals and occidentals alike."

"That's religion you're speaking of," said Laura. "Not a happiness system."

Quite suddenly Sally's face fell apart. She backed away from the cabin door, and Laura could hear her feet moving through the leaves.

Laura cocked an ear, but it was impossible to tell by listening to the rustle of dead leaves whether Sally was advancing deeper into the pine grove toward her cabin or if she had turned back in the direction of the lodge.

"I've hurt Sally's feelings," Laura thought. The brooding expression left her face, and at once a look of gravity and even nobility took its place. She rose to her feet. "I must go and find her."

She pulled a black dress of very thin material over her head and brushed out her stiff hair. Then she set out through the pine grove in search of Sally.

Her gait was a slow rolling one like that of a sailor. Her lips she held parted, and to the gravity of her expression was added a look of wonder which deepened as she approached the lodge. There was no longer any trace of apathy in her countenance. When she reached the dining terrace she stood still and looked about for Sally. The wind was blowing hard, somewhat deadening the roar of the waterfall. Laura saw Sally moving with difficulty between the last row of tables (the row nearest to the precipice) and the heavy chain which separated the dining terrace from its edge.

"Why does she choose to cross there?" Laura asked herself. "There's barely space to get through without brushing against the diners." She hastened across the terrace herself, but at a more convenient place near the lodge steps. Pine groves surrounded the terrace at the other side as well, but through these groves a path had been cut leading to the main road. Laura reached the path first and hid behind a tree until Sally walked past. Then she came out from her hiding place and followed her. Laura knew that Sally was going to Mr. Cassalotti's restaurant in the village. During the last three weeks she had followed Sally several times to the village and joined her there.

Sally's fits of temper and shame were becoming more and more necessary to Laura. They stirred her blood. And while she hated Sally to such an extent at these moments that she wanted to strike her face, her own dignity at once seemed to swoop down upon her like some great and unexpected bird. It was not to comfort Sally, therefore, that she followed her to the village, but to enjoy for a while this calm and noble self born each time out of the other woman's rage.

She kept at a sufficient distance from Sally so that the other did not hear her footsteps. Camp Cataract, although situated in authentically wild country, was not at a very great distance from a little center, which could hardly have been called a town, but which included several stores, a restaurant, and a railroad station.

It was at this restaurant that Sally now stopped and mounted the stairs. She went into the dining room, located at the back of the house and reached only through the store which opened on the front steps. It was a dark room, with only five or six tables. There was no one about, but she could hear the members of the family moving overhead in their apartment. She chose a table next to a glassed-in scene that Mr. Cassalotti had inserted in a large wall niche. The painted drop was of a cottage with lawn and woods and a little stream running to one side of it. Mr. Cassalotti had extended the real lawn by using stage grass, and there were even little trellises about, stuck with old paper roses, too many of them contrasting oddly with the pastel-shaded flowers painted on the drop. Crowding the lawn was an assortment of poorly selected men and women fashioned in different styles and out of different materials, some being brightly painted lead and others carved out of wood. There was also, to complete the pointless staging, a child's miniature orange automobile set down right in the very midst of the lawn gathering and driven by a tiny rubber baby doll. The scene was illuminated from the sides and at this moment supplied the only light in the dining room.

The immediate urge of any diner with even the slightest degree of sensibility, if not to the actual aesthetic offense, then at least to the offense against order and the fulfillment of intention, was to punch through the glass and remove the automobile, if not half the figures. Only to the Cassalotti family and to children there was no disturbing element in this glassed-in scene.

Sally stared for a bit at the familiar lawn group, and even though she was a fanatic with usually one obsession at a time she felt a strong desire to remove the orange truck, which for a second absorbed her completely. She looked around automatically, as everyone else did, for an opening in the glass, although she knew perfectly well that there was none. Then she turned her back upon it and closed her eyes. She was trembling, and the wings of her nostrils were drawn. However, far from taking fright at the hysteria Laura's words had unloosed, or even growing despondent over it, Sally merely underwent the experience very much the way she stood behind the waterfalls each day at Camp Cataract. Far behind her new fit she was smiling to herself, unbeatable and optimistic.

She knew that Laura had intended to upset her by drawing a line between her happiness system and the religions of the world. But it was not the seriousness of this demarcation that Sally was upset about so much as the simple fact that Laura had attacked her at all. Any criticism or show of aggression on Laura's part was enough to set Sally spinning backwards like someone clubbed over the head. This did not alter the fact that Sally considered herself to be the eventual victor. She knew too, without ever having had to reflect upon it, that Laura's connection with the universe was of greater depth and perception than her own—even though Laura was lazy and frankly jeered at life as without purpose. She had merely to speak of a serious subject when immediately the accent of her voice, the expression in her eye, lent to her words the weight of true gold. If Sally had been sincerely interested in becoming a wonderful person, she would have certainly been alarmed at recognizing a deeper accent of truth in Laura's voice than in her own. She would then have known the despair which comes of recognizing that what another understood automatically she herself would have to strive ceaselessly to understand throughout her life, and this would have caused her either to give up her own struggle—even if only temporarily, in a fit of jealous impotence—or, had she the strength, to continue along her own path, but wiser and more humble for her acquaintance with Laura.

She did neither, but instead set herself the task of conquering Laura—although exactly in what sense she meant to conquer her friend she did not herself know. Hers was an instinctive chase with a concealed objective. It is a curious fact that Sally, whose life was a series of tests and rituals of purification imposed upon herself, should have reacted so unscrupulously to the superiority—whether genuine or imagined by herself—of another woman. It was probable that she related the best and most spiritual part of her mind and heart to her life's purpose and only coarser elements in her nature to her friends.

The door opened and Laura entered the dining room. Her beauty was even darker and more mobile than usual, as she stood for a second in the light of the half-open doorway. Sally looked up and noted how the shadows gave to Laura's face its actual dimension, which ordinarily in a cruder light lay behind the features, only half guessed at by the beholder. Now her features and the beauty behind them were the same thing. Sally looked at her beauty but was neither covetous nor jealous. She was conscious only of the effort it cost her to control her own features and even her arms and legs.

"I hate my nervous system," she said to herself, "but I'll get the better of it someday." Laura was approaching slowly toward the table, a look of great sobriety and weariness upon her face. Sally saw this out of the corner of her eye. "That's the way the attack always begins," she commented to herself. "I mustn't let her get started. I'm the one who should attack anyway. But perhaps today is not a very appropriate day for a beginning. Why are the Cassalottis sitting around their rooms in the middle of the afternoon?" Laura was upon her. She could not conceal this from herself any longer.

"Hello, Sally," Laura said to her, and with no further remarks she seated herself at the table. Sally's eyes were stretched wide in their sockets with the strain of attempting to control her nerves while she waited for Laura's assault to begin. These attacks were never overt but on the contrary so disguised that any third person present would not suspect any aggression at all. Even Sally, by some mysterious but compelling rule of conduct, never raised her voice or in any way let it be too apparent in her answers to Laura that she was conscious of any hostility. And although Sally was quite aware that she was being attacked, her temper was held in abeyance by some mysterious rule of manners, and she spoke pleasantly as if she did not understand the hostility behind Laura's words.

Camp Cataract, for so many years a symbol of escape from the strife of difficult human relations, had become since Laura's arrival the very seat of this type of strain for Sally. But it was a strange fact that Sally did not realize this at all. Having divided her life into two parts, she was incapable of including a third, or at least of treating it in a profound manner. With Laura, although she never let this be apparent, she was greedy, belligerent, and without scruple.

Neither one of them spoke for a little, and then Laura asked where the Cassalottis were.

"Hanging around their apartments, Italian style, I guess," said Sally.

"Well, I would like a beer," said Laura. "So I'm going to go and get them down in a minute. Would you like a beer?"

Sally looked straight with glistening round eyes and a little fixed smile on her lips. "You know I don't drink, Laura," she said.

"I forgot," Laura answered, "and anyway, you might change."

"I don't change."

"Really?" Laura pretended surprise. "Well, you should try to see what it's like to behave like somebody else for a change. Why don't you get drunk?" Laura rested her chin in her hand and looked thoughtfully at Sally.

"You want nothing but havoc and destruction around you, isn't that so?" Sally asked.

"Do you think I do?"

"You're a wrecker—look at your cabin. I'm not criticizing, but please don't ask me to be like you." Sally's head began to jerk a little with excitement. "Please don't ask me to be like you," she repeated.

Laura was surprised—Sally had never been so openly antagonistic before.

"I would not want you to be like me, Sally," she said in her sincere voice, with even a note of tenderness in her tone. "I would not want anyone to be like me. I've got melancholia. You know that." Her beautiful eyes were now so warm and solicitous that Sally could not continue to snap at her without making a fool of herself, so she kept her mouth tightly shut.

After a bit Laura spoke again.

"You like to sit in your cabin alone, don't you?" she asked Sally.

"I love it," said Sally.

"Why don't you get a sterno cooker? Then you could heat cans and make little stews for your dinner in the cabin."

"I like to sit on the terrace and watch the waterfall while I eat," said Sally, immediately feeling on her guard.

"Beryl could choose things from the lodge kitchen and bring them to you. A sterno cooker doesn't cost very much."

"I'd just as soon sit on the dining terrace and watch the waterfall while I eat," Sally repeated. She was almost sure the attack was on again, but not positive.

"Those little cookers are not very smelly either," Laura continued. "And Beryl could easily bring you plates and cutlery from the main dining room. You could tip her and she would even wash the plates each day and return them to you."

"I don't want to eat in my cabin," Sally said. But the spirit which had moved her a while ago to reprimand Laura was gone, and instead the familiar sensation of heaviness and impotence invaded her limbs and her head.

"Well, I think you really do," said Laura casually, turning away and glancing about the room, as if to demonstrate that she was losing interest in the conversation, "I suppose you really do but you haven't got a sterno cooker."

Sally half shut her eyes. "This is the attack, all right," she said to herself. "But I'll sit through it this time and not defend myself. It's nearly over anyway, I think."

Sally was correct in her guess that Laura's attack was nearly over. In fact, no sooner had she voiced this opinion to herself than Laura was on her feet.

"I am going upstairs," she said, "to drag the Cassalottis down here. I want my beer. Come with me."

Sally rose a little uncertainly to her feet. It was difficult for her to get up quickly when she was in a nervous state, and for one awful moment she thought she was going to fall back in her chair once more, but she managed to reach Laura's side looking fairly normal. They left the dining room and went into a small dark hallway. Laura, who was very familiar with the Cassalotti house, pulled on a door which opened onto a closed stairway. The walls of the stairway were papered in a small flower pattern and very dirty. They started to mount the stairs —slowly because of their steepness. Sally felt her head turning a little. The air in the stairway was stale. But her dizziness was more the result of Laura's proximity than of the bad air in the stairway. Since there was no bannister, she let the flat of her palm travel along the cold, flower-papered wall. This comforted her to a certain extent until they reached the landing.

The terrible gloom and boredom that had descended upon Laura earlier in the day, back at Camp Cataract, had now completely vanished, not from her memory but from her feelings. At last the day was cluttered with possibilities and adventures. The ascension of the stairs aided her optimism, and by the time she reached the landing a happy excitement was fully upon her.

"Cassalottis!" she called in her husky voice, now ringing with gaiety.

"Hello, Laura Seabrook." Rita Cassalotti's voice was gentle but without warmth.

Laura fairly galloped down the length of the uncarpeted hallway, knocking into a wrought iron stand that supported a trough of ferns on the way. The stand teetered for a moment on its high legs, but it did not fall over.

"I want beer, you bums," Laura shouted as she flung open the Cassalottis' parlor door. Greetings were exchanged while Sally hung back in the hallway, not caring to move forward or backward. She knew that Laura wanted to be rid of her.

"She's moved on to the Cassalottis and everybody else might as well be dead," Sally reflected. "But I'll stay. Certainly I shan't come and go at her convenience." Her head was beginning to ache as a result of the afternoon's complications.

She promised herself that on the following day she would go down into the chasm a mile south of Camp Cataract, where descent was more gradual, and walk along the river bed. She reminded herself too that she had already gone three quarters of the way toward directing her life current, as she termed it, into a peace stream, in spite of her bad nervous system. "Camp Cataract," she said to herself, "is definitely carrying off the honors, and *not* my sister's apartment." This thought cheered her up and she started down the hall toward the parlor, where the girls were laughing and talking so loudly that they did not even notice her entering the room.

Mr. Cassalotti was there, Berenice and Rita—his oldest daughters—an aunt, and some of the younger children. Everyone was dressed, with the exception of Rita Cassalotti, who was wearing a pink wrapper made of an imitation thick velour. There were more ferns here in the upstairs parlor, just like the ones Laura had barely missed knocking over in the hallway. A linoleum stamped with a red and black design covered the floor. The chairs and the sofa were all occupied by the family, with the exception of one odd Victorian chair made of carved black wood in Chinese style, which stood near a window and was seldom used.

Sally seated herself in this chair and folded her hands in her lap. "Now we'll see how far she'll go," she thought, fixing her eyes on Laura, and she felt elated without noticing that she did.

Rita Cassalotti had a small head and eyes a little too close together but she was pretty. Her teeth were very even and the canines beautifully shaped. Men adored her but she was neither vain nor inclined toward flirtation or love-making. She loved the food she got at home, her bedroom furniture and her clothing. Her body was unexpectedly heavier than anyone would have guessed just from seeing her small head and slender neck, but she was not fat, merely soft and round, although only a sensitive man—even if a stranger—might have sensed the coldness lurking in her soft frame.

"What brings you here this afternoon, Laura Seabrook?" Rita questioned her pleasantly.

"I was so bored at Camp Cataract," said Laura, "that I thought the world was coming to an end. Then I remembered that you always cheered me up." This statement was true, at least partially. The Cassalottis did cheer Laura up, but she had forgotten that her original intention had been to pursue Sally and not to visit the Cassalottis.

Rita let out a peal of merry laughter. She always reacted more strongly to what seemed to her the grotesque than to situations or states of feelings that might easily have been included in the content of her own life.

"Do you have a sewing machine, there at Camp Cataract?" Rita asked with a twinkle in her eye.

"No . . . I'm not sure," Laura answered her.

Rita thought this was even more hysterically funny than Laura's first statement.

"Rita! Stop being foolish—you sound like a dope." Her younger sister Berenice silenced her with a look from her big flashing eyes. She was a swarthy, short-legged girl with dark bushy hair and a raucous low voice. Her chin was delicately cleft and her nose was Roman and very beautiful. She was enthusiastic and tempestuous, with a warmth not often encountered in a young girl.

"Why are you talking about machines?" she stormed at Rita.

"Well," said Rita, not in the least disturbed by her sister's outburst. "She said she thought the world was coming to an end, and I thought that if she had a sewing machine she could make some dresses when she didn't know what else to do."

"You're crazy," said Berenice.

"No, I'm not," Rita answered, laughing merrily again. "What's crazy about a sewing machine? You're the one who's on the crazy side, not me."

"Laura's got a lot of trouble," said Berenice. "She wouldn't get no relief from a sewing machine."

"No?" Rita raised her eyebrows and looked questioningly at Laura. "Maybe not," she said with half-hearted interest. The conversation seemed to be losing its grotesque quality and turning on the serious. The very prospect of hearing about anyone else's trouble tired Rita and she yawned.

Mr. Cassalotti, who had not bothered to greet either Laura or Sally, was sitting on a small cane chair and staring ahead of him with hands thrust in his pockets. Without warning he got up from his chair and started toward the door.

"Poppa," said Berenice, "where are you going?"

"I'm going to get the beer out and make raviolis. Come on downstairs and we'll have a little party." He looked back over his shoulder at Laura and nodded to her without changing his expression.

"Just plain havoc, with no thought behind it," Sally was thinking. "That's what she likes, instead of the beautiful. She thinks it's exciting and adventurous to sit indoors in the afternoon with people eating raviolis and drinking beer. She doesn't know where real happiness lies. If she could only be persuaded to stay outdoors a little more. It would be at least a beginning."

Laura was hustling the Cassalottis through the parlor door as hastily as she could, in her eagerness to get at the beer. The children remained always silent and strange whenever Laura appeared. They leaned against the wall looking after her with sober brown eyes.

The Cassalotti sisters, followed by Laura and Sally, started down the steep stairway single file.

"Gee, it's nice you came," said Berenice affectionately to Laura, who was behind her. She turned around and squeezed Laura's leg to emphasize her pleasure. "It will only take Poppa a little while to get the raviolis going, and we can drink beer while we wait anyhow . . ." She gave Rita a little shove and pulled her hair. "Why don't you get dressed, you?" she said.

At that moment Laura's joy at being among the Cassalottis reached its peak—and with it came a familiar chill at the bottom of her heart.

"Oh, God," thought Laura. "I had almost forgotten for a moment. I wish I could be really here, having the kind of fun I think it is to be here."

She was quite accustomed to this cold fright that gripped her heart whenever her pleasure was acute, but it was not fright itself that interested her. She was quite sure that most sensitive people were familiar with this feeling. What disturbed her more than the fright was the chain of questions it always awakened in her mind about whatever she was doing, so that she could never wholeheartedly enter into anything for more than a few seconds at a time.

"How exhausting," she said to herself as she felt the chill settling like a thick fog around her heart. The tormenting question which followed in the wake of her anguish was this: should she consider the anguish to be the natural underlying side of life itself, that side which gives depth and gravity to the sense of living from hour to hour, and which is to be endured simply and accepted, or was it on the other hand a signal for a departure—a signal for a decision? It was this last possibility that she found so upsetting, for she was actually, in her thinking at least, a very conscientious person.

They reached the landing and Laura stood for a second, uncertainly, with Sally waiting behind her on the bottom step.

She wished she had the courage to go out the door onto the wooden porch and thence down the road through the pine woods, instead of sitting down to eat ravioli and to drink beer. The very thought that such an action was incumbent upon her made her feel faint.

"A silly struggle over two silly alternatives—to eat ravioli or to walk in the woods," she whispered to herself, without believing it. She bit her lips hard and a happy thought struck her. "The Cassalottis would be very insulted if I left. How could I have overlooked it?" The relief she felt, having voiced this sentence to herself, was immediate. Her face lost its hunted animal look, and she took long strides in the direction of the dining room.

The others had gone back into the kitchen behind the dining room and were watching Mr. Cassalotti, who was using the ravioli machine. He was very neat and very systematic in his cooking, being a great admirer of both American factory technique and sanitation. He had already selected four cartons and labeled them neatly with the names of friends. "You can take these back to Camp Cataract with you when you go," he said to Laura. "Tell them a ravioli present from Gregorio Cassalotti—and remind them that Wednesday night is Chicken Cassalotti night. Chicken Cacciatore died when Chicken Cassalotti was born." He laughed to himself.

He did not in any way resemble Laura's conception of an Italian, except physically. He was industrious and really only happy when he worked. The girls took the beer into the dining room and they all seated themselves near the glassed-in scene, including Sally, who sat with her chair exaggeratedly far from the table and turned sideways.

"Pull yourself in," said Berenice.

"No, thank you," Sally answered her. "I'm not going to eat or drink. I'm all right here."

Berenice stared at Sally uncomprehendingly, but she felt herself so remote from the other woman that she could not, as she ordinarily would have done, urge her to join them in eating and drinking.

The Cassalotti sisters had brought to the table about fifteen bottles of beer. Laura, so recently released from her small but painful struggle, was giddy as a result of her escape. There still lurked a doubt in her heart but it was a muffled doubt, reserved for a little later. She was determined now to get drunk, and to have the Cassalottis share her renewed gaiety. With Berenice she did not concern herself, for this girl's gaiety, though of a completely different variety (with real joy as its source, rather than pained joy), matched her own. So it was to Rita she addressed herself.

"Rita, do you like Sunday?" she asked her. Rita's face remained closed, and she appeared to have no intention of answering Laura's question at all. Often she did not answer Laura's questions with even so much as a nod of her head. This made Laura all the more determined to find out how Rita felt about everything. She tried formulating her question to Rita differently.

"Do Sundays make you nervous?" she asked this time.

"I don't know," said Rita, without the faintest expression in her voice.

"I like 'em, good weather or bad," put in Berenice. "If it's good weather, I go fishing or hunting for berries and mushrooms, and if it's bad weather I listen to the radio. In the winter, of course, I don't go after berries or mushrooms."

"Do you go after berries and mushrooms too, on Sundays?" Laura asked Rita, interrupting Berenice.

Sally was exasperated with Laura for showing such a keen interest in Rita Cassalotti's Sundays.

"Why doesn't she ask me what I do on Sunday, instead of asking that trollop? She certainly can't do much of any interest if she stays in her wrapper all day."

"If only Berenice would keep her mouth shut for a minute," Laura thought. "I might then be able to drag something out of Rita." She was a little put out with herself for not being able to imagine Rita's attitude toward Sunday. But all the while Berenice continued to fill the glasses with beer the moment they were emptied, so that Laura very soon cared less and less about finding out anything from Rita.

In fact, she was unpleasantly startled when Rita asked Berenice whether she remembered the Sundays at Felicia Kelly's.

"Not as good as you do," said Berenice. "Because I was a little tyke."

"That was ten years ago," Rita said. "I was twenty years old and you were ten. She had her bushes and trees growing so close to the walk there that we used to get soaking wet from the branches after the rain. I used to rub Berenice's hair with a Turkish towel when we got in the house—my own too. It's a mistake to plant them so close." Rita was actually addressing Berenice rather than Laura, for she was never certain that Laura could really understand much of what was said. Berenice, who was interested in almost any topic of conversation, listened attentively.

"She made tutti-frutti ice cream for her family on Sunday, so she always served us some. It was very good quality. You could see the Old Man and the Old Woman on clear days from her kitchen window. I think you could see the Old Man from the parlor window too, but not the Old Woman. I'm sure you couldn't see the Old Woman from the parlor—no, you couldn't have, it wasn't facing right. Berenice used to get a kick out of that. We can't see any mountain peaks from here, just the valley and the woods. But Berenice could see those two peaks very clear from the Kellys', so she was pleased about that, I guess. Do you remember the Old Man and the Old Woman, Berenice?"

Laura was thoroughly bored by the present turn in the conversation, but she felt compelled to question Rita further, since this account about Felicia Kelly's house was a roundabout answer to Laura's original question "Do you like Sundays?", which proved that at least Rita had heard her question, and that the possibility of finding out more concerning Rita and her tastes was not entirely closed to her.

"Did you like going to see Felicia Kelly on Sunday?" Laura asked her, trying to conceal her weariness by tossing her head back and smiling.

Again Rita's face was closed, and instead of answering Laura's question she poured herself some beer very carefully so as to avoid its forming a head.

"Rita doesn't go to see Felicia Kelly any more," said Berenice, and there was such warmth and radiance shining in her eyes even as she made this announcement that Laura felt recompensed, in spite of Rita's queer stubbornness, and was not annoyed with Berenice for interrupting.

"Really?" she said.

"No. One Sunday she went all the way over there—it's about fifteen miles from here—and nobody was home, not even the dog. The cat was there but the dog wasn't. So she never spoke to Felicia Kelly again."

"We drove all the way over there," said Rita, "and then we had to come all the way back without seeing anyone. Poppa was mad too. He used to drive us over there in the truck and call for us every Sunday. She didn't leave a note, either."

"What happened to her?" Laura asked with some degree of real interest.

"I don't know," said Rita. "I never talked to her again."

"She called up once or twice but Poppa just told her Rita wouldn't talk to her, and then he'd hook the receiver on the telephone," put in Berenice.

"Then you never knew why she wasn't home?" Laura asked Rita, looking at her with wonder.

"No," said Rita. "I never talked to her again." She seemed pleased with the end of her story.

At this point Laura gave up thinking about Rita because she was so much of a mystery to her that there seemed to be no hope of her ever understanding any more about how Rita felt than she did that afternoon, even had she persisted in questioning her for the next fifty years. In a sense it was satisfying to know that such mysteries existed and that she did not have to exert herself any further.

Just then, Mr. Cassalotti came in with the raviolis. He had dished out the portions in the kitchen and now carried the full plates over to the table on a tray.

"I got everything ready so all you have to do now is eat. Move your chair in," he said to Sally, putting a plate of raviolis down on the table for her.

They had all forgotten Sally's presence, and looked toward her with surprise. She had moved her chair even further away from the table during the conversation about Felicia Kelly, although no one had noticed it.

"No, thank you," said Sally, her aloof expression changing quickly into one of vivid revulsion. "I'm going home in a minute."

"Not before you eat your ravioli," said Mr. Cassalotti calmly, and going over to her chair he got behind it and lifted her over to the table, where he set her down, chair and all, in front of her raviolis.

Berenice had a hunted, frightened look in her eyes as she watched her father with amazement. Ordinarily she would have laughed heartily at such playfulness, but being extremely sensitive, she felt that Sally was not a person to be lifted through the air even in jest. Rita wasn't either worried or amused.

"Oh, Poppa," she said. "If she don't want to eat don't force her."

Mr. Cassalotti returned to the kitchen and there was silence in the dining room. Even Rita noticed the queer strained look on Sally's face, and she stared at her shamelessly while Laura and Berenice averted their eyes.

Sally was so insulted by Mr. Cassalotti's gesture that, although she wanted to flee from the room, she remained rooted to her chair by such shame and by an anger so burning that it temporarily blotted from her mind its source, so that only the present moment existed for her. Her eye fixed on a red-and-white checked curtain on the wall opposite, and immediately she felt that to draw this curtain was her only hope against suffocation. Then the fear that she would not reach the curtain gradually stole the place of both her shame and her anger, imparting a more pitiful and appealing expression to her eyes.

"It's so hot in here," said Berenice, whose sensitive nature was becoming more and more aroused.

Sally heard the remark and now her heart started to beat with panic lest Berenice reach the window before she did. She felt it was absolutely necessary that she herself draw the curtains and not Berenice.

With what seemed to her superhuman effort, she rose to her feet and then walked like a person lightheaded with fever over to the window. She drew the curtains aside with a shaky hand. Behind them was a black shade which Mr. Cassalotti had hung there so that no daylight would ever penetrate the restaurant. He thought that to eat by electricity was more elegant, and that all restaurateurs should equip their restaurants so as to appear in a land of perpetual night.

Sally lifted the shade and there at last was the window. It had been pouring outside only a moment before, so that streams of rain were still sliding down the window pane. Through the pane the leaves of the elm, whose branches almost brushed against the side of the house, appeared larger and more glistening than they actually were. The grass, a brilliant green in the afterlight of the storm, seemed particularly so around the thick wet trunk of the tree.

Sally felt that she was losing ground faster and faster every minute, a condition which she qualified at calmer moments as "going too fast for myself." But it was not because she was so much of a lady or even particularly dignified that Mr. Cassalotti's gesture had insulted her so deeply. The insult lay in the suddenness of the actual interruption, which had violated abruptly her precarious state of balance.

"I'll have to get out on the ground," she said to herself three or four times. Behind her she could hear the subdued voices of the two other women and Berenice. But they seemed far away, as if they were speaking in a separate room. She felt along the glass several times as if she would find a way of going through the window to get outside, but in a moment she sighed and turned around, scanning the room for the right door. In order to reach it she had to pass the table where the others were sitting. But she kept her head high and was in truth scarcely aware of their presence at all.

Unfortunately Laura was drinking her eighth beer, which suddenly changed her mood into one of lachrymose affection.

"Sally, sweetheart," she called as Sally stalked past the table. "Sally, darling, where are you going?" Sally already had her hand on the knob and was pulling on it, but Laura sprang to her feet and reached Sally's side before she was able to get through the door.

"You have to come and eat your ravioli, because it's delicious, but if you won't eat you can talk to Berenice and Rita and me," Laura said to her. Putting her arms around Sally she searched her face with tenderly swimming eyes.

Sally looked as though she were about to be sick, but with unexpected energy she wrenched herself loose from Laura's embrace and fairly flew out of the room.

The evening air was cold and still, now that the storm had passed, and the sky near the horizon was green, the color green that chills the heart of a person of melancholic or tempestuous nature. But Sally did not even notice it. No natural sight ever depressed her and she did not know what it was to be melancholic.

Pine cones, now soggy and darker-colored after the rain, were scattered about underneath the trees. Sally's sister Henrietta liked to paint pine cones different colors and then heap them into a bowl for decoration.

Sally felt infinitely weary as she looked at these cones, which seemed to be scattered about the grass as far as her eye could see. However (and in spite of the fact that pine cones were abundant in all the surrounding region and lay scattered about even at the very door of her own cabin at Camp Cataract), she felt challenged to gather some, soggy as they were, to take back to her sister. She had nothing but her hat to carry them in, which she determined to use. Squatting down on her heels, she was quickly absorbed in selecting the most perfect cones. In her thoughts there was not a shadow of concern about Laura or the Cassalotti sisters. As far as she was concerned, they did not exist.

Laura had never seen Sally out of control before, and she returned to the table worried and yet excited. Although she was drunk enough to behave carelessly, her instincts forbade her to follow Sally out of doors.

"What do you suppose got into her?" Laura asked.

"A jackass," said Berenice.

Rita reprimanded her sister. "You don't have to use such talk," she said to her.

"She was quite beside herself when she left the room," Laura added, ignoring Berenice's language. Laura knew that she should not be discussing Sally with the Cassalottis, who were certain to interpret her more simply than her unbalanced nature merited.

"She's a stuck-up jackass," Berenice said again. "She doesn't want to associate with us or have you associating with us either. Don't you think I've known it all along? She didn't eat those raviolis just to insult

Poppa. I'd like to see the rotten stinking food they got at her house."

"Fried skunk," said Rita placidly, without a smile.

"That's right." Berenice nodded her approval.

Laura had not expected the conversation about Sally to be on such a low level as this. She was particularly surprised to hear Berenice attack Sally so bitterly, since it had never occurred to her that Berenice could be anything but warmhearted and generous toward everyone.

"Poppa took a lot of trouble making that ravioli for her, and he's a very busy man. I didn't care how the crazy loon acted with us, but she's got to be decent with Poppa. She can't come in here anymore now, that's all. . . . Let her go to a stuck-up place."

"Sally isn't stuck-up," said Laura, who could never be dishonest. "She is high-strung but not stuck-up. High and strict. She's got systems for living."

"So have Rita and me got systems, and one of them is not to look like a rat bit us if we are served food in somebody else's house. We say thank you and we eat our food. So do you, Laura. Don't make excuses for her. Anyway, she hates us."

Berenice was calming down. She scraped at her empty plate with her fork for a little while. Then soon the glow returned to her face, and her eyes were once again shining with warmth and enthusiasm.

"Life is too short . . ." she said, smiling at Laura, and she poured some more beer. But Laura felt ashamed now to have referred to Sally's behavior at all, and she was determined to continue the conversation so as to vindicate in some way the cheapness of her original impulse to gossip.

"I don't think Sally hates you," she said to Berenice. "It's very possible that she loves you."

Berenice opened her eyes wide with incomprehension.

"It's not a bit unusual to love and to hate the same person," Laura continued. Her tone was didactic.

"Unusual," said Berenice. "It's impossible." But she spoke hesitatingly because she was really at sea thus far in the conversation.

"No, no," Laura insisted. "That's partly why living is such trouble. We are likely to love and to hate the very same person at the very same time, and yet neither emotion is more true than the other. You have to decide which you're going to cater to, that's all. Fortunately, if you are at all decent, you manage to keep pushing love a little bit ahead . . . but it can be very, very difficult keeping it that way. I was that way about my mother, and I have been that way about one other person, but particularly my mother."

"Oh, no—" The words escaped Berenice involuntarily.

"Oh, yes!" Laura was vehement. "Sometimes I wanted to hit Mother so hard that it would knock her head right off her body. She's dead now but I think I would feel the same way if she were alive."

Berenice didn't say anything. She clasped both hands tightly around her glass of beer and stared ahead of her. Rita Cassalotti had long since been occupied with some private concern and remained mute.

After a moment Berenice broke the silence. "I've got to go out now," she announced. Cocking her head to one side, she smiled at Laura—a charming smile that showed the dimple in her cheek—and she looked for all the world like a young girl taking leave of her hostess at a tea party.

"But," said Laura, horrified at this unexpected announcement, "I thought we had hours ahead of us still. You didn't say anything. . . ."

Berenice stood up. "I've got to go into town," she said, and once more she tilted her head to one side and smiled enchantingly at Laura, but without meeting Laura's eye.

Berenice was leaving, and Laura knew somehow that she had no appointment, and knew too that no word she could utter would bring Berenice back into the room. Laura's cheeks were hot with shame. She could not bear to have Berenice turn away from her this way, although a moment before she had considered Berenice so shallow that she was ashamed to discuss Sally with her. She was in a panic lest Berenice should cast away their friendship, and her shame sprang from a suspicion that she had ruined something in Berenice's heart—not because of Berenice but because such a misdeed would reflect seriously on her own character.

"Oh, my God," Laura said to herself, "why did I bring up my theory about love and hate? She'll never, never forgive me." Laura had a wild respect for people who were capable of becoming so offended that they rose from their chairs and left the room where they were sitting, and sometimes even the house. And if it was for an ideal that they showed such offense and not for any egoistic personal reason, Laura regarded them as saints.

"She must forgive me," she repeated to herself, "she must, or it will be a real calamity."

She recalled the moment on the bottom step, when she had not obeyed the seemingly mystical challenge to walk through the wet woods instead of sitting down to eat her raviolis. So now, by not having had the courage to heed this compulsion, she had lost the Cassalottis as well. In moments of stress she was very apt to see connections between her intimate world and the actions of other people, as if the adverse behavior of others was dependent at least indirectly upon an earlier wrong decision concerning a private matter of her own. She realized the idiocy of such reasoning but at the same time she thought that everyone else felt that way without noticing it. Certainly nothing was so personal to her as this way of being. In fact it was impossible for her to give it up.

Even so, to witness the shock Berenice had suffered as a result of her own careless remark was to Laura the worst possible punishment, because in the face of Berenice's distress, which overwhelmed this girl so naturally that any question or doubt as to whether she could choose or not choose to overlook her feelings was unthinkable, Laura's own feelings against herself assumed a groteque and petty quality which made her blush. She continued, however, even though humiliated, to suspect that had she not eaten raviolis but really gone walking instead through the woods, she would not have found herself faced by the present quandary. How she was able to feel herself to be grotesque and comical, and at the same time so important that the outcome of her decisions controlled somehow the behavior of people not in the least connected to it, was a puzzle to Laura herself.

She saw all these things and even more, for she was educated enough in psychological matters to conceive that the source of Berenice's own violent reaction to her remarks about hating her mother lay not in what she, Laura, had decided earlier on the bottom step, or even in Berenice's genuine moral indignation, but in a hatred that Berenice might have felt and concealed from herself, at one time or another, toward her own mother. Laura knew about such things but they did not help her one bit when she was in the midst of a calamity.

With all these details very clear in her mind, still (like a person who jumps deliberately into a pit) she was falling deeper and deeper by the second into such an abject terror of Berenice's resentment that she longed for forgiveness more than for anything in the world. She appealed to Rita, hoping that after all she had imagined something amiss in Berenice's behavior while actually everything was really just as it had been a little while before. She had often enough imagined that she had horrified a friend when nothing of the kind had occurred.

"Rita, did Berenice have an appointment?" she asked.

"No, she didn't have no appointment," Rita said, shrugging her shoulders.

"Where did she go then, Rita?" Laura insisted, fixing her eyes on Rita's face.

"She went flying away with the birdies," said Rita Cassalotti, and with sudden animation she stretched out both her arms and moved them up and down in imitation of a bird's flight.

To see Rita thus unconcerned and jesting made Laura feel her plight ever more keenly, for she needed someone's sympathy badly right then. She plucked at Rita's pink sleeve, trying to halt the upward motion of her arm.

"Please stop flying, Rita, and talk to me."

She looked so peculiar that Rita burst out laughing.

"Rita," Laura pleaded, "why do you think she went away?"

Rita shrugged her shoulders. She never paid much attention to Berenice's comings and goings, and had actually scarcely taken notice when Berenice left the table. Rita yawned and got up. "I'm going to get dressed," she said. "I've got a real complete appointment tonight, including dinner, movies, drinks and dancing—with a married guy, too." She started to leave the room and Laura followed behind her. They mounted the stairs together in silence. Laura knew that Rita wanted to be left alone but she was far too nervous to remain by herself and her pride was nonexistent.

"I've got to get dressed," said Rita when she found Laura was behind her even in the bedroom.

"Oh, but please, Rita, let me stay here," Laura begged her, and she searched her mind rapidly for a topic of conversation that might interest Rita. "Rita," she said, her eyes full of concern, "I'm terribly worried about your going around with a married man."

"Why?" Rita asked with no interest. She took off her wrapper and stood before Laura in her bloomers. "I'm not afraid of his wife," she said, thrusting her chin out.

"But morally it's wrong." Laura searched her brain frantically, trying to remember at least one reasonable argument against adultery, but she couldn't think of any.

"If he don't go with me, he'll go with someone else," Rita said flatly. "Not that I give a hoot whether I go with him or anyone else. They're all alike, the men, and I never cared for their company much."

"Why not, Rita?" Laura asked her with great interest.

"I don't know," Rita said, "I just don't care for them. I wish you'd let me dress by myself," she said. "I can't keep my mind on it with you here."

There was nothing left for Laura to do but leave. She thought it was irritating that a dumbbell like Rita Cassalotti needed her privacy at all, and she went out angry as well as forlorn.

"I've ruined everything," she said to herself, descending the stairway slowly, one step at a time.

Not knowing whether it was useless or not to wait for Berenice's return, she wandered aimlessly about the dining room, straightening chairs and stopping now and then to gaze at the glassed-in scene, so provokingly flooded with light when the dining room itself lay in darkness. The orange truck driven by the celluloid baby held her eye. The doll, not designed to sit up, had been tilted against the back of the seat with its legs curled in the air almost over its head.

In spite of the incongruity apparent in this combination, she was overcome with boredom, looking at it as if she were seeing it not for the first but for the thousandth time. She turned herself away, almost in embarrassment, as though she herself were responsible for what she saw in the glass case. She would have liked to ponder on the mysterious effect these two objects had on her, but just then the full realization that Berenice Cassalotti would never have faith in her again seemed, like an ocean wave, to break over her head and wash all other thoughts away.

She hurried out of the dining room and into the store. It was empty. On all other occasions Berenice had taken her to the door flushed with beer and pleasure, and filled with the anticipation of Laura's next visit, for in Berenice's joyous heart even a departure took on the aspect of a return.

Laura closed the door behind her and started toward the road that led out of the village to Camp Cataract. It was a wide sandy road bordered by such tall pine trees that, with the exception of a few sunny hours at midday, the road lay constantly in the shadows. The sandy earth was cold and no grass grew anywhere.

Far ahead of her, out of hearing but not out of sight, Laura could see Sally walking along, her handbag swinging from her wrist. She was walking slowly, with small steps, her head bent, and at a pace suitable to a city street.

Laura had forgotten about her completely.

Late forties to early fifties (?)

THE TIME OF FRIENDSHIP

PAUL BOWLES

THE TROUBLE HAD BEEN growing bigger each year, ever since the end of the war. From the beginning, although aware of its existence, Fräulein Windling had determined to pay it no attention. At first there were only whispered reports of mass arrests. People said: "Many thousands of Moslems have been sent to prison in France." Soon some of her own friends had begun to disappear, like young Bachir and Omar ben Lakhdar, the postmaster of Timimoun, who suddenly one morning were gone, or so she was told, for when she returned the following winter they were not there, and she never had seen them since. The people simply made their faces blank when she tried to talk about it. After the hostilities had begun in earnest, even though the nationalists had derailed the trains and disrupted the trans-Saharan truck service on several occasions, still it was possible to get beyond the disturbed region to her oasis. There in the south the fighting was far away, and the long hours of empty desert that lay between made it seem much farther, almost as though it had been across the sea. If the men of her oasis should ever be infected by the virus of discontent from the far-off north—and this seemed to her almost inconceivable—then in spite of the fact that she was certain that war could bring them nothing but unhappiness, she would have no recourse but to hope for their victory. It was their own land they would be fighting for, their own lives they would be losing in order to win the fight. In the meantime people did not talk; life was hard but peaceful. Each one was aware of the war that was going on in the north, and each one was glad it was far away.

Summers, Fräulein Windling taught in the Freiluftschule in Bern, where she entertained her pupils with tales of the life led by the people in the great desert in Africa. In the village where she lived, she told them, everything was made by the people themselves out of what the desert had to offer. They lived in a world of objects fashioned out of baked earth, woven grass, palmwood and animal skins. There was no metal. Although she did not admit it to the children, this was no longer wholly true, since recently the women had taken to using empty oil tins for carrying water, instead of the goathide bags of a few years before. She had tried to discourage her friends among the village women from this innovation, telling them that the tins could poison the water; they had agreed, and gone on using them. "They are lazy," she decided. "The oil tins are easier to carry."

When the sun went down and the cool air from the oasis below with its sting of woodsmoke rose to the level of the hotel, she would smell it inside her room and stop whatever she was doing. Then she would put on her burnoose and climb the stairs to the roof. The blanket she lay on while she sunbathed each morning would be there, and she would stretch out on it facing the western sky, and feel the departed sun's heat still strong underneath her body. It was one of the pleasures of the day, to watch the light changing in the oasis below, when dusk and the smoke from the evening fires slowly blotted out the valley. There always came a moment when all that was left was the faint outline, geometric and precise, of the mass of mud prisms that was the village, and a certain clump of high date palms that stood outside its entrance. The houses themselves were no longer there, and eventually the highest palm disappeared; and unless there was a moon all that remained to be seen was the dying sky, the sharp edges of the rocks on the hammada, and a blank expanse of mist that lay over the valley but did not reach as far up the cliffs as the hotel.

Perhaps twice each winter a group of the village women would invite Fräulein Windling to go with them up into the vast land of the dunes to look for firewood. The glare here was cruel. There was not even the trace of a twig or a stem anywhere on the sand, yet as they wandered along the crests barefoot the women could spot the places where roots lay buried beneath the surface, and then they would stoop, uncover them, and dig them up. "The wind leaves a sign," they told her, but she was never certain of being able to identify the sign, nor could she understand how there might be a connection between the invisible roots in the sand and the wind in the air above. "What we have lost, they still possess," she thought.

Her first sight of the desert and its people had been a transfiguring experience; indeed, it seemed to her now that before coming here she had never been in touch with life at all. She believed firmly that each day she spent here increased the aggregate of her resistance. She coveted the rugged health of the natives, when her own was equally strong, but because she was white and educated, she was convinced that her body was intrinsically inferior.

All the work in the hotel was done by one quiet, sad-faced man named Boufelja. He had been there when she had first arrived many years ago; for Fräulein Windling he had come to be as much a part of the place as the cliffs across the valley. She often sat on her table by the fireplace after lunch, playing cards by herself, until the logs no longer gave out heat. There were two very young French soldiers from the fort opposite, who ate in the hotel dining-room. They drank a great amount of wine, and it annoyed her to see their faces slowly turning red as they sat there. At first the soldiers had tipped their caps to her as they went out, and they had stopped their laughing long enough to say, "*Bonjour, madame,*" to her, but now they no longer did. She was happy when they had left, and savored the moment before the fire burned out, while it still glowed under the gusts of wind that wandered down the wide chimney.

Almost always the wind sprang up early in the afternoon, a steady, powerful blowing that roared through the thousands of palms in the oasis below and howled under each door in the hotel, covering the more distant village sounds. This was the hour when she played solitaire, or merely sat, watching the burnt-out logs as they fell to pieces before her eyes. Later she would go along the terrace, a high, bright place like the deck of a great ship sailing through the desert afternoon, hurrying into her room for an instant to get her sweater and cane, and start out on a walk. Sometimes she went southward following the river valley, along the foot of the silent cliffs and through the crooked gorges, to an abandoned village built in a very hot place at a turn in the canyon. The sheer walls of rock behind it sent back the heat, so that the air burned her throat as she breathed it in. Or she went farther, to where the cliff dwellings were, with their animals and symbols incised in the rock.

Returning along the road that led to the village, deep in the green shade of the thickest part of the palm forest, she was regularly aware of the same group of boys sitting at the turn of the road, at a place just before it led up the hill to the shops and the village. They squatted on the sand behind the feathery branches of a giant tamarisk, quietly talking. When she came up to them she greeted them, and they always replied, remained silent a moment until she had passed by, and then resumed their conversation. As far as she could tell, there was never any reference to her by word, and yet this year it sometimes seemed to her that once she had gone by, their inflection had subtly altered, as though there had been a modulation into another key. Did their attitude border on derision? She did not know, but since this was the first time during all her years in the desert that the idea had ever suggested itself to her, she put it resolutely out of her mind. "A new generation requires a new technique if one is to establish contact," she thought. "It is for me to find it." Nevertheless she was sorry that there was no other way of getting into the village save along this main road where they invariably gathered. Even the slight tension caused by having to go past them marred the pleasure of her walks.

One day she realized with a slight shock of shame that she did not even know what the boys looked like. She had seen them only as a group from a distance; when she drew near enough to say good-day to them, she always had her head down, watching the road. The fact that she had been afraid to look at them was unacceptable; now, as she came up to them, she stared into the eyes of one after the other, carefully. Nodding gravely, she went on. Yes, they were insolent faces, she thought—not at all like the faces of their elders. The respectful attitudes into which they had been startled were the crudest sort of shamming. But the important thing to her was that she had won: she was no longer preoccupied with having to pass by them every day. Slowly she even grew to recognize each boy.

There was one, she noted, younger than the others, who always sat a little apart from them, and it was this shy one who stood talking to Boufelja in the hotel kitchen early one morning when she went in. She pretended not to notice him. "I am going to my room to work on the machine for about an hour," she told Boufelja. "You can come then to make up the room," and she turned to go out. As she went through the doorway she glanced at the boy's face. He was looking at her, and he did not turn away when his eyes met hers. "How are you?" she said. Perhaps half an hour later, when she was typing her second letter, she raised her head. The boy was standing on the terrace looking at her through the open door. He squinted, for the wind was strong; behind his head she saw the tops of the palms bending.

"If he wants to watch, let him watch," she said to herself, deciding to pay him no attention. After a while he went away. While Boufelja served her lunch, she questioned him about the boy. "Like an old man," said Boufelja. "Twelve years old but very serious. Like some old, old man." He smiled, then shrugged. "It's the way God wanted him to be."

"Of course," she said, remembering the boy's alert, unhappy face. "A young dog that everyone has kicked," she thought, "but he hasn't given up."

In the days that followed, he came often to the terrace and stood watching her while she typed. Sometimes she waved to him, or said: "Good morning." Without answering he would take a step backward, so that he was out of her range. Then he would continue to stand where he was. His behavior irked her, and one day when he had done this, she quickly got up and went to the door. "What is it?" she asked him, trying to smile as she spoke.

"I didn't do anything," he said, his eyes reproachful.

"I know," she answered. "Why don't you come in?"

The boy looked swiftly around the terrace as if for help; then he bowed his head and stepped inside the door. Here he stood waiting, his head down, looking miserable. From her luggage she brought out a bag of hard candy, and handed him a piece. Then she put a few simple questions to him, and found that his French was much better than she had expected. "Do the other boys know French as well as you?" she asked him.

"*Non, madame,*" he said, shaking his head slowly. "My father used to be a soldier. Soldiers speak good French."

She tried to keep her face from expressing the disapproval she felt, for she despised everything military. "I see," she said with some asperity, turning back to her table and shuffling the papers. "Now I must work," she told him, immediately adding in a warmer voice, "but you come back tomorrow, if you like." He waited an instant, looking at her with unchanged wistfulness. Then slowly he smiled, and laid the candy wrapper, folded into a tiny square, on the corner of her table. "*Au revoir, madame,*" he said, and went out of the door. In the silence she heard the scarcely audible thud of his bare heels on the earth floor of the terrace. "In this cold," she thought. "Poor child! If I ever buy anything for him it will be a pair of sandals."

Each day thereafter, when the sun was high enough to give substance to the still morning air, the boy would come stealthily along the terrace to her door, stand a few seconds, and then say in a lost voice that was all the smaller and more hushed for the great silence outside: "*Bonjour, madame.*" She would tell him to come in, and they would shake hands gravely, he afterward raising the backs of his fingers to his lips, always with the same slow ceremoniousness. She sometimes tried to fathom his countenance as he went through this ritual, to see if by any chance she could detect a shade of mockery there; instead she saw an expression of devotion so convincing that it startled her, and she looked away quickly. She always kept a bit of bread or some biscuits in a drawer of the wardrobe; when she had brought the food out and he was eating it, she would ask him for news about the families in his quarter of the village. For discipline's sake she offered him a piece of candy only every other day. He sat on the floor by the doorway, on a torn old camel blanket, and he watched her constantly, never turning his head away from her.

She wanted to know what he was called, but she was aware of how secretive the inhabitants of the region were about names, seldom giving their true ones to strangers; this was a peculiarity she respected because she knew it had its roots in their own prehistoric religion. So she forbore asking him, sure that the time would come when he trusted her enough to give it of his own volition. And the moment happened one morning unexpectedly, when he had just recounted several legends involving the great Moslem king of long ago, whose name was Solomon. Suddenly he stopped, and forcing himself to gaze steadily at her without blinking, he said: "And my name too is Slimane, the same as the king."

She tried to teach him to read, but he did not seem able to learn. Often just as she felt he was about to connect two loose ends of ideas and perhaps at last make a contact which would enable him to understand the principle, a look of resignation and passivity would appear in his face, and he would willfully cut off the stream of effort from its source, and remain sitting, merely looking at her, shaking his head from side to side to show that it was useless. It was hard not to lose patience with him at such moments.

The following year she decided not to go on with the lessons, and to use Slimane instead as a guide, bearer and companion, a role which she immediately saw was more suited to his nature than that of pupil. He did not mind how far they went or how much equipment he had to carry; on the contrary, to him a long excursion was that much more of an event, and whatever she loaded onto him he bore with the air of one upon whom an honor is conferred. It was probably her happiest season in the desert, that winter of comradeship when together they made the countless pilgrimages down the valley. As the weeks passed the trips grew in scope, and the hour of departure was brought forward until it came directly after she had finished her breakfast. All day long, trudging in the open sun and in the occasional shade of the broken fringe of palms that skirted the river-bed, she conversed passionately with him. Sometimes she could see that he felt like telling her what was in his head, and she let him speak for as long as his enthusiasm lasted, often reviving it at the end with carefully chosen questions. But usually it was she who did the speaking as she walked behind him. Pounding the stony ground with her steel-tipped stick each time her right foot went down, she told him in great detail the story of the life of Hitler, showing why he was hated by the Christians. This she thought necessary since Slimane had been under a different impression, and indeed had imagined that the Europeans thought as highly of the vanished leader as did he and the rest of the people in the village. She talked a good deal about Switzerland, casually stressing the cleanliness, honesty and good health of her countrymen in short parables of daily life. She told him about Jesus, Martin Luther and Garibaldi, taking care to keep Jesus distinct from the Moslem prophet Sidna Aissa, since even for the sake of argument she could not agree for an instant with the Islamic doctrine according to which the Savior was a Moslem. Slimane's attitude of respect bordering on adoration with regard to her never altered unless she inadvertently tangled with the subject of Islam; then, no matter what she said (for at that point it seemed that automatically he was no longer within hearing) he would shake his head interminably and cry: "No, no, no, no! Nazarenes know nothing about Islam. Don't talk, madame, I beg you, because you don't know what you're saying. No, no, no!"

Long ago she had kept the initial promise to herself that she would buy him sandals; this purchase had been followed by others. At fairly regular intervals she had taken him to Benaissa's store to buy a shirt, a pair of baggy black cotton trousers of the kind worn by the Chaamba camel-drivers, and ultimately a new white burnoose, despite the fact that she knew the entire village would discuss the giving of so valuable an object. She also knew that it was only the frequent bestowing of such gifts that kept Slimane's father from forbidding him to spend his time with her. Even so, according to reports brought by Slimane, he sometimes objected. But Slimane himself, she was sure, wanted nothing, expected nothing.

It was each year when March was drawing to a close that the days began to be painfully hot and even the nights grew breathless; then, although it always required a strenuous effort of the will to make herself take the step which would bring about renewed contact with the outside world, she would devote two or three days to washing her clothing and preparing for the journey. When the week set for her departure had come, she went over to the fort and put in a call to the café at Kerzaz, asking the proprietor to tell the driver of the next northbound truck to take the detour that would enable her to catch him at a point only about three kilometers from the village.

She and Slimane had come back to the hotel on the afternoon of their last excursion down the valley; Fräulein Windling stood on the terrace looking out at the orange mountains of sand behind the fort. Slimane had taken the packs into the room and put them down. She turned and said: "Bring the big tin box." When he had pulled it out from under the bed he carried it to her, dusting it off with the sleeve of his shirt, and she led the way up the stairs to the roof. They sat down on the blanket; the glow of the vanished sun's furnace heated their faces. A few flies still hovered, now and then attacking their necks. Slimane handed her the biscuit tin and she gave him a fistful of chocolate-covered cakes. "So many all at once?"

"Yes," she said. "You know I'm going home in four days."

He looked down at the blanket a moment before replying. "I know," he murmured. He was silent again. Then he cried out aggrievedly: "Boufelja says it's hot here in the summer. It's not hot! In our house it's cool. It's like the oasis where the big pool is. You would never be hot there."

"I have to earn money. You know that. I want to come back next year."

He said sadly: "Next year, madame! Only Moulana knows how next year will be."

Some camels growled as they rolled in the sand at the foot of the fort; the light was receding swiftly. "Eat your biscuits," she told him, and she ate one herself. "Next year we'll go to Abadla with the caid, *incha'Allah*."

He sighed deeply. "Ah, madame!" he said. She noted, at first with a pang of sympathy and then, reconsidering, with disapproval, the anguish that lent his voice its unaccustomed intensity. It was the quality she least liked in him, this faintly theatrical self-pity. "Next year you'll be a man," she told him firmly. Her voice grew less sure, assumed a hopeful tone. "You'll remember all the things we talked about?"

She sent him a postcard from Marseille, and showed her classes photographs they had taken of one another, and of the caid. The children were impressed by the caid's voluminous turban. "Is he a Bedouin?" asked one.

When she left the embassy office she knew that this was the last year she would be returning to the desert. There was not only the official's clearly expressed unfriendliness and suspicion: for the first time he had made her answer a list of questions which she found alarming. He wanted to know what subjects she taught in the Freiluftschule, whether she had ever been a journalist, and exactly where she proposed to be each day after arriving in the Sahara. She had almost retorted: I go where I feel like going. I don't make plans. But she had merely named the oasis. She knew that Frenchmen had no respect for elderly Swiss ladies who wore woolen stockings; this simply made them more contemptible in her eyes. However, it was they who controlled the Sahara.

The day the ship put into the African port it was raining. She knew the gray terraced ramps of the city were there in the gloom ahead, but they were invisible. The ragged European garments of the dock workers were soaked with rain. Later, the whole rain-sodden city struck her as grim, and the people passing along the streets looked unhappy. The change, even from the preceding year, was enormous; it made her sad to sit in the big, cold café where she went for coffee after dinner, and so she returned to her hotel and slept. The next day she got on the train for Perrégaux. The rain fell most of the day. In Perrégaux she took a room in a hotel near the station, and stayed in it, listening to the rain rattle down the gutter by her window. "This place would be a convenient model for Hell," she wrote to a friend in Basel before going to sleep that night. "A full-blown example of the social degeneracy achieved by forced cultural hybridism. Populace debased and made hostile by generations of merciless exploitation. I take the southbound narrow-gauge train tomorrow morning for a happier land, and trust that my friend the sun will appear at some point during the day. *Seien Sie herzlich gegrüsst von Ihrer Maria.*"

As the train crawled southward, up over the high plateau land, the clouds were left behind and the sun took charge of the countryside. Fräulein Windling sat attentively by the smeared window, enveloped in an increasing sadness. As long as it had been raining, she had imagined the rain as the cause of her depression: the gray cloud light gave an unaccustomed meaning to the landscape by altering forms and distances. Now she understood that the more familiar and recognizable the contours of the desert were to become, the more conscious she would be of having no reason to be in it, because it was her last visit.

Two days later, when the truck stopped to let her out, Boufelja stood in the sun beside the boulders waving; one of the men of the village was with him to help carry the luggage. Once the truck had gone and its cloud of yellow dust had fled across the hammada, the silence was there; it seemed that no sound could be louder than the crunch of their shoes on the ground.

"How is Slimane?" she asked. Boufelja was noncommittal. "He's all right," he said. "They say he tried to run away. But he didn't get very far." The report might be true, or it might be false; in any case she determined not to allude to it unless Slimane himself mentioned it first.

She felt an absurd relief when they came to the edge of the cliffs and she saw the village across the valley. Not until she had made the rounds of the houses where her friends lived, discussed their troubles with them and left some pills here and some candy there, was she convinced that no important change had come to the oasis during her absence. She went to the house of Slimane's parents: he was not there. "Tell him to come and see me," she said to his father as she left the house.

On the third morning after her arrival Slimane appeared, and stood there in the doorway smiling. Once she had greeted him and made him sit down and have coffee with her, she plied him with questions about life in the village while she had been in Europe. Some of his friends had gone to become patriots, he said, and they were killing the French like flies. Her heart sank, but she said nothing. As she watched him smiling she was able to exult in the reflection that Slimane had been reachable, after all; she had proved that it was possible to make true friends of the younger people. But even while she was saying, "How happy I am to see you, Slimane," she remembered that their time together was now limited, and an expression of pain passed over her face as she finished the phrase. "I shall not say a word to him about it," she decided. If he, at least, still had the illusion of unbounded time lying ahead, he would somehow retain his aura of purity and innocence, and she would feel less anguish during the time they spent together.

One day they went down the valley to see the caid, and discussed the long-planned trip to Abadla. Another day they started out at dawn to visit the tomb of Moulay Ali ben Said, where there was a spring of hot water. It was a tiny spot of oasis at the edge of a ridge of high dunes; perhaps fifty palms were there around the decayed shrine. In the shade of the rocks below the walls there was a ruined cistern into which the steaming water dribbled. They spread blankets on the sand nearby, at the foot of a small tamarisk, and took out their lunch. Before starting to eat, they drank handfuls of the water, which Slimane said was famed for its holiness. The palms rattled and hissed in the wind overhead.

"Allah has sent us the wind to make us cool while we eat," Slimane said when he had finished his bread and dates.

"The wind has always been here," she answered carelessly, "and it always will be here."

He sat up straight. "No, no!" he cried. "When Sidna Aissa has returned for forty days there will be no more Moslems and the world will end. Everything, the sky and the sun and the moon. And the wind too. Everything." He looked at her with an expression of such satisfaction that she felt one of her occasional surges of anger against him.

"I see," she said. "Stand over by the spring a minute. I want to take your picture." She had never understood why it was that the Moslems had conceded Jesus even this Pyrrhic victory, the coda to all creation: its inconsistency embarrassed her. Across the decayed tank she watched Slimane assume the traditional stiff attitude of a person about to be photographed, and an idea came into her head. For Christmas Eve, which would come within two weeks, she would make a crèche. She would invite Slimane to eat with her by the fireplace, and when midnight came she would take him in to see it.

She finished photographing Slimane; they gathered up the equipment and set out against the hot afternoon wind for the village. The sand sometimes swept by, stinging their faces with its invisible fringe. Fräulein Windling led the way this time, and they walked fast. The image of the crèche, illumined by candles, occurred to her several times on the way back over the rocky erg; it made her feel inexpressibly sad, for she could not help connecting it with the fact that everything was ending. They came to the point north of the village where the empty erg was cut across by the wandering river valley. As they climbed slowly upward over the fine sand, she found herself whispering: "It's the right thing to do." "*Right* is not the word," she thought, without being able to find a better one. She was going to make a crèche because she loved Christmas and wanted to share it with Slimane. They reached the hotel shortly after sunset, and she sent Slimane home in order to sit and plan her project on paper.

It was only when she began actually to put the crèche together that she realized how much work it was going to be. Early the next morning she asked Boufelja to find her an old wooden crate. Before she had been busy even a half-hour, she heard Slimane talking in the kitchen. Quickly she pushed everything under the bed and went out onto the terrace.

"Slimane," she said. "I'm very busy. Come in the afternoon." And that afternoon she told him that since she was going to be working every morning until after the day of the Christ Child, they would not be making any more long trips during that time. He received the information glumly. "I know," he said. "You are getting ready for the holy day. I understand."

"When the holy day comes, we will have a feast," she assured him.

"If Allah wills."

"I'm sorry," she said, smiling.

He shrugged. "Good-by," he told her.

Afternoons they still walked in the oasis or had tea on the roof, but her mornings she spent in her room sewing, hammering and sculpting. Once she had the platform constructed, she had to model the figures. She carried up a great mass of wet clay from the river to her room. It was two days before she managed to make a Virgin whose form pleased her. From an old strip of muslin she fashioned a convincing tent to house the Mother and the Child in its nest of tiny white chicken feathers. Shredded tamarisk needles made a fine carpet for the interior of the tent. Outside she poured sand, and then pushed the clay camels' long legs deep into it; one animal walked behind the other over the dune, and a Wise Man sat straight on top of each, his white *djellaba* falling in long pointed folds to either side of the camel's flanks. The Wise Men would come carrying sacks of almonds and very small liqueur chocolates wrapped in colored tinfoil. When she had the crèche finished, she put it on the floor in the middle of the room and piled tangerines and dates in front of it. With a row of candles burning behind it, and one candle on each side in front, it would look like a Moslem religious chromolithograph. She hoped the scene would be recognizable to Slimane; he might then be more easily persuaded of its poetic truth. She wanted only to suggest to him that the god with whom he was on such intimate terms was the god worshipped by the Nazarenes. It was not an idea she would ever try to express in words.

An additional surprise for the evening would be the new flashbulb attachment to her camera, which Slimane had not yet seen. She intended to take a good many pictures of the crèche and of Slimane looking at it; these she would enlarge to show her pupils. She went and bought a new turban for Slimane; he had been wearing none for more than a year now. This was a man's turban, and very fine: ten meters of the softest Egyptian cotton.

The day before Christmas she overslept, duped by the heavy sky. Each winter the oasis had a few dark days; they were rare, but this was one of them. While she still lay there in bed, she heard the roar of the wind, and when she got up to look out the window she found no world outside—only a dim rose-gray fog that hid everything. The swirling sand sprayed ceaselessly against the glass; it had formed in long drifts on the floor of the terrace. When she went for breakfast, she wore her burnoose with the hood up around her face. The blast of the wind as she stepped out onto the terrace struck her with the impact of a solid object, and the sand gritted on the concrete floor under her shoes. In the dining-room Boufelja had bolted the shutters; he greeted her enthusiastically from the gloom inside, glad of her presence.

"A very bad day for your festival, alas, mademoiselle!" he observed as he set her coffee pot on the table.

"Tomorrow's the festival," she said. "It begins tonight."

"I know. I know." He was impatient with Nazarene feasts because the hours of their beginnings and ends were observed in so slipshod a manner. Moslem feasts began precisely, either at sundown or an hour before sunup, or when the new moon was first visible in the western sky at twilight. But the Nazarenes began their feasts whenever they felt like it.

She spent the morning in her room writing letters. By noon the air outside was darker with still more sand; the wind shook the hotel atop its rock as if it would hurl it over the tips of the palms below into the river-bed. Several times she rose and went to the window to stare out at the pink emptiness beyond the terrace. Storms made her happy, although she wished this one could have come after Christmas. She had imagined a pure desert night—cold, alive with stars, and the dogs yapping from the oasis. It might yet be that; there was still time, she thought, as she slipped her burnoose over her head to go in to lunch.

With the wind, the fireplace was an unsure blessing: besides the heat it gave, it provided the only light in the dining-room, but the smoke that belched from it burned her eyes and throat. The shutters at the windows rattled and pounded, covering the noise of the wind itself.

She got out of the dining-room as soon as she had finished eating, and hurried back to her room to sit through the slowly darkening afternoon, as she continued with her letter-writing and waited for the total extinction of daylight; Slimane was coming at eight. There would be enough time to carry everything into the dining-room before that, and to set the crèche up in the dark unused wing into which Boufelja was unlikely to go. But when she came to do it, she found that the wind's force was even greater than she had imagined. Again and again she made the trip between her room and the dining-room, carrying each object carefully wrapped in her burnoose. Each time she passed in front of the kitchen door she expected Boufelja to open it and discover her. She did not want him there when she showed the crèche to Slimane; he could see it tomorrow at breakfast.

Protected by the noise of the gale she succeeded in transporting all the parts to the far dark corner of the dining-room without alerting Boufelja. Long before dinner time the crèche was in readiness, awaiting only the lighting of the candles to be brought alive. She left a box of matches on the table beside it, and hurried back to her room to arrange her hair and change her clothing. The sand had sifted through her garments and was now everywhere; it showered from her underwear and stuck like sugar to her skin. Her watch showed a few minutes after eight when she went out.

Only one place had been laid at table. She waited, while the blinds chattered and banged, until Boufelja appeared carrying the soup tureen.

"What a bad night," he said.

"You forgot to prepare for Slimane," she told him. But he was not paying attention. "He's stupid!" he exclaimed, beginning to ladle out the soup.

"Wait!" she cried. "Slimane's coming. I mustn't eat until he comes."

Still Boufelja misunderstood. "He wanted to come into the dining-room," he said. "And he knows it's forbidden at dinner time."

"But I invited him!" She looked at the lone soup plate on the table. "Tell him to come in, and set another place."

Boufelja was silent. He put the ladle back into the tureen. "Where is he?" she demanded, and without waiting for him to reply she went on. "Didn't I tell you he was going to have dinner with me tonight?" For suddenly she suspected that in her desire for secrecy she might indeed have neglected to mention the invitation to Boufelja.

"You didn't say anything," he told her. "I didn't know. I sent him home. But he'll be back after dinner."

"Oh, Boufelja!" she cried. "You know Slimane never lies."

He looked down at her with reproach on his face. "I didn't know anything about mademoiselle's plans," he said aggrievedly. This made her think for a swift instant that he had discovered the crèche, but she decided that if he had he would have spoken of it.

"Yes, yes, I know. I should have told you. It's my fault."

"That's true, mademoiselle," he said. And he served the remaining courses observing a dignified silence which she, still feeling some displeasure with him, did not urge him to break. Only at the end of the meal, when she had pushed back her chair from the table and sat studying the pattern of the flames in the fireplace, did he decide to speak. "Mademoiselle will take coffee?"

"I do want some," she said, trying to bring a note of enthusiasm into her voice. "*Bien,*" murmured Boufelja, and he left her alone in the room. When he returned carrying the coffee, Slimane was with him, and they were laughing, she noted, quite as though there had been no misunderstanding about dinner. Slimane stood by the door an instant, stamping his feet and shaking the sand from his burnoose. As he came forward to take her hand, she cried: "Oh, Slimane, it's my fault! I forgot to tell Boufelja. It's terrible!"

"There is no fault, madame," he said gravely. "This is a festival."

"Yes, this is a festival," she echoed. "And the wind's still blowing. Listen!"

Slimane would not take coffee, but Boufelja, ceding to her pressure, let her pour him out a cup, which he drank standing by the fireplace. She suspected him of being secretly pleased that Slimane had not managed to eat with her. When he had finished his coffee, he wished them good-night and went off to bed in his little room next to the kitchen.

They sat a while watching the fire, without talking. The wind rushed past in the emptiness outside, the blinds hammered. Fräulein Windling was content. Even if the first part of the celebration had gone wrong, the rest of the evening could still be pleasant.

She waited until she was sure that Boufelja had really gone to bed, and then she reached into her bag and brought out a small plastic sack full of chocolate creams, which she placed on the table.

"Eat," she said carelessly, and she took a piece of candy herself. With some hesitation Slimane put out his hand to take the sack. When he had a chocolate in his mouth, she began to speak. She intended to tell him the story of the Nativity, a subject she already had touched upon many times during their excursions, but only in passing. This time she felt she should tell him the entire tale. She expected him to interrupt when he discovered that it was a religious story, but he merely kept his noncommittal eyes on her and chewed mechanically, showing that he followed her by occasionally nodding his head. She became engrossed in what she was saying, and began to use her arms in wide gestures. Slimane reached for another chocolate and went on listening.

She talked for an hour or more, aware as from a distance of her own eloquence. When she told him about Bethlehem she was really describing Slimane's own village, and the house of Joseph and Mary was the house down in the *ksar* where Slimane had been born. The night sky arched above the Oued Zousfana and its stars glared down upon the cold hammada. Across the erg on their camels came the Wise Men in their burnooses and turbans, pausing at the crest of the last great dune to look ahead at the valley where the dark village lay. When she had finished, she blew her nose.

Slimane appeared to be in a state bordering on trance. She glanced at him, expected him to speak, but as he did not, she looked more closely at him. His eyes had an obsessed, vacant expression, and although they were still fixed on her face, she would have said that he was seeing something much farther away than she. She sighed, not wanting to make the decision to rouse him. The possibility she would have liked to entertain, had she not been so conscious of its unlikelihood, was that the boy somehow had been captivated by the poetic truth of the story, and was reviewing it in his imagination. "Certainly it could not be the case," she decided; it was more likely that he had ceased some time back to listen to her words, and was merely sitting there, only vaguely aware that she had come to the end of her story.

Then he spoke. "You're right. He was the King of Men."

Fräulein Windling caught her breath and leaned forward, but he went on. "And later Satan sent a snake with two heads. And Jesus killed it. Satan was angry with Him. He said: 'Why did you kill my friend? Did it hurt you, perhaps?' And Jesus said: 'I knew where it came from.' And Satan put on a black burnoose. That's true," he added, as he saw the expression of what he took to be simple disbelief on her face.

She sat up very straight and said: "Slimane, what are you talking about? There are no such stories about Jesus. Nor about Sidna Aissa either." She was not sure of the accuracy of this last statement; it was possible, she supposed, that such legends did exist among these people. "You know those are just stories that have nothing to do with the truth."

He did not hear her because he had already begun to talk. "I'm not speaking of Sidna Aissa," he said firmly. "He was a Moslem prophet. I'm talking about Jesus, the prophet of the Nazarenes. Everyone knows that Satan sent Him a snake with two heads."

She listened to the wind for an instant. "Ah," she said, and took another chocolate; she did not intend to carry the argument further. Soon she dug into her bag again and pulled out the turban, wrapped in red and white tissue paper.

"A present for you," she said, holding it out to him. He seized it mechanically, placed it on his lap and remained staring down at it. "Aren't you going to open it?" she demanded.

He nodded his head twice and tore open the paper. When he saw the pile of white cotton he smiled. Seeing his face at last come to life, she jumped up. "Let's put it on you!" she exclaimed. He gave her one end, which she pulled taut by walking all the way to the door. Then with his hand holding the other end to his forehead, he turned slowly round and round, going toward her all the time, arranging the form of the turban as it wound itself about his head. "Magnificent!" she cried. He went over to the row of black windows to look at himself.

"Can you see?" she asked.

"Yes, I can see the sides of it," he told her. "It's very beautiful."

She walked back toward the center of the room. "I'd like to take your picture, Slimane," she said, seeing an immediate look of puzzlement appear in his face. "Would you do me a favor? Go to my room and get the camera."

"At night? You can take a picture at night?"

She nodded, smiling mysteriously. "And bring me the yellow box on the bed."

Keeping the turban on his head, he got into his burnoose, took her flashlight and went out, letting the wind slam the door. She hoped the sound had not wakened Boufelja; for an instant she listened while there was no sound but the roar of air rushing through the corridor outside. Then she ran to the dark wing of the room and struck a match. Quickly she lighted all the candles around the crèche, straightened a camel in the sand, and walked back around the corner to the fireplace. She would not have thought the candles could give so much light. The other end of the room was now brighter than the end where she stood. In a moment the door burst open and Slimane came back in, carrying the camera slung over his shoulder. He put it down carefully on the table. "There was no yellow box on the bed," he told her. Then his glance caught the further walls flickering with the unfamiliar light, and he began to walk toward the center of the room. She saw that this was the moment. "Come," she said, taking his arm and pulling him gently around the corner to where the crèche was finally visible, bright with its multiple shuddering points of light. Slimane said nothing; he stopped walking and stood completely still. After a moment of silence, she plucked tentatively at his arm. "Come and see," she urged him. They continued to walk toward the crèche; as they came up to it she had the impression that if she had not been there he would have reached out his hand and touched it, perhaps would have lifted the tiny gold-clad infant Jesus out of His bed of feathers. But he stood quietly, looking at it. Finally he said: "You brought all that from Switzerland?"

"Of course not!" It was a little disappointing that he should not have recognized the presence of the desert in the picture, should not have sensed that the thing was of his place, and not an importation. "I made it all here," she said. She waited an instant. "Do you like it?"

"Ah, yes," he said with feeling. "It's beautiful. I thought it came from Switzerland."

To be certain that he understood the subject-matter, she began to identify the figures one by one, her voice taking on such an unaccustomed inflection of respect that he glanced up at her once in surprise. It was almost as if she too were seeing it for the first time. "And the Wise Men are coming down out of the erg to see the child."

"Why did you put all those almonds there?" asked Slimane, touching some with his forefinger.

"They're gifts for the little Jesus."

"But what are you going to do with them?" he pursued.

"Eat them, probably, later," she said shortly. "Take one if you like. You say there was no yellow box on the bed?" She wanted to take the photographs while the candles were still of equal height.

"There was nothing but a sweater and some papers, madame."

She left him there by the crèche, crossed the room and put on her burnoose. The darkness in the corridor was complete; there was no sign that Boufelja had awakened. She knew her room was in great disorder, and she played the beam of the flashlight around the floor before entering. In the welter of displaced things that strewed the little room there seemed small chance of finding anything. The feeble ray illumined one by one the meaningless forms made by the piling of disparate objects one on the other; the light moved over the floor, along the bed, behind the flimsy curtain of the armoire. Suddenly she stopped and turned the beam under the bed. The box was in front of her face; she had put it with the crèche.

"I mustn't fall," she thought, running along the corridor. She forced herself to slow her pace to a walk, entered the dining-room and shut the door after her carefully. Slimane was on his knees in the middle of the room, a small object of some sort in his hand. She noted with relief that he was amusing himself. "I'm sorry it took me so long," she exclaimed. "I'd forgotten where I'd put it." She was pulling her burnoose off over her head; now she hung it on a nail by the fireplace, and taking up the camera and the yellow box, she walked over to join him.

Perhaps a faint glimmer of guilt in his expression as he glanced up made her eyes stray along the floor toward another object lying nearby, similar to the one he held in his hand. It was one of the Wise Men, severed at the hips from his mount. The Wise Man in Slimane's hand was intact, but the camel had lost its head and most of its neck.

"Slimane! What are you doing?" she cried with undisguised anger. "What have you done to the crèche?" She advanced around the corner and looked in its direction. There was not really much more than a row of candles and a pile of sand that had been strewn with tangerine peel and date stones; here and there a carefully folded square of lavender or pink tinfoil had been planted in the sand. All three of the Wise Men had been enlisted in Slimane's battle on the floor, the tent ravaged in the campaign to extricate the almonds piled inside, and the treasure sacks looted of their chocolate liqueurs. There was no sign anywhere of the infant Jesus or his gold-lamé garment. She felt tears come into her eyes. Then she laughed shortly, and said: "Well, it's finished. Yes?"

"Yes, madame," he said calmly. "Are you going to make the photograph now?" He got to his feet and laid the broken camel on the platform in the sand with the other debris.

Fräulein Windling spoke evenly. "I wanted to take a picture of the crèche."

He waited an instant, as if he were listening to a distant sound. Then he said: "Should I put on my burnoose?"

"No." She began to take out the flash-bulb attachment. When she had it ready, she took the picture before he had time to strike a pose. She saw his astonishment at the sudden bright light prolong itself into surprise that the thing was already done, and then become resentment at having been caught off his guard; but pretending to have seen nothing, she went on snapping covers shut. He watched her as she gathered up her things. "Is it finished?" he said, disappointed. "Yes," she replied. "It will be a very good picture."

"Incha' Allah."

She did not echo his piety. "I hope you've enjoyed the festival," she told him.

Slimane smiled widely. "Ah yes, madame. Very much. Thank you."

She let him out into the camel-square and turned the lock in the door. Quickly she went back into her room, wishing it were a clear night like other nights, when she could stand out on the terrace and look at the dunes and stars, or sit on the roof and hear the dogs, for in spite of the hour she was not sleepy. She cleared her bed of all the things that lay on top of it, and got in, certain that she was going to lie awake for a long time. For it had shaken her, the chaos Slimane had made in those few minutes of her absence. Across the seasons of their friendship she had come to think of him as being very nearly like herself, even though she knew he had not been that way when she first had met him. Now she saw the dangerous vanity at the core of that fantasy: she had assumed that somehow his association with her had automatically been for his ultimate good, that inevitably he had been undergoing a process of improvement as a result of knowing her. In her desire to see him change, she had begun to forget what Slimane was really like. "I shall never understand him," she thought helplessly, sure that just because she felt so close to him she would never be able to observe him dispassionately.

"This is the desert," she told herself. Here food is not an adornment; it is meant to be eaten. She had spread out food and he had eaten it. Any argument which attached blame to that could only be false. And so she lay there accusing herself. "It has been too much head and high ideals," she reflected, "and not enough heart." Finally she traveled on the sound of the wind into sleep.

At dawn when she awoke she saw that the day was going to be another dark one. The wind had dropped. She got up and shut the window. The early morning sky was heavy with clouds. She sank back into bed and fell asleep. It was later than usual when she rose, dressed, and went into the dining-room. Boufelja's face was strangely expressionless as he wished her good morning. She supposed it was the memory of last night's misunderstanding, still with him—or possibly he was annoyed at having had to clean up the remains of the crèche. Once she had sat down and spread her napkin across her lap, he unbent sufficiently to say to her: "Happy festival."

"Thank you. Tell me, Boufelja," she went on, changing her inflection. "When you brought Slimane back in after dinner last night, do you know where he had been? Did he tell you?"

"He's a stupid boy," said Boufelja. "I told him to go home and eat and come back later. You think he did that? Never. He walked the whole time up and down in the courtyard here, outside the kitchen door, in the dark."

"I understand!" exclaimed Fräulein Windling triumphantly. "So he had no dinner at all."

"I had nothing to give him," he began, on the defensive.

"Of course not," she said sternly. "He should have gone home and eaten."

"Ah, you see?" grinned Boufleja. "That's what I told him to do."

In her mind she watched the whole story being enacted: Slimane aloofly informing his father that he would be eating at the hotel with the Swiss lady, the old man doubtless making some scornful reference to her, and Slimane going out. Unthinkable, once he had been refused admittance to the dining-room, for him to go back and face the family's ridicule. "Poor boy," she murmured.

"The commandant wants to see you," said Boufelja, making one of his abrupt conversational changes. She was surprised, since from one year to the next the captain never gave any sign of being aware of her existence; the hotel and the fort were like two separate countries. "Perhaps for the festival," Boufelja suggested, his face a mask. "Perhaps," she said uneasily.

When she had finished her breakfast, she walked across to the gates of the fort. The sentry seemed to be expecting her. One of the two young French soldiers was in the compound painting a chair. He greeted her, saying that the captain was in his office. She went up the long flight of stairs and paused an instant at the top, looking down at the valley in the unaccustomed gray light, noting how totally different it looked from its usual self, on this dim day.

A voice from inside called out: "*Entrez, s'il vous plait!*" She opened the door and stepped in. The captain sat behind his desk; she had the unwelcome sensation of having played this same scene on another occasion, in another place. And she was suddenly convinced that she knew what he was going to say. She seized the back of the empty chair facing his desk. "Sit down, Mademoiselle Windling," he said, rising halfway out of his seat, waving his arm, and sitting again quickly.

There were several topographical maps on the wall behind him, marked with lavender and green chalk. The captain looked at his desk and then at her, and said in a clear voice: "It is an unfortunate stroke of chance that I should have to call you here on this holiday." Fräulein Windling sat down in the chair; leaning forward, she seemed about to rest her elbow on his desk, but instead crossed her legs and folded her arms tight. "Yes?" she said, tense, waiting for the message. It came immediately, for which she was conscious, even then, of being grateful to him. He told her simply that the entire area had been closed to civilians; this order applied to French nationals as well as to foreigners, so she must not feel discriminated against. The last was said with a wry attempt at a smile. "This means that you will have to take tomorrow morning's truck," he continued. "The driver has already been advised of your journey. Perhaps another year, when the disturbances are over. . . ." ("Why does he say that?" she thought, "when he knows it's the end, and the time of friendship is finished?") He rose and extended his hand.

She could not remember going out of the room and down the long stairway into the compound, but now she was standing outside the sentry gate beside the wall of the fort, with her hand on her forehead. "Already," she thought. "It came so soon." And it occurred to her that she was not going to be given the time to make amends to Slimane, so that it was really true she was never going to understand him. She walked up to the parapet to look down at the edge of the oasis for a moment, and then went back to her room to start packing.

All day long she worked in her room, pulling out boxes, forcing herself to be aware only of the decisions she was making as to what was to be taken and what was to be left behind once and for all.

At lunchtime Boufelja hovered near her chair. "Ah, mademoiselle, how many years we have been together, and now it is finished!" "Yes," she thought, but there was nothing to do about it. His lamentations made her nervous and she was short with him. Then she felt guilt-stricken and said slowly, looking directly at him: "I am very sad, Boufelja." He sighed "Ay, mademoiselle, I know!"

By nightfall the pall of clouds had been blown away across the desert, and the western sky was partly clear. Fräulein Windling had finished all her packing. She went out onto the terrace, saw the dunes pink and glowing, and climbed the steps to the roof to look at the sunset. Great skeins of fiery storm-cloud streaked the sky. Mechanically she let her gaze follow the meanders of the river valley as it lost itself in the darkening hammada to the south. "It is in the past," she reminded herself; this was already the new era. The desert out there looked the same as it always had looked. But the sky, ragged, red and black, was like a handbill that had just been posted above it, announcing the arrival of war.

It was a betrayal, she was thinking, going back down the steep stairs, running her hand along the familiar rough mud wall to steady herself, and the French of course were the culprits. But beyond that she had the irrational and disagreeable conviction that the countryside itself had connived in the betrayal, that it was waiting to be transformed by the struggle. She went into her room and lit the small oil lamp; sitting down, she held her hands over it to warm them. At some point there had been a change: the people no longer wanted to go on living in the world they knew. The pressure of the past had become too great, and its shell had broken.

In the afternoon she had sent Boufelja to tell Slimane the news, and to ask him to be at the hotel at daybreak. During dinner she discussed only the details of departure and travel; when Boufelja tried to pull the talk in emotional directions, she did not reply. His commiseration was intolerable; she was not used to giving voice to her despair. When she got to her room she went directly to bed. The dogs barked half the night.

It was cold in the morning. Her hands ached as she gathered up the wet objects from around the washbowl on the table, and somehow she drove a sliver deep under the nail of her thumb. She picked some of it out with a needle, but the greater part remained. Before breakfast she stepped outside.

Standing in the waste-land between the hotel and the fort, she looked down at the countryside's innocent face. The padlocked gasoline pump, triumphant in fresh red and orange paint, caught the pure early sunlight. For a moment it seemed the only living thing in the landscape. She turned around. Above the dark irregular mass of palm trees rose the terraced village, calm under its morning veil of woodsmoke. She shut her eyes for an instant, and then went into the hotel.

She could feel herself sitting stiffly in her chair while she drank her coffee, and she knew she was being distant and formal with Boufelja, but it was the only way she could be certain of being able to keep going. Once he came to tell her that Slimane had arrived bringing the donkey and its master for her luggage. She thanked him and set down her coffee cup. "More?" said Boufelja. "No," she answered. "Drink another, mademoiselle," he urged her. "It's good on a cold morning." He poured it out and she drank part of it. There was a knocking at the gate. One of the young soldiers had been sent with a jeep to carry her out to the truck-stop on the trail.

"I can't!" she cried, thinking of Slimane and the donkey. The young soldier made it clear that he was not making an offer, but giving an order. Slimane stood beside the donkey outside the gate. While she began to speak with him the soldier shouted: "Does he want to come, the *gosse?* He can come too, if he likes." Slimane ran to get the luggage and Fräulein Windling rushed inside to settle her bill. "Don't hurry," the soldier called after her. "There's plenty of time."

Boufelja stood in the kitchen doorway. Now for the first time it occurred to her to wonder what was going to become of him. With the hotel shut he would have no work. When she had settled her account and given him a tip which was much larger than she could afford, she took both his hands in hers and said: "*Mon cher* Boufelja, we shall see one another very soon."

"Ah, yes," he cried, trying to smile. "Very soon, mademoiselle."

She gave the donkey-driver some money, and got into the jeep beside the soldier. Slimane had finished bringing out the luggage and stood behind the jeep, kicking the tires. "Have you got everything?" she called to him. "Everything?" She would have liked to see for herself, but she was loath to go back into the room. Boufelja had disappeared; now he came hurrying out, breathless, carrying a pile of old magazines. "It's all right," she said. "No, no! I don't want them." The jeep was already moving ahead down the hill. In what seemed to her an unreasonably short time they had reached the boulders. When Fràulein Windling tried to lift out her briefcase the pain of the sliver under her nail made the tears start to her eyes, and she let go with a cry. Slimane glanced at her, surprised. "I hurt my hand," she explained. "It's nothing."

The bags had been piled in the shade. Sitting on a rock near the jeep, the soldier faced Fräulein Windling; from time to time he scanned the horizon behind her for a sign of the truck. Slimane examined the jeep from all sides; eventually he came to sit nearby. They did not say very much to one another. She was not sure whether it was because of the soldier with them, or because her thumb ached so constantly, but she sat quietly waiting, not wanting to talk.

It was a long time before the far-off motor made itself heard. When the truck was still no more than a puff of dust between sky and earth, the soldier was on his feet watching; an instant later Slimane jumped up. "It is coming, madame," he said. Then he bent over, putting his face very close to hers. "I want to go with you to Colomb-Bechar," he whispered. When she did not respond, because she was seeing the whole story of their friendship unrolled before her, from the its end back to its beginning, he said louder, with great urgency: "Please, madame."

Fräulein Windling hesitated only an instant. She raised her head and looked carefully at the smooth brown face that was so near. "Of course, Slimane," she said. It was clear that he had not expected to hear this; his delight was infectious, and she smiled as she watched him run to the pile of bags and begin carrying them out into the sunlight to align them in the dust beside the edge of the trail.

Later, when they were rattling along the hammada, she in front beside the driver and Slimane squatting in the back with a dozen men and a sheep, she considered her irresponsible action in allowing him to make this absurd trip with her all the way to Colomb-Bechar. Still, she knew she wanted to give this ending to their story. A few times she turned partially around in her seat to glance at him through the dirty glass. He sat there in the smoke and dust, laughing like the others, with the hood of his burnoose hiding most of his face.

It had been raining in Colomb-Bechar; the streets were great puddles to reflect the clouded sky. At the garage they found a surly Negro boy to help them carry the luggage to the railway station. Her thumb hurt a little less.

"It's a cold town," Slimane said to her as they went down the main street. At the station they checked the bags and then went outside to stand and watch a car being unloaded from an open freight train: the roof of the automobile was still white with snow from the high steppes. The day was dark, and the wind rippled the surface of the water in the flooded empty lots. Fräulein Windling's train would not be leaving until late in the afternoon. They went to a restaurant and ate a long lunch.

"You really will go back home tomorrow?" she asked him anxiously at one point, while they were having fruit. "You know we have done a very wicked thing to your father and mother. They will never forgive me." A curtain seemed to draw across Slimane's face. "It doesn't matter," he said shortly.

After lunch they walked in the public garden and looked at the eagles in their cages. A fine rain had begun to be carried on the wind. The mud of the paths grew deeper. They went back to the center of the town and sat down on the terrace of a large, shabby modern café. The table at the end was partly sheltered from the wet wind; they faced an empty lot strewn with refuse. Nearby, spread out like the bones of a camel fallen on the trail, were the rusted remains of an ancient bus. A long, newly-felled date palm lay diagonally across the greater part of the lot. Fräulein Windling turned to look at the wet orange fiber of the stump, and felt an idle pity for the tree. "I'm going to have a Coca-Cola," she declared. Slimane said he, too, would like one.

They sat there a long time. The fine rain slanted through the air outside the arcades and hit the ground silently. She had expected to be approached by beggars, but none arrived, and now that the time had come to leave the café and go to the station she was thankful to see that the day had passed so easily. She opened her pocket-book, took out three thousand francs, and handed them to Slimane, saying: "This will be enough for everything. But you must buy your ticket back home today. When you leave the railway station. Be very careful of it."

Slimane put the money inside his garments, rearranged his burnoose, and thanked her. "You understand, Slimane," she said, detaining him with her hand, for he seemed about to rise from the table. "I'm not giving you any money now, because I need what I have for my journey. But when I get to Switzerland I shall send you a little, now and then. Not much. A little."

His face was swept by panic; she was perplexed.

"You haven't got my address," he told her.

"No, but I shall send it to Boufelja's house," she said, thinking that would satisfy him. He leaned toward her, his eyes intense. "No, madame," he said with finality. "No. I have your address, and I shall send you mine. Then you will have it, and you can write to me."

It did not seem worth arguing about. For most of the afternoon her thumb had not hurt too much; now, as the day waned, it had begun to ache again. She wanted to get up, find the waiter, and pay him. The fine rain still blew; the station was fairly far. But she saw Slimane had something more to say. He leaned forward in his chair and looked down at the floor. "Madame." he began.

"Yes?" she said.

"When you are in your country and you think of me you will not be happy. It's true, no?"

"I shall be very sad," she answered, rising.

Slimane got slowly to his feet and was quiet for an instant before going on. "Sad because I ate the food out of the picture. That was very bad. Forgive me."

The shrill sound of her own voice exclaiming, "No!" startled her. "No!" she cried. "That was good!" She felt the muscles of her cheeks and lips twisting themselves into grimaces of weeping; fiercely she seized his arm and looked down into his face. "*Oh, mon pauvre petit!*" she sobbed, and then covered her face with both hands. She felt him gently touching her sleeve. A truck went by in the main street, shaking the floor.

With an effort she turned away and scratched in her bag for a handkerchief. "Come," she said, clearing her throat. "Call the waiter."

They arrived at the station cold and wet. The train was being assembled; passengers were not allowed to go out onto the platform and were sitting on the floor inside. While Fräulein Windling bought her ticket Slimane went to get the bags from the checkroom. He was gone for a long time. When he arrived he came with his burnoose thrown back over his shoulders, grinning triumphantly, with three valises piled on his head. A man in ragged European jacket and trousers followed behind carrying the rest. As he came nearer she saw that the man held a slip of paper between his teeth.

The ancient compartment smelled of varnish. Through the window she could see, above some remote western reach of waste-land, a few strips of watery white sky. Slimane wanted to cover the seats with the luggage, so that no one would come into the compartment. "No," she said. "Put them in the racks." There were very few passengers in the coach. When everything was in place, the porter stood outside in the corridor and she noticed that he still held the slip of paper between his teeth. He counted the coins she gave him and pocketed them. Then quickly he handed the paper to Slimane, and was gone.

Fräulein Windling bent down a bit, to try and see her face in the narrow mirror that ran along the back of the seat. There was not enough light; the oil lantern above illumined only the ceiling, its base casting a leaden shadow over everything beneath. Suddenly the train jolted and made a series of crashing sounds. She took Slimane's head between her hands and kissed the middle of his forehead. "Please get down from the train," she told him. "We can talk here." She pointed to the window and began to pull on the torn leather strap that lowered it.

Slimane looked small on the dark platform, staring up at her as she leaned out. Then the train started to move. She thought surely it would go only a few feet and then stop, but it continued ahead, slowly. Slimane walked with it, keeping abreast of her window. In his hand was the paper the porter had given him. He held it up to her, crying: "Here is my address! Send it here!"

She took it, and kept waving as the train went faster, kept calling: "Good-by!" He continued to walk quickly along beside the window, increasing his gait until he was running, until all at once there was no more platform. She leaned far out, looking backward, waving; straightway he was lost in the darkness and rain. A bonfire blazed orange by the track, and the smoke stung in her nostrils. She pulled up the window, glanced at the slip of paper she had in her hand, and sat down. The train jolted her this way and that; she went on staring at the paper, although now it was in shadow; and she remembered the first day, long ago, when the child Slimane had stood outside the door watching her, stepping back out of her range of vision each time she turned to look at him. The words hastily printed for him on the scrap of paper by the porter were indeed an address, but the address was in Colomb-Bechar. "They said he tried to run away. But he didn't get very far." Each detail of his behavior as she went back over it clarified the pattern for her. "He's too young to be a soldier," she told herself. "They won't take him." But she knew they would.

Her thumb was hot and swollen; sometimes it seemed almost that its throbbing accompanied the side-to-side jolting of the coach. She looked out at the few remaining patches of colorless light in the sky. Sooner or later, she argued, he would have done it.

"Another year, perhaps," the captain had said. She saw her own crooked, despairing smile in the dark window-glass beside her face. Maybe Slimane would be among the fortunate ones, an early casualty. "If only death were absolutely certain in wartime," she thought wryly, "the waiting would not be so painful." Listing and groaning, the train began its long climb upwards over the plateau.

Tangier, 1962

THE GARDEN

PAUL BOWLES

A MAN WHO LIVED in a distant town of the southern country was working in his garden. Because he was poor his land was at the edge of the oasis. All the afternoon he dug channels, and when the day was finished he went to the upper end of the garden and opened the gate that held back the water. And now the water ran in the channels to the beds of barley and the young pomegranate trees. The sky was red, and when the man saw the floor of his garden shining like jewels, he sat down on a stone to look at it. As he watched, it grew brighter, and he thought: "There is no finer garden in the oasis."

A great happiness filled him, and he sat there a long time, and did not get home until very late. When he went into the house, his wife looked at him and saw the joy still in his eyes.

"He has found a treasure," she thought; but she said nothing.

When they sat face to face at the evening meal, the man was still remembering his garden, and it seemed to him that now that he had known this happiness, never again would he be without it. He was silent as he ate.

His wife too was silent. "He is thinking of the treasure," she said to herself. And she was angry, believing that he did not want to share his secret with her. The next morning she went to the house of an old woman and bought many herbs and powders from her. She took them home and passed several days mixing and cooking them, until she had made the medicine she wanted. Then at each meal she began to put a little of the *tseuheur* into her husband's food.

It was not long before the man fell ill. For a time he went each day to his garden to work, but often when he got there he was so weak that he could merely sit leaning against a palm tree. He had a sharp sound in his ears, and he could not follow his thoughts as they came to him. In spite of this, each day when the sun went down and he saw his garden shining red in its light, he was happy. And when he got home at night his wife could see that there was joy in his eyes.

"He has been counting the treasure," she thought, and she began to go secretly to the garden to watch him from behind the trees. When she saw that he merely sat looking at the ground, she went back to the old woman and told her about it.

"You must hurry and make him talk, before he forgets where he has hidden the treasure," said the old woman.

That night the wife put a great amount of *tseuheur* into his food, and when they were drinking tea afterward she began to say many sweet words to him. The man only smiled. She tried for a long time to make him speak, but he merely shrugged his shoulders and made motions with his hands.

The next morning while he was still asleep, she went back to the old woman and told her that the man could no longer speak.

"You have given him too much," the old woman said. "He will never tell you his secret now. The only thing for you to do is go away quickly, before he dies."

The woman ran home. Her husband lay on the mat with his mouth open. She packed her clothing and left the town that morning.

For three days the man lay in a deep sleep. The fourth day when he awoke, it was as if he had made a voyage to the other side of the world. He was very hungry, but all he could find in the house was a piece of dry bread. When he had eaten that, he walked to his garden at the edge of the oasis and picked many figs. Then he sat down and ate them. In his mind there was no thought of his wife, because he had forgotten her. When a neighbor came by and called to him, he answered politely, as if speaking to a stranger, and the neighbor went away perplexed.

Little by little the man grew healthy once more. He worked each day in the garden. When dusk came, after watching the sunset and the red water, he would go home and cook his dinner and sleep. He had no friends, because although men spoke to him, he did not know who they were, and he only smiled and nodded to them. Then the people in the town began to notice that he no longer went to the mosque to pray. They spoke about this among themselves, and one evening the imam went to the man's house to talk with him.

As they sat there, the imam listened for sounds of the man's wife in the house. Out of courtesy he could not mention her, but he was thinking about her and asking himself where she might be. He went away from the house full of doubts.

The man went on living his life. But the people of the town now talked of little else. They whispered that he had killed his wife, and many of them wanted to go together and search the house for her remains. The imam spoke against this idea, saying that he would go and talk again with the man. And this time he went all the way to the garden at the edge of the oasis, and found him there working happily with the plants and the trees. He watched him for a while, and then he walked closer and spoke a few words with him.

It was late in the afternoon. The sun was sinking in the west, and the water on the ground began to be red. Presently the man said to the imam: "The garden is beautiful."

"Beautiful or not beautiful," said the imam, "you should be giving thanks to Allah for allowing you to have it."

"Allah?" said the man. "Who is that? I never heard of him. I made this garden myself. I dug every channel and planted every tree, and no one helped me. I have no debts to anyone."

The imam had turned pale. He flung out his arm and struck the man very hard in the face. Then he went quickly out of the garden.

The man stood with his hand to his cheek. "He has gone mad," he thought, as the imam walked away.

That night the people spoke together in the mosque. They decided that the man could no longer live in their town. Early the next morning a great crowd of men, with the imam going at the head of it, went out into the oasis, on its way to the man's garden.

The small boys ran ahead of the men, and got there long before them. They hid in the bushes, and as the man worked they began to throw stones and shout insults at him. He paid no attention to them. Then a stone hit the back of his head. He jumped up quickly. As they ran away, one of them fell, and the man caught him. He tried to hold him still so he could ask him: "Why are you throwing stones at me?" But the boy only screamed and struggled.

And the townspeople, who were on their way, heard the screaming, and they came running to the garden. They pulled the boy away from him and began to strike at the man with hoes and sickles. When they had destroyed him, they left him there with his head lying in one of the channels, and went back to the town, giving thanks to Allah that the boy was safe.

Little by little the trees died, and very soon the garden was gone. Only the desert was there.

Asilah, 1963

MEJDOUB

PAUL BOWLES

A MAN WHO SPENT his nights sleeping in cafés or under the trees or wherever he happened to be at the time when he felt sleepy, wandered one morning through the streets of the town. He came to the market place, where an old mejdoub dressed in rags cavorted before the populace, screaming prophecies into the air. He stood watching until the old man had finished and gathered up the money the people offered him. It astonished him to see how much the madman had collected, and having nothing else to do, he decided to follow him.

Almost before he got out of the market he was aware that small boys were hurrying from under the arcades to run alongside the mejdoub, who merely strode forward, chanting and waving his sceptre, and from time to time threatening the children who came too close. Walking at some distance behind, he saw the old man go into several shops. He came out each time with a banknote in his hand, which he promptly gave to one of the small boys.

It occurred to him then that there was much he could learn from this mejdoub. He had only to study the old man's behavior and listen carefully to the words he uttered. Then with practice he himself could make the same gestures and shout the same words. He began to look each day for the mejdoub and to follow him wherever he went in the town. At the end of a month he decided that he was ready to put his knowledge to use.

He travelled south to another city where he had never gone before. Here he took a very cheap room by the slaughterhouse, far from the center of town. In the flea-market he bought an old and tattered djellaba. Then he went to the iron-mongers and stood watching while they made him a long sceptre like the one the mejdoub had carried.

The next day, after practicing for a while, he went into the town and sat down in the street at the foot of the largest mosque. For a while he merely looked at the people going past. Slowly he began to raise his arms to the sky, and then to gesture with them. No one paid him any attention. This reassured him, as it meant that his disguise was successful. When he began to shout words the passers-by looked toward him, but it was as if they could not see him, and were only waiting to hear what he had to say. For a time he shouted short quotations from the Koran. He moved his eyes in a circular motion and let his turban fall over his face. After crying the words *fire* and *blood* several times he lowered his arms and bent his head, and said no more. The people moved on, but not before many of them had tossed coins on the ground in front of him.

On succeeding days he tried other parts of the city. It did not seem to matter where he sat. The people were generous to him in one place the same as in another. He did not want to risk going into the shops and cafés until he was certain that the town had grown used to his presence. One day he stormed through the streets, shaking his sceptre to the sky and screaming: Sidi Rahal is here! Sidi Rahal tells you to prepare for the fire! This was in order to give himself a name for the townspeople to remember.

He began to stand in the doorways of shops. If he heard anyone refer to him as Sidi Rahal, he would step inside, glare at the proprietor, and without saying a word, hold out his hand. The man would give him money, and he would turn and walk out.

For some reason no children followed him. He would have been happier to have a group of them with him, like the old mejdoub, but as soon as he spoke to them, they were frightened and ran away. It's quieter like this, he told himself, but secretly it bothered him. Still, he was earning more money that he ever had thought possible. By the time the first rains arrived, he had saved up a large sum. Leaving his sceptre and ragged djellaba in his room by the slaughterhouse, he paid the landlord several months' rent in advance. He waited until night. Then he locked the door behind him and took a bus back to his own city.

First he bought a great variety of clothing. When he was richly dressed he went out and looked for a house. Soon he found one that suited him. It was small and he had enough money left to pay for it. He furnished two rooms and prepared to spend the winter eating and smoking kif with all his old friends.

When they asked him where he had been all summer, he spoke of the hospitality and generosity of his wealthy brother in Taza. Already he was impatient for the rains to stop. For there was no doubt that he truly enjoyed his new work.

The winter finally came to an end. He packed his bag and told his friends that he was going on a business trip. In the other town he walked to the room. His djellaba and sceptre were there.

This year many more people recognized him. He grew bolder and entered the shops without waiting in the doorways. The shopkeepers, eager to show their piety to the customers, always gave a good deal more than the passers-by.

One day he decided to make a test. He hailed a taxi. As he got in he bellowed: I must go to Sidi Larbi's tomb! Fast! The driver, who knew he was not going to be paid, nevertheless agreed, and they rode out to a grove of olive trees on a hill far from the town.

He told the driver to wait, and jumped out of the taxi. Then he began the long climb up the hill to the tomb. The driver lost patience and drove off. On the way back to the town he missed a curve and hit a tree. When he was let out of the hospital he spread the word that Sidi Rahal had caused the car to go off the road. Men talked at length about it, recalling other holy maniacs who had put spells on motors and brakes. The name of Sidi Rahal was on everyone's lips, and people listened respectfully to his rantings.

That summer he amassed more money than the year before. He returned home and bought a larger house to live in, while he rented out the first one. Each year he bought more houses and lands, until finally it was clear that he had become a very prosperous man.

Always when the first rains fell he would announce to his friends that he was about to travel abroad. Then he would leave secretly, never allowing anyone to see him off. He was delighted with the pattern of his life, and with the good luck he had been granted in being able to continue it. He assumed that Allah did not mind if he pretended to be one of His holy maniacs. The money was merely his reward for providing men with an opportunity to exercise their charity.

One winter a new government came to power and announced that all beggars were to be taken off the streets. He talked about this with his friends, all of whom thought it an excellent thing. He agreed with them, but the news kept him from sleeping at night. To risk everything by going back, merely because that was what he wanted to do, was out of the question. Sadly he resigned himself to spending the summer at home.

It was not until the first few weeks of spring had gone by that he realized how close it had been to his heart, the starting out on a fine starry night to go in the bus to the other city, and what a relief it had been each time to be able to forget everything and live as Sidi Rahal. Now he began to understand that his life here at home had been a pleasure only because he had known that at a certain moment he was going to leave it for the other life.

As the hot weather came on he grew increasingly restless. He was bored and lost his appetite. His friends, noticing the change in him, advised him to travel, as he always had done. They said that men had been known to die as a result of breaking a habit. Again he lay awake at night worrying, and then secretly he determined to go back. As soon as he had made the decision he felt much better. It was as though until then he had been asleep, and suddenly had awakened. He announced to his friends that he was going abroad.

That very night he locked up his house and got onto a bus. The next day he strode joyously through the streets to sit in his favorite spot by the mosque. Passers-by looked at him and remarked to one another: He's back again, after all. You see?

He sat there quietly all day, collecting money. At the end of the afternoon, since the weather was very hot, he walked down to the river outside the gates of the town, in order to bathe. As he was undressing behind some oleander bushes, he glanced up and saw three policemen coming down the bank toward him. Without waiting he seized his slippers, threw his djellaba over his shoulder, and began to run.

Sometimes he splashed into the water, and sometimes he slipped in the mud and fell. He could hear the men shouting after him. They did not chase him very far, for they were laughing. Not knowing this, he kept on running, following the river, until he was breathless and had to stop. He put on the djellaba and the slippers, thinking: I can't go back to the town, or to any other town, in these clothes.

He continued at a slower gait. When evening came he was hungry, but there were no people or houses in sight. He slept under a tree, with only the ragged djellaba to cover him.

The next morning his hunger had grown. He got up, bathed in the river, and set out again. All that day he walked under the hot sun. In the late afternoon he sat down to rest. He drank a little water from the river and looked around him at the countryside. On the hill behind him stood a partially ruined shrine.

When he was rested, he climbed up to the building. There was a tomb inside, in the center of the big domed room. He sat down and listened. Cocks crowed, and he heard the occasional barking of dogs. He imagined himself running to the village, crying to the first man he met: Give me a piece of bread, for the love of Moulay Abdelqader! He shut his eyes.

It was nearly twilight when he awoke. Outside the door stood a group of small boys, watching him. Seeing him awaken, they laughed and nudged one another. Then one boy tossed in a piece of dry bread, so that it fell beside him. Soon they were all chanting: He's eating bread! He's eating bread!

They played the game for a while, throwing in clods of earth and even uprooted plants along with the scraps of bread. In their faces he could read wonder, malice and contempt, and shining through these shifting emotions the steady gleam of ownership. He thought of the old mejdoub, and a shiver ran through him. Suddenly they had gone. He heard a few shrill cries in the distance as they raced back to the village.

The bread had given him a little nourishment. He slept where he was, and before it grew light he set out again along the river, giving thanks to Allah for having allowed him to get beyond the village without being seen. He understood that heretofore the children had run from him only because they knew that he was not ready for them, that they could not make him theirs. The more he thought about this, the more fervently he hoped never to know what it was like to be a true mejdoub.

That afternoon as he turned a bend in the river, he came suddenly upon a town. His desperate need for food led him straight to the market. Paying no heed to the people's stares, he went into a stall and ordered a bowl of soup. When he had finished it and paid, he entered another stall for a dish of stew. In a third place he ate skewered meat. Then he walked to the bread market for two loaves of bread to carry with him. While he was paying for these, a policeman tapped him on the shoulder and asked for his papers. He had none. There was nothing to say. At the police station they locked him into a small foul-smelling room in the cellar. Here in this closet he passed four days and nights of anguish. When at the end of that time they took him out and questioned him, he could not bring himself to tell them the truth. Instead he frowned, saying: I am Sidi Rahal.

They tied his hands and pushed him into the back of a truck. Later in the hospital they led him to a damp cell where the men stared and shivered and shrieked. He bore it for a week, and then he decided to give the officials his true name. But when he asked to be taken before them, the guards merely laughed. Sometimes they said: Next week, but usually they did not answer at all.

The months moved by. Through nights and days and nights he lived with the other madmen, and the time came when it scarcely mattered to him any more, getting to the officials to tell them who he was. Finally he ceased thinking about it.

Tangier, 1974

THE FQIH

PAUL BOWLES

ONE MIDSUMMER AFTERNOON a dog went running through a village, stopping just long enough to bite a young man who stood on the main street. It was not a deep wound, and the young man washed it at a fountain nearby and thought no more about it. However, several people who had seen the animal bite him mentioned it to his younger brother. You must take your brother to a doctor in the city, they said.

When the boy went home and suggested this, his brother merely laughed. The next day in the village the boy decided to consult the fqih. He found the old man sitting in the shade under the figtree in the courtyard of the mosque. He kissed his hand, and told him that a dog no one had ever seen before had bitten his brother and run away.

That's very bad, said the fqih. Have you got a stable you can lock him into? Put him there, but tie his hands behind him. No one must go near him, you understand?

The boy thanked the fqih and set out for home. On the way he determined to cover a hammer with yarn and hit his brother on the back of the head. Knowing that his mother would never consent to seeing her son treated in this way, he decided that it would have to be done when she was away from the house.

That evening while the woman stood outside by the well, he crept up behind his brother and beat him with the hammer until he fell to the floor. Then he fastened his hands behind him and dragged him into a shed next to the house. There he left him lying on the ground, and went out, padlocking the door behind him.

When the brother came to his senses, he began a great outcry. The mother called to the boy: Quick! Run and see what's the matter with Mohammed. But the boy only said: I know what's the matter with him. A dog bit him, and the fqih said he has to stay in the shed.

The woman began to pull at her hair and scratch her face with her fingernails and beat her breasts. The boy tried to calm her, but she pushed him away and ran out to the shed. She put her ear to the door. All she could hear was her son's loud panting as he tried to free his hands from the cords that bound them. She pounded on the wood and screamed his name, but he was struggling, his face in the dirt, and did not reply. Finally the boy led her back to the house. It was written, he told her.

The next morning the woman got astride her donkey and rode to the village to see the fqih. He, however, had left that morning to visit his sister in Rhafsai, and no one knew when he would be back. And so she bought bread and started out on the road for Rhafsai, along with a group of villagers who were on their way to a souq in the region. That night she slept at the souq and the following morning at daybreak she started out again with a different group of people.

Each day the boy threw food in to his brother through a small barred window high above one of the stalls in the shed. The third day he also threw him a knife, so he could cut the ropes and use his hands to eat with. After a while it occurred to him that he had done a foolish thing in giving him the knife, since if he worked long enough with it he might succeed in cutting his way through the door. Thus he threatened to bring no more food until his brother had tossed the knife back through the window.

The mother had no sooner arrived at Rhafsai than she fell ill with a fever. The family with whom she had been travelling took her into their house and cared for her, but it was nearly a month before she was able to rise from the pallet on the floor where she had been lying. By that time the fqih had returned to his village.

Finally she was well enough to start out again. After two days of sitting on the back of the donkey she arrived home exhausted, and was greeted by the boy.

And your brother? she said, certain that by now he was dead.

The boy pointed to the shed, and she rushed to the door and began to call out to him.

Get the key and let me out! he cried.

I must see the fqih first, aoulidi. Tomorrow.

The next morning she and the boy went to the village. When the fqih saw the woman and her son come into the courtyard he raised his eyes to heaven. It was Allah's will that your son should die as he did, he told her.

But he's not dead! she cried. And he shouldn't stay in there any longer.

The fqih was astounded. Then he said: But let him out! Let him out! Allah has been merciful.

The boy however begged the fqih to come himself and open the door. So they set out, the fqih riding the donkey and the woman and boy following on foot. When they got to the shed, the boy handed the key to the old man, and he opened the door. The young man bounded out, followed by a stench so strong that the fqih shut the door again.

They went to the house, and the woman made tea for them. While they sat drinking the fqih told the young man: Allah has spared you. You must never mistreat your brother for having shut you away. He did it on my orders.

The young man swore that never would he raise his hand against the boy. But the boy was still afraid, and could not bring himself to look at his brother. When the fqih left to return to the village, the boy went with him, in order to bring back the donkey. As they went along the road, he said to the old man: I'm afraid of Mohammed.

The fqih was displeased. Your brother is older than you, he said. You heard him swear not to touch you.

That night while they were eating, the woman went to the brazier to make the tea. For the first time the boy stole a glance at his brother, and grew cold with fear. Mohammed had swiftly bared his teeth and made a strange sound in his throat. He had done this as a kind of joke, but to the boy it meant something very different.

The fqih should never have let him out, he said to himself. Now he'll bite me, and I'll get sick like him. And the fqih will tell him to throw me into the shed.

He could not bring himself to look again at Mohammed. At night in the dark he lay thinking about it, and he could not sleep. Early in the morning he set out for the village, to catch the fqih before he began to teach the pupils at the msid.

What is it now? asked the fqih.

When the boy told him what he feared, the old man laughed. But he has no disease! He never had any disease, thanks to Allah.

But you yourself told me to lock him up, sidi.

Yes, yes. But Allah has been merciful. Now go home and forget about it. Your brother's not going to bite you.

The boy thanked the fqih and left. He walked through the village and out along the road that led finally to the highway. The next morning he got a ride in a truck that took him all the way to Casablanca. No one in the village ever heard of him again.

Tangier, 1974

YOU HAVE LEFT YOUR LOTUS PODS ON THE BUS

PAUL BOWLES

A TRAVEL ESSAY *included in the Black Sparrow edition of* The Collected Stories of Paul Bowles.

I SOON LEARNED not to go near the windows or to draw aside the double curtains in order to look at the river below. The view was wide and lively, with factories and warehouses on the far side of the Chao Phraya, and strings of barges being towed up and down through the dirty water. The new wing of the hotel had been built in the shape of an upright slab, so that the room was high and had no trees to shade it from the poisonous onslaught of the afternoon sun. The end of the day, rather than bringing respite, intensified the heat, for then the entire river was made of sunlight. With the redness of dusk everything out there became melodramatic and forbidding, and still the oven heat from outside leaked through the windows.

Brooks, teaching at Chulalongkorn University, was required as a Fulbright Fellow to attend regular classes in Thai; as an adjunct to this he arranged to spend much of his leisure time with Thais. One day he brought along with him three young men wearing the bright orange-yellow robes of Buddhist monks. They filed into the hotel room in silence and stood in a row as they were presented to me, each one responding by joining his palms together, thumbs touching his chest.

As we talked, Yamyong, the eldest, in his late twenties, explained that he was an ordained monk, while the other two were novices. Brooks then asked Prasert and Vichai if they would be ordained soon, but the monk answered for them.

"I do not think they are expecting to be ordained," he said quietly, looking at the floor, as if it were a sore subject all too often discussed among them. He glanced up at me and went on talking. "Your room is beautiful. We are not accustomed to such luxury." His voice was flat; he was trying to conceal his disapproval. The three conferred briefly in undertones. "My friends say they have never seen such a luxurious room," he reported, watching me closely through his steel-rimmed spectacles to see my reaction. I failed to hear.

They put down their brown paper parasols and their reticules that bulged with books and fruit. Then they got themselves into position in a row along the couch among the cushions. For a while they were busy adjusting the folds of their robes around their shoulders and legs.

"They make their own clothes," volunteered Brooks. "All the monks do."

I spoke of Ceylon; there the monks bought the robes all cut and ready to sew together. Yamyong smiled appreciatively and said: "We use the same system here."

The air-conditioning roared at one end of the room and the noise of boat motors on the river seeped through the windows at the other. I looked at the three sitting in front of me. They were very calm and self-possessed, but they seemed lacking in physical health. I was aware of the facial bones beneath their skin. Was the impression of sallowness partly due to the shaved eyebrows and hair?

Yamyong was speaking. "We appreciate the opportunity to use English. For this reason we are liking to have foreign friends. English, American; it doesn't matter. We can understand." Prasert and Vichai nodded.

Time went on, and we sat there, extending but not altering the subject of conversation. Occasionally I looked around the room. Before they had come in, it had been only a hotel room whose curtains must be kept drawn. Their presence and their comments on it had managed to invest it with a vaguely disturbing quality; I felt that they considered it a great mistake on my part to have chosen such a place in which to stay.

"Look at his tattoo," said Brooks. "Show him."

Yamyong pulled back his robe a bit from the shoulder, and I saw the two indigo lines of finely written Thai characters. "That is for good health," he said, glancing up at me. His smile seemed odd, but then, his facial expression did not complement his words at any point.

"Don't the Buddhists disapprove of tattooing?" I said.

"Some people say it is backwardness." Again he smiled. "Words for good health are said to be superstition. This was done by my abbot when I was a boy studying in the *wat*. Perhaps he did not know it was a superstition."

We were about to go with them to visit the *wat* where they lived. I pulled a tie from the closet and stood before the mirror arranging it.

"Sir," Yamyong began. "Will you please explain something? What is the significance of the necktie?"

"The significance of the necktie?" I turned to face him. "You mean, why do men wear neckties?"

"No. I know that. The purpose is to look like a gentleman."

I laughed. Yamyong was not put off. "I have noticed that some men wear the two ends equal, and some wear the wide end longer than the narrow, or the narrow longer than the wide. And the neckties themselves, they are not all the same length, are they? Some even with both ends equal reach below the waist. What are the different meanings?"

"There is no meaning," I said. "Absolutely none."

He looked to Brooks for confirmation, but Brooks was trying out his Thai on Prasert and Vichai, and so he was silent and thoughtful for a moment. "I believe you, of course," he said graciously. "But we all thought each way had a different significance attached."

As we went out of the hotel, the doorman bowed respectfully. Until now he had never given a sign that he was aware of my existence. The wearers of the yellow robe carry weight in Thailand.

A few Sundays later I agreed to go with Brooks and our friends to Ayudhaya. The idea of a Sunday outing is so repellent to me that deciding to take part in this one was to a certain extent a compulsive act. Ayudhaya lies less than fifty miles up the Chao Phraya from Bangkok. For historians and art collectors it is more than just a provincial town; it is a period and a style—having been the Thai capital for more than four centuries. Very likely it still would be, had the Burmese not laid it waste in the eighteenth century.

Brooks came early to fetch me. Downstairs in the street stood the three bhikkus with their book bags and parasols. They hailed a cab, and without any previous price arrangements (the ordinary citizen tries to fix a sum beforehand) we got in and drove for twenty minutes or a half-hour, until we got to a bus terminal on the northern outskirts of the city.

It was a nice, old-fashioned, open bus. Every part of it rattled, and the air from the rice fields blew across us as we pieced together our bits of synthetic conversation. Brooks, in high spirits, kept calling across to me: "Look! Water buffaloes!" As we went further away from Bangkok there were more of the beasts, and his cries became more frequent. Yamyong, sitting next to me, whispered: "Professor Brooks is fond of buffaloes?" I laughed and said I didn't think so.

"Oh, he was saying: 'Go into second gear,' or 'We are coming to a bridge," or 'Be careful, people in the road.' Whatever he saw."

Since neither Brooks nor I appeared to have understood, he went on. "All the buses must have a driver's assistant. He watches the road and tells the driver how to drive. It is hard work because he must shout loud enough for the driver to hear him."

"But why doesn't he sit up in front with the driver?"

"No, no. There must be one in front and one in the back. That way two men are responsible for the bus."

It was an unconvincing explanation for the grueling sounds we had heard, but to show him that I believed him I said: "Aha! I see."

The taxi drew up in front of the hotel and I got out. When I said good-by to Yamyong, he replied, I think with an shade of aggrievement: "Good-by. You have left your lotus pods on the bus."

Tangier, 1971

THINGS GONE AND THINGS STILL HERE

PAUL BOWLES

An essay on Moroccan legends and beliefs included in the Black Sparrow edition of The Collected Stories of Paul Bowles.

TANGIER—if I were to move into the house at Ain Chqaf I should go to great expense to have the workmen install a fountain in the center of the courtyard. The water would fall into a marble basin and run out along marble troughs into a ditch. Running water, they say, rests the soul before the hour of prayer. On occasion, perhaps too much. An example: the familiar story of Hadj Allal, who came to grief through no fault of his own.

"As if he had stepped on a mine," explained one divinity student. "Only the mine was invisible and made no sound when it exploded. No one knew anything about it. He was there looking into the stream. Then he came into the mosque. For all of us he had been out there perhaps five minutes. But in the place where he had fallen two years had gone by. He tried to explain it to us. We took him home and told his wife to put him to bed and cover him up."

There is the tale of the fqih who taught in a local mosque some two centuries ago. No trace of his passage through life would remain now had it not been for an inexplicable psychic misadventure: the man must have stumbled upon one of those rare fissures in time—an open fault, as it were, in the surface of time—and fallen in.

Another fqih, this one in Hajra den Nahal, is said to have slipped between two instants and fallen into a deep well of time. The accident occurred while he was washing in the stream outside the mosque. As he squatted by the running water two tolba passed by on their way into the mosque to pray. They were having a conversation. Later the fqih stated that he had heard only one phrase: "in the twinkling of an eye." That seems to have been the signal. Everything around him stopped existing and he was in darkness.

In all versions the entry into this bubble in time is decisive for the protagonist. The two false years, according to the Nahali's story, were spent by him in India in a state of invisibility. During that time he did nothing but observe a famous goldsmith at work. When he was cast out of the time trap and returned to the stream by the mosque, he had brought with him all the Indian master's secrets, knowledge which he immediately put to use by becoming a goldsmith himself. His fame as a master artisan spread throughout Islam, so that the Indian goldsmith, on hearing of it, could not rest until he had visited Morocco and seen the designs himself. Unwisely, he traveled with his wife. The dénouement and meaning of the story for those who tell it is the Nahali's double victory. Not only did the Indian see all his own designs improved upon by the Moroccan, but he also lost his wife to him.

Another unfortunate fqih passed his sojourn in the time bubble as a woman, but returned to the world with greater wisdom.

A brilliant account could be written of the saga of the Haddaoua and their destruction. The patron saint sat smoking kif in a nargilah all day every day, it is said; even seven or eight years ago adepts could still be found smoking beside the ruined tomb. The brotherhood has been painstakingly eradicated by the authorities. Sometimes you see a lone man walking along the road wearing the dusty rags and wild hairdo of a Haddaoui, but since the cult no longer exists (and, perhaps more importantly, has no headquarters) such a man no longer deserves the respect which being a member of a brotherhood would give him, and so for most citizens he slips into the category of ordinary madman.

In the eyes of the government, the Haddaoua were not a religious sect at all, but an organized group of brigands to be finished off with bullets. Apart from their uncanny powers over goats, which made it possible for them to arrange the wholesale theft of these animals all over northern Morocco, and their use of magic spells as a threat in order to extort money from the rural populace, there would seem to be no valid reason for their persecution and extermination. Perhaps it was the fact that they built a fortress and kept a good many women shut into the cellars. They claimed that the women had come of their own volition and asked to be taken in as adepts. Whether or not that was the case, once the women had been present at the rituals they were not permitted to leave the premises, but were locked into the basement where they performed domestic duties.*

The Haddaoua placed great stress on food. Each meal was a banquet. This emphasis on eating may have been the result of the vast quantities of cannabis the men ingested each day, but the meals themselves were made possible by the easy availability of edible livestock. A Haddaoui could go out alone into the countryside and return in a few days with hundreds of goats following him in single-file formation. This alone was enough to strike fear into the hearts of the peasants. No one appears to know exactly how they imposed their will on the animals, but all agree that it was a special art which took time and patience to learn. When you consider that the men learned the technique by lying down among the animals and conversing with them at night during their sleep, it does not seem so improbable. The Haddaoui lying in the Marrakech dust forty years ago "became" a goat while I watched, and there in front of me was a man's body with a goat inside it, as if the goat had been able to assume the visible form of a man, while at the same time it remained unmistakably a goat. Whatever it was that they stumbled upon in the way of esoteric knowledge, their misuse of it was their undoing.

For people living in the country today the djinn is an accepted, if dreaded, concomitant of daily life. The world of djenoun is too close for comfort. Among the Moroccans it is not a question of summoning them to aid you, but simply of avoiding them. Their habitat is only a few feet below ours, and is an exact duplication of the landscape above-ground. Each tree, rock and house has its identical counterpart beneath the earth's surface. The only difference is that there the sky is made of earth instead of air, and so it is totally dark. But since the lower world is a faithful reproduction of the upper world, it follows that the djenoun are perfectly equipped for life down there, and actually prefer it to our world. The trouble occurs when they emerge and take on human or animal form, for they are our traditional enemies, an alien tribe always on the lookout for an opportunity to infiltrate our ranks, and they do this merely by establishing contact with us.

Once a djinn has revealed himself to you your life changes. You can suspect his influence or presence whenever things have not gone as they should have, whenever there is a suspect or inexplicable ele-

* This is the legend. A recent examination of the place, however, proved to me that there are no cellars beneath any of the structures in the sanctuary.

ment in a situation, whenever, in short, you are confronted with anything you don't understand. This is your warning; you begin to look for the djinn, and sooner or later you come across it and recognize it, no matter in what form you find it. What counts is your behavior and method of dealing with it at that point. Losing out in your struggle with a djinn can involve you in years of harassment or illness; it can also be fatal.

Above all you must guard against becoming emotionally involved with a djinn or a djinniya. There are many instances of miscegenation, but these are usually not discovered until after one partner has killed the other. "I watched her for months and I noticed that she never ate anything with salt in it. That was how I knew she was not a woman."

The open points along the frontier between the two worlds can conceivably occur anywhere, but exist generally in caves and under water, particularly under running water. If your itinerary involves crossing a stream, best have something made of steel (or at least iron) handy. City people often say there are no djenoun, not any more, or in any case not in the city. In the country, where life is the same as before and where there are not many automobiles and other things containing iron, they admit that djenoun probably still exist. But they add that the automobiles will eventually drive them all away, for they can't stand the proximity of iron and steel. Then it will be only in the distant mountains and the desert where you will need to worry about them.

Notwithstanding the rationalizations, djenoun continue to raise havoc now and then in the very center of the city by coming suddenly out of sink drains and attacking housewives. With this in mind, many women will not allow any hot water to fall into the sink, which means they must wash the dishes in cold water for fear of burning the possible inhabitant of the pipe. Djenoun have been known to be extremely vindictive in such cases, and commonly retaliate by causing paralysis in the offender.

If you go to the outskirts of any town, to where the fields begin and sheep are grazing, and dig in the earth under certain trees, you will come upon a knife. If you dig somewhere a few yards away from there, you may find another. There are many of them, all of the folding sort, and each one is clasped shut on a scrap of paper. Even though you open every knife you find, each time releasing a man from the spell of some accursed woman, still you are not going to spend all your time doing good turns for a whole group of men you have never known and never will meet. There would be no reason in the first place to go and dig for knives unless you suspect that a woman has shut a knife on you. Then, depending on who you think it might have been and where she would be most likely to go in order to bury it, you get busy and start to dig.

Sometimes you come upon other men digging, and when they see you they look ashamed and pretend to be looking for some change they have dropped. Often they stand up, shrug, and walk away. But if you go some distance and wait, they come back and start again to dig. Where is the justice in a world in which a woman with a simple folding knife can make so much trouble for a man?

"Twice I've found folded knives deep in the water at the bottom of the cliffs along the strait. The women who do this are even worse than the ones who bury them in the ground. They are willing to walk all the way to the cliffs so they can ruin the lives of the men they hate. There is not much chance of these knives being found and opened. And even if the paper where the curse was written has dissolved in the water, the man can have no sort of life again until the blade is opened. It's the shutting of the blade on the curse that keeps a man from being able to get hard. If I ever come across a woman burying a knife, she'll never get back home."

Tangier, 1975

A GUATEMALAN IDYLL

JANE BOWLES

Excised from the novel that became Two Serious Ladies, *the following selection was published in 1944 as a separate story, "A Guatemalan Idyll."*

When the traveler arrived at the pension the wind was blowing hard. Before going in to have the hot soup he had been thinking about, he left his luggage inside the door and walked a few blocks in order to get an idea of the town. He came to a very large arch through which, in the distance, he could see a plain. He thought he could distinguish figures seated around a far-away fire, but he was not certain because the wind made tears in his eyes.

"How dismal," he thought, letting his mouth drop open. "But never mind. Brace up. It's probably a group of boys and girls sitting around an open fire having a fine time together. The world is the world, after all is said and done, and a patch of grass in one place is green the way it is in any other."

He turned back and walked along quickly, skirting the walls of the low stone houses. He was a little worried that he might not be able to recognize a door of his pension.

"There's not supposed to be any variety in the U.S.A.," he said to himself. "But this Spanish architecture beats everything, it's so monotonous." He knocked on one of the doors, and shortly a child with a shaved head appeared. With a strong American accent he said to her: "Is this the Pension Espinoza?"

"*Sí!*" The child led him inside to a fountain in the center of a square patio. He looked into the basin and the child did too.

"There are four fish inside here," she said to him in Spanish. "Would you like me to try and catch one of them for you?"

The traveler did not understand her. He stood there uncomfortably, longing to go to his room. The little girl was still trying to get hold of a fish when her mother, who owned the pension, came out and joined them. The woman was quite fat, but her face was small and pointed, and she wore glasses attached by a gold chain to her dress. She shook hands with him and asked him in fairly good English if he had had a pleasant journey.

"He wants to see some of the fish," explained the child.

"Certainly," said Señora Espinoza, moving her hands about in the water with dexterity. "Soon now, soon now," she said, laughing as one of the fish slipped between her fingers.

The traveler nodded. "I would like to go to my room," he said.

• • •

The American was a little dismayed by his room. There were four brass beds in a row, all of them very old and a little crooked.

"God!" he said to himself. "They'll have to remove some of these beds. They give me the willies."

A cord hung down from the ceiling. On the end of it at the height of his nose was a tiny electric bulb. He turned it on and looked at his hands under the light. They were chapped and dirty. A barefoot servant girl came in with a pitcher and a bowl.

In the dining room, calendars decorated the walls, and there was an elaborate cut-glass carafe on every table. Several people had already begun their meal in silence. One little girl was speaking in a high voice.

"I'm not going to the band concert tonight, mamá," she was saying.

"Why not?" asked her mother with her mouth full. She looked seriously at her daughter.

"Because I don't like to hear music. I hate it!"

"Why?" asked her mother absently, taking another large mouthful of her food. She spoke in a deep voice like a man's. Her head, which was set low between her shoulders, was covered with black curls. Her chin was heavy and her skin was dark and coarse; however, she had very beautiful blue eyes. She sat with her legs apart, with one arm lying flat on the table. The child bore no resemblance to her mother. She was frail, with stiff hair of the peculiar light color that is often found in mulattoes. Her eyes were so pale that they seemed almost white.

As the traveler came in, the child turned to look at him.

"Now there are nine people eating in this pension," she said immediately.

"Nine," said her mother. "Many mouths." She pushed her plate aside wearily and looked up at the calendar beside her on the wall. At last she turned around and saw the stranger. Having already finished her own dinner, she followed the progress of his meal with interest. Once she caught his eye.

"Good appetite," she said, nodding gravely, and then she watched his soup until he had finished it.

"My pills," she said to Lilina, holding her hand out without turning her head. To amuse herself, Lilina emptied the whole bottle into her mother's hand.

"Now you have your pills," she said. When Señora Ramirez realized what had happened, she dealt Lilina a terrible blow in the face, using the hand which held the pills, and thus leaving them sticking to the child's moist skin and in her hair. The traveler turned. He was so bored and at the same time disgusted by what he saw that he decided he had better look for another pension that very night.

"Soon," said the waitress, putting his meat in front of him, "the musician will come. For fifty cents he will play you all the songs you want to hear. One night would not be time enough. *She* will be out of the room by then." She looked over at Lilina, who was squealing like a stuck pig.

"Those pills cost me three *quetzales* a bottle," Señora Ramirez complained. One of the young men at a nearby table came over and examined the empty bottle. He shook his head.

"A barbarous thing," he said.

"What a dreadful child you are, Lilina!" said an English lady who was seated at quite a distance from everybody else. All the diners looked up. Her face and neck were quite red with annoyance. She was speaking to them in English.

"Can't you behave like civilized people?" she demanded.

"You be quiet, you!" The young man had finished examining the empty pill bottle. His companions burst out laughing.

"O.K., girl," he continued in English. "Want a piece of chewing gum?" His companions were quite helpless with laughter at his last remark, and all three of them got up and left the room. Their guffaws could be heard from the patio, where they had grouped around the fountain, fairly doubled up.

"It's a disgrace to the adult mind," said the English lady. Lilina's nose had started to bleed, and she rushed out.

"And tell Consuelo to hurry in and eat her dinner," her mother called after her. Just then the musician arrived. He was a small man and he wore a black suit and a dirty shirt.

"Well," said Lilina's mother. "At last you came."

"I was having dinner with my uncle. Time passes, Señora Ramirez! *Gracias a Dios*!"

"*Gracias a Dios* nothing! It's unheard-of, having to eat dinner without music."

The violinist fell into a chair, and, bent over low, he started to play with all his strength.

"Waltzes!" shouted Señora Ramirez above the music. "Waltzes!" She looked petulant and at the same time as though she were about to cry. As a matter of fact, the stranger was quite sure that he saw a tear roll down her cheek.

"Are you going to the band concert tonight?" she asked him; she spoke English rather well.

"I don't know. Are you?"

"Yes, with my daughter Consuelo. If the unfortunate girl ever gets here to eat her supper. She doesn't like food. Only dancing. She dances like a real butterfly. She has French blood from me. She is of a much better type than the little one, Lilina, who is always hurting; hurting me, hurting her sister, hurting her friends. I hope that God will have pity on her." At this she really did shed a tear or two, which she brushed away with her napkin.

"Well, she's young yet," said the stranger. Señora Ramirez agreed heartily.

"Yes, she is young." She smiled at him sweetly and seemed quite content.

Lilina meanwhile was in her room, standing over the white bowl in which they washed their hands, letting the blood drip into it. She was breathing heavily like someone who is trying to simulate anger.

"Stop that breathing! You sound like an old man," said her sister Consuelo, who was lying on the bed with a hot brick on her stomach. Consuelo was small and dark, with a broad flat face and an unusually narrow skull. She had a surly nature, which is often the case when young girls do little else but dream of a lover. Lilina, who was a bully without any curiosity concerning the grown-up world, hated her sister more than anyone else she knew.

"Mamá says that if you don't come in to eat soon she will hit you."

"Is that how *you* got that bloody nose?"

"No," said Lilina. She walked away from the basin and her eye fell on her mother's corset, which was lying on the bed. Quickly she picked it up and went with it into the patio, where she threw it into the fountain. Consuelo, frightened by the appropriation of the corset, got up hastily and arranged her hair.

"Too much upset for a girl of my age," she said to herself patting her stomach. Crossing the patio she saw Señora Córdoba walking along, holding her head very high as she slipped some hairpins more firmly into the bun at the back of her neck. Consuelo felt like a frog or a beetle walking behind her. Together they entered the dining room.

"Why don't you wait for midnight to strike?" said Señora Ramirez to Consuelo. Señorita Córdoba, assuming that this taunt had been addressed to her, bridled and stiffened. Her eyes narrowed and she stood still. Señora Ramirez, a gross coward, gave her a strange idiotic smile.

"How is your health, Señorita Córdoba?" she asked softly, and then feeling confused, she pointed to the stranger and asked him if he knew Señorita Córdoba.

"No, no; he does not know me." She held out her hand stiffly to the stranger and he took it. No names were mentioned.

Consuelo sat down beside her mother and ate voraciously, a sad look in her eye. Señorita Córdoba ordered only fruit. She sat looking out into the dark patio, giving the other diners a view of the nape of her neck. Presently she opened a letter and began to read. The others all watched her closely. The three young men who had laughed so heartily before were now smiling like idiots, waiting for another such occasion to present itself.

The musician was playing a waltz at the request of Señora Ramirez, who was trying her best to attract again the attention of the stranger. "Tra-la-la-la," she sang, and in order better to convey the beauty of the waltz she folded her arms in front of her and rocked from side to side.

"Ay, Consuelo! It is for her to waltz," she said to the stranger. "There will be many people in the plaza tonight, and there is so much wind. I think that you must fetch my shawl, Consuelo. It is getting very cold."

While awaiting Consuelo's return she shivered and picked her teeth.

The traveler thought she was crazy and a little disgusting. He had come here as a buyer for a very important textile concern. Having completed all his work, he had for some reason decided to stay on another week, perhaps because he had always heard that a vacation in a foreign country was a desirable thing. Already he regretted his decision, but there was no boat out before the following Monday. By the end of the meal he was in such despair that his face wore a peculiarly young and sensitive look. In order to buoy himself up a bit, he began to think about what he would get to eat three weeks hence, seated at his mother's table on Thanksgiving Day. They would be very glad to hear that he had not enjoyed himself on this trip, because they had always considered it something in the nature of a betrayal when anyone in the family expressed a desire to travel. He thought they led a fine life and was inclined to agree with them.

Consuelo had returned with her mother's shawl. She was dreaming again when her mother pinched her arm.

"Well, Consuelo, are you coming to the band concert or are you going to sit here like a dummy? I daresay the Señor is not coming with us, but *we* like music, so get up, and we will say good night to this gentleman and be on our way."

The traveler had not understood this speech. He was therefore very much surprised when Señora Ramirez tapped him on the shoulder and said to him severely in English: "Good night, Señor. Consuelo and I are going to the band concert. We will see you tomorrow at breakfast."

"Oh, but I'm going to the band concert myself," he said, in a panic lest they leave him with a whole evening on his hands.

Señora Ramirez flushed with pleasure. The three walked down the badly lit street together, escorted by a group of skinny yellow dogs.

"These old grilled windows are certainly very beautiful," the traveler said to Señora Ramirez. "Old as the hills themselves, aren't they?"

"You must go to the capital if you want beautiful buildings," said Señora Ramirez. "Very new and clean they are."

"I should think," he said, "that these old buildings were your point of interest here, aside from your Indians and their native costumes."

They walked on for a little while in silence. A small boy came up to them and tried to sell them some lollipops.

"Five *centavos*," said the little boy.

"Absolutely not," said the traveler. He had been warned that the natives would cheat him, and he was actually enraged every time they approached him with their wares.

"Four *centavos* . . . three *centavos*. . . ."

"No, no, no! Go away!" The little boy ran ahead of them.

"I would like a lollipop," said Consuelo to him.

"Well, why didn't you say so, then?" he demanded.

"No," said Consuelo.

"She does not mean no," explained her mother. "She can't learn to speak English. She has clouds in her head."

"I see," said the traveler. Consuelo looked mortified. When they came to the end of the street, Señora Ramirez stood still and lowered her head like a bull.

"Listen," she said to Consuelo. "Listen. You can hear the music from here."

"Yes, mamá. Indeed you can." They stood listening to the faint marimba noise that reached them. The traveler sighed.

"Please, let's get going if we *are* going," he said. "Otherwise there is no point."

The square was already crowded when they arrived. The older people sat on benches under the trees, while the younger ones walked round and round, the girls in one direction and the boys in the other. The musicians played inside a kiosk in the center of the square. Señora Ramirez led both Consuelo and the stranger into the girls' line, and they had not been walking more than a minute before she settled into a comfortable gait, with an expression very much like that of someone relaxing in an armchair.

"We have three hours," she said to Consuelo.

The stranger looked around him. Many of the girls were barefoot and pure Indian. They walked along holding tightly to one another, and were frequently convulsed with laughter.

The musicians were playing a formless but militant-sounding piece which came to many climaxes without ending. The drummer was the man who had just played the violin at Señora Espinoza's pension.

"Look!" said the traveler excitedly. "Isn't that the man who was just playing for us at dinner? He must have run all the way. I'll bet he's sweating some."

"Yes, it is he," said Señora Ramirez. "The nasty little rat. I would like to tear him right off his stand. Remember the one at the Grand Hotel, Consuelo? He stopped at every table, señor, and I have never seen such beautiful teeth in my life. A smile on his face from the moment he came into the room until he went out again. This one looks at his shoes while he is playing, and he would like to kill us all."

Some big boys threw confetti into the traveler's face.

"I wonder," he asked himself. "I wonder what kind of fun they get out of just walking around and around this little park and throwing confetti at each other."

The boys' line was in a constant uproar about something. The broader their smiles became, the more he suspected them of plotting something, probably against him, for apparently he was the only tourist there that evening. Finally he was so upset that he walked along looking up at the stars, or even for short stretches with his eyes shut, because it seemed to him that somehow this rendered him a little less visible. Suddenly he caught sight of Señorita Córdoba. She was across the street buying lollipops from a boy.

"Señorita!" He waved his hand from where he was, and then joyfully bounded out of the line and across the street. He stood panting by her side, while she reddened considerably and did not know what to say to him.

Señora Ramirez and Consuelo came to a standstill and stood like two monuments, staring after him, while the lines brushed past them on either side.

• • •

Lilina was looking out of her window at some boys who were playing on the corner of the street under the street light. One of them kept pulling a snake out of his pocket; he would then stuff it back in again. Lilina wanted the snake very much. She chose her toys according to the amount of power or responsibility she thought they would give her in the eyes of others. She thought now that if she were able to get the snake, she would perhaps put on a little act called "Lilina and the Viper," and charge admission. She imagined that she would wear a fancy dress and let the snake wriggle under her collar. She left her room and went out of doors. The wind was stronger than it had been, and she could hear the music playing even from where she was. She felt chilly and hurried toward the boys.

"For how much will you sell your snake?" she asked the oldest boy, Ramón.

"You mean Victoria?" said Ramón. His voice was beginning to change and there was a shadow above his upper lip.

"Victoria is too much of a queen for you to have," said one of the smaller boys. "She is a beauty and you are not." They all roared with laughter, including Ramón, who all at once looked very silly. He giggled like a girl. Lilina's heart sank. She was determined to have the snake.

"Are you ever going to stop laughing and begin to bargain with me? If you don't I'll have to go back in, because my mother and sister will be coming home soon, and they wouldn't allow me to be talking here like this with you. I'm from a good family."

This sobered Ramón, and he ordered the boys to be quiet. He

took Victoria from his pocket and played with her in silence. Lilina stared at the snake.

"Come to my house," said Ramón. "My mother will want to know how much I'm selling her for."

"All right," said Lilina. "But be quick, and I don't want them with us." She indicated the other boys. Ramón gave them orders to go back to their houses and meet him later at the playground near the Cathedral.

"Where do you live?" she asked him.

"Calle de las Delicias number six."

"Does your house belong to you?"

"My house belongs to my Aunt Gudelia."

"Is she richer than your mother?"

"Oh, yes." They said no more to each other.

There were eight rooms opening onto the patio of Ramón's house, but only one was furnished. In this room the family cooked and slept. His mother and his aunt were seated opposite one another on two brightly painted chairs. Both were fat and both were wearing black. The only light came from a charcoal fire which was burning in a brazier on the floor.

They had bought the chairs that very morning and were consequently feeling lighthearted and festive. When the children arrived they were singing a little song together.

"Why don't we buy something to drink?" said Gudelia, when they stopped singing.

"Now you're going to go crazy, I see," said Ramón's mother. "You're very disagreeable when you're drinking."

"No, I'm not," said Gudelia.

"Mother," said Ramón. "This little girl has come to buy Victoria."

"I have never seen you before," said Ramón's mother to Lilina.

"Nor I," said Gudelia. "I am Ramón's aunt, Gudelia. This is my house."

"My name is Lilina Ramirez. I want to bargain for Ramón's Victoria."

"Victoria," they repeated gravely.

"Ramón is very fond of Victoria and so are Gudelia and I," said his mother. "It's a shame that we sold Alfredo the parrot. We sold him for far too little. He sang and danced. We have taken care of Victoria for a long time, and it has been very expensive. She eats much meat." This was an obvious lie. They all looked at Lilina.

"Where do you live, dear?" Gudelia asked Lilina.

"I live in the capital, but I'm staying now at Señora Espinoza's pension."

"I meet her in the market every day of my life," said Gudelia. "Maria de la Luz Espinoza. She buys a lot. How many people has she staying in her house? Five, six?"

"Nine."

"Nine! Dear God! Does she have many animals?"

"Certainly," said Lilina.

"Come," said Ramón to Lilina. "Let's go outside and bargain."

"He loves that snake," said Ramón's mother, looking fixedly at Lilina.

The aunt sighed. "Victoria . . . Victoria."

Lilina and Ramón climbed through a hole in the wall and sat down together in the midst of some foliage.

"Listen," said Ramón. "If you kiss me, I'll give you Victoria for nothing. You have blue eyes. I saw them when we were in the street."

"I can hear what you are saying," his mother called out from the kitchen.

"Shame, shame," said Gudelia. "Giving Victoria away for nothing. Your mother will be without food. I can buy my own food, but what will your mother do?"

Lilina jumped to her feet impatiently. She saw that they were getting nowhere, and unlike most of her countrymen, she was always eager to get things done quickly.

She stamped back into the kitchen, opened her eyes very wide in order to frighten the two ladies, and shouted as loud as she could: "Sell me that snake right now or I will go away and never put my foot in this house again."

The two women were not used to such a display of rage over the mere settlement of a price. They rose from their chairs and started moving about the room to no purpose, picking up things and putting them down again. They were not quite sure what to do. Gudelia was terribly upset. She stepped here and there with her hand below her breast, peering about cautiously. Finally she slipped out into the patio and disappeared.

Ramón took Victoria out of his pocket. They arranged a price and Lilina left, carrying her in a little box.

• • •

Meanwhile Señora Ramirez and her daughter were on their way home from the band concert. Both of them were in a bad humor. Consuelo was not disposed to talk at all. She looked angrily at the houses they were passing and sighed at everything her mother had to say. "You have no merriment in your heart," said Señora Ramirez. "Just revenge." As Consuelo refused to answer, she continued. "Sometimes I feel that I am walking along with an assassin."

She stopped still in the street and looked up at the sky. "*Jesu Maria*!" she said. "Don't let me say such things about my own daughter." She clutched at Consuelo's arm.

"Come, come. Let us hurry. My feet ache. What an ugly city this is!"

Consuelo began to whimper. The word "assassin" had affected her painfully. Although she had no very clear idea of an assassin in her mind, she knew it to be a gross insult and contrary to all usage when applied to a young lady of breeding. It so frightened her that her mother had used such a word in connection with her that she actually felt a little sick to her stomach.

"No, mamá, no!" she cried. "Don't say that I am an assassin. Don't!" Her hands were beginning to shake, and already the tears were filling her eyes. Her mother hugged her and they stood for a moment locked in each other's arms.

Maria, the servant, was standing near the fountain looking into it when Consuelo and her mother arrived at the pension. The traveler and Señorita Córdoba were seated together having a chat.

"Doesn't love interest you?" the traveler was asking her.

"No . . . no . . ." answered Señorita Córdoba. "City life, business, the theater. . . ." She sounded somewhat halfhearted about the theater.

"Well, that's funny," said the traveler. "In my country most young girls are interested in love. There are some, of course, who are interested in having a career, either business or the stage. But I've heard tell that even these women deep down in their hearts want a home and everything that goes with it."

"So?" said Señorita Córdoba.

"Well, yes," said the traveler. "Deep down in your heart, don't you always hope the right man will come along some day?"

"No . . . no . . . no. . . . Do you?" she said absentmindedly.

"Who, me? No."

"No?"

She was the most preoccupied woman he had ever spoken with.

"Look, señoras," said Maria to Consuelo and her mother. "Look what is floating around in the fountain! What is it?"

Consuelo bent over the basin and fished around a bit. Presently she pulled out her mother's pink corset.

"Why, mamá," she said. "It's your corset."

Señora Ramirez examined the wet corset. It was covered with muck from the bottom of the fountain. She went over to a chair and sat down in it, burying her face in her hands. She rocked back and forth and sobbed very softly. Señora Espinoza came out of her room.

"Lilina, my sister, threw it into the fountain," Consuelo announced to all present.

Señora Espinoza looked at the corset.

"It can be fixed. It can be fixed," she said, walking over to Señora Ramirez and putting her arms around her.

"Look, my friend. My dear little friend, why don't you go to bed and get some sleep? Tomorrow you can think about getting it cleaned."

"How can we stand it? Oh, how can we stand it?" Señora Ramirez asked imploringly, her beautiful eyes filled with sorrow. "Sometimes," she said in a trembling voice, "I have no more strength than a sparrow. I would like to send my children to the four winds and sleep and sleep and sleep."

Consuelo, hearing this, said in a gentle tone: "Why don't you do so, mamá?"

"They are like two daggers in my heart, you see?" continued her mother.

"No, they are not," said Señora Espinoza. "They are flowers that brighten your life." She removed her glasses and polished them on her blouse.

"Daggers in my heart," repeated Señora Ramirez.

"Have some hot soup," urged Señora Espinoza. "Maria will make you some—a gift from me—and then you can go to bed and forget all about this."

"No, I think I will just sit here, thank you."

"Mamá is going to have one of her fits," said Consuelo to the servant. "She does sometimes. She gets just like a child instead of getting angry, and she doesn't worry about what she is eating or when she goes to sleep, but she just sits in a chair or goes walking and her face looks very different from the way it looks at other times." The servant nodded, and Consuelo went in to bed.

"I have French blood," Señora Ramirez was saying to Señora Espinoza. "I am very delicate for that reason—too delicate for my husband."

Señora Espinoza seemed worried by the confession of her friend. She had no interest in gossip or in what people had to say about their lives. To Señora Ramirez she was like a man, and she often had dreams about her in which she became a man.

The traveler was highly amused.

"I'll be damned!" he said. "All this because of an old corset. Some people have nothing to think about in this world. It's funny, though, funny as a barrel of monkeys."

To Señorita Córdoba it was not funny. "It's too bad," she said. "Very much too bad that the corset was spoiled. What are you doing here in this country?"

"I'm buying textiles. At least, I was, and now I'm just taking a little vacation here until the next boat leaves for the United States. I kind of miss my family and I'm anxious to get back. I don't see what you're supposed to get out of traveling."

"Oh, yes, yes. Surely you do," said Señorita Córdoba politely. "Now if you will excuse me I am going inside to do a little drawing. I must not forget how in this peasant land."

"What are you, an artist?" he asked.

"I draw dresses." She disappeared.

"Oh, God!" thought the traveler after she had left. "Here I am, left alone, and I'm not sleepy yet. This empty patio is so barren and so uninteresting, and as far as Señorita Córdoba is concerned, she's an iceberg. I like her neck though. She has a neck like a swan, so long and white and slender, the kind of neck you dream about girls having. But she's more like a virgin than a swan." He turned around and noticed that Señora Ramirez was still sitting in her chair. He picked up his own chair and carried it over next to hers.

"Do you mind?" he asked. "I see that you've decided to take a little night air. It isn't a bad idea. I don't feel like going to bed much either."

"No," she said. "I don't want to go to bed. I will sit here. I like to sit out at night, if I am warmly enough dressed, and look up at the stars."

"Yes, it's a great source of peace," the traveler said. "People don't do enough of it these days."

"Would you not like very much to gc to Italy?" Señora Ramirez asked him. "The fruit trees and the flowers will be wonderful there at night."

"Well, you've got enough fruit and flowers here, I should say. What do you want to go to Italy for? I'll bet there isn't as much variety in the fruit there as here."

"No? Do you have many flowers in your country?"

The traveler was not able to decide.

"I would like really," continued Señora Ramirez, "to be somewhere else—in your country or in Italy. I would like to be somewhere where the life is beautiful. I care very much whether life is beautiful or ugly. People who live here don't care very much. Because they do not think." She touched her finger to her forehead. "I love beautiful things: beautiful houses, beautiful gardens, beautiful songs. When I was a young girl I was truly wild with happiness—doing and thinking and running in and out. I was so happy that my mother was afraid I would fall and break my leg or have some kind of accident. She was a very religious woman, but when I was a young girl I could not remember to think about such a thing. I was up always every morning before anybody except the Indians, and every morning I would go to market with them to buy food for all the houses. For many years I was doing this. Even when I was very little. It was very easy for me to do anything. I loved to learn English. I had a professor and I used to get on my knees in front of my father that the professor would stay longer with me every day. I was walking in the parks when my sisters were sleeping. My eyes were so big." She made a circle with two fingers. "And shiny like two diamonds, I was so excited all the time." She churned the air with her clenched fist. "Like this," she said. "Like a storm. My sisters called me wild Sofía. At the same time they were calling me wild Sofía, I was in love with my uncle, Aldo Torres. He never came much to the house before, but I heard my mother say that he had no more money and we would feed him. We were very rich and getting richer every year. I felt very sorry for him and was thinking about him all the time. We fell in love with each other and were kissing and hugging each other when nobody was there who could see us. I would have lived with him in a grass hut. He married a woman who had a little money, who also loved him very much. When he was married he got fat and started joking a lot with my father. I was glad for him that he was richer but pretty sad for myself. Then my sister Juanita, the oldest, married a very rich man. We were all very happy about her and there was a very big wedding."

"You must have been brokenhearted, though, about your uncle Aldo Torres going off with someone else, when you had befriended him so much when he was poor."

"Oh, I liked him very much," she said. Her memory seemed suddenly to have failed her and she did not appear to be interested in speaking any longer of the past. The traveler felt disturbed.

"I would love to travel," she continued, "very, very much, and I think it would be very nice to have the life of an actress, without children. You know it is my nature to love men and kissing."

"Well," said the traveler, "nobody gets as much kissing as they would like to get. Most people are frustrated. You'd be surprised at the number of people in my country who are frustrated and good-looking at the same time."

She turned her face toward his. The one little light bulb shed just enough light to enable him to see into her beautiful eyes. The tears were still wet on her lashes and they magnified her eyes to such an extent that they appeared to be almost twice their normal size. While she was looking at him she caught her breath.

"Oh, my darling man," she said to him suddenly. "I don't want to be separated from you. Let's go where I can hold you in my arms." The traveler was feeling excited. She had taken hold of his hand and was crushing it very hard.

"Where do you want to go?" he asked stupidly.

"Into your bed." She closed her eyes and waited for him to answer.

"All right. Are you sure?"

She nodded her head vigorously.

"This," he said to himself, "is undoubtedly one of those things that you don't want to remember next morning. I'll want to shake it off like a dog shaking water off its back. But what can I do? It's too far along now. I'll be going home soon and the whole thing will be just a soap bubble among many other soap bubbles."

He was beginning to feel inspired and he could not understand it, because he had not been drinking.

"A soap bubble among many other soap bubbles," he repeated to himself. His inner life was undefined but well controlled as a rule. Together they went into his room.

"Ah," said Señora Ramirez after he had closed the door behind them, "this makes me happy."

She fell onto the bed sideways, like a beaten person. Her feet stuck out into the air, and her heavy breathing filled the room. He realized that he had never before seen a person behave in this manner unless sodden with alcohol, and he did not know what to do. According to all his standards and the standards of his friends she was not a pleasant thing to lie beside.

She was unfastening her dress at the neck. The brooch with which she pinned her collar together she stuck into the pillow behind her.

"So much fat," she said. "So much fat." She was smiling at him very tenderly. This for some reason excited him, and he took off his own clothing and got into bed beside her. He was as cold as a clam and very bony, but being a truly passionate woman she did not notice any of that.

"Do you really want to go through with this?" he said to her, for he was incapable of finding new words for a situation that was certainly unlike any other he had ever experienced. She fell upon him and felt his face and his neck with feverish excitement.

"Dear God!" she said. "Dear God!" They were in the very act of making love. "I have lived twenty years for this moment and I cannot think that heaven itself could be more wonderful."

The traveler hardly listened to this remark. His face was hidden in the pillow and he was feeling the pangs of guilt in the very midst of his pleasure. When it was all over she said to him: "That is all I want to do ever." She patted his hands and smiled at him.

"Are you happy, too?" she asked him.

"Yes, indeed," he said. He got off the bed and went out into the patio.

"She was certainly in a bad way," he thought. "It was almost like death itself." He didn't want to think any further. He stayed outside near the fountain as long as possible. When he returned she was up in front of the bureau trying to arrange her hair.

"I'm ashamed of the way I look," she said. "I don't look the way I feel." She laughed and he told her that she looked perfectly all right. She drew him down onto the bed again. "Don't send me back to my room," she said. "I love to be here with you, my sweetheart."

The dawn was breaking when the traveler awakened next morning. Señora Ramirez was still beside him, sleeping very soundly. Her arm was flung over the pillow behind her head.

"Lordy," said the traveler to himself. "I'd better get her out of here." He shook her as hard as he could.

"Mrs. Ramirez," he said. "Mrs. Ramirez, wake up. Wake up!" When she finally did wake up, she looked frightened to death. She turned and stared at him blankly for a little while. Before he noticed any change in her expression, her hand was already moving over his body.

"Mrs. Ramirez," he said. "I'm worried that perhaps your daughters will get up and raise a hullabaloo. You know, start whining for you, or something like that. Your place is probably in there."

"What?" she asked him. He had pulled away from her to the other side of the bed.

"I say I think you ought to go into your room now the morning's here."

"Yes, my darling, I will go to my room. You are right." She sidled over to him and put her arms around him.

"I will see you later in the dining room, and look at you and look at you, because I love you so much."

"Don't be crazy," he said. "You don't want anything to show in your face. You don't want people to guess about this. We must be cold with one another."

She put her hand over her heart.

"Ay!" she said. "This cannot be."

"Oh, Mrs. Ramirez. Please be sensible. Look, you go to your room and we'll talk about this in the morning . . . or, at least, later in the morning."

"Cold I cannot be." To illustrate this, she looked deep into his eyes.

"I know, I know," he said. "You're a very passionate woman. But my God! Here we are in a crazy Spanish country."

He jumped from the bed and she followed him. After she had put on her shoes, he took her to the door.

"Good-bye," he said.

She couched her cheek on her two hands and looked up at him. He shut the door.

She was too happy to go right to bed, and so she went over to the bureau and took from it a little stale sugar Virgin which she broke into three pieces. She went over to Consuelo and shook her very hard. Consuelo opened her eyes, and after some time asked her mother crossly what she wanted. Señora Ramirez stuffed the candy into her daughter's mouth.

"Eat it, darling," she said. "It's the little Virgin from the bureau."

"Ay, mamá!" Consuelo sighed. "Who knows what you will do next? It is already light out and you are still in your clothes. I am sure there is no other mother who is still in her clothes now, in the whole world. Please don't make me eat any more of the Virgin now. Tomorrow I will eat some more. But it is tomorrow, isn't it? What a mix-up. I don't like it." She shut her eyes and tried to sleep. There was a look of deep disgust on her face. Her mother's spell was a little frightening this time.

Señora Ramirez now went over to Lilina's bed and awakened her. Lilina opened her eyes wide and immediately looked very tense, because she thought she was going to be scolded about the corset and also about having gone out alone after dark.

"Here, little one," said her mother. "Eat some of the Virgin."

Lilina was delighted. She ate the stale sugar candy and patted her stomach to show how pleased she was. The snake was asleep in a box near her bed.

"Now tell me," said her mother. "What did you do today?" She had completely forgotten about the corset. Lilina was beside herself with joy. She ran her fingers along her mother's lips and then pushed them into her mouth. Señora Ramirez snapped at the fingers like a dog. Then she laughed uproariously.

"Mamá, please be quiet," pleaded Consuelo. "I want to go to sleep."

"Yes, darling. Everything will be quiet so that you can sleep peacefully."

"I bought a snake, mamá," said Lilina.

"Good!" exclaimed Señora Ramirez. And after musing a little while with her daughter's hand in hers, she went to bed.

• • •

In her room Señora Ramirez was dressing and talking to her children.

"I want you to put on your fiesta dresses," she said, "because I am going to ask the traveler to have lunch with us."

Consuelo was in love with the traveler by now and very jealous of Señorita Córdoba, who she had decided was his sweetheart. "I daresay he has already asked Señorita Córdoba to lunch," she said. "They have been talking together near the fountain almost since dawn."

"*Santa Catarina!*" cried her mother angrily. "You have the eyes of a madman who sees flowers where there are only cow turds." She covered her face heavily with a powder that was distinctly violet in tint, and pulled a green chiffon scarf around her shoulders, pinning it together with a brooch in the form of a golf club. Then she and the girls, who were dressed in pink satin, went out into the patio and sat together just a little out of the sun. The parrot was swinging back and forth on his perch and singing. Señora Ramirez sang along with him; her own voice was a little lower than the parrot's.

Pastores, pastores, vamos a Belén
A ver a María y al niño también.

She conducted the parrot with her hand. The old señora, mother of Señora Espinoza, was walking round and round the patio. She stopped for a moment and played with Señora Ramirez's seashell bracelet.

"Do you want some candy?" she asked Señora Ramirez.

"I can't. My stomach is very bad."

"Do you want some candy?" she repeated. Señora Ramirez smiled and looked up at the sky. The old lady patted her cheek.

"Beautiful," she said. "You are beautiful."

"Mamá!" screamed Señora Espinoza, running out of her room. "Come to bed!"

The old lady clung to the rungs of Señora Ramirez's chair like a tough bird, and her daughter was obliged to pry her hands open before she was able to get her away.

"I'm sorry, Señora Ramirez," she said. "But when you get old, you know how it is."

"Pretty bad," said Señora Ramirez. She was looking at the traveler and Señorita Córdoba. They had their backs turned to her.

"Lilina," she said. "Go and ask him to have lunch with us . . . go. No, I will write it down. Get me a pen and paper."

"Dear," she wrote, when Lilina returned. "Will you come to have lunch at my table this afternoon? The girls will be with me, too. All the three of us send you our deep affection. I tell Consuelo to tell the maid to move the plates all to the same table. Very truly yours, Sofía Piega de Ramirez."

The traveler read the note, acquiesced, and shortly they were all seated together at the dining-room table.

"Now this is really stranger than fiction," he said to himself. "Here I am sitting with these people at their table and feeling as though I had been here all my life, and the truth of the matter is that I have only been in this pension about fourteen or fifteen hours altogether—not even one day. Yesterday I felt that I was on a Zulu island, I was so depressed. The human animal is the funniest animal of them all."

Señora Ramirez had arranged to sit close beside the stranger, and she pressed her thigh to his all during the time that she was eating her soup. The traveler's appetite was not very good. He was excited and felt like talking.

After lunch Señora Ramirez decided to go for a walk instead of taking a siesta with her daughters. She put on her gloves and took with her an umbrella to shield her from the sun. After she had walked a little while she came to a long road, completely desolate save for a few ruins and some beautiful tall trees along the way. She looked about her and shook her head at the thought of the terrible earthquake that had thrown to the ground this city, reputed to have been once the most beautiful city in all the Western Hemisphere. She could see ahead of her, way at the road's end, the volcano named Fire. She crossed herself and bit her lips. She had come walking with the intention of dreaming of her lover, but the thought of this volcano which had erupted many centuries ago chased all dreams of love from her mind. She saw in her mind the walls of the houses caving in, and the roofs falling on the heads of the babies . . . and the mothers, their skirts covered with mud, running through the streets in despair.

"The innocents," she said to herself. "I am sure that God had a perfect reason for this, but what could it have been? *Santa María*, but what could it have been! If such a disorder should happen again on this earth, I would turn completely to jelly like a helpless idiot."

She looked again at the volcano ahead of her, and although nothing had changed, to her it seemed that a cloud had passed across the face of the sun.

"You are crazy," she went on, "to think that an earthquake will again shake this city to the earth. You will not be going through such a trial as these other mothers went through, because everything now is different. God doesn't send such big trials any more, like floods over the whole world, and plagues."

She thanked her stars that she was living now and not before. It made her feel quite weak to think of the women who had been forced to live before she was born. The future too, she had heard, was to be very stormy because of wars.

"Ay!" she said to herself. "Precipices on all sides of me!" It had not been such a good idea to take a walk, after all. She thought again of the traveler, shutting her eyes for a moment.

"*Mi amante! Amante querido!*" she whispered; and she remembered the little books with their covers lettered in gold, books about love, which she had read when she was a young girl, and without the burden of a family. These little books had made the ability to read seem like the most worthwhile and delightful talent to her. They had never, of course, touched on the coarser aspects of love, but in later years she did not find it strange that it was for such physical ends that the heroes and heroines had been pining. Never had she found any difficulty in associating nosegays and couplets with the more gross manifestations of love.

She turned off into another road in order to avoid facing the volcano, constantly ahead of her. She thought of the traveler without really thinking of him at all. Her eyes glowed with the pleasure of being in love and she decided that she had been very stupid to think of an earthquake on the very day that God was making a bed of roses for her.

"Thank you, thank you," she whispered to Him, "from the bottom of my heart. Ah!" She smoothed her dress over her bosom. She was suddenly very pleased with everything. Ahead she noticed that there was a very long convent, somewhat ruined, in front of which some boys were playing. There was also a little pavilion standing not far away. It was difficult to understand why it was so situated, where there was no formal park, nor any trees or grass—just some dirt and a few bushes. It had the strange static look of a ship that has been grounded. Señora Ramirez looked at it distastefully; it was a small kiosk anyway and badly in need of a coat of paint. But feeling tired, she was soon climbing up the flimsy steps, red in the face with fear lest she fall through to the ground. Inside the kiosk she spread a newspaper over the bench and sat down. Soon all her dreams of her lover faded from her mind, and she felt hot and fretful. She moved her feet around on the floor impatiently at the thought of having to walk all the way home. The dust rose up into the air and she was obliged to cover her mouth with her handkerchief.

"I wish to heaven," she said to herself, "that he would come and carry me out of this kiosk." She sat idly watching the boys playing in the dirt in front of the convent. One of them was a good deal taller than the others. As she watched their games, her head slumped forward and she fell asleep.

No tourists came, so the smaller boys decided to go over to the main square and meet the buses, to sell their lollipops and picture postcards. The oldest boy announced that he would stay behind.

"You're crazy," they said to him. "Completely crazy."

He looked at them haughtily and did not answer. They ran down the road, screaming that they were going to earn a thousand *quetzales*.

He had remained behind because for some time he had noticed that there was someone in the kiosk. He knew even from where he stood that it was a woman because he could see that her dress was brightly colored like a flower garden. She had been sitting there for a long time and he wondered if she were not dead.

"If she is dead," he thought, "I will carry her body all the way into town." The idea excited him and he approached the pavilion with bated breath. He went inside and stood over Señora Ramirez, but when he saw that she was quite old and fat and obviously the mother of a good rich family he was frightened and all his imagination failed him. He thought he would go away, but then he decided differently, and he shook her foot. There was no change. Her mouth, which had been open, remained so, and she went on sleeping. The boy took a good piece of the flesh on her upper arm between his thumb and forefinger and twisted it very hard. She awakened with a shudder and looked up at the boy, perplexed.

His eyes were soft.

"I awakened you," he said, "because I have to go home to my house, and you are not safe here. Before, there was a man here in the bandstand trying to look under your skirt. When you are asleep, you know, people just go wild. There were some drunks here too, singing an obscene song, standing on the ground, right under you. You would have had red ears if you had heard it. I can tell you that." He shrugged his shoulders and spat on the floor. He looked completely disgusted.

"What is the matter?" Señora Ramirez asked him.

"Bah! This city makes me sick. I want to be a carpenter in the capital, but I can't. My mother gets lonesome. All my brothers and sisters are dead."

"Ay!" said Señora Ramirez. "How sad for you! I have a beautiful house in the capital. Maybe my husband would let you be a carpenter there, if you did not have to stay with your mother."

The boy's eyes were shining.

"I'm coming back with you," he said. "My uncle is with my mother."

"Yes," said Señora Ramirez. "Maybe it will happen."

"My sweetheart is there in the city," he continued. "She was living here before."

Señora Ramirez took the boy's long hand in her own. The word sweetheart had recalled many things to her.

"Sit down, sit down," she said to him. "Sit down here beside me. I too have a sweetheart. He's in his room now."

"Where does he work?"

"In the United States."

"What luck for you! My sweetheart wouldn't love him better than she loves me, though. She wants me or simply death. She says so any time I ask her. She would tell the same thing to you if you asked her about me. It's the truth."

Señora Ramirez pulled him down onto the bench next to her. He was confused and looked out over his shoulder at the road. She tickled the back of his hand and smiled up at him in a coquettish manner. The boy looked at her and his face seemed to weaken.

"You have blue eyes," he said.

Señora Ramirez could not wait another minute. She took his head in her two hands and kissed him several times full on the mouth.

"Oh, God!" she said. The boy was delighted with her fine clothes, her blue eyes, and her womanly ways. He took Señora Ramirez in his arms with real tenderness.

"I love you," he said. Tears filled his eyes, and because he was so full of a feeling of gratitude and kindness, he added: "I love my sweetheart and I love you too."

He helped her down the steps of the kiosk, and with his arm around her waist he led her to a sequestered spot belonging to the convent grounds.

• • •

The traveler was lying on his bed, consumed by a feeling of guilt. He had again spent the night with Señora Ramirez, and he was wondering whether or not his mother would read this in his eyes when he returned. He had never done anything like this before. His behavior until now had never been without precedent, and he felt like a two-headed monster, as though he had somehow slipped from the real world into the other world, the world that he had always imagined as a little boy to be inhabited by assassins and orphans, and children whose mothers went to work. He put his head in his hands and wondered if he could ever forget Señora Ramirez. He remembered having read that the careers of many men had been ruined by women who because they had a certain physical stranglehold over them made it impossible for them to get away. These women, he knew, were always bad, and they were never Americans. Nor, he was certain, did they resemble Señora Ramirez. It was terrible to have done something he was certain none of his friends had ever done before him, nor would do after him. This experience, he knew, would have to remain a secret, and nothing made him feel more ill than having a secret. He liked to imagine that he and the group of men whom he considered to be his friends, discoursed freely on all things that were in their hearts and in their souls. He was beginning to talk to women in this free way, too—he talked to them a good deal, and he urged his friends to do likewise. He realized that he and Señora Ramirez never spoke, and this horrified him. He shuddered and said to himself: "We are like two gorillas."

He had been, it is true, with one or two prostitutes, but he had never taken them to his own bed, nor had he stayed with them longer than an hour. Also, they had been curly-headed blond American girls recommended to him by his friends.

"Well," he told himself, "there is no use making myself into a nervous wreck. What is done is done, and anyway, I think I might be excused on the grounds that: one, I am in a foreign country, which has sort of put me off my balance; two, I have been eating strange foods that I am not used to, and living at an unusually high altitude for me; and, three, I haven't had my own kind to talk to for three solid weeks."

He felt quite a good deal happier after having enumerated these extenuating conditions, and he added: "When I get onto my boat I shall wave goodby to the dock, and say good riddance to bad rubbish, and if the boss ever tries to send me out of the country, I'll tell him: 'not for a million dollars!' " He wished that it were possible to change pensions, but he had already paid for the remainder of the week. He was very thrifty, as, indeed, it was necessary for him to be. Now he lay down again on his bed, quite satisfied with himself, but soon he began to feel guilty again, and like an old truck horse, laboriously he went once more through the entire process of reassuring himself.

• • •

Lilina had put Victoria into a box and was walking in the town with her. Not far from the central square there was a dry-goods shop owned by a Jewish woman. Lilina had been there several times with her mother to buy wool. She knew the son of the proprietress, with whom she often stopped to talk. He was very quiet, but Lilina liked him. She decided to drop in at the shop now with Victoria.

When she arrived, the boy's mother was behind the counter stamping some old bolts of material with purple ink. She saw Lilina and smiled brightly.

"Enrique is in the patio. How nice of you to come and see him. Why don't you come more often?" She was very eager to please Lilina, because she knew the extent of Señora Ramirez's wealth and was proud to have her as a customer.

Lilina went over to the little door that led into the patio behind the shop, and opened it. Enrique was crouching in the dirt beside the washtubs. She was surprised to see that his head was wrapped in bandages. From a distance the dirty bandages gave the effect of a white turban.

She went a little nearer, and saw that he was arranging some marbles in a row.

"Good morning, Enrique," she said to him.

Enrique recognized her voice, and without turning his head, he started slowly to pick up the marbles one at a time and put them into his pocket.

His mother had followed Lilina into the patio. When she saw that Enrique, instead of rising to his feet and greeting Lilina, remained absorbed in his marbles, she walked over to him and gave his arm a sharp twist.

"Leave those damned marbles alone and speak to Lilina," she said to him. Enrique got up and went over to Lilina, while his mother, bending over with difficulty, finished picking up the marbles he had left behind on the ground.

Lilina looked at the big, dark red stain on Enrique's bandage. They both walked back into the store. Enrique did not enjoy being with Lilina. In fact, he was a little afraid of her. Whenever she came to the shop he could hardly wait for her to leave.

He went over now to a bolt of printed material which he started to unwind. When he had unwound a few yards, he began to follow the convolutions of the pattern with his index finger. Lilina, not realizing that his gesture was a carefully disguised insult to her, watched him with a certain amount of interest.

"I have something with me inside this box," she said after a while.

Enrique, hearing his mother's footsteps approaching, turned and smiled at her sadly.

"Please show it to me," he said.

She lifted the lid from the snake's box and took it over to Enrique.

"This is Victoria," she said.

Enrique thought she was beautiful. He lifted her from her box and held her just below the head very firmly. Then he raised his arm until the snake's eyes were on a level with his own.

"Good morning, Victoria," he said to her. "Do you like it here in the store?"

This remark annoyed his mother. She had slipped down to the other end of the counter because she was terrified of the snake.

"You speak as though you were drunk," she said to Enrique. "That snake can't understand a word you're saying."

"She's really beautiful," said Enrique.

"Let's put her back in the box and take her to the square," said Lilina. But Enrique did not hear her, he was so enchanted with the sensation of holding Victoria.

His mother again spoke up. "Do you hear Lilina talking to you?" she shouted. "Or is that bandage covering your ears as well as your head?"

She had meant this remark to be stinging and witty, but she realized herself that there had been no point to it.

"Well, go with the little girl," she added.

Lilina and Enrique set off toward the square together. Lilina had put Victoria back into her box.

"Why are we going to the square?" Enrique asked Lilina.

"Because we are going there with Victoria."

Six or seven buses had converged in one of the streets that skirted the square. They had come from the capital and from other smaller cities in the region. The passengers who were not going any farther had already got out and were standing in a bunch talking together and buying food from the vendors. One lady had brought with her a cardboard fan intended as an advertisement for beer. She was fanning not only herself, but anyone who happened to come near her.

The bus drivers were racing their motors, and some were trying to move into positions more advantageous for departing. Lilina was excited by the noise and the crowd. Enrique, however, had sought a quiet spot, and was now standing underneath a tree. After a while she ran over to him and told him that she was going to let Victoria out of her box.

"Then we'll see what happens," she said.

"No, no!" insisted Enrique. "She'll only crawl under the buses and be squashed to death. Snakes live in the woods or in the rocks."

Lilina paid little attention to him. Soon she was crouching on the edge of the curbstone, busily unfastening the string around Victoria's box.

Enrique's head had begun to pain him and he felt a little ill. He wondered if he could leave the square, but he decided he did not have the courage. Although the wind had risen, the sun was very hot, and the tree afforded him little shade. He watched Lilina for a little while, but soon he looked away from her, and began to think instead about his own death. He was certain that his head hurt more today than usual. This caused him to sink into the blackest gloom, as he did whenever he remembered the day he had fallen and pierced his skull on a rusty nail. His life had always been precious to him, as far back as he could recall, and it seemed perhaps even more so now that he realized it could be violently interrupted. He disliked Lilina; probably because he suspected intuitively that she was a person who could fall over and over again into the same pile of broken glass and scream just as loudly the last time as the first.

By now Victoria had wriggled under the buses and been crushed flat. The buses cleared away, and Enrique was able to see what had happened. Only the snake's head, which had been severed from its body, remained intact.

Enrique came up and stood beside Lilina. "Now are you going home?" he asked her, biting his lip.

"Look how small her head is. She must have been a very small snake," said Lilina.

"Are you going home to your house?" he asked her again.

"No. I'm going over by the cathedral and play on the swings. Do you want to come? I'm going to run there."

"I can't run," said Enrique, touching his fingers to the bandages. "And I'm not sure that I want to go over to the playground."

"Well," said Lilina. "I'll run ahead of you and I'll be there if you decide to come."

Enrique was very tired and a little dizzy, but he decided to follow her to the playground in order to ask her why she had allowed Victoria to escape under the buses.

When he arrived, Lilina was already swinging back and forth. He sat on a bench near the swings and looked up at her. Each time her feet grazed the ground, he tried to ask her about Victoria, but the question stuck in his throat. At last he stood up, thrust his hands into his pockets, and shouted at her.

"Are you going to get another snake?" he asked. It was not what he had intended to say. Lilina did not answer, but she did stare at him from the swing. It was impossible for him to tell whether or not she had heard his question.

At last she dug her heel into the ground and brought the swing to a standstill. "I must go home," she said, "or my mother will be angry with me."

"No," said Enrique, catching hold of her dress. "Come with me and let me buy you an ice."

"I will," said Lilina. "I love them."

They sat together in a little store, and Enrique bought two ices.

"I'd like to have a swing hanging from the roof of my house," said Lilina. "And I'd have my dinner and my breakfast served while I was swinging." This idea amused her and she began to laugh so hard that her ice ran out of her mouth and over her chin.

"Breakfast, lunch, and dinner and take a bath in the swing," she continued. "And make *pipi* on Consuelo's head from the swing."

Enrique was growing more and more nervous because it was getting late, and still they were not talking about Victoria.

"Could I swing with you in your house?" he asked Lilina.

"Yes. We'll have two swings and you can make *pipi* on Consuelo's head, too."

"I'd love to," he said.

His question seemed more and more difficult to present. By now it seemed to him that it resembled more a declaration of love than a simple question.

Finally he tried again. "Are you going to buy another snake?" But he still could not ask her why she had been so careless.

"No," said Lilina. "I'm going to buy a rabbit."

"A rabbit?" he said. "But rabbits aren't as intelligent or as beautiful as snakes. You had better buy another snake like Victoria."

"Rabbits have lots of children," said Lilina. "Why don't we buy a rabbit together?"

Enrique thought about this for a while. He began to feel almost lighthearted, and even a little wicked.

"All right," he said. "Let's buy two rabbits, a man and a woman." They finished their ices and talked together more and more excitedly about the rabbits.

On the way home, Lilina squeezed Enrique's hand and kissed him all over his cheeks. He was red with pleasure.

At the square they parted, after promising to meet again that afternoon.

• • •

It was a cloudy day, rather colder than usual, and Señora Ramirez decided to dress in her mourning clothes, which she always carried with her. She hung several strands of black beads around her neck and powdered her face heavily. She and Consuelo began to walk slowly around the patio.

Consuelo blew her nose. "Ay, mamá," she said. "Isn't it true that there is a greater amount of sadness in the world than happiness?"

"I don't know why you are thinking about this," said her mother.

"Because I have been counting my happy days and my sad days. There are many more sad days, and I am living now at the best age for a girl. There is nothing but fighting, even at balls. I would not believe any man if he told me he liked dancing better than fighting."

"This is true," said her mother. "But not all men are really like this. There are some men who are as gentle as little lambs. But not so many."

"I feel like an old lady. I think that maybe I will feel better when I'm married." They walked slowly past the traveler's door.

"I'm going inside," said Consuelo suddenly.

"Aren't you going to sit in the patio?" her mother asked her.

"No, with all those children screaming and the chickens and the parrot talking and the white dog. And it's such a terrible day. Why?"

Señora Ramirez could not think of any reason why Consuelo should stay in the patio. In any case she preferred to be there alone if the stranger should decide to talk to her.

"What white dog?" she said.

"Señora Espinoza has bought a little white dog for the children."

The wind was blowing and the children were chasing each other around the back patio. Señora Ramirez sat down on one of the little straight-backed chairs with her hands folded in her lap. The thought came into her mind that most days were likely to be cold and windy rather than otherwise, and that there would be many days to come exactly like this one. Unconsciously she had always felt that these were the days preferred by God, although they had never been much to her own liking.

The traveler was packing with the vivacity of one who is in the habit of making little excursions away from the charmed fold to return almost immediately.

"Wow!" he said joyfully to himself. "I sure have been giddy in this place, but the bad dream is over now." It was nearly bus time. He carried his bags out to the patio, and was confused to find Señora Ramirez sitting there. He prompted himself to be pleasant.

"Señora," he said, walking over to her. "It's goodby now till we meet again."

"What do you say?" she asked.

"I'm taking the twelve o'clock bus. I'm going home."

"Ah! You must be very happy to go home." She did not think of looking away from his face. "Do you take a boat?" she asked, staring harder.

"Yes. Five days on the boat."

"How wonderful that must be. Or maybe it makes you sick." She put her hand over her stomach.

"I have never been seasick in my life."

She said nothing to this.

He backed against the parrot swinging on its perch, and stepped forward again quickly as it leaned to bite him.

"Is there anyone you would like me to look up in the United States?"

"No. You will be coming back in not such a long time?"

"No. I don't think I will come back here again. Well. . . ." He put out his hand and she stood up. She was fairly impressive in her black clothes. He looked at the beads that covered her chest.

"Well, good-bye, señora. I was very happy to have met you."

"*Adios*, señor, and may God protect you on your trip. You will be coming back maybe. You don't know."

He shook his head and walked over to the Indian boy standing by his luggage. They went out into the street and the heavy door closed with a bang. Señora Ramirez looked around the patio. She saw Señorita Córdoba move away from the half-open bedroom door where she had been standing.

1940–1941

A DAY IN THE OPEN

JANE BOWLES

Excised from the novel that became Two Serious Ladies, *the following selection was published in 1945 as a separate story, "A Day in the Open."*

In the outskirts of the capital there was a low white house, very much like the other houses around it. The street on which it stood was not paved, as this was a poor section of the city. The door of this particular house, very new and studded with nails, was bolted inside and out. A large room, furnished with some modern chromium chairs, a bar, and an electric record machine, opened onto the empty patio. A fat little Indian boy was seated in one of the chairs, listening to the tune *Good Night, Sweetheart*, which he had just chosen. It was playing at full volume and the little boy was staring very seriously ahead of him at the machine. This was one of the houses owned and run by Señor Kurten, who was half Spanish and half German.

It was a gray afternoon. In one of the bedrooms Julia and Inez had just awakened. Julia was small and monkey-like. She was appealing only because of her extraordinarily large and luminous eyes. Inez was tall and high-breasted. Her head was a bit too small for her body and her eyes were too close together. She wore her hair in stiff waves.

Julia was moaning on her bed.

"My stomach is worse today," she said to Inez. "Come over and feel it. The lump on the right side is bigger." She twisted her head on the pillow and sighed. Inez was staring sternly into space.

"No," she said to Julia. "I cannot bear to feel that lump. *Santa*

María! With something like that inside me I should go wild." She made a wry face and shuddered.

"You must not feel it if you do not want to," said Julia drowsily. Inez poured herself some *guaro*. She was a heavy drinker but her vitality remained unimpaired, although her skin often broke out in pimples. She ate violet lozenges to cover the smell of liquor on her breath and often popped six or seven of them into her mouth at once. Being full of enterprise she often made more money outside the whorehouse than she did at her regular job.

Julia was Mexican and a great favorite with the men, who enjoyed feeling that they were endangering her very life by going to bed with her.

"Well," said Inez, "I think that this afternoon I will go to the movies, if you will lend me a pair of your stockings. You had better lie here in your bed. I would sit here with you but it makes me feel very strange now to stay in this room. It is peculiar because, you know, I am a very calm woman and have suffered a great deal since I was born. You should go to a doctor," she added.

"I cannot bear to be out in the street," said Julia. "The sun is too hot and the wind is too cold. The smell of the market makes me feel sick, although I have known it all my life. No sooner have I walked a few blocks than I must find some park to sit in, I am so tired. Then somebody comes and tries to sell me orchids and I buy them. I have been out three times this week and each time I have bought some flowers. Now you know I can't afford to do this, but I am so weak and ill that I am becoming more like my grandmother every day. She had a feeling that she was not wanted here on this earth, either by God or by other people, so she never felt that she could refuse anyone anything."

"Well, if you are going to become like your grandmother," said Inez, "it will be a sad mistake. I should forget this sort of thing. You'll get to the doctor. Meanwhile, sit in the sun more. I don't want to be unkind. . . ."

"No, no. You are not unkind," Julia protested.

"You sit in this dark room all day long even when there is sun and you do not feel so sick."

Julia was feeling more desperately lonely than she had ever felt before in her life. She patted her heart. Suddenly the door pushed open and Señor Kurten came into the room. He was a slight man with a low forehead and a long nose.

"Julia and Inez," he said. "Señor Ramirez just telephoned that he is coming over this afternoon with a friend. He is going to take you both out to the country on a picnic and you are to hurry up and be ready. Try to bring them back to the bar in the evening."

"Hans," said Julia. "I am sick. I can't see Señor Ramirez or anyone else."

"Well, you know I can't do anything if he wants to see you. If he was angry he could make too much trouble. I am sorry." Señor Kurten left the room, closing the door slowly behind him.

"He is so important," said Inez, rubbing some eau de cologne over Julia's forehead. "So important, poor child. You must go." Her hand was hard and dry.

"Inez—" Julia clutched at Inez's kimono just as she was walking away. She struggled out of bed and threw herself into the arms of her friend. Inez was obliged to brace herself against the foot of the bed to keep from being knocked over.

"Don't make yourself crazy," said Inez to Julia, but then Inez began to cry; the sound was high like the squeal of a pig.

"Inez," said Julia. "Get dressed and don't cry. I feel better, my little baby."

They went into the bar and sat down to await the arrival of Señor Ramirez and his friend. Julia's arm was flung over the side of the chair, and her purse was swinging from her hand on an unusually long strap. She had put a little red dot in the corner of each eye, and rouged her cheeks very highly.

"You don't look very good," said Inez. "I'm afraid in my heart for you."

Julia opened her eyes wide and stared fixedly ahead of her at the wall. The Indian boy was polishing a very large alarm clock with care.

Soon Señor Ramirez stuck his head through the doorway. He had a German face but there was something very Spanish in the angle of his slouched fedora hat. His mustaches were blond and abundant. He had just shaved, and the talcum powder was visible on his chin and on his cheeks. He wore a pink shirt and a light tweed jacket, and on the fourth finger of each hand a heavy gold ring studded with a jewel.

"Come on, daughters," he said. "The car is waiting outside, with my friend. Move along."

Señor Ramirez drove very quickly. Julia and Inez sat uncomfortably on the edge of the back seat, hanging onto the straps at the side.

"We are going on a picnic," shouted Señor Ramirez. "I've brought with me five bottles of champagne. They are in the back of the car and they were all packed in ice by my cook. There is no reason why we should not have everything we want with us. They are inside a basket in the back. She wrapped the ice in a towel. That way it doesn't melt so quickly, but still we have to get there in a pretty short time. I drink nothing but American whiskey, so I brought along a quart of it for myself. What do you think of that?"

"Oh, how nice," said Julia.

"I think we shall have a wonderful time," said Inez.

Señor Ramirez's friend Alfredo looked ill and disgruntled. He did not say anything himself, nor did the angle of his head indicate that he was listening to a word that anyone else was saying.

It was a cold day and the parasols under which the policemen stood were flapping in the wind. They passed a new yellow brick building, high at the top of six or seven flights of yellow brick steps.

"That is going to be a new museum," said Señor Ramirez. "When it opens we are all going to have a big dinner there together. Everyone there will be an old friend of mine. That's nothing. I can have dinner with fifty people every night of my life."

"A life of fiesta," put in Inez.

"Even more than that. They are more than just fiestas," he said, without quite knowing what he meant himself.

The sun was shining into Julia's lap. She felt lightheaded and feverish. Señor Ramirez turned the radio on as loud as he could. They were broadcasting *Madame Butterfly* as the car reached the outskirts of the city.

"I have three radios at home," said Señor Ramirez.

"Ah," said Inez. "One for the morning, one for the night and one for the afternoon." Julia listened to Inez with interest and wonder. They were on the edge of a deep ravine, going round a curve in the road. The mountainside across the ravine was in the shade, and some Indians were climbing toward the summit.

"Walk, walk, walk . . ." said Julia mournfully. "Oh, how tired it makes me feel to watch them."

Inez pinched her friend's arm. "Listen," she whispered to her. "You are not in your room. You daren't say things like that. You must not speak of being tired. It's no fun for them. They wouldn't like it."

"We'll be coming to that picnic spot in a minute," said Señor Ramirez. "Nobody knows where it is but me. I like to have a spot, you know, where all my friends won't come and disturb me. Alfredo," he added, "are you hungry?"

"I don't think this Alfredo is very nice, do you?" Inez asked very softly of Julia.

"Oh, yes," said Julia, for she was not quick to detect a mean nature in anybody, being altogether kind and charitable herself. At last, after driving through a path wide enough for only one car, they arrived at the picnic spot. It was a fair-sized clearing in a little forest. Not far from it, at the bottom of a hill, was a little river and a waterfall. They got out and listened to the noise of the water. Both of the women were delighted with the sound.

"Since it is so sunny out, ladies," said Señor Ramirez, "I am going to walk around in my underpants. I hope that my friend will do the same if he wants to."

"What a lucky thing for us," said Inez in a strident voice. "The day begins right." Señor Ramirez undressed and slipped on a pair of tennis shoes. His legs were very white and freckled.

"Now I will give you some champagne right away," he said to them, a little out of breath because he had struggled so quickly out of his clothes. He went over to where he had laid the basket and took from it a champagne bottle. On his way back he stumbled over a rock; the bottle fell from his hand and was smashed in many pieces. For a moment his face clouded over and he looked as though he were about to lose his temper; instead, seizing another bottle from the basket, he flung it high into the air, almost over the tops of the trees. He returned elated to his friends.

"A gentleman," he said, "always knows how to make fun. I am one of the richest businessmen in this country. I am also the craziest. Like an American. When I am out I always have a wonderful time, and so does everyone who is with me, because they know that while I am around there is always plenty. Plenty to eat, plenty to drink, and plenty of beautiful women to make love to. Once you have been out with me," he pointed his finger at Julia and Inez, "any other man will seem to you like an old-lady schoolteacher."

He turned to Alfredo. "Tell me, my friend, have you not had the time of your life with me?"

"Yes, I have," said Alfredo. He was thinking very noticeably of other things.

"His mind is always on business," Señor Ramirez explained to Julia. "He is also very clever. I have gotten him this job with a German concern. They are manufacturing planes." Alfredo said something to Señor Ramirez in German, and they spoke no longer on the subject. They spread out their picnic lunch and sat down to eat.

Señor Ramirez insisted on feeding Julia with his own fingers. This rather vexed Inez, so she devoted herself to eating copiously. Señor Ramirez drank quantities of whiskey out of a tin folding cup. At the end of fifteen or twenty minutes he was already quite drunk.

"Now, isn't it wonderful to be all together like this, friends? Alfredo, aren't these two women the finest, sweetest women in the world? I do not understand why in the eyes of God they should be condemned to the fires of hell for what they are. Do you?"

Julia moaned and rose to her feet.

"No, no!" she said, looking up helplessly at the branches overhead.

"Come on," said Señor Ramirez. "We're not going to worry about this today, are we?" He took hold of her wrist and pulled her down to the ground beside him. Julia hid her face in her hands and leaned her head against his shoulder. Soon she was smiling up at him and stroking his face.

"You won't leave me alone?" she asked, laughing a little in an effort to bring him to terms with her. If anyone were to be pitted successfully against the Divine, she thought, it would certainly be someone like Señor Ramirez. The presence of such men is often enough to dispel fear from the hearts of certain people for whom God is more of an enemy than a friend. Señor Ramirez's principal struggle in life was one of pride rather than of conscience; and because his successes were numerous each day, replenishing his energy and his taste for life, his strength was easily felt by those around him. Now that he was near her, Julia felt that she was safe from hell, and she was quite happy even though her side still hurt her very badly.

"Now," said Inez, "I think that we should all play a game, to chase gloomy thoughts out of this girl's head."

She rose to her feet and snatched Señor Ramirez's hat from where it lay beside him on the ground, placing it a few feet away upside down on the grass. Then she gathered some acorns in the picnic basket.

"Now," she said. "We will see who can throw these acorns into the hat. He will win."

"I think," said Señor Ramirez, "that the two women should be naked while we are playing this; otherwise it will be just a foolish children's game."

"And we are not children at all," said Inez, winking at him. The two women turned and looked at Alfredo questioningly.

"Oh, don't mind him," said Señor Ramirez. "He sees nothing but numbers in his head."

The two girls went behind some bushes and undressed. When they returned, Alfredo was bending over a ledger and trying to explain something to Señor Ramirez, who looked up, delighted that they had returned so quickly, so that he would not be obliged to listen.

"Ah," he said. "Now this looks much more like friends together, doesn't it, Alfredo?"

"Come on," said Inez. "We will all get into line here with this basket and each one will try to throw the acorn into the hat."

Señor Ramirez grew quite excited playing the game; then he began to get angry because he never managed to get the acorn into the hat. Inez screeched with laughter and threw her acorn wider and wider of the mark, each time purposely, in order to soothe, if possible, the hurt pride of Señor Ramirez. Alfredo refused to play at all.

"Games don't interest me," said Señor Ramirez suddenly. "I'd like to play longer with you, daughters, but I can't honestly keep my mind on the game."

"It is of no importance at all, really," said Inez, busily trying to think up something to do next.

"How are your wife and children?" Julia asked him.

Inez bit her lip and shook her head.

"They are well taken care of. I have sent them to a little town where they are staying in a pension. Quiet women—all three of them—the little girls and the mother. I am going to sleep." He stretched out under a tree and put his hat over his face. Alfredo was absorbed in his ledger. Inez and Julia sat side by side and waited.

"You have the brain of a baby chicken," Inez said to Julia. "I must think for both of us. If I had not had a great deal of practice when I had to keep count of all the hundreds of tortillas that I sold for my mother, I don't know where we would be."

"Dead, probably," said Julia. They began to feel cold.

"Come," said Inez. "Sing with me." They sang a song about leaving and never returning, four or five times through. When Señor Ramirez awakened he suggested to Julia that they go for a walk. She accepted sweetly, and so they started off through the woods. Soon they reached a good-sized field where Señor Ramirez suggested that they sit for a while.

"The first time I went to bed with a woman," he said, "it was in the country like this. The land belonged to my father. Three or four times a day we would come out into the fields and make love. She loved it, and would have come more often if I had asked her to. Some years later I went to her wedding and I had a terrible fight there. I don't even remember who the man was, but in the end he was badly hurt. I can tell you that."

"If you put your arms around me," said Julia, "I will feel less cold. You don't mind my asking you to do this, but I love you very much and I feel very contented with you."

"That's good," said Señor Ramirez, looking off at the mountains and shielding his eyes from the sun. He was listening to the sound of the waterfall, which was louder here. Julia was laughing and touching various parts of his body.

"Ah," she said. "I don't mind my side hurting me so badly if I can only be happy the way I am now with you. You are so sweet and so wonderful."

He gave her a quick loud kiss on the mouth and rose to his feet.

"Listen," he said. "Wouldn't you like to come into the water with me?"

"I am too sick a woman to go into the water, and I am a little bit afraid."

"In my arms you don't have to be afraid. I will carry you. The current would be too strong for you to manage anyway." Señor Ramirez was now as gay as a lark, although he had been bored but a moment before. He liked nothing better than performing little feats that were assured of success from the beginning. He carried her down to the river, singing at the top of his voice.

The noise of the falls was very loud here, and Julia clung tightly to her escort.

"Don't let go, now," she said. But her voice seemed to fly away behind her like a ribbon caught in the wind. They were in the water and Señor Ramirez began to walk in the direction of the falls.

"I will hold tight, all right," he said. "Because the water runs pretty swiftly near the falls." He seemed to enjoy stepping precariously from one stone to another with Julia in his arms.

"This is not so easy, you know. This is damned hard. The stones are slippery." Julia tightened her grip around his neck and kissed him quickly all over his face.

"If I let you go," he said, "the current would carry you along like a leaf over the falls, and then one of those big rocks would make a hole in your head. That would be the end, of course." Julia's eyes widened with horror, and she yelled with the suddenness of an animal just wounded.

"But why do you scream like that, Julia? I love you, sweetheart." He had had enough of struggling through the water, and so he turned around and started back.

"Are we going away from the waterfall?"

"Yes. It was wonderful, wasn't it?"

"Very nice," she said.

He grew increasingly careless as the current slackened, with the result that he miscalculated and his foot slipped between two stones. This threw him off his balance and he fell. He was unhurt, but the back of Julia's head had hit a stone. It started to bleed profusely. He struggled to his feet and carried her to the riverbank. She was not sure that she was not dying, and hugged him all the more closely. Pulling her along, he walked quickly up the hill and back through the woods to where Inez and Alfredo were still sitting.

"It will be all right, won't it?" she asked him a bit weakly.

"Those damn rocks were slippery," he growled. He was sulky, and eager to be on his way home.

"Oh, God of mine!" lamented Inez, when she saw what had happened. "What a sad ending for a walk! Terrible things always happen to Julia. She is a daughter of misfortune. It's a lucky thing that I am just the contrary."

Señor Ramirez was in such a hurry to leave the picnic spot that he did not even want to bother to collect the various baskets and plates he had brought with him. They dressed, and he yelled for them all to get into the car. Julia wrapped a shawl around her bleeding head. Inez went around snatching up all the things, like an enraged person.

"Can I have these things?" she asked her host. He nodded his head impatiently. Julia was by now crying rhythmically like a baby that has almost fallen asleep.

The two women sat huddled together in the back of the car. Inez explained to Julia that she was going to make presents of the plates and baskets to her family. She shed a tear or two herself. When they arrived at the house, Señor Ramirez handed some banknotes to Inez from where he was sitting.

"*Adios*," he said. The two women got out of the car and stood in the street.

"Will you come back again?" Julia asked him tenderly, ceasing to cry for a moment.

"Yes, I'm coming back again," he said. "*Adios*." He pressed his foot on the accelerator and drove off.

The bar was packed with men. Inez led Julia around through the patio to their room. When she had shut the door, she slipped the banknotes into her pocket and put the basket on the floor.

"Do you want any of these baskets?" she asked.

Julia was sitting on the edge of her bed, looking into space. "No, thank you," she said. Inez looked at her, and saw that she was far away.

"Señor Ramirez gave me four drinking cups made out of plastic," said Inez. "Do you want one of them for yourself?"

Julia did not answer right away. Then she said: "Will he come back?"

"I don't know," Inez said. "I'm going to the movies. I'll come and see you afterwards, before I go into the bar."

"All right," said Julia. But Inez knew that she did not care. She shrugged her shoulders and went out through the door, closing it behind her.

1940–1941

SEÑORITA CÓRDOBA

JANE BOWLES

A FRAGMENT FROM *an excised section of* Two Serious Ladies, *the following selection was first published in 1985.*

ONE MORNING Señorita Córdoba received a letter from her mother. She sat beside the fountain reading it.

My Dear Violeta—
I do hope you are enjoying every minute of your stay in the city of Antigua. It is a great miracle to think that Antigua has been destroyed once by fire and once by water. My father pointed out the beauty of this city to me at an early age. He said to me, "When you go to Europe, you need not bow your head in shame that you have come from a country inhabited almost entirely by Indians, as many Europeans are wont to believe. But say to them proudly, "If Europe were a crown and in this crown one jewel were missing—the most beautiful jewel of all—you would find it in my country situated between two volcanoes and surrounded by hills. Its name is Antigua." At that age I loved to sit among the ruins, but Aunt Mercedes (who has come to agree with me), Aunt Mercedes and I still think it a little unwise for you to have taken such a trip at this particular moment. I realize it is only a few hours away, of course. Did you say that your board was fifty cents a day? For that they should serve you all the chicken you wanted and if they don't I hope you will be sure to demand your just rights. The lady of the pension will understand. I think perhaps that I as your mother have been a little

too spiritual all my life. I do not want you to be the same. Perhaps, though, spiritual would not be the correct term to apply to you. Aunt Mercedes and I have been contenting ourselves with eggs and beans. The meat has been unusually hard this week and so very dear. I don't want you to worry about this or let it spoil your lovely holiday. You might try to buy a picture of the All Saints Day parade from someone who has a camera. Try not to buy it—ask for it, nicely. Señora Sanchez was in the other evening. She was riding by on a horse and she stopped in. She was complaining bitterly about prices, and insulted me grossly, I thought, by handing me half a chicken enveloped in some newspaper, which I handed over to the servants, of course. Aunt Mercedes didn't think that was quite wise. She is a great chicken eater, while I myself am more or less indifferent to all foods, as you know. Aunt Mercedes thought it dreadful that she should be riding on a horse, so soon after her husband's death. We send you our best wishes for an agreeable holiday. May the Lord bless you and keep you well.

Your mother

Señorita Córdoba frowned and looked into the fountain. "Such an old-fashioned letter," she thought to herself. "My mother and my aunt are living like cliff dwellers. Such people write a letter about a chicken." She took a pencil from her bag and made some figures on a piece of paper. She knew just about how much money she needed to get back to Paris and to live there for a little while, while she was starting her dress establishment. She was going to make dresses with a Latin spirit. There was only one way for her to get hold of this money, she was certain, and that was through a man. She had seen a lot of this going on in Paris, and she thought that she would know how to handle such a situation if she could possibly meet a man rich enough in Guatemala. "It would all be in a first-class way," she had assured herself.

On the following morning Señorita Córdoba overheard Señora Ramirez telling the children that their father would arrive that day. She was delighted to hear this, because she knew Señor Ramirez to be one of the richest men in the country . . . and a great lady lover. It was on the chance that he would come to Antigua to visit his wife and children that she herself had decided to spend the Holy Week in Señora Espinoza's pension. She knew that Señora Ramirez had been spending the Semana Santa there now for many years, or so she had heard tell from her mother and her mother's friends, who had never understood why Señor Ramirez did not send his wife to a more expensive touristic hotel. He had never been seen at the pension with her until the previous year, when he had suddenly appeared in Antigua and stayed there for several days. However, most people said that he had come to spend his time with his friend Alfonso Gutierres, who had opened an unfrequented but very elegant hotel which was reputed to have the best wine cellar and hard liquor stock in the country. Señorita Córdoba, having heard of his former visit, had been very much in hopes that he would return again this season. She had thought the short journey well worth the risk, particularly as she was tired of helping her mother with the coffee finca and the house—two things which interested her less than anything in the world. She was delighted that he was arriving so promptly. She was never able to relax or enjoy anything that was not concerned directly with the making of her life. Now she was in a feverish state, pulling her dresses out of her trunk and examining them for holes. The figure that she had decided was the minimum sum which she would demand for her trip and to cover the initial investment in her dress shop, and of course her first six months living in Paris, she had marked down on a pad which lay on the bureau. She went over and looked at the pad now, and her cheeks were quite flushed with the intensity of her figuring. She stood there for a long time and then she changed the number on the pad. She made it a little lower.

She picked up a long silk ball dress that she had not worn for many years. It was pink, and to the bodice were pinned some shapeless silk flowers. She decided to wear this to dinner, as it was the fanciest thing she had and was certain to please a Spanish man. She lay down on the bed. Her face was strained and stiff. She shut her eyes for a moment and thought of the name of her shop. It was to be called "Casa Córdoba." "Now," she said to herself, "for what the French call beauty sleep. No thoughts—no thoughts—just rest." She could hear marimba music playing over the radio. She loved listening to music, and it made her think of all the things which she considered beautiful—Venice and the opera and the hall of mirrors in the palace at Versailles. To her, luxury and beauty (beauty there was none without at least the luxury of past splendor) were synonymous with morality, and when people lived well she considered them to be good people and when they lived really luxuriously she considered them to be saints. The marimba music and her memory of Venice and her walk through the hall of mirrors gave her such a feeling of the goodness of God that she crossed herself and decided to buy a candle in the church after her siesta.

The diners had all taken their places when Señorita Córdoba entered the room. The Ramirez daughters, Consuelo and Lilina, were seated on either side of their father, wearing their fiesta dresses. The servant stood in confusion before Señor Ramirez because he had ordered her not to bother with the soup but to bring him instead a large portion of meat and some beer right away.

"Wouldn't you like some soup first?" Maria asked him. Ramirez was beginning to lose his temper when he saw Señorita Córdoba enter the room. She had brightened her cheeks with some rouge, and on the whole she looked quite beautiful. Señor Ramirez's mouth hung open. He turned completely around in his chair and stared at Violeta. The traveler rose at the same time and rushed over to Señorita Córdoba as though he had never seen her before. She blushed a bright pink and her eyebrow twitched. To get away from all this attention she went over to the English lady in the corner and began to talk to her. The English lady was very much surprised because she had never received more than a curt nod from Miss Córdoba before this moment.

"Miss," said Violeta, "I wish you would take a walk with me some morning. I think it is a shame that we haven't become better acquainted with one another."

"Yes, it is, isn't it," answered the English lady. Miss Córdoba's armpits were wet with nervous sweat. She was terribly embarrassed since she had entered the room in her ball dress. She was bending over the English lady with one hand placed flat on the table, and she noticed that the English lady was looking into her bodice, a faint expression of disgust visible in her face, the disgust of an English person who does not like to be near to a foreigner.

"You Spanish girls all have such beautiful olive skin," she said. This was a completely hysterical thing for her to say because Violeta's skin was whiter than her own. She continued, "I would be very glad to take a walk with you but I am sure you will still be in the arms of Morpheus when I have already eaten my breakfast and written my letters for the day. I can't walk after ten because the sun tires me so. I have as a matter of fact covered the ground here thoroughly but I am looking forward to the processions. A friend described them to me so beautifully that I've been longing to see them ever since. A wonderful gift, to make other people see things. I am more or less mute myself. I have been impressed by the colors here. What a sense of color the Indians have. They are famous for it, aren't they?"

"Oh yes, very famous. I will see you then soon?"

"Perhaps."

Señorita Córdoba had nothing to do but to go back to the table and submit to the stares of Señor Ramirez and the appraising glances of the traveler. Out of exuberance Señor Ramirez decided to focus his attention on his older, eleven-year-old child, Consuelo.

"Now I think it would do you some good if you drank a big glass of beer," he said. "The Germans always give their children beer and look what a fine race of people they are."

"I don't want any beer, thank you, papa."

"You've never tried it so you don't know whether or not you like it." He poured her some beer and put it in front of her but she made no attempt to drink it. "You heard papa say that he wanted you to drink some beer."

"What kind of a crazy idea is this?" asked Señora Ramirez.

"What kind of a crazy girl is that that she won't drink beer?" answered Señor Ramirez.

"Yes, drink, Consuelo," said Señora Ramirez. "What is the matter with you?" She pushed the glass up to her daughter's lips but Consuelo refused to drink, although her mouth was covered with foam. The girl's eyes were beginning to shine. With a sudden jerking of her arm she knocked the glass out of her mother's hand, and the beer flowed over the table. Then she jumped up and down and screamed. Señorita Córdoba turned halfway around in her chair and looked at her bitterly. And partly for this reason, and partly because Consuelo was herself in love with the traveler and certain that the traveler in turn loved Señorita Córdoba, Consuelo lunged toward her and started to scratch Señorita Córdoba's face and to tear her coiffure apart. Violeta, with an icy smile on her face, stuck her leg out in order to trip Consuelo, but in so doing she miscalculated and slid off her chair onto the floor. Consuelo ran from the room, and both the traveler and Señor Ramirez helped Violeta up from the floor. She leaned her head on her hand and cried a little because the incident had so unnerved her. Señor Ramirez ordered a glass of beer for Señorita Córdoba.

"You drink that, Señorita," he said, "and when I am finished eating I will beat my daughter. I promise you that."

"I hope that you will," said Señorita Córdoba.

"Never before," said the English lady, "have I met three such horrid people. The daughter is a real Fury, unable to control herself, the father a child-beater, and the young woman full of revenge, willing to have the child beaten. My digestion is spoiled." She threw her napkin onto the table and left the room.

"Who is that one?" Señor Ramirez asked his wife.

"A tourist who eats here every day."

"She takes everything hard," said the traveler, turning to Señorita Córdoba. "Single women of her age do, you know. In our country we call them old maids."

"What is the difference what she is," said Señorita Córdoba. "To me she is no more than a flea."

"That's right," said Señor Ramirez. "That's right. Most people are fleas—fleas with big stomachs but nothing in their heads."

"But those big stomachs have to be fed," said the traveler, thinking that this was going to be a political discussion. "Or do you believe in letting them eat cake?"

"Cake? I don't care what they eat." The traveler decided not to explain about Marie Antoinette. Señorita Córdoba had composed herself completely by now, and she turned to Señor Ramirez.

"I am Señorita Violeta Córdoba," she said to him, disregarding all traditions of ladylike behavior, for she had always been able to throw tradition to the four winds without being in the least revolutionary. "Thank you for having lifted me from the floor onto my seat."

"And what about me?" said the traveler. "Don't I count in this at all?" Señorita Córdoba nodded to him without smiling. Ramirez stood up and toasted Señorita Córdoba with his beer. "To a beautiful lady," he said, "as beautiful as a red rose." They were speaking together in English.

"A thousand thanks," said Señorita Córdoba quickly. "Let us hope that you mean what you say, and are not just a poet."

"I can be a poet when I want to be, but it is only one of twenty or thirty things that I can do."

Señor Gutierres' hotel was austere but very elegant. The patio around which it was built was very small and almost always very dark. Looking down into it from the third floor, it was hard to distinguish the bushes and the few flower beds. Each bedroom was decorated in order to look as much like the bedroom of a Spanish king or nobleman as possible. The beds were on raised daises and the monogram of the hotel was on each pillow slip. The walls were rough and decorated with crossed sabres and blue or gold banners. The chairs were made of a very dark wood with carved narrow backs and little satin cushions tied to the seats by means of four tassels. Off the patio were two small dining rooms for those guests who preferred not to eat in the presence of strangers, and one large dining room that was public. In the public living room there was a veritable collection of sabres with fancy hilts, and chairs with backs that reached halfway up the wall. It was impossible to see in this room at all during the day, and at night the weak electric lamps left the corners of the room in total darkness.

Señor Gutierres was a gloomy businessman born in Spain who claimed to have noble blood. He was out in the back court, a place to which the guests had no access, wrangling with the cook about a chicken which he was holding by its feet and pinching. He was very thin and had deep circles under his eyes. There were a great many badly made rabbit hutches around and a tremendous chicken coop. He was one of the few people in the country who kept his chickens in a coop. However, there were three large holes in the wiring and the chickens stepped in and out of the coop freely. The courtyard was a mess and it was just beginning to drizzle when Señor Ramirez came out and clapped his friend on the shoulder. "How about coming down to the bar and having a drink with me?" Señor Gutierres nodded and smiled for a second and together they went to the bar, which was underground and smelled very strongly of new wood. The bar stools were made of barrels. Señor Ramirez sat down on one of these and Señor Gutierres dropped the chicken, which he was still holding, onto the floor. The chicken began to strut around the shiny wooden floor, pecking at whatever it saw.

"How do you like my bar now that it is completed?"

"I will like your brandy even better when I have completed a bottle of that."

"Do you like my bar?" Señor Gutierres said again, determined to get an answer out of Señor Ramirez.

"Beautiful."

"I have designed the whole hotel for movie actresses and actors when they are on their vacations. They will be coming down over that highway like flies when it is finished." He looked at Señor Ramirez to see if he was of the same opinion, but his friend was staring hard at the labels on the bottles.

"A lot of people on their honeymoons, too. Rich people who like to go far, far away when they get married." He took down a bottle of brandy from the shelf and served himself and Señor Ramirez.

"You don't think much about this new highway. I dream about it by day and by night. You will see a difference in the hotels in this country when it is built. You won't recognize the place you were born in inside of five years. No?"

Señor Gutierres could never get it through his head that Norberto Ramirez was not interested in anything but having a good time and wielding a certain amount of power. He had inherited most of his money and was successful because he had the character of a bully. Señor Gutierres could not imagine that anyone as important and as impressive as Señor Ramirez should not be interested in business. He believed that his friend's disinclination to talk on any subject of interest was merely a ruse, which he had long ago decided to ignore.

"I have built my hotel purposely so soon because later it will not be so cheap. I have already quite a few guests who come here because they know they get good quality. They are all quality people. Everything has to be right for them. It is just as cheap to be right as to be wrong, my friend, you know that, and with a war coming in Europe, all those with quality who used to go to Biarritz will come here. And I am not going to make cheap prices for them. They mustn't pay anything different from what they were paying in Biarritz, otherwise they will say to themselves, Look, what is this? There is something wrong—so cheap, and they will even get to worry that there might be lower-class people in the same hotel. No, they must be taken like sleeping babies from one bed to another, quietly, so they don't wake up. A little Spanish decoration for a change will be all right. But if you notice this hotel is made to remind you more or less of a palace."

One of the Indian servants appeared in the doorway. She looked to be about forty and she was nursing a baby at her breast and smiling. "What do you want, Luz?" asked Señor Gutierres.

"I have come for the chicken, Señor. He must feel very sad for he is estranged from the other chickens, his brothers and his sisters, and the poor little thing cannot find anything to eat here." She started to chase it. The chicken spread its wings and ran as fast as it could around and around the room. The baby started to howl.

"Stop it, stop it!" shouted Señor Gutierres. "You can come and get him later."

"No, wait a minute, man," said Señor Ramirez, climbing down from his stool. "I will get this chicken." He spread his arms out and chased it from corner to corner, making terrible scratches in the wooden floor with the heels of his shoes, to the horror of Señor Gutierres, who began to rub his nose nervously with the back of his hand. Señor Ramirez was quite red in the face by now and beginning to lose his balance. He made a lunge toward the chicken and managed to corner it, but in so doing he fell sideways onto the floor and managed to crush the chicken beneath him.

"Ay," said the servant. "Now it is dead we shall have to cook it for tomorrow night's supper."

"Take it away, for the love of God," said Señor Gutierres, lifting his friend to his feet and handing the bloody chicken to the servant.

"What a shame, what a shame." The servant shook her head and left the room. They had another brandy together and did not bother to clean up the blood and the feathers which stuck both to one side of Señor Ramirez' coat and to the floor.

Señorita Córdoba meanwhile had had enough of waiting around the patio for the problematic return of Señor Ramirez. "My God," she said to herself, "I have no time to lose. I am behaving like a person with not a brain in her head." Besides, it had begun to rain and it was incredibly gloomy sitting there under the eaves, which projected a little bit from the house for the purpose of protecting one from the sun and from the rain. She went into her room, painted her face a bit more, and changed to a short dress. Then she decided to knock on Señor Ramirez' door and by some ruse try to find out where this lady's husband was likely to be. This she did and at first received no answer.

She knocked a little harder. "Come in," said Señora Ramirez in a voice that was caught in her throat. Señorita Córdoba opened the door and saw that Señora Ramirez and the two girls were lying on their beds, in a row. Consuelo's dark eyes showed intense suffering as she rolled them slowly in the direction of the door. Lilina, seeing that it was Señorita Córdoba, pulled her pillow out from behind her head and buried her face beneath it. Señora Ramirez' eyes were swollen with sleep and she looked very much as though nothing would ever interest her again. Señorita Córdoba decided to ignore the mood that was in the room and she went hastily to the foot of Señora Ramirez' bed.

"I thought perhaps that you would be feeling rather badly as a result of this afternoon's events, and I came in to tell you more or less not to brood about it, and to ask you whether or not I could help you with anything."

Señora Ramirez nodded her head, and closed her eyes. Señorita Córdoba was growing impatient. She looked down at Consuelo. "You, young girl," she said, "you should apologize to me." Consuelo shook her head from side to side. "No," she said, "no, you are a very bad woman." She patted her heart.

"Well, Señora Ramirez, your daughter is a maniac. I am a religious woman and I am a very busy woman. That is all that anybody can say of me."

"Certainly," agreed Señora Ramirez, opening her eyes. "That is all anyone can say. And of me they can say that I am a mother of two children, and also a woman with a great many heartaches."

"I suppose you are wondering where your husband is at this very moment."

"No, no," said Señora Ramirez. "He is always outside somewhere."

Señorita Córdoba was exasperated. "But *where*? Where could he be?"

"With Gutierres, drinking."

"Who is Gutierres?"

"He is the owner of a hotel. It is called the Hotel Alhambra. My husband has never taken me to meet him and I shall probably never meet him before the day that I die."

Having gathered the information that she had been seeking, Señorita Córdoba hurriedly took her leave, warning Consuelo at the door that she had better repent shortly. And then she was on her way, with an even and decided gait, like someone who has been sent on an important mission by the head of an organization. She was not a person who envisioned failure often, but only the interminable steps towards success.

When she arrived at the hotel she found a servant in the patio and inquired of her where she could find Señor Gutierres. "He is in the bar," said the servant, leading the way slowly.

"Good evening," said Señorita Córdoba, entering the room. "I hope that I have not interrupted a serious business conversation. Women have a very bad habit of doing this."

"Women have no bad habits," said Señor Ramirez, climbing down from his stool and taking her by the arm a little roughly.

"I got it into my head," said Señorita Córdoba, "that I would like to look at some rooms here."

"I am sure you will take great pleasure in seeing them." Señor Gutierres had bounded to the door in his eagerness, but Señor Ramirez held his hand up in the air.

"Before the rooms," he said, "we are all going to have a drink together to celebrate the arrival of a lady. Champagne for her, Gutierres. Sit down, Señorita."

Señorita Córdoba complied with this request only too willingly and took her seat at the bar.

"How delightful," she said. "I always like to drink champagne because it reminds me of Paris, where I belong."

"Paris is a very gay city. The night life there is very beautiful," said Señor Gutierres, believing that he was dealing with an elegant client. "Here in this hotel there is everything to remind you of Paris. I have letters from there asking for reservations. Your father no doubt owns a finca, and you no doubt have lived all your life in Paris and in Biarritz. And now you find this country strange, like the jungle—*bien*?"

"This lady," said Señor Ramirez, "lives in the pension where I always put my wife and my two girls. That is how I know her."

Gutierres' face fell. He had hardly expected to draw his customers from Señora Espinoza's pension, which he considered a step below the large touristic hotels.

"I know the lady who owns the pension," he said sadly, "but very little, only to speak to. I know very few people in this town. My servants buy for me, so why should I speak to anyone?"

"You are better off keeping your life to yourself," said Señorita Córdoba, "than having companions that are doing nothing but just sitting and trying to find someone to laugh with."

A shadow seemed to pass across the face of Señor Ramirez. For a moment he thought of going back to the capital right away. "Here, here," he shouted. "What is all this about your life alone? Let's be together, friends—like baby chickens under the wings of the mother hen."

Señor Gutierres was now just a little bit drunk, and he was beginning to wander on to things that he scarcely knew he thought about. "No," he said, "no—no chickens under one wing. Each man alone, proud, acting as he has been taught to act by his family, never living in a house that is lower than the house in which he was born. Each man remembering his father and his mother and what he has been taught is sacred."

"The only thing that is sacred, my poor boy, is money," said the pleasure-seeking Norberto.

"No, it is one's class," insisted Señor Gutierres. "We must love our own class. I cannot talk and be friendly with people whose childhood I know has been different from mine, who did not have the same silver on the table when they sat down to eat."

"You would be glad to talk with me, Gutierres, even if I ate with pigs when I was a little boy."

"No, no, I would not. There is real friendship only between men who have always been used to the same things. Between two such men no words need be spoken, because each one knows that the other will do nothing to disgust him or upset him, and the pleasure of being with such a friend is quite enough. I have such a friend here, who knows the value of every piece of furniture in the Alhambra. And there is no wine that is familiar to me that is not familiar to him. We don't have to say anything to each other. Each of us remembers the same things. His family and my family come from the same part of Spain. I feel so close to him that I might say that I would even wear his underclothes. Forgive me, Señorita." He bowed his head.

"But *my* underwear you would not put on for five thousand quetzales, eh, señor?" said Ramirez, throwing his chest out.

Señor Gutierres, having started off talking about his thin code which he considered to be a universal and important ideology, had necessarily to go on further. His astute business sense was completely obliterated by the fanaticism that all men feel about whatever it is they believe makes the world an orderly and respectable place in which to live. "No, señor," he said, "I would not wear your underwear, for your education is far below mine and your family, as I know, were not much more than peasants before they came to this country."

"Oh, how rude you are," said Señorita Córdoba, taking hold of Señor Ramirez' hand. "And I am sure it is not true."

"Certainly it is true," said Señor Ramirez, "and this monkey will soon find out what else is true." Señorita Córdoba was surprised that Señor Ramirez had as yet not kicked the bar stools over, but apparently his family was not a sensitive point with him, and perhaps also he was having a very pleasurable reaction from the drinks and was not inclined to fight.

"Let him kiss his chairs," continued Señor Ramirez, "and see how many women he will get to kiss. He is probably a miserable eunuch anyway. Kiss me." He put his hand under Señorita Córdoba's chin and kissed her full on the mouth. Señorita Córdoba wondered whether or not she should resist this kiss, and decided very quickly that it was wiser to pretend to enjoy it. She passed a fluttering hand over his ear, which was one of the few love gestures she knew about.

"This woman is a trollop," said Señor Gutierres in a trembling voice. Señor Ramirez could not possibly let this remark pass so he stopped kissing Señorita Córdoba and gave Gutierres a sock on the jaw that knocked him off his stool and onto the floor, where he lay unconscious.

"Now," he said to Señorita Córdoba, lifting her down from her stool, "let us find an agreeable place in this beautiful Alhambra Hotel." He spat on the floor.

"Oh, well," said Señorita Córdoba, deciding that it was time for her to be a little bit shy. "Shall we stand in the patio a little bit and then go home?"

"No," he said. "I want to go where I can see your beautiful face." He led her upstairs, and with his foot he kicked open the door to one of the bedrooms, and turned on the light. She went and sat down on one of the chairs which Señor Gutierres considered to be beautiful and folded her hands in her lap. "I have always been interested to know a man like you," she said, "with such a wonderful way of knowing how to live."

"There are no disappointments in my life," said Señor Ramirez, "and I love it. I can show you some wonderful things."

"My life is a terrible disappointment to me," said Señorita Córdoba, and her heart beat very quickly as she felt she was approaching her goal.

The room was badly lighted and she searched his eyes avidly to see what effect her words had made on him. It seemed to her that they had a slightly blank look, like the eyes of anyone who is gazing at a particular object without really seeing it.

"You have not had the right kind of love," he said.

"That is not the only reason," said Señorita Córdoba, shaking her head vigorously. Señor Ramirez was feeling suddenly very drunk and he threw himself down on the bed.

"You must not go to sleep," she said nervously, rising to her feet.

"Who in the devil is going to sleep?" Señor Ramirez leaned on his elbows and looked at her like an angry bull.

"Listen," she said, "I'm so miserable on that finca where I am living that I think that if it goes on any longer I will certainly drown myself in the river."

"Drowning is no good," said Ramirez. "That's only good for scared fools, like those little dogs that shiver all the time—they have them in Mexico. You are not on your finca now. Come here on the bed and stop talking so much." He put his arm out and caught at the air with his hand.

"I want to go away to Paris, where I have friends, and start a dress shop."

"Sure," said Señor Ramirez.

"But I have not got any money."

"I have so much money."

"I need five thousand dollars."

He started to unbutton his pants. Señorita Córdoba remembered that many men were not interested in ladies nearly as much after they had made love to them as they were beforehand, so she decided that she had better make sure that she received a check first. She did not know how to do this tactfully but her own greed and the fact that he was drunk, and that she thought him a coarse person anyway, made her believe that she would be successful. She walked quickly to the window and stood with her back to him.

"What are you looking at outside the window?" asked Señor Ramirez, in a thick voice, smelling trouble.

"I am not looking at anything. On the contrary, I am just thinking about you, and how little you are really interested in whether or not I will open a dress shop."

"You can open a thousand dress shops, my beautiful woman. What is the matter with you?"

"You lie. I cannot even open one dress shop." She turned around and faced him.

"Wildcat," he said to her. She tried to look more touching.

"You will not help me to open a dress shop. Must it be someone else that will help me?"

"I am going to help you open fifty dress shops—tomorrow."

"I would not ask you for fifty, only for one. Would you make me happy and give me a check tonight so that I know when I go to sleep I will have my dress shop? I would like to sleep in peace just for once and know that I am not going to have to go back to that terrible finca, and listen to the dogs howling and my mother praying out loud. This one check would banish all these horrible things from my mind right away and I would be eternally grateful to you. I would be so glad that it had been you who did it, too."

"Well, then, come here."

She sat down on the bed beside him and he kissed her, but while he was kissing her she pushed him away and said to him, "Give me the check now."

"What is this?" asked Señor Ramirez. "Are you still talking about this damn foolish check?"

"Yes," said Señorita Córdoba, seeing that it was no use any longer to employ tact. "I will not go to bed with you unless you first give me a check for five thousand quetzales, or a piece of paper saying that you owe this sum of money to me."

Certainly this remark was not having the right effect on Señor Ramirez, who struggled with difficulty down from the bed and buttoned his trousers. She watched him attentively and noticed that the glands in his neck were moving. "Angry again," she said to herself, but she could think of nothing to say that would calm him except "Where are you going?" which she asked in a rather ironical tone of voice, all her false ardor dampened now by her own conviction that she would fail to get her money. Señor Ramirez was trembling and very red in the face. She stood still and appeared to be very calm even when he finally stumbled out of the room, but when she heard him clambering down the stairs she walked out onto the balcony and looked down over the railing into the patio. One light was burning and in a moment Señor Ramirez came into the patio and picked up what she saw was a large urn with a tall plant growing out of it. This he threw to the ground not very far from his feet, because it was very heavy. It smashed in many pieces, but made less noise than she expected to hear because the dirt inside the urn muffled the sound that it would otherwise have made.

She could not understand his fury, knowing so little about deeply outraged feelings and the fact that so much of people's violence is spent in the elaborate and grim protection of a personality as underdeveloped as a foetus yet grown quickly to tremendous proportions, like a giant weed. Being stupid herself, she did not recognize the danger inherent in all those whose self-protective instincts are far greater than the personality they are protecting, because their armor can only be timeworn and made up of the most stagnating of human impulses. Señorita Córdoba was unwounded if unintelligent, and her rages were unimportant nervous discharges.

Señor Ramirez was struggling with the big wooden doors that led into the street and making a terrible racket shaking the heavy iron chains, but it was to no avail because the doors were locked from the inside. She could only hear him now without being able to see him, since the bulb threw no light into the front of the patio. Suddenly he stopped rattling the chains and she heard him walking back in the direction of the staircase.

"My God," she thought, "he has murder in his heart, certainly," and she sneaked around to another side of the balcony. Fortunately the servant who had before been looking for the chicken was awakened by the noise and she now came into the patio to find out what the trouble was. "The door is locked," Ramirez shouted at her.

"Yes," she whispered. "I'll fetch the key."

She returned with the key and let Señor Ramirez out of the patio into the street. Señorita Córdoba decided to wait a little while before returning to the pension herself. She was thinking very hard of a way to redeem herself on the following day. She was like certain mediocre politically minded persons upon whose minds failure leaves no deep impression, not because of any burning belief in the ideal for which they are fighting, but rather because they are accustomed to thinking only of what to do next. These people are often valuable but at the same time so removed from reality that they are ridiculous. After sitting a while in the gloomy Spanish bedroom Señorita Córdoba went downstairs and in turn awakened the Indian servant, who let her out.

1940–1941

ALLAL

PAUL BOWLES

HE WAS BORN in the hotel where his mother worked. The hotel had only three dark rooms which gave on a courtyard behind the bar. Beyond was another smaller patio with many doors. This was where the servants lived, and where Allal spent his childhood.

The Greek who owned the hotel had sent Allal's mother away. He was indignant because she, a girl of fourteen, had dared to give birth while she was working for him. She would not say who the father was, and it angered him to reflect that he himself had not taken advantage of the situation while he had had the chance. He gave the girl three months' wages and told her to go home to Marrakech. Since the cook and his wife liked the girl and offered to let her live with them for a while, he agreed that she might stay on until the baby was big enough to travel. She remained in the back patio for a few months with the cook and his wife, and then one day she disappeared, leaving the baby behind. No one heard of her again.

As soon as Allal was old enough to carry things, they set him to work. It was not long before he could fetch a pail of water from the well behind the hotel. The cook and his wife were childless, so that he played alone.

When he was somewhat older he began to wander over the empty table-land outside. There was nothing else up here but the barracks, and they were enclosed by a high blind wall of red adobe. Everything else was below in the valley: the town, the gardens, and the river winding southward among the thousands of palm trees. He could sit on a point of rock far above and look down at the people walking in the alleys of the town. It was only later that he visited the place and saw what the inhabitants were like. Because he had been left behind by his mother they called him a son of sin, and laughed when they looked at him. It seemed to him that in this way they hoped to make him into a shadow, in order not to have to think of him as real and alive. He awaited with dread the time when he would have to go each morning to the town and work. For the moment he helped in the kitchen and served the officers from the barracks, along with the few motorists who passed through the region. He got small tips in the restaurant, and free food and lodging in a cell of the servants' quarters, but the Greek gave him no wages. Eventually he reached an age when this situation seemed shameful, and he went of his own accord to the town below and began to work, along with other boys of his age, helping to make the mud bricks people used for building their houses.

Living in the town was much as he had imagined it would be. For two years he stayed in a room behind a blacksmith's shop, leading a life without quarrels, and saving whatever money he did not have to spend to keep himself alive. Far from making any friends during this time, he formed a thorough hatred for the people of the town, who never allowed him to forget that he was a son of sin, and therefore not like others, but *meskhot*—damned. Then he found a small house, not much more than a hut, in the palm groves outside the town. The rent was low and no one lived nearby. He went to live there, where the only sound was the wind in the trees, and avoided the people of the town when he could.

One hot summer evening shortly after sunset he was walking under the arcades that faced the town's main square. A few paces ahead of him an old man in a white turban was trying to shift a heavy sack from one shoulder to the other. Suddenly it fell to the ground, and Allal stared as two dark forms flowed out of it and disappeared into the shadows. The old man pounced upon the sack and fastened the top of it, at the same time beginning to shout: Look out for the snakes! Help me find my snakes!

Many people turned quickly around and walked back the way they had come. Others stood at some distance, watching. A few called to the old man: Find your snakes fast and get them out of here! Why are they here? We don't want snakes in this town!

Hopping up and down in his anxiety, the old man turned to Allal. Watch this for me a minute, my son. He pointed at the sack lying on the earth at his feet, and snatching up a basket he had been carrying, went swiftly around the corner into an alley. Allal stood where he was. No one passed by.

It was not long before the old man returned, panting with triumph. When the onlookers in the square saw him again, they began to call out, this time to Allal: Show that berrani the way out of the town! He has no right to carry those things in here. Out! Out!

Allal picked up the big sack and said to the old man: Come on.

They left the square and went through the alleys until they were at the edge of town. The old man looked up then, saw the palm trees black against the fading sky ahead, and turned to the boy beside him.

Come on, said Allal again, and he went to the left along the rough path that led to his house. The old man stood perplexed.

You can stay with me tonight, Allal told him.

And these? he said, pointing first at the sack and then at the basket. They have to be with me.

Allal grinned. They can come.

When they were sitting in the house Allal looked at the sack and the basket. I'm not like the rest of them here, he said.

It made him feel good to hear the words being spoken. He made a contemptuous gesture. Afraid to walk through the square because of a snake. You saw them.

The old man scratched his chin. Snakes are like people, he said. You have to get to know them. Then you can be their friends.

Allal hesitated before he asked: Do you ever let them out?

Always, the old man said with energy. It's bad for them to be inside like this. They've got to be healthy when they get to Taroudant, or the man there won't buy them.

He began a long story about his life as a hunter of snakes, explaining that each year he made a voyage to Taroudant to see a man who bought them for the Aissaoua snake-charmers in Marrakech. Allal made tea while he listened, and brought out a bowl of kif paste to eat with the tea. Later, when they were sitting comfortably in the midst of the pipe-smoke, the old man chuckled. Allal turned to look at him.

Shall I let them out?

Fine!

But you must sit and keep quiet. Move the lamp nearer.

He untied the sack, shook it a bit, and returned to where he had been sitting. Then in silence Allal watched the long bodies move cautiously out into the light. Among the cobras were others with markings so delicate and perfect that they seemed to have been designed and painted by an artist. One reddish-gold serpent, which coiled itself lazily in the middle of the floor, he found particularly beautiful. As he stared at it, he felt a great desire to own it and have it always with him.

The old man was talking. I've spent my whole life with snakes, he said. I could tell you some things about them. Did you know that if you give them majoun you can make them do what you want, and without saying a word? I swear by Allah!

Allal's face assumed a doubtful air. He did not question the truth of the other's statement, but rather the likelihood of his being able to put the knowledge to use. For it was at that moment that the idea of actually taking the snake first came into his head. He was thinking that whatever he was to do must be done quickly, for the old man would be leaving in the morning. Suddenly he felt a great impatience.

Put them away so I can cook dinner, he whispered. Then he sat admiring the ease with which the old man picked up each one by its head and slipped it into the sack. Once again he dropped two of the snakes into the basket, and one of these, Allal noted, was the red one. He imagined he could see the shining of its scales through the lid of the basket.

As he set to work preparing the meal Allal tried to think of other things. Then, since the snake remained in his mind in spite of everything, he began to devise a way of getting it. While he squatted over the fire in a corner, he mixed some kif paste in a bowl of milk and set it aside.

The old man continued to talk. That was good luck, getting the two snakes back like that, in the middle of the town. You can never be sure what people are going to do when they find out you're carrying snakes. Once in El Kelaa they took all of them and killed them, one after the other, in front of me. A year's work. I had to go back home and start all over again.

Even as they ate, Allal saw that his guest was growing sleepy. How will things happen? he wondered. There was no way of knowing beforehand precisely what he was going to do, and the prospect of having to handle the snake worried him. It could kill me, he thought.

Once they had eaten, drunk tea and smoked a few pipes of kif, the old man lay back on the floor and said he was going to sleep. Allal sprang up. In here! he told him, and led him to his own mat in an alcove. The old man lay down and swiftly fell asleep.

Several times during the next half hour Allal went to the alcove and peered in, but neither the body in its burnous nor the head in its turban had stirred.

First he got out his blanket, and after tying three of its corners together, spread it on the floor with the fourth corner facing the basket. Then he set the bowl of milk and kif paste on the blanket. As he loosened the strap from the cover of the basket the old man coughed. Allal stood immobile, waiting to hear the cracked voice speak. A small breeze had sprung up, making the palm branches rasp one against the other, but there was no further sound from the alcove. He crept to the far side of the room and squatted by the wall, his gaze fixed on the basket.

Several times he thought he saw the cover move slightly, but each time he decided he had been mistaken. Then he caught his breath. The shadow along the base of the basket was moving. One of the creatures had crept out from the far side. It waited for a while before continuing into the light, but when it did, Allal breathed a prayer of thanks. It was the red and gold one.

When finally it decided to go to the bowl, it made a complete tour around the edge, looking in from all sides, before lowering its head toward the milk. Allal watched, fearful that the foreign flavor of the kif paste might repel it. The snake remained there without moving.

He waited a half hour or more. The snake stayed where it was, its head in the bowl. From time to time Allal glanced at the basket, to be certain that the second snake was still in it. The breeze went on, rubbing the palm branches together. When he decided it was time, he rose slowly, and keeping an eye on the basket where apparently the other snake still slept, he reached over and gathered together the three tied corners of the blanket. Then he lifted the fourth corner, so that both the snake and the bowl slid to the bottom of the improvised sack. The snake moved slightly, but he did not think it was angry. He knew exactly where he would hide it: between some rocks in the dry river bed.

Holding the blanket in front of him he opened the door and stepped out under the stars. It was not far up the road, to a group of high palms, and then to the left down into the oued. There was a space between the boulders where the bundle would be invisible. He pushed it in with care, and hurried back to the house. The old man was asleep.

There was no way of being sure that the other snake was still in the basket, so Allal picked up his burnous and went outside. He shut the door and lay down on the ground to sleep.

Before the sun was in the sky the old man was awake, lying in the alcove coughing. Allal jumped up, went inside, and began to make a fire in the mijmah. A minute later he heard the other exclaim: They're loose again! Out of the basket! Stay where you are and I'll find them.

It was not long before the old man grunted with satisfaction. I have the black one! he cried. Allal did not look up from the corner where he crouched, and the old man came over, waving a cobra. Now I've got to find the other one.

He put the snake away and continued to search. When the fire was blazing, Allal turned and said: Do you want me to help you look for it?

No, No! Stay where you are.

Allal boiled the water and made the tea, and still the old man was crawling on his knees, lifting boxes and pushing sacks. His turban had slipped off and his face ran with sweat.

Come and have tea, Allal told him.

The old man did not seem to have heard him at first. Then he rose and went into the alcove, where he rewound his turban. When he came out he sat down with Allal, and they had breakfast.

Snakes are very clever, the old man said. They can get into places that don't exist. I've moved everything in this house.

After they had finished eating, they went outside and looked for the snake between the close-growing trunks of the palms near the house. When the old man was convinced that it was gone, he went sadly back in.

That was a good snake, he said at last. And now I'm going to Taroudant.

They said good-bye, and the old man took his sack and basket and started up the road toward the highway.

All day long as he worked, Allal thought of the snake, but it was not until sunset that he was able to go to the rocks in the oued and pull out the blanket. He carried it back to the house in a high state of excitement.

Before he untied the blanket, he filled a wide dish with milk and kif paste, and set it on the floor. He ate three spoonfuls of the paste himself and sat back to watch, drumming on the low wooden tea-table with his fingers. Everything happened just as he had hoped. The snake came slowly out of the blanket, and very soon had found the dish and was drinking the milk. As long as it drank he kept drumming; when it had finished and raised its head to look at him, he stopped, and it crawled back inside the blanket.

Later that evening he put down more milk, and drummed again on the table. After a time the snake's head appeared, and finally all of it, and the entire pattern of action was repeated.

That night and every night thereafter, Allal sat with the snake, while with infinite patience he sought to make it his friend. He never attempted to touch it, but soon he was able to summon it, keep it in front of him for as long as he pleased, merely by tapping on the table, and dismiss it at will. For the first week or so he used the kif paste; then he tried the routine without it. In the end the results were the same. After that he fed it only milk and eggs.

Then one evening as his friend lay gracefully coiled in front of him, he began to think of the old man, and formed an idea that put all other things out of his mind. There had not been any kif paste in the house for several weeks, and he decided to make some. He bought the ingredients the following day, and after work he prepared the paste. When it was done, he mixed a large amount of it in a bowl with milk and set it down for the snake. Then he himself ate four spoonfuls, washing them down with tea.

He quickly undressed, and moving the table so that he could reach it, stretched out naked on a mat near the door. This time he continued to tap on the table, even after the snake had finished drinking the milk. It lay still, observing him, as if it were in doubt that the familiar drumming came from the brown body in front of it.

Seeing that even after a long time it remained where it was, staring at him with its stony yellow eyes, Allal began to say to it over and over: Come here. He knew it could not hear his voice, but he believed it could feel his mind as he urged it. You can make them do what you want, without saying a word, the old man had told him.

Although the snake did not move, he went on repeating his command, for by now he knew it was going to come. And after another long wait, all at once it lowered its head and began to move toward him. It reached his hip and slid along his leg. Then it climbed up his leg and lay for a time across his chest. Its body was heavy and tepid, its scales wonderfully smooth. After a time it came to rest, coiled in the space between his head and his shoulder.

By this time the kif paste had completely taken over Allal's mind. He lay in a state of pure delight, feeling the snake's head against his own, without a thought save that he and the snake were together. The patterns forming and melting behind his eyelids seemed to be the same ones that covered the snake's back. Now and then in a huge frenzied movement they all swirled up and shattered into fragments which swiftly became one great yellow eye, split through the middle by the narrow vertical pupil that pulsed with his own heartbeat. Then the eye would recede, through shifting shadow and sunlight, until only the designs of the scales were left, swarming with renewed insistence as they merged and separated. At last the eye returned, so huge this time that it had no edge around it, its pupil dilated to form an aperture almost wide enough for him to enter. As he stared at the blackness within, he understood that he was being slowly propelled toward the opening. He put out his hands to touch the polished surface of the eye on each side, and as he did this he felt the pull from within. He slid through the crack and was swallowed by darkness.

On awakening Allal felt that he had returned from somewhere far away. He opened his eyes and saw, very close to him, what looked like the flank of an enormous beast, covered with coarse stiff hair. There was a repeated vibration in the air, like distant thunder curling around the edges of the sky. He sighed, or imagined that he did, for his breath made no sound. Then he shifted his head a bit, to try and see beyond the mass of hair beside him. Next he saw the ear, and he knew he was looking at his own head from the outside. He had not expected this; he had hoped only that his friend would come in and share his mind with him. But it did not strike him as being at all strange; he merely said to himself that now he was seeing through the eyes of the snake, rather than through his own.

Now he understood why the serpent had been so wary of him: from here the boy was a monstrous creature, with all the bristles on his head and his breathing that vibrated inside him like a far-off storm.

He uncoiled himself and glided across the floor to the alcove. There was a break in the mud wall wide enough to let him out. When he had pushed himself through, he lay full length on the ground in the crystalline moonlight, staring at the strangeness of the landscape, where shadows were not shadows.

He crawled around the side of the house and started up the road toward the town, rejoicing in a sense of freedom different from any he had ever imagined. There was no feeling of having a body, for he was perfectly contained in the skin that covered him. It was beautiful to caress the earth with the length of his belly as he moved along the silent road, smelling the sharp veins of wormwood in the wind. When the voice of the muezzin floated out over the countryside from the mosque, he could not hear it, or know that within the hour the night would end.

On catching sight of a man ahead, he left the road and hid behind a rock until the danger had passed. But then as he approached the town there began to be more people, so that he let himself down into the seguia, the deep ditch that went along beside the road. Here the stones and clumps of dead plants impeded his progress. He was still struggling along the floor of the seguia, pushing himself around the rocks and through the dry tangles of matted stalks left by the water, when dawn began to break.

The coming of daylight made him anxious and unhappy. He clambered up the bank of the seguia and raised his head to examine the road. A man walking past saw him, stood quite still, and then turned and ran back. Allal did not wait; he wanted now to get home as fast as possible.

Once he felt the thud of a stone as it struck the ground somewhere behind him. Quickly he threw himself over the edge of the seguia and rolled squirming down the bank. He knew the terrain here: where the road crossed the oued, there were two culverts not far apart. A man stood at some distance ahead of him with a shovel, peering down into the seguia. Allal kept moving, aware that he would reach the first culvert before the man could get to him.

The floor of the tunnel under the road was ribbed with hard little waves of sand. The smell of the mountains was in the air that moved through. There were places in here where he could have hidden, but he kept moving, and soon reached the other end. Then he continued to the second culvert and went under the road in the other direction, emerging once again into the seguia. Behind him several men had gathered at the entrance to the first culvert. One of them was on his knees, his head and shoulders inside the opening.

He now set out for the house in a straight line across the open ground, keeping his eye on the clump of palms beside it. The sun had just come up, and the stones began to cast long bluish shadows. All at once a small boy appeared from behind some nearby palms, saw him, and opened his eyes and mouth wide with fear. He was so close that Allal went straight to him and bit him in the leg. The boy ran wildly toward the group of men in the seguia.

Allal hurried on to the house, looking back only as he reached the hole between the mud bricks. Several men were running among the trees toward him. Swiftly he glided through into the alcove. The brown body still lay near the door. But there was no time, and Allal needed time to get back to it, to lie close to its head and say: Come here.

As he stared out into the room at the body, there was a great pounding on the door. The boy was on his feet at the first blow, as if a spring had been released, and Allal saw with despair the expression of total terror in his face, and the eyes with no mind behind them. The boy stood panting, his fists clenched. The door opened and some of the men peered inside. Then with a roar the boy lowered his head and rushed through the doorway. One of the men reached out to seize him, but lost his balance and fell. An instant later all of them turned and began to run through the palm grove after the naked figure.

Even when, from time to time, they lost sight of him, they could hear the screams, and then they would see him, between the palm trunks, still running. Finally he stumbled and fell face downward. It was then that they caught him, bound him, covered his nakedness, and took him away, to be sent one day soon to the hospital at Berrechid.

That afternoon the same group of men came to the house to carry out the search they had meant to make earlier. Allal lay in the alcove, dozing. When he awoke, they were already inside. He turned and crept to the hole. He saw the man waiting out there, a club in his hand.

The rage always had been in his heart; now it burst forth. As if his body were a whip, he sprang out into the room. The men nearest him were on their hands and knees, and Allal had the joy of pushing his fangs into two of them before a third severed his head with an axe.

Tangier, 1976

KITTY

PAUL BOWLES

KITTY LIVED IN a medium-sized house with a big garden around it. She loved some things, like picnics and going to the circus, and she hated other things, like school and going to the dentist's.

One day she asked her mother: "Why is my name Kitty?"

"Your name is really Catherine," her mother said. "We just call you Kitty."

This reply did not satisfy Kitty, and she decided that her mother did not want to tell her the truth. This made her think even more about her name. Finally she thought she had the answer. Her name was Kitty because some day she was going to grow up into a cat. She felt proud of herself for having found this out, and she began to look into the mirror to see if perhaps she was beginning to look like a cat, or at least like a kitten.

For a long time she could see nothing at all but her own pink face. But one day when she went up to the glass she could hardly believe what she saw, for around her mouth tiny gray whiskers were beginning to sprout. She jumped up and down with delight, and waited for her mother to say something about them. Her mother, however, had no time for such things, and so she noticed nothing.

Each day when Kitty looked at her reflection she saw more wonderful changes. Slowly the whiskers grew longer and stood out farther from her face, and a soft gray fur started to cover her skin. Her ears grew pointed and she had soft pads on the palms of her hands and the soles of her feet. All this seemed too good to be true, and Kitty was sad to find that nobody had said a word about the marvelous change in her. One day as she was playing she turned to her mother and said: "Meow. I'm Kitty. Do you like the color of my fur?"

"I don't know," her mother said. "What color is it?"

"It's gray!"

"Oh, gray. Very pretty," said her mother, and Kitty saw with a sinking heart that she did not care what color the fur was.

After that she tried to make several neighbors remark on her fine whiskers, her velvety ears and her short fluffy tail, and they all agreed that these things were very nice, and then paid no more attention to them. Kitty did not care too much. If *they* could not see how different she had become, at least she herself could.

One summer morning when Kitty awoke, she discovered that her fingernails and toenails had been replaced by splendid new pearly gray claws that she could stick out or pull in as she chose. She jumped out of bed and ran into the garden. It was still very early. Her mother and father were asleep, but there were some birds walking around on the lawn.

She slipped behind some bushes and watched. After a long time she began to crawl forward. The branches caught her nightgown, so she tore it off. When one of the birds came very close to her, she sprang forward and caught it. And at that moment she knew that she was no longer a girl at all, and that she would never have to be one again.

The bird tasted good, but she decided not to eat it. Instead, she rolled on her back in the sun and licked her paws. Then she sat up and washed her face. After a while she thought she would go over to Mrs. Tinsley's house and see if she could get some breakfast. She climbed up to the top of the wall and ran quickly along it to the roof of the garage. From there she scrambled down the trellis into Mrs. Tinsley's backyard. She heard sounds in the kitchen, so she went up to the screen door and looked in. Then she said: "Meow." She had to keep saying it for quite a while before Mrs. Tinsley came and saw her.

"Well, if that isn't the cutest kitten!" Mrs. Tinsley said, and she called to her husband and her sister. They came and saw the small gray kitten with one paw raised, scratching at the screen. Of course they let her in, and soon Kitty was lapping up a saucer full of milk. She spent the day sleeping, curled up on a cushion, and in the evening she was given a bowl of delicious raw liver.

After dinner she decided to go back home. Mr. Tinsley saw her at the kitchen door, but instead of opening the door for her, he picked her up and locked her into the cellar. This was not at all what Kitty wanted, and she cried all night.

In the morning they let her go upstairs, and gave her a big bowl of milk. When she had drunk it she waited in the kitchen until Mrs. Tinsley opened the door to go out into the yard. Then she ran as fast as she could between Mrs. Tinsley's feet, and climbed up onto the roof of the garage. She looked down at Mrs. Tinsley, who was calling: "Kitty, Kitty, Kitty." Then she turned and ran the other way. Soon she was in her own garden. She went up to all the doors and looked in. There were policemen inside the house with her mother and father. They were holding Kitty's torn nightgown in their hands, and her mother was crying and sobbing. No one paid the slightest attention to Kitty.

She went sadly back to Mrs. Tinsley's house, and there she stayed for many weeks. Sometimes she would go over to her own house and peek again through the doors, and often she saw her mother or her father. But they looked very different from the way they had looked before, and even if they noticed her, they never came to the door to let her in.

It was nice not having to go to school, and Mr. and Mrs. Tinsley were very good to her, but Kitty loved her mother and father more than she could love anyone else, and she wanted to be with them.

Mr. and Mrs. Tinsley let her go out whenever she pleased now, because she always came back. She would go to her house at night and look in through the window to see her father sitting alone reading the paper. This was how she knew that her mother had gone away. Even if she cried and pushed her claws against the window, her father paid no attention to her, and she knew that he would never let her in. Only her mother would do that. She would come and open the door and take her in her arms and rub the fur on her forehead and kiss her.

One day several months later when Kitty climbed over the wall into her own garden, she saw her mother sitting in a chair outside. She looked much better, almost the way she had used to look. Kitty walked slowly toward her mother over the grass, holding her tail in the air. Her mother sat up straighter, watching as she came nearer. Then she put out her hand and wriggled her fingers at Kitty. "Well, the pretty pussycat," she said. "Where did *you* come from?"

Kitty went near enough so that her mother could rub her head and scratch her cheeks. She waved her tail and purred with delight as she felt her mother's fingers stroking her fur. Then she jumped up into her mother's lap and lay curled up there, working her claws joyously in and out. After a long time her mother lifted her up and held her against her face, and then she carried her into the house.

That evening Kitty lay happily in her mother's lap. She did not want to try her father's lap because she was afraid he might push her off. Besides, she could see that it would not be very comfortable.

Kitty knew that her mother already loved her, and that her father would learn to love her. At last she was living exactly the life she always had wished for. Sometimes she thought it would be nice if she could make them understand that she was really Kitty, but she knew there was no way of doing that. She never heard them say the word *Kitty* again. Instead, because her fur was so long and fine that when she moved she seemed to be floating, they named her Feather. She had no lessons to worry about, she never had to go to the dentist's, and she no longer had to wonder whether her mother was telling her the truth or not, because she knew the truth. She was Kitty, and she was happy.

Tangier, 1977

HERE TO LEARN

PAUL BOWLES

I

MALIKA NEEDED NO ONE to tell her she was pretty. From the beginning of her memory people had murmured about her beauty, for even when she was a baby girl the symmetry of her head, neck and shoulders was remarkable. Before she was old enough to go to the spring to fetch water she knew she had eyes like a gazelle and that her head was like a lily on its stalk. At least, these were the things older people said about her.

On a hill above the town stood a large building with palm-shaded walks leading up to it. This belonged to the Hermanas Adoratrices. Certain of these nuns, upon catching sight of Malika, had gone to her father, offering to take her in charge and teach her to speak Spanish and to embroider. Enthusiastically he had agreed. Allah has sent us here to learn, he would say. Malika's mother, who disapproved of her daughter's spending her time with Nazarenes, did her utmost to make him change his mind. Nevertheless Malika stayed with the sisters for five years, until her father died.

Malika's grandmother was fond of saying that when she had been Malika's age she had looked exactly like her, and that if it were possible for her to become a little girl again and stand beside Malika, no one would be able to tell them apart. At first Malika found this impossible to believe; she studied the old woman's ravaged face and straightway rejected the idea. After her grandmother had died, she began to understand what the old woman had meant when she said: Only Allah remains the same. One day she would no longer be pretty, but now she was. Thus, when she was able to go by herself to the spring and carry back two full pails of water, it meant nothing to her if the older boys and the young men called to her and tried to speak with her. They would do better, she thought, to say all those flattering things to girls who needed such reassurance.

A barracks full of soldiers stood just outside the town. The men were rough and brutal. When she caught sight of one of them, even in the distance, Malika would hide until he had disappeared. Fortunately the soldiers seldom strayed into the arroyo that lay between her house and the spring; they preferred to saunter in groups up and down the main road leading through the town.

There came a day when her mother insisted that she go to sell a hen at the market on the main highway. Her older sister always had done this, but she was at a neighbor's house helping prepare for a wedding. Malika begged her mother to lend her her haïk so she could cover her face.

Your sister's been a thousand times. She never wears a haïk.

Malika knew this was because no one paid any attention to her sister, but she could not say it to her mother. I'm afraid, she said, and burst into tears. Her mother had no patience with the silly behavior of girls, and refused to let her take the haïk. As Malika ran out of the house, holding the hen by its legs, she snatched up a soiled bathtowel. As soon as she was out of sight, she wrapped it loosely around her head, so that when she got to the highway she could pull it down and cover at least a part of her face.

Several dozen women lined one side of the road, each sitting on the ground with her wares spread out around her. Malika went to the end of the row, which was opposite a small park where the soldiers sat on benches. People wandered past and picked up the hen to squeeze it and shake it, so that it constantly squawked and fluttered. She had pulled the towel down so far over her eyes that she could see only the earth at her feet.

After an hour or so had gone by, a woman came along who began to discuss the price of the hen with her. Eventually she bought it, and Malika, once she had tied the coins up in a piece of cloth, jumped to her feet. The towel slipped over her face and fell to the ground. She picked it up and started to hurry along the highway.

II

The town was derelict; it smelled of the poverty in which its people were accustomed to live. Nor was there any indication that in some past era something more had existed. The wind from the sea raised the dust of the streets high into the air and showered it angrily over the countryside. Even the leaves of the fig trees were coated white. The hot sand flying stung the skin on the backs of her legs as she turned the corner of the side street that led to the lower end of the gully. She draped the towel over her head and held onto it with one hand. It had never occurred to her to hate the town, for she assumed that anywhere else would be more or less the same.

The street was scarcely more than an alley, with walls on either side. All at once she heard the sound of heavy boots pounding the earth behind her. She did not turn around. Then a hard hand seized her arm and pushed her roughly against the wall. It was a soldier, and he was smiling. He braced his arms against the wall on each side of her so she could not escape.

Malika said nothing. The man stood gazing at her. He was breathing deeply, as though he had been running. Finally he said: How old are you?

She looked directly into his eyes. Fifteen.

He smelt of wine, tobacco and sweat.

Let me go, she said, and she tried desperately to duck under the barricade. The pain she felt as he twisted her arm made her open her eyes very wide, but she did not cry out. Two men in djellabas were approaching from the direction of the gully, and she fixed her eyes on them. The soldier turned, saw them, and began to walk quickly back toward the highway.

When she got home, she tossed the bit of cloth with the money in it onto the taifor, and indignantly showed her mother the marks on her arm.

What's that?

A soldier grabbed me.

Her mother dealt her a stinging blow across the face. Malika had never seen her in such a rage.

You young bitch! she screamed. That's all you're good for!

Malika ran out of the house and down into the gully, where she sat on a rock in the shade, wondering if her mother might be going mad. The unexpectedness and injustice of the sudden blow had removed all thought of the soldier from her mind. She felt that she must find an explanation of her mother's behavior; otherwise she would hate her.

That night at dinner things were not much better; her mother would not look at her, and directed all her remarks to her other daughter. This proved to be the pattern for the days that followed. It was as if she had decided that Malika no longer existed.

Good, thought Malika. If I'm not here, then she's not here. She's not my mother and I do hate her.

This silent war between them did not mean that Malika was exempt from having to continue to go to the market. Nearly every week she would be sent off to sell a hen or a basket of vegetables and eggs. She had no further trouble with the soldiers, perhaps because she now stopped on her way down the gully each time and smeared a little mud over her face. It was always dry by the time she reached the highway, and although the women there sometimes stared at her with surprise, the men paid her no attention. On her way home, going up the gully, she would wash her face.

There was always suspicion in her mother's glance now when she returned to the house. If you get into trouble, she said, I swear I'll kill you with my own hands. Malika sniffed and left the room. She knew what her mother meant, but it astonished her to see how little she knew about her own daughter.

III

One day as Malika sat in the front row of women and girls in the market on the highway, a long yellow car without a top drove up silently and stopped. There was only one man in it, and he was a Nazarene. The women began to murmur and cry out, for the man held a camera in his hands and was pointing it at them. A girl sitting next to Malika turned to her and said: You speak Spanish. Tell him to go away.

Malika ran over to the car. The man lowered his camera and stared at her.

Señor, you mustn't take pictures here, she said, looking at him gravely. She pointed back at the row of indignant women.

The Nazarene was big, with light-colored hair. He understood and smiled. *Muy bien, muy bien*, he said good-naturedly, still looking fixedly at her. She was suddenly conscious of the dirt on her face. Without thinking she rubbed her cheek with the back of her hand. The man's smile became broader.

Will you let me take your picture?

Malika's heart began to beat painfully. No! No! she cried, aghast. Then by way of explanation she added: I have to go and sell my eggs.

The Nazarene looked more pleased than ever. You have eggs for sale? Bring them over.

Malika went and fetched the little packet of eggs, tied in a cloth. A group of boys had caught sight of the dazzling yellow car, and now they surrounded it, demanding money. The Nazarene, trying to wave them away, opened the door for Malika and pointed to the empty seat. She laid the bundle on the leather cushion and bent to undo the knot, but the arms of the boys kept pushing in front of her and jostling her. The Nazarene shouted angrily at the urchins in a foreign language, but this deterred them only for an instant. Finally, in a rage, he said to Malika: Get in. She lifted the eggs and obeyed, seating herself with the bundle on her lap. The man reached in front of her and slammed the door shut. Then he raised the window. But two beggars now had joined the boys, and they were able to reach over the top of the window.

Without warning the Nazarene started up the motor with a great roar. The car shot forward. Startled, Malika turned to see some of the boys sprawling in the road. When she looked again, they were almost out of the town. The Nazarene still seemed to be very angry. She decided not to ask him how far he was going before he stopped and bought the eggs. Her emotions hovered between delight at being in the fine car and anxiety about walking back to the town.

The trees were going by very fast. It seemed to her that she had always known something strange like this would happen to her one day. It was a comforting thought, and it kept her from feeling actual fear.

IV

Soon they turned onto a dirt road that burrowed deep into a eucalyptus grove. Here in the dubious shade the Nazarene shut off the motor and turned to Malika with a smile. He took the bundle of eggs from her lap and put it into the back of the car. From a basket behind her seat he brought out a bottle of mineral water and a napkin. He poured a little water onto the napkin and with one hand on her shoulder set to work wiping the streaks of mud from her cheeks. She let him rub, and she let him remove the towel wrapped around her head, so that her hair fell to her shoulders. Why shouldn't he see me? she thought. He's a good man. She had already noticed that he did not smell at all, and his gentleness with her gave her a pleasant sensation.

Now shall I take your picture?

She nodded. There was no one to witness the shameful act. He made her sit lower in the seat, and held the camera above her. It clicked so many times, and he looked so peculiar with the big black apparatus in front of his face, that she began to laugh. She thought he might stop then, but he seemed even more pleased, and went on clicking the camera until it would click no more. Then he spread a blanket on the ground and set a basket of food in the center of it. They sat with the basket between them and ate chicken, cheese and olives. Malika was hungry, and she thought this great fun.

When they had finished, he asked her if she wanted him to take her back to the market. It was as if darkness had fallen over the world. She thought of the women there, and of what they would say when they saw her. She shook her head vigorously. The present moment was real; she would not help it to end. No, not yet, she said lightly.

He looked at his watch. Shall we go to Tetuan?

Her eyes brightened. It was less than an hour's ride from her town, but she had only heard about it. The trees sped by again. Here a stiff breeze blew in from the Mediterranean, and Malika was chilly. The man took out a soft camel's hair cape and put it around her shoulders.

Tetuan was very exciting with all its traffic. The guards in scarlet and white stood at attention in front of the Khalifa's palace. But she would not get out of the car and walk with him in the street. They were parked there in the Feddane, where the hot afternoon sun beat down on them. Finally the man shrugged and said: Well, if I'm going to get to Tangier tonight, I'd better take you back home.

Malika made a strange sound. She seemed to have become very small inside the cape.

What's the matter?

I can't!

The man stared at her. But you've got to go back home.

Malika began to wail. No, no! she cried. The man glanced nervously at the passersby, and tried to comfort her with words. But a possibility had just revealed itself to her, and at that moment the idea was powerful enough to occupy her totally. Seeing her too immersed in inner turmoil even to hear him, he started the car and slowly made his way through the throng of people to the other side of the plaza. Then he drove along the principal street to the outskirts of the city, stopped the car by the side of the road, and lighted a cigarette.

He turned to her. One would almost have said that on the seat beside him there was nothing but the cape. He tugged at it, and heard a sob. Gently slipping his hand inside, he smoothed her hair for a moment. Finally she began to push herself upward into a sitting position, and her head appeared.

I'm going to take you with me to Tangier, he said. She made no reply to this, nor did she look at him.

They sped westward, the late afternoon sun in front of them. Malika was conscious of having made an irrevocable choice. The results, already determined by destiny, would be disclosed to her one by one, in the course of events. It was only slowly that she became aware of the landscape around her and of the summer air rushing past.

They came to a tiny café, alone on the mountainside, and stopped. Come in and we'll have some tea, he said. Malika shook her head, pulling the cape more tightly around her.

The man went inside and ordered two glasses of tea. A quarter of an hour later a boy carried them to the car on a tray. The tea was very hot, and it took them a while to drink it. Even when the boy had come and taken away the tray, they went on sitting there. Eventually the man switched on the headlights, and they started down the mountainside.

V

Malika was frightened by the elevator, but she relaxed somewhat when the man had shown her into the apartment and shut the door behind them. There were thick rugs and soft couches piled with pillows, and lights that could be turned on and off by pushing a button. Most important of all, the Nazarene lived there by himself.

That night he showed her to a room, telling her it was to be hers. Before he said goodnight he took her head in his hands and kissed her on the forehead. When he had gone she wandered into the bathroom and amused herself for a long time turning the hot and cold taps on and off, to see if sooner or later one of them would make a mistake. Finally she undressed, put on the muslin gandoura the man had left for her, and got into the bed.

A pile of magazines lay on the table beside her, and she began to look at the pictures. There was one photograph which caught her attention and held it. The picture showed a luxurious room, with a beautiful woman lying back in a chaise longue. A wide collar of diamonds flashed from her neck, and in her hand she held a book. The book was open but she was not looking at it. Her head was raised, as though someone had just come into the room and found her reading. Malika studied the photograph, glanced at others, and returned to it. To her it illustrated the perfect pose to adopt when receiving guests, and she resolved to practice it by herself, so that when the time came she could put it to use. It would be a good idea to be able to read, too, she thought. One day she would ask the man to show her how.

They had breakfast on the terrace in the morning sun. The building overlooked a spacious Moslem cemetery. Beyond it was the water. Malika told him it was not good to live so near to a graveyard. Later, she looked over the railing, saw the elaborate domed mausoleum of Sidi Bou Araqia, and nodded her head in approval. As they sat over their coffee, he answered more of her questions. His name was Tim, he was twenty-eight years old, but he had no wife and no children. He did not live in Tangier all the time. Sometimes he was in Cairo and sometimes in London. In each of these places he had a small flat, but he kept his car in Tangier because that was where he came when he was not working.

As they sat there Malika heard sounds inside the apartment. Presently a fat black woman in a yellow zigdoun came onto the terrace. *Bonjour*, she said, and she began to carry out the dishes. Each time she appeared Malika sat very straight, looking fixedly out across the water at the mountains in Spain.

Someone would be coming in a little while, Tim said, an Italian woman who was going to take her measurements and make some clothes for her.

Malika frowned. What kind of clothes?

When he said: Whatever you want, she jumped up and went to her room, returning with a copy of *The New Yorker*, which she opened at a page showing a girl in a knit sports suit standing by a set of matched luggage. Like this one, she said. An hour or so later the Italian woman came in, very businesslike, tickled Malika with her tape measure for a while, and left, notebook in hand.

VI

Late that afternoon when the black woman had gone, Tim took Malika into her bedroom, pulled the curtains across the windows, and very gently gave her her first lesson in love. Malika did not really want this to happen then, but she had always known it would sooner or later. The slight pain was negligible, but the shame of being naked in front of the man was almost more than she could bear. It never had occurred to her that a body could be considered beautiful, and she did not believe him when he told her she was perfect in every part. She knew only that men used women in order to make children, and this preoccupied her, as she had no desire for a child. The man assured her that he was not hoping for children either, and that if she did as he told her there was no danger of having any. She accepted this as she accepted everything else he said. She was there in order to learn, and she intended to learn as much as possible.

When, during the next few weeks, she finally consented to go with him to the houses of his friends, he did not guess that she agreed to appear in public only because she had studied herself in the new clothes, and had found them sufficiently convincing to act as a disguise. The European garments made it possible for her to go into the streets with a Nazarene and not be reviled by other Moroccans.

After taking Malika to a photographer's studio and making several lengthy visits to the authorities, Tim returned triumphant one day, waving a passport at her. This is yours, he said. Don't lose it.

Nearly every day there were parties on the Mountain or picnics on the beach. Malika particularly loved the night picnics around a fire, with the sound of the waves breaking on the sand. Sometimes there were musicians, and everyone danced barefoot. One evening eight or ten of the guests jumped up and ran shouting toward the breakers to swim naked in the moonlight. Since the moon was very bright, and there were men and women together, Malika gasped and hid her face. Tim thought this amusing, but the incident caused her to question the fitness of the people in Tangier to be her models for the elegance she hoped to attain.

One morning Tim greeted her with a sad face. In a few days, he told her, he had to go to London. Seeing her expression of chagrin, he quickly added that in two weeks he would be back, and that she would go on living in the flat just as though he were there.

But how can I? she cried. You won't be here! I'll be all alone.

No, no. You'll have friends. You'll like them.

That evening he brought two young men to the apartment. They were handsome and well-dressed, and very talkative. When Malika heard Tim address one of them as Bobby, she burst into laughter.

Only dogs are called Bobby, she explained. It's not a man's name.

She's priceless, said Bobby. A teen-age Nefertiti.

Absolute heaven, agreed his friend Peter.

After they had gone, Tim explained that they were going to keep Malika company while he was in England. They would live in the apartment with her. On hearing this, she was silent for a moment.

I want to go with you, she said, as if anything else were inconceivable.

He shook his head. *Ni hablar.*

But I don't want love with them.

He kissed her. They don't make love with girls. That's why I asked them. They'll take good care of you.

Ah, she said, partially reassured, and at the same time thinking how clever Tim was to have been able to find two such presentable eunuchs with so little apparent effort.

As Tim had promised, Bobby and Peter kept her amused. Instead of taking her out to parties they invited their friends in to meet her. Soon she realized that there were a good many more eunuchs in Tangier than she had suspected. Since, according to Bobby and Peter, these tea-parties and cocktail hours were given expressly for Malika, she insisted on knowing exactly when the guests would be coming, so she could receive them in the correct position, lying back on the cushions of the divan with a book in her hand. When the new arrivals were shown in, she would raise her head slowly until its noble proportions were fully evident, fix her gaze on a point far behind anything in the room, and let the beginning of a smile tremble briefly on her lips before it vanished.

She could see that this impressed them. They told her they loved her. They played games and danced with each other and with her. They tickled her, nuzzled her, took her on their laps and fussed with her hair. She found them more fun to be with than Tim's friends, even though she was aware that the things they said had no meaning. To them everything was a game; there was nothing to learn from them.

VII

Tim had been gone for more than a week when they first brought Tony to the flat. He was a tall, noisy Irishman for whom the others of the group seemed to have a certain respect. At first Malika assumed that this was because he was not a eunuch like them, but quickly she discovered that it was only because he had far more money to spend than they did. Tony's clothing always smelled delicious, and his car, a green Maserati, attracted even more attention than Tim's. One day he came by at noon, while Bobby and Peter were still at the market. The black woman had received orders from Bobby to let no one in under any circumstances, but Tony was an expert in getting around such things. Malika had been playing a record of Abdelwahab's; now she quickly silenced it and gave all her attention to Tony. In the course of their dialogue, he remarked casually that her clothes were pretty. Malika smoothed her skirt.

But I'd like to see you in some other clothes, he went on.

Where are they?

Not here. In Madrid.

They heard the door slam, and knew that Bobby and Peter had returned. The two had quarreled and were communicating only in acid monosyllables. Malika saw that the game of dominoes they had promised to play with her when they got back would not take place. She sat and sulked for a while, turning the pages of one of Tim's financial magazines. Eunuchs were extremely childish, she reflected.

Bobby came into the room and stood at the other end, arranging books on the bookshelves in silence. Soon the black woman appeared in the doorway and announced to him in French that Monsieur Tim had telephoned from London and would not be in Tangier until the eighteenth.

When Tony had translated the information into Spanish, Malika merely sat staring at him, an expression of despair on her face.

Bobby hurried out of the room. Ill at ease, Tony stood up and followed him. A moment later Bobby's sharp voice cried: No, she can't go out to eat with you. She can't go out at all, anywhere, unless we go along. One of Tim's rules. If you want to eat here, you can.

Very little was said at lunch. In the middle of the meal Peter flung down his napkin and left the room. Afterward the black woman served coffee on the terrace. Bobby and Peter were arguing farther back in the flat, but their shrill voices were strangely audible.

For a while Malika sipped her coffee and said nothing. When she spoke to Tony, it was as if there had been no interruption to their earlier conversation. Can we go to Madrid? she said.

You'd like that? He grinned. But you see how they are. And he pointed behind him.

A mí me da igual cómo son. I only promised to stay with them for two weeks.

The next morning, while Bobby and Peter were at the market buying food, Tony and Malika put some valises into the Maserati and drove to the port to catch the ferry to Spain. Tony had left a short note for Bobby, saying that he had borrowed Malika for a few days, and would see to it that she telephoned.

VIII

They slept in Córdoba the first night. Before setting out for Madrid in the morning, Tony stopped at the cathedral to show it to her. When they walked up to the door, Malika hesitated. She peered inside and saw an endless corridor of arches extending into the gloom.

Go on in, said Tony.

She shook her head. You go. I'll wait here.

Driving out of the city, he scolded her a bit. You should look at things when you have the chance, he told her. That was a famous mosque.

I saw it, she said firmly.

The first day in Madrid they spent at Balenciaga's, morning and afternoon. You were right, Malika said to Tony when they were back in the hotel. The clothes here are much better.

They had to wait several days for the first items to be ready. The Prado was almost next door to the hotel, but Tony decided against making the attempt to entice Malika into it. He suggested a bullfight.

Only Moslems know how to kill animals, she declared.

They had been in Madrid for more than a week. One evening as they sat in the bar downstairs at the Ritz, Tony turned to her and said: Have you called Tangier? No, you haven't. Come.

Malika did not want to think of Tangier. Sighing, she rose and went with Tony up to his room, where he put in the call.

When finally he heard Bobby at the other end of the wire, he gestured and handed the telephone to Malika.

At the sound of her voice, Bobby immediately began to reproach her. She interrupted him to ask for Tim.

Tim can't get back to Tangier quite yet, he said, and the pitch of his voice rose as he added: But he wants *you* to come back right now!

Malika was silent:

Did you hear what I said? yelled Bobby. *Oíste?*

Yes, I heard. I'll let you know. She hung up quickly so as not to hear the sounds of outraged protest at the other end.

They went several more times to Balenciaga for fittings. Malika was impressed by Madrid, but she missed the comforting presence of Tim, particularly at night when she lay alone in her bed. While it was pleasant to be with Tony because he paid so much attention to her and constantly bought her gifts, she knew he did this only because he enjoyed dressing her the way he wanted her to look when they went out together, and not because he cared about her.

Although the deliveries continued to be made, and the gowns and ensembles were perfect, Malika's pleasure was somewhat lessened by her discovery that the only places where people really looked at what she was wearing were two restaurants and the bar downstairs. When she remarked about this to Tony, he laughed.

Ah! What you want is Paris. I can see that.

Malika brightened. Can we go there?

When the last garment had arrived, Tony and Malika ate a final dinner at Horcher, and started early the next morning for Paris. They spent the night in Biarritz, where the streets were rainswept and empty.

IX

Paris was far too big. She was frightened of it even before they arrived at the hotel, and she determined not to let Tony out of her sight unless she was safe in her room. At the Hôtel de la Trémoaille she watched him lying back on his bed, making one telephone call after the other while he joked, shouted, waved his legs, and screamed with laughter. When he was through telephoning he turned to her.

Tomorrow night I'm going to take you to a party, he said. And I know just what you'll wear. The oyster-colored satin number.

Malika was excited by the sumptuous house and the guests in evening clothes. Here at last, she was certain, she had reached a place where the people were of the ultimate degree of refinement. When she found that they looked at her with approval, she was filled with a sense of triumph.

Soon Tony led her up to a tall, pretty girl with flashing black eyes. This is my sister Dinah, he announced. She speaks better Spanish than I do.

Indicating Malika, he added: And this is the new Antinea. He left the two together and disappeared into another room.

Dinah's manner with her made her feel that they had been friends for a long time. When they had chatted for a few minutes, she led her over to a group of South Americans. The women were covered with jewels and some of them carried the pelts of animals over their shoulders. Even the men wore huge diamonds on their fingers. Malika suspected that Tim would disapprove of these people, but then it occurred to her that perhaps he could not be relied upon as an arbiter of taste in a city like this.

Paris es muy grande, she said to a man who smiled at her invitingly. I never saw it until yesterday. I'm afraid to go out. Why did they make it so big?

The man, smiling more broadly, said he was at her service, and would be delighted to go with her wherever she wished, whenever it suited her.

Oh, she said, looking pensive. That would be nice.

Mañana?

Somehow Dinah had caught the end of their dialogue. Not tomorrow, I'm afraid, she said briskly, taking Malika's arm. As she led her away she whispered furiously: His wife was standing there watching you.

Malika stole a frightened glance over her shoulder. The man was still smiling at her.

During the next few days Dinah, who lived nearby in the Avenue Montaigne, came regularly to the hotel. She and Tony had long discussions while Malika listened to Radio Cairo. One afternoon when Tony had gone out and Malika was bored, she asked Dinah to put in a call to Bobby in Tangier. A half hour later the telephone rang, and she heard Bobby's voice.

Hola, Bobby!

Malika! His voice was already shrill. You can't do this to me! Why are you in Paris? You've got to come back to Tangier.

Malika was silent.

We're waiting for you. What will Tim say if you're not here?

Tim! she said with scorn. Where is Tim?

He's coming back next week. I want to speak to Tony.

Tony's gone out.

Listen to me! Bobby shouted. What hotel are you in?

I don't know its name, she said. It's in Paris. It's a nice hotel. *Adiós.*

One morning not long afterward Tony announced abruptly that he was leaving for London in an hour. Dinah came in shortly before he set out. They seemed to be involved in a dispute, which ended only when he kissed each of them good-bye. After he had gone, Malika nodded her head sagely. London, she mused. He won't come back.

X

The day after Malika moved into Dinah's flat the weather turned rainy and cold. Dinah often went out, leaving her alone with the housemaid and cook. She was just as glad to stay indoors where it was warm. Her wardrobe, impressive as it was, failed to include any kind of covering for cold weather. Dinah had told her that the cold was just beginning, and that it would not be warm again for many months. It seemed to Malika that somewhere in Paris there must be a *joteya*, where she could take two or three evening gowns and exchange them for a coat, but Dinah shook her head when she asked her about it.

The apartment was spacious, and there were plenty of magazines to study. Malika spent her time curled up on a divan, examining the details in the fashion photographs.

Tony called from London, postponing his return for a few days. When Dinah gave her the news, Malika smiled and said: *Claro.*

I'm having lunch today with a friend. She has mountains of clothes, said Dinah. I'll see if I can't get a coat for you.

What she brought back that afternoon was a mink coat badly in need of repairs. Malika gazed at the rips with visible distaste.

You haven't any idea of how lucky you are, Dinah told her. She shrugged.

When the garment had been fitted at the furrier's and the skins resewn, it looked completely new, as if it had just been made for Malika. She ran her fingers over its glistening surface and examined herself in the mirror, and quickly decided that it was a very fine coat after all.

Dinah's friend came to lunch. Her name was Daphne. She was not very pretty and she tried to speak Italian with Malika. During the course of the meal she invited them both to a house-party at Cortina d'Ampezzo.

Dinah was enthusiastic. She brought out an album of photographs after Daphne had left, and spread it in Malika's lap. Malika saw that the ground was white and the people, whose clothing was not at all elegant, wore long boards on their feet. She was doubtful, but the strange white landscape and the groups of festive people intrigued her. It might be more interesting than Paris, which in the end had turned out to be rather dull.

They went to the office to book plane passage. Have you any money at all? Dinah asked her as they waited.

Malika was suddenly very much ashamed. Tony never gave me any.

It's all right, Dinah told her.

Before they left there was a lively argument between them as to whether Malika should take all her valises with her on the plane to Milano.

But you won't need all those clothes there, Dinah objected. And besides, it would cost so much.

I have to take everything, Malika said.

All of her belongings went with them on the plane. They had bad weather on the way to Milano, where Daphne's car met them. She was already in Cortina.

Malika had not enjoyed the plane ride. She did not understand why people with cars took planes. There was nothing to see but clouds, and the rocking of the plane made some of the passengers sick, so that by the end of the flight everyone seemed to be nervous and unhappy. For a while as they sped along the autostrada Malika thought she was back in Spain.

According to the driver, there were already so many friends staying at Daphne's chalet that no place was left for them. Daphne was putting them up in a hotel. Dinah received this news in silence; presumably she was displeased. Malika, when she understood the situation, secretly rejoiced. There would be many more people in the hotel than in the house.

XI

It was cold in Cortina. At first Malika would not go out of the hotel. The air is like poison, she complained. Then she began to experiment a bit, finally discovering that it was an agreeable kind of cold.

She would sit with the others on the terrace of the hotel in the brilliant sunshine, wearing her warm coat, sipping hot chocolate while they had their cocktails. The red-cheeked jollity of the people around her was a new experience, and the snow never ceased to fascinate her. Each morning when Daphne and her guests came to fetch Dinah, Malika would watch the noisy group rush out toward the ski fields. Then she would wander through the public rooms. The employees were polite, and often smiled at her. There was a shop in the hotel that sold skis and the clothes that had to be worn when using them. The window displays were changed daily, so that Malika was often to be seen standing outside the door, inspecting the merchandise through the glass.

Twice a tall young man had sauntered up to the shop windows as she stood there, giving the impression that he was about to speak to her. Both times she had turned away and resumed her aimless meandering. Tony and Dinah had warned her repeatedly against entering into conversation with strangers, and she thought it better to observe the etiquette they considered so important. She had discovered that Otto the barman spoke Spanish, and in the morning when the bar was often empty she would go in and talk with him. One morning he asked her why she never went out to ski with her friends.

I can't, she said in a muffled voice.

At that moment, in the mirror behind the bar, she saw the tall young man come into the room and remain standing by the door, as if he were listening to their conversation. She hoped Otto would not continue it, but he did.

That's no reason, he said. Take lessons. There are plenty of good skiing professors in Cortina.

Malika shook her head slowly several times.

The young man stepped to the bar, saying, in Spanish: He's right, our friend Otto. That's what Cortina's for. Everybody skis here.

Now he leaned on the bar and faced Malika. I spend a lot of time south of the border myself, he said as though in confidence. I have a little hacienda down in Durango.

Malika stared at him. He was speaking in Spanish, but she had no idea of what he was talking about. He misunderstood her expression and frowned. What's the matter. Don't you like Durango?

She looked at Otto and back at the tall young man. Then she burst into laughter, and the sound filled the bar agreeably. The tall young man's face seemed to melt as he heard it.

She slid down from the barstool, smiled at him, and said: I don't understand. *Hasta luego*, Otto. While the young man was still making a visible effort to collect his thoughts, she turned and walked out of the bar.

This marked the beginning of a new friendship, one which grew to substantial proportions later that same day. At the end of the afternoon Malika and the young man, who said his name was Tex, went for a walk along the road outside the hotel, where the snow had been packed down. The peaks of the mountains around them were turning pink. She sniffed the air with enthusiasm.

I like it here, she said, as though the subject had been under discussion.

You'd like it more if you learned to ski, he told her.

No, no!

She hesitated, then went on quickly: I can't pay for lessons. I haven't any money. They don't give me any.

Who's they?

She walked on beside him without answering, and he took her arm. By the time they got back to the hotel she had agreed to let Tex pay for lessons, skis and clothes, on condition that the clothes be bought at a shop in the town and not at the hotel.

Once she had been fitted out, the lessons were begun, Tex being always present. Dinah did not like the idea at all. She said it was unheard-of, and she asked Malika to point Tex out to her.

Malika, who had felt no resentment at being left each day to her own devices, could not understand Dinah's objections. She was delighted with her new friend, and arranged for Dinah to meet him in the bar, where she sat for a half hour listening to them speak in English. Later that night Dinah told her Tex was uncivilized. Malika did not understand.

He's an idiot! Dinah cried.

Malika laughed, for she took this to mean that Dinah also liked him. He has a good heart, she replied calmly.

Yes, yes. You'll see that good heart soon enough, Dinah told her with a crooked smile.

Having observed that Tex's interest in her was due in part to the mystery with which she seemed to be surrounded, Malika offered him as little information about herself as possible. He was still under the impression that she was Mexican and a member of Dinah's family, and that for one reason or another Dinah was in charge of her. His misconception amused Malika, and she did nothing to correct it. She knew Dinah and Daphne were persuaded that she and Tex were having an affair, and this pleased her, too, since it was not true.

Sometimes, in spite of Malika's efforts to restrain him, Tex drank too much whiskey. This generally happened in the bar after dinner. At such moments his face often took on an expression that made her think of a fish dragged up onto the beach. His eyes bulging, his jaw slack, he would take one of her hands in both of his, and groan: Oh, Honey! To Malika this was an expression of momentary despair. She would sigh and shake her head, and try to comfort him by saying that he would feel better in a little while.

The lessons were going very well; Malika spent most of the daylight hours on the snow with Tex. She would have eaten at his table, too, if Dinah had not indignantly forbidden it.

One day at lunch Dinah lit a cigarette and said: You're going to have your last skiing lesson tomorrow. We're leaving for Paris on Thursday.

Malika saw that she was watching her closely to observe the effect of her announcement. She decided to look slightly crestfallen, but not enough to give Dinah any satisfaction.

It's been a marvelous holiday, Dinah went on, and we've all had a fine time, but now it's over.

Así es la vida, murmured Malika with lowered head.

XII

That afternoon when the lesson was over, Malika and Tex sat side by side in the snow, looking out across the valley in the fading light. All at once she found that she was sobbing. Tex stared at her in consternation, then drew her to him, trying to comfort her. Through her sobs, she repeated what Dinah had told her at lunch.

When she felt his arms around her, she knew that the only reason for her unhappiness was that she did not want to leave him. She leaned her head on his chest and sobbed: *Me quiero quedar contigo, Tex, contigo.*

These words transformed him. He began to glow. While he soothed her with gestures, he told her he would do anything in the world for her. If she wanted him to, he would take her away that very night. She stopped weeping and listened.

Before they rose from the snowbank, they had agreed upon the following morning for their departure, while Dinah would be out skiing. Tex was determined to have no further meeting with Dinah, but Malika made him leave a note behind for her, which she dictated.

> *Dinah, I don't want to go to Paris now. Thank you and thank Daphne. I loved Cortina. Now I'm going to learn to ski. I'll be in Switzerland for a while. Good luck, Malika.*

Tex had made arrangements to have a chauffeur-driven car large enough to hold Malika's many valises pick them up at the hotel at half past nine in the morning. Everything went off smoothly. Malika handed the note for Dinah to the receptionist. He did not mention the subject of her bill, which she had feared he might do, but merely nodded gravely.

As they left Cortina behind them, Malika said: Dinah's going to be very angry.

I'm thinking of that, said Tex. Will she make trouble?

She can't do anything. She never saw my passport. She doesn't even know my name.

Tex appeared to be stunned by this information, and began to put a whole series of questions to her, but she, being happy to see the beautiful white landscape outside, replied without answering them, seized his hand now and then to draw his attention to a detail in the landscape, and, by taking gentle command, succeeded in putting him off without his being aware of it.

They had lunch at a small restaurant in Mezzolombardo. The waiter brought a bottle of wine and poured out two glasses. No, said Malika, pushing it away.

Your friend Dinah's not here now, Tex reminded her. You can do whatever you like.

Dinah! she scoffed. What's Dinah beside the words of God?

He stared at her, mystified, without pursuing the matter further, and drank the bottle of wine by himself, so that he was in a happy and relaxed state when they got back into the car. As they rolled southward on the autostrada he devoted himself to crushing her hand in his, nuzzling her neck with his lips, and finally kissing her feverishly on the lips. Malika could not have hoped for more.

XIII

At dinner that night in Milano she watched him drink two bottles of wine. Later in the bar he had several whiskeys. At Cortina she would have begged him to stop, but this night she affected not to notice that he was resolutely sliding into a drunken state. Instead, she began to tell him a complicated story she had known since her childhood, about a female ghoul that lived in a cave and unearthed newly buried corpses to extract their livers. Seeing his expression of total bewilderment, she stopped halfway through the tale.

He shook his head. What an imagination! he said.

I want to learn how to speak English, Malika went on, leaving the ghoul behind. That's what I'm going to do in Switzerland.

Tex was drunk by the time they went upstairs. She regretted this, for she liked him much better when he was sober. But she suspected that he was going to want to sleep with her and she thought it wiser for their first time together that he be in a state of befuddlement. It was imperative that he believe himself to be the first to have had her.

In the morning when he awoke staring, trying to remember, she confided that it had not been as painful as she had expected. Tex was contrite; he nearly wept as he begged her forgiveness. She smiled and covered him with kisses.

Having won this much, she pressed on, not with any specific purpose in mind, but simply to gain a stronger foothold. While he was still in the slough of early-morning remorse, she made him promise to abjure whiskey.

At the Grand Saint Bernard, as the police handed back their passports, Malika saw Tex stare at hers briefly with astonishment. When they were in the car, he asked to see the passport again. The Arabic characters seemed to cause him great excitement. He began to ask her questions about Morocco which she could not have answered even if she had been in the mood for such conversation. She assured him it was like any other country. Now I'm looking at Switzerland, she said.

They arrived in Lausanne at sunset and took rooms in a large hotel by the lake, at Ouchy. It was far grander than the hospice at Cortina, and the people living there, not being dressed for skiing, seemed to Malika much more elegant.

I like it here, she said to Tex that night at dinner. How long can we stay?

The next morning, at Malika's insistence, they went together to the Berlitz School for intensive language courses: she in English and he in French. She saw that Tex imagined she would soon tire of the strict schedule, but she was determined not to leave Lausanne before she could converse in English. They spent each morning in their respective classes, had lunch together, and returned to the school at three for further tutoring.

Every Friday afternoon Tex would rent a car, and they would drive to Gstaad, stopping to have dinner on the way. Saturdays and Sundays if no snow fell, they skied at Wasserngrat or Eggli. Sometimes he would insist on staying over until Monday, even though it meant missing their morning classes. Malika could see that if she had let him have his way he always would have done this, and very likely would have extended the weekends further and further. He approved of Malika's learning English, but he could not fathom her obsessive preoccupation with it. Nor, had he asked her, could she have explained it to him. She knew only that unless she kept on learning she was lost.

XIV

During the winter there in Lausanne they made no friends, being entirely satisfied with each other's company. One day as they were coming out of the Schweizerische Kreditanstalt, where Tex had opened an account for Malika, he turned to her and apropos of nothing asked her if she had ever thought of being married.

She looked at him wonderingly. I think of it all the time, she said. You know it makes me happy to be married to you.

He stared at her as if he had understood nothing she had said. After a moment he seized her arm and pulled her to him. It makes me happy, too, he told her. She could see, however, that something was on his mind. Later when they were alone, he said that of course it was true that they were married, but that what he had been speaking of was marriage with papers.

With papers or not with papers! It's the same thing, isn't it? If two people love each other, what have papers got to do with it?

It's the governments, he explained. They like married people to have papers.

Of course, she agreed. In Morocco, too. Many people are married with papers.

She was about to add that papers were important if you expected to produce children, but she checked herself in time, sensing that the observation bordered on dangerous ground. Already, from certain questions he had put to her, she suspected that he had begun to wonder if she were pregnant. His questions amused her, based as they were on the supposition that there had been no Tim before Tex, to show her how always to be safe.

One morning in early spring when she complained of feeling tired, he asked her outright.

You think Moroccan women don't know anything? she cried. If they want to make children they make them. If they don't, they don't make them.

He nodded dubiously. Those home remedies don't always work.

She saw that she was safe. He knew nothing about Morocco. Mine does, she said.

If she never mentioned America to him or asked about his family, it was because she could not envisage his life there with enough clarity to be curious about it. For his part, he spoke of America with increasing frequency. Never before had he stayed away for so long, he said. Malika interpreted these remarks as warnings that he had had enough of his present life and was contemplating a change. The thought struck terror to her heart, but she would not let him perceive this.

From time to time she would catch him in the act of staring at her, an expression of utter incomprehension on his face. By now, at Malika's insistence, they often spoke together in English. She thought it suited him much better than Spanish; he seemed to have an altogether different voice.

Would you like to be married? With papers, I mean.

Yes, if you want to.

And you? he insisted.

Of course I want to, if you want to.

They were married in the rectory office of a Protestant minister, who remarked in an aside to Tex that personally he was not in favor of marriage where the bride was as young as Malika. In my experience, he said, very few such unions prove to be permanent.

To Malika the episode was a bit of nonsense of the sort that Nazarenes appear so much to enjoy. Nevertheless she saw clearly that it was a matter of great importance to Tex. Indeed, his character seemed to have undergone a subtle metamorphosis since the ceremony, in that he was now more self-assertive. She liked him rather better this way, and concluded that secretly he was a very devout man. The papers were obviously a requirement of the Nazarene religion; now that he had them he felt more secure.

It was only a fortnight later that Tex, after drinking a little more wine than was his habit, announced to her that they were going home. Malika received the news with a sinking sensation. She could see that he was glad to be leaving the world of hotels and restaurants, and she suspected that life in a house would be very different and not nearly so much fun.

Once again she saw nothing from the plane, but this time the journey went on for such a long time that she grew worried. Tex was sleepy, nevertheless she disturbed him several times to ask: Where are we?

Twice he answered jovially: In the air. The next time he said: Somewhere over the ocean, I suppose. And he stole a glance at her.

We're not moving, she told him. We're standing still. The plane is stuck.

He only laughed, but in such a way that she realized she had made a mistake of some sort. I don't like this plane, she said.

Go to sleep, Tex advised her.

She shut her eyes and sat quietly, feeling that she had gone much too far away—so far that now she was nowhere. Outside the world, she whispered to herself in Arabic, and shivered.

XV

Being in Los Angeles persuaded Malika that she was right, that she had left behind everything that was comprehensible, and was now in a totally different place whose laws she could not know. They went from the airport to the top of the mountain, where a house was hidden in the woods. Tex had told her about it, but she had imagined something very different, like the Mountain in Tangier, where the villas had big gardens around them. This house was buried among the trees; she could not see the rest of it even when they went up to the door.

In the middle of the forest, she said wonderingly.

An ugly little Filipino in a white jacket opened the door for them. He bowed low and made a short formal speech of welcome to Malika. She knew he was speaking English, but it was not the English she had been taught in Lausanne. At the end she thanked him gravely.

Later she asked Tex what the little man had been saying.

He was hoping you'd be happy here in your new house, that's all.

My house? But it's your house, not mine!

Of course it's yours! You're my wife, aren't you?

Malika nodded. She knew, no matter what anyone pretended, that when men grew tired of their wives they put them out, and took new ones. She loved Tex and trusted him, but she did not expect him to be different from other men. When the time came, she knew he would find a pretext to rid himself of her. The important point was to know how to fight off the fatal moment, to make it come as late as possible. She nodded again and said with a smile: I like this house, Tex.

The rooms had irregular shapes, with unexpected alcoves and niches where there were soft couches with piles of cushions. As she inspected the house she noted with satisfaction that the windows were barred with iron grillwork. She had already seen the massive front door with its heavy bolts.

That night as they sat in front of the fireplace they heard the yapping of coyotes.

Jackals, murmured Malika, turning her head to listen. Very bad.

She found it incomprehensible that anyone should waste money building such a pretty house in a place so far from everything. Above all she could not understand why the trees had been left growing so close to the house. Silently she determined never to go outside unless Tex accompanied her, and never under any circumstances to remain in the house without him.

The next morning, when Tex was about to drive down into the city, Malika began to run from room to room, crying: Wait! I'm going with you.

You'd be bored, he told her. I've got to go to a lawyer's office. You stay here with Salvador.

She could not let Tex know that she was afraid to stay in the house; it would be an unforgivable affront. No, no, no. I want to see the town, she said.

He kissed her and they set out for the city. It was a bigger car than the one he had rented at the airport the day before.

I always want to go with you no matter where you go, she confided, hoping that this declaration would aid in establishing a precedent.

During these weeks, when she watched the life in the streets, she could find no pattern to it. The people were always on their way somewhere else, and they were in a hurry. She knew better than to imagine that they were all alike; still, she had no way of knowing who was who. In Morocco, in Europe, there had been people who were busy doing things, and there had been others watching. Always, no matter where one was or what one was doing, there were watchers. She had the impression that in America everyone was going somewhere and no one sat watching. This disturbed her. She felt herself to be far, far away from everything she had ever known. The freeways inspired her with dread, for she could not rid herself of the idea that some unnameable catastrophe had occurred, and that the cars were full of refugees fleeing from the scene. She had ample opportunity to observe the miles of small houses set side by side, and compare these simple dwellings with the house on the mountain. As a result it occurred to her that perhaps she was fortunate to live where she did. One day as they drove into the city she turned to Tex and said: Do you have more money than these people?

What people?

She moved her hand. The ones who live in these houses.

I don't know about other people's money, he said. I know I never have enough of my own.

She looked out at the rows of frail wooden houses with their dusty shrubbery, and could not believe him. You *do* have more money, she declared. Why don't you want to say it?

This made him laugh. Whatever I have, I made myself. The day I was twenty-one my father handed me a check and said: Here. Let's see what you can do with this. In three years I changed it into four and a half times as much. Is that what you meant, Dad? I asked him. That's what I meant, son, he said.

Malika thought a moment, saying finally: And now when he needs money you give it to him.

Tex looked sideways at her and said gravely: Of course.

She wanted to ask him if he had no friends in Los Angeles. Since their arrival she had not met anyone, and she thought this strange. It could be a custom here for recently married couples to keep strictly to themselves during a specified period. Or perhaps Tex's friends here were all girls, which would automatically preclude her knowing them. When she asked him, he said he seldom came to Los Angeles. I'm generally with my family in Texas, he said, or down at the hacienda.

There was a studio upstairs with a wide sun-deck that was not hidden by trees in the middle of the day. Malika did not feel entirely at ease sitting out there, with nothing between her and the dark forest. She suspected that the trees harbored dangerous birds. Sometimes she and Tex sat up here between dips in the pool, which, being below inside the closed patio, she considered safe. Tex would observe her as she lay stretched on a mattress, and assure her she was more beautiful than ever. She had noticed this herself, but she was pleased to know that he too had seen it.

XVI

One day Tex told her that a man named F. T. was coming to dinner. F. T. was an old friend of his father's, who managed his financial affairs for him. Malika was interested to hear what such work entailed, so Tex made an effort to explain the mechanics of investment. She was quiet for a while. But then you can't make money unless you already have it, she said.

That's about it, Tex agreed.

F. T. was middle-aged and well-dressed, with a small gray moustache. He was delighted with Malika, and called her Little Lady. This struck her as vaguely insulting, but since she could see that he was a pleasant and well-behaved man otherwise, she made no objections. Besides, Tex had told her: Remember. If you should ever need anything, anything at all, just call F. T.'s number. He's like my father.

During dinner she decided that she really liked F. T., even though he seemed not to take her very seriously. Afterward he and Tex talked together for a long time. The words went on for so long that Malika fell asleep on a divan and awoke only after F. T. had gone. She was apologetic for having been rude, but she blamed Tex for allowing it to happen.

He threw himself down beside her. F. T. thought you were great. He says you're beyond a doubt the most beautiful girl he's ever seen.

He's a nice man, she murmured.

Ever since her arrival in California, her life had seemed static. When she thought back about it, she decided that it had stopped moving when she had left the Berlitz School. Innocently, she asked Tex if she might continue the lessons here. To her astonishment he ridiculed the suggestion, claiming that all she needed was practice in conversation. Because he was not in the habit of refusing her anything, she did not take him at his word, and continued to dwell on her desire for further instruction. All at once she saw that he was going to be firm; he seemed to consider her dissatisfaction a criticism of him. Finally she realized that he was angry.

You don't understand! she cried. I have to study English more before I can study anything else.

Study!

Of course, she said calmly. I'm always going to study. You think I want to stay like this?

I hope you do, Honey, for my sake. You're perfect.

He took hold of her, but she wriggled free.

That evening Tex said to her: I'm going to get an extra woman in the kitchen and let Salvador give you lessons in cooking. That's something you should learn, don't you think?

Malika was silent. Do you want me to learn? You know I want to make you happy.

She began to spend several hours each day in the kitchen with Salvador and Concha, a Mexican girl of whose work the little Filipino was scornful. It was a pleasant enough room, but the number of strange machines and the little bells that kept sounding as Salvador rushed from one spot to another awed and confused her. She was even a bit afraid of Salvador, because his face never changed its fixed expression—that of a meaningless grin. It seemed to her that when he was annoyed the grin became even wider. She took care to pay strict attention to everything he told her. Soon he had her making simple dishes which they ate at lunch. If the recipe called for a béchamel or a chasseur, he made it himself and incorporated it, since the timing was more than Malika could manage. It gratified her to see that Tex thought her food good enough to be served at table. She continued to spend two hours in the kitchen each morning, and another hour or so before dinner in the evening. Sometimes she helped Salvador and Concha prepare a picnic hamper, and they went to the beach. She would have liked to tell Tex about the picnics on the beach at Tangier, but there was no way of doing that.

XVII

Occasionally, despite Malika's entreaties, Tex would take advantage of her morning session in the kitchen to drive the small car into the city on an errand. She would be uneasy until he returned, but he was always back in time for lunch. One morning he failed to appear at the usual hour. The telephone rang. Salvador wiped his hands and stepped into the butler's pantry to answer it, while Malika and Concha went on chatting together in Spanish. In a moment Salvador reappeared in the doorway, and with a radiant smile told Malika the police had called to say that Mister Tex had met with an accident and was in a hospital in Westwood.

Malika rushed at the little man and seized him by the shoulders. Telephone to F. T.!

She hopped up and down while he searched for the number and dialed it. As soon as she saw that he was speaking to F. T., she snatched the telephone from his hand.

F. T.! Come and get me! I want to see Tex.

She heard F. T.'s voice, calm and reassuring. Yes. Now you just wait quietly for me. I'll be there as soon as I can. Don't you worry. Let me speak to Salvador again.

She left Salvador talking into the telephone and rushed upstairs to the studio, where she began to walk back and forth. If Tex was in the hospital, he probably would not be home to sleep that night, and she would not stay in the house without him. She went out onto the sun-deck and stared at the trees. Tex is dead, she thought.

It was mid-afternoon before F. T.'s car drew up at the door. He found her in the studio lying face down on a couch. When she heard his voice she sprang up, wide-eyed, and ran to him.

That night Malika slept at F. T.'s house. He had insisted upon taking her home with him and leaving her in the care of his wife. For it was true that Tex was dead; he had succumbed not long after reaching the hospital.

F. T. and his wife did not commiserate with Malika. Mrs. F. T. said a show of sympathy could induce hysteria. Malika merely talked on and on, weeping intermittently. Sometimes she forgot that her listeners did not know Arabic or Spanish, until at their prompting she would go back into English. She had sworn to accompany Tex whenever he went out, and she had not done so, therefore he had been killed, he was the only being in the world she loved, and she was far from home, and what was going to become of her here alone?

That night as she lay in the dark listening to the occasional passing wail of a police siren, she was assailed afresh by the sensation she had felt on the plane—that of having gone too far for the possibility of return. Being with Tex had made it possible to accept the strangeness of the place; now she saw herself as someone shipwrecked on an unknown shore peopled by creatures whose intentions were unfathomable. And no one could come to rescue her, for no one knew she was there.

She slept at F. T.'s house for several nights. During the days she visited supermarkets and other points of interest with Mrs. F. T. You've got to keep busy, her hostess told her. We can't have you brooding.

There was no way, however, of preventing Malika from worrying about what was to become of her, stranded in this unlikely land without a peseta to buy herself bread, and only the caprice of F. T. and his wife between her and starvation.

XVIII

One morning F. T. himself drove Malika to his office. Out of respect for him she had dressed with great care in a severe gray silk suit from Balenciaga. Her entrance into the office with F. T. caused a stir of interest. When she sat facing him across his desk in a small inner room, he pulled a sheaf of papers from a drawer. As he leafed through them he began to talk.

Betty tells me you're worried about money.

Seeing Malika nod, he went on. I take it you haven't any at all. Is that right?

She felt in her handbag and pulled out a crumpled twenty dollar bill that Tex had given her one day when they were shopping.

Only this, she said, showing him.

F. T. cleared his throat.

Well, I want you to stop worrying. As soon as we get everything cleared up you'll have a regular income. In the meantime I've opened a checking account for you at the bank downstairs in this building.

He saw anxiety flitting across her face, and added hastily: It's your money. You're his sole beneficiary. After taxes and all the rest, you'll still have a substantial capital. And if you're wise, you'll leave it all just where it is, in certificates of deposit and treasury notes. So stop worrying.

Yes, she said, understanding nothing.

I never let Tex play with stocks, F. T. went on. He had no head for business.

She was shocked to hear F. T. denigrate poor Tex in this way, but she said: I see.

When we get everything straight and running smoothly, you ought to have around fifty thousand a month. Possibly a little more.

Malika stared at F. T. Is that enough? she asked cautiously.

He shot a quick glance at her over his spectacles. I think you'll find it's enough.

I hope so, she said with fervor. You see, I don't understand money. I never bought anything myself. How much does a thing cost? I don't know. Only in my own country.

Of course. F. T. pushed a checkbook along the top of the desk toward her. You understand, this is a temporary account for you to draw on now, until all the legal work is finished. I hope you won't overdraw. But I'm sure you won't.

He smiled encouragingly at her. Remember, he went on. There are only twenty-five thousand dollars there. So be a good girl and keep track of your checks.

But I can't do what you tell me! she exclaimed. Please do it for me.

F. T. sighed. Can you write your name? he asked very quietly.

Tex showed me in Lausanne, but I've forgotten.

In spite of himself, F. T. raised his arms. But my dear lady, how do you expect to live? You can't go on this way.

No, she said miserably.

F. T. pushed back his chair and stood up. Well, he said jovially, what you don't know you can always learn. Why don't you come up here every morning and study with Miss Galper? She's as smart as a whip. She'll teach you everything you need to know. That's my suggestion for you.

He was not prepared for her vehement response. She jumped up and hugged him. Oh, F. T.! That's what I want! That's what I want!

XIX

The following day Malika moved her luggage into a hotel in Beverly Hills. Under F. T.'s advice she kept Salvador on, living in the house, but now functioning solely as chauffeur. Each morning he called at the hotel for her and drove her to F. T.'s office. She found this routine stimulating. Miss Galper, a pleasant young woman with glasses, would spend the forenoon working with her, after which they generally went to lunch together. There had not been much glamor in Miss Galper's life, and she was fascinated by Malika's accounts of Europe and Morocco. There remained a basic mystery in her story, nevertheless, since she never explained how she came to be living at Tim's flat in Tangier. In her version, she might have come into being during a picnic on the beach at Sidi Qacem.

When after two months F. T. saw that Malika was, if anything, even more serious and determined about pursuing her practical education, he suggested that the lessons continue at the hotel. Now it was Miss Galper whom Salvador drove to and from Beverly Hills. Occasionally they went shopping—small expeditions to Westwood that delighted Malika because for the first time she was aware of prices, and could gauge the buying power of her money. F. T. had told her that with what Tex had left for her she would be able to live better than most people. At the time she had supposed this was a part of his attempt to comfort her, but now that she understood the prices she realized that he had been stating a fact. She said nothing to Miss Galper of her surprise at finding the cost of goods so low. Instead, she overwhelmed her with a constant flow of small gifts.

You've got to stop this, Malika, Miss Galper told her.

The first month they had done nothing but arithmetic. After that there was the telling of time, the names of the days and the months. With some difficulty Miss Galper taught her to sign the two forms of her name: *Malika Hapgood* and *Mrs. Charles G. Hapgood.* By the time the lessons were moved to the hotel, Malika had begun to practice writing out in words complicated sums given her in figures. They went back to dates, and she had to learn to write them correctly.

You can leave everything else to a secretary, Miss Galper told her. But you've got to take care of your money yourself.

To this end she gave Malika a course in reading bank statements, and another in spacing the purchase of securities to assure regular turnover.

As the months went by and Malika's insight into the functioning of the world around her grew, she began to understand the true extent of her ignorance, and she conceived a passionate desire to be able to read the texts of newspapers and magazines.

I'm not an English teacher, Miss Galper told her. F. T. doesn't pay me for that. We can get you a good professor whenever you want.

Malika, being persuaded that she could learn only from Miss Galper, consulted F. T. about it. After a certain amount of deliberation, he devised a plan which delighted Malika and pleased Miss Galper as well. He would give Miss Galper a year's holiday with salary if Malika wanted to take her on as a paid companion during that time. In this way, he implied to Malika, she would be able to get the reading lessons she wanted. He added that he did not think Miss Galper was the person to give them, but since Malika had her heart set on being taught by her, this seemed to him a viable strategy.

It was Miss Galper's idea to make a tour of Europe. F. T. suggested they buy a big car, put it on a freighter, and take Salvador along with them to pick it up over there and drive it. When Malika heard this, she asked why they could not all go on the ship with the car. It might be possible, F. T. told her.

Eventually F. T. had arranged to get Malika a new passport, had even helped Miss Galper and Salvador expedite theirs, and, accompanied by Mrs. F. T., had bidden them a lengthy farewell at the dock in San Pedro. It was a comfortable Norwegian freighter bound for Panama and eventually for Europe.

The ship was already in tropical waters. Malika said she had imagined it could be this hot only in the Sahara, and certainly not on the sea. She had nothing to do all day. Salvador spent most of his time sleeping. Miss Galper sat in a deck chair reading. She had refused to give Malika any kind of lessons while they were on the ship. It would make me seasick, she assured her. But she noticed Malika's boredom, and talked with her for long periods of time.

XX

Malika could not sit, as Miss Galper could, looking at the sea. The flat horizon on all sides gave her much the same sensation of unreality she had experienced on the plane with Tex. Panama came as a relief, making it clear that the ship had not been static during all those days, and that they had reached a very different part of the world.

It took all day to go through the canal. Malika stood on deck in the sun, waving back to the men working along the locks. But from Panama on, her restlessness increased daily. She was reduced to playing endless games of checkers with a yawning Salvador each afternoon in the narrow passengers' lounge. They never spoke during these sessions. From the beginning of the voyage the captain had urged Malika to visit the bridge. At some point Miss Galper had mentioned that he had the power to seize anyone on the ship and have him locked into a dark cell somewhere below. When Malika finally accepted his invitation she took Miss Galper along.

Standing at the prow, Malika stared ahead at the white buildings of Cadiz. As the ship moved into the port, the combination of the light in the air, the color of the walls and the odors on the wind told her that she was back in her part of the world and close to home. For a long time she had refused to think about the little house above the gully. Now that it no longer frightened her, she was able to imagine it almost with affection.

It was her duty to go and visit her mother, however hostile a reception she might get from her. She would try to give her money, which she was certain she would refuse to take. But Malika was ready with a ruse. If her mother spurned the money, she would tell her she was leaving it next door with Mina Glagga. Once Malika was out of the way, her mother would lose no time in going to claim it.

Miss Galper had hoped to spend the night in Cadiz, but Malika insisted on driving straight to Algeciras. Now that she was so near home, she wanted to get there as soon as she could. I must see my mother, she said. I must see her first.

Of course, said Miss Galper. But you haven't seen her in two years or more and she isn't expecting you. One day sooner or later?

We can come back. Now I have to go and see my mother.

In Algeciras at the hotel that night they saw Salvador eating at the other end of the long dining room. He had changed from his uniform into a gray flannel suit. Malika observed him carefully, and said: He's drinking wine.

He'll be all right tomorrow, Miss Galper told her. They always drink, Filipinos.

He was at the door grinning when they came out of the hotel in the morning to be driven to the dock. Most of the passengers going to Tangier were Moroccans. Malika had forgotten the shameless intensity with which her countrymen stare at women. Now she was back among her own kind. The realization startled her; she felt both excitement and apprehension.

XXI

After they had settled into their quarters at the hotel, Malika went down to the desk. She hoped to visit her mother in the evening, when she was sure to be in the house, and when there would be a valid excuse for not staying too long. She intended to reserve two rooms in Tetuan for the night, one for Salvador and one for herself, and return to Tangier in the morning. In the lobby they told her of a new hotel on the beach only a mile or so from her town. She asked them to telephone for reservations.

Miss Galper's room was down the corridor from hers. Malika knocked on her door and told her she would be leaving about five o'clock, in order to get to the hotel before dark.

Miss Galper looked at her searchingly. I'm glad you're doing it now and getting it over with, she said.

You can have a good time, Malika told her. There are bars where you can go.

No, thank you. The men here give me the creeps. They all try to talk to you.

Malika shrugged. What difference does it make? You can't understand what they're saying.

This was fortunate, she thought. The brutally obscene remarks made by the men to women passing in the street disgusted and infuriated her. Miss Galper was lucky not to know any Arabic.

She said a lame good-bye and hurried to her room. The prospect of seeing her mother had unsettled her. Mechanically she put a few articles of clothing into an overnight bag. On the way out she cashed some traveler's checks at the office, and soon she and Salvador were on the road to Tetuan.

The mountains had scarves of white cloud trailing outward from their summits. Salvador criticized the narrow highway. Malika scarcely heard his complaints. Her heart was beating unusually fast. It was true that she was going back to help her mother; she was going because it was included in the pattern. Since the day she had run away, the vision of the triumphant return had been with her, when she would be the living proof that her mother had been mistaken, that she was not like the other girls of the town. Now that the moment was drawing near, she suspected that the visit was foredoomed to failure. Her mother would feel no pleasure at seeing her—only rancor and bitterness at the thought that she had been with Nazarenes.

Salvador said: In Pilipinas we got better roads than this one.

Don't go fast, she told him.

They skirted Tetuan and turned to the left along the road that led to her town. The sea wind rushed through the car. *Bismil'lah*, she murmured under her breath, for now she was entering the crucial part of the journey.

She did not even know they had reached the town until they were in the main street. It looked completely different. There were big new buildings and bright lights. The idea that the town might change during her absence had not occurred to her; she herself would change, but the town would remain an unmoving backdrop which would help her define and measure her transformation.

A moment later they had arrived at the new hotel, spread out along the beach in a glare of green floodlights.

XXII

Malika soon discovered that it was not a real hotel. There was no room service, and in the dining room they served only snack-bar food. Before eating, she changed into blue jeans, bought in Los Angeles at Miss Galper's suggestion. She wore a sweater and wrapped a silk kerchief tightly around her head. In this costume she felt wholly anonymous.

Salvador was already eating at the counter in the comedor. She sat on a stool near him and ordered pinchitos. Her stomach rebelled at the thought of eating, but she chewed and swallowed the meat because she had learned that to feel well she must eat regularly. Through the rasping of a transistor radio at the end of the counter she heard the dull, repeated sound of the waves breaking over the sand below. If her mother flew into a rage and began to beat her, she would go directly to Mina Glagga and give her the money, and that would finish it. She signed the chit and went out into the wind to the car.

The town's new aspect confused her. They had moved the market; she could not see it anywhere, and she felt a wave of indignation at this betrayal. Salvador parked the car at the service station and they set out on foot up the narrow street that led to the house. There were street lights only part of the way; beyond, it would have been dark had it not been for the moon. Salvador glanced ahead and said it would be better to turn around and come again in the morning.

You wait here, she said firmly. I'll come back as soon as I can. I know the way. And she quickly went on, before he could argue about it.

She made her way up along the empty moonlit street until she came to a small open square from which, in the daytime at least, her mother's house was visible ahead, at the edge of the barranca. Now as she looked, the moon's light did not seem to strike it at all; she could see no sign of it. She hurried on, already assailed by a nightmarish premonition, and then she stopped, her mouth open in disbelief. The house was not there. Even the land where it had stood was gone. Mina Glagga's and all the houses bordering on the gully had disappeared. Bulldozers had made a new landscape of emptiness, a great embankment of earth, ashes and refuse that stretched downward to the bottom of the ravine. The little house with its garden had been just below where she now stood. She felt her throat tighten painfully as she told herself that it no longer existed.

Ceasing finally to stare at the meaningless terrain, she turned and went back to the square, where she knocked at the door of one of the houses. The woman who opened the door was a friend of her mother's whose name she had forgotten. She eyed Malika's blue jeans with distaste and did not ask her inside. They talked standing in the doorway. In an expressionless voice the woman told her that her mother had died more than a year earlier, during Ramadan. It was fortunate, she added, that she had not lived to see them destroy her house in order to build the new road. She thought Malika's sister had gone to Casablanca, but she was not certain.

By now the woman had pushed the door so that it was nearly shut. Malika thanked her and said good night.

She went over and stood at the edge of the landfill, staring down at the uniform surface of the hillside, unreal even in the careful light dropped over it by the moon. She had to force her eyes shut to clear them of the tears that kept forming, and she found it strange, for she had not felt tenderness for her mother. Then she saw more clearly. It was not for her mother that she felt like weeping; it was for herself. There was no longer any reason to do anything.

She let her gaze wander over the dim expanse toward the mountains beyond. It would be good to perish here in the place where she had lived, to be buried along with the house under the hateful mass. She pounded the edge of it with her heel, lost her footing, and slid downward some distance through mounds of ashes and decayed food. In that instant she was certain it was happening, as a punishment for having wished to be dead a moment ago; her weight had started a landslide that would roll her to the bottom, leaving her under tons of refuse. Terrified, she lay still, listening. There were faint stirrings and clinks around her, but they quickly died away into silence. She scrambled up to the roadbed.

A cloud had begun to move across the moon. She hurried down the hill toward the street light where Salvador waited.

Tangier, 1978

NEXT TO NOTHING

PAUL BOWLES

At first there was mud, and the sound of breathing.
and no one was sure of where we were.
When we found out, it was much too late.
Now nothing can happen save as it has to happen.
And then I was alone, and it did not matter.
Only because by that time nothing could matter.

The next year there were knifing matches in the stadium.
I think the people are ready for it, the mayor said.
Total involvement. A new concept in sports.
The loser does not leave the ring alive.

But no one can know where he is until he knows where he has been.
I sat quietly, and the air changed then, and I looked up.
And the black branches trailing in the living water
stirred slowly with the change of air.
Piropos, you said. El aire les hace piropos.

> *Have you change for this banknote?*
> *It is closed off for the time being.*
> *Take me to the other end of the city*
> *where they slice up the sharks on the sand.*
>
> *The double tariff applies after sundown.*
> *It is forbidden to pass beyond this railing.*
> *Take me to the other end of the city*
> *where nobody wants to go.*

Yes, I said we would need the machine-guns by next March,
but I also warned against saying life was easy.
I mixed hoops and coffins, cradles and needles
while the lights twinkled on far-off Monte Tomás.
We sat in a park that smelled of pine trees,
and that night there were voices in the corridors
and I remembered the empty face of the blind man as he sang.
Tu misma tienes la culpa
de lo que has hecho conmigo.

You will find yourself among people.
There is no help for this
nor should you want it otherwise.
The passages where no one waits are dark
and hard to navigate.
The wet walls touch your shoulders on each side.
When the trees were there I cared that they were there.
And now they are gone, does it matter?
The passages where no one waits go on
and give no promise of an end.
You will find yourself among people,
Faces, clothing, teeth and hair
and words, and many words.
When there was life, I said that life was wrong.
What do I say now? You understand?

Something is going on these recent days.
The clouds that lie in trees
Can skim your head as you run uphill.
After sunset birds fly down
push inside the grill and eat the plants.
Seafog swells across the lowlands
and the slow ships moan.

Yes, something is going on.
You said you saw them together
but they were not together.

Who loves the fog?
Why do the birds come?
As to the clouds, you may be innocent.

Living branches trail in black water. Nothing moves.
And how do I know what you are to me?
Our theories are untested. You must not laugh.
We thought there were other ways.
Probably there are, but they are hidden
and we shall never find them.

What's his name?
God forbid.
Where does he live?
Nobody knows.
How do we get there?
Ask the conductor.
That's his face?
Nobody knows.
Now shall I ask him?
God forbid.

Take me to the other end of the city
where no one knows the difference between you and me.
I went back. I did not find him.
And what do I say now? You understand?

The woman pointed.
That's the model we
should have had with us.
We thought about it,
hung back and didn't.

Wished a thousand times we had.
But that's the way those things go.

You never can know
until afterwards.
Roads of nothing but
sharp pebbles and stones.

And they say there are
snakes behind the rocks.
You see no snakes but
you know they are there.

And after you've gone
down into seven
empty valleys, one
after the other,

you find that you've been
quietly crying
for the past half hour.
Or at least I did.

Because there was no
connection. No more
connection to any-
thing at all. Nothing.

It might not have been
such an awful trip
if we'd had that one.

The woman pointed.
That's the model we
ought to have chosen.

It will be raining up there by the time you arrive.
Try to get through quickly. The forest's cold green breath
is best left undisturbed, coiled close to the boughs.
In open country again you can breathe.
That is the theory, but our theories are untested.
Things are not the way they were.
How can we be sure? New laws apply,
and who knows the difference between the law and the wind?
And who knows the difference between you and me?
Y tu misma tienes la culpa
de lo que has hecho conmigo.

I should like to see the bottom of the fountain.
Do not go too near the edge.
Does this path lead to the artificial lake?
The band concert has been posponed.
Is there a waterfall behind these rocks?
The guardian is not on duty.

I have no idea of what is going to happen
or in which parts the pain will be.
We are only in spring, and spring has a twisting light.

Spring's images are made of crystal and cannot be
recalled.
There will be suffering, but you know how to coax it.
There will be memories, but they can be deflected.
There will be your heart still moving
in the wind that has not stopped flying westward,
and you will give a signal. Will someone see it?

We thought there were other ways.
The darkness would stay outside.
We are not it, we said. It is not in us.

Yes, yes, go with her. The old man smiled.
You will be back. You will not find me.

There was a time when life moved on a straighter line.
We still drank the water from the lake,
and the bucket came up cold
and sweet with the smell of deep water.
The song was everywhere that year, an absurd refrain:
It's only that it seems so long, and isn't.
It's only that it seems so many years,
and perhaps it's one.
When the trees were there I cared that they were there,
and now they are gone.
On our way out we used the path that goes around the swamp.
When we started back the tide had risen.
There was another way, but it was far above and hard to get to.
And so we waited here, and everything is still the same.

There were many things I wanted to say to you
before you left. Now I shall not say them.
Though the light spills onto the balcony
making the same shadows in the same places,
only I can see it, only I can hear the wind
and it is much too loud.

The world seethes with words. Forgive me.
I love you, but I must not think of you.
That is the law. Not everyone obeys it.
Though time moves past and the air is never the same
I shall not change. That is the law, and it is right.

Yes, yes, I went with her. Yes.
In the shine of morning and the glow of afternoon.

Piropos, you said. El tiempo te hace piropos.
There will never be a way of knowing.
I did go back. The old man was gone.

Do no thinking, give no reasons,
have no sensations, make no apologies.
The anguish was not real enough,
the age of terror too short-lived.
They thought all that was finished, left behind.
They were sure there must be other ways.

I am the spider in your salad, the bloodsmear on your bread.
I am the rusted scalpel, the thorn beneath your nail.
Some day I shall be of use to you, as you can never be to me.
The goats leap from grave to grave, and nibble at last year's thistles.
In the name of something more than nothing, of Sidi Bouayad,
and all who have wisdom and power and art,
I am the wrong direction, the dead nerve-end, the unfinished scream.
One day my words may comfort you, as yours can never comfort me.

Tangier, 1976

Grateful acknowledgment is made for permission to reprint the following copyrighted works:

"Call at Corazón," "How Many Midnights," and "You Are Not I" from *The Delicate Prey* by Paul Bowles. © 1945, 1946, 1947, 1948, 1949, 1950 by Paul Bowles. First published by The Ecco Press in 1972. Reprinted by permission of the publisher.

"Plain Pleasures," "Camp Cataract," "A Stick of Green Candy," "A Guatemalan Idyll," and "A Day in the Open" from *The Collected Works of Jane Bowles.* Copyright © 1966 by Jane Bowles. Reprinted by permission of Farrar, Straus & Giroux, Inc.

"Pages from Cold Point" and "A Man Must Not Be Very Moslem" from *Too Far from Home: The Selected Writings of Paul Bowles.* © 1993 by The Ecco Press. Reprinted by permission of The Ecco Press.

Selection from *The Sheltering Sky* by Paul Bowles. © 1949, renewed 1977 by Paul Bowles. First published by The Ecco Press in 1978. Reprinted by permission of the publisher.

Selection from *Let It Come Down* by Paul Bowles. Copyright © 1952, 1980 by Paul Bowles. By permission of Black Sparrow Press.

"Emmy Moore's Journal," "The Iron Table," and "Going to Massachusetts" from *Feminine Wiles* by Jane Bowles. Copyright © 1976 by Paul Frederic Bowles. Reprinted with the permission of Black Sparrow Press.

"The Children's Party," "East Side: North Africa," "Curls and a Quiet Country Face," "Looking for Lane," "Laura and Sally," and "Señorita Córdoba" by Jane Bowles. By permission of Paul Bowles.

Letter dated June 1954 ("Letter 58") from *Out in the World: Selected Letters of Jane Bowles 1935–1970.* Copyright © 1985 by Paul Frederic Bowles. Reprinted with the permission of Black Sparrow Press.

Selection from *The Spider's House* by Paul Bowles. Copyright © 1955 by Paul Bowles. By permission of Black Sparrow Press.

THE VIKING PORTABLE LIBRARY

The Portable Sherwood Anderson
Edited by Horace Gregory

The Portable Beat Reader
Edited by Ann Charters

The Portable Blake
Edited by Alfred Kazin

The Portable Cervantes
Edited by Samuel Putnam

The Portable Chaucer
Edited by Theodore Morrison

The Portable Chekhov
Edited by Avrahm Yarmolinsky

The Portable Conrad
Edited by Morton Dauwen Zabel

The Portable Conservative Reader
Edited by Russell Kirk

The Portable Malcolm Cowley
Edited by Donald W. Faulkner

The Portable Stephen Crane
Edited by Joseph Katz

The Portable Dante
Edited by Paolo Milano

The Portable Emerson
Edited by Carl Bode and Malcolm Cowley

The Portable Faulkner
Edited by Malcolm Cowley

The Portable Greek Historians
Edited by M. I. Finley

The Portable Greek Reader
Edited by W. H. Auden

The Portable Graham Greene
Edited by Philip Stratford

The Portable Hawthorne
Edited by Malcolm Cowley

The Portable Henry James
Edited by Morton Dauwen Zabel

The Portable Thomas Jefferson
Edited by Merrill D. Peterson

The Portable James Joyce
Edited by Harry Levin

The Portable Jung
Edited by Joseph Campbell

The Portable Kipling
Edited by Irving Howe

The Portable D. H. Lawrence
Edited by Diana Trilling

The Portable Abraham Lincoln
Edited by Andrew Delbanco

The Portable Machiavelli
Edited by Peter Bondanella and Mark Musa

The Portable Karl Marx
Edited by Eugene Kamenka

The Portable Medieval Reader
Edited by James Bruce Ross and Mary Martin McLaughlin

The Portable Arthur Miller
Edited by Harold Clurman

The Portable Milton
Edited by Douglas Bush

The Portable Nietzsche
Edited by Walter Kaufmann

The Portable North American Indian Reader
Edited by Frederick Turner

The Portable Dorothy Parker
Edited by Brendan Gill

The Portable Plato
Edited by Scott Buchanan

The Portable Poe
Edited by Philip Van Doren Stern

The Portable Romantic Poets
Edited by W. H. Auden and Norman Holmes Pearson

The Portable Renaissance Reader
Edited by James Bruce Ross and Mary Martin McLaughlin

The Portable Roman Reader
Edited by Basil Davenport

The Portable Shakespeare
Edited by Marshall Best

The Portable Bernard Shaw
Edited by Stanley Weintraub

The Portable Steinbeck
Edited by Pascal Covici, Jr.

The Portable Swift
Edited by Carl Van Doren

The Portable Thoreau
Edited by Carl Bode

The Portable Tolstoy
Edited by John Bayley

The Portable Mark Twain
Edited by Bernard De Voto

The Portable Twentieth-Century Russian Reader
Edited by Clarence Brown

The Portable Victorian Reader
Edited by Gordon S. Haight

The Portable Voltaire
Edited by Ben Ray Redman

The Portable Walt Whitman
Edited by Mark Van Doren

The Portable Oscar Wilde
Edited by Richard Aldington and Stanley Weintraub

The Portable World Bible
Edited by Robert O. Ballou

"Then?"

I said that in America there were no buffaloes in the fields, and that was why Brooks was interested in seeing them. There were no temples in the landscape, either, I told him, and added, perhaps unwisely: "He looks at buffaloes. I look at temples." This struck Yamyong as hilarious, and he made allusions to it now and then all during the day.

The road stretched ahead, straight as a line in geometry, across the verdant, level land. Paralleling it on its eastern side was a fairly wide canal, here and there choked with patches of enormous pink lotuses. In places the flowers were gone and only the pods remained, thick green disks with the circular seeds embedded in their flesh. At the first stop the bhikkus got out. They came aboard again with mangosteens and lotus pods and insisted on giving us large numbers of each. The huge seeds popped out of the fibrous lotus cakes as though from a punchboard; they tasted almost like green almonds. "Something new for you today, I think," Yamyong said with a satisfied air.

Ayudhaya was hot, dusty, spread-out, its surrounding terrain strewn with ruins that scarcely showed through the vegetation. At some distance from the town there began a wide boulevard sparingly lined with important-looking buildings. It continued for a way and then came to an end as abrupt as its beginning. Growing up out of the scrub, and built of small russet-colored bricks, the ruined temples looked still unfinished rather than damaged by time. Repairs, done in smeared cement, veined their façades.

The bus's last stop was still two or three miles from the center of Ayudhaya. We got down into the dust, and Brooks declared: "The first thing we must do is find food. They can't eat anything solid, you know, after midday."

"Not noon exactly," Yamyong said. "Maybe one o'clock or a little later."

"Even so, that doesn't leave much time," I told him. "It's quarter to twelve now."

But the bhikkus were not hungry. None of them had visited Ayudhaya before, and so they had compiled a list of things they most wanted to see. They spoke with a man who had a station wagon parked nearby, and we set off for a ruined *stupa* that lay some miles to the southwest. It had been built atop a high mound, which we climbed with some difficulty, so that Brooks could take pictures of us standing within a fissure in the decayed outer wall. The air stank of the bats that lived inside.

When we got back to the bus stop, the subject of food arose once again, but the excursion had put the bhikkus into such a state of excitement that they could not bear to allot time for anything but looking. We went to the museum. It was quiet; there were Khmer heads and documents inscribed in Pali. The day had begun to be painful. I told myself I had known beforehand that it would.

Then we went to a temple. I was impressed, not so much by the gigantic Buddha which all but filled the interior, as by the fact that not far from the entrance a man sat on the floor playing a *ranad* (pronounced *lanat*). Although I was familiar with the sound of it from listening to recordings of Siamese music, I had never before seen the instrument. There was a graduated series of wooden blocks strung together, the whole slung like a hammock over a boat-shaped resonating stand. The tones hurried after one another like drops of water falling very fast. After the painful heat outside, everything in the temple suddenly seemed a symbol of the concept of coolness—the stone floor under my bare feet, the breeze that moved through the shadowy interior, the bamboo fortune sticks being rattled in their long box by those praying at the altar, and the succession of insubstantial, glassy sounds that came from the *ranad*. I thought: If only I could get something to eat, I wouldn't mind the heat so much.

We got into the center of Ayudhaya a little after three o'clock. It was hot and noisy; the bhikkus had no idea of where to look for a restaurant, and the prospect of asking did not appeal to them. The five of us walked aimlessly. I had come to the conclusion that neither Prasert nor Vichai understood spoken English, and I addressed myself earnestly to Yamyong. "*We've got to eat.*" He stared at me with severity. "We are searching," he told me.

Eventually we found a Chinese restaurant on a corner of the principal street. There was a table full of boisterous Thais drinking *mekong* (categorized as whiskey, but with the taste of cheap rum) and another table occupied by an entire Chinese family. These people were doing some serious eating, their faces buried in their rice bowls. It cheered me to see them: I was faint, and had half expected to be told that there was no hot food available.

The large menu in English which was brought us must have been typed several decades ago and wiped with a damp rag once a week ever since. Under the heading SPECIALITIES were some dishes that caught my eye, and as I went through the list I began to laugh. Then I read it aloud to Brooks.

"Fried Sharks Fins and Bean Sprout
Chicken Chins Stuffed with Shrimp
Fried Rice Birds
Shrimps Balls and Green Marrow
Pigs Lights with Pickles
Braked Rice Bird in Port Wine
Fish Head and Bean Curd"

Although it was natural for our friends not to join in the laughter, I felt that their silence was not merely failure to respond; it was heavy, positive.

A moment later three Pepsi-Cola bottles were brought and placed on the table. "What are you going to have?" Brooks asked Yamyong.

"Nothing, thank you," he said lightly. "This will be enough for us today."

"But this is terrible! You mean no one is going to eat *anything*?"

"You and your friend will eat your food," said Yamyong. (He might as well have said "fodder.") Then he, Prasert, and Vichai stood up, and carrying their Pepsi-Cola bottles with them, went to sit at a table on the other side of the room. Now and then Yamyong smiled sternly across at us.

"I wish they'd stop watching us," Brooks said under his breath.

"They were the ones who kept putting it off," I reminded him. But I felt guilty, and I was annoyed at finding myself placed in the position of the self-indulgent unbeliever. It was almost as bad as eating in front of Moslems during Ramadan.

We finished our meal and set out immediately, following Yamyong's decision to visit a certain temple he wanted to see. The taxi drive led us through a region of thorny scrub. Here and there, in the shade of spreading flat-topped trees, were great round pits, full of dark water and crowded with buffaloes; only their wet snouts and horns were visible. Brooks was already crying: "Buffaloes! Hundreds of them!" He asked the taxi driver to stop so that he could photograph the animals.

"You will have buffaloes at the temple," said Yamyong. He was right; there was a muddy pit filled with them only a few hundred feet from the building. Brooks went and took his pictures while the bhikkus paid their routine visit to the shrine. I wandered into a courtyard where there was a long row of stone Buddhas. It is the custom of temple-goers to plaster little squares of gold leaf onto the religious statues in the *wats*. When thousands of them have been stuck onto the same surface, tiny scraps of the gold come unstuck. Then they tremble in the breeze, and the figure shimmers with a small, vibrant life of its own. I stood in the courtyard watching this quivering along the arms and torsos of the Buddhas, and I was reminded of the motion of the bô-tree's leaves. When I mentioned it to Yamyong in the taxi, I think he failed to understand, for he replied: "The bô-tree is a very great tree for Buddhists."

Brooks sat beside me on the bus going back to Bangkok. We spoke only now and then. After so many hours of resisting the heat, it was relaxing to sit and feel the relatively cool air that blew in from the rice fields. The driver of the bus was not a believer in cause and effect. He passed trucks with oncoming traffic in full view. I felt better with my eyes shut, and I might even have dozed off, had there not been in the back of the bus a man, obviously not in control, who was intent on making as much noise as possible. He began to shout, scream, and howl almost as soon as we had left Ayudhaya, and he did this consistently throughout the journey. Brooks and I laughed about it, conjecturing whether he was crazy or only drunk. The aisle was too crowded for me to be able to see him from where I sat. Occasionally I glanced at the other passengers. It was as though they were entirely unaware of the commotion behind them. As we drew closer to the city, the screams became louder and almost constant.

"God, why don't they throw him off?" Brooks was beginning to be annoyed.

"They don't even hear him," I said bitterly. People who can tolerate noise inspire me with envy and rage. Finally I leaned over and said to Yamyong: "That poor man back there! It's incredible!"

"Yes," he said over his shoulder. "He's very busy." This set me thinking what a civilized and tolerant people they were, and I marvelled at the sophistication of the word "busy" to describe what was going on in the back of the bus.

Finally we were in a taxi driving across Bangkok. I would be dropped at my hotel and Brooks would take the three bhikkus on to their *wat*. In my head I was still hearing the heartrending cries. What had the repeated word patterns meant?

I had not been able to give an acceptable answer to Yamyong in his bewilderment about the significance of the necktie, but perhaps he could satisfy my curiosity here.

"That man in the back of the bus, you know?"

Yamyong nodded. "He was working very hard, poor fellow. Sunday is a bad day."

I disregarded the nonsense. "What was he saying?"